MATTERHORN

A graduate of Yale University and a
Rhodes Scholar at Oxford, Karl Marlantes
served as a marine in Vietnam, where he was
awarded the Navy Cross, the Bronze Star, two
Navy Commendation Medals for Valor, two
Purple Hearts, and ten Air Medals. He and his
wife Anne live on a small lake in western
Washington State. *Matterhorn* is his first novel.

This novel is dedicated to my children,
who grew up with the good and
bad of having a Marine combat
veteran as a father.

Shame and honor clash where the courage of a steadfast man is motley like the magpie. But such a man may yet make merry, for Heaven and Hell have equal part in him.

Wolfram von Eschenbach
"Parzival"

A glossary explaining slang, military jargon, and technical terms has been provided at the back of the book.

Chain of Command and Principal Characters
(Radio call signs in italics)

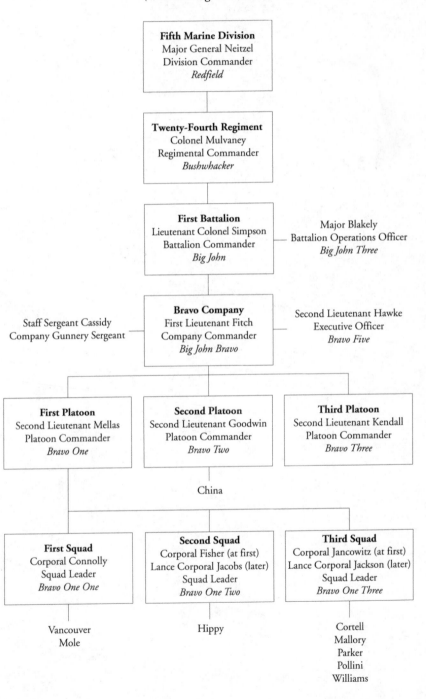

Fifth Marine Division
Major General Neitzel
Division Commander
Redfield

Twenty-Fourth Regiment
Colonel Mulvaney
Regimental Commander
Bushwhacker

First Battalion
Lieutenant Colonel Simpson
Battalion Commander
Big John

Major Blakely
Battalion Operations Officer
Big John Three

Staff Sergeant Cassidy
Company Gunnery Sergeant

Bravo Company
First Lieutenant Fitch
Company Commander
Big John Bravo

Second Lieutenant Hawke
Executive Officer
Bravo Five

First Platoon
Second Lieutenant Mellas
Platoon Commander
Bravo One

Second Platoon
Second Lieutenant Goodwin
Platoon Commander
Bravo Two

Third Platoon
Second Lieutenant Kendall
Platoon Commander
Bravo Three

China

First Squad
Corporal Connolly
Squad Leader
Bravo One One

Second Squad
Corporal Fisher (at first)
Lance Corporal Jacobs (later)
Squad Leader
Bravo One Two

Third Squad
Corporal Jancowitz (at first)
Lance Corporal Jackson (later)
Squad Leader
Bravo One Three

Vancouver
Mole

Hippy

Cortell
Mallory
Parker
Pollini
Williams

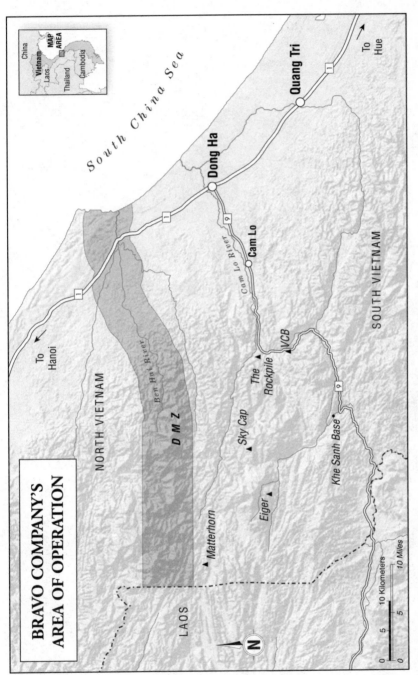

South China Sea

To Hanoi

NORTH VIETNAM

D M Z

Ben Hai River

LAOS

Matterhorn ▲

Eiger ▲

Sky Cap ▲

The Rockpile ▲

▲ VCB

Khe Sanh Base •

Cam Lo River

Cam Lo

Dong Ha

Quang Tri

To Hue

SOUTH VIETNAM

N

0   5   10 Kilometers
0   5   10 Miles

China
Vietnam
Laos
Thailand
Cambodia
MAP AREA

Matterhorn, Eiger, and Sky Cap are fictional places; the other locations are real.

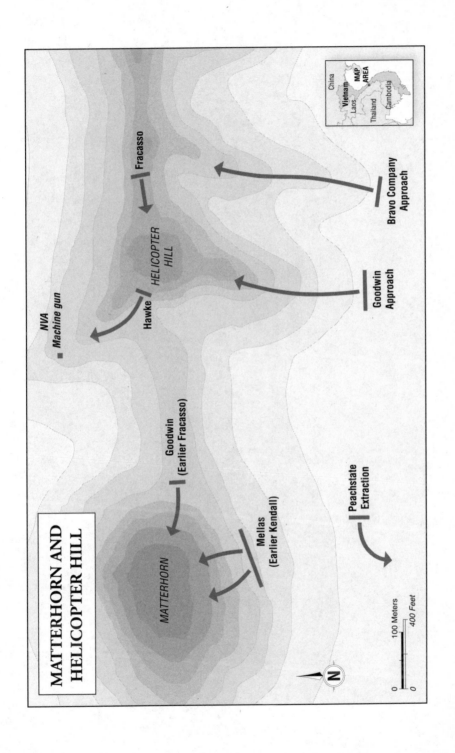

MATTERHORN AND
HELICOPTER HILL

MATTERHORN

Goodwin
(Earlier Fracasso)

Mellas
(Earlier Kendall)

NVA
Machine gun

Hawke

HELICOPTER
HILL

Fracasso

Goodwin
Approach

Bravo Company
Approach

Peachstate
Extraction

0   100 Meters
0   400 Feet

N

China
Vietnam
Laos
Thailand
Cambodia
MAP
AREA

MATTERHORN

CHAPTER
ONE

Mellas stood beneath the gray monsoon clouds on the narrow strip of cleared ground between the edge of the jungle and the relative safety of the perimeter wire. He tried to focus on counting the other thirteen Marines of the patrol as they emerged single file from the jungle, but exhaustion made focusing difficult. He also tried, unsuccessfully, to shut out the smell of the shit, which sloshed in the water that half-filled the open latrine pits above him on the other side of the wire. Rain dropped from the lip of his helmet, fell past his eyes, and spattered onto the satiny olive cloth that held the armor plating of his cumbersome new flak jacket. The dark green T-shirt and boxer shorts that his mother had dyed for him just three weeks ago clung to his skin, heavy and clammy beneath his camouflage utility jacket and trousers. He knew there would be leeches clinging to his legs, arms, back, and chest beneath his wet clothes, even though he couldn't feel them now. It was the way with leeches, he mused. They were so small and thin before they started sucking your blood that you rarely felt them unless they fell on you from a tree, and you never felt them piercing your skin. There was some sort of natural anesthetic in their saliva. You would discover them later, swollen with blood, sticking out from your skin like little pregnant bellies.

When the last Marine entered the maze of switchbacks and crude gates in the barbed wire, Mellas nodded to Fisher, the squad leader, one of three who reported to him. "Eleven plus us three," he said. Fisher nodded back, put his thumb up in agreement, and entered the wire. Mellas followed him, trailed by his radio operator, Hamilton.

The patrol emerged from the wire, and the young Marines climbed slowly up the slope of the new fire support base, FSB Matterhorn, bent over with fatigue, picking their way around shattered stumps and dead trees that gave no shelter. The verdant underbrush had been hacked down with K-bar knives to clear fields of fire for the defensive lines, and the jungle floor, once veined with rivulets of water, was now only sucking clay.

The thin, wet straps of Mellas's two cotton ammunition bandoleers dug into the back of his neck, each with the weight of twenty fully loaded M-16 magazines. These straps had rubbed him raw. All he wanted to do now was get back to his hooch and take them off, along with his soaking boots and socks. He also wanted to go unconscious. That, however, wasn't possible. He knew he would finally have to deal with the nagging problem that Bass, his platoon sergeant, had laid on him that morning and that he had avoided by using the excuse of leaving on patrol. A black kid—he couldn't remember the name; a machine gunner in Third Squad—was upset with the company gunnery sergeant, whose name he couldn't remember either. There were forty new names and faces in Mellas's platoon alone, and almost 200 in the company, and black or white they all looked the same. It overwhelmed him. From the skipper right on down, they all wore the same filthy tattered camouflage, with no rank insignia, no way of distinguishing them. All of them were too thin, too young, and too exhausted. They all talked the same, too, saying fuck, or some adjective, noun, or adverb with fuck in it, every four words. Most of the intervening three words of their conversations dealt with unhappiness about food, mail, time in the bush, and girls they had left behind in high school. Mellas swore he'd succumb to none of it.

This black kid wanted out of the bush to have his recurrent headaches examined, and some of the brothers were stirring things up in support. The gunnery sergeant thought the kid was malingering and should have his butt kicked. Then another black kid refused to have his hair cut and people were up in arms about *that*. Mellas was supposed to be fighting a war. No one at the Basic School had said he'd be dealing with junior Malcolm X's and redneck Georgia crackers. Why couldn't the Navy corpsmen just decide shit like whether headaches were real or not? They were supposed to be the medical experts. Did the platoon commanders on Iwo Jima have to deal with crap like this?

As Mellas plodded slowly up the hill, with Fisher next to him and Hamilton automatically following with the radio, he became embarrassed by the sound his boots made as they pulled free of the mud, fearing that it would draw attention to the fact that they were still shiny and black. He quickly covered for this by complaining to Fisher about the squad's machine gunner, Hippy, making too much noise when Fisher had asked for the machine gun to come to the head of the small column because the point man thought he'd heard movement. Just speaking about the recent near-encounter with an enemy Mellas had not yet seen started his insides humming again, the vibration of fear that was like a strong electric potential with no place to discharge. Part of him was relieved that it had been a near miss but another part acted peeved that the noise might have cost them an opportunity for action, and this peevishness in turn irked Fisher.

When they reached the squad's usual position in the company lines, Mellas could see that Fisher could barely contain his own annoyance by the way he nearly threw to the ground the three staves he'd cut for himself and a couple of friends while out on the patrol. These staves were raw material for short-timer's sticks, elaborately carved walking sticks, roughly an inch and a half in diameter and three to five feet long. Some were simple calendars, others works of folk art. Each stick was marked in a way that showed how many days its owner had survived on his thirteen-month tour of duty and how many days were left to go. Mellas had also been anxious about the sound Fisher had made cutting the three staves with a machete, but he had said nothing. He was still in a delicate position: nominally in charge of the patrol, because he was the platoon commander, but until he was successfully broken in he was also under the orders of Lieutenant Fitch, the company commander, to do everything Fisher said. Mellas had accepted the noise for two reasons, both political. Fitch had basically said Fisher was in charge, so why buck Fitch? Fitch was the guy who could promote Mellas to executive officer, second in command, when Second Lieutenant Hawke rotated out of the bush. That

would put him in line for company commander—unless Hawke wanted
it. A second reason was that Mellas hadn't been sure if the noise was dangerous, and he was far more worried about asking stupid questions than
finding out. Too many stupid comments and dumb questions at this stage
could make it more difficult to gain the respect of the platoon, and it was
a lot harder to get ahead if the snuffs didn't like you or thought you were
incompetent. The fact that Hawke, his predecessor, had been nearly
worshipped by the platoon did not help matters.

Mellas and Hamilton left Fisher at Second Squad's line of holes and
slowly climbed up a slope so steep that when Mellas slipped backward
in the mud he barely had to bend his knee to stop himself. Hamilton,
bowed nearly double with the weight of the radio, kept poking its antenna into the slope in front of him. The fog that swirled around them
obscured their goal: a sagging makeshift shelter they had made by snapping their rubberized canvas ponchos together and hanging the ponchos over a scrap of communication wire strung only four feet above
the ground between two blasted bushes. This hooch, along with two
others that stood just a few feet away from it, formed what was called,
not without irony, the platoon command post.

Mellas wanted to crawl inside his hooch and make the world disappear, but he knew this would be stupid and any rest would be short.
It would be dark in a couple of hours, and the platoon had to set out
trip flares in case any soldiers of the North Vietnamese Army—the
NVA—approached. After that, the platoon had to rig the claymore
mines, which were placed in front of their fighting holes and were command detonated by electric wire; they delivered 700 steel balls in a fan-
shaped pattern at groin height. In addition, the uncompleted sections
of the barbed wire had to be booby-trapped. If Mellas wanted to heat
his C-rations he had to do so while it was still daylight, otherwise the
flame would make a perfect aiming point. Then he had to inspect the
forty Marines of his platoon for immersion foot and make sure everyone took the daily dose of dapsone for jungle rot and the weekly dose
of chloroquine for malaria.

He and Hamilton stopped just in front of Bass, the platoon sergeant, who was squatting outside the hooches in the rain making coffee
in a number-ten can set over a piece of burning C-4 plastic explosive.
The C-4 hissed and left an acrid smell in the air but was preferred to
the eye-burning stink of the standard issue trioxane heat tabs. Bass was
twenty-one and on his second tour. He emptied several small envelopes
of powdered C-ration coffee into the boiling water and peered into the
can. The sleeves of his utility jacket were neatly rolled into cuffs just
below his elbows, revealing forearms that were large and muscular.
Mellas, watching Bass stir, set the M-16 he had borrowed from Bass
against a log. It had taken very little coaxing from Bass to convince
Mellas that it was stupid to rely on the standard-issue .45 pistols the
Marine Corps deemed sufficient for junior officers. He pulled off the
wet cotton ammunition bandoleers and let them fall to the ground:
twenty magazines, each filled with two interwoven rows of bullets. Then
he shrugged out of his belt suspenders and dropped them to the mud,
along with their attached .45 automatic, three quart-size plastic canteens,
pistol ammunition, his K-bar, battlefield compresses to stop bleeding,
two M-26 fragmentation hand grenades, three smoke grenades, and his
compass. Breathing deeply with relief, he kept watching the coffee, its
smell reminding him of the ever-present pot on his mother's stove. He
didn't want to go check the platoon's weapons or clean his own. He
wanted something warm, and then he wanted to lie down and sleep. But
with dark coming there was no time.

He undid his steel-spring blousing garters, which held the ends of
his trousers tightly against his boots as protection against leeches. Three
leeches had still managed to get through on his left leg. Two were attached and there was a streak of dried blood where a third had engorged
itself and dropped off. Mellas found it in his sock, shook it loose onto
the ground, and stepped on it with his other foot, watching his own blood
pop out of its body. He took out insect repellant and squeezed a stream
onto the other two leeches still attached to his skin. They twisted in pain
and dropped off, leaving a slow trickle of blood behind.

Bass handed him some coffee in an empty C-ration fruit cocktail
can and then poured another can for Hamilton, who had dumped his

radio in front of his and Mellas's hooch and was sitting on it. Hamilton took the coffee, raised the can to Bass in a toast, and wrapped his fingers around the can to warm them.

"Thanks, Sergeant Bass," Mellas said, careful to use the title Bass had earned, knowing that Bass's goodwill was crucial. He sat down on a wet, rotting log. Bass described what had happened while Mellas was out on patrol. FAC-man, the company's enlisted forward air controller, had once again not been able to talk a resupply chopper down through the clouds, so this had been the fourth day without resupply. There was still no definitive word on the firefight the day before between Alpha Company and an NVA unit of unknown size in the valley below them, but the rumor that four Marines had been killed in action was now confirmed.

Mellas tightened his lips and clenched his teeth to press back his fear. He couldn't help looking down onto the cloud-covered ridges that stretched out below them into North Vietnam, just four kilometers away. Down there were the four KIAs, four dead kids. Somewhere in that gray-green obscurity, Alpha Company had just been in the shit. Bravo's turn was coming.

That meant his turn was coming, something that had been only a possibility when he had joined the Marines right out of high school. He had entered a special officer candidate program that allowed him to attend college while training in the summers and getting much-needed pay, and he had envisioned telling admiring people, and maybe someday voters, that he was an ex-Marine. He had never actually envisioned being in combat in a war that none of his friends thought was worth fighting. When the Marines landed at Da Nang during his freshman year, he had to get a map out to see where that was. He had wanted to go into the Marine Air Wing and be an air traffic controller, but each administrative turning point, his grades in college, his grades in Basic School, and the shortage of infantry officers had implacably moved him to where he was now, a real Marine officer leading a real Marine rifle platoon, and scared nearly witless. It occurred to him that because of his desire to look good coming home from a war, he might never come home at all.

He fought back the fear that surged through him whenever he realized that he could die. But now the fear had started his mind churning again. If he could get into Hawke's position as executive officer, then he'd be safe inside the perimeter. There would be no more patrols; he'd handle admin and be next in line for company commander. For him to get Hawke's position, the current company commander, Lieutenant Fitch, would have to rotate home and Hawke would have to take Fitch's place. That was actually quite likely. Everyone loved Hawke, up the chain of command and down. Still, Fitch was new to the job. That meant a long wait, unless of course Fitch was killed or wounded. As soon as this idea went through his head, Mellas felt terrible. He didn't want anything bad to happen to anyone. He tried to stop thinking, but he failed. Now it occurred to him that he'd have to wait for Hawke to rotate home, unless something happened to Hawke. Mellas was amazed and ashamed. He realized that part of him would wish anything, and maybe even do anything, if it meant getting ahead or saving his own skin. He fought that part down.

"How's the wire coming?" Mellas asked. He didn't really care about the task of stringing the barbed wire in front of the holes, but he knew he should appear interested.

"Not bad, sir," Bass said. "Third Squad's been working on it all day. We're close to finished."

Mellas hesitated. Then he plunged into the problem he'd avoided that morning by going out on patrol. "That kid from Third Squad come to see you about going to the rear again?" He was still overwhelmed, trying to remember everyone's name.

"Name's Mallory, sir." Bass snorted. "Malingering fucking coward."

"He says he has headaches."

"And I've got a pain in the ass. There's two hundred good Marines on this hill want to go to the rear, better ones than that piece of shit. He's had a headache ever since he came out to the bush. And don't give me any of that 'Watch out 'cause he's a brother' shit, because there's a lot of good splibs out here that don't have headaches. He's chickenshit." Bass took a long drink and then exhaled steam into the cool damp air. "And, uh," Bass added, a slight smile on his lips, "Doc Fredrickson has him up by his hooch. He's been waiting for you to get back."

Mellas felt the hot sweet coffee move down his throat and settle into his stomach. He wriggled his water-wrinkled toes to keep from nodding off. The warmth of the coffee through the can felt good against his hands, which were beginning to run pus, the first symptoms of jungle rot. "Shit," he said to no one in particular. He placed the cup against the back of his neck where the strap of the magazine bandoleer had rubbed it raw.

"Drink it, Lieutenant," said Bass. "Don't make love to it." Bass took out his pocketknife and began carving another elaborate notch on his short-timer's stick. Mellas looked at it with envy. He had 390 days left to go on his own tour.

"Do I have to deal with it now?" Mellas asked. He instantly regretted asking the question. He knew he was whining.

"You're the lieutenant, sir. RHIP." Rank has its privileges.

Mellas was trying to think of a witty comeback when he heard a scream from Second Squad's area. "Jesus! Get the squid! Get Doc Fredrickson!" Bass immediately threw down his stick and ran toward the voice. Mellas sat there, so stupid with exhaustion he couldn't will himself to move. He looked at Hamilton, who shrugged and finally took a sip of his coffee. He watched Jacobs, the fire team leader with the stutter from Second Squad, run up the hill and disappear inside Fredrickson's hooch. Mellas sighed and started pulling his bloody socks and wet boots back on as Jacobs and Fredrickson, the Navy medical corpsman, went sliding and skidding back down the hill. Several minutes later, Bass came walking slowly up the hill, stonily impassive.

"What is it, Sergeant Bass?" Mellas asked.

"You'd better go have a look, Lieutenant. It's the damnedest thing I ever saw. Fisher's got a leech right smack up the hole in his cock."

"God," Hamilton said. He looked up at the clouds and then back down at the steaming coffee in his hands. He raised the coffee. "Here's to fucking leeches."

Mellas felt revulsion, but also relief. No one could hold him responsible for something like that. Without lacing the boots, he headed down the hill toward Second Squad's position, slipping in the mud,

worrying about how he would replace a seasoned squad leader like
Fisher when he knew hardly anyone in the platoon.

An hour earlier, Ted Hawke had also been worrying about replacing
an experienced leader. But Hawke was worrying about Mellas, who had
replaced him as First Platoon commander when Hawke had been moved
up to the company's number two spot, executive officer. Hawke had been
in-country long enough to be accustomed to being scared—that came
with every operation—but he was not used to being worried, and that
worried him.

He picked up a splintered stick and began to doodle absentmind-
edly in the mud, tracing the pattern of a five-pointed star over and over
again, a habit from grade school days that he fell into when he was trying to think. The stick was one of thousands, all that remained of the
huge trees that had once stood on this jungle hilltop, just three kilometers from Laos and two from the DMZ. The hill, one of many similar
unnamed hills in the area, all of them over a mile high and shrouded by
cold monsoon rain and clouds, had the misfortune of being just a little
higher than the others. For this reason, a staff officer sitting fifty-five
kilometers to the east at Fifth Marine Division headquarters in Dong
Ha had picked it to be flattened and shorn of vegetation to accommodate an artillery battery of 105-millimeter howitzers. The same officer
had also named it Matterhorn, in keeping with the present vogue of
naming new fire support bases after Swiss mountains. The orders soon
worked their way down through regiment to the First Battalion, whose
commanding officer selected the 180 Marines of Bravo Company to
carry them out. This decision dropped Bravo Company and its weary
second in command, Lieutenant Theodore J. Hawke, into an isolated
valley south of Matterhorn. From there it took a three-day slog through
the jungle to reach the top of the hill. Over the course of the next week
they turned it, with the help of nearly 400 pounds of C-4 plastic explosive, into a sterile wasteland of smashed trees, tangled logging slash,
broken C-ration pallets, empty tin cans, soggy cardboard containers,

discarded Kool-Aid packages, torn candy bar wrappers—and mud. Now they were waiting, and Hawke was worrying.

There were smaller worries than the competence of Lieutenant Mellas. One was that the hill was at the extreme range of the lone 105-millimeter howitzer battery at Fire Support Base Eiger, over ten kilometers to the east. This problem was somewhat related to the waiting, because before they could be dropped into the valley to the north of Matterhorn, they had to await the arrival of Golf Battery, the artillery unit that was supposed to occupy Matterhorn's now bald hilltop in order to cover infantry patrols operating beyond the protective cover of the howitzers on Eiger. It was all very simple back at headquarters. Alpha and Charlie companies go into the valley first. When they get beyond the artillery cover from Eiger, Golf Battery moves to Matterhorn. Bravo and Delta companies replace Charlie and Alpha companies down in the valley, but they are now under the cover of artillery on Matterhorn. All of this allows the First Battalion to push farther north and west, continuing its mission of attacking the intricate web of roads, trails, supply dumps, and field hospitals that support the NVA's 320th and 312th steel divisions.

What wasn't in the plan was the NVA unit that shot down, with the accurate fire of a .51-caliber machine gun, the first CH-46 supply chopper that tried to reach Matterhorn. The chopper crashed in flames on an adjacent hill that the Marines in Bravo Company immediately named Helicopter Hill. The entire crew died.

Since then the clouds had lifted only one other time, four days earlier, when another helicopter from Marine Air Group 39, struggling in the thin mountain air, worked its way up to Matterhorn's landing zone from the valley to the south. It arrived with some food and replacements and departed with a number of new .51-caliber holes and a wounded crew chief. Soon afterward, word came down that MAG-39 wanted the gook machine gun eliminated before Golf Battery was brought in, particularly since the operation would entail dangling ponderous howitzers on cables beneath choppers already straining because of the altitude—choppers that would hardly be able to dodge bullets. This problem, along with another of Hawke's worries—the monsoon rain and clouds that had made air support impossible and resupply almost impossible—had thrown off the operation's timetable by three full days and brought down the wrath of Lieutenant Colonel Simpson, radio call sign Big John Six, First Battalion's commanding officer.

Hawke stopped doodling and stared down the steep hillside. Wisps of fog obscured the gray wall of jungle just beyond the twisted rolls of barbed wire at the edge of the cleared ground. He was standing just behind the line of fighting holes that belonged to First Platoon, which he had just turned over to the main source of his worry, Second Lieutenant Waino Mellas, United States Marine Corps Reserve. One of the company's outposts had radioed in that Mellas's patrol had just passed it on the saddle between Matterhorn and Helicopter Hill and would be coming in shortly. Hawke was here to get some feel for Mellas when he was exhausted after the adrenaline-pumping tension of a patrol that hadn't found anything. Hawke had learned long ago that what really mattered in combat was what people were like when they were exhausted.

Hawke was twenty-two, with freckled skin and thick dark hair with an undertone of red that matched his large red mustache. He wore a green sweatshirt, turned inside out so the nap showed matted and dirty, like old fustian. It was stained with sweat and had dark smudges from his armored flak jacket. His trousers were caked with mud and had a hole in one knee. He wore a billed cap, eschewing the floppy camouflage bush hats as being pretentiously gunjy. He kept scanning the tree line, his eyes darting back and forth in the search pattern of the combat veteran. The hillside was steep enough that he could see over the trees to the top of a dark layer of cloud that hid a valley far below him. That valley was bounded by another ridge of high mountains to its north, just like the ridge to Matterhorn's south. Somewhere in that valley to the north, Alpha Company had just taken four killed and eight wounded. It had been too far from Eiger for effective artillery support.

Hawke sighed heavily. Tactically, the company was out on a limb. It was a long way from help and was about to go into combat with all three of its platoons being led by corn-fed rookies. Very quietly he said, "Fuck it," whirled, and launched the splintered stick into the mass of pushed-over trees and brush that separated the landing zone from the line of holes protecting it. Then the bluegrass tune that had been invading his mind all day came back again. He kept hearing the Country Gentlemen—high harmonies, Charlie Waller's fast wrists flat-picking his guitar—singing about an entire expedition that had died in an early attempt to climb the Matterhorn in Switzerland. When Hawke put his hands to his ears to stop it, pus from an open jungle rot sore on his hand got smeared on his right ear. He wiped his hand on his filthy trouser leg, blending new pus with old pus, blood from squashed leeches, grease from a spilled can of spaghetti and meatballs, and the damp clay and greasy plant matter that coated the rotting cotton of his camouflage jungle utilities.

The patrol emerged one by one from the jungle, the Marines bent over, drenched with sweat and rain. Hawke gave a silent snort of approval when he saw that Mellas was right behind Corporal Fisher, where he was supposed to be until Lieutenant Fitch, the CO, said that Mellas was ready to take the lead. Hawke didn't know how to react to Mellas. He was someone you expected to be in the wrong place, but here he was in the right place. Top Seavers, the company first sergeant, had passed the word over the battalion radio net from Quang Tri that Mellas had gone to some fancy private college and graduated second in his class at the Basic School. The fancy college fit with the good grades from the Basic School, but it made Hawke worry that they might have inherited someone who thought that school smarts trumped experience and heart. More worrisome was Top Seavers's comment that when Mellas had first shown up at division personnel on New Year's Day, just six days ago, he had asked for a weapons platoon instead of a rifle platoon. Seavers had concluded that Mellas was trying to avoid going out on patrols, but Hawke wasn't sure. He read Mellas not as a coward but possibly just as a politician. The commander of the weapons platoon, which traditionally had the three 60-millimeter mortars and the company's nine machine guns, lived with the company command group. So he had constant contact with the company commander—unlike the rifle platoon commanders, who were isolated down on the lines. But there weren't enough lieutenants to cover even the rifle platoons now, and with most of the action involving only a platoon or a smaller unit the machine guns were permanently farmed out to the rifle platoons, one to a squad, leaving only the mortars, which could be handled by a corporal. But Mellas didn't fit the stereotype of an ambitious officer. For starters, he didn't look any older than the kids he was supposed to command. Also, he didn't look particularly squared away, everything in its proper place, sails at perfect right angles to the wind, cultivating what an ambitious officer would call command presence. On the other hand, looking careless could just be privileged give-a-shit Ivy League attitude, like wearing duct tape on loafers and jeans with holes in them, knowing all along that they were headed straight to Wall Street or Washington and three-piece suits. Mellas was also handsome to the point of bearing what Hawke's Irish uncle, Art, would have called the marks of God's own handiwork, a plus in civilian life but almost a handicap in the Marine Corps. Moreover, he stood in marked contrast to the other new second lieutenant, Goodwin, a much easier read. Goodwin's record at the Basic School was undistinguished, but Hawke knew he had a natural hunter on his hands. That judgment had been made during the first ten seconds he'd seen the two new lieutenants. The chopper that delivered them to the hill had taken machine-gun fire all the way into the zone. Both lieutenants had come barreling out of the back and dived for the nearest cover, but Goodwin had popped his head up to try to figure out where the NVA machine gun was firing from. Hawke's problem with Goodwin, however, was that while good instincts were necessary, in modern war they weren't sufficient. War had become too technical and too complex—and this one in particular had become too political.

Doc Fredrickson had Fisher flat on his back with his trousers pulled down, in the mud in front of Fisher's hooch. Those Marines from Second Squad who weren't on hole watch were standing in a semicircle behind Fredrickson. Fisher was trying to joke but his grin was very tight. Doc Fredrickson turned to Jacobs, Fisher's most senior fire team leader. "Go tell Hamilton to radio for the senior squid. Tell him we'll probably need an emergency medevac."

"E-e-emergency," Jacobs repeated, his stutter more pronounced than usual. He immediately started up the hill. Fredrickson turned to Mellas, his eyes serious and intent in his narrow face. "Fisher's got a leech in his penis. It crawled up the urethra during the patrol and I don't think I can get it out."

Fisher was lying back with his hands folded behind his head. Like most bush Marines he wore no underwear, in order to help stave off crotch rot. It had now been several hours since he had peed.

Mellas looked up at the swirling fog and then down at Fisher's wet smiling face. He forced a laugh. "You would have to find a perverted leech," he said. He checked the time. Less than two hours until dark. A night medevac this high up and in this weather would be impossible.

"You might as well put your trousers on, Fisher," Fredrickson said. "Don't drink any water. It'd be a bad place to have to amputate."

Jacobs came slipping back down the hill, breathing hard. He was stopped by Bass, just outside of the immediate circle of Fisher's curious friends. "I p-passed the word, Sergeant Bass."

"OK," Bass said. "Get Fisher's gear packed up. Split up his ammo and C-rats. Give the lieutenant his rifle so he doesn't have to keep borrowing mine. Did he have a listening post tonight or anything?"

"N-no, we had the p-patrol today," Jacobs said. His long but normally tranquil face now had a worried look and his broad shoulders had slumped forward. He'd been a fire team leader a few seconds before; now he had the squad.

Mellas opened his mouth to say that the decision about who would temporarily take over the squad was up to him, but he could see that it had already been made by Bass. He shut his mouth. Mellas knew that if he pulled rank he'd lose what little authority he seemed to have.

Fredrickson turned to Mellas. "I think we ought to move him up to the LZ. He'll be starting to feel it pretty soon. No telling when the chopper's going to make it in." He looked up at the dark swirling mist. "If it don't get here quick, I don't know what's going to happen. I guess something inside's got to give and if it screws up the kidney or busts loose inside of him . . ." He shook his head and looked down at his hands. "I just don't know that much about people's insides. We never got it in Field Med."

"What about the senior squid?" Mellas asked, referring to Hospital Corpsman Second Class Sheller, the company-level corpsman, Fredrickson's boss.

"I don't know. He's an HM-2 but I think he worked in a lab the whole time. He's only out here because he pissed someone off at the Fifth Med. He's been out here a week longer than you."

"He's worthless," Bass spat.

"Why do you say that?" Mellas asked.

"He's a fat fucker."

Mellas made no reply, wondering what it took to get on Bass's good list. On the first day Mellas had arrived, desperately wanting everyone to like him, Bass hadn't made it easy. Bass had been running the platoon for close to a month without any lieutenant, and he was quick to point out that he had been doing his first tour in Vietnam when Mellas was starting college.

"That's him there," Fredrickson said. Sheller, who like all company corpsmen went by the nickname Senior Squid, came huffing down the hill, his new jungle boots still black like Mellas's, his utilities not yet bleached pale by the constant rain and exposure. His face was round and he wore black-rimmed Navy-issue glasses and a new bush cover on his head. He looked conspicuously out of place among the thin, rangy Marines.

"What's the problem?" he asked cheerily.

"It's Fisher," Fredrickson replied. "He's got a leech inside his urethra."

Sheller pursed his lips. "Doesn't sound good. No way of getting to it, I suppose. Can he urinate?"

"No," Fredrickson said. "That's how we found out."

"If he could piss we wouldn't need you," Bass growled.

Sheller looked briefly at Bass and then quickly shifted his eyes to the ground. "Where is he?" he asked Fredrickson.

"He's down there packing his gear."

Sheller headed toward where Fredrickson pointed. Fredrickson turned to Bass and Mellas and shrugged his shoulders as if to say "You tell me" and turned to follow him. Bass snorted in disgust. "Fat fucker."

Sheller had Fisher drop his trousers again. He asked how long it had been since he last urinated and then glanced up at the sky and down to his watch. He turned to Mellas. "He'll have to be medevaced. Emergency. I'll go see the skipper."

"Move it, Fisher," Bass said. "You're getting out of the bush. Get your ass up to the LZ."

Fisher grinned and started back toward his hooch, pulling on his trousers as he went. Bass turned toward the holes and shouted through his cupped hands. "Any of you people got mail to go out, give it to Fisher. He's getting medevaced." A general scurry took place immediately. Bodies disappeared into hooches and fighting holes, digging into the packs and plastic bags the men used to keep their letters dry.

"Jacobs," Bass shouted, "tell that goddamn Shortround, Pollini, to change shirts with Fisher. He looks like Joe Shit the ragpicker. And tell Kerwin in Third Squad to trade trousers." Jacobs, grateful for something to do, moved off and began collecting the most worn-out clothing in the squad to replace it with Fisher's less worn-out clothing.

Sheller came back up to Bass and Mellas and dropped his voice. "He's going to be in a lot of pain. I can dope him up, but I don't know what will happen to his bladder or kidneys."

"Well, we don't either," Bass said, "but we ain't been to no fancy Navy medical school." Sheller looked at Bass and started to say something but changed his mind. Bass's perpetual scowl, broad shoulders, and thick arms didn't invite back talk.

"Do what you can for him," Mellas said quickly, trying to ease the tension between the two of them. Mellas turned to Bass. "You going to finally put that novel of yours in the mailbox?"

Bass laughed. He had fallen in love with Fredrickson's cousin, a high school senior, from a yearbook photograph. He had been writing a letter to her for several days and it was already fifteen pages long. The two of them headed back to Mellas's hooch.

"I can't believe it," Mellas said. "Almost Staff Sergeant Bass, hard-ass, falling in love by mail."

"Just 'cause you ain't got nobody to write to except your mother," Bass fired back.

The dart hurt. Mellas remembered Anne, that last night when she turned her back on him in bed. He remembered a trip they took to Mexico, her crying on a village square, pushed beyond her limit by his drive to explore the next place. He had watched her in confusion, loving her, not knowing what to do.

Mellas crawled into the hooch and rummaged for some stationery and a pen. He decided to try to write to her. The letter came out as a cheery "Here we are in a place called Matterhorn. I'm fine, etc." He pasted together the gummed parts of the special envelope. In the jungle there was so much moisture that normal envelopes would stick together before anyone could use them, and in the summer water was so precious that people absolutely loathed licking anything.

"Hey, Mr. Mellas." Every so often Bass used the formal, traditional naval form of address, to emphasize that Mellas was still a boot lieutenant.

Mellas could make no objection. Bass was perfectly correct. "Yes, Sergeant Bass."

"If the bird doesn't make it in and Fisher can't piss, then what happens? Does he just fill up and bust?"

"I don't know, Sergeant Bass. I suppose something like that."

"It's a pisser," Bass muttered. "I got to go see if Skosh is still awake."

Mellas didn't smile at what he knew was an unconscious pun. He crawled after Bass into the dark interior of his hooch, where Bass's eighteen-year-old radio operator, Skosh, was on radio watch. He was so slight that Mellas wondered how he managed to pack the heavy radio on patrols. Skosh had a dark green towel wrapped around his neck and was reading a pornographic book that looked as if it had passed through the hands of every radio operator in the battalion.

"Find out what's the word on the medevac," Bass said. He moved to the back of the hooch. Mellas followed him, crawling over smelly quiltlike nylon poncho liners, his knees hitting hard ground as they sank into Bass's rubber air mattress.

Skosh didn't answer but picked up the handset and started talking. "Bravo Bravo Bravo, Bravo One."

"This is the Big B," the radio hissed out. "Speak."

"What's the story on the medevac? Over."

"Wait one." There was a brief pause. Mellas watched Skosh, who was reading his book again and listening to the faint hiss of the receiver. There was a burst of static as someone on the other end keyed the handset. A new voice came over the air. "Bravo One, this is Bravo Six Actual. Put on your actual." Mellas knew that Six Actual was the skipper, Lieutenant Fitch, and he was asking to speak to Mellas personally—to First Platoon's actual commander, not just anyone tending the radio.

Mellas took the handset from Skosh and keyed it, a little nervous. "This is Bravo One Actual. Over."

"It looks dim for your bird. The valley's souped in from Fire Support Base Sherpa on out. They had one bird try to get out and couldn't find us. Since we've got a couple of hours before your character Foxtrot gets too bad, they'll wait at Sherpa to see if it clears. Over."

"I thought it was an emergency medevac," Mellas answered. "Over."

"We sent it in as a priority. It won't be upgraded to an emergency until it gets so bad he'll die unless they get him out. Over."

Mellas knew they didn't want to risk the bird and the crew when they could hold on for a couple of hours and maybe get better weather. "Roger, Bravo Six. I got you. Wait one." Bass had been signaling Mellas. Mellas released the transmit key on the handset.

"Ask him if we got an order in for any class six," Bass asked.

"What's class six?"

"Just ask him."

Mellas rekeyed the handset. "Bravo Six, One Assist wants to know if we're getting any class six in. Over."

When Fitch rekeyed the handset Mellas heard laughter dying out. "Tell One Assist we got it on order."

"Roger. Thanks for the info. Out."

Mellas turned to Bass. "What's class six?"

"Beer, sir." Bass's face was stonily innocent.

Mellas felt foolish and unprofessional. His jaw muscles tightened in anger. He'd looked bad in front of the whole command post group.

Bass simply looked at him and smiled. "You've got to keep reminding them, Lieutenant, otherwise they forget about you."

Hawke watched Corporal Connolly, leader of Mellas's First Squad, struggling up the hill through the mud and blasted stumps on his short powerful legs. He guessed that Connolly would put out that much effort for only one thing: beer.

Connolly stopped to catch his breath and then shouted, "Hey, Jayhawk. You just get to stand around now that they made you XO?"

Hawke smiled at hearing his own Boston accent. He let out a deep-throated growl and raised his right hand, curling his fingers over like talons in what everyone in the company knew as the hawk power sign, a parody of the black power fist or the antiwar protesters' peace sign, depending on which political movement Hawke wished to satirize at the time. He roared, "Conman, I can do anything I want. I'm a second lieutenant." He started shadowboxing and then raised both fists above him like a winning prizefighter and shouted, "I'm Willy Pep. I'm in round thirteen of my famous comeback fight." Then he went into a dance, arms above his head, first and second fingers still curved like talons.

A few Marines on the lines down below him turned their heads. Once they saw it was Jayhawk doing the hawk dance they went back to staring over their rifle barrels at the wall of jungle, quite used to him.

Hawke stopped his antics. His eyes went blank. The bluegrass tune came back to him: "Men have tried and men have died to climb the Matterhorn." The five-string banjo would come on strong behind the wailing fiddle and the high-pitched Appalachian voices would rise in an east Tennessee lament, "Matterhorn. Matterhorn." Hawke wanted out of the bush. He wanted to hold a girl who smelled nice and felt soft. He wanted to go home to his mom and dad. He knew, however, that he wouldn't leave Fitch and the rest of Bravo Company with three boot butterbars until they were safely broken in or dead, the only two possibilities for new second lieutenants in combat.

Connolly finally reached Hawke and, gasping for air, asked, "Hey, when we going to get in some class six?"

"Conman, I knew it. Do I look like a fortune-teller to you?"

"The chopper going to make it in?"

"You must really think I do look like a fortune-teller," Hawke answered. "And if your squad could do something besides litter the jungle with Kool-Aid packages and Trop bar wrappers, maybe we'd find that gook machine gun so the zoomies will fly us in some Foxtrot Bravo."

"I don't want to find no gook machine gun."

"I could hardly have guessed."

"Hey, Jayhawk."

"What?" Hawke never minded being called by his nickname, as long as they were out in the bush.

"Troops got to have mail."

"Thanks. You fucking Dear Abby or something?"

"I *wish* I was fucking Dear Abby."

"She's too old for you. Get back to your herd, Connolly."

"You get your ass promoted to XO and suddenly we're cattle."

"Suck out."

"How come they didn't make you skipper? You got more time in the bush than Fitch."

"Because I'm a second lieutenant and Fitch is a first lieutenant."

"That don't cut no ice with me."

"Well, you're not Big John Six, so no one cares what you think. And you won't be Big John Bravo One-One Actual if you don't quit pestering me."

"So relieve me of my command and send me home in disgrace." Connolly turned away, heading downhill, hitching his too-large trousers up around his waist. The dragging cuffs were ragged and filthy from being stepped on.

Hawke smiled affectionately at Connolly's back. But then he thrust his hands into his pockets, and the smile turned to a wince as the pocket edges scraped the jungle rot. He watched Connolly heading back to the lines in the gloom, passing Mellas, who was climbing up toward him. He sighed and, methodically but very firmly, began to smash the stick against a log until it broke. What he really wanted to do was crawl out of his wet, filthy clothes and curl up into a small unconscious ball. Then the song came back.

Mellas knew Hawke had seen him coming up to talk, but Hawke had turned away to climb the short distance to the flattened landing zone, the LZ, without him. He felt a twinge of anger at the unfairness with which guys like Hawke and Bass treated him, just because they'd gotten here before he had. Everyone had to be new sometime. Feeling like a kid trying to catch up with his older brother, he continued to climb. He saw Hawke join the small group of Marines who had gathered around Fisher and someone he thought he recognized as the company gunny: Staff Sergeant . . . somebody. God, the names. He should be putting them in a notebook to memorize.

When he reached the LZ, panting for breath, Mellas could see that Fisher was in severe pain. Fisher would sit on his pack, then lie on his side next to it, then stand up, then repeat the motions again. Hawke was telling a story and had everyone laughing except Fisher, though Fisher was smiling gamely. Mellas envied Hawke's ease with people. He hesitated, not sure how to announce his presence. Hawke solved his problem by greeting him first. "Hey, Mellas. Just had to see how Fisher managed to get himself medevaced without getting a scratch on him, huh?" Fisher forced a smile. "I know you've met the gunny, Staff Sergeant Cassidy." Hawke indicated a man who Mellas thought must be in his late twenties, given his hard-used face and rank. Cassidy had cut himself, and the infected cut was oozing watery pus. Putting together the pepperish red skin tone, the name, and the hillbilly accent, Mellas pegged him as redneck Scots-Irish.

Cassidy simply nodded at Mellas and looked at him with narrow blue eyes, obviously appraising him.

Hawke turned to the others. "For those of you not in First Herd, this is Lieutenant Mellas. He's an oh-three." When Mellas's request to be an air traffic controller with the air wing had been turned down he'd been assigned his military occupational specialty, or MOS: 0301, infantry officer, inexperienced. If he was still alive in six months he would be anointed 0302, infantry officer, experienced. All Marine infantry specialties were designated by zero-three followed by different pairs of numbers: 0311, rifleman; 0331, machine gunner. Zero-three, called "oh-three," was dreaded by many Marines because it meant certain combat. Every other MOS was designed to support oh-three. It was the heart and soul of the Marine Corps. Few attained senior command who didn't hold it.

There were polite murmurs of "Sir" and "Hello, sir" and obvious relief that Mellas was an infantry officer and not another supply or motor transport officer. General Neitzel, the current commanding general, had decided that since every Marine was a trained rifleman, it followed logically that every Marine officer should have experience as a rifle platoon commander for at least ninety days. The flaw in the general's logic was that after a non-infantry officer had made the inevitable mistakes of any new officer in combat, all of which were paid for by the troops under his command, he would be transferred back to his primary military occupation in the rear, subjecting the troops to breaking in yet another new officer and dying because of the new officer's mistakes.

Mellas knew that Hawke had done him a favor by telling the group that he was a grunt like them. Some of his earlier annoyance at Hawke dissipated. He was beginning to learn that this was a typical reaction to Hawke; people just couldn't stay mad at him very long.

Mellas joined Hawke and Cassidy, looking down at Fisher. Hawke went on talking quietly, but now only to Mellas and Cassidy, even though everyone, including Fisher, could hear him. "I just sent Fredrickson down to ask for an emergency medevac. If we don't get him out in a couple of hours I don't know what will happen." Fisher was watching Hawke and Mellas intently.

Mellas turned to Fisher. "Hang in there, Tiger." Mellas was trying to be jolly but couldn't repress a feeling of annoyance that he was losing an experienced squad leader.

"I'm hanging, Lieutenant. I sure would like a piss, though. At least I'm finally getting Lindsey here out to Hong Kong." Fisher was referring to a forlorn-looking Marine from Third Platoon, also clothed in rotting castoffs.

Lindsey smiled at Fisher. He had been sitting on the landing zone for three days, waiting for a helicopter to take him on his R & R. "You'd have to have your insides shot out and a will made out to the pilot before one of them would come out to this cocksucking mountain."

"There it is," Fisher replied. The phrase was much-used by stoic grunts everywhere. He'd bitten off the last word in a spasm and now he began to moan. Mellas turned away. Lindsey watched Fisher. It was clear he'd seen pain before.

Hawke squatted down next to Fisher. "You'll be OK, man. Hurts, doesn't it? We just put you down for an emergency. They'll get a bird out here now. You don't think one of those zoomies would miss his movie back at the airfield in Quang Tri, do you?"

Fisher smiled and then arched his back in an uncontrollable spasm, trying to take the pressure off.

"Why the hell did they take so long calling in an emergency?" Mellas asked.

Hawke looked at him, a slight smile on his face. "Whoa. Peevish this afternoon." He softened. "You call in too many emergencies and you get a reputation for crying wolf. The dispatcher turns your emergencies into priorities and the priorities become routines. Then when you really do have an emergency, you don't get any birds. If you think I'm kidding just stick around awhile."

"Do I have any choice?"

"My boy, you're green but you learn fast." It came out as an imitation of W. C. Fields, which irritated Mellas, but clearly the kids liked it.

"I always was quick."

Hawke turned to the Marine waiting for his R & R. "Hey, Lindsey, go down and get the senior squid."

Lindsey wearily got to his feet and looked down at Fisher. "What'll I tell him?" he asked Hawke.

"Tell him Fisher's getting bad." Hawke didn't seem to mind explaining what Mellas considered to be fully apparent facts.

Lindsey jogged off down the hill toward the command post.

"How come Lindsey gettin' out of the bush and not Mallory?" The Marine who asked the question was round-faced, black, with a droopy

Ho Chi Minh mustache and small light patches on his face from some skin problem. Everything got quiet. Mellas's political antenna was fully extended.

"You say 'sir' when you're talking to an officer," Cassidy said. His voice held the authority of a Marine drill instructor combined with plain dislike.

The Marine swallowed, hesitated. Hawke cut in quickly, looking at him steadily. "China, this isn't the time or place."

"That's right. They's never no time, no place for the black man."

"Sir," Hawke said quietly, before Cassidy could say anything. Mellas could see that Cassidy was angry but keeping his mouth closed because Hawke had taken control.

There was a moment of inner battle on China's part. "Sir," he finally answered.

Hawke was silent. He simply looked at China. China stood his ground, obviously waiting for an answer to his question. Two of Fisher's friends, who were black and stood nearby, unconsciously moved closer together.

"*Sir*," China said. "With all due respect, *sir,* the Marine is askin' why Lance Corporal Mallory, who is sufferin' from headaches and possible brain damage, isn't being skyed out a here with Lance Corporal Lindsey, who is sufferin' from lack of female companionship."

The question hung in the darkening gray air. Cassidy put his knuckles on his hips and leaned slightly forward, about to explode, when Hawke broke into a chuckle, shaking his head. Someone else tittered. "China, goddamn it, why are you breaking our balls up here in the fucking rain when you know full well that"—Hawke held up a finger—"first, none of us are sure if Mallory actually has headaches, including you, unless you got a medical degree recently and I missed it, and second"—he held up a second finger—"even if he did, he can still function fully in combat, or at least as fully as Mallory was ever able to function in combat, and three"—now his thumb was added—"as I was saying about calling in medevacs when they aren't really needed, and four"—he folded his thumb back and switched to four fingers—"adding an extra hundred-sixty pounds plus his gear at this altitude with no idea what the loading is on the bird already could mean risking that no one gets out of the bush."

"Lindsey weigh a hundred sixty pounds."

"Sir," Hawke added. Hawke's insistence on the "sir" had as little personal animosity in it as a mother's insistence on "may I" in place of her child's "can I."

"Sir," China said.

"He's kind of got a point," Mellas said. It couldn't hurt to have the blacks know he wasn't prejudiced.

Hawke turned to look at Mellas, his mouth dropping open. China looked at Mellas, too, his own surprise evident but better concealed. Still, Mellas could see that he'd scored a point there. He could also see that he'd lost one with the gunny, Cassidy. Cassidy's face had paled and his eyes looked like small blue stones.

Hawke did not try to conceal his exasperation. He addressed both Mellas and China. "Lindsey's been in the bush eleven months, Mallory three. Lindsey's been waiting on the LZ for three days and if he doesn't get out before we push off on the op, he'll miss his R & R altogether. Lindsey's never complained about shit and all we've heard from Mallory is nothing but complaints. If we let Mallory go, then anyone else can go to the rear anytime *they tell us* that they hurt someplace. Christ, we all hurt someplace. You know as well as I do why it ain't gonna nevah hoppin." Hawke's last three words, a parody of a Vietnamese accent, were spoken slowly and directly to China.

Mellas felt his face redden and wished it wouldn't, making it redden even more. He saw China glance quickly at the two brothers, but he could see that they had gone neutral. Then China looked at him. Mellas kept his face expressionless, his lips pressed shut.

After a moment's hesitation, China gave in. "Just pointin' out a inconsistency, Lieutenant Hawke," China said.

"Yeah, I heard."

Fisher began to moan and Hawke and China both turned to look at him, glad to use the moaning to pull back from the confrontation. Cassidy turned his back on the group and walked off the LZ.

"Oh, goddamn it, Lieutenant Hawke, I have to piss bad. Oh, shit.

Why aren't they here?" Fisher was barely short of crying. "Oh, fuck those bastards. Fuck those bastards." He tried to rise, attempting to relieve the pressure, then gave a short fierce cry that he clamped off with his teeth. Hawke caught him before he fell over. Fisher grimaced and said, "Shit. I can't stand up or lay down neither."

"Hang on, Fisher, they'll have you out in no time," Hawke said. He sat down on Fisher's pack, putting his hands under Fisher's armpits, supporting him halfway between lying and standing, taking most of Fisher's weight.

Mellas felt left out again—and stupid. He knew full well why he had stuck his foot in his mouth, but he hadn't thought ahead that by putting in his two cents' worth of racial equity he would invite Hawke's rather solid rebuke in front of so many people. Still, he guessed that his comment would work its way around the company. He didn't regret that he'd laid out his politics; he just regretted that he'd been so inept. Then he started to question whether it would look better to be up on the LZ with Fisher or back down on the lines with his platoon or doing something with the company commander, Lieutenant Fitch, to help the medevac. He decided that it would be best to keep quiet and not ask too many questions.

Hawke looked anxiously at the lowering clouds, then down the hill toward the lines. "Got all your mail ready to go?" he asked without looking at Mellas.

It took a moment for Mellas to realize that Hawke was talking to him. "Yeah," he said. "You're sitting on it. It's all in Fisher's pack."

A few minutes later Sheller, the senior squid, and Lieutenant Fitch, the skipper, came up on the LZ from the company command post. Fitch looked small, almost catlike, next to Sheller. When they reached Fisher, Fitch looked at him briefly and then turned to Mellas and Hawke. He was wearing his half-merry, half-mischievous look, accentuated by the dapper mustache he was cultivating. "Looks like Fisher's gone and fucked himself up good, doesn't it?" he said. He turned to Fisher. "How'd you manage to do this after what you brought back in your dick from

Taipei? I've heard of being a carrier, but you're something else." He turned back and waited with the others as Sheller timed Fisher's pulse.

When Sheller joined them, his face was troubled. "Skipper, if we don't get him out in another hour it's going to be dark and he's going to come apart. His heart is already racing, even with the morphine. I don't have anything to give him except more morphine and, well, too much of it . . . you know. So I'm holding off on a second syrette. In case."

"In case what?" Fitch asked.

"In case I have to do something here."

No one said anything until Fitch broke the silence. "What do you do if the chopper doesn't make it?" he asked.

"The only thing I can think of is try and cut a hole so's he can relieve the pressure. He isn't going to like that."

"I don't think in another hour he'll care very much," Hawke said.

"What's the story on the bird?" Mellas asked.

"Same-same," Fitch replied. "The only way they'll get here is to flat-hat under the clouds right up the side of the mountain. Let's hope they have enough room." He paused. "And light," he added softly.

"I'm going to need a place to work on him that's cleaner than the LZ, Skipper," Sheller said. "I can't do it in the mud." He looked pale and was breathing shallowly. "Also, I'll need lots of light, so it'll have to be pretty lightproof."

"Use my hooch. Snik and I can rig something else if he has to stay the night," Fitch said, referring to Relsnik, the battalion radio operator.

"Oh, Jesus no, Skipper." It was Fisher, who had been listening to them all along. "They got to get me out."

"Don't worry," Fitch said. "If we have to operate we'll take a picture of it before we start. That way you'll have some proof to back up your stories." Fisher managed to grin. Mellas was fidgeting, moving his weight from foot to foot.

Fitch turned to Mellas. "It'll be dark pretty soon. We'd better have our actuals meeting in about zero five so we can at least see to write."

"OK, Skipper," Mellas said, again feeling unsure whether he should stay with Fisher or go with Fitch. He took another look at Fisher. "You take it easy, Fisher," he said. Fisher nodded. Mellas followed Fitch.

* * *

They slid sideways on their boots, skiing in the mud down the steep hill, and arrived in front of the company command post. The CP was a hooch like all the others, two ponchos draped over communication wire. This one, however, was distinguished from the rest by dirt piled up against its lower edges to stop wind and light leaks, and by a large two-niner-two radio antenna waving slightly in the monsoon air.

Fitch was combing his hair before a steel shaving mirror wedged in a crack in a blasted tree stump. Rain started to fall with more intensity. Fitch put the comb in his back pocket and crawled into the entrance of the hooch, followed immediately by Hawke. Mellas hesitated, unsure if he was invited.

"Jesus Christ, Mellas," Hawke shouted. "Ain't you got enough sense to come out of the fucking rain?"

Mellas squeezed into the small shelter. Two radio operators were also inside, one manning the battalion radio net, the other the company net. A single candle cast flickering shadows on the sagging poncho roof. Three rubber air mattresses covered with camouflage poncho liners lay side by side. The edges of the hooch were filled with rifles, canteens, ammunition, and packs. A *Seventeen* magazine, a month-old *Time,* and a Louis L'Amour western lay scattered near the radios. Mellas didn't know where to put his muddy boots. He eventually sat back against a pack with his feet sticking out of the hooch's opening.

Fitch introduced the two radiomen to Mellas, who immediately forgot their names, and asked one of them to call the platoon commanders for the actuals meeting. The subsequent radio exchange between the company headquarters and the three platoons, from Fitch's request to its completion, took less than twenty seconds. Mellas, who had been feeling that the company radio operators needed more discipline, was impressed.

Hawke turned to Fitch. "Conman just slipped me the word that China's stirring up the brothers again and just now I had a little one-on-one with him up at the LZ." He looked at Mellas. "Along with some help." Mellas looked down at the mud.

"Ahh, fuck," Fitch said. "What now?"

"Right now, R & R quotas. It's all bullshit." Hawke turned to Mellas. "Hey, Mellas, did Top Seavers say anything to you about Top Angell over at Charlie Company swapping two Taipeis for a Bangkok for Parker?"

Mellas's stomach gave a lurch. He vaguely remembered Seavers asking him to pass along something about R & R quotas to Hawke, but at the time it had been meaningless and he didn't want to look foolish by asking to clear it up. "No, I don't recall him saying anything about it," he lied coolly. He also didn't want to look foolish again in front of Hawke.

"Huh. Well, maybe we can get through to him on Big John Relay tonight."

"Have you had racial problems here in the company?" Mellas asked, switching the subject.

"Naw, not really," Hawke answered. "Oh, a couple of numbnuts bitch a lot and keep things stirred up. Out here the splibs can't bitch any more than the chucks. We're all fucking niggers as far as I can tell."

"Who's this China?"

"He's our local H. Rap Brown, our very own black radical," Fitch said, smiling, "otherwise known as Lance Corporal Roland Speed. But he doesn't like anyone to call him that. Cassidy hates him, but he's a good machine gunner and he hasn't caused any real trouble yet. We got our white bigots, too." Fitch was looking at his two radio operators.

The operator who talked to the battalion, Relsnik, looked at Fitch. "I can't help it, sir. You didn't grow up next to them like me and Pallack did back in Chicago. If you did, you'd hate 'em too. I mean most of the black guys out here are decent. I even like some of them. But they're individuals. As a race, I hate 'em."

Fitch shrugged his shoulders and looked at Mellas. "You can't beat the position for logic."

The two radiomen went back to their magazines.

Down at the lines, Private First Class Tyrell Broyer, who had come in on the same chopper as Mellas and Goodwin, threw his small folding shovel into his fighting hole and gave it the finger. His hands and fingers, still not hardened to the bush, were cut from stringing barbed wire, blistered from hacking with the machete, and crisscrossed with infected cuts made by sharp jungle grasses. He'd returned from stringing wire down below the line of fighting holes to find his own hole half filled with a small mudslide.

He looked up at the darkening sky, readjusting his heavy plastic glasses on the bridge of his nose. Fear that he would be caught without protection in the dark quickly moved him back into the hole. He immediately felt ashamed of his fear. He could be lying up on the LZ like that poor guy from Second Squad. He resumed shoveling, trying to ignore the pain from a ripped fingernail, until he sensed that someone was squatting on the ground above his hole. He turned to find a pair of bleached-out jungle boots. His eyes moved upward to a dark-skinned knee showing through a small hole in faded utilities. His gaze stopped on the face of a stocky black Marine with a drooping Ho Chi Minh mustache. The visitor clenched his right fist and greeted him, and they went through the handshake dance that was the common greeting between all black Marines, an elaborate rhythmic touching of fists, both knuckles and tops and bottoms, that lasted several seconds.

"Where you from, brother?" the visitor asked when they had finished.

"Baltimore." Broyer looked down at his very small hole, feeling pressure to get it dug before the light faded and he would be left exposed. His plastic glasses slipped down his nose again and he quickly pushed them back up.

"Don't worry about the fuckin' hole, man. You dig enough of those motherfuckers in the next thirteen months to fill a lifetime. Got a cigarette?"

"Yeah." Broyer reached into his pocket and pulled out a small C-ration cigarette package. He offered it to the stranger, who was smiling at him as if enjoying some sort of joke. He noticed that the stranger was afflicted with vitiligo, which left pigmentless white patches on his face and arms.

"M' name's China," the stranger said. "Just thought I'd get around seein' some a the new brothers." China lit the cigarette and took in a slow breath. "What's you name, brother?"

"Broyer."

"Shit, man. You real name, not you slave name."

"Tyrell," Broyer said, wondering if that was a slave name, too. He was relieved when China said nothing. "You in First Platoon?" Broyer asked.

"Naw. Second Herd. Gun Squad. I get around a lot, though. Sort of the welcome wagon, you know?" China laughed a wheezy giggle. "What you think of those two chuck lieutenants come in with you the other day?"

"Don't know them. They came into VCB on the chopper after we already got there on the convoy."

"Figures," China said offhandedly. He waited for Broyer to go on.

"They didn't seem too bad. The one's sort of a country dude, talking about hunting and stuff. The other one seems decent. Sort of has a stick up his rear though. Joe College dude."

"Uh-huh." China looked out at the jungle, barely ten meters downhill from where they were talking. Broyer followed China's gaze to the wall of foliage. It was being laboriously pushed back with K-bars and entrenching tools by other members of Broyer's platoon. A few stood guard in their holes, rifles and magazines carefully laid out in front of them, scanning the dark tree line.

"You think we'll get hit here?" Broyer asked.

"Shit, man. You think the gooks crazy 'nough to want this motherfuckin' place? They got better things to do with they time. Shit, man." China smiled at him.

Broyer laughed softly, looking down at his entrenching tool.

"Look brother," China said. "Don'chew worry. I got one more new brother to see 'fore the actuals meeting is over and I gotta get back to my poz, but I see you later, OK? You settle down soon. We all scared, but you get used to bein' scared. You need to talk with a brother, you come on over." They went through the handshake dance. Broyer was glad he'd asked a friend at boot camp to teach it to him one night when they were both on fire watch and everyone else was asleep.

*   *   *

The actuals assembled in the twilight outside First Lieutenant Fitch's hooch. A light mist obscured the distinction between their shadowy silhouettes, further intensifying Mellas's discomfort in not being able to remember their names.

Mellas had barely spoken to the Third Platoon commander, Second Lieutenant Kendall, recently of the Fifteenth Motor Transportation Battalion. This was not by any choice of his own: there simply had been no time to talk. Kendall had sandy curly hair and wore yellow-tinted wraparound glasses that he kept touching as he talked. Mellas noted that he wore a simple gold wedding band.

Second Lieutenant Goodwin, who had been with Mellas at the Basic School and had come in with him on the chopper, was jostling up against his platoon sergeant, Staff Sergeant Ridlow, muffling a guffaw about something. Goodwin was wearing a bush cover on his head. Mellas felt a small pang of envy. The first day Mellas and Goodwin had drawn their gear in Quang Tri, Goodwin had exchanged his stateside billed cap for the floppy camouflage bush cover and looked as if he'd worn it all his life. Mellas had put one on, too, stared at himself in the mirror, and, feeling he looked foolish, stuffed it in a seabag to take home as a souvenir if he made it back. Several days later, just moments after they had arrived at Matterhorn, Mellas again confronted his envy of Goodwin. It happened when the skipper, Lieutenant Fitch, crisply announced that Mellas would go with Sergeant Bass. Fitch added that Bass had done a hell of a job running the platoon in the interim between Hawke's moving up to executive officer and Mellas's arrival. Fitch then assigned Goodwin to Second Platoon with Staff Sergeant Ridlow, whom he described as competent but a little lax. Mellas knew instantly that Fitch thought Goodwin was the better officer because he'd given Goodwin the tougher assignment. Fitch hadn't even asked about their Basic School records, where they went to college, or anything else. It seemed unfair.

Mellas was brought back to the present when he noticed a pale ash-colored German shepherd with odd reddish ears that was lying in the mud panting, head up, and staring at him. The dog's handler, a lean Marine with a large drooping mustache like that of an ancient Celtic warrior, was asleep next to the dog, a camouflage bush cover pulled over his eyes. Others in the CP group—the enlisted forward air controller, always called FAC-man; the senior squid, Sheller; and the enlisted artillery forward observer, Daniels—were sitting in a small group, eating C-rations, just close enough to hear what was going on in the actuals meeting but far enough away to not be part of it.

"All right, let's get going," Hawke said. "The weather forecast is more of the same shit." Hawke paused. "Again." People laughed. "We still don't know what the fuck Alpha and Charlie companies are doing in the bush, or when Delta and us are supposed to flip-flop with them. You've all probably got the word that Alpha did take four Coors." Coors was radio code for dead. "Don't know any names yet. Word is they got hit strung out in a river." Hawke hurried on, paging through a pocket-size hard-covered green notebook. "No word on R & R quotas yet. Who's got palace guard tomorrow? I nearly got drowned in the trash when the wind picked up this afternoon."

Kendall raised his hand.

"OK, Kendall. Police it up. We'll have rats if we don't." Hawke looked up at the sky, squinting against the drizzle. "Correction. More rats. It's already Rat Alley up here." He looked down at his notebook, sheltering it close against his damp sweatshirt. "I hear battalion wants to set up here once we get the cannon cockers in, so get everyone shaved and looking decent before they show up and start screaming."

Goodwin's platoon sergeant, Ridlow, exploded. "If they'd fly in some fucking water maybe we'd be more likely to clean up." His gravelly voice faded off into a mutter about how fucked up it was to always be short of water in a fucking monsoon, and how fucking fucked up the fucking country was. He spat at the ground and wiped a week's growth of beard with the back of one large hand. His other hand rested on his hip next to his Smith & Wesson .44 Magnum revolver. The first thing Goodwin had done when they'd been introduced was ask to see it; they'd hit it off immediately.

Hawke was looking at the sky, letting Ridlow get it out of his system. "Well," he said, "since there's no *pertinent* comments, I guess that's about all I've got. Oh, yeah, get your needs lists in to Gunny Cassidy so when the birds do start bringing in the arty battery we can get some supplies. Gunny Cassidy?"

"Nothing, sir," Cassidy said. "Just you people give me your head count before you leave."

"Senior Squid?" Hawke asked.

"Uh, no, sir. Just make sure the platoon corpsmen get their medical supply needs down on your lists so I can get the battalion aid station to put them on the chopper."

Bass snorted. "They do that automatically."

Sheller looked at Bass and pressed his lips together tightly. In the moment of hesitation Hawke cut in. "OK, any bitches, gripes, grievances, needs, or solicitations before the skipper goes?"

"Mallory wants to request mast again," Bass said. "Says he's got a headache that won't go away and the squids are fucking with him by keeping him in the bush."

"If the puke didn't play that goddamned jungle music so loud he wouldn't have a sore head," Cassidy muttered.

"That's Jackson with the music," Bass said. "From my herd. He's a good Marine." Cassidy looked steadily at Bass, and Bass looked steadily back at Cassidy. Cassidy said nothing more but gave an almost imperceptible nod that said, If you say it's so, Sergeant Bass, then it's so. Mellas, his antennae up, knew instantly that these two men were cut from the same green cloth.

"Maybe we ought to just do Mallory a favor and break his head all the way for him," Ridlow muttered. He looked quickly at his platoon commander, Goodwin, and then broke into a cackle. The other sergeants and Goodwin did as well. Mellas smiled, although he didn't like the overtones.

Fitch sighed, realizing he'd have to deal with it. "I'll talk to Mallory," he said. "But you warn him, Mellas, that he'd better have a good story."

"Mallory's already up for the Pulitzer Prize for fiction with his last story," Hawke said. Hawke looked around. "Anything else?" No one said anything. He turned to Goodwin. "Try and keep your machine gunner, China, busy. OK? The less visiting time he has the better."

Cassidy snorted. "They want to see black power? Tell them to look down the black barrel of my fucking Smith & Wesson Model 29." Ridlow cackled again.

Hawke looked wearily at Cassidy and Ridlow. "China may be a dumb kid, but I'd take him seriously." Ridlow glanced sideways at Goodwin, then over to Cassidy. No one said anything. "It's all yours, Skipper," Hawke said.

"Right." Fitch's head came up. He'd been sitting on a log, dangling his feet. His small, handsome face looked tired. "Big John Six went bugfuck over the radio again about the gook machine gun." Big John Six was Lieutenant Colonel Simpson, the battalion commander and Fitch's boss. He'd promised his own boss, Colonel Mulvaney, the regimental commander, that Mulvaney could move a howitzer battery to a secure zone. Losing the supply chopper after he said the zone was safe was embarrassing enough, but he'd then promised he'd fix the problem pronto and it was now two full days after the promised date and the zone was still not secure.

"What's he going to do?" Ridlow boomed out. "Cut your hair off and send you to Vietnam?"

Fitch laughed politely at the standard retort, looking down at his swinging feet. "I suppose he could banish me to Okinawa." Okinawa was universally known as the worst possible place to get for R & R. Relations with the Japanese had gotten so tense that the brass had forbidden nearly every activity for which anyone went on R & R. When the laughter died down, Fitch pointed into the fog that swirled over the trees to the southwest and said, referring to the enemy, "I think Nagoolian is going to head over to that ridgeline tomorrow. He used it on the first day, and he's never used the northwest one, so he probably figures we'll be looking on the northwest one for him. Bass, you were down there. What's that southwest finger look like?"

"It's like the rest of the fucking place. Took us three hours to make eight hundred meters. Had to use machetes to get through. Pretty goddamn hard to sneak up on someone like that."

"That's why he'll be there. Mellas, send a baseball team over the top of the ridge and look around. If you don't find them, at least it'll move them out away from the main approach path."

"Aye, aye, Skipper." Mellas was jotting down notes in his own green notebook and mentally reviewing the current company radio code, which was often used for direct conversation. A baseball team was a squad of twelve men, a basketball team was a fire team of four men, a football team a platoon of forty-three men. "Can I get some maps for my squad leaders?"

Everyone burst into laughter. Mellas reddened.

"Mellas," Hawke said, "it'd be easier for you to date Brigitte Bardot than to get any more maps than we've got. You don't want to know what I had to trade for the one you've got, and I don't want to have to say it in front of the skipper."

"It's true," Fitch added. "Maps are in short supply. Sorry. Just another inch of the green dildo." He quickly went on. "Goodwin?"

"Yeah, Jack?" Mellas winced at Goodwin's casualness in addressing the company commander as Jack, especially since that wasn't his name. If Fitch noticed, he didn't let on.

"I want one of your baseball teams out on the south finger, then work up the draw between there and the east ridge. I want you to check out the crashed bird on Helicopter Hill on the way back. See if Nagoolian's been nosing around. You other two platoon commanders send your red dogs out wherever you want," he said, using the radio brevity code for any squad-size patrol.

Fredrickson broke in on the circle, breathing hard. "He's starting to scream. Lindsey's got a shirt stuffed in his mouth. It'll be too loud to keep down in a few minutes. We're going to have to cut."

Mellas looked at Fitch and then over at Sheller, whose throat was working underneath his double chin. Sheller rubbed his hands together as if to warm them. Fitch was looking at him, hard, his lower lip over his upper.

"It's got to be done, Jim," Hawke said quietly.

Fitch nodded, still looking at the senior squid. "How do you feel, Sheller?" Mellas was surprised to hear the senior squid called by his name.

"I don't have a catheter, Skipper, and trying to ram something up the urethra to clean out the leech would just make a mess of it. The only thing I can think to do is cut into the penis from the bottom side. Two cuts. You can see where his urethra's swollen right up to the leech. Cut one is just up from there on the bladder side to relieve the pressure. I'd try to keep it small. Stick in a piece of IV tubing to keep the cut open and keep him drained until we get him out of here." Sheller fished into his pockets and brought out a freshly cut piece of tubing. "I'll need to sterilize it and have some floor space to work on, sir. I can grease it with bacitracin to help it slide into the cut."

"That's only one cut," Fitch said.

"Yeah. OK." Sheller swallowed. "Cut two. I'd cut into the leech to bleed it and kill it. We don't want it moving upstream." He looked at the silent group, realizing it was all on him. "I'll use Fredrickson. It'll make Fisher feel better if it's a squid he's used to."

Hawke looked grimly satisfied. Bass kept looking at Sheller and then back to the skipper with no emotion on his face.

"OK, Squid. Go ahead on it." Fitch spoke crisply with no hint of doubt. He turned to Hawke. "Ted, go up and tell those guys to move Fisher down here."

Sheller moved off and crawled into the CP hooch without saying anything. He started to clear it out. The others, except Mellas, Hawke, Fitch, and Cassidy, returned to their positions.

The entire hill was quiet, on the 100 percent alert that happened every dusk and dawn. Mellas watched Fredrickson and Lindsey talking to Fisher as they began to move him off the landing zone on a stretcher made by wrapping a poncho between two tree limbs. Fisher suddenly cried out and Lindsey cursed quietly. Hawke, who was walking alongside the stretcher, quickly stifled Fisher's cry by placing his hand over his mouth. Mellas walked beside them, figuring it was better to say nothing.

When they reached the CP they pulled Fisher inside the small hooch. Sheller was laying out his kit and lighting candles. Fredrickson removed Fisher's filthy trousers and folded them carefully. Outside the hooch the two radio operators huddled next to their equipment while

Fitch tried to make the entrance lightproof. Hawke and Cassidy sat on the ground, quietly talking.

Inside, Doc Fredrickson looked at Sheller, whose chin was trembling slightly underneath the fat. Fisher was writhing in pain and trying not to scream. Fredrickson crawled behind Fisher, putting his knees on each side of Fisher's head. He then leaned over and put his hands and full weight on Fisher's shoulders. The candles flickered in the draft, casting shadows across the draped ponchos.

"It's going to be OK, Fisher," Fredrickson whispered, bending close to Fisher's face. "It's going to be OK."

"Oh, fuck, Doc, stop it. Stop it from hurting."

"It's going to be OK."

Fredrickson was looking intensely at Sheller, willing him to do it. The senior squid finished lubricating the IV tube, switched it to his left hand, and looked back at Fredrickson across Fisher's body. He picked up a small knife in his right hand and, using his elbows, he spread Fisher's legs and crawled between them. He looked up at Fredrickson again. With anguish on his face he silently mouthed, "I don't know if I'm right."

Fredrickson nodded his head in encouragement. "Do it," he mouthed silently. "Do it."

Fisher started moaning again, arching his back, trying to get his bladder and kidneys off the floor. The senior squid put the knife in the candle flame. Then he poured alcohol on it. There was a slight hiss and the alcohol smell filled the hooch. He lifted Fisher's penis back, pushing it firmly against his stomach. Even that pressure made Fisher scream.

Fredrickson leaned his whole body over Fisher's face, muzzling him, pressing down on his shoulders and upper arms.

Sheller pushed the blade into Fisher's penis. Fisher screamed and Fredrickson put all of his weight on him to keep him from rolling. Blood and urine streamed over the knife blade, the initial burst spraying Sheller's hands and chest. Then Sheller pushed the makeshift catheter up the smooth side of the knife into the incision and quickly slipped the blade out. Urine coursed out of the catheter, flowing over Fisher's hips and crotch, filling the tent with its hot smell, running onto the mud, soaking the nylon poncho liners under Fisher's body.

"Goddamn. Goddamn. Oh, goddamn," Fisher cried, but each "goddamn" lessened in intensity with the lessening force of the coursing urine, until all that could be heard was Fisher's ragged panting and the deep breathing of Fredrickson and Sheller.

Fisher broke the silence. "What would I say if this was a movie?"

Fredrickson shook his head back and forth and snorted a laugh. "Shit, Fisher," he said. Sheller, still breathing hard, merely nodded at Fisher.

Fisher winced and took in a shaky breath. He held it, then let it out all at once and turned his head to the side, looking at the floor of the hooch. "Kind of a mess."

Sheller nodded. "Yeah. Kind of a mess," he said. He was covered in blood and urine. He flicked a glance at Fredrickson, who nodded very slightly. Then Fredrickson suddenly bore down on Fisher with his full weight. Senior Squid took Fisher by surprise and quickly punctured his penis again, this time to pierce the leech and kill it.

Fisher bucked his hips upward, screaming. "Jesus Christ, Squid. What the fuck?" Fredrickson kept his full body weight on him, trying to keep him still.

"Sorry," Sheller said. Blood from the swollen leech was running along the flat of the knife. He pulled it out and took a deep breath. Dark blood oozed from the second cut, mixing with the redder blood and urine from the first.

Sheller sat back on his haunches, his knees under him.

"You fucking done?" Fisher asked.

Sheller nodded yes.

The small hooch, filled with the three young men, the light from the candles, and the warm smell of urine, was quiet.

From outside they could hear FAC-man, the forward air controller, shouting. "Get him up to the LZ. The bird's coming in."

"Now what?" Fisher asked.

"I don't know," Sheller answered. "They get you to Charlie Med. The usual repair work. Infection's the main problem around here. We don't know what got carried in by the leech or on the knife for that matter."

"No, I mean . . ." Fisher hesitated. "You know, later. Back home."

FAC-man poked his head through the ponchos. "I've got the fucking chopper. Get him up on the LZ. What the fuck you waiting for?" He ran off into the dark with his radio on his back, talking to the pilot.

Sheller rolled out of the way as Fitch and Hawke came through the opening of the hooch and grabbed the stretcher. He didn't answer Fisher, using the interruption as an excuse. What would scar tissue do? Infection? Had he cut tubes he didn't even know about? He honestly didn't know what would happen and was fully aware he might have doomed Fisher to be not only childless, but impotent.

Mellas watched the shadows moving back up the hill. The familiar washboard thumping could be heard in the valley below them as the chopper fought for altitude, skimming over the tops of trees beneath the low cloud cover. Then the NVA .51 opened up. It was followed almost immediately by the chopper's two .50-caliber machine guns, firing blindly into the dark jungle to try to suppress the fire. The chopper loomed out of the darkness and slammed into the zone; its crew chief immediately jumped out and yelled at the Marines to get the stretcher on board.

Cassidy, Hawke, Fitch, and FAC-man ran across the LZ with the stretcher and up the ramp of the chopper, the sound of the NVA .51's bullets cracking through the air. Mellas crouched to the ground, thankful he was just below the lip of the LZ, defiladed from the fire. The chopper was moving before the four stretcher bearers were even out of it. It was already airborne as the last dark figure jumped for the ground and ran for the lip of the LZ.

The shadowy bulk of the chopper merged into darkness, the faint glow of its instrument panel disappearing with it into the night. The firing stopped. Mellas rose to a half crouch and glanced back inside the CP hooch. The senior squid was still kneeling over the now deserted space, the front of his utility shirt soaked with urine and blood, his knife in his hand. He was crying and praying at the same time.

CHAPTER
TWO

The light died. Voices were silenced. Darkness and fear replaced light and reason. The whisper of a leaf scraping on bark would make heads turn involuntarily and hearts gallop. The surrounding blackness and the unseen wall of dripping growth left no place to run. In that black wet nothingness the perimeter became just a memory. Only imagination gave it form.

Mellas shivered in his hooch and listened to the whispers of the company communications network. Through the mud he could feel Hamilton shaking but couldn't see him, curled up in a greasy nylon poncho liner. Mellas's own wet undershirt clung to him. At home, he'd snapped at his mother for dyeing it too pale a color. "I'll be spotted a mile away." She had bit her lip to hold back the tears. Mellas had wanted to hug her but didn't.

He had hole-check at 2300 and 0300 to make sure those on watch were awake. Meanwhile, he sat like someone who needs to urinate but doesn't want to leave a warm bed. A rat crept through the vegetation, and Mellas could hear it rustling through discarded C-ration containers. He imagined it dragging its wet belly on the ground. He watched the minute hand on his watch creep its luminous route toward eleven. At exactly eleven, far to the east, he heard what he surmised was an Arc Light mission, B-52s from Guam, flying far to the east and so high they couldn't be seen, dropping hundreds of 500- and 1,000-pound bombs. The bombing could make a small area of suspected enemy troop concentration a furnace of pain and death, but to Mellas it seemed like only sterile thunder without rain. He watched the minute hand creep past eleven. The inner voice of duty won. He strapped on his pistol, put on his helmet, and crawled outside.

Invisible rain struck his cheeks. The warmth from his poncho liner drifted away like a thin cry over stormy water. He headed downhill, slipping in the mud. Then, after groping his way for what seemed far too long a time, he grew frightened that he would overshoot the lines and be killed by his own men. He tripped face forward over a root, grunting, hurting his wrist as he broke his fall. Cold water from the mud worked through his clothing. Blinded, he crept forward on hands and knees, hoping to find the machine-gun position directly downhill from his own hooch. He tried to imagine its occupant, Hippy, who had questionably regulation hair and wore, hanging from his neck, a silver peace medallion that looked curiously like a passenger jet.

A voice, barely audible, floated through the darkness: "Who's that?"

"It's me," Mellas whispered. "Character Mike." He was afraid that if he said "lieutenant" a North Vietnamese soldier lurking just outside the lines would fire on him.

"Who the fuck's character Mike?" the voice whispered back.

"The new lieutenant," Mellas responded, frustrated and realizing that he'd probably made enough noise to be shot anyway. Mellas crawled toward the voice. Suddenly his hand encountered freshly turned clay. He must be near a fighting hole. He felt, rather than saw, a shadowy shape inside his small circle of awareness, barely a foot from his eyes.

"How's everything?" Mellas whispered.

"I keep hearing something down the finger."

"How far?"

"Can't tell."

"If it gets close and you want to throw a Mike-26, make sure you tell me or Jake." Jacobs had replaced Fisher as leader of Mellas's Second Squad.

"I'm in Third Squad."

Mellas was suddenly confused. He peered intently in the direction of the man's face but couldn't make out who it was.

"Who've I got here?" Mellas finally whispered.

"Parker, sir."

Mellas was aghast. He'd crawled in a totally different direction from what he had intended. He tried to visualize Parker and then he remembered that Parker was the one who felt he'd been passed over for his R & R in Bangkok. Sullen.

Then both of them were silent, trying to see in the dark. The spattering rain precluded any hope of hearing somebody moving in the jungle. Mellas felt it plastering his shirt to his back and began to shiver. The noise of his shivering made hearing even harder. Parker shifted his weight impatiently.

Mellas tried to think of something to say to make a connection. "Where you from, Parker?" he whispered.

Parker didn't answer.

Mellas hesitated. He didn't know if Parker was being defiant or was simply afraid to make any more noise. He made a choice, though.

"Parker, I asked you a question."

Parker waited a full three seconds before answering. "Compton."

Mellas didn't know where that was. "Oh," he said. "Is it nice there?"

"I wouldn't call it that."

"Sir," Mellas appended.

"I wouldn't call it that, *sir.*"

Mellas didn't know how to answer. He felt the chance to make a connection with Parker slipping away. He gave it a last shot. "I'm from Oregon, a little logging town on the coast called Neawanna."

"Neawanna?" There was a hesitation. "Sir."

"Yeah. Funny name, huh? Indian name."

Silence.

"I've got to move on," Mellas whispered, sensing Parker's discomfort. "Who's in the next hole to your right?"

Parker did not respond immediately, and Mellas wondered if he too was having a problem keeping all the names straight. Finally Parker whispered, "Chadwick."

"Thanks, Parker." Mellas crawled off toward the next hole. That hadn't gone well, he thought. He felt awkward and incompetent.

The rain, propelled by a sudden gust of wind, blew into his face briefly and then subsided into a slow, steady patter on his helmet. He was crawling through mud on his hands and knees in total darkness, knowing that he had missed his first and second squads completely and would have to double back to pick them up. He sensed another mass. "Chadwick?" he whispered, hoping that Parker had told him the right name. No answer. "Chadwick, it's me, Lieutenant Mellas." His whisper floated across the silence.

It was greeted with a clearly audible sigh of relief. "Jesus fuck, sir, I thought I'd die. I was about to blow your ass away."

It took two hours to cover his platoon's 140 meters of the perimeter. He came back exhausted, his clothing soaked and clotted with mud, leeches clinging to his arms and legs. Twice a night, 389 nights to go.

Several hours later the leader of Mellas's Third Squad, Corporal Jancowitz, watched gray gradually infiltrate the blackness. He was not happy to see morning, because he knew he had to go out on patrol. But he wasn't unhappy, either, because it meant one less day until his R & R in Bangkok, where he'd see Susi again. It also meant that the predawn 100 percent alert was over and he could fix breakfast. He told the squad to stand down and stationed his third fire team on watch.

He took out a can of chopped eggs, added some chocolate from a Hershey Trop bar—a high-melting-point chocolate developed for the jungle—and mixed in some Tabasco and A1 sauce, both of which he'd carefully hoarded from his last R & R. Then he added apricot juice, throwing the apricots and the can into the jungle. He ripped off a small piece of C-4 plastic explosive, placed it on the ground, set the can on top, and lit the explosive. A white hissing flame enveloped the can. Thirty seconds later Jancowitz was spooning the contents into his mouth and thinking about Susi, the Thai bar girl for whom he had extended his tour another six months. The extension had earned him thirty days' leave in Bangkok. They were the best thirty days of his life. Now he'd been back in Nam long enough to earn another week of R & R with

Susi, just days away. When he got back he'd up for his second six-month extension. That would get him thirty more days with Susi. Six months after that and he'd be done, really done, out of the Crotch—the corps— and married, with more than two years' savings to start them out.

Here he was, nineteen, a corporal, and a squad leader. He was up for meritorious promotion to sergeant for the Wind River op. The Jayhawk said he'd try and get his ass sent back to the rear to serve out his second extension, and that looked a lot better than going home to the assholes waving signs and shouting at him. Besides, there wasn't going to be anybody waiting for him. Three months stateside to muster out, then back to Bangkok with nearly three years of pay. Things could be worse. Bass had even said he was counting on Jancowitz to help break in the new lieutenant, now that Fisher was gone.

The new lieutenant was breaking in his new .45 by working the action back and forth. His radio operator, Hamilton, was eating breakfast: ham and lima beans mixed with grape jelly. Mellas wasn't hungry.

"Don't worry, sir, it'll work," Hamilton said, his mouth full.

Mellas looked at the weapon, then put it back in his holster.

"Besides," Hamilton went on, pointing at it with a white plastic spoon, "it ain't worth a fart in a shit fight. I'd have a sawed-off twelve-gauge if I could get one."

Mellas didn't know how to answer. The standard table of equipment, the document that authorized which weapons went to which military occupation specialty, allocated only pistols to officers, on the theory that officers were supposed to be thinking, not shooting. He looked down at his pistol and then over at Fisher's carefully oiled M-16 and bandoleers of magazines, each with eighteen bullets. A magazine was supposed to hold twenty, but kids had died learning that the springs came from the factory too weak to properly feed into the rifle the twenty that were specified. The standard table of equipment was beginning to look impractical. Mellas took Fisher's rifle and started working the mechanism.

"Don't worry, sir, it'll work too," Hamilton said.

Mellas flipped him the bird.

Hamilton ignored this. He chewed contemplatively for a moment and then reached into his pack for the highly treasured Pickapeppa sauce that had been mailed to him from home. He carefully added two drops to the cold ham, grape jelly, and lima beans, stirred them in, and retasted. The new lieutenant still wasn't hungry.

By the time Jancowitz came trudging up the slope to Mellas's hooch, Mellas had his gear on: three canteens, two filled with Rootin' Tootin' Raspberry and one with Lefty Lemon; five hand grenades; two smoke grenades; a compass; a map coated with plastic shelving paper from home; bandages, battle dressing, and halazone; water purification tablets; his pistol; two bandoleers of M-16 magazines; and food cans stuffed into extra socks that were in turn stuffed into the large pockets on the sides of his utility trousers. Some people just hung the socks filled with cans on their backpacks.

He carefully bloused his trousers against his boots with the steel springs to keep the leeches out and stuck a plastic bottle of insect repellent into the wide rubber band circling his new green camouflage helmet cover. He looked at his watch as the tail end of Goodwin's patrol disappeared into the jungle below. He'd never convince Fitch that he was any good if his patrol didn't leave on time.

Jancowitz grinned at Mellas. "Sir, I'd, uh . . ." He hesitated and then tapped the side of his soft camouflage bush cover.

Mellas looked at Hamilton. "The insect repellent," Hamilton said. "The white stands out in the bush. Makes a great target."

"Then what's the rubber band for?" Mellas asked, shoving the bottle into his pocket.

"Beats me, sir," Hamilton answered. "Holds the fucking helmet together, I guess."

"You could put things in it like branches for camouflage," Jancowitz said carefully.

Hamilton giggled, and Mellas smiled tightly. It wasn't fair. He'd seen Marines on television with squeeze bottles of repellent strapped to their helmets. He'd carefully noted the details. Suddenly it dawned on him that the television shots were all around villages, where the people with cameras were more likely to be, and there was no wall of dark green jungle on all sides.

"We're all set, sir," Jancowitz said. "Just waiting for Daniels." Lance Corporal Daniels was the enlisted FO, the artillery battery's forward observer. Fitch assigned him to the patrols that he felt might need what little support they could get from Andrew Golf, the distant battery at fire support base Eiger.

As Jancowitz led the way down to Third Squad's sector, the sound of Marvin Gaye singing "I Heard It Through the Grapevine" broke the morning stillness. Mellas could see the Marines of Third Squad standing around, some nervously fiddling with their gear, all apparently ready before Jancowitz had gone to get Mellas. A group of black Marines were huddled together smoking cigarettes. At their center was a well-built, serious-looking young man who was squatting over a portable 45-rpm record player.

"OK, Jackson, cut the sounds," Jancowitz said briskly.

Without looking up, Jackson raised his hand, palm toward Jancowitz. "Hey, man, cool off. The a.m. show ain't over yet."

Several of the group laughed softly, including Jancowitz, who quickly glanced at Mellas to see if Mellas objected.

Mellas didn't know whether he should object or not. He looked back at Jancowitz and Hamilton for a cue.

Bass broke the momentary impasse by walking up behind them. "Why don't you play real music, like Tammy Wynette, instead of that fucking jungle music?"

"Beats washtubs and broomsticks," Jackson said, waiting for the laughter that followed. Mellas joined in awkwardly. Jackson looked up, hearing an unfamiliar voice. Recognizing Mellas, he immediately turned off the record player and stood up. The small group got serious, attentive, all business, crushing cigarettes in the mud.

"Sorry, sir," Jackson said. "I didn't know you were there."

What struck Mellas about Jackson was that he clearly wasn't sorry. He was just being polite. He looked at Mellas with an openness that declared he was quite capable of defending himself, without being defensive. Mellas smiled. "That's OK. Hate to stop the show."

Bass, satisfied that Mellas was in good hands with Jancowitz, grunted and moved off to join Second Squad to bird-dog Jacobs on his first day leading a patrol.

"Where's Shortround?" Jancowitz asked, looking around.

Jackson sighed and pointed toward a pair of ponchos that covered a hole dug into the side of the hill. "He had listening post last night. I guess he's still eating."

"Shortround!" Jancowitz shouted. "Goddamn it. Get your ass down here."

There was a grunt. A head, still unseen, poked clumsily into the low-hung poncho. Two short legs, covered by large dirty trousers, backed out of the hooch. A short kid with curly brown hair and an over-size nose grinned at Jancowitz. Spaghetti sauce was smeared on his face. He wiped it off with large hands stained dark brown with ingrained dirt.

"Hi, Janc," Shortround said brightly, grinning.

Jancowitz turned to Mellas. "Sir, this is Pollini, only we call him Shortround. And it ain't because he's small and fat." A short round was an artillery shell that fell short by mistake, often killing its own men.

Pollini quickly stuffed several Trop bars into his pockets, grabbed his rifle, and joined the group just as Daniels came down the hill from the CP, carrying his radio on his back. Jancowitz introduced him to Mellas, then took the handset from Hamilton's radio and called the CP. "Bravo, this is Bravo One Three. We're moving."

The squad wound its way into the jungle in one long snake—Jancowitz three from the front; Mellas behind him, watching Jancowitz's every move; Daniels behind Mellas. No one spoke. Mellas was thinking that Jancowitz had been in the bush nearly nineteen months. He probably knew more about staying alive than anyone else in the company.

Once the kids were under the trees, the leeches started dropping on them. They tried to knock each leech off before it dug in and drew blood but were usually too late because they were focusing more attention on the jungle, straining to hear, see, or smell the clue that would give them, and not the North Vietnamese, the first shot.

The leeches made full use of their victims. Mellas watched some fall onto the kids' necks and slide under their shirts like raindrops. Other leeches would wriggle on the damp humus of the jungle floor, attach to a boot, then go up a trouser leg, turning from small wormlike objects to bloated blood-filled bags. Occasionally someone would spray insect repellent on a leech and it would fall squirming to the ground, leaving blood trickling down the kid's arm, leg, or neck. During the patrol, Mellas began to take great pleasure in killing the little bastards and watching his own blood spurt out of their bodies.

The fourteen-man snake moved in spasms. The point man would suddenly crouch, eyes and ears straining, and those behind him would bunch up, crouch, and wait to move again. They would get tired, let down their guard. Then, frightened by a strange sound, they would become alert once again. Their eyes flickered rapidly back and forth as they tried to look in all directions at once. They carried Kool-Aid packages, Tang—anything to kill the chemical taste of the water in their plastic canteens. Soon the smears of purple and orange Kool-Aid on their lips combined with the fear in their eyes to make them look like children returning from a birthday party at which the hostess had shown horror films.

They stopped for lunch, setting up a small defensive perimeter. Jancowitz, Mellas, and Hamilton lay flat on the ground next to the radio, eating C-rations. They littered the jungle with the empty cans. Flies and mosquitoes materialized from the heavy air. Mellas doused himself again with repellent. It stung fiercely as it got into his cuts and bites. He found two leeches on his right leg. He burned them alive with paper matches while he ate canned peaches.

Already tired from lack of sleep, Mellas now struggled with physical fatigue from fighting his way through nearly impenetrable brush, slipping up muddy slopes to gain a ridgeline, searching for tracks, searching for clues. He was wet from both sweat and rain. Effort. Weight. Flies. Cuts. Vegetation.

He no longer cared where they were or why. He was glad he was new and Jancowitz was still more or less in charge, though he was ashamed of feeling that way. Three hundred eighty-nine days and a wake-up to go.

At one point they hit a wall of bamboo they couldn't avoid. It lay between them and a checkpoint, a ridgeline where the NVA machine gun might be. They had to hack through it. All security was lost as the kid on point took out a machete and smashed a hole in the bamboo. Soon they were in a bamboo tunnel. The ground sloped upward. It got steeper. They began to slip. The kid with the machete tired and another took his place. They needed an hour to go about 200 meters.

Suddenly, Williams, the point man, went rigid, then slowly sank to one knee, rifle at his shoulder. Steam rose from his back. Everyone froze in position, ears straining, trying to stop the noise of their own breathing. Jancowitz quietly moved forward to find out what was happening. Hamilton, a good radioman, moved up too, as if he were part of Jancowitz's body. Mellas followed.

"You hear that, Janc?" Williams whispered. He was trembling and his forehead was tight with tension. They had stopped on the side of a ridge. A rivulet trickled through thick brush and plants with broad leaves. Mellas strained to hear over the sound of his breath and his pounding heart. Soon he could distinguish soft snorts, muffled coughlike noises, and a cracking and tearing of branches.

"What is it?" Mellas whispered.

"Gook trucks, sir," Daniels said softly. He had slipped up behind Mellas, so quietly that this whisper frightened him. Mellas saw that Daniels was grinning and his mouth was smeared red with Choo Choo Cherry, which heightened the flush of his cheeks.

"Gook trucks?" Mellas asked. "What are you talking about?" He turned to Jancowitz, who was watching him with mild amusement.

"Elephants, sir," Jancowitz said.

"The gooks use them to carry shit," Daniels said.

By this time everyone had relaxed, and the squad was already in the inboard-outboard defense position, every two men alternating the direction of sight. Jancowitz pointed at Pollini and Delgado, a gentle-eyed Chicano kid whom everyone called Amarillo, because it was his hometown. These two reluctantly heaved themselves to their feet and crept out, one on each side of the squad, to act as outposts.

"So?" Mellas asked. He was uncomfortably aware that trouble was coming his way.

"Don't you think we ought to call in a mission, sir?" Daniels asked.

"A fire mission? On some elephants?"

"They're gook transportation, sir."

Mellas looked at Jancowitz. He remembered a major at the Basic School telling him to trust sergeants and squad leaders—they'd been there. The major hadn't mentioned that the sergeants were nineteen-year-old lance corporals.

"He's right, sir," Jancowitz said. "They do use them for hauling shit."

"But they're wild," Mellas said.

"How do you know, sir?"

At this point Daniels chimed in. "We shoot them all the time, sir. You deny the gooners their transportation system."

"But we're at extreme range."

"It's an area target, sir," Daniels answered. An area target was one that covered a general location, such as troops in the field, so accuracy was less of an issue than for a single-point target, like a bunker.

Mellas looked at Hamilton and at Tilghman, who carried the M-79 grenade launcher. They both just stared back. Mellas didn't want to look sentimental or foolish in front of the squad. It was war, after all. Nor did he want to buck a standard operating procedure when he wasn't really sure of his ground. He'd been told to trust his squad leaders. "Well," he began slowly, "if you really do shoot them . . ."

Daniels grinned. He already had his map out, and now he reached for the handset of his radio.

"Andrew Golf, this is Big John Bravo. Fire mission. Over."

In his imagination, Mellas saw the battery scrambling into action as the call for a fire mission came crackling in to its fire control center.

Moments after Daniels relayed the map coordinates and compass bearings, the first shell came through the jungle, sounding like a train speeding through a tunnel. There was a dull thud transmitted through the ground, then a louder shattering crash through the air. Then there was the sound of brush cracking and the movement of heavy frightened bodies. Daniels made a quick adjustment, and a second shell roared. Again the earth moved and the air shattered. After that, the muffled sounds could be heard no more.

Daniels called off the mission. "They'll be to fuck and gone by now," he said, smiling with satisfaction.

Jancowitz didn't want to bother checking for results, since it meant going all the way down in the ravine. To climb back out again would take hours. Mellas agreed.

When they finally struggled back inside the company perimeter, the squad immediately began cleaning weapons and fixing dinner, getting ready for the evening alert and the long night of watch. Jackson started his record player and Wilson Pickett's voice floated across the tiny man-made clearing in the jungle. "Hey, Jude, don't make it bad . . ."

Mellas could barely drag himself up to the CP to report to Fitch. He simply wanted to collapse and sleep. Bass was already in with nothing to report—as was Goodwin, except for some tiger tracks. Ridlow, Goodwin's platoon sergeant, however, had discovered some footprints near a stream. It was impossible to tell how many people had left them. He figured they couldn't be more than two days old; otherwise, the rain would have washed them away.

Mellas listened while Fitch relayed the negative reports to battalion. An entire day of patrols, and all they had proved was that someone was in the jungle, as if a downed helicopter and a bunch of dead crewmen hadn't already proved that. He also listened while Fitch turned in the coordinates of the footprints to the artillery battery for harassment and interdiction—H & I.

When Fitch got off the hook, Mellas asked, "What happens if it's a montagnard?" referring to the indigenous people who had been pushed into the mountains centuries earlier by the invading Vietnamese.

Fitch pursed his lips. "If it is," Fitch said carefully, "then he's got to be working for the NVA. Otherwise, he'd have cleared out or come in to the position."

"I don't know. Maybe," Mellas said.

Hawke was listening while he poured powdered coffee and sugar into a battered cup that he had fashioned from a C-ration pear can by leaving the lid attached and folding it back to make a handle. He poured water from his canteen into the can and placed it on a small wad of C-4 plastic explosive. The cup's lower half had turned steel blue from many heatings.

"There's leaflets all over the fucking place telling people it's a free-fire zone," Fitch said.

"You know they can't read," Mellas said petulantly.

"Shit, Mellas," Hawke cut in. "He knows it. You going to call off your H & I because it might fuck up some lost mountain man?"

"I don't know. I'm the new guy around here," Mellas snapped. He was so tired that he was beginning to regret he'd even brought the subject up.

Hawke lit the C-4 and a brilliant white flame engulfed the can, turning it cherry red and bringing the water to a rapid boil almost instantly. The action stopped the conversation until the flame died. Hawke gingerly touched the makeshift cup, now filled with boiling coffee. "Well, I'll tell you, then," Hawke said. "You don't. Jim's fucked either way. If we get attacked, and he didn't call in H & I, he's shit-canned. If he does call them in and kills a montagnard, he's shit-canned too. Things have changed since Truman left. The buck's sent out here now."

Fitch smiled, thankful for Hawke's support.

Mellas looked at the ground, sorry he'd lost his temper. "You never did say why," he said.

"So you don't get your fucking ass blown away, that's why," Hawke said, softening when he saw Mellas look at the ground. He dabbed at the handle of the cup again and, feeling that it was safe, picked it up with his thumb and forefinger.

"You call off H & I," Fitch said, "and the gooks have access to this mountain like a freeway ramp. It's my fucking troops over any lost mountain man, and it'll stay that way. I decided that a long time ago." Fitch looked quickly up at the darkening sky, seemingly embarrassed over his sudden speech.

Hawke held the steaming coffee up toward Mellas. "Here. Take it."

"No, it's yours," Mellas said.

"I make the fastest cup of coffee in I Corps. This little cup's been with me ever since I got here. It's the ever-flowing source of all that's good and the cure of all ills." He smiled and gestured again for Mellas to take it. "It even cures hot tempers."

Mellas had to smile. He took the cup. The coffee was sweet and good.

Later that night, outside the perimeter in the blackness, Private First Class Tyrell Broyer of Baltimore, Maryland, on his first listening post, lay shivering, flat on his stomach, the rain seeping through his poncho. Jancowitz had paired him with Williams, from Cortell's fire team, a steady kid who'd been raised on a ranch in Idaho. Williams's muddy boots were next to Broyer's face and vice versa, so they protected each other's backs. "What's that noise?" Broyer whispered.

"The wind. Shut up."

Broyer was tempted to start keying the radio's handset frantically, just so someone would talk to them. He didn't care if he made one of the lieutenants mad at him for getting scared. He shivered again. There was a whirring noise. Instantly the two of them stiffened, their rifles pushing out slowly.

"What *is* that noise?" Broyer whispered. "High in the air."

"Don't know. Bats? Shut up, goddamn it."

Williams shifted and his boot hit Broyer's face. Broyer stifled a curse and pushed his glasses back on his nose, aware of an irony—he couldn't see a thing anyway. He slowly pushed Williams's boot away. He put his forehead on his fists to keep his glasses clear of the ground and smelled the damp earth, feeling the cold edge of his helmet against his neck. He grabbed a handful of clay and squeezed it as hard as he could. He wanted to squeeze his fear into the clay so he could throw it away. A gust of wind hit his wet utility shirt, sending a cold shiver along his back. He started praying, asking God to stop the wind and the rain so he could just hear something. It was then that Williams reached out a hand in the dark and gently patted him on the back.

That night, God didn't stop the wind or the rain. The next day, however, the rain did stop for two hours, and six choppers made it in without incident, dumping Marines who were returning from sick leave and R & R, replacements, water, food, and ammunition. Along with that came a large amount of C-4 explosive to help prepare the top of the hill for the arrival of Golf Battery, which was why Bravo Company was on Matterhorn in the first place.

Mellas grew accustomed to the tense monotony of patrolling. Days slid by, mercifully without enemy contact. Eventually the artillery battery came in, blasting out gun pits from the clay, digging in bunkers for their fire control center. Matterhorn was barren, shorn of trees. Nothing green was left in what was slowly turning into a wasteland of soggy discarded cardboard C-ration boxes, cat-hole latrines, buried garbage, burned garbage, trench latrines, discarded magazines from home, smashed ammunition pallets, and frayed plastic sandbags. Whole stretches of what had formerly been thick jungle were now exposed, the shattered limbs and withered stumps turning ashen like bones of dead animals under the overcast sky above. A small bulldozer made the top of the hill perfectly flat. Then came the howitzers, which were flown in dangling from helicopters like fishing weights. Within hours of their arrival the big guns were firing, their harsh explosions hurting ears, thudding through bodies, and, at night, shattering precious sleep.

An intense salvo of the entire battery firing a single time-on-target jerked Mellas awake. It had been just over an hour since he had crawled into his hooch after the last hole-check of the night. Adrenaline pumped through his body. He tried to slow it down, taking deep slow breaths. Rain fell in heavy sheets in the total darkness, and the comm-wire moorings of the hooches snapped with each gust of wind. Mellas pulled his soggy nylon poncho liner tighter around him, rolled over on one side, and tucked his knees up against his chest, trying to keep what remained of the warm dampness from disappearing into the dark.

No patrol today. It was like a reprieve.

The arrival of the battery had considerably increased the payoff for an attack by the NVA, so Fitch had increased the patrolling radius to cover more territory. This forced the patrols to leave at dawn and left them almost no daylight when they returned. The combination of tension from the possibility of making contact and the stultifying fatigue left everyone drained and irritable by nightfall. Kids were falling asleep on watch. To fight the boredom, Mellas found himself making up patrol routes just to see various features of the terrain. He paid less and less attention to where an NVA sniper or observation team might be hiding. In fact, he was torn: he didn't know whether to plan his patrols to avoid finding anyone or to find the NVA machine gun and bring himself to the notice of the colonel. He shifted to his other side, still not wanting to leave the poncho liner. He saw himself taking an NVA machine-gun team by surprise while they were eating their rice, surrounding them silently, and capturing the entire group. Then he was marching them back, finding out a great deal of information, and afterward being commended in front of the colonel and his staff. Perhaps there would be a newspaper story at home about the exploit—name recognition was important—and a medal. He wanted a medal as much as he wanted the company.

Another salvo ripped sound through the ground and air, breaking off his daydream. He stared into the blackness, now totally awake, his mind focused on the problem of replacing Jancowitz, who was about to go on R & R. He had map classes to teach, jungle to clear, and more barbed wire to lay, but no patrol. No patrol today.

He threw aside the thin nylon liner and sat up, his head touching the ponchos strung above him. The greasy camouflage liner smelled like urine. He did, too. Mellas smiled. He untied his soggy bootlaces in the dark and pulled at a wet boot. It came loose, leaving a damp sock, parts of it stiff with decaying blood from old leech wounds. He pulled the sock off carefully—especially in places where the wool, skin, and blood had clotted together over the leech bites and jungle rot. He imagined, from the feel of his foot, that it must look like the underside of a mushroom. A sudden gust of wind spattered more rain against the hooch. He began rubbing his feet, trying to stave off immersion foot. He'd seen pictures of it during training. When the foot was constantly in cold water, blood deserted it. Then it died, still attached to the leg, and rotted until either it was amputated or gangrene killed the rest of the body. He felt guilty suddenly for not having checked the platoon's feet. It would look bad on his fitness report if he had a lot of cases of immersion foot.

Two hours later Mellas was leading a map-reading class for Third Squad, feeling good about being in his own element.

"All right," he said, "who knows the contour interval?" A couple of hands shot up. Mellas was pleased; the kids seemed to enjoy the class. "OK, Jackson."

Jackson looked around shyly at his friends. "Uh, it's twenty meters, sir."

"Right. If you went across three contour lines, then how far would you have walked?"

Parker, not to be outdone by Jackson, raised his hand. "That'd be sixty meters." He smiled, pleased with himself.

Jackson snickered. "You got no brain whatsoever. Sixty meters, shit. Man, you are a stupid individual."

"What is it then, smart-ass?" Parker shot back.

"No way you can tell. Contours go up and down. You maybe went up sixty or maybe down sixty, but you maybe walked to fucking Hanoi before you did." The rest of the squad was laughing, and Parker finally joined in.

Mellas envied Jackson's natural ability to blunt the harshness of his words simply by the way he delivered them. How could you get mad at someone who neither needed to attack nor was at all worried about being able to defend? It was like getting mad at Switzerland. Mellas watched Jackson throughout the rest of the class, seeing that the blacks gravitated toward him for more than his portable record player.

Later that afternoon, Mellas crawled into Bass's hooch. Skosh was reading *Seventeen* magazine by candlelight and wearing an Incredible Hulk sweatshirt. Bass was lying on top of his air mattress, generally called a rubber lady, writing another long letter to Fredrickson's cousin.

"Heavy stuff, Skosh," Mellas said.

"Hey, Lieutenant, look at her," Skosh said quietly, showing Mellas a teenage girl modeling winter fashions, her face glowing beneath tossed-back satin hair. "You think if I wrote the magazine they'd tell me who she was?"

"Are you shitting me, Skosh? Every horny bastard in the United States would be writing to those girls if magazines did that."

Skosh withdrew the magazine and continued to look at the girl. "Maybe if they knew we was over here in Vietnam and couldn't do no harm or nothing . . ."

"Skosh, they don't give a shit where you are," Mellas said softly. He thought about Anne.

"I suppose not. Before I quit high school last year there was this girl looked just like her. Of course she was a senior, and me a junior, so I couldn't ever really, you know," his voice trailed off, "get to know her or anything."

"Hang in there, Skosh," Mellas said, "You'll be home—"

"In a hundred eighty-three fucking days and a wake-up," Skosh said quietly.

Mellas settled himself cross-legged on the end of Bass's rubber lady. The luxury of having one of the rare air mattresses was reserved for those with more rank or time in-country. Everyone else slept on the ground. "Class went pretty well today," he started off. "They seemed interested."

"Even fucking grunts get tired of digging holes."

Mellas nodded, smiling. "Hey, I'm thinking of Jackson for squad leader when Janc goes on R & R." He felt he might as well come to the point right away.

"I don't like it, Lieutenant. I don't want him and his fucking buddies all buddy-buddying each other around their jungle music all the time. He's too buddy-buddy, sir."

"You mean he's a brother." Mellas looked at Bass closely to see how he would react. There wasn't a flicker on Bass's face.

"Yes, sir, but not like you think. There ain't one color in the Marine Corps but green, and I believe that. I don't think Jackson does. I mean, I think he'd favor the splibs."

"Yeah, but he's smart. People like him. Chucks and splibs both."

"You don't want a squad leader people like," Bass said emphatically.

"Bullshit, Sergeant Bass. You get a squad leader they don't like and you've got a shitty squad."

"People didn't like me too much when I became a platoon sergeant."

"You're different."

"He's a fucking lifer," Skosh put in.

Mellas laughed.

"You stick to your fucking radio or I'll volunteer your ass for CAG," Bass retorted. "You'll wish you had some fucking lifers around when the fucking gooks desert you."

Skosh hunched his shoulders and went back to his magazine. "I should be so lucky," he mumbled. Radio operators had it easier in set positions, mainly because they were able to stand their night watches inside whatever shelter they managed to build. The longer they were in a set position, the better their shelters. On the patrols and operations, however, they more than made up for that comfort. Not only did they have to pack the heavy radios in addition to the ammunition and equipment that everyone else packed, but they were primary targets because they were the communication links and walked next to the leaders, the other primary targets.

"What's CAG?" Mellas asked.

"Some harebrained cluster fuck thought up by some asshole civilian in an air-conditioned office in Washington."

Mellas waited. Skosh wasn't listening.

"It means combined action group, sir," Bass continued. "Good fucking Marines are supposed to fight with South Gook militia and defend the villages. Only what happens is good Marines end up fighting all by themselves when the South Gooks dee-dee on them."

"I heard that tagging Marines alongside the villagers was working. Or had been, anyway," Mellas said. He suddenly felt very far away from his government; he had a gnawing suspicion that he, too, could be out in the jungle, abandoned like those Marines.

He forced the qualm down and assumed a "let's get back to business" tone of voice. "Anyhow, what do you think about Jackson, Sergeant Bass?" He rushed on without letting Bass reply. "I don't think he'd be too buddy-buddy. You can talk to him about it. Besides, who else have we got? With Fisher gone I've got to use Jake to fill in for him at

Second Squad. Vancouver won't do anything but walk point, you know that." Bass nodded. Everyone knew that Vancouver, a big kid who'd actually left Canada to volunteer for the Marines, was probably the best fighter in the company. He just always refused leadership roles, preferring to be the first man in the column, the most dangerous job in any rifle company. Everyone else reluctantly took point only when it was their turn. Mellas made one more effort. "Jackson already knows everyone." He stopped. He could see that Bass wasn't really listening. He was just politely waiting for Mellas to finish.

"Lieutenant, I think a lot of guys are going to think you put him there because he's a brother."

"What do you think?" Mellas asked.

"I think it entered your mind." Bass looked at him, waiting for Mellas's reply.

"All right, it did. I don't want China having any footholds," he said, almost mumbling the last words.

Bass looked at him a moment. "I don't like this fooling around with people because of their color. We could get in deep shit over it." He looked down at the half-finished letter and sighed, as if wishing himself home. "But maybe you're right. It ain't like it used to be, that's for damned sure. When I signed on in 'sixty-four it was protecting American citizens and property. This shit . . ." He suddenly became aware of Skosh and broke off. "Skosh, get on the hook and see if any Class Six is coming in."

"I asked them this morning, Sergeant Bass."

"Ask—them—again," Bass said, enunciating each word very clearly.

Skosh began raising the CP and Mellas looked at Bass. "You agree on Jackson, then?"

"Yeah, I agree. But no fucking buddy-buddy."

Mellas laughed, more out of relief than humor. "OK. No buddy-buddy."

Mellas slipped back outside into the drizzle. The faint sounds of James Brown doing "Say It Loud" floated from the lines. He saw Hawke coming down the hill with a cigar in his mouth. Hawke's red mustache looked incongruous beneath his wet black hair. Mellas waited for him.

"Whatever you were about to do," Hawke said, "don't."

"Why not?"

"Now that the arty battery's here, the battalion CP group won't be far behind. Fitch wants your lines cleaned up."

Mellas flared. "My lines are cleaner than anybody else's. What am I supposed to do, put out a goddamned red carpet so the colonel can promenade on it?"

"Hey, cool it down." Hawke looked sideways at Mellas. "You really do have a temper, don't you?"

"I'm just tired. I usually don't."

"You mean you don't usually show it. All Fitch wants is the fucking gumball wrappers and Kool-Aid packages put in one spot so it doesn't look like a garbage dump down here. And nobody said anything about you being better or worse than anyone else." Hawke took a long pull on his cigar. "In fact, if you must know, your lines are probably cleaner than the other platoons'." Mellas smiled. "But then you've got Sergeant Bass."

Mellas laughed. "Get back, Hawke. Is that what you came to tell me?"

"Well, not all of it." Hawke closed one eye and looked sideways at Mellas, tasting the tobacco on his lips. "I thought you might want to hear how Fisher came out. Or have you been too busy?"

"How is he?" Mellas said enthusiastically, but he felt his face reddening. He hadn't thought about Fisher in any way except as leaving a hole to fill.

"They sent him to Japan for more surgery."

"What's the prognosis?"

"Don't know. Worst case, I guess, is he'll never get it up again."

"It's the shits," Mellas said. He looked away from Hawke down toward Second Squad's fighting holes. "I still have to replace him." He said it to himself as much as to Hawke.

Hawke surveyed Mellas coolly. "If you don't relax, Mellas, you'll never learn to love it out here."

The joke broke Mellas's mood, and he laughed.

"Who you got in mind?" Hawke asked, blowing a careful cloud of smoke.

"Jackson." Mellas looked for reaction. None came. "He's got some brains."

"Might be all right, and then again it might not be."

"Why not?"

"He's a brother. He's fucking *black*, Mellas."

"So."

"All the brothers in Third Squad look up to him, right?" Hawke said.

"Yeah, that's why I picked him."

"So he sells out to the man and what do all his brothers think of him then?"

"Shit." Mellas said flatly. "Shit." He felt hemmed in by a force like a magnetic field. He couldn't see it, but he could feel it tightening.

A voice shouted down from the CP. "Hey, Five, we got a bird coming up the valley."

Hawke ran up the hill, leaving Mellas alone.

When Vancouver heard the chopper coming up the valley, he stuck the machete in the earth and left it quivering as he ran up the hill.

"Vancouver, where the fuck you going?" Conman yelled. He was pulling on the end of a roll of razor wire.

"My fucking gook sword's come in," Vancouver shouted, still running. "I know it has."

"What the fuck good is it to be a squad leader with someone like that around?" Conman muttered under his breath. He couldn't follow Vancouver, because he was supplying the tension for Mole—a black machine gunner from Conman's squad—to stake in the razor wire. "Hurry the fuck up, Mole, goddamn it. I got better things to do than get the fuck cut out of me by this shit." The wire had indeed cut through several of the scabs that formed over the jungle rot on Conman's hands, and the blood and pus were slowly oozing over the wire, making it difficult to hold.

Mole gave Conman the finger and continued staking in the wire as methodically as he cleaned his machine gun. "I ain't gonna fuck up this wire job 'cause you want to go read you fucking mail." Mole looked up the hill at the chopper that was now settling down on the LZ, the roar of its turbines nearly drowning out his last words. The chopper touched earth, bouncing slightly on its big wheels. A few new kids ran out carrying the red mailbags.

Vancouver reached the LZ just as the chopper began to shudder and whine for its takeoff. He towered over a new kid and reached for the bag the kid carried. "This First Platoon's mail?" he shouted. The sound was lost in the chopper's takeoff and the mad whirl of air. The kid clutched at the bag. He'd been told in no uncertain terms its value and what would happen to him if he failed to deliver it.

"Give me that fucking thing," Vancouver shouted. He grabbed the bag and started opening its drawstrings.

"Vancouver, what the fuck are you doing?"

Vancouver looked over his shoulder and saw Staff Sergeant Cassidy's red face. He stood up and looked down at him. "Oh, hi, Gunny. I'm looking for my gook sword. I ordered the fucking thing two months ago." The new kid slowly took back the mailbag, his glance vacillating between Vancouver and Cassidy.

"Vancouver," Cassidy said in mock weariness, "go back down to the lines and let me take care of the mail, OK? Because if you don't, and if I ever see that fucking sword of yours, I'll break it over your fucking head. Is that clear?"

"You wouldn't really do that, would you, Gunny?" Vancouver asked.

"Try me."

Vancouver turned and headed down the hill.

Cassidy watched him go with obvious affection. He had intercepted the sword with its ornate scabbard and complicated straps three weeks earlier and hidden it in Bravo Company's supply tent in order to keep Vancouver from getting killed trying to use it. He turned to face the five new kids who had come in on the chopper. "What the fuck you staring at?" Cassidy asked, his smile suddenly gone. "Do I look pretty to you?"

* * *

While most of the platoon was reading the mail for the third time, Mellas was preparing supper. He told himself it would be a while before his mail caught up with him. He was adding Tabasco sauce, grape jam, and powdered lemon tea to his can of spaghetti and meatballs when he became aware of Doc Fredrickson watching him.

"Can I talk to you a minute, Lieutenant?" Fredrickson asked.

"Sure. Beats eating."

"It's about Mallory, sir."

"Ahh, fuck. I thought you and Bass took care of that."

"He's still complaining about headaches," Fredrickson said. "I give him all the Darvon he can handle and he keeps coming back for more."

"Is that shit addictive?" Mellas asked.

"I don't know, sir. It's just what they give us. I think it's fucking useless." Fredrickson leaned over and looked into the can of spaghetti. "Maybe you ought to put some of that fake coffee cream stuff in it. It'd smooth it out."

"You stick to medicine."

"Anyway, I ain't sure Mallory even has headaches. But I've been watching him close, and on patrol yesterday he looked like he was hurting."

"Him and everyone else. I've got headaches too."

"Maybe you ought to talk to him. I talked to the senior squid, and he says sometimes people get psychosomatic stuff and it really does hurt them even if it's all in their heads anyway. It's also possible that there's really something wrong with him."

"What—you want me to decide?"

"You're the platoon commander. If you think he's telling the truth, maybe we ought to send him back to VCB to see a doctor. Just in case something really is wrong with him."

"OK."

"He's over in my hooch now."

Mellas looked at Fredrickson out of the corner of his eye. "All right."

Fredrickson left and returned with Mallory, a small-boned kid with narrow hips, a thin graceful neck, and a rather large head.

"Hi, Mallory," Mellas said, trying to be friendly. "Doc says you're still having trouble with headaches."

"My fucking head hurts," Mallory said. "I eat all that Darvon and it don't do shit."

"How long you had the headaches?"

"Ever since they humped us without water on the DMZ operation. I think I got heat-stoked or something." Mallory looked quickly over at Fredrickson to see how the corpsman was reacting. Fredrickson had his poker face on.

Mellas took a spoonful of spaghetti and chewed it while he thought. "Well, shit, Mallory, I don't know what it is. Doc's stumped. You have them all the time?"

"I tell you my fucking head hurts," Mallory whined.

"I believe you, Mallory. It's just that there's not much we can do about it. I suppose we could send you back to VCB for a checkup." Mellas watched for a reaction, but Mallory only bent his head over his knees, holding it in his hands.

"My fucking head hurts."

Mellas looked at Fredrickson, who shrugged his shoulders. "Tell you what, Mallory," Mellas said. "I'll see if we can't get you back to VCB for a couple of days to see the doctor. Right now you'll just have to bear with it for a while, OK?"

Mallory moaned. "I can't stand it. It fucking hurts all the time."

Mellas hesitated, then sighed. "I'll go up and talk with the senior squid," he said.

"I already seen him. He didn't do nothing."

"Well, maybe we can get you out. Just hang in there for a while."

"OK, sir." Mallory stood up and dragged himself down the hill toward the lines.

Fredrickson asked, "What do you think, sir?"

"I don't know. I think he probably has headaches. The question is, how bad." Mellas poked at the remains of the spaghetti. "I'd hate to have it be some sort of brain problem and not get it checked out. We could get in deep shit."

Up at Sheller's hooch, Mellas met with some resistance—not from Sheller, but from Hawke and Cassidy, who were playing pinochle with him.

"He's a fucking malingerer," Cassidy growled.

"How do you know that?" Mellas asked.

"I can smell 'em. Half the Marines on this hill have headaches and gut aches and all sorts of fucking aches, but they don't keep asking to go back to VCB."

"Suppose he has a tumor or something. You want to risk that?"

"All he needs is a kick in the ass."

"I think Cassidy's right," Hawke said. "Mallory tried to get out of the DMZ op, but we never let him. He was fine after that. No complaints until now. Everyone knows we got to go down into the valley as soon as Charlie and Alpha Company are pulled out. So all of a sudden, up come the headaches."

"Maybe it's psychosomatic," Mellas said. "I mean, maybe it's true he's scared. Maybe that's what gives him headaches."

Cassidy folded his cards in his hands. "What the fuck's psychosomatic except another fancy word for someone who doesn't want to do something that's hard and scary? Nerves don't break down—they give up. I've got a psychosomatic pain in the ass with all these fucking yardbirds. Go watch the sick bay the day before we shove off on an operation. Every nigger in the battalion's waiting in line. Mallory ain't no different."

Mellas's jaw set at the remark, but he said nothing.

"They don't all go, Gunny," Hawke said. "In fact, hardly any of them. But I'll grant you that Mallory probably would."

Cassidy sighed. "It's your fucking platoon, Lieutenant," he said to Mellas.

"And I'll send him to VCB."

"Fine, sir. I'll let you know when the next bird comes in. Get his ass up to the LZ. Don't be too surprised if he doesn't come back until after we go into the valley."

A chopper bringing in water for the artillery battery came in the next morning, and Mallory flew to Vandegrift Combat Base, VCB. He returned three days later, along with a note to the senior squid from the battalion's navy surgeon, Lieutenant Selby. "I see nothing wrong with this Marine that would keep him from performing his normal duties." Sheller walked it down to Mellas and Fredrickson, and Mellas called Mallory up and handed it to him.

"Sheeit," Mallory said after reading it. "Sheeit. I tell you my fucking head aches." He avoided looking at Mellas.

Mellas wanted to ask why one visit to the battalion aid station had taken three days. But he let it go, since Jancowitz had already dressed Mallory down in front of the whole squad and put him on listening post two nights to make up for the two days he'd probably fucked off back in the rear smoking dope. "You'll just have to live with it, Mallory," Mellas replied. "It's probably psychosomatic. We all get afraid of things and sometimes the body tries to keep us from doing them. You'll just have to get over it."

"You're saying it's in my fucking head?" Mallory whined. His tone of voice was an accusation that lumped Mellas with all the others who wouldn't help. "I tell you it's real, man. It fucking hurts me so I can't hardly think."

"Mallory, it's psychosomatic. You'll just have to get used to it. We can't do anything for you. We tried."

"Sheeit." Mallory turned away, still holding the doctor's note in his thin hand.

CHAPTER
THREE

The battalion's coming in tomorrow," Fitch said tightly. "Let's get 'em cleaned up." A loud salvo from the arty battery exploded behind them, making everyone flinch. "That means haircuts, shaves, the works. No mustaches unless they're corporals or higher. Big John Six's orders."

Mellas wearily walked back to the platoon. Hamilton saw him coming and shouted down to the holes below for the squad leaders. Another salvo rocked the hill, obliterating all other sounds. He reached his hooch and sat down, staring blankly into the fog. Eventually the three squad leaders arrived. Jancowitz, filthy, was still in his gear from a patrol. On his face, sweat mixed with fine drops of precipitation. Connolly squatted down with his hands resting across his knees, Vietnamese style. Jacobs, still nervous about his job as temporary squad leader, already had a green notebook and a ballpoint pen ready. The next to arrive was Bass, breathing hard from chugging up the slope. He squatted on the ground, looking over toward Doc Fredrickson's hooch, annoyed because Fredrickson hadn't made it to the meeting on time. "He's up at the LZ with Senior Squid," Mellas said. "They're counting pills for a reorder when the battalion gets here."

"Battalion?" Bass asked, cocking his right eye.

"Tomorrow. The birds are already fragged. That means we've got to get everyone squared away."

Jancowitz and Connolly nodded, having been through it before.

Jacobs was scratching away in his notebook. "H-h-haircuts, Lieutenant?" he asked.

"Yes, Jake," Mellas said, with just a tinge of sarcasm.

"With what? Our fucking K-bars?" Bass asked.

Jancowitz giggled. "I thought you fucking lifers just grew short hair."

"You keep mouthing off," Bass replied, "and I'll cut yours with a goddamn E-tool and then shove it so far up your butt you'll be eating pussy with the blade."

"I don't see why in hell not," Jancowitz replied, undaunted. "We manage to do everything else with our E-tools."

"Rumor has it," Mellas broke in, "that Cassidy managed to get some clippers from the arty people that'll get passed around, and they've got plenty of water, too. So everyone shaves. And about the shaving—no stashes unless you're E-5 or above."

"Bullshit, sir!" Jancowitz looked betrayed. "I'm a fucking squad leader and squad leaders can have stashes. It's always been that way." He'd written to Susi about it.

"Janc, the word is E-5 and above."

"No one can see yours now," Bass said. "Why do you care?"

"I promise you I won't go anywhere near the LZ. No one'll see me." He looked at Bass and Mellas. Neither one could help him.

"Cut off the stashes and get anyone who needs a haircut a haircut," Mellas said quickly, giving no chance for rebuttal. "That's that. Who's got the patrols tomorrow?" Connolly and Jacobs each raised a finger. "OK, I'll be going with Conman. Bass will be going with Jacobs." Mellas outlined the patrol routes and together they targeted preparation fires by the artillery and mortars. Mellas was good with maps, he knew it, and it didn't go unnoticed by the platoon—their lives depended on it. Fredrickson showed up and handed out the daily dose of malaria tablets, and they split up.

Mellas was eating some glutinous C-ration beef and potatoes mixed with applesauce and some of Bass's carefully rationed Worcestershire sauce when Jancowitz came trudging back up the hill, this time with

Parker behind him. Bass, who was heating water for coffee, looked over at Mellas. "I'll bet you a can of peaches that Parker doesn't want his hair cut," he said.

"Shit," Mellas said.

"RHIP," Bass said, smiling, with half-closed eyes.

The two arrivals reached the little level spot that the platoon CP group shared. Mellas swallowed another spoonful before acknowledging their presence.

"OK, Janc, what's the problem?"

"Parker wants to request mast, sir."

"How come, Parker?" Mellas asked, looking at him.

"I ain't getting no haircuts."

"What the fuck did you say?" Bass stood up, jaw thrust out, the tin can of hot water in his hand. "You're talking to the lieutenant, Parker." To Mellas, it hardly seemed the time to enforce military etiquette, but he let Bass go on.

"Sir, I don't need no haircuts and I want to see the skipper for mast, *sir*," Parker repeated.

Bass sat down. Requesting mast with the skipper was every Marine's privilege. Mellas looked at Parker's hair. It was curly, nearly an Afro. There was very little doubt that the battalion CP would find it too long, not just because of the Marine Corps' preference for extremely short hair, but also because of the political implications. "OK, Janc," he said, "I'll take it from here. Thanks."

Jancowitz nodded and headed back down the hill, where Hippy, clippers in hand, was sizing up another customer who was sitting on his gun emplacement with a towel around his neck. Mellas motioned toward a piece of broken ammunition pallet. "Sit down, Parker. Let me finish dinner." Parker sat down, somewhat hesitantly, looking at Bass. Almost everyone was afraid of Bass because of his unpredictable temper. Bass finished his coffee and moved off toward his hooch without saying anything.

"You know, Parker, that the skipper will have to tell you to get your hair cut."

"Why's that?" he said, looking at the thick mud on his boots.

"Because it's too *long,* Parker. We got the battalion coming in tomorrow and that's the way it's got to be."

"I requested mast, and I got my right to see the skipper, and you can't stop me."

"Jesus Christ, Parker. I'm not trying to stop you from seeing the skipper. I'm just trying to save you a walk up the hill."

"I request mast."

"Let's go, then." Mellas threw the remaining glob of food into an empty cardboard box whose sides were collapsing from constant exposure to the rain. He turned to Parker for one last try. "Parker, the skipper works under the same rules as everyone else. It's going to have to get cut."

Parker took off his bush cover and grabbed at a few strands of his hair. "It ain't no longer than Bass's. He just greases the shit down. His motherfucking hillbilly hair could be five feet long and no one say shit about that." Something told Mellas that if he were a good officer he'd never let Parker get away with talking that way to him. Still, Parker's argument was valid, even though a losing one.

"Let's go see the skipper," Mellas said tautly. He turned and continued up the hill, slipping in the mud, aware of Parker watching his clumsy progress.

Fitch, Hawke, and the two radio operators, Pallack and Relsnik, were jammed together under the ponchos playing jungle bridge. It was their forty-fifth game in a series of 300, officers versus enlisted men. Sergeant Cassidy sat nearby on an ammo box. He was just outside the opening of the hooch carving on the stave Fisher had brought back, indifferent to the rain.

"What's the trouble, Lieutenant?" Cassidy asked.

Fitch looked out of the opening and started to rise.

"Oh, no, you don't, Skipper," Pallack said, turning to Parker. "Hey, Parker, you got to hold on. D' enlisted are about to take another game off d' officers." He turned back to the game and slapped down a card, hard. "You fucking dummies. Hee, hee. Look at dat queen." Parker's jaws were working beneath his dark cheeks. Fitch grimaced and threw down a card.

Parker spoke up. "Sir, I got the right for mast."

"You got the *privilege,* Parker," Cassidy growled. "You don't just walk in on the company commander and tell him you want mast."

Parker stood his ground. "I got the right for mast." Cassidy stood up. Hawke quickly threw a card and Pallack swooped up the little pile and then slapped down another, laughing. Hawke looked at Fitch and shrugged. Fitch threw in the rest of his cards, and Pallack and Relsnik shook hands and pulled out their pens and notebooks, both recording the score so there was no chance of error, making cracks about how anyone could be so dumb at playing cards and still manage to become an officer. The card game had eased the tension between Cassidy and Parker by giving Cassidy a chance to look away, which he took.

Fitch crawled out of the hooch and stood. "OK, Parker. Let's go inside Hawke's hooch and talk things out." Fitch's manner was easy and direct, and Parker seemed to relax a little. They crawled into Hawke's hooch.

Mellas walked back to his own hooch. People were out by the wire setting in trip flares for the night. A late cooking fire was visible down at Conman's squad, and Mellas shouted for it to be put out. It disappeared. The lines were quiet.

Mellas started to write a letter in the remaining twilight but was interrupted by Skosh, who'd packed the radio over with him. "It's the Six," he said. He squatted down and casually began reading Mellas's letter, which Mellas snatched away from him.

Fitch's voice crackled over the net. "Your character Pappa who was just up here has twenty minutes to get his fucking hair cut. Then I want to see him. You copy?"

"I copy." Mellas sighed and handed Skosh the hook. "Why do I have to fart around with goddamned haircuts in the middle of the jungle because some colonel is going to show up?"

Skosh shrugged his shoulders. "Just another inch of green dildo, sir."

Mellas walked down to Jancowitz's area. Parker was talking with Mole who, like many of the brothers in the battalion, wore a noose of heavy khaki nylon rope around his neck. Mellas guessed that it had something to do with lynching but was afraid to ask. The rest of the blacks from Third Squad stood around them. They fell silent when they saw Mellas approaching.

Everyone's hair had been cut except Parker's. Jackson spoke up, his broad face relaxed, his eyes calmly engaging with Mellas's. "Sir, I think they're fucking with the brothers over these haircuts." It was stated with no apparent anger.

Mellas tried hard for the same tone. "Jackson, no one has any choice in the matter. Curly hair doesn't look regulation and we've got the Big Six coming in tomorrow and Lieutenant Fitch is on the spot. I really don't want to hear anything more about it."

"Yes, sir," Jackson said, turning away.

Mellas looked at Parker. "You know you've got about fifteen minutes, right?"

"Yes, sir," Parker mumbled.

"OK. Get it done and get up to the skipper and we'll forget the whole goddamn silly thing."

It was almost dark when PFC Tyrell Broyer saw Gunny Cassidy and Sergeant Ridlow from Lieutenant Goodwin's platoon coming down the hill. Cassidy was holding a pair of hair clippers. Broyer nervously adjusted his glasses even though they didn't need adjusting. He glanced at Parker, who shared their two-man fighting hole. Cassidy and Ridlow disappeared into Bass's hooch and Broyer heard them laughing.

Parker, his hair still uncut, leaned against the rear of the fighting hole, staring into the jungle. His rifle rested on a plastic sandbag and his arms were crossed in front of him.

"Hey, brother," Broyer said quietly, "I think we got trouble coming down the hill about your hair."

Parker grunted and spat. "God and country bigot motherfuckers."

Broyer looked back at the hooch above him. Sergeant Bass was crawling out, his beefy arms showing below his neatly rolled-up sleeves. Cassidy emerged behind Bass, his face set hard. Next came Ridlow. Parker gave a quick sideways glance over his shoulder and immediately turned away, stone-faced. Broyer wanted to run for help but didn't know where to go. He excused his inaction by recalling that he couldn't leave his hole during the evening 100 percent alert. He shifted his feet nervously.

The group of sergeants gathered silently around them.

"It's time, Parker," Cassidy said. "I see you decided you'd rather have it done by a pro."

Parker clenched his teeth.

"You fucking answer, turd, when you're spoken to," Bass said.

Bass had moved in front of the fighting hole and was glaring directly into Parker's face. Ridlow stood to his right, his boots next to Parker's face. Cassidy was to Bass's left. Bass motioned for Broyer to get out of the hole and Broyer scrambled out, still not knowing where to go. He saw the rest of the squad watching in silence.

"Did you fucking hear me, you puke?" Cassidy asked.

"Yes sir," Parker mumbled.

"I didn't hear you, Parker," Bass said, smiling.

"Yes, *sir*," Parker spat out.

"How would you like it, Parker?" Cassidy asked. "Parted on the left? What do you think, Sergeant Bass? What would Sassoon do?"

"Maybe on the left," Bass said. "No, make it down the center. A reverse Mohawk."

"I think we ought to take his fucking head off," Ridlow growled.

Cassidy squatted down and leaned forward to whisper in Parker's ear. "Parker, you fucking turd, so help me God if you make one fucking wrong move I'm gonna screw your head off and shit in it. I don't know what the fuck's wrong with these fucking officers in this company to take the crap that pukes like you hand out all the time, but if I had my way I'd have your ass strung up to the nearest fucking tree. You don't request mast about a fucking haircut. You request mast when something is really wrong. And you don't disobey orders. Now you sit up real nice on the edge of this hole and get your hair cut like a man, or so help me God I'll personally beat holy fuck out of you and leave you for the fucking maggots where you belong. You understand?"

Bass had also squatted down to look directly at him. Parker glanced around. The others in the squad were peering at him from their holes. They had all gotten their hair cut. Broyer heard the sound of Cassidy squeezing the hair clippers. He looked at Bass's heavy forearms. His knees were shaking and there was a racing feeling inside him.

"I just want to say my hair ain't no longer than some chuck that grease it down. That's all I want to say."

"Good. Now you've said it," Cassidy said. "And I want to say I don't want a puke like you in my Marine Corps. I just want to say that. You aren't worthy of the name. Now, I'll give you three counts to sit your ass on the edge of this fighting hole. One . . ."

Parker moved.

Broyer, still standing next to the fighting hole, took a breath. He looked around. He saw the lieutenant standing by Bass's hooch. Like everyone else, he was watching Cassidy clip Parker bald.

As soon as they stood down from the evening alert Broyer took off for Second Platoon to find China. It was the first time he'd been in another platoon's area, and he was a little surprised to see trash lying around the fighting holes. Walking by a hooch he heard a loud guffaw and then a hearty laugh. Lieutenant Goodwin's blond head stuck out of the hooch. Broyer scurried by, feeling out of place and hoping to avoid a confrontation. He walked up to a brother he didn't know, pushed his glasses back up on his nose, walked up to the man, and went through the now familiar handshake. He asked where China hung out. The brother pointed toward a small hooch, half hidden beneath a huge felled tree, barely two feet from a machine-gun position. He went over and saw China and two brothers leaning against the trunk of the tree on the side away from the hooch. They were eating supper. Their voices reminded him of summer nights in Baltimore.

China greeted him, going through the handshake. "Hey, brother, glad you could come by. Meet my friends."

One of them offered Broyer a C-ration can filled with hot coffee. He took it and sat down, gingerly holding the folded-down lid so the heat wouldn't burn his fingers. When he started to tell them about the haircut, he was surprised at the anger that spilled out. "And then the chickenshit motherfuckers shaved him bald. They shaved him fucking *bald.* And we just stood there and watched those motherfuckers."

When Broyer finished, China sprang to his feet. "You tell Parker get his ass over here soon as he can. And don't worry, we won't be standin' 'round much longer no more. We got the power." He was pounding his fist on the log. "We got the power. We gonna do some fuckin' over our own pretty soon."

Broyer hurried away, feeling understood, feeling China's will and strength.

China sat down against the log and sighed. He reached out to heat up another cup of coffee. The two others, knowing that China would speak when he had something to say, began to talk to each other, extinguishing the fire when darkness finally fell.

Broyer relayed China's message to Parker, and when Parker got off watch that night he made his way over to Second Platoon's area. He had to half-crawl, half-crouch up to the top of the LZ and then head back down to Second Platoon to avoid being shot by accident. In the blackness it took him about an hour.

When he reached China's hooch, the brother China shared it with was asleep and alone. He angrily told Parker to go down to the hole below them. He did, and after identifying himself, he slipped into China's two-man fighting hole.

"Shhh," China said, pretending to hear something, trying to think. The wind moved up the hill toward them, smelling of wet earth and moss. Brush, unseen, just ten meters in front of them, whispered beneath creaking trees.

"You said you wanted to see me," Parker finally whispered.

"Yeah." China was still thinking.

"They fucked with me this afternoon. Fucked with me bad, man."

"You stupid shit, shut the fuck up," China whispered fiercely.

"Hey, what's with you, man?"

"What's with *me*?" China whispered. "What's with you makin' a jive-assed flaky scene over a fuckin' haircut?"

"Hey, you told me, man—"

"I told you we'd wait to pick our ground and then we'd have a *cause*. Now I got every brother in the company wonderin' what the fuck I'm gonna do over a jive-assed fuckin' haircut. I ought to take you fuckin' head off. I just get the brothers sendin' parts to me and you got to blow shit up."

"They fucking castrated me right in front of my brothers and you be saying *I* fucked up?" Parker's lips curled back; his anger was barely under control. China felt it but knew he could handle Parker.

"Hey, brothers, cool it, huh?" China's hooch mate was whispering from the open flap. "Ridlow be checking lines anytime and he light big fire to our asses if you don't cool it."

Parker cooled down slightly, and China shifted his feet.

"Look," China said, "the racist motherfuckers gonna be taught a lesson, but you gotta do it up right. You hear me? You gotta do it up right. We don't keep the power unless we keep our brains. You hear me? And the brothers back home need weapons—*real* weapons."

"I hear you," Parker said sullenly. "I'll kill the motherfucker myself."

"You don't kill nobody without my say-so."

"I'll kill any fucking pig I want."

"You listen a me, Parker. We need you. You know that. Right? You know that. You brothers need you. But we don't need you doing no killin' unless it's a real showdown. We don't need you doin' that. You let me and Henry decide that stuff. We get it together next time we in VCB."

"Shit. We ain't seen VCB in two months. What makes you think we see VCB now? Henry rotate home before you see him. Sheeit."

"We see him, Parker. You just learn to bide time. We got time. Now you let me think how I'm gonna handle this, OK? And no fuckin' around with it. You just let me think about this tonight and I'll start seein' the brothers in the morning. OK?"

"OK."

"You did fine, brother. It took a lot of guts to stand up like that. I'm sorry I jumped on you. It's just we playin' for really big stakes here. You hear me? Big stakes. Can be no *mis*-takes." China cackled, leaving Parker nothing to say.

Parker went to all fours to feel his way back to his own fighting hole, leaving China in total blackness. China spent the rest of his watch and even took his hooch mate's watch trying to figure out how to handle the situation. He had to move the emphasis from something trivial like haircuts. Cassidy seemed the likely target. Cassidy, not the fucking haircut, was the key to the situation. He'd see the brothers first thing in the morning before patrol.

China did see the brothers first thing in the morning. Mellas, worried, watched him talking. When Mellas went down to join First Squad for the patrol, Mole was conspicuously late, still cleaning his machine gun in full view of the assembled squad, picking away at minuscule pieces of lint. The heavy noose hung from his coffee-colored neck.

Mole, who was six-two and very well built, didn't look like a mole. He'd received the nickname on the DMZ operation. Connolly's squad had been pinned down, and Mole had moved so low to the ground behind rocks and bushes to flank the enemy that the rest of the squad swore he'd gone underground. He'd opened up on the NVA, killing two and scattering the rest. The skipper had put him up for a Bronze Star.

"You going to burp it too, Mole?" Mellas asked, trying to make his voice light.

Mole continued cleaning the weapon. "Gun's gotta be babied, sir," he mumbled, "'specially when we can't get the fucking parts we order."

Mellas squatted down next to him. "You pissed off about something, Mole?"

"No, sir. Just doing my job." Mole scrutinized the gun's heavy receiver.

Not wanting to confront the haircut issue, Mellas looked at his watch. "Look, Mole, we're five minutes late already. Try and hurry it up, OK?"

Mole grunted and clamped the belt-feeder assembly into place.

Mellas joined Connolly and Vancouver, as well as Daniels, the artillery FO; the German shepherd, Pat; and Corporal Arran, Pat's handler. They were all checking their weapons, adjusting straps, stuffing favorite C-rations into pockets for lunch, and taking final drinks of water before topping off their canteens—all the nervous rituals one does to keep the ego functioning in the face of imminent death.

Mellas felt a surge of pride that Vancouver was in his platoon. Although he hadn't known who Vancouver was at the time, he remembered clearly their first encounter. It had been at VCB while he was waiting for a helicopter to take him and Goodwin out to Matterhorn. It was mostly a time of cold drizzle, boredom, and nervous energy amid rifled boxes of C-rations gone soggy and the smell of JP-4 fuel and urinal pipes stuck in sodden clay, but Mellas could have spent the rest of his days lying there in the mud. That squalid landing zone at VCB was a place where he could stay alive, where the dreaded bush lay in the future, beyond the helicopter's ramp. At VCB you could watch the helicopters leave without you. There, you never had to step through the dark aluminum-ringed portal to the unknown terror of the bush.

Still, by midafternoon, even Goodwin had been worn down by the rain and the boredom. They all dozed in the gray light, drizzle falling on them, stupefied by waiting and by their desire to forget what they were waiting for. Then the monotony broke.

A single Marine jumped off the back of an incoming helicopter and walked slowly across the landing zone toward the dirt road that led to the regiment's rear area. The Marine stood six-three or six-four, but his size wasn't nearly as interesting as the sawed-off M-60 machine gun dangling from two web belts hung over his shoulders. An M-60 usually took two men to operate. The book assigned a crew of three. A crude handle had been welded onto the barrel so the Marine could control the kick without resting it on a bipod. Two cans of machine-gun ammo lay against his chest, suspended from his shoulders. In addition to all this weight, Mellas guessed that he also carried the usual full pack of the bush Marine: sleeping gear, food, extra clothes, hand grenades, books, letters, magazines, ponchos for shelter from the rain, shovel, claymore mines, bars of C-4 plastic explosive, trip flares, handmade stove, pictures of girlfriends, toilet articles, insect repellent, cigarettes, rifle-cleaning gear, WD-40, jars of freeze-dried coffee, and maybe a package or two of long-rats: freeze-dried trail food designed as rations for long-range patrols but more often used by the grunts for special occasions. On the Marine's head was an Australian bush hat, left brim folded up at the side. Matted blond hair, discolored with grime, showed beneath it. His uniform was a mass of tattered holes and filth. One trouser leg had been torn off just below the knee, revealing pasty white flesh covered with infected leech bites and jungle rot. His hands, face, and arms were also covered with jungle rot and open sores. You could smell him as he walked by. But he walked by as if the LZ belonged to him, seemingly unaware of the hundred or more pounds he carried. He was a bush Marine, and Mellas wanted fervently to be just like him.

What Mellas didn't know then, but knew now, was that Vancouver had made the usual swap for the most tattered clothing in his platoon—he would be able to get all new clothing back in the rear—and that Lieutenant Fitch, acting on Fredrickson's recommendation, had sent him to VCB to clean up his NSU—nonspecific urethritis. Vancouver had contracted this medical problem when the company was at VCB some weeks before, waiting to lift out on the next operation. Instead of staying where he should have been, he had sneaked off one night through seven kilometers of unsecured territory to a Buru village near Ca Lu. Rumor had it that Vancouver was secretly married to a girl there.

The memory of seeing Vancouver at VCB gave Mellas a deep yearning to be back in its comparative safety. From VCB, Matterhorn had looked like the bush. Now Matterhorn itself felt like VCB. In the distant valley below Mellas were unseen trails, connecting base camps and supply dumps, crisscrossing the border into North Vietnam and Laos, a spidery network that carried the supplies and replacements for the NVA's operations against the population centers in the south and along the coast. The battalion's job was to stop them. Soon, he knew, he'd be down there—no perimeter, no artillery battery, no landing zones, no Matterhorn. The real bush.

*   *   *

Mellas's mind snapped back to the task at hand. They were going on another routine patrol to protect the artillery battery.

When Mole finished cleaning his machine gun, he walked over to Connolly and nodded. Connolly broke into activity, calling out the starting order of the fire teams in the patrol. Vancouver moved quietly down toward the intricate maze that was the only way through the barbed wire. Skosh, normally Bass's radio operator, had been sitting against a stump with his eyes closed the whole time. He rose and joined Mellas behind the first team. He and Hamilton had traded jobs to help relieve boredom. The scout dog, Pat, sniffed at each Marine as he went by, memorizing his smell. Once in the jungle, Pat would be alert to any smell that was different. Arran said Pat could memorize well over a hundred individual scents.

In five minutes they were down the steep hill into the jungle, away from the litter, tangled wire, garbage, and barren mud. A bird called. They heard its wings as it flapped away from the squad's path. The canopy rose high above them, 100 to 150 feet, blocking out sunlight, casting the squad into shadow. Down they went, like divers in a gray-green sea.

Pat was alert almost immediately, but Mellas and Corporal Arran were both expecting one of three two-man outposts that sat outside the company perimeter during the day. The squad wound silently by Meaker and Merritt from Second Platoon, acknowledging them with silent smiles. Outpost, or OP, duty was easy except that the OP was likely to be sacrificed warning the company of an attack.

The squad continued down the trail. The OP disappeared behind them. About ten minutes later, Arran went down on one knee, his hand on Pat's quivering back, trying to read Pat's message. The squad halted, and everyone tensed, looking to the sides of the trail. Arran pointed off the trail to the right and then pointed down. Mellas raised an eyebrow to Conman, and Conman nodded. Mellas put his thumb up—OK—and Conman tapped the kid in front of him and pointed right. The squad slipped off the trail that followed the crest of the finger and began working down a steep draw toward the valley floor. Suddenly, they were engulfed in bamboo. The top of the bamboo was about three feet above their heads, and they had to thread their way cautiously, moving aside stalks to build their own tunnel through the solid green mass.

Vancouver, on point, started going too far into the bottom of the draw. Mellas threw a pebble at Conman. Conman turned, and Mellas gave him a negative sign and pointed upslope. The word passed up front to Vancouver, and the squad quit going downhill into the draw, staying mid-slope on the finger that led down to the valley. Walking down a draw was an invitation to an ambush.

The sign came for the machetes. One was passed up from behind Mellas and soon everyone could hear the dull thwack of the blade as an impassible tangle was cut away so the squad could move again. With each sound, rifles were held tighter, and eyes and ears strained a little more. Finally the sound ceased. The squad began moving again, everyone ready to fire at the slightest noise or movement in the jungle.

The squad crawled, slid, sweated, and muttered its way through the dark jungle. Machetes had to be passed forward again. Again their dull thwacking echoed down the line. Kids bit their lower lips, fingered their safeties off and on. Yet without the machetes they couldn't move; and if they couldn't move, they couldn't return to the safety of the perimeter.

Conman rotated the lead fire team as each team became exhausted from the tension of being on point and the backbreaking work of swinging the machetes. Everyone, even Mellas, took his turn with a machete. Mellas knew it was foolish for him—it hindered tactical control—but he wanted to show that he could share some of the burden. He was acutely aware that the squad could be heard hundreds of meters away. Yet the patrol was going to certain checkpoints to make sure the NVA were kept well away from approach paths to Matterhorn. This literal bushwhacking let the patrol accomplish its mission without walking down established trails where the odds of getting ambushed were greatly increased. As he was finding out, no strategy was perfect. All choices were bad in some way.

Within minutes Mellas's hands were raw and blistered, and his arm felt weighted down. The whole time he was hacking at the bamboo he felt naked, aware that his rifle was in his left hand, and that his finger was not on the trigger. If he was fired on he would have to rely on the

kid behind him to take out the enemy. Finally, after an eternity, someone tapped him on the shoulder and he dropped back behind Conman,
where Skosh was with the radio. Mellas was sweating profusely, from
both his labor and his fear. A voice within his head began mocking him,
asking him why in hell any NVA would be anywhere near the middle
of this damned bamboo patch they'd stumbled into.

Two more hours went by before they were out of the bamboo and
back into the relative ease of walking through jungle, sweating, fighting
insects, groping, as blind as the leeches against which they waged their
real war. Lieutenant Fitch asked for pos reps—position reports—every
twenty minutes or so. Mellas dutifully radioed them in, feeling frustrated
and useless because they barely changed. In two hours the patrol had
gone perhaps 300 meters.

Then, in an instant, the dullness and fatigue were swept away,
leaving clean, cold terror.

Conman dived to the dirt in front of Mellas. Skosh too hit the dirt,
before Mellas could even fold his knees. The entire squad was flat on
the ground, rifles alternating sides all along the line, as they were assigned. Conman peered intently forward, then he started to hunch and
wriggle backward on his belly and forearms toward Mellas. He turned
and held up three fingers, then held out an open palm with a questioning look on his face. At least three, maybe more. Mellas's heart started
to pound painfully in his throat. He was trying to remember what he'd
been told to do, back at Quantico. His mind seemed empty. Conman
squirmed back farther. Mellas could see no one else. All alone. All alone,
and maybe about to die.

"Pat alerted," Conman whispered. "Arran says at least three gooks,
by the way Pat's acting. Probably more."

"Maybe it's the machine-gun team," Mellas whispered, thinking,
Why me?

Conman shrugged. "What'll we do, Lieutenant?"

Mellas didn't have the slightest idea.

He wanted to radio Bass and the Jayhawk and ask them. At the same
time, he knew that this idea was ridiculous. His mind was turning over
possibilities so fast that he felt dizzy. Meanwhile, Conman waited,

open-mouthed, for Mellas to come up with a plan of action. If it was just three, he could send in the squad on line and wipe them out. If it was a three-man OP, an outpost for a larger unit, that unit could be anything from a platoon to a company. If he went in with the squad, they'd walk right into the deep shit and be lucky to come out with anybody alive. Then again, if it was only three there would be no excuse for not going after them. But someone would probably get killed. It might be Mellas, unless he sent two fire teams in without him. But what would the others think of that? He'd have to go. But *he* could get killed. It was only three. How could he be afraid? The odds were so much in their favor. Mellas suddenly saw himself and the fourteen squad members lined up against a wall, facing a firing squad of fifteen men, only one of whom had a bullet in his rifle. The odds would be very much in his favor there as well. But suppose the one bullet hit him. He suddenly knew that odds became meaningless when everything was at stake.

Mellas decided to assume it was an outpost for a larger group until he knew otherwise. That meant he'd have to find out. His training took over. His mind started inventorying his available weapons.

"Gun up," he whispered to Skosh. The word went back to invisible kids lying on the jungle floor. "Set it in here," Mellas whispered to Conman. "Put Vancouver with his machine gun one-eighty from it."

"He won't like it."

"To hell with him. Send a fire team around to the left. We'll cover with Mole if they get into the shit. Who do you want to go?"

Now it was Conman's turn to play God, at age nineteen. He shut his eyes. "Rider."

So some are chosen to die young.

Mellas turned to Skosh. "Rider up." Skosh crawled back toward the next man. "Rider up." The whisper passed along.

"Your seventy-nine man have any shotgun rounds?" Mellas asked Conman.

Conman held up three fingers.

Mellas cursed under his breath. The rounds, so useful in the jungle where nothing could be seen, were always in short supply. The M-79 men hoarded them like misers.

"He'll go with the team."

Conman nodded.

"Set the gun in so Rider can get his ass back if he runs into trouble. I'll go and pick him up."

"What about artillery?" Conman asked.

Mellas felt a sudden sinking in his stomach. He'd forgotten all about it. "I'll see Daniels on the way down," he said, saving face.

Conman gave him a thumbs-up and started crawling to the nearest person to set up the perimeter.

Mellas passed Skosh. "Stick with Conman. I'll be with Daniels and on the arty frequency if the Six wants me." Mellas continued crawling down the line of intense questioning faces. He kept whispering, "Three gooks. Maybe more. Conman'll set you in," all the while motioning them forward. He met Mole and Young, Mole's assistant gunner, moving forward, both of them sweating heavily. Mole looked grim. Young gave a wan smile, dragging the heavy machine-gun ammunition beside him on the ground, trying very hard to move without making noise.

"You'll block for Rider," Mellas whispered to Mole. "See Conman." Mole nodded, continuing in a low crawl, the large gun cradled across his arms as he worked his way forward. Rider came crawling forward behind Mole and Young, his face glistening, his eyes slightly wild. The two frightened kids in his fire team crawled behind him. Yet no one questioned that they would do what they were told. "Three gooks," Mellas whispered. "We have to find out if that's all. Could be an OP. Tell Connolly that I said for you to take Gambaccini and his M-79 with you."

Rider licked his lips and looked quickly at his two friends. One nodded. The other was staring into the jungle as if the intensity of his gaze could reveal its secret. But the undergrowth revealed nothing. The secret could be revealed only by crawling into the jungle and meeting it there.

Rider nodded and pointed uphill, looking at his team. The three of them crawled toward the head of the column, disappearing almost immediately. Mellas continued down the line, sending kids forward to form the perimeter.

Daniels crawled up, his radio slipping awkwardly from side to side on his back.

"The angle is the shits for Golf Battery," Daniels whispered. "The ridge is between them and the gooners. The one-oh-fives will have to shoot nearly straight up to come straight down on them and Golf is so far away the rounds won't reach. If they shoot a flatter trajectory to make the distance, they'll hit the ridge's front side or fly right over the target. I think you ought to use the company's sixties. The rounds are a tenth the weight, but they'll hit the target. I've got them up on the net now."

Mellas nodded his head, thankful for Daniels's foresight. "Good," he said.

Daniels started forward again, twisting the frequency knob at the same time to tell his battery to stand by, that he'd be using the mortars; then he switched frequencies again and started talking to the company mortar squad. Mellas and Daniels met Vancouver lying in front of them, his own machine gun cradled on a rotten limb. Skosh was crawling toward Mellas, holding out the handset. Mellas grabbed it, waiting for Daniels to finish with the mortars. He noticed that Rider's fire team and Gambaccini and his M-79 grenade launcher were already gone. "It's the skipper," Skosh whispered.

"I'll need a pos rep," Fitch said. "Over."

"We haven't moved squat since the last one," Mellas whispered. "Over."

"Bravo One, I want a pos rep. You copy?"

"Wait one." Mellas's hands were shaking as he dug out his map. The jungle made it impossible to see any landmarks. He tried to remember the terrain they'd walked over, estimate the distances. It was like navigating underwater. He stabbed a finger at the most likely spot, still feeling it was the same place he'd radioed in last time. He looked at Daniels, raising his eyebrows. Daniels moved his finger to a point on his own map with his own peculiar pencil marks and dogears, not trusting anyone else's. He looked at where Mellas was pointing on his own map. Thumbs-up. Mellas radioed in the position. If he was wrong, the shells could hit Rider's team, or them, instead of the enemy.

Fitch got off the hook and let Corporal Devon, the squad leader of the 60-millimeter mortars, come back up on the net.

Daniels started talking. "Bravo Whiskey, Bravo One One, fire mission. Over."

And Mellas had nothing to do.

He sat down while Daniels called in the mission. He noticed that there were ants on the ground where they had set in. He could barely see the backs of some of the kids as they lay beneath the foliage. A bird chirped. He didn't know if the whole thing wasn't just a foolish exercise.

The thunk of mortar shells leaving the tube jarred him. For all the hours they'd walked, he was surprised to hear the sounds of tubing so close to him. There was a sudden rush and a loud crash as the 60-millimeter shells came nearly straight down. The sounds were muffled and seemed far away. Mellas wondered if they'd read the map that badly.

"Right fifty. Drop one hundred," Daniels whispered, correcting by sound alone. The second salvo came down right on the ridge above them. The sounds were magnified tenfold, no longer masked by the earth. Daniels called for four salvos. Then he adjusted to the right and called in four more. Mellas was amazed: it was all mechanical, yet people were probably getting killed.

Pat was lying quietly next to Arran, who was sitting against a log. The dog was panting and so seemed to be grinning. His odd reddish ears were standing up.

The radio whispered. Skosh handed Mellas the handset. "I have to know the word on the basketball team." It was Fitch, using the radio code for a fire team. "Big John Six wants to know. Also Golf Six wants to know why he's standing by and not firing the mission. Over."

"Tell him character Delta thinks the angle is bad. We're masked by a ridge and the mortars have a better shot at it. And I can't walk out and ask the damned basketball team what the score is because I don't exactly know where they are. Which is another reason why we don't want the artillery right now. Over."

Fitch came back up laughing. "OK. Let me know ASAP. Six out."

An ant bit Mellas, who suppressed a yelp. He noticed Pat pressing his paws on the ground, holding his head back as if to push the ants away. Several of the kids were squirting insect repellent on their faces and legs. He looked at his wristwatch. Only five minutes had passed. More mortar shells crumped into the jungle; the explosions moved the ground beneath them yet seemed somehow far away. Mellas slapped at a fly and missed. It circled off and landed on Skosh, who did exactly the same thing. Two more minutes went by. Daniels told the mortars to hold off for a minute. One of the kids was cautiously moving his leg back and forth, probably trying to get the blood back into a foot that had fallen asleep. The fly landed on Mellas again. Then the jungle ripped apart.

It was as if someone had torn a sheet of solid sound. The M-16s, on full automatic, screamed, making Mellas wince and shut his eyes. Just a few meters in front of him he could hear the slower, more solid hammering of the heavier-caliber NVA AK-47s. Mellas, who had buried his face in the earth, now raised his eyes, trying to see through the jungle to where the sound originated. Quick bursts from the lighter, higher-velocity M-16s of Rider's fire team were going off; the bursts alternated as one rifleman would cover for another who was slamming in a new magazine. The blurred screams of the M-16s on full automatic answered the slower and heavier slapping of the AK-47s. The AK bullets cracked overhead, cutting branches in two. Leaves, bark, and splinters rained down on the men's helmets and backs. There was a short explosive pop followed almost immediately by the thud of a much louder explosion as Gambaccini got off a grenade round. Uphill from them, someone was shouting. There were crashing sounds in the jungle. The radio was screaming. "What the fuck's going on? You being hit? Over."

Mellas could scarcely talk because of the blood pounding in his throat. The air was crazy with the ear-hammering noise of automatic weapons. "That's a neg." Mellas was unaware that he was shouting. "It's the basketball team. Over."

"Where are they? Give me a pos rep. Over." Fitch's voice steadied Mellas, who had to cover one ear with his hand to hear what Fitch was saying. "About twenty-five meters bearing zero-four-five. Maybe less. I don't know. I can't see shit." Mellas's words were coming out in gasps.

"Get your arty cranked up. You want the sixties dropped in closer? Over."

"That's a neg." Mellas gasped for air. "Don't know where the team is." Panting. "Character Delta's going up on the arty net now. Over."

Mellas was bewildered by the suddenness of it all. It had been so methodical, so easy. Now he couldn't even tell where the fire was coming from. Should he go after Rider or wait for him? Questions rattled through his head, but no answers came. He decided to stay put.

An AK-47 bullet with just enough energy left to keep moving after it exited from a thick brush stem fluttered over Mellas's head with a high-pitched whine and lost itself in the dense jungle behind him.

Then there was silence. It was as if the last shattering burst had killed all sound. Everyone was breathing rapidly. Mole was digging his toes into the earth behind the machine gun, the stock pulled in tight to his shoulder, staring down the barrel as if trying to cut through the jungle with his eyes.

There were no sounds from the forest.

Mellas crawled up next to Connolly and whispered, "We've got to get in touch with Rider."

Connolly nodded. He cupped his hands and called out in a strangled half whisper, "Rider?" His voice carried through the silence like a shaft of light through a dark cave. No answer. An insect started to chirrup again. "Rider, get your ass back in here. Call my name when you get close so we'll know it's you." Connolly turned to Mellas. "He ain't hardly going to yell back, sir."

The radio hissed with static. Mellas knew what was coming. "This is Bravo Six. We need a sit rep. Big John is creaming his jeans. Over."

"Six, this is One Actual. No change yet. Over."

There was a long pause. Fitch knew as well as anyone that, at the moment, to go looking for Rider would be insane. He'd be shooting anything that moved. So would any number of NVA. The radio hissed again. "I copy. But you've got to get me a sit rep ASAP. Over."

"I copy. We're working on it. Over."

"Roger that. Bravo Six out."

Three long minutes went by. Then they heard a sound in the bushes. Rifles moved in unison, focusing on the single sound. Connolly's hand was up, holding the fire. A whisper cut through the bush. "Conman?"

Rifles relaxed.

"Here," Conman whispered back.

A brief commotion followed, then Rider came scrambling into the perimeter, crouched low, followed by his two team members and Gambaccini with the M-79 still smoking from the barrel. They threw themselves to the ground.

Rider crawled over to Mellas. He was breathing hard. His face was streaked with dirt and sweat. His utility shirt reeked. "Two gooks," he said. "Maybe more. We saw each other at the same time." His chest heaved, trying to pull in more air. "We both opened up. We hit the deck. Shot shit out of everything. I may have hit one. They dee-deed."

"Which way?"

Rider shook his head negatively. "Fuck if I know. Downhill."

"That'd be south," Mellas said, pulling out his map. He pulled the squad back while Daniels worked over the area south and east of them with artillery and mortar fire, controlling the 105-millimeters from his own radio and the 60-millimeters from Skosh's radio. After about fifteen minutes the squad moved into the worked-over area, everyone on the alert, Pat quivering with excitement but under perfect control by Arran.

Pat picked up a trail and started tracking. The squad followed Pat down into the valley. They worked through thicker and thicker growth, occasionally seeing a torn bush, a broken tree limb, or fresh dirt from the artillery. Other than these small signs and the smell of the explosive, the half-hour fire mission and fight had made no impression on the jungle at all. The Marines began to grow weary.

The radio cracked. "Bravo One, this is Bravo Six. Big John wants an after-action report. He can't wait any longer. He's got to see Bushwhacker Six. I've also got Golf Six on my back wanting to know how his artillery did. Over."

"Wait one," Mellas said. He sighed, holding the handset in front of his mouth, thinking. Mellas wanted to believe something had happened, something good that he could report. They'd shot up a quarter of an hour's worth of shells. Rider had done an incredible job checking out the alert. No one had been hurt. It was a good job. Mellas wanted to believe they'd done well. He wanted to, so he did.

"Bravo Six, this is Bravo One. Our character Romeo feels certain he got one right when he opened up. He only saw two gooks, but from the sound of things there had to be more than that. We got a probable for sure. Over."

There was a pause. "What about the artillery damage assessment? Over."

Mellas looked at Skosh. Skosh shook his head and spat, still leaning over. "I don't know. I'm just the fucking radioman."

Conman spoke up. "Give them a fucking probable and get the arty off the skipper's back. They'll never leave us alone if we don't, sir."

"I can't give them a goddamn probable," Mellas said. "What evidence have I got?"

"They don't need fucking evidence. They need an artillery damage assessment. Tell them there's all sorts of blood trails around here. They always like that."

Mellas looked at Daniels. Daniels held up both hands, palms out, and shrugged. He didn't give a shit.

Mellas keyed the radio. "Bravo Six, this is Bravo One Actual. We got one probable. That's all. Over." He wasn't going to lie so that an artillery officer could feel good.

So the one probable became a fact. Fitch radioed it in to battalion. Major Blakely, the battalion operations officer, claimed it for the battalion as a confirmed, because Rider said he'd seen the guy he shot go down. The commander of the artillery battery, however, claimed it for his unit. The records had to show two dead NVA. So they did. But at regiment it looked odd—two kills with no probables. So a probable got added. It was a conservative estimate. It only made sense that if you killed two, with the way the NVA pulled out bodies, you had to have some probables. It made the same sense to the commander of the artillery battalion: four confirmed, two probables, which is what the staff would report to Colonel Mulvaney, the commanding officer of Twenty-Fourth Marines, at the regimental briefing. By the time it reached Saigon, however, the two probables had been made confirms, but it didn't make sense to have six confirmed kills without probables. So four of those got added. Now it looked right. Ten dead NVA and no one hurt on our side. A pretty good day's work.

CHAPTER
FOUR

Colonel Mulvaney, the regimental commander, ponderously made his way up the single aisle between the captains, majors, and lieutenant colonels who stood at attention waiting for him to reach his empty place at the front of the rows of folding chairs. The humid air in the tent smelled of mothballs. When he reached his chair, Mulvaney grunted to Major Adams, who crisply asked the men to take their seats.

Mulvaney picked up the briefing sheets that had been placed on his chair and shuffled through them. His mind was on the recent discussion with the division chief of staff about the coming combined cordon and search operation at Cam Lo. It "must use ARVN troops and the local militia." It would be "highly conspicuous and highly political" —and, in Mulvaney's view, highly impractical. He'd been asked to give two battalions. After his vehement argument against it, including a colorful analysis of the effectiveness of ARVN, the Army of the Republic of Vietnam, he'd been ordered to give two battalions.

Major Adams cleared his throat. Mulvaney sighed, eased his large body back into the chair, and nodded at Adams, who immediately turned to a large map and indicated with a pointer.

"Contact occurred today at eleven-forty-seven hours, at grid coordinates 689558, between a squad-size unit from Bravo Company One Twenty-Four on a routine security patrol, and an estimated ten to fifteen Vietnamese. Two confirmed kills, one probable. No injuries reported from Bravo Company. Artillery fire was called in with two confirmed kills and one probable reported. The weather prohibited air strikes." The major turned to face Mulvaney.

Mulvaney knew he should ask a question. It annoyed him that Adams kept saying One Twenty-Four all the time, as if after twenty-six years in the Marine Corps he wouldn't know that Bravo Company of his own regiment was in the first battalion. He nevertheless kept his temper, remembering his wife, Maizy, who even at the airport had cautioned him again to keep his temper, not only for the sake of the men under him but also for the sake of his career. A fucking combined operation with the South Gooks. Sitting around a goddamned village while their goon squads went in and roughed up the civilian political opposition. Again he remembered that people were expecting a question.

"Any intelligence gathered?" he asked. "Weapons recovered?"

Major Adams hadn't covered that question. He quickly looked down at the second row of seats, where Lieutenant Colonel Simpson and Major Blakely, First Battalion's commanding officer and operations officer, were leaning forward in their chairs behind Mulvaney. Blakely, immediately recognizing that Adams wasn't prepared for Mulvaney's question, quickly shook his head no, his lips pursed tightly. Adams, with hardly a pause, answered the colonel's question. "That's a negative, sir. Immediately after contact was made the friendly unit withdrew to bring in artillery fires."

Mulvaney grunted again. Even though it had been a quarter of a century ago, it seemed to him that only last weekend he himself had been leading patrols in the jungle. If he'd been leading the goddamned patrol and had run into a unit of unknown size, he could very well imagine getting his ass out of the area and not bothering to collect papers.

Two kills for Bravo Company and two more for Golf Battery—with no casualties—was good enough for one day's action. It entered his mind that with a body count of four it might be more than good enough, but he decided not to ask any questions that might put Simpson in a bad light—or himself, for that matter, for not trusting his officers. He watched Simpson writing in a notebook, his face even redder than usual, and wondered if Simpson was still drinking. When he'd been in First Division at Camp Pendleton, after Korea, Simpson had been drinking quite heavily, but then who didn't after that damned war. They'd returned home as if they'd been on some goddamned exercise. Blakely he didn't know. Good-looking guy. Kind you'd see at an embassy. Too young for Korea, so no combat experience. Not his fault. Still, he wished Blakely did have experience. But his record looked good. Good fitness reports. Probably champing at the bit for a battalion. Keep an eye on him. He saw Blakely whisper something to Simpson, and Simpson again wrote in the notebook.

The intelligence briefing droned on. Sensor readings picked up at coordinates 723621. An AO, air observer, spotted two NVA in the open at coordinates 781632. Elements of Hotel Company, Two Twenty-Four, uncovered two rice caches of fifty kilos each at coordinates 973560. Mulvaney's thoughts drifted. Why in hell is it always "elements" and not men? Who should he pick for the combined operation? He became aware of a silence and knew it was time for him to ask another question or two.

After intelligence came the regimental Three on operations, then the medical officer, then supply, then the adjutant, then artillery, then air, then Red Cross liaison from Quang Tri, then the congressional inquiries, and finally the commanders of the battalions.

Mulvaney watched closely as Simpson strode quickly to the front of the tent: a small man, his jungle camouflage neatly starched, his red face and hands contrasting oddly with the green material. Mulvaney knew that Simpson had been a young lieutenant in Korea at the same time he himself had been there, although they hadn't known each other then. Simpson had apparently done a fine job—earning a Silver Star and a Purple Heart—and his fitness reports were all excellent. But the scuttlebutt was that there'd been a painful divorce along with the drinking problem. But then, hell, divorces and drinking weren't exactly uncommon problems in the Marine Corps. Mulvaney watched Simpson pick up Adams's pointer and turn to face him, waiting for a nod. Mulvaney could see that, as usual, Simpson was nervous as hell. You could tell right away when Simpson didn't know what he was talking about.

Simpson turned to the map and began speaking. After showing the dispositions of the companies, he paused a moment for effect. "As you

can see, sir, with my companies spread in an arc, here, here, and here"—
the pointer whapped the map crisply at each *here*, fixing in place 175 to
200 Marines at each whap—"and with Bravo Company providing security for Golf Battery here on Matterhorn"—*whap*—"I have decided
it expedient that I move my tactical headquarters immediately to
Matterhorn to personally direct operations. With Bravo Company
making contact here"—*whap*—"and Alpha Company here"—*whap*—
"I'm certain we have a sizable NVA unit operating in this area. The
supply and ammunition cache found three days ago by Charlie Company here"—*whap*—"as well as the bunker complex that Alpha uncovered last week here"—*whap*—"all indicate that this area will soon be
highly productive. I intend to be right on the spot when the shit hits the
fan. That's why I've already ordered my staff to begin planning for
moving my headquarters to Matterhorn."

Mulvaney looked blankly at Simpson. Just when he was thinking
of using Simpson in the combined operation down in the flatlands, the
son of a bitch had decided to get gunjy and move to the fucking bush.
As if being out in the goddamned jungle and not being able to see his
men was any better than being at VCB and not being able to see his men.
Yet Mulvaney couldn't talk about the operation yet. It would keep his
commanders on pins and needles wondering who was going to have to
pull up stakes and head for the flats while the South Gooks fiddle-farted
around with their wasted goddamned villages, and his old friend and
now commander of the division General Neitzel could tell the Army
three-star in charge of I Corps, who could report to Abrams in Saigon,
that the Marines had "cooperated fully" with the government of the
Republic of Vietnam.

Several people coughed. Simpson seemed unsure what to do and
looked back at Blakely for a sign. Blakely brought his eyebrows together
and nodded slightly, assuring him that it was OK just to wait.

"That's fine, Simpson, fine," Mulvaney said. Bravo Company. He
searched his memory. Bravo Company. Wasn't Bravo commanded by a
young first lieutenant? Fitch, wasn't it? He'd been the one who'd found
an ammo dump and all those 122-millimeter rockets on the Laotian
border by Co Roc. Now Mulvaney remembered. He, Neitzel, and some

of the bigger Army brass had flown out there to get in a couple of pictures, and Simpson had been hovering around the edge of the group being ignored while the brass were falling all over themselves patting Fitch on the back. Maybe Simpson just couldn't stand not being in the limelight. Mulvaney could easily move Simpson back if he needed to. That young Fitch was lucky. Luck was one of the attributes Napoleon considered necessary for a good officer. Napoleon knew his shit. That had been the second time Fitch's picture was in *Stars and Stripes*. The first time was just after he'd taken over the company from Black, when Black lost his leg. The kid had fought the company out of a real shit sandwich up on the DMZ. Jesus, that was a bum deal, Black losing his leg. A good career officer. Fitch was a reservist, if Mulvaney remembered right. Christ, they're almost all reservists now. The regulars were all being chewed up by this . . . *thing* over here. Still, the kid *was* lucky. So far. As for Simpson's sudden hots to get out into the bush, it never hurt to reward initiative, even if initiative came at an inopportune time. And Simpson could be right. That arc of recent firefights . . . Maybe he could compromise, pull back only two of Simpson's companies. Who knew or cared if Simpson was going up there to control his men better or just get into the limelight? In war, action mattered, not motives. "Just don't get your ass shot by any gook machine guns when you fly in, Simpson."

Mellas found Hawke making coffee in his battered cup on a stove devised from a number ten can. He was using heat tabs, which even at a distance made Mellas's nasal passages sting.

"I'd like to put Rider and his team in for some sort of medals," Mellas said. "They did a hell of a job today."

Hawke didn't answer right away. He was watching the small bubbles forming at the bottom of the cup and wiping at the slight tears caused by the heat tab. "This isn't the Air Force, Mellas."

"No shit it isn't. We did a hell of a job out there today." As soon as he said it, Mellas knew he'd slipped. He felt his face starting to redden. "I didn't mean—"

"The fuck you didn't mean." Hawke looked up quickly at Mellas, eyes flashing for a moment. He resumed watching the can. Mellas knew that Hawke was letting him squirm. Then, without looking up, Hawke said, "Look, Mellas, in the Navy or Air Force they give you a medal for what the Marines consider just doing their job. In the Marines you only get a medal for being braver than just doing your job." Then he looked at Mellas. "You get in fixes where medals are handed out because you were unlucky and had to fix things or because you were stupid and had to fix things. Be careful about what you're wishing for."

"I don't want to get on your bad side," Mellas said. "I was just—"

"Stow it, huh?" Hawke turned to Mellas. In a very even voice he said, "Mellas, I don't give a fuck which side of me you're on. I just want to find out whether you're going to kill any of my friends or not, and right now I'm not too fucking sure."

The hissing of the heat tab in the stove seemed very loud.

Mellas was the first to break. "OK, I wanted a medal. That doesn't mean Rider and Conman shouldn't have one."

Hawke eased a little in response to this honesty. "Well, you don't lack for persistence." He sighed. "Look. Everyone wants a medal. That's no sin. When I first got here, I wanted one, too. It's just that after you've been out here long enough to see what they cost, they don't seem so fucking shiny." He looked up briefly, to see if Mellas got the point. Then he poured two packages of instant coffee and two packages of sugar into the boiling water. He stirred it with a stick.

"Sorry," Mellas said.

Hawke visibly softened. He handed up the steaming cup and smiled. "Shit, Mellas, drink this. It cures all ills, even vainglory and ambition. The only thing that hurts about a rebuke is the truth."

Mellas took the coffee and smiled. "Benjamin Franklin."

"Fuck no. My uncle Art, the poet."

"Benjamin Franklin. Art copped a lick."

"Yeah? Typical. You can never tell with Uncle Arthur. We're not even certain Grandma had him with Grandpa."

The two were silent while Mellas took a sip.

"Maybe we can get Rider a meritorious promotion to lance corporal," Hawke said. "That will at least get him some more money. Of course you'll have to write it up like it was fucking Chapultepec and Belleau Wood combined and Rider's a potential Chesty Puller."

"How long should it be?"

"Do I look like a fucking English teacher?"

"Can't I ask you a serious question?"

"Why are you so fucking serious?" Hawke asked.

"I'm not all the time."

"Neither am I."

The two of them stood there, looking at each other, suddenly seeing through their formal relationship.

"Goodwin said you went to Harvard," Hawke said.

"I went to Princeton."

"They're all the fucking same. Same guys with tassels on their fucking loafers, same communist fucking courses." He passed the coffee back to Mellas.

Mellas took two sips, trying not to burn his lips on the hot metal. He handed the cup back to Hawke. "Where did you go to college?" Mellas asked, feeling uncertain of how to proceed.

Hawke took a careful sip and licked his upper lip. "C to the Fourth."

"Huh?"

"Cape Cod Community College. I finished my last two years at U Mass."

Mellas nodded, squatting on his haunches, unconsciously imitating all the other bush Marines who did this to avoid getting their trouser seat wet.

"What the fuck you doing in the Crotch anyway?" Hawke asked. "All you fucking Ivy Leaguers got enough money to get out. Doctors, psychiatrists, graduate schools, homosexual tendencies. Jesus." He looked at Mellas suspiciously. "Are you and Goodwin shitting me about where you went to school?"

Mellas paused for his usual careful weighing of answers. "I joined when I was eighteen, before I went to college. I grew up in a little logging town in Oregon and any guy worth a shit does his time in the service. That's what everyone called it—the service. There wasn't any war then and I got to go to college on a scholarship and got paid in the summers. They made me a lance corporal in the reserves and I didn't have to do Navy ROTC."

"You still could have gotten out when the war started. Your kind must have all sorts of fucking pull with draft boards and congressmen."

"Not really."

"Bullshit."

Mellas hesitated. Most of his friends from Princeton did indeed have the kind of pull Hawke was talking about. He and his friends from Neawanna Union High School did not. He wanted to tell Hawke that going to Princeton was different from having a father who went to Princeton, but he didn't. "I don't know. It just seemed that all the other guys were going."

"And the president doesn't lie. He must know something we don't."

"Right," Mellas said.

"You still could have switched to the Navy. All the rest of your hoity-toity buddies joined the Navy, didn't they? At least the ones that weren't screwing their brains out and smoking dope at some peace rally."

"Yeah. Mostly. The ones who joined anything. A couple joined the CIA," he added, feeling somewhat defensive about his friends. Hawke handed Mellas the steaming pear can. Mellas, smiling at the ribbing he was getting, juggled the can from hand to hand. "Maybe I'm just a fool for wanting to be different. There are so many guys trying to get into Navy OCS, the Navy'll have fucking ensigns scraping paint pretty soon."

"Yeah. Real happy ensigns."

Mellas laughed, took another sip, and then handed the cup back to Hawke.

Hawke took a sip of coffee and eyed Mellas shrewdly over the brim of the tin can cup. "You know, I bet you're thinking you're going to run for fucking Congress as an ex-Marine."

*　*　*

At the actuals meeting that night, Fitch told everyone about the plan to move the battalion headquarters group to Matterhorn as soon as possible. Bravo Company's part of the plan was nailing the NVA machine gun.

Goodwin spoke voluntarily for the first time. "Hey, Jack. I got this hunch I want to try out tomorrow."

"Have at it," Fitch said. He handed Goodwin his map.

"This fucking gook machine-gun team," Goodwin said. "Both times they fire from the east side, right? And when Mellas runs into them, they dee-dee south. But south is downhill and nothing but bamboo and elephant grass. North is cliffs and shit. That means they work around the south side of the hill and are over there." Goodwin pointed west. "Between us and Laos, but not too far, because they'd lose too much altitude. They ain't no dumber than we are and I sure as shit wouldn't want to hump a machine gun up this fucking mountain every day just to get a chance to shoot at a chopper. But I wouldn't be so high I had to hump for water either."

Mellas envied Goodwin's practical logic.

"OK, Goodwin," Fitch said, "turn in your route and we'll prep it for you just before you go."

"No prep, Jack."

"You're sure?"

"I don't want no tip-offs. I'm going right where they are, Jack." Goodwin pulled Fitch's map over a little. He squinted at it, then his large finger pointed to a small offshoot of a larger ridge. "Right here."

Everyone looked at the spot. Mellas looked questioningly at Hawke. Hawke shrugged.

Goodwin left before dawn with one of his three squads, heading west toward Laos. Mellas went south with Jacobs and Second Squad from his platoon, down a long finger that led onto the valley floor below them.

They were moving slowly in thick jungle along the crest of the finger when they heard the firefight start. Even though they were a good two kilometers south of Goodwin, the noise of the M-16s was so loud that everyone hit the dirt.

Mellas grabbed the hook from Hamilton and listened.

". . . Goddamn it, I don't know how many there are, Jack. I'm busy."

"Bravo Two, Bravo Two, this is Bravo Six. Big John's got to have your position report. Over."

Nobody answered. Suddenly there was complete silence.

"Bravo Two, you get back on this fucking net. Over."

Firing erupted again, and the sound rolling over them was now intermingled with the thump of hand grenades.

Mellas pulled out his compass and took a bearing on the sound. It was an endless ear-shattering explosion that set his heart racing. Mellas keyed the handset. "Bravo Six, this is One Actual. I've got a bearing on the sound of three four zero. My pos is six seven one five one niner. Over." Mellas and Fitch both knew that Mellas had just risked exposing his own unit to NVA mortar or artillery fire by revealing his position over the radio in order to give Fitch the second compass bearing that would pinpoint Goodwin's location.

Fitch's voice returned. "I copy three four zero." There was a brief pause. "He's just where he said they'd be. You know the spot? Over."

"I'm on my way." Mellas suddenly felt useful, important, rushing to help his friend.

The rush soon turned to frustration as the Marines cursed and hacked at the indifferent jungle. Mellas pushed them, swinging the machete himself when his turn came. The firing died down. Then it stopped altogether.

They linked up about an hour later. Both squads were exhausted, but Goodwin's squad was carrying one SKS rifle, an AK-47, and a long-barreled Russian DShKM .51-caliber machine gun, plus several steel boxes of linked cartridges and a heavy, spider-legged tripod. They also had the usual belt buckles, water pipes, helmets, and military insignia and buttons, useful for trading. One of the kids had been hit seriously enough to have to hobble between two friends, but he wasn't in any real danger. Goodwin himself had been creased across the right ear with a bullet. It had taken out a small piece of flesh and cartilage and left a thin bloody track down his neck.

"Hey, Jack," he boomed out to Mellas, pulling on his ear. His voice was unnaturally loud because of the temporary hearing loss. He was tugging on his bloody earlobe. "Look at this. A fucking Purple Heart." He laughed with delight and adrenaline. "Two more and I'm out of this fucking hole."

Mellas forced a smile. It was well known that after three wounds the Marine Corps considered the recipient too nervous, too unlucky, or too stupid to remain effective in combat. The kids in both squads laughed. Those from Second Platoon couldn't stop talking about how Goodwin had taken the small machine-gun team by surprise, crawling up on their position, firing, throwing grenades over their crude log barrier. They'd killed three. The rest had fled.

By the time they reached the perimeter all the kids were calling Goodwin Scar.

Mellas was aware of how plain and ordinary, perhaps even hesitant, he must look next to Goodwin. He couldn't quite use the word chickenshit, but deep down inside, unnamed, the fear of it was there.

The next day, the battalion staff flew into Matterhorn.

Lieutenant Hawke stood outside Fitch's hooch, his hands in the pockets of his field jacket. He felt invaded. Bravo had walked to Matterhorn through virgin jungle and had pushed the jungle back to form a crown of open space around Matterhorn's crest, all under the constant harassment of the machine-gun team. Now the battalion CP group was flying in on choppers, trundling in bag after bag of gear, canned goods, radios, alcohol, and magazines. Hawke wanted to believe it was coincidental that they came the day after Goodwin had bagged the gook machine gun.

The enlisted men, mostly radio operators and supply clerks, were digging out large bunkers and filling sandbags. Hawke knew that they were all just doing what they were told, but he resented them. Even more, he resented the way Fitch had combed his hair and shaved a second time that day to meet the colonel and the Three, Blakely.

"Shit," he said out loud and crawled back inside the hooch to find a cigar. Relsnik and Pallack were both there, playing gin and monitoring the radios.

"Anything new on our red dogs?" Hawke asked, automatically shifting his frame of reference to the map in his head, where he constantly knew the positions of the company's security patrols.

"Naw," Pallack answered. "Except fucking Lieutenant Kendall turned in a pos rep that was about a klick off d' one Daniels turned in just after him, so I put 'em where Daniels said." He turned back to his hand.

This wasn't the first time that Kendall had made a mistake reading a map, and Hawke knew as well as Pallack that Daniels was probably right. He also knew that Daniels had probably turned in the position report to show Kendall up. He decided not to pursue the discrepancy on the radio. He'd talk to Kendall and Daniels about it separately. He crawled back outside into the gray afternoon and lit his second-to-last cigar. He took a long slow puff, savoring every sensation, especially the warm dryness of the smoke. "Shit," he said again, thinking of the constant rain. Then it occurred to him that with the battalion moving in, there ought to be someone up there he could buy cigars from. He smiled, his eyes roving over the lines, taking in the terrain and thinking about the positions of the patrols at the same time.

Fitch had previous patrols, not current ones, on his mind. As he made his way slowly up the slope he was rehearsing his arguments about why it took so long to get the gook machine gun. He lifted his stateside utility cover from his head, pushed down his hair, and replaced the cover neatly. When he saw Simpson and Blakely conferring over a map and occasionally looking down into the valley, he gave a short sigh and walked across the LZ to join them.

"You wanted to see me, sir?" he asked, saluting both of them.

"No salutes, Lieutenant," Simpson said jauntily. "We don't want Blakely here picked off by another gook machine gun, do we?" Fitch lowered his hand and Blakely laughed. "It's good to be out in the bush," Simpson said almost absently. He put his field glasses to his eyes and scanned the valley.

"You doing OK, Tiger?" Blakely asked.

"Yes sir," Fitch said.

Finally the field glasses came down and Simpson turned toward him. "You know what to do when you kill gooks, Lieutenant?"

Fitch was at a loss for an answer. "Sir?"

Enunciating each word as if speaking to a child, Simpson repeated, "What do you do when you kill gooks, Lieutenant?"

"I, uh, sir?"

"You don't know, do you?"

"Uh, no, sir. I mean, I'm not sure what the colonel is asking."

"I'm asking about fucking intelligence, Lieutenant. *Fuck-ing in-tel-li-gence.* You know what that is?"

"Yes sir, I do. Sir."

"Well, it doesn't look like it." Simpson turned to Blakely as if sharing a secret. Blakely nodded, and Simpson went on: "Let me help you out. You know, you don't always have Marine Corps photographers to record your after-action reports for you." He smiled, but apparently not with good humor. Blakely did the same. Fitch smiled back uncertainly. "Intelligence, Lieutenant," Simpson went on, "is built up by the fastidious collection of minutiae. You understand that, don't you? It isn't the result of spectacular finds. It's the result of hard work, constant attention to detail—to minutiae. *Mi-nu-tiae.*"

"Yes sir."

"When you get dead gooks, you collect everything. Wallets, shoulder patches, letters, everything. You empty their pockets. You bring in their weapons, their backpacks. You smell their fucking breath to see what they've been eating for lunch. You following me, Lieutenant?"

"Yes sir."

"Good. I don't want any more intelligence lapses."

"Yes sir."

"I'm glad to see you finally got that fucking gook machine-gun team. How many patrols you running a day?"

"Three, sir."

"Not enough, was it? Two fucking weeks."

"Sir. We were trying to put in a firebase and build up the lines at the same time."

"Everyone has problems, Skipper."

"Sir, we did *get* the machine gun. And didn't lose anyone doing it. We also brought it in along with an AK and an SKS."

"And what unit were they from?"

Fitch licked his lip. "I don't know, sir," he finally answered. He knew that since the battalion had turned in Mellas's one probable as a confirmed, there would be no sense telling Simpson there was no body to search. On the other hand, Goodwin had definitely killed three, but he'd come back in with weapons and trading material—crowing like a rooster, the kids calling him Scar—and no intelligence. Fitch almost smiled at the memory, in spite of the fact that he was getting dressed down for it now. Fuck, he thought, they're all from the 312th fucking steel division anyway and everyone knows it, including you, Simpson.

"You see, Lieutenant, you not only failed to be aggressive in your patrolling, you neglected your defenses."

"Sir?"

"Your lines, Lieutenant. Your lines. They're totally exposed to artillery attack."

"Sir, uh. The closest gook artillery is at Co Roc, as far as we know. That's even farther than our own was at Eiger."

"You're the one who found all the fucking 122s."

"I know, sir. But the gooks don't usually waste those on small in-fantry positions. They're for taking out bigger stuff."

"You read Giap's mind now?"

"No sir. I wasn't trying to say—I mean, I know nothing is for sure, but—"

"Exactly. Nothing is for sure. It takes you fucking forever to find that machine gun that has Bushwhacker Six all over my ass, and I get out here and your fucking lines are a shambles and totally exposed to an artillery attack."

"Sir, are you saying we should put covers on the fighting holes?"

"Well, Blakely," Simpson said, turning to his Three and smiling. "It appears the Basic School still teaches standard infantry defense tactics."

"Yes sir," Blakely said.

Simpson turned back to Fitch. "That's right, Lieutenant Fitch. I want those lines prepared for an artillery attack. *Artillery*, Lieutenant. And rockets, not just mortars. You've got three days."

"Sir, the troops are right at the edge. We don't have chain saws, big shovels, any steel matting. Hell, even sandbags are hard to come by. I mean with you people and the arty people using them—"

"That's right. Preparing for an artillery attack." Simpson looked out at the valley again through his field glasses. "In Korea the gooks always hit us with artillery before they attacked. Don't worry about sandbags, Lieutenant. We've got them on order. I'm sure you can figure some way to put in the roofs."

Fitch knew he was being dismissed, but he made one last try. "Sir, if I might say. I mean, I know you're right about arty. We'd be a lot safer with overheads, but . . . Well sir, the men in the company get a little spooked if they can't see and hear, and we sort of feel, I mean, even when Captain Black had the company before me, we always chose to maximize the hearing and sight and take the small risk of getting hit by arty. It's sort of SOP, sir."

"Standard operating procedure just changed, Lieutenant. I'm not going to lose good fucking Marines to artillery because of laziness."

"Sir?"

"What?"

"Sir, they're not lazy. They're tired."

"I wasn't talking about the snuffys, Lieutenant."

"Yes sir."

"Now I want to see those fucking fighting holes covered. Three days, Skipper."

"Yes sir."

*   *   *

Halfway through his second-to-last cigar, Hawke saw Fitch sliding his way down the side of the hill. "How'd it go?" he asked.

Fitch told him.

"Did you argue with him?"

Fitch hesitated, looking down at the ground. "Sure."

"Ah, fuck, Jim. Not hard enough. Why don't we build the fucking Siegfried Line? No, the Pyramid of Cheops. We've got all the slave labor."

Hawke left Fitch squatting alone in the drizzle and stalked off to find Cassidy.

Cassidy's hooch was neat and orderly. His rifle and ammunition were hung on carefully whittled pegs stuck into the wooden ammunition crates that formed one wall. Cassidy was gazing at a picture of his wife and three-year-old son when Hawke stuck his head into the entry. He waved him in and Hawke filled him in on the bunker problem.

Cassidy didn't answer right away. He showed Hawke the picture. "Think he'll be a Marine someday?"

"Sure, Gunny." Hawke knew he should say something more, but he couldn't think of anything. There was an awkward silence. Hawke broke it. "So I wondered if maybe you couldn't go see the sergeant major. I hear he's been in combat. Maybe he can talk to the colonel about it."

Cassidy grunted. "I don't want to go looking like no fucking crybaby, Lieutenant, not in front of the sergeant major."

"But that's what he's for, isn't he? Doesn't he represent the enlisted man's point of view? Cassidy, these kids are fucking *tired*."

"Yeah, but . . ." Cassidy rolled over on his rubber lady and stared at the poncho, which was ruffling in the damp breeze. "You get the reputation for a crybaby and you're fucking finished." He looked at Hawke, almost pleading. "If I make E-7, we can have another kid, maybe a piano."

Hawke was disappointed in Cassidy. "OK, Gunny, I see your point. Just thought I'd see what you thought of the idea." He backed out of the hooch.

Cassidy lay there a long time listening to rain spattering against the poncho. He was an acting company gunny in a combat outfit, while only a staff sergeant, E-6. That meant a lot toward promotion to gunnery sergeant, E-7. His wife would be proud. His son. But if he complained to the sergeant major . . . A staff sergeant on the wrong side of the battalion sergeant major would stay a staff sergeant for a very long time.

"Fuck!" he finally shouted, and crawled out of the hooch.

Cassidy found Sergeant Major Knapp supervising the building of the command bunker. Knapp's utilities were clean, his boots shiny and black. He looked like a business executive doing weekend reserve duty. Yet Cassidy knew that as a teenager the sergeant major had been at Tarawa.

After the usual small talk, Cassidy said he had a problem. "It's about the order to cover the fighting holes with roofs."

"I hadn't heard about that."

"The colonel told the skipper that we had three days to cover the fighting holes with roofs. Wants them sandbagged, leave slits for the rifles and M-60s. You know. *Guns of Navarone.*" The sergeant major sat there, watching him. Cassidy fidgeted. "Well, goddamn it, Sergeant Major, it's a stupid fucking order. You got to hear and see and you can't do either in a fucking cave, not with rain beating on the roof. Fucking gooners can crawl right around and hit us blind on our backsides if we can't hear them. Our men are fucking exhausted. We've been patrolling the shit out of this place, building the fucking LZ, laying goddamned wire, clearing fields of fire, and all we get to work with is our fucking K-bars and E-tools. Our goddamned hands are full of pus."

"You're talking about your commanding officer, Staff Sergeant Cassidy," Knapp said quietly.

Cassidy swallowed. "Yes, Sergeant Major." He felt his face burning. "If we get hit, it's going to be by sappers sneaking up on us at night. The gooks won't hit us with artillery. They ain't going to waste ammo that they hauled through air strikes over four hundred miles at night on a fucking hill like this." The sergeant major listened impassively. Listening to junior NCOs was part of his job. Cassidy's voice intensified as he saw Knapp's indifference. "They sneak up on you, goddamn it. You've got to listen for the little bastards. I don't see why these men got to build their own fucking coffins."

"So what do you want me to do about it?"

"I ain't no fucking crybaby, Sergeant Major, and we got a good fucking company of Marines. We can do what we're told, and no griping, but I think the colonel don't understand the situation, that's all. This ain't fucking Korea. Maybe you could talk to him."

"Why doesn't Lieutenant Fitch do that?"

"I guess he tried."

"Then what can I do?"

Cassidy could see that the sergeant major wasn't about to use up chits to help out a young staff sergeant who felt overworked and underpaid.

Knapp patted Cassidy on the shoulder. "Tell you what, Staff Sergeant Cassidy, I'll see if I can't spare you some men to help after we get done setting up the CP area. I might even be able to secure a chain saw or two. My God, anything we can do to help. Just ask."

Cassidy walked wearily down the hill, knowing he had damaged his standing with the sergeant major and failed the kids in the company as well. He cursed his temper.

By the next morning a full storm was hurling itself against the hill. The platoon moved in slow motion all day, buffeted by the wind, hampered by cold hands that made grasping E-tools and knives even more difficult than normal. It seemed cruelly unnecessary to Mellas to have to return to the backbreaking work of digging and chopping just when they had reached the point where they could start working on their own living quarters. Yet they dug and chopped, finding the meaning of their actions within the small prosaic tasks, casting from their minds the larger questions that would only lead them to despair.

Vancouver and Conman alternated filling sandbags, one holding a bag open while the other one shoveled in the sticky clay. To Vancouver each sandbag was just that, nothing more—one filled sandbag to be followed by the next. The small E-tool burned his blisters and sores. He watched the blood and pus from the jungle rot on his fingers and wrists smear in with the mud and rainwater. He paused occasionally to wipe his hands on his trousers, not even thinking that he had to sleep in them. Everything soon had the same greasy consistency anyway, mixing in with the urine that he couldn't quite cut off because he was so cold, the semen from his last wet dream, the cocoa he'd spilled the day before, the snot he rubbed off, the pus from his skin ulcers, the blood from the popped leeches, and the tears he wiped away so nobody would see that he was homesick. Except for his size and the role that he'd taken on, or fallen into, Vancouver was no different from any other teenager in the platoon. He knew that the role gave the others heart and he had to admit that he liked playing it, because of what it did for his friends and for himself. He liked the respect—hell, he was almost a celebrity. But he was not ignorant of what it cost. Being on point scared him every time he took it, yet something compelled him to take it every time.

Broyer figured he needed sixteen of the small logs to complete their bunker. He knelt before the first one, squinting at it through his glasses, not wanting to start. His hand was swollen. He'd cut it on razor grass two days earlier and it had become infected. He'd seen the squid about it, but all Fredrickson could do was paint it with some red shit and give him some Darvon for the pain. When he touched the handle of his K-bar the pain made him want to pull his hand away and hold it under his armpit, nursing it with the warmth of his body.

He hacked at the log with the knife. The pain was intense. The K-bar bounced back from the hard wood, leaving only a small nick. He stared at the nick. He took his left hand and tried again. He was ineffectual left-handed; the K-bar merely bounced off the wood instead of biting at it.

"You've got to get mad at it," Jancowitz said, coming up behind Broyer unexpectedly. "Like this." He took the K-bar from Broyer's hand and attacked the log, cursing it. He smashed the large knife against the wood again and again. He screamed filthy language. Small chips began to come out of the wood. Janc suddenly stopped and smiled. He threw the K-bar into the wood, point first, and left it there quivering. "Eight fucking days until I see Susi in Bangkok," he said. He walked off down the line.

When Second Squad returned from patrol, Jacobs immediately noticed how far behind his squad was in building the bunkers, even though Lieutenant Mellas and Sergeant Bass both had promised him that the squads not on patrol would work equally hard on the entire platoon sector. Hippy's machine-gun position did have the beginning of a wall around it, as well as some rather crooked logs, which Jake guessed were rejects from the other squads. He sat down heavily in the mud, legs dangling inside the hole.

Hippy took off his wire-rimmed glasses and wiped them on his shirt. He held them up to the rain and looked through them. He put them back on, and then slowly took off his boots, grimacing. He carefully peeled his wet socks from his feet, which were discolored and puffy.

"Those look ugly," Jake said.

Hippy grunted. He began massaging his feet. "There it is." He rubbed a few minutes more, then put his boots back on, wincing, and started taking apart the gun to clean out the dirt and vegetation.

Jake wished desperately that Fisher were back, but Fisher was gone. Just like that, taken away, and now here he was, feet dangling in Hippy's machine-gun position, everyone tired, the fucking rain beating into the earth, his squad without bunkers, and only two days left to complete them.

"No one did shit for us today," Jake said. He kicked at the side of Hippy's hole, and a glob of mud splashed into the water. He saw Lieutenant Mellas approaching him from Conman's section.

Mellas squatted down next to the hole. "Thought I'd save you the trouble of walking uphill to give me the after-action report."

Jake noticed that Mellas, too, was dirty and tired, and it made him feel good to think that the lieutenant had been working on the lines as well. "Nothing, sir. Nothing but rain and fucking jungle."

"No footprints? Nothing?"

"You've been out there. Nothing."

Rain suddenly slashed down on them in heavy sheets. Water ran off Jake's helmet onto his nose and neck in tiny cascades. Jake looked at the lines. "I see they got a lot done on our bunkers today, sir."

Mellas looked away briefly. "They did the best they could. As far as they were concerned you guys got to screw off with a walk in the park."

Hippy slammed home the bolt of the machine gun, startling both Jake and Mellas. "Tell me something, Lieutenant," Hippy said. "Just tell me where the gold is."

"Gold?" Mellas looked puzzled, but Jake knew that Hippy was struggling with something deep. He could see Hippy's jaw muscles trying to control the frustration and exhaustion.

"Yes, the gold, the fucking gold, or the oil, or uranium. Something. Jesus Christ, something out there for us to be here. Just anything, then I'd understand it. Just some fucking gold so it all made sense."

Mellas didn't answer. He stared at the jungle for a long time. "I don't know," he finally said. "I wish I did."

"There it is," Jake said. He lifted the butt of his rifle to the earth beside him and pushed himself to his feet.

Mellas stood with him. "Look, Jake, I know it's tough, but we've got some daylight left. Get some food and see if you can't fill some sandbags for foundations for the roofs before dark."

Jake looked at Mellas dully, trying to comprehend it all. He turned without saying a word to pass the order down to the fire team leaders.

The light began to fade and the lines grew quiet as the company went on the evening stand-to. Williams and Cortell, who had been working next to Johnson on their own bunker, were cleaning their M-16s in what light remained. These two had been together ever since they came in-country. Cortell, the leader of Jancowitz's second fire team, was small and, had he been better fed, would have been round. His slightly receding hairline made him look older than his nineteen years. Williams, tall and rangy, with the big hands of a rancher, was almost Cortell's physical opposite. What they had in common, besides the Marine Corps and eight months in combat, was farmwork, although for the one it was cotton in the Mississippi delta and for the other Herefords and hay.

Cortell liked this kid from Idaho. Until he joined the Marines, Cortell had never spoken with a white boy other than to excuse himself or conduct business. Even in boot camp, the whites and blacks had pretty much kept to themselves for the brief moments the Marine Corps allowed any of them time to themselves. Now here they were. He could never quite get used to it, expecting Williams to refuse to sit next to him one day or suddenly go off on him for no good reason. But Williams never did. Today, however, Cortell could feel something different about Williams, nothing dangerous or ill-willed, but something self-conscious and hesitant. He took a chance.

"Somethin' on you mind, Will?"

Williams held up the trigger assembly to inspect it.

"Yeah, but . . ."

"But what?"

"I don't know."

Cortell waited. He knew that waiting was often the best thing.

"I mean, I know that Cassidy and Ridlow and Bass are always getting on you about it. But . . . I mean I think you do. I mean congregating. You always go off by yourselves back at VCB. Even out here, you're always hanging out with Jackson and the other Negroes."

"We ain't Negroes any more," Cortell cut in, not unkindly.

"Well, whatever you are. I mean . . . that shit isn't going to get you anywhere."

Cortell carefully snapped the barrel of the M-16 in place. "I bet you think we over there doing some kind of voodoo or somethin'. Hatchin' up black power plots."

"I don't know," Williams said. "I'm not there."

"Well, hate to disappoint you dumb cowboy ass, but we don't even think 'bout white folks when we be *con*gregatin'." Cortell gave his characteristic chuckle. "You ever hear that story 'bout the ugly ducklin'?"

"I may be from Idaho, but our mommas do tell us fairy tales." He pointed the barrel of his M-16 toward the waning light and peered through the back side, checking for dirt. Satisfied, he began reassembling the rifle.

"Well. You know Jesus," Cortell said. "He spoke in parables. You know why? Because when you speak in parables it's the listener comes up with the right answer, not what the talker think is the right answer. You with me here?"

Williams nodded.

"I bet you think that story be about some ugly little kid that no one like because he be a plug*ugly* little kid and then he grow up and he not ugly anymore because he ain't no duck. He be a *swan*. Whoa. And of course the swans be all white and the ducks all dark, but I'm not gon' go there with this sermon."

Williams smiled. Cortell was always getting kidded about preaching when he got excited. He took the ribbing, not without a little pride.

"Well, let me tell you what *I* think that story be about. It be about this little duck can't grow up. Can't grow up to be a big duck 'cause he ain't a duck. But he don't know what he's 'sposed to grow up *to*." Cortell looked carefully to be sure he wasn't losing Williams. "I mean, you don't know what you supposed to grow up *to*, that make it pretty hard to grow up." He waited a moment. "So, we ain't *congregating*, we just hangin' out with people best we can to figure out where *to* is. You with me here? *To* ain't with the white folk 'cause we be black folk and tryin' to find *to* hangin' out with you chucks just a dead end for us. When I hang out with you chucks, I'm a black man first and who I really am come next. When I hang out with the splibs, I'm *me* first and there ain't no black man at all. It got nothin' to do with white folk. It's just the way it is. Ain't no voodoo conspiracy. We just hangin' out and movin' on best we can."

Williams, who had been holding his breath, let it out. "Yeah. There it is."

"There it is," repeated Cortell.

"I think it scares people," Williams said.

"Scare you?"

"Yeah. Naww." He worked the bolt on his rifle. "I don't know."

"We get scared, too," Cortell said. He looked out at the jungle and back home to Four Corners, Mississippi. "Seems the only way I ever talk with a white man is to be just a little scared." He came back to Matterhorn and looked over at Williams. "Till you, brother."

Williams slammed home the bolt and stood up. "Aww . . ." He shook his head sideways. Then he smiled, looking down at his chest.

Cortell laughed. "Sit down here, m' man. You ain't got phase two of my sermon yet."

Williams sat down. "Speak, Reverend."

"We ain't Negroes any more."

"You were when I was in high school and that was only last spring."

"We ain't Negroes any more. We blacks."

Williams only half-suppressed a smile, knowing Cortell would see he was amused. "So if we were whites last spring are we supposed to be called Blancos or Caucasios or something now?"

"Get back."

"No, really. I mean, what did you folks used to be called?"

"Niggers," Cortell said, opening his eyes wide.

"Not that. Fuck you. I know that's an insult. You know what I mean. I mean what did you folks called *yourselves*."

"Don't give me any 'you folks' stuff either. You talkin' to one man here."

"OK, then. What did blacks used to call yourselves?"

Cortell thought a moment. "Well, Negro a lot, actually. The Reverend King called us that. But he dead. It seem too close to nigger now, or *ni*gra." His mind raced through an image of southern aristocracy and then any possible connective root between the words *genteel* and *gentile,* which he quickly dismissed. His mind was always doing that to him. "Negro doesn't have that, you know, pride thing." He held up the bolt of his M-16, trying to catch the last of the light on it to see if he'd missed anything. "Sometimes we called ourselves people of color."

"People of color. Never heard that one."

"Yeah, but you from *I*daho."

Williams gave Cortell the finger and went back to wiping down the barrel of his own M-16 with another oiled patch.

"Anyway," Cortell went on, "we blacks now. Ever'one be some color. Even *white* is a color." Now it was Cortell's turn to let Williams know he was suppressing a smile. "But it be a pretty dull go-nowhere do-nothin'-for-you insipid color."

"Whoa, Cortell. In-*sip*-id."

"What, you think I'm some dumb cotton chopper with no vocabulary just because I talk like I live in Mississippi?"

Williams smiled at him. "People of color," he said. "Pee-oh-cee." He paused, then said, "Poc." He waited just a moment, then, "Poc, poc." It had the sound of a coffee percolator just starting to boil.

Cortell shook his head, smiling at the foolishness.

Williams was suddenly on his feet again. "Poc, poc, poc." His head was thrown back and now the sound was like a chicken squawking in a barnyard. "Poc poc pocpocpoc." He was walking half-crouched, his neck poking forward, hands tucked under his armpits with his elbows out. "Poc, poc, poc, poc." He crowed and strutted. Heads turned from up and down the line and then turned back to what they were doing.

Cortell hung his head, trying very hard not to laugh. "You do that shit 'round some of the other brothers they wring you chicken neck."

"Poc." Williams sat down. "Poc, poc."

"I know you a dumb Blanco from Idaho so I don't have to kill you," Cortell said, "but you make fun of somethin' serious and do some that poc poc stuff in front of the wrong brothers and you be in some serious shit."

"Serious shit?" Williams said. "Serious shit?" He raised his arms and indicated everything around him. "*This* is serious shit. Everything else is horseshit."

They resumed assembling their rifles. It had never occurred to Cortell, until now, that friendship, not just getting along with someone, was possible. It had never occurred to him that friendship was not possible, either. It had just never been there as a thought at all. Williams had simply been a fact, like the jungle or the rain. He started to muse on this. How could something occur to him that had never been in his mind before? It had to have been there before—otherwise, it wouldn't have popped up—but it must have been hiding someplace. Where was that someplace in the mind where all that stuff hid? Was that what people meant when they said "the mind of God"? But then, that meant God's mind was inside him someplace—and Cortell got a little scared at where his head was taking him. He'd have to get someplace quiet, the way he always did when these kinds of questions scared him, and talk with Jesus about it. Maybe he could go talk with the battalion chaplain someday when they got out of the bush. He wondered if the new lieutenant knew the answer. Someone said he'd been to college, and they had to teach them something about God there, didn't they? Then he started wondering who *they* were.

"Or maybe chickenshit," Cortell replied to Williams. As usual, the time lapse between someone's last words and his own reply had been filled with all these thoughts, but they came so fast that the person he was talking with wouldn't even notice a pause. Cortell assumed it happened like that to everyone.

After a while Williams said, "So, I mean, about growing up *to* someplace. Or someone. I don't know. I mean, you got somebody in mind? Martin Luther King or Cassius Clay or somebody?"

Cortell looked up at the darkening clouds. "Nope. I got Jesus. He's my *to*."

"Yeah, but Jesus is white."

"Nope. He be a brown Jew. God got it just right."

While working on the bunkers, Mellas caught glimpses of Simpson and Blakely, but neither of them ever came down to the lines so it was impossible to meet them without appearing obvious. Midway through the next day the storm slacked off to the usual drizzle, and at lunch break Mellas tried another path.

When he reached the top of the hill, some artillerymen were grunting one of the heavy 105-millimeter howitzers into the center of a new gun pit. All the trees were gone. The top of the hill was stacked with cannons, crates, and machinery. Matterhorn looked like an aircraft carrier in a jungle sea.

Mellas spotted the cluster of radio antennae above the new battalion combat operations bunker and ducked down through the small opening. Two hissing Coleman lanterns lighted the gloomy interior; the air was warm and smelled of their fuel. A lieutenant was moving markers on a map. The lieutenant frowned. Mellas quickly identified himself as an officer. "Hi," he said. "Lieutenant Mellas, Bravo One." He put on his nicest smile.

The watch officer brightened. "Bif Stevens, arty liaison, Twenty-Second Marines." He held out his hand and Mellas took it, noticing how soft and clean it was. They chatted, Mellas asking intelligent questions, Stevens responding, apparently glad to see that at least one of the grunts actually cared about what he did for them. Mellas thought about asking, as his own private joke, if Stevens had any booze, just to make it look as if that was the real reason for showing interest, but he decided against it. He kind of liked the guy.

"Are there many guys like Fitch?" Mellas eventually asked. "I mean, lieutenants running companies?"

"Not a lot," Stevens answered. "Maybe one to a battalion for the line companies. Some mustangs for headquarters and supply companies. It's all luck."

"How's that?"

"You know. Right place at the right time. Being the company executive officer when the CO gets killed or transferred. That sort of thing."

"You think Hawke will get Bravo when Fitch goes?"

"Like I said, it's timing—and if he's crazy enough to want to stay in the bush. He's overdue now for the rear. Policy is to get as many lieutenants exposed to combat as possible. They'll rotate Hawke someplace soon as we get some. Same policy for captains. Of course we're short of captains."

"Yeah, they all got killed when they were lieutenants," Mellas quipped.

Mellas stored Stevens's information about transfer and command policy in the part of his mind that dealt with power. This was as automatic for him as it would be for a farmer to store the morning's weather report and the smell of the air, and then to harvest a week early and beat the unseasonable rains.

Two men pushed through the blanket over the entrance, spilling light and cold air inside. One was neat and good looking, even handsome, and wore the gold leaves of a major. The other was small, wizened, and tough, his face both young and old, marked by lines and the strain of a body that had seen extreme use and maybe too much alcohol. Silver leaves gleamed from a neatly starched collar. Mellas felt excited. It was Lieutenant Colonel Simpson, Big John Six.

Simpson gave Mellas a puzzled look. Major Blakely, on the other hand, returned Mellas's smile. "Who do we have here, Stevens?" he asked.

"Lieutenant Mellas from Bravo Company, sir," Stevens replied.

"Ahhh. One of our new tigers. I'm Major Blakely, the battalion Three. Meet Lieutenant Colonel Simpson, our commanding officer." Blakely shook Mellas's hand. Mellas felt dirty and unkempt.

Simpson reached out a small hand. His grip was surprisingly strong. He grunted. "Welcome aboard, Mellas. You an oh-three?" he asked, referring to the military occupational specialty, or MOS, for infantry.

"Yes sir," Mellas replied, laughing. "Looks like you're stuck with me a lot longer than ninety days."

"Good," Simpson said with a grunt, satisfied. "You a regular?"

"No sir, not yet." Mellas paused, giving a "young man at a crossroads" look. "I'm thinking about it, but I'm also thinking about law school."

"High-paid fucking clerks," Simpson said. "Pussies, too." He walked over to the map and started asking Stevens about the disposition of Alpha and Charlie companies in the valley to the north.

"The Marine Corps needs lawyers, too," Blakely said.

"I know, sir. But for me there's only one reason to stay in the Marine Corps—to lead men. That's why I'm an oh-three." Mellas noted that Blakely wore a Naval Academy ring and Simpson wore no ring. "Of course, most of my friends from Princeton are going to law school," he added, knowing Blakely would pick up on it.

"Jesus Christ," Simpson said with a snort, "how'd we ever let someone with a fucking communist education into the Marine Corps?" Blakely and Mellas both gave the expected laugh, as did Stevens.

"Well, sir," Mellas said, "you know how low standards have slipped since you joined."

"Jesus, don't I," Simpson said.

Mellas knew he'd connected. He also knew that this moment was the perfect time to leave, but he wasn't through. He turned to Blakely. "I don't know how law school could compare with having a platoon. Being a platoon commander has to be the greatest experience of my life. I suppose only running a company could have it beat." Blakely nodded. Mellas could see that he was anxious to be with the colonel. "I was really lucky to get Lieutenant Hawke's old platoon. He's one of the best. We'll really miss him when he gets out of the bush."

Blakely raised his eyebrows. "He due out soon?"

"Overdue. And is he *ready*." Mellas laughed. "He's been in the bush nearly ten months. It's a pisser, though, losing all the experience so new lieutenants like myself can pick it up. It's hard on the men." Mellas paused, then brightened. "You must snap up guys like Hawke as soon as you can."

Blakely smiled smugly. "We manage to hang on to our good ones." He and Mellas were dancing, but as far as they were concerned it was just chatting. Like most good dancers, they made it look easy.

At the three-day deadline the bunkers were only half finished. Because the battery now offered a much more tempting target to the NVA, the security patrols had to be pushed out farther from the hill, and so they took much more time and effort to complete. The Marines would return, already exhausted, to start blasting trees into logs with C-4 and hacking at the logs with their K-bars. Unremitting physical effort combined with the monsoon rains, the mud, and the ceaseless hammering of the artillery battery left them nearly in a stupor.

But they kept at it, digging their fighting holes deeper into the rootbound clay. The bunker roofs had to be raised high enough above the fighting holes so a man could stand on a ledge and fire above the hole's parapet. The roofs had to be set on supporting walls formed from sandbags filled with clay. These walls, and their new exits and entrances, were eventually several feet high on the downhill side and barely aboveground on the uphill side.

The defensive lines grew more distinguishable. No longer were they made up of holes that blended in with the earth and the mass of torn limbs and brush. The holes had been transformed into naked, angular structures, stark against the denuded hillside, looking like sturdy little boxes poking out from the slope.

Mellas worked hard like the rest of them, learning from Jancowitz the subtleties of bunker construction. Don't use rocks, because they splinter into deadly shards. Dig pits and shelves to keep feet and ass free of standing water. Interlace hard material with soft to absorb blast energy. Soon Mellas was not only helping with the hacking and hauling but enjoying the intricate planning of the total defense. He carefully walked the ground from the jungle upward, finding how the lay of the land channeled attackers into natural avenues of approach. Then he set the bunkers so that the avenues of approach would be filled with machine-gun bullets. Pegs were carefully driven into the ground so that the swing of the machine-gun barrel would be limited and the fire would be directed into the avenue of approach even in total darkness. More barbed wire came in by chopper, and the exhausting, hand-bloodying work of stretching it tautly below the bunkers continued.

Hawke and Fitch both recognized a natural defensive engineer in Mellas and soon had him coming with them whenever they toured the perimeter. Solving the intricacies of setting bunkers so that each bunker was defended by at least two others was an exercise in iterative geometry that came naturally to Mellas. Move one bunker, and all the bunkers around it had to be moved. Getting it right before the bunker was built was the trick, because if one fire team finished a bunker without considering all those around it, a critical weakness could be created in the interlocking system. Mainly because of Hawke's natural feel for the probable pattern of assault and Mellas's ability to figure out placement, only three half-finished bunkers proved to be misplaced and had to be destroyed and rebuilt just a few feet from their previous positions, to the exasperation of those who had built them.

Every hand in the company ran with pus from jungle rot. Bacteria invaded the cuts and open blisters. Old gloves—even gloves with holes in them—brought more cash than had been paid for them originally. Eventually, though, these transactions dwindled. Any gloves, with or without holes, became as precious as mail and no market price could be struck. Going out on patrol, which used to be a dreaded duty, became a longed-for holiday.

It took six spirit-breaking days to finally complete the bunkers. No one celebrated. On the seventh day the kids rested by doubling the patrols. That evening, Fitch opened the actuals meeting with a terse announcement. "We're heading into the valley at first light. The battery and the battalion CP group will start pulling out simultaneously. Charlie Company will be where they drop us and take the same choppers back here. They'll provide security for battalion staff and the artillery during the shift. Then they're all heading for the lowlands. Some big fucking operation around Cam Lo."

"We just finish the bunkers and they're pulling everyone off?" Mellas grabbed a lone surviving plant and savagely uprooted it, flinging it down the hill. "Jesus Christ," he hissed, his teeth clenched. "Just like that. We're pulling out." He had grown proud of the job they'd done—of himself, his platoon, all of them—in spite of the fact that it made them more vulnerable at night. Given enough ammunition, he felt they could hold off a regiment.

"We and Delta flip-flop missions with Alpha and Charlie," Fitch continued slowly. "Relsnik has it from a battalion radio operator that regiment gave Big John Six one last chance to prove he's got lots of gooks out here. We've also got responsibility for blowing the ammo cache Charlie Company uncovered. They ran out of C-4."

"You mean we're going out in the jungle just to look around?" Mellas asked. "A whole damned company?"

"Two damned companies," Hawke corrected.

"Well, I'm not telling those guys down on the lines that we're leaving after what they've been put through. You get the colonel or that goddamned Three down there to explain why we whipped their asses into the ground so we could pull out the second we built the goddamned Rock of Gibraltar in the middle of goddamned nowhere."

"Look, Mellas," Fitch said tightly, "simmer the fuck down. We leave at first light. You just get your platoon ready to move."

The rest of the actuals were silent. Kendall fiddled with his wedding ring and his wraparound yellow sunglasses. Goodwin, looking drawn and haggard, squatted on his heels toying with a stick. His constant clowning had been a source of relief during the construction. He had said nothing during the entire meeting.

After the meeting, Mellas made his way slowly down the hill, wondering how he'd break the news that they'd built the bunkers for no purpose. It also surprised him, after all the days of looking into the valley, wondering what it was like down there, worrying about going, that now it was time to go, just like that. His entire world had been instantly transformed at the word of a man he barely knew. The platoon could be ready to go in half an hour. All they needed was to pack their food and ammunition. But he felt there should be more time, some ritual of getting ready, before they plunged into that dark valley.

When Mellas reached his hooch, everyone was already there. It was obvious that everyone knew. Jackson, now leader of the Third Squad, had his pocket notebook out and his pen ready; he looked very serious. Bass had presented Jackson with the decision to make him acting squad leader in Janc's absence and had given no alternatives, just telling Jackson he was it. This was the best they could do to alleviate the problem of Jackson's worrying about reactions from the brothers. Connolly, the leader of the First Squad, was looking down at Mellas's C-ration box, his legs apart and his hands on his hips. He kept spitting into the box, seemingly unconscious of what he was doing. Occasionally he would look out at the valley and curse; his Boston twang was just loud enough to be heard. "Fuckin' A, man, the fuckin' Crotch. There it is." Then he'd spit into the box again, making Mellas cringe because he'd probably have to open one of the packets that Connolly had spat on. He said nothing, however, feeling this wasn't the time. Jacobs, who had taken Second Squad from Fisher, was also staring into the fog below them. He turned to look at Mellas, his eyes flashing. "F-fucking bunkers. F-for nothing." Then he turned again to the fog, saying nothing more. Mellas knew the company history as well as any of them. Bravo Company had never been on an op without at least three deaths.

"There it is, you unhappy motherfuckers," Jancowitz crowed. "Another inch of the green dildo. I'm going to Bangkok and Susi's going to screw my brains out. Hee hee."

"You were screwed brainless when you extended your tour," Connolly said.

Mellas quickly opened his notebook. "That will do, Conman." He began to pass on all the information he'd received at the actuals meeting.

"Who's going into the zone first?" Bass asked. He was notching another day into his short-timer's stick.

"Scar," Mellas replied, chagrined that Fitch had chosen Goodwin over him for the important task of securing the landing zone in the valley. He'd wanted to volunteer to go first, even though he was afraid, just so Fitch would know he was a decent guy.

"Good," Bass grunted. "We had it last time."

Mellas went on handing out coordinates, call signs, changes in radio brevity codes, all the minutiae that make up the day-to-day operation of an infantry unit.

Bass immediately organized work parties in the darkness at the top of the LZ where the company's 60-millimeter mortar squad was set in. There he passed out the mortar shells, each weighing a little over three pounds. The Marines tied two each to their packs. Even the radio operators slung one beneath their radios. That gave the company more than 400 mortar rounds, making it a formidable small artillery force.

Mellas placed two of the mortar shells—still wrapped in their neat cardboard tubes—under the bottom of his pack, tying them in place with wire. By the time he'd finished stuffing all the food he could into his pack, it weighed almost sixty pounds. In addition, he had his grenades, two bandoleers of ammunition, and four canteens of water. Still, Mellas's burden was lighter than that of most of the kids. He didn't have to share the machine-gun ammunition, extra C-4, trip flares, claymore mines, and rope. The machine gunners and radio operators carried very heavy loads, and the mortar squad carried even more, each man lugging his own rifle and personal gear as well as seven or eight mortar shells and a heavy part of the disassembled mortars, which included sixteen-pound bipods and awkward thirteen-pound steel base plates as well as the long heavy mortar tubes themselves.

That night, the faint glow of red-lens flashlights shone beneath poncho liners as last letters home were written. Mellas wrote too, trying to sound cheerful. But leaving Matterhorn filled him with cold foreboding.

CHAPTER
FIVE

The mood on the landing zone at the battalion CP was different. Lieutenant Colonel Simpson had opened a second bottle of Wild Turkey and was generously passing out shots to the pared-down staff that had come up the hill with him.

"I smell 'em, goddamn it," Simpson said, pouring Blakely and Stevens another shot. "I smell 'em." Light from the hissing Coleman lanterns flickered against the walls of the bunker, casting the shadows of the five officers huddled around the C-ration boxes that served as a low map table. Blakely took his bourbon neat, but Stevens didn't much like the stuff and mixed his with enough 7-Up to kill the taste. When the colonel started drinking, there was no clear stopping point until the colonel stopped drinking. Junior officers didn't stop first—that was protocol. Captain Bainford, the air liaison officer, and Captain Higgins, the intelligence officer, sat wearily on the ground with their backs against the bunker wall, not really in the group around the map. They were trying to stay awake. The battalion radio operators also had shots of whiskey—Simpson was certainly not unfair to enlisted men—but they kept their distance and were quiet, monitoring the desultory radio traffic of the night.

"Well, sir," Blakely mused aloud, "we got a compromise. Can't complain."

"By God, we can't, can we," Simpson said. "Two companies in the bush is better than none." He paused, took another quick drink, sighed, and smacked his lips. "Goddamn, that's good whiskey."

"Yes, sir," Blakely agreed, taking another, smaller sip of his own. He knew that if they did find something in the valley during the next few days, it would be very unlikely that General Neitzel could resist doing something about known enemy troops operating just north of them. Matterhorn anchored the west end of Mutter's Ridge, an avenue of attack into the populated lowlands. No matter how intensely he felt the political pressure that was diverting nearly the whole regiment to the Cam Lo operation, he'd have to respond. Blakely's mind drifted to an imaginary scene at division headquarters, where he was chief of staff, advising the general on the political complications and how they interacted with the strategic complications. He smiled at his daydream. Simpson was right. This damned Wild Turkey got smoother and smoother.

Blakely mentally reviewed the flip-flop plan again. Originally it had been easy. Continue the original mission with two companies in the valley snooping and pooping. Charlie flip-flops with Bravo on Matterhorn, and Alpha flip-flops with Delta on Eiger. Then comes the idea of the Cam Lo cluster fuck with everyone pulling back to VCB to get ready for that. So that plan had to be changed. Then comes Mulvaney's compromise with Simpson. So now Bravo and Delta are going out to the valley instead of to VCB. So *that* plan had to be changed. A question flickered in his mind. When was the last ration resupply for Delta on Eiger? It hadn't mattered before, because Delta was originally going back to VCB with everyone else. Then it occurred to him that with Charlie moving back to VCB instead of to Matterhorn, that left Golf Battery and battalion headquarters exposed, albeit just briefly, during the time of the flip-flop. This pushed the question of Delta's food supply out of his mind.

"Sir," he said to Simpson. "I'm just thinking about covering the battery. They'll be exposed without Bravo Company for a while until we get them moved back to VCB."

"What are we talking about? A couple of hours? Blakely, they're Marines. If the gooks are dumb enough to attack us, the battery'll hold them off, and instead of dropping Delta into the valley we'll drop 'em back here and kill gooks from both sides." He put his arm around Blakely's shoulders. "You're a hell of a staff officer, Blakely, but you're a worrywart." He took Blakely's glass and poured more Wild Turkey into it. "Now relax. That's an order." He handed a full glass to Blakely.

Blakely smiled at him and took it. "Can't disobey an order, sir."

"Goddamn right you can't."

Blakely took a drink. Damn, Simpson could sure pick a good whiskey. The glow was moving from his stomach through his arms and legs. He felt good. The battery did have only a small window of vulnerability during which it had to protect itself. He was being a worrywart—Simpson was right. For a brief moment Blakely wondered who was blowing the abandoned bunkers on Matterhorn, but just then the other officers broke into laughter. Simpson had pulled out another bottle of Wild Turkey from someplace and was grinning widely as he opened it. He's got to be just as tired as me, Blakely thought. The colonel was right about something else—Blakely should relax more. Besides, it would do nothing for his fitness reports if he looked like a stick-in-the-mud and got on Simpson's wrong side. No one liked stick-in-the-muds. Simpson needed him, too. Simpson had lots of guts; Silver Stars don't come easily in the Marine Corps. But Simpson wasn't up to handling the details. Of course, that's why Simpson had him. Blakely took another sip, savoring it. He had to hand it to the old man: Simpson could pick whiskey. It had been a fucking nightmare to get everything rescrewed around once Simpson got the word he could put two companies in the valley instead of taking the whole battalion into the flats. One small change, just one, and all that fucking food and ammunition, all set up to go one way, had to be turned around to go somewhere else. Good staff work was complicated. Blakely's mind wandered; he was half-listening to the jokes and stories of the other officers. He wished he were home. He wished he were asleep. He slugged the rest of the whiskey. What was wrong with relaxing when he could? If everyone was getting drunk before the Cam Lo operation kicked off, why be left behind? You want to be seen as a team player.

Before first light, Bravo Company assembled in heli teams at the LZ. The kids, fully loaded, heavy, encumbered, crouched in a single line that stretched below the crest of the hill, waiting for the choppers to come with the daylight. The artillerymen went about their business of packing up their gear, stepping between and sometimes over the infantrymen sitting on the ground. Some looked at the infantrymen curiously, but most tried to ignore them, not wanting to be caught up in their fate.

When Vancouver strolled across the LZ in the predawn semi-darkness, however, even the studied indifference of the artillerymen was broken.

"Where the fuck did *he* come from?"

"A fucking movie. Didn't you know the Crotch was making a fucking movie out of this op?"

"They couldn't get John Wayne so they got him."

"Naww, fuck. They're shooting background for Huntley-Brinkley."

"Did you see what that mother was carrying? A fucking sawed-off M-60. Jesus Christ."

"He'd never be able to hit a thing with it. It's a bunch of gunjy bullshit."

"I don't know, man."

"It's bullshit. You couldn't control it."

"Who the fuck *cares* if you can control a fucking M-60?"

Mellas kept walking around to check each heli team, asking if everything was all right. He approached the last team, Bass's. Skosh was lying on the ground with his eyes half closed, a green towel wrapped around his neck.

"I guess we're all set, Sergeant Bass," Mellas said.

Bass looked at him. "I guess we are, Lieutenant."

Embarrassed by his obvious anxiety, Mellas walked over to where Goodwin lay on his back, eyes shut, head cradled in his helmet.

Mellas whispered, so the others wouldn't hear, "Hey, Scar."

Goodwin grunted.

"Did you pack any underwear?"

"Naw, shit, Jack. All it does is give you crotch rot."

"Yeah," Mellas whispered. He fingered the pale green T-shirt that his mother had dyed for him.

"How come you call everyone Jack?"

Goodwin opened his eyes and looked at him. "It's easier to remember their names that way."

"Oh," Mellas said. "Sure."

Goodwin closed his eyes again.

Mellas walked over to where Jackson was lying with his team. Jackson looked up at Mellas, craning his neck over his immense pack. His record player was tied on top with communication wire. "All set, Jackson?" Mellas asked for the third time.

"Yes sir." Jackson, with that nothing-to-hide look of his, held Mellas's eyes. Then he broke eye contact to look down the line of tired bodies in his squad. Mellas could see that everyone in the squad had cultivated a bored waiting-for-a-bus expression that concealed all emotions.

"Couldn't go without your sounds, huh?" Mellas asked.

"No sir. Not hardly."

"How much does it weigh?"

Cortell, the leader of the second fire team, who was sitting next to his friend Williams, chuckled. "Man," Cortell said, "you can't carry nothin' lighter than music."

Jackson flipped a thick middle finger in Cortell's direction. "Easy for you to say, you ain't carryin' it." He turned back to Mellas. "The suffering I endure so my men can have music, and Cortell makes light of it."

"Jesus make all your burdens light," Cortell said.

"Yeah, well he ain't here today, Preacher."

"Where two or more are gathered in his name, Jesus be there." Cortell was used to the banter about his Christianity and gave back as good as he received.

Mellas had caught Jackson's pun, and it made him feel more secure with Jackson as a squad leader. "Why didn't you get a little tape recorder?" he asked Jackson.

Jackson paused, thinking. "I guess I just like to see the record go around."

Mellas laughed but knew what Jackson meant. Somehow the cassette was foreign—Japanese—or futuristic. A forty-five record was probably as near to home as anyone could get in the jungle.

Corporal Arran walked by with Pat tagging just behind and to his right, obviously not on heel, sniffing at whatever was of interest to him, turning his head, panting happily in response to the various greetings of the Marines. He sniffed at Mellas's trouser leg, then trotted over to where Williams was sitting against his pack, his large rancher's hands cradling the back of his head. Williams sat up and reached out to tousle the dog's reddish ears, smiling, obviously pleased that Pat had singled him out. "I like dogs," he said to Mellas. "They seem to know it." He turned back to the dog, grabbed the loose skin on Pat's neck, and gently wagged the dog's head back and forth. "Hey, big fella. Hey. What you doing in Vietnam?" The dog licked Williams's hand and then his cheek and Williams giggled. "You don't know why you're here any more than me, do you, big guy?"

Arran gave a quick low whistle and Pat trotted off after him. Mellas continued down the line of Marines, stopping when he reached Pollini, who was retying his mortar rounds to the top of his pack. He reminded Mellas of a mouse busily trying to set things right in a cluttered nest.

Pollini looked up at him. "Hello, Lieutenant Mellas, sir." He had his big grin on. His face was smeared with grime.

"Pollini, don't you ever wash?" Mellas asked quietly.

Pollini reached a grimy hand to his face, rubbed it down his cheek, then looked at it, but of course the hand showed nothing new. His hands were the large ones of an old carpenter, with big yellow nails, yet his face under his mop of curly black hair looked like that of a choirboy who'd fallen in the mud. He looked up at Mellas, grinning again. "I washed this morning, sir, and shaved too."

Jackson had walked over, mild annoyance showing on his face because Pollini wasn't ready to go. "Shortround, you didn't shave this morning." Jackson said. "You ain't never shaved."

"I did too." Pollini stood up. "Ask Cortell." He turned to Mellas. "I did shave."

Jackson knelt down beside Pollini's mangled pack and started tightening wire and tying down objects. "Shortround, goddamn it," he said, pushing a wire into place. "Lieutenant, I swear he was all wired up about three minutes ago."

"I had to get a . . ." Pollini said.

Jackson stopped tying. "You had to get a what?"

"Just something."

"Shortround, you eating your food?"

Pollini grinned. Grinning was his main defense against all bigger and more competent people. "Well, just a can of peaches. I was on LP last night and missed breakfast."

"Why did you miss breakfast?" Jackson turned to Mellas. "I gave him twenty minutes while we were taking down our trip flares and claymores, sir."

"It's all right, Jackson." Mellas turned to Pollini. "You know you're going to need all the food you can carry. Why didn't you just go get some out of the boxes lying around the area?"

"I don't know, sir."

"You don't know because you're fucking stupid," Jackson said. "Now get your gear back together. Where are the peaches?"

Pollini dug into a large pocket. His size-small jungle utilities fit him like a clown suit. He pulled out the can and handed it to Jackson, who stuck it back in Pollini's jammed pack, angrily making room for it.

Pollini suddenly looked as though he was going to cry. "I'm not stupid," he said.

"You're fucking stupid," Jackson said.

"That's enough, Jackson," Mellas said.

He turned to Pollini. "Shortround, you're just going to have to learn to think about things. The choppers are due in about five minutes and here you are farting around and eating up your food besides."

"I didn't get any breakfast." Pollini was getting stubborn, his back to the wall.

Mellas felt his nerves, already jangling, begin to fray despite the enforced coolness. "Make sure he's ready to go, Jackson," he said, deciding it would be better to drop the subject. He walked away and settled back on the ground. He shut his eyes, hoping to look as if he'd gone to sleep. He gradually became aware of a plane droning overhead, lost above the clouds. He knew it was an airplane and not a helicopter because of the smoothness of the drone and the absence of the flat slapping thud a helicopter's rotors made against the air. He looked up from where he lay, seeing nothing, scanning the area where the sound was coming from with the interest of any bored person in a distraction. For a moment he caught a glimpse of a large plane, a quick leaden flash amid the cloud cover. Then it disappeared again. It seemed to be circling in lower. When it finally broke out of the cloud cover, it was far off to the northeast, over the valley into which they were to be dropped. It was a large propeller-driven aircraft.

"Looks like a transport plane," Mellas said to Hamilton. "What do you think he's doing?"

"Fucked if I know, sir." Hamilton didn't even bother to look. He was memorizing radio frequencies and codes.

The plane turned in a lazy circle, gaining altitude up above the ridgeline that extended from Matterhorn to Helicopter Hill and into the east. When it swung around again it was directly in line with the ridge, heading straight toward them. It kept coming. Quite a few people were watching it by now. A fine faint plume fell from behind it, a darker grayish silver cloud, hardly distinguishable from the overcast backdrop. The drone grew louder. The plane continued straight on. A few more Marines rose to their feet.

"What the hell?" said Mellas. He too stood up.

The plane roared overhead, its U.S. Air Force markings clearly visible, the sound of its four turboprops deafening. Within seconds they were enveloped in a chemical mist. People were coughing, wheezing, shouting obscenities. Mellas could see Fitch, tears running from his eyes, shouting over Relsnik's radio to battalion, demanding to know what was going on and trying to get battalion to stop it. The plane was dwindling into a speck to the southwest, climbing for altitude over the Laotian border until it was lost in the clouds. The only evidence of its passing was that the whole hill reeked, as if covered with mosquito repellent.

Hamilton raised an imaginary glass to the air. "Here's to the fucking Air Force."

Mellas, his eyes still tearing, walked over to where the company CP group was sitting. Fitch was holding on to the hook, clearly waiting for a reply from battalion. "I've got Bainford, the battalion forward air controller, on it," he said when Mellas got within speaking distance.

About a minute later the handset squawked and Mellas could hear a tinny voice saying, "It's a defoliant. We put an order in for it for tomorrow, but it looks like we got a fuckup someplace. Sorry about that. It won't hurt you. It's just to kill plants. It's called Agent Orange. It's so the trees won't give any shelter to the enemy. The Air Force has used it a lot, and it won't bother humans."

"Well, it bothers me," Mellas said loudly. Fitch ignored him.

"Roger that. Bravo Six out."

Fitch turned to Mellas. "You heard him—it's for killing plants. Zoomies. God damn them." Fitch kept muttering curses as he wiped his eyes.

Hawke walked up and handed Fitch his pear-can cup, steaming with coffee.

The sound of the birds coming in from the south finally broke the nervous lethargy. Mellas rushed into his gear, rechecking ammunition and weapons, then realized that Goodwin would be going in first and sat down again.

The first bird came in fast. Its roar filled the air and its blades lashed the puddles of water in the muddy clay. Goodwin rushed across the open ground with his heli team. He slapped their backs, counting them, as he moved them into the opening jaws of the chopper's rear. The tailgate closed and he was gone. Almost immediately a second bird flew in, and then a third. Mellas saw Sergeant Ridlow, his big .44 strapped to his hip, run across the LZ. Then Mellas too was running across the LZ, Hamilton scrambling beside him, his radio buried under all his other gear. Mellas counted his team into the bird. He gave a thumbs-up to the crew chief, and they were swallowed and sliding off into space, the chopper dropping down from the hilltop to pick up airspeed. Mellas had his compass out, continually checking directions so that when they hit the ground he'd be oriented immediately.

Off to their right the looming black ridgeline that had been their constant companion on the hill, and had required a full day's effort to reach, slid by in seconds. Below it were steep jungle-covered slopes carved by large streams. The jungle stopped when it hit the valley floor and elephant grass took over. The map was a confused series of contour lines. In several places the contour lines didn't even join—the mapmakers had given up.

The deck tilted and the pitch of the blades changed. The roar of the engine increased. Mellas's throat was throbbing again. The grass rushed up toward them, changing from its illusory smoothness to its ten-foot-tall reality. The chopper hit with a crash, throwing everyone back on his rear end. The doors opened and they scrambled out, hitting the mashed grass beneath their feet at a full run. Mellas immediately headed to the left and began placing everyone in his assigned place in the zone.

Nothing happened. Smiles broke out over rifle barrels pointing outward into the grass. A few minutes later Mellas saw Fitch and Hawke running across the LZ toward the Charlie Company CP group. Mellas walked over to join them. As he did, he saw that the kids of Charlie Company were nearly exhausted and their clothing, dark and wet, was clinging to their bodies. Their jungle rot was even worse than what Mellas had seen at Matterhorn.

Mellas saw a radioman and walked toward someone who was lying on the ground but looked like a platoon commander. He looked up at Mellas wearily. His face was wide and he had a short thick mustache. There was no way of identifying rank except by intuition, but this man seemed to be in charge. "Hello. I'm Lieutenant Mellas. First Platoon Bravo Company. You guys look tired."

The man scratched his ear and grimaced. He reached out a beefy hand. "I'm Jack Murphy. Charlie One. We died two days ago and I'm having post-death hallucinations about sitting on an LZ waiting to get out of this fucking place. This is Somerville." He indicated the radioman. "He's not really here either." Then Murphy's face twitched and his head gave a brief jerk. He seemed unaware of it, as did his radio operator.

"They fucking humped us to death," said Somerville.

"What's the terrain like?"

"Awful," Murphy said. Again there was the quick sideways jerk of the head and the facial twitch. "Fucking mountains. Cliffs. Covered in fucking clouds."

Mellas pretended not to see the tic. "Hard resupply, I suppose."

"No. It was easy."

"Oh?"

"There wasn't any."

"Oh." Mellas decided Jack Murphy didn't feel like talking. But Mellas wanted information. "I heard you got hit."

"Yeah."

"What happened?"

Murphy grunted and raised himself to a sitting position. He brought his pack up with him as if it were simply part of his body. Then he lurched to his feet. He was about two inches taller than Mellas. He pointed into the elephant grass, indicating something unseen. "Out over that way the country gets real steep, lots of fucking streams and shit. You got ropes?"

"Yeah. We carry one per squad."

"Good," Murphy said. "Well, about four days from here, maybe less if you follow where we went and risk getting ambushed, there's a steep fucking hill. The gooks have dug steps out of it, so they've obviously had plenty of time to prepare bunkers. The point man and one other started up and all shit broke loose. The gooks got both of them and two others."

"You get any?"

"Who the fuck knows?" Murphy told Mellas the story. They had been strung out along a river that ran just below a hill. The terrain wasn't suitable for goats. Under the cover of their M-79 grenade launchers, they pulled the bodies back and didn't go any farther. They had to build a landing zone quickly in order to get the wounded medevaced in time. They were socked in by the monsoon and there was no good place in that impossible terrain anyway, so they humped downhill as fast as they could to get out of the cloud cover. One more died on the way down.

Murphy suddenly sat down again, worn out. "Save your fucking food." He twitched two times.

"Thanks," Mellas said. Murphy only grunted in reply.

Mellas moved on. He joined Fitch and Hawke and someone he guessed was Charlie Six, Charlie Company's commanding officer. The man wore a battered pair of glasses with tape wrapped around them. His utilities were black with water and rotten elephant grass. They clung to his body. He kept glancing nervously at the sky.

"Mellas," Fitch greeted him, unfolding his map, "just who we want to see."

"Your enthusiasm is hardly contagious," Mellas answered. Fitch didn't smile.

Hawke broke in, imitating W. C. Fields, "My boy, you do learn fast."

Fitch laughed nervously.

The conversation with Murphy had left Mellas on edge, and the W. C. Fields imitation, a form of humor he had always considered low-brow, grated on his nerves.

"Enough, Jayhawk," he said.

"Yes, *sir.*"

Mellas immediately regretted having said anything.

Fitch, licking his lips nervously, was oblivious of the exchange. He pointed to the map that he had laid out on the ground, and they all knelt over it. "This is about where the ammo cache is," he said. "Captain Coates here figures it's about three days if we follow their trail and risk ambush. Four or five if we take the safer way up along the ridgeline here." He bit his lip, suddenly silent. Then he looked up at Mellas. "I want First Platoon on point. We're going to make our own trail so I need someone who's good with a map. Right now we've got to clear out of the LZ fast. The gooks are probably already setting up their mortars. Follow Charlie Company's trail until I say otherwise." He licked his lips. "Tell your point man that Alpha's coming down the fucking trail with a body so don't get trigger-happy." Fitch's voice trailed off, and he gazed uncertainly into the damp rustling elephant grass. Mellas could feel Fitch's uneasiness. It was his first major operation commanding the entire company.

Captain Coates was sound asleep, slumped on his pack next to his radio operator, who was also asleep.

Mellas felt a stirring of hope. Here were two company commanders, one unsure of himself, the other giving in to exhaustion, yet both
had received commands. Then why not himself? He saw himself telling people back home he had commanded a company in action, 212 men.
No, 212 Marines. He looked over at Hawke, feeling Hawke's presence
as an impediment, knowing the company would go to Hawke and not
himself unless a captain showed up when Fitch rotated, in which case it
still wouldn't go to him. He simply needed more time.

Hawke, mistaking Mellas's look for a silent question, nodded toward
the sleeping commander of Charlie Company and began to fill in Fitch's
instructions. "Charlie Six could only describe the cache area. He couldn't
actually locate it on the map, because the map's inaccurate. So where the
battalion says it is ain't necessarily so. Coates says the map is a good six
hundred meters off in some places. Tonight we're going to try to make an
old gook base camp they found, up here." Hawke circled his finger around,
indicating a broad area. "The jungle's so thick he wasn't sure exactly where
he was, but it sounds like a good defensive position. Your first sign will be
brush cuttings. Either that or you'll hit Charlie's trail from the uphill side.
You start seeing signs, stop and give Jim a call and he'll come up and take
a look. I'll be humping *way* in the rear with Staff Sergeant Samms." Mellas
knew that Samms, Third Platoon's platoon sergeant, was regarded as
competent. But Samms was saddled with Lieutenant Kendall's poor map-
reading skills until they could get Kendall over his mandatory ninety days
in the bush and get him back to his motor transportation unit.

"What about the Kit Carsons?" Mellas asked, referring to the scouts
assigned to the company for the operation, former NVA soldiers who
had deserted and taken better pay with the Americans.

"They're on fucking strike," Hawke said. "They'll just hump along
with the CP group."

"You want me to pull out now?" Mellas asked.

Fitch came back to the present and told Mellas to take his platoon
about 200 meters up Charlie's and Alpha's trail and then wait for the
rest of the company to wind out of the landing zone. Mellas was surprised when Fitch told him that it took about half an hour for a company to snake single file out of a zone.

"Where you walking?" Hawke asked Mellas.

"Number five." The point man would lead, followed by the dog, Pat, and Corporal Arran; another rifleman and the squad leader were at positions three and four; and then came Mellas, followed by Hamilton and the radio.

"Good. I don't want the company going off on a fucking bear hunt because some squad leader can't read his compass. You'd better know where the fuck you are all the time."

"Yes, *sir*." Mellas said, smiling and trying to understand why Hawke was suddenly so testy.

"Just keep on your fucking toes." Hawke wasn't smiling. "And keep your fucking compass hidden when you check it. Man with a compass is a dead giveaway for a leader."

"Sure, Hawke."

Mellas rejoined the platoon. Everyone stood up, anxious to get out of the zone, feeling exposed to enemy mortars attracted by the helicopters. Bass and all three squad leaders pointed out with some passion that First Platoon had had point at the end of the last operation. Mellas stopped the argument by saying Fitch had ordered First Platoon on point because of the critical need to navigate to the NVA base camp. They all knew that with the possible exception of Daniels, Mellas was the best one with a map and compass and accepted their fate.

There was no argument among the squads that it was Conman's squad's turn to have point for the platoon. Vancouver was eating a package of Kool-Aid powder, waiting for the go-ahead. Everyone had given up trying to argue Vancouver out of taking point for the squad.

Mellas radioed Fitch. "Bravo Six, this is Bravo One. We're ready to roll. Just follow in trace of my Bugs Bunny Grape. Over."

"One, Bravo," Pallack answered. "Skipper says to make hat. Over."

"Roger. One out." Mellas looked at Vancouver and pointed into the elephant grass. Vancouver, who had purple smeared all around his mouth, took a last pull at the torn package and handed the remainder to Mellas. He chambered a round into his sawed-off machine gun and walked into the tall grass, following Charlie Company's path. Mellas looked at the package, purple powder smeared on the torn edges, wet from Vancouver's saliva. He shrugged, downed a mouthful, and made a face at Hamilton. "God, how do you stand this shit?" His eyes squinted at the tartness, and then he felt saliva gushing into his mouth. He shook his head and moved out, Hamilton following.

Almost immediately the hubbub of the landing zone was cut off from view and hearing. The tall grass whispered around them. Soon they passed Charlie Company's two-man outpost. One bedraggled kid called out, "I hope they don't hump you like they humped us."

"Me too," Mellas called back to him. "Here, I hate this flavor." He tossed the Bugs Bunny Grape to him and the kid smiled, holding it up in the air. Then he was lost to view.

There was no sun, just gray drizzle and the wet sighing elephant grass towering above them, its lower portions already rotting, making more soil to grow more elephant grass. As they twisted and turned along the trail of smashed grass, Mellas continually checked his compass. He kept it close to his hip.

Bass, with the tail-end squad, radioed that he was just now passing Charlie's outpost. Mellas was both surprised and disconcerted by how slowly they must be going, and the platoon was less than a third of the company. He went on farther, trying to estimate how far he'd have to go in order to put enough trail behind him to accommodate the entire company. Eventually he told Connolly to stop. Word passed up to Vancouver, who was on point, and Mellas motioned everyone down, alternating directions inboard-outboard to watch both sides of the trail. He waited for Fitch's word that the company had gotten its tail out of the zone and he could move forward again. He felt isolated, seeing only one person on the trail ahead of him and no one behind him because of the elephant grass, taking it on faith that the company was indeed still there. The drizzling rain and the wet elephant grass soaked his clothes through.

The radio hissed faintly. "Move it. Over."

"Roger. Moving," Hamilton answered. "Out." Hamilton motioned to Connolly, and everyone climbed to his feet without any word from Mellas. A good radioman and squad leader functioned without the need of a lieutenant, and Hamilton and Connolly had been together for months. Mellas was occupied with a leech he'd picked up. He kept kicking at his left leg with his right foot, hoping to kill it or knock it off without having to stop and squeeze insect repellent on it.

The company jerked forward, the radio alternately telling it to stop and go. It moved like an inchworm, slowly building up a contraction somewhere in the middle, then slowly stretching out until one kid lost sight of another. Word would then pass forward or back to the nearest radio. "Break in the column." Then the radioman would call forward to the point platoon: "Hold it. We lost you." Everyone would stop. People would fume.

Then the whole rear of the column would pile up on the kids who were stopped. Word would pass up and down until it reached a radio. "We're back in contact." Then the front of the inchworm would move blindly off. Slowly each part would feel the tug of the one in front of it and each Marine would start walking again, boots barely lifted from the mud of the trail, steps short and slow. Meanwhile the back would still be piling up and stopping. By the time the back of the column would get unpiled and moving, there would be another break in the front.

"Bravo One, Bravo." The radio's curt message ended in a burst of static as Pallack's transmitter key was let up. "Alpha figures dey're four hundred to five hundred meters from d' zone, so you ought to be close. Over."

"Roger. Bravo One out."

Hamilton looked at Mellas. In the silence of the elephant grass Mellas had heard the entire conversation, even though Hamilton was the one using the handset. Mellas nodded and moved up behind Connolly, who was at number four. "Alpha's close," he whispered. Connolly passed the word up to Corporal Arran, who was walking with a much-coveted twelve-gauge shotgun at the ready next to Pat. Vancouver, who was in front of Pat and Arran, was completely out of sight in the narrow twisting confines of the muddy trail.

Everyone grew tenser. There was only a split second to decide whether the slight movement on the trail in front was friendly or unfriendly. Deciding wrong could mean death, or the death of a fellow Marine in the approaching unit.

The company pressed on in the tunnel of grass, the sky visible only directly above them, the light poor. Vancouver scarcely dared breathe. Pat moved his red-brown ears nervously, sensing the Marines' tenseness. Suddenly Pat's silvery-white hair stood up, his tail went rigid, his nose pointed, and his red ears were angled forward. Mellas motioned everyone down. Silently, the column sank into the grass. Vancouver lay down next to the trail, his gun pointed to where the trail turned a corner. Everyone waited to see whether a Marine or an NVA soldier would come around the corner. Soon the fire team on point heard the sound of someone slipping in the mud. Then a few more footsteps. Then there was an eerie silence. No movement. No sound.

Connolly, eyebrows raised, turned to look at Mellas. Mellas nodded *yes*. Connolly whispered, "Hey, Alpha. This is Bravo here."

A voice whispered back, "Whoa, man. Am I glad to hear you." The voice rose to a soft speaking tone. "We're there. I just heard Bravo Company." Alpha's point man emerged cautiously around the corner of the trail, crouched low to the ground, eyes darting. Vancouver raised his hand, and the kid relaxed. He pushed his rifle's selector switch off full automatic. He was drawn, and the jungle rot on his face was very bad. He didn't smile as he shuffled past the quiet Marines from Bravo Company. Soon another kid emerged around the bend, then another. Eventually a radio operator came along. With him was a tall, thin, young-looking lieutenant, his camouflage utilities clinging to his body. He was trembling with early-stage hypothermia. He stopped in front of Mellas and let his platoon go by.

"Charlie in the zone still?" His voice was hoarse, weary.

"Some were when we left," Mellas answered. "They may have all flip-flopped back to VCB by now. I didn't hear any more birds come in."

"They probably forgot we're still here. Shit. First they tell us Charlie's going to Matterhorn and we're going to Eiger. Then we heard everyone was going to VCB. Some fucking cluster fuck around Cam Lo. Now the word is we're going to Eiger again. Fucked if I can keep up. Hey, you know that fucking Irishman, Jack Murphy?"

"Just met him."

"He owes me fifty bucks' worth of bourbon. He said there was no way we could get fucked over worse than on the DMZ operation. You got a cigarette?"

"No, sorry."

Hamilton casually pulled out his own plastic container, opened the lid, and offered both the lieutenant and his radioman a cigarette. Their hands shook as they gratefully lit up. Mellas was appalled at the lack of security. A person could smell cigarette smoke for miles. The tall lieutenant blew a large cloud and sighed. He turned to one of the weary figures going by. "Who's got the fucking stiff?"

"I don't know, sir."

"Shit." He turned to Mellas. Clearly close to a collapse, he took another long draw on his cigarette. "We haven't eaten in four days." It was a flat sincere statement. Just then, around the bend in the trail came four Marines. They carried a heavy burden slung between them in a poncho hanging from two poles. One kid looked angry; the other three seemed to be in a daze, faces drawn, wet, muddy. A white, slightly puffy arm stuck up into the air from the poncho. The bearers dumped their load on the ground, breathing hard. With the poles on the ground, the poncho lay open between them, exposing a naked corpse. The angry-looking Marine spat out his words between harsh breaths.

"How much farther, Lieutenant?"

He directed the words at the tall lieutenant, but Mellas answered.

"About six hundred meters."

"Six hundred! Fuck me in the mouth. Why don't we just hump him to VCB? Dumb cocksuckers."

"Cool down," the tall lieutenant said wearily.

"They killed him, Lieutenant. They fucking humped him to death and you want me to calm down. Well, fuck you." The kid's neck showed rows of taut cords. The lieutenant handed him his cigarette, not saying anything. "Thanks," the kid said. He sat down and took a deep draw while the other members of the company stepped over him and the body; then he handed the cigarette to one of the men with him. Mellas kept staring at the body, pale and bloated against the dark mud of the trail.

"How did he die?" Mellas asked.

"Officially, it's pneumonia," the lieutenant answered. "Couldn't get him medevaced. No birds."

"Bullshit. They humped him to death." The kid said it softly.

"Pneumonia. Jesus." Mellas whistled under his breath. "And you couldn't get him out? Doesn't make sense."

"No fucking shit, doesn't make sense." The lieutenant gently toed the body. "He was a good fucking kid, too. The squid hasn't a clue. All we know is his temperature shot up over a hundred six and he started screaming. We took all his clothes off to get it down. Didn't work. We'd called for an emergency medevac when it hit a hundred four. Doc thought it was flu or something. Battalion said it wasn't an emergency." He snickered, nearly losing control. "I guess we were right."

He turned to the angry kid who was finishing the cigarette. "Who's supposed to take over?"

"Maki's team."

"OK. Leave him here. I'll tell Maki to pick him up."

The kid rounded up his fire team and they trudged down the trail. Another team arrived, slung their rifles over their backs against their packs, and picked up the two poles. They struggled down the trail, the swaying body pulling them off balance.

"Thanks for the cigarette," the tall lieutenant said to Hamilton.

"It's OK, sir."

He turned and walked down the trail, his radioman following. Mellas looked at Hamilton, who was watching them disappear. Tired kids continued to file past.

"Jesus," Mellas said.

"There it is, sir," Hamilton answered.

Mellas's insides were humming. A soft wind snaked its way through the grass, turning his wet clothing cold.

CHAPTER
SIX

Y ou've never been out on a rampage before, have you?" Fitch
        peered at Mellas over his can of pears. He was sitting cross-
        legged on a tuft of wet moss. Rampage was the brevity code
for an ambush.

"Sure I have," Mellas replied. "We ambushed three cows in Virginia one night."

"Oh, yeah." Fitch laughed, spooning another pear into his mouth.
"I heard about that. It was just before we graduated." He continued
gulping down his pears. "Big John Six figures we can ambush some gooks
who might be heading for the base camp tonight and don't know we're
here."

"I kind of doubt it," Mellas said. They had reached the abandoned
North Vietnamese base camp just an hour before. Everyone was digging in. "It must sound like a herd of water buffalo at a barn dance around
here."

Fitch chuckled and tossed the can into the bushes. "You see those
big cat tracks when we came in?" he asked.

"He was probably sniffing at the shit Charlie Company left
around."

Fitch laughed. "The way they looked, I don't think they left him
very much."

Mellas took a quick look at the jungle. He was in no mood to talk
about wildlife. Ambushes could go wrong, and they'd be way outside
the lines alone in the dark.

Fitch pulled out his map and showed Mellas a crayon mark where battalion wanted to ambush. "You don't have to take it out yourself. Bass or Conman can set up a good ambush." He pulled his K-bar out of its sheath and began cleaning his fingernails with it.

Mellas knew the offer was another test. "Naw, I'll go. Nothing else to do." He began unfolding his own map, hoping Fitch wouldn't see that his hands were trembling.

Hawke walked up to them. "I had to jump on fucking Kendall for not getting his men clearing brush." Hawke sighed and squatted down. "You got any fucking coffee?"

"Hell, you're the XO, Jayhawk, coffee is your job," Fitch replied. "What did Kendall say?"

"Said he was sorry and he'd get on it. What do you mean *my* fucking job?"

"What else you got to do?" Mellas put in.

"Well, one thing I don't have to do is take any fucking lip from wise-ass boot lieutenants, that's for damn sure."

Mellas laughed but regretted his dumb quip. At the same time, he was desperately trying to recall all the mechanics of that aborted ambush of cows back in Virginia.

Fitch continued cleaning his nails, then spoke up. "I'm sending a squad from First Platoon out on a rampage."

"What for?" Hawke said.

"The Three called me on the hook and said he wants it."

"What for?" Hawke persisted.

"Says the Six and he both think it's a good chance to kill some gooks."

"You mean a good chance to impress fucking regiment with how gung ho we are."

"Maybe."

Fitch remained quiet, knowing that there was no way out, but Hawke had to have a chance to let everyone know that he disagreed. He turned to Mellas and sighed. "There it is," he said. "I'll get Two and Three to move in and take a couple of your holes since you'll have a squad out. You going out with them?"

Again the test, and the very real temptation to tell Connolly or Bass to do it. He fought it down. "Yeah. No time like the present."

"What? You a fucking Buddhist or something?" Hawke said.

Mellas did a double take at Hawke's comment and then filed it, reevaluating Hawke once again. He laughed. "Naw. Lutheran. We got all eternity, but we feel guilty about it."

"What the fuck you guys talking about?" Fitch asked, genuinely puzzled. He looked at his watch. "You better get set in before it gets too dark to see."

In spite of his fear, the thought of springing an ambush excited Mellas. Battalion would know immediately who had led it. He might even get a medal if they killed enough. And if he was going to lie out in the rain and cold all night, he might as well get the satisfaction of killing someone. As soon as the thought crossed Mellas's mind, he reproached himself for his callousness. He also knew he didn't have the nerve to ask anyone else to lead the ambush.

Mellas had just finished briefing Jackson's squad about the ambush —it was their turn—when Hamilton called over that there was to be an actuals meeting.

"Right now? I just left the place."

"Right now, sir."

Mellas walked back to Fitch's hooch, fuming. Everyone else was already there, including the two Kit Carson scouts. Their value supposedly lay in knowing the NVA intimately. Unfortunately, no one in the company spoke Vietnamese, and they spoke no English, and no Marine would trust a deserter anyway. They were another example of a brainstorm that looked good in Washington, 10,000 miles from reality.

The two Kit Carsons were squatting down trying to listen to Vietnamese music on their transistor radio.

"Hey, Arran," Cassidy growled at the dog handler, "tell them two fucking dinks to turn off the damned noise." Arran knew about seven words in Vietnamese—more than anyone else knew—so he always talked with the Kit Carsons. He motioned to the radio and made cutting noises with his hands. Eventually, the huskier of the two small men got the message and clicked it off. His arm was horribly scarred. The Marines figured the injury had happened when he was on the other side. He held up the radio and grinned.

"Numbah one."

Arran glowered at him, "Radio number ten. Number ten." He pointed to the sky. "Dark, NVA. Number ten."

The Kit Carson nodded. "Numbah ten."

"Yeah, that's right, you stupid fucker," Cassidy growled. No one really wanted them along, but they were assigned by Division S-2, so Fitch had let them hump along with the headquarters group in the middle of the column. The two Kit Carson's resumed talking Vietnamese in low musical voices. Fitch stood up, and everyone forgot they were there.

"As you know, Delta was following in our trace all afternoon." Fitch looked at the ground and scuffed it. "None of you are going to like this, but I've been talking with Delta Six on the hook and it seems battalion didn't tell him until the last minute that he was coming into the valley with us. They were low on food as it was, but they thought they were going back to VCB." He put his hands in his back pockets and looked into the jungle. "Anyway, they didn't get a chance to draw any extra rations." He looked back at the group. "So battalion told them to hook up with us and take half of ours."

Mellas exploded, surprising himself. "No, goddamn it. They aren't getting any of mine."

"It isn't their fault, Mellas," Hawke said. "I know how you feel, though."

"What are we supposed to do, go on half rations because battalion can't get its shit together?" Mellas knew he sounded like a quarrelsome child, but he didn't care. He was tired, he had an ambush to set up, and he was already slightly hungry. He'd been trying to ration the food he had to make it last through the operation.

"You'll each collect two days' rations from everyone and leave them here." Fitch was obviously accepting no bullshit, so no one argued. "And I want it done randomly. No unloading the crap. If you were in their shoes you'd want some decent food."

"I'll be damned," Mellas said caustically. "The law of universability."

Goodwin looked at Mellas. "What the fuck you talking about, Jack?"

"Moral philosophy for the Golden Rule."

"Yeah, sure," Goodwin said. "Do unto others before they do you—that's the fucking Golden Rule out here, Jack." Everyone laughed.

Mellas walked back to where he and Bass had set up the platoon command post. The bantering had relaxed his anger, but now it was coming back.

"So we got to give Delta our long rats, Lieutenant?" Bass asked as Mellas approached them. Mellas had long since given up trying to spring news on any of them. Everyone was still digging holes, except Doc Fredrickson, who was counting out malaria tablets, his own small hole already finished. If they were hit, he wouldn't use it much anyway, since he'd be tending the wounded.

"Yeah. Shit. *Coordinate with Bravo Company concerning food resupply.*" His mocking tone brought a few smiles. "And Fitch doesn't want us creaming the good stuff either."

Hamilton looked ruefully at his pack. "Do I give them my peaches or my pound cake?"

"Just one more glorious day in the corps," said Bass, "where every day's a holiday and every meal's a feast."

"Lifer," Fredrickson retorted.

"Loyal, industrious, freedom-loving, efficient, rugged," Bass shot back quickly.

"Lazy, ignorant fucker expecting retirement," Fredrickson replied.

Mellas burst out laughing.

"No fucking comments from the junior officer section," Bass said.

"Well, this junior officer is taking out a rampage so an almost staff sergeant can get his much-needed rest and keep up with the company tomorrow. So if you'd kindly kiss the platoon good night for me, I'll take the radio and be on my way."

"Aye, aye, Mr. Mellas." Bass picked up one of the radios that lay next to the ponchos where he and Skosh were going to erect their shelter. He handed it to Mellas. "You got a code name?"

Mellas thought a moment. "Vagina."

"Can't have it."

"Why not?"

"Can't be cluttering up the airways with filth."

"Nothing filthy about the vaginas I know. I don't know about the ones you know."

"You ain't been around enough to know what one is."

Mellas slung the radio over one shoulder. He picked up his rifle. "I don't have to get around to know what one is," he said cockily, "they come to me."

"Whooo."

Mellas laughed, but he was laughing to cover the hurt of Bass's jibes. He was twenty-one and still a virgin, a fact that shamed him deeply. Anne was the only woman he'd been really intimate with, and she never wanted to have intercourse. He never pushed it. They would roll around madly until Mellas ejaculated and fell asleep. He'd wake up feeling bad because she never climaxed the way he did. One night, she did own up to feeling guilty because she wouldn't allow intercourse. But Mellas also felt guilty, because he didn't know what to do and was afraid to ask questions.

The mood over at Jackson's squad was subdued. Mallory was slowly working the bolt back and forth on the M-60 machine gun, making a smooth metallic clicking. He would stop periodically to hold his hands to his head as if to stop it from bursting. Williams seemed nervous. He kept switching feet, his big hands buttoning and rebuttoning a single button on his camouflage utility jacket.

"Hey, Williams," Jackson kidded him softly, "it'll stay buttoned. Don't worry."

Williams grinned, embarrassed. "Yeah, I guess it will." He stopped but almost immediately began toying with it again. Broyer gave Williams a reassuring thumbs-up sign, hidden so no one else could see it, and then pushed his glasses up on his nose with the same hand. Williams nodded. A little smile flickered briefly on his face.

Parker and Cortell were baiting Pollini as he fumbled to put his rifle back together after cleaning it. "No, Shortround, you put it in *t' other* way," Cortell said, his round face merry.

"Yeah, the *other* way," Parker repeated.

Pollini was grinning and trying to fix the rifle, but he kept looking up at the two of them and wasn't concentrating on what he was doing.

"Shit, Shortround," Parker said, "you'd fuck up a wet dream, wouldn't you?"

"No, I wouldn't," Pollini said, grinning.

"You such a fuckup, Shortround, you ought to be declared a national disaster and you mother taken off the streets and given relief," Parker cackled.

"At least I didn't get shaved bald," Pollini retorted. Parker stopped smiling. The look on Pollini's face made it clear that he knew he'd made a mistake.

Parker took a slow step forward. "What's that, Snowflake?" he said quietly.

Pollini looked around hesitantly. "I said at least I'm smart enough not to get shaved bald."

Parker pulled out his K-bar.

"Hey, man," Cortell said, "put away that shit."

"I don't take no shit like that," he said to Cortell, but stayed focused on Pollini. "Maybe you and Jesus do."

Pollini started to back away, looking for help. He fell backward into a partially dug fighting hole. Parker was on him instantly, knocking the wind from him with his knees. Pollini gasped in tiny ineffectual breaths, his face contorted. "What's the matter white boy, not smart enough to breathe?" Parker had the point of his K-bar's blade pressed against Pollini's Adam's apple. Every time Pollini tried to gasp for air, the motion would jab the knife's point against it.

There was the sound of a round being chambered and then Williams's calm cowboy voice. "Parker, I'll shoot you if you don't get off of him."

"That's right," Parker said, still holding the knife to Pollini's throat. "You protect you little sawed-off brother here." He looked around him, angry. "Where my own brothers, huh?"

Mallory laid his M-60 on the ground and pulled his .45 from its holster. He shoved back the action and let it snap forward, chambering a round. His hand was shaking, but the pistol pointed at Williams.

"Now there," Parker said. "We even up, ain't we, Williams?"

At this point Jackson intervened. He quietly said, "OK, you two, put the shit down. This between Parker and Shortround, not between chucks and splibs."

"It *might* not be between chucks and splibs," Parker said, his knife still on Pollini's Adam's apple.

In a tight constricted whisper Pollini wheezed, "I take it back. I didn't mean nothing, Parker."

"Oh, you didn't, huh? I ought to cut you nuts off for what you said. But I'm going let you go because you so fucking stupid. But I don't forget things." He looked up at Williams, who stood his ground with the M-16.

"Come on, you two," Jackson said, ignoring Parker and address-ing Mallory and Williams. "Put the shit down. We got an ambush to run tonight." Then he moved into the line of fire between the two of them.

Williams flicked his eyes quickly at Jackson, then lowered his rifle and put the safety on. Mallory eased the hammer of the .45 forward.

"It just between you and me now, Shortround," Parker said. "And I'm going to let you go, 'cause you so stupid." He pushed back from Pollini, smiling, and stood up. Then he jumped in the air and stomped hard on Pollini's stomach with his boot. Pollini cried out in pain and Williams immediately ran for Parker, slamming his rifle against the side of his head. Parker came around in a low crouch swinging the knife, just missing Williams. Jackson tackled Williams, rolling him away from Parker's knife as they hit the ground, knocking the rifle aside. He stayed on top of Williams, who struggled to get free, and turned his head to Parker. "You keep the fuck back," he said.

They heard the sound of running feet. Bass had his heavy short-timer's stick and was shouting. "What the fuck's going on around here?" The lieutenant was just behind him.

Parker put his K-bar back in its sheath.

"What the fuck's going on, Jackson?" Bass asked. Pollini was retching in the partially dug hole.

"Nothing, Sergeant Bass," Jackson said. "Williams and I got into an argument."

Mellas went over to Pollini. "Who the hell got into an argument with Shortround?" he asked. He put his hand on Pollini's shoulder. "Who was it?"

"No one, sir," Pollini answered. He was doubled over, tears running into the vomit on his chin. "I fell in this fucking hole. Honest, sir."

Bass turned to Parker. "Listen, you fucking puke—"

"It's OK, Sergeant Bass," Mellas said quickly.

"Sir, I know this fucking excuse for a man—"

"It's *OK*, Sergeant Bass."

"I'd string him up by his nuts."

"We'll handle this with office hours." Mellas looked around. "Everybody here. Fighting while on duty. We'll take care of it when we get in. Goddamn it, I'll bust every one of you."

Williams and Jackson got up off the ground. Williams checked his rifle for dirt, brushing it off, moving the mechanism. Pollini struggled to his feet. Bass picked up Pollini's rifle, now covered with mud, and handed it to him. "You better get it cleaned up," he growled. He stalked back to his hole.

Mellas looked around at everyone. Mallory was trying to look as though he was inspecting his .45. "I don't care what happened right now," Mellas said. "We'll deal with it later. We got an ambush to set up in about twenty minutes."

Pollini stifled a groan. He had his rifle in two pieces. "You able to go on the ambush, Shortround?" Mellas asked.

"Yes sir." Pollini suddenly grinned at Mellas and held up the two muddy halves of the rifle. "I thought I'd get it real clean so it'd open right up when we sprang the ambush, sir."

"That was good thinking, Pollini."

"Yeah, Shortround, he a real sharp dude."

"Knock it off, Parker," Mellas said. "You're in enough trouble." He turned to Jackson. "I want this squad ready to go in ten minutes. Get the shine off their faces."

When Mellas returned, Cortell was rubbing unnecessarily large amounts of mud and charcoal onto Pollini's face. Mellas wanted to say something right away but was reluctant to show favoritism.

Pollini was trying to be a good sport. "Hey, Lieutenant," he said, "make him stop."

Mellas couldn't help laughing. Pollini was just funny to look at. "Go a little easy on him, Cortell," Mellas finally said. Cortell stopped rubbing it in so hard.

Jackson arrived.

"Don't look so worried," Mellas said to him. "It's bad enough with me looking worried."

Jackson smiled, but his anxiety was clear to Mellas, who hadn't really thought about the ambush yet. Suddenly Mellas realized he still didn't know what he was doing. His mind started to churn through all the relevant points he'd been taught about ambushes: front and rear security, assembly points, initiating signals, communications wire or string to tug on for silent signals, kill zones. The mechanics of sudden death were as complex as they were violent.

The Marines of Third Squad collected around Mellas, waiting nervously in silence. Mellas began figuring. "I'm guessing the trail will take a bend somewhere. We'll set up an L-shaped ambush. Mallory, you'll be on the little end of the L with the M-60 and shooting straight down the trail so if you miss someone in front, you'll hit someone behind him. Just make sure you get the gun pegged in so you don't shoot off the trail in the dark and hit one of us." Mallory nodded.

"Tilghman, you'll be next to me with shotgun rounds. We'll need two men each, for front and rear security. You got a team for that, Jackson?"

Jackson thought a moment. "Yeah. Cortell, you can lay out in the boonies for a while."

Cortell groaned. His friend Williams cleared his throat and looked into the jungle. Cortell spoke up. "Shit, Jackson, you get some power and you turn on you friends just like that." He snapped his fingers. Jackson nodded his head in affirmation and smiled at him. Cortell looked at Mellas. "What can I say, sir?"

"Nothing." Mellas waited a second. "Who you want in front and who you want in back?" It was Cortell's fire team—it was his choice.

"I'll take Williams up front with me. Parker and Chadwick can go behind." Mellas was relieved. For a moment he feared that Pollini was in Cortell's team with Parker. Then he remembered—Pollini was with the team headed by Amarillo, the kid who kept doggedly telling everyone that if they had to nickname him something that meant yellow in Spanish, the least they could do was pronounce it correctly. Of course no one did. It had become a running joke.

"OK, then. No one makes a move or fires a shot until I do. If the unit is too big for us to handle, I'm going to just put my head down and hope like hell they walk on by." Mellas turned to Cortell. "The warning will be three tugs on the comm-wire. We'll give three back. Then you give a pull for every man you count going by you. Same for you, Parker. Everybody got it?" They all nodded. "OK. I'll select the assembly area, about twenty meters off the trail. We'll move into position from there. Everyone meets there afterward. If you get separated, we'll wait ten minutes. If you don't make it back by then, we'll assume you're hit. Don't move. We'll get you if it takes the whole company."

Jackson spoke up. "The code word tonight is Monkey-Cat, so if any of you dudes gets lost, make sure you holler Monkey before you try and come home." He grinned. Williams and Amarillo let out brief bursts of air, just short of laughter. With night encroaching, voices all around the perimeter were dropping to whispers.

Mellas looked around at the group. They were all carrying poncho liners, ammunition, and grenades. Their faces were black, and their bush covers were pulled down low or crumpled. Helmets weren't used on ambushes, because the profile was too easily recognizable.

As the squad filed past the holes in the twilight, the rest of the company was still digging in. Mellas selected an ambush site about 200 meters down the trail and located the assembly area, and they moved into position quietly, stringing wire from hand to hand and out to the security teams. Mellas chose a very dense part of the jungle on a slight downhill slope, figuring that anyone coming uphill bearing a load would probably have his head down and be breathing hard, making it harder to see and hear. The trail curved sharply, and at the bend Mallory and Barber, the A gunner, set up the machine gun. Mellas took the middle of the long side, next to Jackson, who had taken the radio. They settled in to wait.

It got dark: black, sightless dark. Mellas could no longer see the trail in front of him. The darkness seemed to push down on him from the clouds. He heard Jackson breathing next to him. His own wristwatch sounded like an alarm clock. He tried to stuff it under his belly, but the effort itself made noise, so he stopped.

It occurred to him that if the NVA could hear his wristwatch, they deserved to live. But did they deserve to die if they couldn't hear it? It was a zero-sum game. One side won only if the other side lost. Mellas was starting to nod off.

He struggled to alertness and gave one tug on the wire. Everyone awake? There was a tug back from both sides. Everyone was awake. Mellas shivered. Goddamn the cold and the dark. Impenetrable blackness. He was blind. He felt the fog settle in low through the thick jungle, whispering about them. The radio, set on the company frequency at its lowest volume, made a quiet hiss. "If you're all secure, key your handset two times." It was Bass, back inside the company's position, on the radio. Mellas keyed twice, having taken the handset from Jackson, who was lying close enough to pass it back and forth. It was so dark that Mellas felt suffocated. He couldn't see Jackson even though he could touch him. Mellas leaned his head on the cold dewy top of his rifle, the steel feeling cool and comforting against his forehead. The rest of his body ached with cold and damp. Only six hours until daylight. He wished he were back on the hill or back home in bed with the trees rustling outside the window. The school bus will be here pretty soon. Mommy will have breakfast ready.

An anguished scream jerked Mellas awake, but it choked off immediately. It had come from the forward security post.

"What the hell?" Mellas whispered. The entire squad was tense. He could feel the others, but no one could see a thing. They heard a grunting sound, a gruff cough that chilled Mellas through, and then the sound of brush crackling. Then nothing. Suddenly the wire on Mellas's wrist was being tugged furiously again and again; there was no order, just wild tugging. Then they heard Cortell's voice. He was nearly hysterical, but he was still careful to whisper. "I'm comin' in. I'm comin' in. Oh, Jesus Christ. Oh, Lord Jesus." They could hear him crawling along, hitting bushes in the dark. He was trying to follow the trail. "Oh, my Lord Jesus. Lieutenant? Jackson? Where are you?"

"Over here, Cortell," Mellas said in a normal voice, trying to control his fear. The radio net burst into activity. The whole company had heard the scream, and Fitch was trying to determine what was happening.

Mellas answered. "It was us. I don't know what's happening yet. We're aborting the rampage. Over."

"Roger that."

Someone reached out and pulled Cortell in. He was panting in short gasps. Jackson and Mellas crawled toward the sound, Mellas holding on to the handset and Jackson leading the way, the radio on his back. Both still had their poncho liners wrapped around them.

"Hey, man," Jackson said, "what's the matter?"

"Oh, Jesus, Jackson, it's Williams," Cortell gasped out. "A tiger got him."

"He all right?"

"He ate him, man. He jumped him and dragged him off and ate him. Lord God, we was just layin' there and all a sudden there's Williams screamin' and I hear this tiger bat him, like across the neck or somethin', and then crunch him right through the head." Mellas couldn't see Cortell as he talked, but Cortell's voice conveyed his horror. "Oh, Lord God, sweet Jesus."

Jackson moved over, held on to Cortell, and talked to him in low tones. "Hey, man, it's all right. There's nothin' you can do. Hey, man, take it easy, huh? Be cool."

Mellas keyed the handset. "Bravo, this is Bravo One Actual. Our security was attacked by a tiger. We think he's dead. Can't see a goddamned thing. Over."

"Jesus Christ," Fitch's voice answered. "See if you can find him. Maybe he's just mauled. Over."

"I tell you we can't see shit out here. I can't even see my radio and I'm using the goddamned thing. Over."

"Roger that. Wait one."

Mellas waited, sightless. "Jackson, tell everyone to set in tight and keep their ears open. Get Parker and Broyer in."

"Right, sir." Jackson slipped off the radio and crawled away, using the wire to guide him.

"You all right, Cortell?" Mellas asked into the blackness.

"Yes sir," Cortell's voice came back. "I'm OK now. Jesus, sir, I hope he ain't dead, but I heard his head go. I think it just popped open, sir."

The radio hissed a static burst. Fitch's voice came out of the handset. "We can shoot you some illumination rounds. Maybe it'll scare the cat off and you can find your man. Over."

"Sounds fine. Go ahead on it. Over."

"Roger that. Out."

Routine procedures like talking on radios seemed out of place to Mellas. Yet they didn't change, even if a tiger attacked. Mellas couldn't have been sure that anyone was still around him if it hadn't been for the sound of breathing. "Well," he whispered into nothingness, "nothing to do but wait. No sense getting all split up."

They waited five minutes. Then Fitch said "Shot" over the radio.

"Shot. Out," Mellas repeated. Soon they heard the funny whiffling noise of the illumination shell. There was a pop high in the air to their south as the tiny parachute deployed. Then they could hear the hiss of burning phosphorus. The trail and jungle were cast into eerie quavering relief. Jackson's and Cortell's faces shone through the mud and charcoal covering them. Jackson slipped back into the radio's carrying straps and Mellas rose.

"Let's go. Cortell, you lead."

Cortell led off, rifle at the ready, Mellas directly behind him, followed by Jackson and the rest.

They came to where Cortell and Williams had lain. The ground was slightly depressed, and both of their poncho liners were there as well as Williams's rifle. There was a dark stain of blood on the grass.

They heard another illumination round, whiffling unseen with the sound of a small Fourth of July rocket. Everything grew brighter again. As the round fell, vague diffuse shadows changed position.

They came across Williams's bush cover almost immediately. It was wet and stained with blood. It was also torn through. Mellas wondered if tigers defended their food and how far they dragged it to eat it. They kept looking, occasionally seeing a bit of blood. They fired off some rounds to frighten the tiger away. They had covered 100 meters when they came on Williams's body. His legs and backside had been ripped open and partially eaten. It looked as though he'd been killed with one quick blow to the skull, breaking his neck. Puncture wounds from long sharp teeth were sunk deeply into his face and temples.

They wrapped the mess in Williams's poncho liner and moved back up the trail toward the company, sweating and stumbling through the eerie light.

CHAPTER
SEVEN

Until dawn, Fitch pleaded for a helicopter. No choppers were flying. The rain and fog had shut down operations all over northern I Corps. It would be suicidal to try to find Bravo Company in the mountains. The order to blow the ammo cache stood.

The squad threw fingers to divide up Williams's food and ammunition. Pollini won the throw for his poncho liner.

Fredrickson and Bass wrapped Williams's body with comm-wire to keep the torn pieces together. The body looked like beef in a cold storage locker, hardened blood mixed with pale skin and exposed meat. They tied the ankles, knees, elbows, and wrists closely together and then wrapped the torso in a poncho, leaving the arms and legs out. They tied the arms and legs to a long pole so they could carry the body, swinging, beneath it. Fredrickson wired Williams's head, which had been lolling loose inside the poncho, next to the pole so it wouldn't throw the carriers off balance.

As the platoon sat waiting for Kendall's platoon to wind out of the perimeter, taking point, followed by Goodwin's platoon, Hawke came and sat quietly next to Bass and Mellas. The executive officer always walked with the last platoon in the column, tail-end Charlie, lowering the risk that both he and the skipper would be killed at the same time. They were all aware of Williams's body in the olive drab cocoon.

"Why couldn't it have been one of the worthless fuckers?" Bass asked. His jaw began to tremble. He stood up quickly and started shouting at Skosh to get his ass in gear.

Mellas looked at Hawke. "Because the world's not fair," he said quietly.

"There it is," Hawke answered.

Eventually First Platoon's own point men began to move, falling in behind Goodwin's last fire team. Mellas set off numbly, thankful not to have any responsibility for finding their way.

He passed the pile of food supplies left for Delta. Then he was deep in jungle. The entire history of their stay—the holes they'd dug so laboriously, the hooches they'd set up, the place where he'd heated a cup of cocoa and talked with Hawke and Hamilton, the spot where he'd pissed—had been swallowed so totally that his memories seemed to be of dreams, not reality. The company left no more mark on the jungle than a ship's wake on the sea.

By the second day the body was little more than an inconvenience. The belly had swollen, and gas escaped occasionally from one end or the other. Rigor mortis had set in. The kids cursed it beneath their breath when they stumbled with it or slipped. "Goddamn you, Williams, you fat poag. You always ate too fucking much."

Whenever the company reached a relatively open space, Fitch asked for a chopper to come over and lower a hook so they could get rid of the body. He always got the same answer—no—though the reasons varied. Other priorities. Poor weather. Once they sprang loose a Huey slick, but in the low clouds with rain slashing through the trees the small chopper was unable to locate them, let alone get down close enough to lower a rope.

The carriers would curse and pick Williams up, and he'd swing from side to side down the trail with them, like a dead deer, his discolored hands bloated and puffed up around the wire. Skin had started to come loose from the muscles and slide down the fingers and arms, collecting where the fingers joined the hands and at the elbows, translucent and puckered like discarded surgical gloves.

In the darkness, in the rain, they would lay him just inside the perimeter behind Third Squad's sector. During his watch, Cortell would talk quietly to the body, remembering what Mama Louisa had once told him back in Four Corners—that the soul could stay around three or four days before departing, getting used to the idea that it was dead.

On the third night Cortell crawled to the body and put his hands on the lump that was the head. "Williams, I'm sorry. I might have done somethin' but run. I didn't know. I was so scared. You know how scared you can get. You and me been scared like that. You know. I'm sorry, Williams. Oh, Jesus, I'm so sorry." Cortell started to sob.

Jackson, in the next hole, crawled across the ground and gently pulled Cortell away from the body, urging him silently back into his fighting hole, getting him to stop. The sobs could be heard too clearly, delineating the perimeter's position.

And truly, on the fourth day, what was slung beneath the pole had no soul. It stank.

Late that same afternoon, the company was stopped cold. Everyone sat down inboard-outboard and leaned back wearily against his pack. The kids took swigs of plastic-tasting water from their canteens or started de-leeching. Some dozed off. It was soon apparent from the radio conversation that Lieutenant Kendall was lost again.

Mellas pulled out his map. There was nothing to take bearings on. Clouds hid anything the jungle didn't hide. Mellas carefully reconstructed the terrain they'd passed through, dead-reckoning their position. Finally, when he could stand it no longer, he slipped out of his pack and walked back along the line of tired Marines to find Hawke and Bass.

Hamilton didn't get up to go with him. He closed his eyes and fell asleep.

Mellas found Hawke and Bass already heating coffee in the old pear can, which Hawke carried tied to the outside of his pack for ready access. Hawke, who was squatting Vietnamese style on the path next to the burning C-4, glanced up. "Cut me some fucking slack, Mellas." Hawke turned to Bass. "I don't believe he smelled the coffee all the way up front."

"It's funny about him," Bass said. "I never seen him make his own cup of coffee, but he always knows when someone else is making one."

Mellas laughed and sat down in the mud with them. He started unfolding his map. Just then a static-riddled voice came from the radio handset, hooked on the strap of Skosh's pack. It was Kendall. "Best I can figure, Bravo Six, we're at"—there was a pause—"from Chevrolet, up one point two and right three point four. Over."

Fitch's taut voice returned. "I copy." Fitch was already a full day late in reaching the next geographic checkpoint that had been assigned to him by Lieutenant Colonel Simpson.

Mellas pulled the map over to where Bass and Hawke could see it. The day's radio code used cars for position reports. He found the prearranged coordinates of Chevrolet and traced out Kendall's reported position. "He's crazy. We'd have to be over this ridgeline. We're by this riverbed, even if we've never seen it. You can feel the way the ground slopes."

Hawke looked at the map, grunted approval, and put the finishing touches on the coffee.

The radio came to life again as someone keyed his handset. In the silence of the jungle they all could clearly hear the person breathing. "I don't think so, Bravo Three." It was Fitch. "I see us just about a klick south of there by the blue line. Over."

There was a long silence. An error could bring their own artillery down on them. Worse, it could mean hours of extra walking.

"What a dingbat," Mellas said.

Hawke took a gulp of coffee, then handed the cup to Bass, who took a deep pull and handed it to Mellas, who did the same and passed it over to Skosh. The coffee burned delightfully all the way into Mellas's stomach, where he felt it radiate heat to his body. Sharing the cup felt good. It reminded him of passing around a joint.

Hawke took another drink, put the steaming can on the mud, and took the radio handset. "Bravo Six, this is Bravo Five. Over."

"Yeah, Five," Fitch returned.

"Bravo One Actual and I are back here with Bravo One Assist, and we've decided you're both fucked up. We're down zero point three and right four point five. Over."

Daniels's voice crackled over the air. "That's affirmative, Skipper."

There was short pause, and Fitch came up on the hook again. "OK, I'll buy that. You copy that, Bravo Three? Over."

"Roger, I copy," said Kendall. "If that's where we are, I got to come back out of this little draw because we're headed the wrong direction. Over."

"Jesus Christ," Bass muttered.

"Bravo Two, this is Bravo Six. You copy our pos? Over."

"Fuck, yes, Jack. Over."

"Look, Scar, I know you're not due to walk point until tomorrow, but could you take it this afternoon so Three can join our tail as we go by? Over."

There was short pause while Goodwin weighed the request against the additional danger.

"OK, Jack. Bravo Two, out."

Mellas left Hawke and Bass and worked his way forward to Hamilton, who gave him the handset. "Skipper wants to talk to you," Hamilton said. From the tone of his voice, Mellas felt something had gone wrong.

"Bravo Six, this is Bravo One Actual. Over."

"Bravo One, where the fuck you been? You don't go anyplace without your radio. Is that clear? Do you copy that? Over."

Mellas flushed and looked angrily at Hamilton, who had averted his eyes and was adjusting the heavy radio to ride better on his back.

"Roger, I copy that." Mellas knew that everyone on the radio net was aware of his mistake. He gave the handset back to Hamilton, saying nothing.

"I should have gone with you," Hamilton mumbled. "Sorry, sir. I won't let you down again."

"Sorry won't get it," Mellas snapped. He reached down for his heavy pack and heaved it into place. He readjusted his ammunition bandoleers and took a long pull of brackish halazoned water. "Oh, hell. I should have known better myself," he said. He handed Hamilton his open canteen.

With Goodwin leading the way, Bravo Company lurched forward. Soon they were passing the disgusted-looking Marines from Kendall's platoon, who sat back in the low brush, rifles at the ready, watching the rest of the company file by. With Goodwin's platoon up front, they made faster progress, but it was still not fast enough for Colonel Simpson or Major Blakely, who began to ask Fitch for position reports almost hourly.

By nightfall the company was still four kilometers short of the ammunition site. The colonel radioed that the ammo was to be blown by noon the next day or he'd have Fitch relieved. This left Fitch with the alternative he'd dreaded—moving the company down into the river valley and taking the trail on which Alpha had been ambushed.

As he checked holes that night, Mellas felt a subtle change in the atmosphere. A pocket of warm air, isolated in the monsoon, was going slowly toward the China Sea. By the time they were moving the next morning, heading down off the high ridgeline that afforded some breeze and the coolness of altitude, the air felt like a wool blanket pulled over their heads.

To get down to the trail they had to break out their ropes. Hands burned red and blisters erupted as they dangled down steep cliffs with heavy loads on their backs. Sweat stung their eyes. Tempers flared. Mellas felt as if he were having an asthma attack in a stuffy automobile.

After two hours they reached the trail that ran down the valley floor. It formed a narrow muddy tunnel in the thick growth. Light barely penetrated the ceiling of overhanging vegetation. Goodwin waved the two Kit Carsons out in front and the company jerked its way forward. The rate of progress was now nearly double what it had been off the trail—however, so was the danger.

There was no longer any need to hack through bush and bamboo, but the fear of ambush still kept the pace agonizingly slow. Mellas fumed, wondering why blowing the dump by noon was better than blowing it that night. He wished they were up on the ridge where it was cooler and safer and the going was not much slower.

After two more hours Goodwin's platoon moved off the trail to allow Mellas's to take point. When he saw Goodwin, Mellas was too hot and tired to do anything except roll his eyes and let his tongue hang out. "You ain't fucking wrong, Jack," Goodwin said in an almost normal tone of voice. It seemed very loud. Those who heard him smiled.

An hour later the entire column had stopped. The kids stood dumbly in the heat, sweating, reeking, not wanting to move forward, yet wanting to get the day over with. Then some of them sat down. Soon the entire column was taking five with no one having given the word.

Fitch came forward. "What the fuck's going on?"

Mellas didn't know. He knew he should have known. He crawled forward, determined to get back in Fitch's good graces. He reached Jackson. Jackson didn't know. Mellas crawled on, Hamilton crawling after him. A small clearing opened up. The two Kit Carsons were cooking a meal, listening to their transistor radio.

Mellas was enraged. The lead Marine must have seen the Kit Carsons stop, but he hadn't been ordered to take point. Being on point was the Kit Carsons' bad luck. He wasn't about to volunteer to push past them and risk getting killed, especially since it meant walking across an open clearing. If the Kit Carsons weren't supposed to be cooking their meal, then an officer would probably wonder why the whole column had stopped and come up and investigate—as in fact happened.

Mellas strode out of the cover of the jungle into the small patch of light. "Goddamn you fucking gook assholes." He kicked the pot of water, scattering the burning C-4. "Get out of my goddamn sight." One of them reached for the pot, the other for his rifle. Mellas was too angry to feel threatened. "Get the fuck out of here!" he screamed, shoving them toward the rear. "Back. You go to CP, you stupid motherfucker. Back. Me no want you. You numbah ten."

He radioed Fitch that he was sending the Kit Carsons back and didn't want to see them up front again. "I don't want any fucking deserters fucking up my men," he shouted over the radio.

Fitch sighed. "Just get us moving, OK? Out."

Mellas's contempt for anything Vietnamese grew.

Fitch sent Arran and Pat forward in hopes that Pat's nose would help speed things along. It didn't.

An hour later Mellas saw Mallory sitting at the edge of the trail, his machine gun across his knees, holding his head and moaning with pain. "Come on, Mallory," Mellas said. "We've only got a few more hours to go, then we'll blow the shit up and get our asses out of here." The column filed wearily past them.

"My head aches, Lieutenant," Mallory said, nearly screaming.

"I know. We're going to try and get you to a psychologist. Maybe he'll be able to help."

A loud groan escaped Mallory before he could cut it off. "A psychologist? Oh, shit, man. I tell you it hurts. I'm not crazy."

Mellas held out his hand and Mallory struggled to his feet and humped up the trail, trying to regain his position in the line.

Within minutes they were again stopped dead. No one knew why. Mellas wanted to sit down and guzzle water. A leech groped its way toward him, one end anchored to the ground while the other end arched up, blindly sensing the air. Mellas began torturing it with his bottle of insect repellent. Disgusted with himself, he killed it with his boot.

Hamilton walked up and offered the handset to Mellas. "It's the skipper," he said.

Fitch's voice was testy. "What's the fucking holdup now? Over."

"I'm finding out now," Mellas lied.

"Well, hurry the fuck up."

Mellas groaned and struggled to his feet. Hamilton followed. They reached Jacobs, whose squad was now on point.

"What's the story?" Mellas whispered.

"P-Pat alerted."

"Don't you ever pass the damned word back?"

"S-sorry, sir." He gave Hamilton a quick knowing look, which was returned. Mellas caught the exchange. One more peevish lieutenant.

He calmed down and moved forward with Hamilton creeping

behind him, sweating under the load of the radio. They reached the dog and Arran. Arran squatted beside Pat, holding Pat's thick neck, his shotgun at the ready. Pat's tongue stuck out. The dog's lungs worked rapidly, trying to expel the heat. One of his reddish ears was folded half down, as if it had wilted.

"Small alert, sir," Arran whispered. "Robertson and Jermain are checking it out." There was an uncertain pause. "Uh, sir. Pat's done in. We been on point two hours now."

Mellas only nodded and continued forward, feeling more exposed with each step. He reached Jermain, the M-79 man, who was lying prone on the trail, trying to peer through the thick bamboo all around them. Mellas and Hamilton crawled up to him. "Where's Robertson?" Mellas whispered. Robertson was the leader of Jacobs's first fire team.

Jermain turned his face, red with the heat and excitement, toward Mellas, and motioned with his hands in a wide arc. Robertson had chosen to move around to come up behind any possible enemy.

"He went by himself?" Mellas whispered. Jermain nodded and shrugged, still looking straight ahead. Mellas was struck by Robertson's bravery.

The radio hissed. Hamilton quickly muffled the handset against his shirt, but he listened to the words. He tapped Mellas's boot. "It's the skipper. He wants to know what the fucking holdup is."

Mellas grabbed the handset. "Bravo Six, we're checking it out, goddamn it. Over." He had barely controlled the volume of his voice.

"Roger, Bravo One. I got Big John on my ass about the ammo getting blown. I'll give you five more minutes. Over."

"Roger. Out." Mellas gave Hamilton the handset. "The colonel's in a hurry," he said to Hamilton bitterly. "Start moving forward, Jermain."

Jermain turned to look at him in surprise. "We got to cover for Robertson," he said, exasperated. "Someone's got to care."

Mellas started crawling forward past Jermain, who took a deep breath and crawled out in front of him, his honor having been challenged.

"Jermain?" a voice whispered from the jungle ahead of them.

"Yeah. Right here," Jermain whispered back.

There was a rustle in the bushes, and then Robertson's sweating face emerged. He was duckwalking. "Oh, hi, Lieutenant," he said, and smiled. He remained there in a squat, his little body looking perfectly at ease in its folded-up position.

Mellas turned to look at Hamilton. "'Hi, Lieutenant,' he says." He shook his head and turned to Robertson. "See anything?" he asked.

Robertson shook his head, obviously unfazed by Mellas's sarcastic tone. "I got the feeling, though, that they're just in front of us keeping tabs somehow."

Mellas became serious. "Why do you feel that?"

"I don't know. Little things. I just feel it."

Mellas reached for the handset. "Bravo Six, this is Bravo One Actual. We checked out negative up here. I'll be rotating squads and then we'll be moving. I'm sending Arran back. Pat's done and we'll have big Victor"—he meant Vancouver—"on point anyway. Over." Fitch acknowledged and Mellas stood up in the trail. "Pass the word back for Conman's squad to move up. You guys take tail-end Charlie," he told Jake. "Tell Arran to wait on the CP group."

Pretty soon Vancouver's large frame could be seen moving up the trail, his modified M-60 hanging from his neck. Connolly was just two men behind him. Mellas told the lead fire team and Connolly about the situation and the need for haste. "But don't go any faster than feels OK, Vancouver," he added. "I don't care how much of a hurry the colonel is in to move his little pins in the map."

"I got you, sir."

Vancouver stared down the trail, constantly scanning it, his eyes jerking with tension. Walking down a trail to save time, he knew, was an invitation for an ambush. Also, Robertson had smelled something. He was a good fire team leader and had been around a while. If Robertson was being cautious, there was good reason. But on point there are always good reasons to be cautious, even if there's no hurry. The point man is all alone. It makes no difference if there's a fire team or an entire battalion behind him. He sees no one—only shadows. At every turn lurks the possible ambush—and the point man is the first to go. Or, if the ambushers are particularly successful, they let the point man by and cut him off when they open up on the lieutenant and the radio operator. It's like walking a hundred feet up on a bending two-by-four with the wind blowing in sporatic gusts from different directions. There's no help. No rope. No friend to lean on. The point man is also blindfolded by the jungle. His ears are confused by every tiny sound behind him, obscuring the one sound that might save him. He wants to scream for the whole world to shut up. His hands sweat, making him worry that he won't be able to pull the trigger. He wants to piss even if he just pissed five minutes ago. His heart thumps in his throat and chest. He waits out the eternity before the squad leader says it's time to rotate back into safety.

Vancouver stopped thinking. Fear and exposure drove thought from his head. Only survival remained.

It was the oddly bent piece of bamboo about ten meters down the trail that caused the rush of dread that saved him. Vancouver dropped to his knees and opened up. The roar of the machine gun and the spewing of hot casings turned the silent world of the jungle upside down. Everything was motion—Marines rolling off the trail, seeking cover in the foliage, scrambling, praying, crawling for their lives. Vancouver saw only shadows, but the shadows were screaming back at him with AK-47 automatic rifles. Bullets spun past him in the trail, kicking up mud, churning the place where the Marines had been a split second before. Connolly rolled into the brush, coming faceup on his back, his M-16 clutched to his chest. He was holding his fire, just as they had discussed so many times.

The sawed-off M-60 stopped firing. The belt had run out. Vancouver dived for the side of the trail, and Connolly rolled over into it on his stomach. He let loose on automatic just as an NVA soldier emerged from the wall of jungle to finish Vancouver off. Connolly's bullets caught the NVA soldier full in the chest and face. The back of the man's head exploded. Connolly rolled over again, fumbling wildly for another magazine. An M-16 opened up on Vancouver's right, almost on top of him, the bullets screaming past his right ear. Then another M-16 followed almost immediately to his left. Vancouver was crawling backward, along with Connolly, as fast as he could. Connolly was pushing a second magazine into place, shouting for Mole. "Gun up! Gun up! Mole! Goddamn it!"

Vancouver pulled another belt of ammunition from the metal box on his chest and slapped it into the gun's receiver. He heard Connolly shouting for Gambaccini, the M-79 man, and Rider, his first fire team leader. He saw the lieutenant, who'd moved forward and was shouting something at Hamilton and reloading a magazine himself. Then Gambaccini popped up and let loose with a grenade over Vancouver's head. There was a crashing sound in the brush to his left. He almost fired, but it was Rider moving his team up; all four were abreast and to the left of the trail in the jungle. They began laying down disciplined fire, pouring bullets into the unseen enemy.

To Mellas, the whole thing happened so quickly that he didn't even remember thinking. There was the sudden burst of Vancouver's machine gun, and Mellas dived for the ground and immediately started crawling forward to find out what was happening. Automatically, he started shouting for Mole to get the gun up front and heard the command being relayed back down the line. Fitch's excited voice was screaming over the radio. Mellas shouted at Hamilton—"Tell him I don't know. I don't know"—and crawled furiously forward.

He had just crawled around a bend in the trail when Vancouver's gun stopped and he saw Connolly roll out, firing in front of him while Vancouver was scrambling backward. Mellas shoved his face into the dirt just behind Vancouver's right knee, poked his rifle blindly down the trail, and opened up over Vancouver's head. Almost simultaneously, it seemed, the M-79 grenade launcher shot off a solid thump that sent a round of fléchettes down the trail. Then a whole fire team crashed through the jungle on his left and opened up on full automatic. All this time, Connolly was also shouting for Mole and the machine gun, crawling backward.

Mole came scrambling up the trail, gun cradled in his arms, crawl-ing crablike, awkwardly, but very fast. His A gunner, Young, the only white kid in the machine-gun teams except for Hippy, crawled behind him, dragging the heavy steel boxes of machine-gun belts. Mole slammed the gun down on its bipod just off the trail and immediately started lay-ing disciplined bursts of fire down the dark green corridor. Tracers sped down the tunnel of jungle like the taillights of receding cars. Young crawled up next to the barrel, fresh belt in hand, eyes wide with fear, ready to reload.

Mellas rolled back and grabbed the hook from Hamilton, panting for air. "Ambush. I knew this fucking trail. Death trap. Vancouver spot-ted them. Before we got into the kill zone. I think they dee-deed. Over."

"Casualties? Over."

"That's a neg. Over."

"Thank God," Fitch replied, forgetting radio procedure.

Mellas was quivering with excitement and with a strange exulta-tion, as if his team had just won a football championship. No casualties. He'd done well. It was over too quickly, though. Somehow, it should be prolonged. He wanted to tell Fitch and Hawke all about it. He wanted to go running down the long line of excited Marines, telling the story of the fight over and over again. They'd broken up an ambush. His pla-toon. Killed two, maybe three of the enemy, and suffered not a scratch. A perfect job.

"Bravo Six, this is Bravo One. Over."

"Bravo Six," Fitch answered.

"We need artillery," Mellas pleaded excitedly. "The goddamned gooners are dee-deeing right out of the fucking area. Where's the goddamn mortars? Let's *get* some."

"Roger that, Bravo One. Character Delta's working up an arty mission right now. It's a little hard on the mortar squad to fire shells into the tree limbs over their heads. You copy? Over." Mellas was too ex-cited to notice Fitch's sarcasm.

He crawled over to where Connolly was lying beside Mole, peer-ing down the shadowy trail. Connolly, too, was quivering and breath-ing hard. Vancouver was to Connolly's left, and Rider's fire team to the left of Vancouver, pulled back now in echelon, forming the left side of a wedge. The rest of the squad, without being told, had formed the right side of the wedge at the head of the column to get maximum fire in the direction of the ambush but still allow fire to their sides to protect their flanks.

"I think they drug the body away, sir," Connolly said. "Just as we was crawling back, I thought I caught some movement. Did you see them?"

"Yeah," Mellas lied, without intending to. "You're right." In his imagination, fueled by the excitement, this mention of an NVA soldier pulling a body back into the cover of the jungle was enough to convince him that he'd actually seen it happen. "Why doesn't the skipper send a platoon around in an envelopment?" he asked, staring down the trail.

Connolly looked at Mellas. "In this shit?"

Mellas stopped gazing straight ahead and looked at Connolly. For some reason, that comment had brought him down. Once more he saw tangled jungle on both sides of a narrow muddy path. "Yeah, it'd take forever. They'd be sitting ducks. You'd hear them for miles."

"There it is, sir."

"Maybe we can get it on with the artillery." Mellas wanted to keep talking about the incident. "You're sure about the gook you zapped in the head?" he asked.

"I saw his fucking face disappear," Connolly said grimly.

"We'll call it a confirmed, even if we don't have the body. I mean, there's no way the gooner can still be alive. Vancouver must have greased at least another one or two." Mellas turned to Vancouver. "Hey, Vancouver, how many you think you got?"

Vancouver looked down at his steaming weapon. "Jeez, sir, all I saw was fucking bushes and all this shit came flying at me. I maybe hit a couple of them, though."

"We'll look for blood trails soon as the arty mission's over. But we must have got at least one confirmed and two probables."

Mellas turned around to where Hamilton was lying with the heavy radio pressing him into the dirt, its small bent antenna waving in the still air. He proudly reported the score. "Bravo this is One. We got one confirmed up here and two probables. Over."

"Roger, one confirmed and two probables," Pallack's voice answered. "Heads down. I just heard character Delta say 'shot.' He'll be working it in close. Over."

"Incoming," Mellas called out in a loud voice. "Friendly incoming."

He looked around to see if his men were reasonably safe. Then it occurred to him that everybody already had his head down and had been that way for the past three minutes. He buried his own head in the earth as the first anguished scream of the 105s came through the sky from Eiger.

It was again Third Squad's turn to take point. They handed off Williams's body to Second Squad and moved quietly forward. Cortell kept taking his helmet off and putting it on, rubbing his high, glistening forehead. Everyone hurried through the would-be kill zone, breathing a thank-you for Vancouver's eyes and reaction time.

Jackson found two rice cakes hanging from a man's bloody web belt that had been removed and tossed beside the trail. He happily stuffed them into his large trouser pockets, as all of his squad's food was gone. He quickly cut the brass buckle with its red star from the belt, knowing it would bring some good money from souvenir hunters in Da Nang, and passed it back to Vancouver. A little farther down the trail they found a bloody cap. That also was passed back to Vancouver, who silently gave it to Connolly. Connolly stuffed it into his pocket.

Mellas's whole body was zinging. His hands quivered. He started at nearly every noise and talked too rapidly, and too much, on the radio. He kept mentally replaying the scene, wondering how he could have reacted faster and killed more of them, wondering if Connolly was aware that, while he was changing magazines, Mellas had saved him by firing. He wondered if people outside the company would hear about his action and how his platoon had succeeded when Alpha Company had lost so many in a similar ambush. He remained charged up until they reached the ammunition dump that afternoon as the light began to fade from the gray sky.

At the dump, Mellas was bitterly disappointed.

He couldn't believe that all the reports he'd read about the Air Force and Navy destroying bunkers had referred to what he saw before him: three large holes dug in the dank ground, covered with logs and earth.

Inside the three bunkers were ten 120-millimeter rockets, several hundred 82-millimeter mortar shells, eighty small 61-millimeter mortar shells, enough AK-47 ammunition to supply a platoon for one firefight, and a few medical supplies donated by the English Red Cross.

Hawke seemed strangely happy. He broke into the hawk dance, then climbed on top of one of the bunkers and tossed bandage rolls in the air like streamers, shouting at the top of his lungs, "The fucking English! I knew it was the fucking English behind this war!" He laughed and tossed another bandage, looping it in the trees. The whiteness looked out of place against the dark canopy.

The company mostly shrugged at the Jayhawk's antics. Cassidy organized a work party, and soon the ammunition was hauled into a pit where he, Samms, Bass, and Ridlow joyfully collaborated in blowing it up.

Everyone buried his head in the earth and they set off the charge. There was a tremendous explosion, but not even a quarter of the ammunition went off. The rest twisted skyward, tumbling end over end, and scattered across the area. The kids booed. Cassidy laughed and immediately put the booers to work collecting the ammunition. The Marines on the work detail grumbled. "We must have the only fucking lifers in the Crotch that can't blow up a fucking ammo dump." They waited for an hour to make sure there were no cook-offs in the pit and once more set the charges. This time they covered the ammo with rocks and earth to contain the explosion.

The platoon sergeants themselves were laughing about the incongruity of the situation. Most people would think they couldn't light a match around an ammo dump without setting it off. Basically, every-one was happy. They would probably clear an LZ the next morning and sky out by afternoon, their mission accomplished with no casualties other than Williams.

Mellas, however, felt a curious malaise, anxiety, and an emptiness beyond hunger—he had been on half rations for five days and had eaten nothing at all today. Four thoughts kept hammering at him. First, how could the English, seemingly the most civilized of people, the people with whom they'd fought side by side against the Nazis, be aiding their enemy, the North Vietnamese Army? Every penny that the North Viet-namese saved by receiving donations could be spent on ammunition that could kill him. Every life saved was a life that could kill him, too. Mellas felt betrayed. Second, he was still trying to reconcile those tiny log-covered pits referred to as bunkers with the images in his mind of bombs smashing concrete and steel, the Siegfried Line, the *Guns of Navarone.* Third, why in hell had they walked all this way, sacrificed Williams, and nearly killed the entire First Squad but for Vancouver's uncommon alertness, for no more ammunition than could be hauled off with a couple of trucks?

These thoughts nagged at him as he struggled to dig his hole for the night. When he finished, he sat down to face the fourth question. Should he make his last cup of coffee now or in the morning? The pla-toon was just about out of food. He decided to wait. He went off to find Hawke and Fitch to talk about medals for the action, half hoping that maybe he'd get one, too, but at the same time realizing that all he'd really done was show up for the party. He also hoped Hawke and Fitch would be fixing coffee.

Fitch was on the hook with the Three, who had questions of his own—to which Fitch had the wrong answers.

"I was informed that there were three ammunition bunkers in this complex. These numbers you've given us just don't jibe. Over."

Fitch took a deep breath and looked at Hawke before answering. Pallack rolled his eyes.

"That's affirmative. Three bunkers. We got them all. The num-bers you got are everything that's in them. They're *little* bunkers. Over."

"I copy." There was a burst of static as Blakely released his transmitting button. Fitch waited nervously. Static burst out again. "Stand by for a frag order, Bravo Six. Over."

"Roger your last. Bravo Six out."

"A fragment order on the original?" Mellas asked, uneasy about any change. "Does that mean we're not skying out tomorrow?"

Fitch shrugged. "Maybe something to do with Delta Company over the ridge. Hell, we can't go far with everyone out of food."

"Not quite everyone," Hawke said, digging into the side pocket of his utility trousers. He held up a single can of apricots. Everyone looked at it longingly. "And I ain't opening it." Hawke stuffed it back into his pocket. "I got a bad feeling about that frag order."

At the regimental briefing that afternoon, Major Adams was particularly snappy. *Whap.* "And at coordinates 768671, elements of Bravo One Twenty-Four destroyed the ammunition dump uncovered by Alpha Company and believed to be one of the supply sources for elements of the Three Hundred Twelfth steel division now known to be operating in our TAOR. Approximately five tons of ammunition consisting of one-hundred-twenty-millimeter rockets, small arms and automatic weapons ammunition, and mortar rounds were destroyed along with approximately one thousand pounds of medical supplies."

"Better leave the medical supplies out of the report," Mulvaney said. "No sense getting somebody riled up about destroying medical supplies." Somehow the public felt it was OK to kill men with tumbling bullets and flaming jelly, but to kill them by denying them medical supplies was against some societal notion of decency.

"Aye, aye, sir," Adams answered.

Mulvaney turned stiffly in his chair to look back at Colonel Simpson and Major Blakely, who were seated behind him. "Maybe you do have some gooks out there, Simpson," he said.

Blakely smiled and looked up at Adams, whose face revealed a twinge of jealousy. Mulvaney turned back to face the briefing officer. He was trying to figure how many men and how long it would take to haul five tons to such a remote location. Through terrain like that, it was quite an accomplishment. He had to admire the North Vietnamese Army. But why were they stacking ammunition there? Was it a way station for moving the ammunition farther south? They could hit Hue again. Now that would be a fucking propaganda disaster. Let the politicians chew on that for a while. But then they might also be preparing a move in force straight across Mutter's Ridge, where they'd control Route 9 and then starve out VCB. Now that they'd abandoned Matterhorn to get enough troops to do the stupid fucking Cam Lo political operation, that would be what he'd do if he were a gook. He suddenly felt, in the middle of his back, the uneasiness that had saved him so often in Korea and the Pacific. Then he noticed Major Adams waiting nervously to continue, sighed, and nodded his large head. He couldn't cover everywhere.

Whap. The pointer moved to the left, three-quarters of an inch, the distance it had taken Bravo Company half a day to move. "As the colonel is aware, Bravo made point-to-point contact with an undetermined-size unit of North Vietnamese Infantry at grid coordinates 735649 earlier today. Two confirmed kills and three probables with no casualties suffered by Bravo Company. The bodies were searched with negative findings."

Mulvaney turned to look at Blakely and Simpson. "Someone must have really been on their toes out there," he said. "Was it a point-to-point or an ambush?" In fact Mulvaney already knew that it was the big blond Canadian kid with the sawed-off M-60 who had busted up an ambush. His jeep driver had the story from one of the First Battalion radio operators. Bravo's skipper must have been in an awful hurry to be barrel-assing down a trail another company had already been hit on. That young lieutenant *was* lucky. Probably hadn't learned when to charge and when not to. Mulvaney would have to talk to him about it if he got the chance.

Simpson cleared his throat, his face reddening. "In answer to your question, sir, Bravo's point man apparently fired first and the lead squad pulled back and set up. We called it a point-to-point contact because it seemed the most conservative."

Mulvaney grunted and turned to endure the remainder of the briefing. Why in fuck Simpson should worry about breaking up an ambush was beyond him.

After suffering through hearing the Navy doctor tell how many Marines went through his sick bay, the congressional inquiries officer tell how many letters he'd handled from upset congressmen responding to letters from upset mothers and wives, and the Red Cross liaison man tell about dependents who were not getting pay allotments, Mulvaney could finally rise from his chair to address his officers.

"As you already know, gentlemen, the Fifth Marine Division continues to be involved in a combined cordon and search operation with the First ARVN Division. Our major objective, as you also know, continues to be Cam Lo." Mulvaney turned to the large map and began outlining the next day's plan of the ongoing operation, all the while feeling that somehow he had let his regiment down. Working with the goddamned gooks wasn't his idea of fighting a war, particularly when all that would probably happen was a few old political scores would get settled in Cam Lo. Some SEAL teams had been operating in the villages for several years now, assassinating "known Vietcong leaders," but where the fuck did *that* information come from? Supposedly from the CIA, but then none of those spooks were hanging out in the villages. Christ, they're all six-foot-two white boys from Yale. So where did the spooks get their information? Probably from one of the damned secret societies who were just fingering a leader of another secret society over the control of some drug market and getting their dirty work done courtesy of the United States Navy. Any Vietcong leadership, if the Vietcong existed in any force there at all after their buddies from the north set them up to be obliterated by American firepower during Tet, would be long gone by the time all the security leaks from the ARVN trickled down. Yes, Mulvaney mused, power in the secret societies would definitely shift after Cam Lo, and the spooks would be played for suckers, and his Marines would pay the price. He wanted to kick the CIA's ass and break the fucking ARVN's scrawny necks.

"Simpson," he said. "I'm going to have to disappoint you. We'll have to abandon the Matterhorn area for good. I can't afford to give up any of Mutter's Ridge. Lookout and Sherpa keep me covered in the Khe Sanh region. Division wants a new fire support base opened at Hill 1609 just beneath Tiger's Tooth. We'll have to bring in those two companies in the Matterhorn area and then send one of them out close enough to open 1609."

"But, sir." Simpson stood up, excited, already believing the numbers he'd "estimated" for his report. "We're just beginning to find what's really up there." He turned to look to Blakely for support.

Blakely didn't miss his cue. "I'm sure the regimental commander realizes," Blakely began, "that with the latest findings of Bravo Company, combined with the intelligence estimates of division, there's a high probability that the NVA is becoming quite active in the far northwest. It would be a real shame after having given those reports to division to have no follow-through on them."

Mulvaney almost exploded. The last goddamned thing on his mind was following up on some fucking report he'd turned in to division. Then he remembered his wife. He counted to five. Then he counted five more.

His mind went back to that night at Camp Lejeune—it must have been 1954 or 1955; he was still a captain in any case; he had Alpha Company, Second Marines. Maizy had come back from bridge with Neitzel's wife, Dorothy, and some of her cronies. Neitzel was already a major and was heading for Amphibious Warfare School and a big staff job. Mulvaney had been painting the living room, little James slung in a beach towel hanging from his neck.

"My God, Mike," Maizy said. "You're getting paint all over him—and the fumes. The girls' bedroom must be full of them." She was smiling and shaking her head, at the same time removing her impeccable white gloves and placing them where they always resided, in her grandmother's crystal bowl, the only thing she had ever inherited. She grabbed the apron that always hung on the kitchen door hook, and tossed it over her shoulder to protect her only suit. She took the baby from him. "Wouldn't sleep again?" she asked.

"Eeyep."

"Girls go to bed on time?"

"Eeyep."

"Can you put the roller down?"

"Uh-oh. Serious scuttlebutt." He put the roller in the tray and watched her watching little James so that she wouldn't have to look him in the eye. He knew that she never wanted to hurt his feelings, but he also knew that she didn't shirk from delivering bad news if it meant a better life for her kids. That same drive had her memorizing bidding rules, with him quizzing her from a book while she ironed clothes so she "wouldn't make a damned fool of herself in front of the other wives." That same anxiety had also had her agonizing with her sister at Christmastime about what suit to buy when she had first been invited to the bridge table, as if her sister knew more about suits than Maizy did because she worked in a real office.

"Dorothy Neitzel did it as a favor, so I don't want you to take it in the wrong way. She really is trying to help."

He watched her glance up at him and then quickly back down at James. "Help how?" Might as well get it over.

"You know, what do you guys call it, back-channel communication."

"Gossip."

She laughed. "That's what *we* call it." Then she looked at him seriously. "Oh, Mikey," she said, her eyes pleading. "Dorothy says you stood up for that awful alcoholic First Sergeant Hanford who got caught trying to divert base water to some sort of . . . some sort of swimming hole or something that he'd dug out with a bulldozer that he'd, what do you call it, requisitioned, from the engineering battalion without asking them for it. We call that stealing."

"It gets goddamned hot in those stupid squad bays, and those kids loved it. I told the colonel that all Hanford needed was an off-the-record chewing out. Instead they busted him. He's got four kids. All he was doing was looking out for the troops. You know what I told you that day you picked me up from the hospital."

"Yes, I know. That you'd always take the side of the bush Marine." She sighed. "Mikey, of course you're right, but on that very same day, in my father's 1939 Chevy—I was driving because your leg still wouldn't work from Okinawa—I told you that there might be times that you could be a little more circumspect. You can do a lot more good for your bush Marines as a colonel than as a captain."

He took a quick God-help-me look at the ceiling. "Hanford did the right thing the wrong way. No harm, no foul."

"The harm, Michael, was telling the colonel that if he ever got his fat ass out of his air-conditioned office he'd understand what Hanford was trying to do."

Mulvaney tightened his lips and folded his arms across the chest.

"Don't you get stubborn with me, Michael Mulvaney. You were wrong to do it. Can't you think of your own family, your own kids, for once?"

"That's unfair."

She breathed, softened. "Yes, it was." She reached out to touch his arm. "But Mikey, please, you've got to hold your temper." His temper had been an issue ever since he'd gotten back from the Pacific. She moved her hand back to the baby. "Do you want to know what else Dorothy told me?"

"I can't wait."

"She is doing us a favor, Mikey, for God's sake."

Mulvaney sat down on the tarp-covered couch and looked up at her. "Go ahead. All ready on the firing line."

She sat down beside him, scrunching sideways, her tight skirt riding up to show the welt of her stocking, something that always distracted Mulvaney. She tugged, unsuccessfully, at the skirt with her right hand, trying to keep James on her shoulder with her left and Mulvaney on task. She solved both problems by putting the baby and the apron across her lap. She pointed a finger at him, eyes merry. "You are always horny."

"So? I'm on the firing line anyway. Shoot me."

"Later." She smiled down at the baby and said in a quiet singsong, "Daddy wants to make you a little sister." Then she looked up at Mulvaney, her large green eyes suddenly serious. "Dorothy says that they all think you're . . ." She hesitated.

"Go on."

"That you're some kind of a throwback to World War II. The word is that Mulvaney will never get out of the jungle, but he's good in a fight."

"That's bad?"

"Oh, Mikey, don't be deliberately dense. You know as well as I do that it's the planners that get ahead, not the fighters."

"And the politicians."

"Yes!" She stamped one black pump on the floor and rose to her feet. Putting the baby back on her shoulder, she walked quickly into their bedroom where the crib was next to the bed, her two-inch heels punctuating every step.

He had watched the way her tight wool skirt beautifully molded her rear end.

The briefing room swam back into consciousness, a layer above the memory of his home and his wife. God, how he missed her now. He saw everyone waiting for him to say something.

He knew Blakely was right. With promising reports coming in from Bravo Company, it would look foolish not to follow through. "But where in hell am I supposed to get the men to follow up on your fucking reports?" he asked. He was uncomfortably aware that his strangled anger at Blakely and the ARVNs made his voice sound petty and whining.

Blakely thought quickly. "Why not let Bravo Company sweep the area and move up to 1609 on foot, sir."

Mulvaney looked at the map. It looked like a little over twenty kilometers as the crow flies, but the small squares were almost completely brown with the thick mass of twenty-meter contour intervals. They could barely fit next to each other and still be distinguishable. He remembered parts of Korea that looked like this, and he shuddered—there hadn't been any jungle there. "What's their condition?" he asked Simpson. "They've been out in the bush a long time, if I remember."

"Top-notch, sir. They could be there in four days."

If Simpson said four days, then it would probably take eight. "Food? Power sources for the radios? Ammo? With this Cam Lo op, you know I'm short on birds for resupply."

"No problem, sir," Simpson replied, enjoying the chance to show the other battalion commanders how ready his battalion was.

Blakely paled and swallowed. He hadn't bothered to tell Simspon that Bravo had given half its food to Delta almost a week ago to cover the error of pushing Delta off inadequately supplied.

"What do you think, Major Blakely?" Mulvaney asked.

Blakely didn't hesitate. "One Twenty-Four can do the job, sir. You know what they say about the impossible."

"Yes," Mulvaney said quietly, turning to look at the map. "It takes a little longer." Sick, frostbitten Marines crowded into his memory, struggling up frozen hills, their backs bent under mortars and ammunition, the wounded strapped on litters bound to fenders and in the backs of jeeps and small trucks, clenching their teeth at each painful jolt. Then his mind contrasted that image with one of thin, sore-ridden bodies with barely enough energy to fight the jungle, let alone fight the Japanese. He forced his mind back to the brightly lit briefing room and the map in front of him. He figured it would be a fucking hump at that. Still, he could live with it. They had ten days before 1609 had to be secured. That left Bravo two real days of wiggle room. Something, however, nagged at him. It was like a lump beneath a sleeping bag that he couldn't quite flatten. But with that much ammo in that dump, and if he didn't follow through on it as Blakely had suggested . . . He knew he had a reputation for being too impetuous. In this new Marine Corps of careful staff work and covering your ass with paper, it just wasn't the same. His old friend Neitzel had blended right in with the new Corps; that was why Neitzel had a division and Mulvaney didn't. If they hit pay dirt, it couldn't hurt his chances of becoming a general. He smiled, imagining his wife pinning on his stars. "Oh, hell," he growled at himself.

"Sir?" Major Adams responded.

"Nothing, Adams. OK, Simpson, you're on. Don't let me down."

The frag order that appended their original order to destroy the supply dump reached Bravo Company one hour after the regimental briefing broke up. It consisted of a series of checkpoints and times of arrival, nothing more, some in deep draws, others high on ridges. The line of march took no heed of the wild terrain.

Hawke began the actuals meeting. "Gentlemen, I'd like to introduce you to our new leader, Captain Meriwether Lewis. My name is Clark, but you can call me Wm for short. We won't be skying out for a while."

Fitch explained the frag order. "We've got about three hours of daylight left, so we might as well get a couple of hours humping. Otherwise there's no chance of making checkpoint Alpha."

"Shit," Mellas said. "We just dug in. That body stinks and my platoon's out of food."

"You ain't the Lone Ranger, Mellas," Hawke said, "but you might be Sacajawea. You still got point."

Mellas gritted his teeth and took his map out of his pocket, but he had to smile at Hawke's joke. "I don't see any point in it, that's all," he said. People groaned and Mellas felt better. "What about this funny-looking three-cornered hill for a position for tonight?" he said. "We might make it before dark. Jesus, though, the river looks like it runs right through a fucking canyon."

They discussed it briefly and Fitch gave the go-ahead. He ordered the food redistributed but would allow anyone to keep one C-ration can if he had one, mitigating any resentment on the part of those who had saved their rations. Most of the kids, like Mellas, had already eaten all the food they had. The platoon sergeants collected everything that remained. The redistributed food, now held in common, equaled about three-quarters of a can per person. Twenty minutes after redistributing the food, the company wound out of the ammunition dump, Jacobs's squad leading, Jackson's struggling with Williams's body.

They moved slowly northeastward, following a rushing stream, higher into the mountains, closer to the DMZ. The terrain grew wildly beautiful, with steep jungle-covered peaks and rushing torrents of water from the monsoon rains. Occasionally, someone would slip on a glassy, water-smoothed rock and his entire body would be covered in swift white water that immediately soaked into his pack, wetting his poncho liner. Unable to regain his feet against the force of the stream because of all his heavy gear, he would be pulled up by laughing companions. Those who got soaked, however, knew that they'd be fighting the cold all that night, trying to use body heat to dry their clothes and poncho liners.

The trees grew larger and the forest darker as they gained altitude. At one point a large flat outcropping of rock opened the jungle enough to afford them a view of their line of march. Directly in front of them was a dark, narrow valley filled with clouds, which hung close to dark peaks of barren rock. The peaks guarded a narrow, twisting river. Each Marine who passed that open viewpoint made some nervous gesture: tightening his equipment, pausing to spray repellent on a leech, whistling aloud. The rain, which up to now had been falling in a misty drizzle from high clouds, suddenly intensified. It pounded the earth, bringing a rush of cold air.

By the time they reached the three-cornered hill, Mellas had an intense headache because of his depleted blood sugar. His body had been drained by onslaughts of adrenaline, hunger, and the constant sucking cold of wet clothing. Feeling like a sick animal, he dragged himself along by will alone.

The hill rose impossibly high in the gloom.

Jacobs looked upward. "Who the f-fuck p-picked this?" Water from the stream at the base of the hill was dripping from his trousers.

Mellas closed his eyes. "I did, asshole."

The point man sighed, then started crawling up the slope, pushing his rifle in front of him, grabbing roots and rocks.

Partway up Mellas heard a commotion behind him. He turned to see Hippy looking helplessly up the hill as he slid backward, his heavy machine gun held in front of his face. He started knocking into people behind him, who in turn starting to slide and knock into others. The whole slow-motion scene came to a halt against a tree and everyone untangled himself, cursing Hippy. They started upward again.

It took Mellas's platoon an hour to reach the top while the rest of the company waited in the rushing river, freezing, exposed to attack, as the light faded completely. Mellas, as the first officer in, was responsible for setting in the defense for the company and guiding the Marines into positions as they arrived. He thrashed his way through the dark jungle with a machete, outlining the perimeter. It was all he could do to keep from falling to the forest floor, never to move again. Tangled growth slapped his face, tore at his exposed skin, hid the terrain from his eyes. He kept trying to remember all the rules about placing his machine guns. His E-tool, the small folding entrenching shovel attached to his pack, caught on a branch, and the sudden imbalance with the immense weight of his pack almost pulled him over backward. He struck out at the limb, breaking it, hurting his hand and opening the scab over a jungle-rot sore on his arm. In a frenzy, he took out his K-bar and hacked the bush to pieces. Afterward his face felt hot and flushed but his back was damp and cold. His hands were swollen, and his fingers did not want to move. He pulled down his trousers and shit watery feces that spattered on his bare legs and boots. He retched at the smell, unable to throw up because his stomach was empty.

He headed back down the hill to guide his weary platoon in. It took the rest of the company an hour to get to the top because First Platoon's trail had turned into a mudslide. When Mellas finally was able to return to his own position, he found Hamilton with the dry heaves from exhaustion and lack of food, retching painfully over the beginnings of a shallow hole.

Mellas watched him, realizing that he'd have to dig the entire hole himself. "Here, give me that," Mellas said bitterly, taking the small entrenching tool. "Why don't you go see if you can rig our ponchos up for some sort of hooch?" he said more gently.

Hamilton tried to smile but began retching again. "I'll be OK in a while, sir," he gasped. "Don't worry, I'll help with the hole."

"Forget it," Mellas said. He started digging. When Hamilton turned away, Mellas began silently crying, hacking at the damp earth in impotent fury.

Fitch had said there would be a full moon that night, and indeed the monsoon clouds had lightened just enough to permit an eerie glow above the trees when Mellas did his first hole-check. He found Hippy sitting silently on the edge of his hole. His bare feet dangled into the darkness below him and his ragged bleached-out boots sat next to the hole. "You'd better cover those boots, Hippy," Mellas whispered. "I homed in on them like an airport beacon."

"Thanks, sir," Hippy replied. He took his boots and put them in the hole. "Just trying to let them air a little. Thought maybe it'd keep the gooks away if they was downwind."

Mellas laughed and sat down beside Hippy. "Anything going on?" he whispered.

"Here? You shitting me, Lieutenant?"

Mellas smiled. He kicked his boot out to adjust his position and hit Hippy's foot. Hippy winced. "Hey. You got foot trouble, Hippy?"

"Naw. Nothing serious, sir."

"Let me see them."

"It ain't nothing, sir. Just some blisters."

"Uh-huh," Mellas replied. "Let's see one, Hippy."

Hippy drew his left foot up to the edge of the hole. Even in the ghostly light, Mellas could see that it was grotesquely swollen and discolored. It repelled him. He took a deep breath. The other foot was no different. "The squid seen these?"

"No sir."

Mellas exploded. "Why the fuck not?"

Hippy hung his head.

"Hippy, you're a fucking cripple. Shit."

"I can make it, Lieutenant," he answered.

"Shit." Mellas stood up. "Sure you can, if you extend six months." Mellas took a breath and tried to cool down. Where in the fuck was he going to find another gun-squad leader as good as Hippy? "There must be some way we can get a bird to get your ass out of here."

"Sorry, sir," Hippy said.

"Sorry don't get it," Mellas barked, immediately wishing he hadn't. "Who do you want to take over the gun squad?"

Hippy touched the butt plate of the machine gun. "I humped that motherfucker a long ways, sir. I want to hump it in. It's got good karma."

"Hippy, they'll goddamned amputate. You ever hear of gangrene?"

Hippy looked down at his feet, then giggled. "They're pretty fucking bad, aren't they, Lieutenant?"

"Yeah. Pretty fucking bad." Mellas waited a moment. "Who, Hippy?"

"Mole. And let Young hump my gun." Hippy reached down and toyed with the silver peace medallion that hung around his neck. "This is my last op, sir. My twelve and twenty's in nine days and I'm out of the bush. Ten days after that, I sky out for home. I'm so short what you're hearing now is a tape recording."

"We'll get you out. They've got to bring us some fucking food sometime and pick Williams up."

In the blackness in front of Fitch's hooch the conversation was also about helicopters and food. Fitch was on the hook with the battalion watch officer.

"What's the word on our resupply?" Fitch said tightly. "We're already on our spare power sources and we're fucking hungry. Over."

"We're trying, but the Whiskey Oscar at MAG-Thirty-Nine says they got all the birds tied up in some big to-do in the flatlands and all the heavies are in bed, so we can't alter the priorities. Can you wait a couple of days? Over."

Hawke, who was sitting across from Fitch, winced at the security breach about the upcoming operation.

"Wait a couple of days? Goddamn it, we haven't eaten for a couple of days already and we've been on half rations the entire time we've been out here because some dumb son of a bitch sitting on his fat ass back at Victor Charlie Bravo forgot to give Delta time to get organized. Now I want a fucking chopper out here with some food on it or by God there'll be hell to pay when I get in. Now. I mean it, Stevens."

"Don't use my name over the net, Bravo Six," Stevens replied. "You know the gooners monitor our nets. I don't want them using my name, writing weird stuff home to my wife. Over."

"Sorry, character Sierra," Fitch replied, realizing that if he argued with Stevens their chances for resupply would be worse. "Look, help us out. We're starving to death. At least tell us what the fuck we're supposed to be doing out here. Over."

"I don't know what to do about the birds, Bravo Six. Honest. As far as what you're doing out there I thought that would be obvious. If you found that much ammunition, there must be more around there someplace. Hell, division public relations put out a news release about Alpha's fight for it and everything. Over."

"Fight for it? They were fucking ambushed." Fitch unkeyed the handset and looked at Hawke and Cassidy. "News story?" he said. His stomach felt weak.

"Well, that isn't the way I heard it." Stevens started to say something else but was cut off.

"Shut the fuck up and let me think, goddamn it," Fitch shouted back into the receiver, interrupting Stevens's transmission and probably not being totally received. Stevens apparently received enough of it to get the message, though.

"We got to have food, Jim," Hawke said. He had been doodling a pentangle star in the mud. "Even Lewis and Clark could hunt buffalo on the way."

"Yes, sir," Cassidy said, "and I caught a couple of kids limping. I think we got some immersion foot cases that we ought to medevac. Otherwise we'll cripple some good Marines."

"OK," Fitch said. He put the receiver back to his ear and keyed it. "Big John, this is Bravo Six. Make the bird request a priority, and if I don't get it tomorrow, then you tell them the next day it'll be an emergency. I got some bad cases of immersion foot we've got to take care of ASAP. Over."

"Oh. The Six isn't going to like that. You know what he thinks about immersion foot. Over."

"Let me worry about Big John Six. You worry about fragging us a fucking bird. Pri-or-it-y," he enunciated. "We'll have a zone cleared by noon. Over."

"Noon? How are you going to make checkpoint Alpha tomorrow?"

"Frag the fucking bird," Fitch said between clenched teeth. "Bravo Six out."

There was a pause, then the radio hissed again. "Don't get sore, Bravo Six. I was just trying to tell you the score, that's all. Over."

Fitch stared into the darkness, holding the handset away from his mouth. After a long wait, the radio hissed again.

"OK, Bravo Six. I'll see what I can do. No need to get sore. Big John out."

The next morning they drew straws to see who would clear away enough jungle to make a landing zone. Mellas lost. Still shivering with the wet and cold, he walked dejectedly back to tell the platoon. Kendall and Goodwin went back to prepare security patrols.

The only possible place for an LZ was a small level spot just off the crest of the hill. It was, however, covered with a formidable mass of matted bamboo and elephant grass. Mellas felt physically ill. His small K-bar and dull E-tool seemed useless in the face of this clotted, dense plant life. He looked at his hands, feeling the sores of jungle rot. He looked at Jackson, knowing he could tell Jackson to start clearing while he went back to sit with Bass and monitor the single radio they now shared. He'd ordered the other radio turned off to save power. He knew, however, that he couldn't leave these kids and ever earn their respect. Still, he didn't know what to do in the face of this overwhelming green wall. He sensed Jackson beside him, getting mad. Mellas simply stared at the impossible task. His mind wouldn't focus. Clear the jungle—with no tools and no food. He closed his eyes.

Then he heard Jackson scream.

"Fucking no-good shit!" Jackson went snarling past Mellas. Mellas looked dumbly at him, thinking Jackson had cracked. Jackson threw himself like a football player making a cross-body block into the wall of bamboo and grass. The mass yielded slightly. Jackson ran back to the group, let out a whoop, and again hurled himself at the tangled mass. It bent. He backed off and jumped into it feet first, cursing it. He began jumping up and down on it, shouting an exultant chant. The bamboo broke. The grass sagged and fell. Broyer, shielding his glasses with his arms, gave a whoop and ran headlong at the dent made by Jackson.

Mellas took only a second to realize that he'd just had his first lesson in real leadership. He then charged forward, headfirst, as if going off tackle. The mass of vegetation let his head in but stopped his shoulders. He was followed by Tilghman, the M-79 man, and then Parker and Cortell. Mellas ran back, turned around, snarled, and did it again. Jacobs's and Connolly's squads, infected with the excitement of the game, went crashing into the grass too. Vancouver actually picked Connolly up and threw him like a log into the mess. Uniforms turned black with the wet rot. Hands and arms ran with blood from the rasping razor grass. But the landing zone grew.

By eleven that morning the zone was cleared. The kids lay flat on their backs, exhausted, staring at the gray swirling clouds. An hour later the clouds touched the earth. Both the landing zone and the waiting Marines looked ghostly and unreal. By late afternoon they were all shivering with the cold, dejected, quiet, still waiting for the bird. The food was all gone. Many had eaten only three-quarters of a can in the last forty-eight hours. Fog was all around them. Even Jackson could not crush the fog.

Fitch sent Kendall and Goodwin out on squad-size patrols to provide security for the landing zone, just in case. Kendall got lost and had to fire a pop-up flare for Daniels and Fitch to get a bearing on him. Everyone grumbled that the flare would tell the NVA where the Marines were, and among themselves the kids started calling Kendall Pop-Up. Kendall's platoon sergeant, Samms, sat down with Bass and bitched for nearly an hour about Kendall and the policy of having every officer get experience by commanding a rifle platoon. Goodwin radioed in that he'd found something, but it was a surprise. Fitch offered Hawke twenty dollars for his can of apricots. Hawke refused.

In midafternoon, Cortell and Jackson walked up to see Hawke about the next R & R quotas. When they reached the center of the perimeter they found Lieutenant Goodwin, still loaded with hand grenades and ammunition, fondling two baby tigers. Senior Squid and Relsnik were watching Sergeant Cassidy poke playfully at the blind kittens, a smile on his face.

Cortell, who'd shared a fighting hole with Williams since they'd arrived in-country eight months earlier, saw the two tigers differently. He broke away from Jackson and walked over to the group.

"I don't think they ought to be here," he said. His heart was starting to pound, but he was vowing to do something for Williams—anything to ease the guilty feeling that he had let Williams down.

"Well, fuck me," Cassidy said, standing up. "You don't think they ought to be here, do you? Do you remember me asking for your opinion?"

Cortell said nothing, wishing Jackson would speak up.

"You just walk up to your fucking superiors and tell them what you think all the time?" Cassidy asked.

"No sir," Cortell said. The old fear of the Deep South returned, weakening his knees.

"Then I suggest you mind your own business. I thought you'd fucking like jungle animals."

Cortell's nostrils flared and his face went pallid. His hands and legs burned. He felt Jackson's hand on his elbow, pulling him gently back, away from Cassidy and away from an inner precipice. Cortell was breathing hard, staring at Cassidy, who was staring right back at him. "I'll kill those motherfuckers," Cortell said.

"Over my dead body," Cassidy said.

"You want it that way?"

"You threatening to kill me, Cortell?" Cassidy asked.

"Come on, Cortell," Jackson said. Cortell heard him as if through a long tunnel. Jackson turned to Cassidy and added quietly, "He ain't threatening to kill you, Gunny. It's about Williams, his fucking friend."

Cortell slapped angrily at Jackson's hand, pulling himself from its grip.

"Come *on*, Cortell," Jackson hissed. "You gonna get your ass locked up." Jackson pulled him around, Cortell jerking back and Jackson jerking him forward. Cortell somehow managed to break free of his rage by stepping outside himself. He became aware of himself being angry. Then he realized that he and Jackson were pulling at each other. His mind went spinning through images of Jesus and the money changers, Peter cutting the servant's ear, Jesus hanging on the cross, God crying for his lost child. He remembered who he was and where he was and allowed Jackson to grip his elbow and walk him down the hill, leaving Cassidy standing in front of the silent group.

Then he remembered Four Corners, Mississippi, and Gilead, four miles down the dirt road, where the white people lived. He remembered driving down the tree-lined streets, trying to look inconspicuous in his grandfather's old 1947 Ford, carefully wiped clean of dust. He remembered his grandmother having made sure his shirt was white and ironed. Then he remembered his older cousin, Luella, walking back home on the dusty road from Gilead, hot and exhausted in her housemaid's uniform, to nurse her baby who'd been left with Luella's mother the whole fourteen hours of her absence, aching to ease her breasts and her heart. Then he remembered hours and hours of holding his urine and the white high school boys who stared at him with hard eyes when he came to the cotton storage shed without "proper business," only wanting to pass a message to his uncle who worked in the yard out back. In his memory now they all looked like Cassidy.

Cortell started running for the lines. Jackson watched him go. Then he shouted, "Cortell, you stupid mother." When Cortell reached his fighting hole he grabbed his M-16 and pulled back the action to chamber a round. He turned around, his eyes wild, and started running toward the top of the hill. Jackson tackled him from above, sending the M-16 flying.

"I'll kill the motherfuckers," Cortell screamed. "I'll kill the motherfuckers." He kicked and writhed under Jackson's hold, scratching at Jackson's eyes, trying to claw his way back to his weapon. Jackson held on tight.

Mellas was watching Bass make a cup of coffee with the last envelope of instant coffee in the platoon when they heard Cortell scream. They immediately started running. Mellas jumped on top of both Jackson and Cortell, tearing Jackson away. Cortell started to scramble to his feet, but

Bass fell on him, pinning him to the ground. Cortell's wide, normally pleasant face was contorted with pain and rage.

Jackson, much more under control, didn't struggle with Mellas. "I'm all right," he said. "It's Cortell." Mellas looked into his eyes, then rolled off. Jackson stood and began brushing himself off, looking down at Cortell, pinned under Bass's solid body.

"What the fuck's the matter with you?" Mellas asked Cortell.

"The Gunny," Cortell said. "I'll kill him." He was under control, however, and it was obvious he did not mean it.

Bass, seeing that Cortell had regained control of himself, got up, reached out a hand, and helped him off the ground. "What'd Cassidy do?" Bass asked.

Jackson spoke up. "Scar brought back two baby tigers and the Gunny's up playing with them."

"So?" Bass asked.

"So I told him to get them out of here," Cortell said. "A tiger killed Williams, or don'chew remember either?"

Bass's face registered the pain the statement caused, but he said nothing.

Mellas cut in. "You just can't go telling the Gunny to do what you want. I know how you feel. You've got to know he'd react to that. He probably doesn't know how it affects you."

"He told Cortell he ought to like jungle animals," Jackson said quietly.

Mellas's head sank and he turned away momentarily. Bass muttered under his breath, then turned, heading toward the CP.

Mellas stopped him. "It's my problem," he said. "Let's get our story straight, then I'll go up and talk to Scar about it. That'll be easier than talking to Cassidy."

Jackson and Cortell told their side of the story. When they'd finished, Mellas looked at Cortell. "You still figure you're going to kill old Cassidy?" he asked, smiling.

Cortell smiled back, his nose running a little. "No, I guess I let him go home. Somebody stupid back there must want him." He laughed shakily and Mellas joined in.

*   *   *

Mellas found Goodwin over by his platoon area. "It's just a couple of little baby tigers. Hey, look at them." He knelt down to let one lick his finger. "Wouldn't harm no one. Shit, Jack, I can't kill 'em."

Mellas looked at the two tiny kittens. "Jesus, no, don't kill them," he said, solemnly. "We'd have mama outside the lines in a second. You've got to take them back to where you found them."

"Fuck I do, Jack. That's a couple of fucking klicks."

"I'll take them back," Mellas said.

"It's OK by me, Jack. But you don't know where to go, do you?" Goodwin smiled, enjoying Mellas's temporary loss of composure.

"No. I don't."

"Well then, fuck." Goodwin picked up one of the kittens. "I'll take them back." He paused a moment, thinking. "Ain't no fucking gooks stupid enough to be out here anyway."

"Thanks, Scar," Mellas said, truly grateful. "I owe you one."

"Naw. I got nothing better to do. Shouldn't have brought them back in the first place. I didn't think nothing about that guy of yours getting eaten."

Vancouver volunteered to go with Goodwin, along with several of Goodwin's men, and they left the kittens just outside the entrance of the cave where they had found them. The group returned well after midnight, slowed by the darkness, silent and bent with exhaustion.

While Goodwin was out, Mellas, filled with self-righteous anger, confronted Cassidy at the actuals meeting. Cassidy, forced again into the role of villain, responded to Mellas's attack with anger of his own. "I just told the dumb fucker he ought to like the fucking animals because they're both from the fucking jungle in the first place. They are, ain't they? They're so fucking proud of all this black power bullshit and if they're supposed to be big bad African warriors, they ought to be proud about where they come from."

Mellas didn't answer.

"This Marine Corps' gone to shit since this fucking war," Cassidy continued. "Maybe I popped off. But a fucking private first class ain't got no right barging in on an officer and a staff sergeant telling them his worthless opinion. No fucking discipline. No fucking pride. And they keep fucking us career professionals by sending us out into the bush for the millionth time while the fat-asses and fucking shirkers can refuse to go out in the bush any time they want. Well, I'm getting the fuck out."

There was an embarrassed silence. Mellas suddenly felt sorry for this man for whom the world was changing too quickly. "I guess I was a little quick too, Sergeant Cassidy," Mellas said. "Maybe if you just told Cortell you were sorry."

"I ain't fucking sorry, Lieutenant."

"Cassidy, things could get bad. They're already pissed about Parker's haircut. This on top of it isn't going to sit too well."

"If they want to try any of that black power bullshit on me, Lieutenant, I'll black power their black asses to fucking hell. They don't scare me. I've handled punks before."

Mellas dropped it, glancing at Fitch to let him know. Fitch quickly moved on with the actuals meeting. The only news he had was that the batteries were getting so low that, in addition to all second radios being turned off, the actuals' radios were to be turned on only when the company was moving and at night. Battalion's last order was to make up the time lost; reach today's checkpoint, Alpha, by late morning tomorrow; hit checkpoint Bravo by midafternoon; and be back on schedule at checkpoint Charlie by tomorrow night. There would be no resupply. The LZ had been built for nothing.

CHAPTER
EIGHT

When they moved out in the darkness the next morning, Goodwin's platoon was on point. Mellas's platoon had the relative safety of the middle of the column. Resigned to humping out instead of flying, the kids put one foot in front of the other in the endless dance of the infantry. For those not on point, thoughts turned to memories of better times, meals they had eaten, girls they had known or wished they had known better. For those on point, there was no past; there was only the frightening now.

Hunger dominated people's minds, nagging at the point men and at Goodwin, who tried to ignore his pounding brain and concentrate on the task at hand. They walked with a constant feeling of irritation and frustration. A piece of gear catching on a branch became a monstrous injustice. Bumping into someone from behind because of fatigue-dulled senses brought out unreasonable anger rather than the usual sarcastic comment.

They reached checkpoint Alpha one hour after dusk, now a full day behind schedule. Checkpoint Alpha turned out to be the top of a hill covered with jungle, nothing more. They had eaten nothing all day, the last three-quarters can of food having been eaten the day before. It had been three days since anyone had eaten even a half ration.

All through dinner, Lieutenant Colonel Simpson looked distracted. Major Blakely assumed that he was worried about how he'd explain the delay to Colonel Mulvaney at the next day's briefing. He hardly seemed to notice when the enlisted waiter removed his plate and refilled his coffee cup. He only halfheartedly joined Major Blakely and Captain Bainford, the forward air control officer, in telling tales and laughing over cigars. Simpson reached for the bottle of Mateus that they'd nearly consumed during the meal and poured himself another glass, ignoring the coffee. He drank it quickly. He reached into his pocket for another cigar but found the thin cardboard box empty.

"Cigar, Colonel?" Blakely asked, reaching for one of his own.

Simpson lit it from the candle on the table, worked up a good start with some quick inward puffs, then relaxed. Blakely lit one of his own, leaned back, and looked out of the wire mesh that protected the interior of the officers' and staff NCOs' small mess tent from the insects hovering just outside. At sunset, VCB was not a pretty place to have a meal. Enlisted men stood in ragged bunches in the chow line outside the mess tent. The ground was muddy. The night air stank of kerosene and burning barrels of shit collected from the latrines. A lone Huey, returning to Quang Tri, rose from the rough airstrip, was lost momentarily against the gray-green of the hills, and then emerged silhouetted against the dying light.

"This is no fucking place to be, Blakely," Simpson growled. He took what seemed like an angry puff of his cigar.

"Sir?"

"We ought to be in the bush. We got three companies sitting on their asses in the flatlands and one fucking off up in the mountains. Can't control them. Can't kick ass when we need to."

"I agree, sir, but with the battalion split like it is, companies all over the map even when we do have an operation, how are you going to control them?"

"Matterhorn. I want to be back on Matterhorn. We'd have the whole northwest corner of the country tied up. Keep the companies down in the jungle disrupting the gooks, hitting their supply lines, destroying their caches." He spat a piece of tobacco to the floor. "Who knows, even forays into Laos. This bombing bullshit just don't get it.

You drop a bomb and a grunt gets up and walks right through the crater, and the NVA are a bunch of grunts, some of the best. That's why
we got to send our grunts out after them."

"I agree," Blakely said carefully, looking at the forward air controller with a sideways glance, "but with the goddamned political re-
strictions what can you do? But, I do agree, goddamn it. You go where
the action is." Blakely didn't ask the colonel what the difference was
between running four companies by radio from Matterhorn and running four companies by radio from VCB. He knew the real difference
was psychological, at least for the people back at division. With One
Twenty-Four's command post on the map at Matterhorn—all by itself,
in the most exposed position—people back at division would constantly
be reminded that the officers who ran One Twenty-Four were bush
Marines, not staff personnel hidden in thick bunkers. Blakely knew the
value of image. It wouldn't hurt at all if they got shelled every so often.
He had to have real combat on his record, the kind with Purple Hearts
and medals. It was the best route, maybe the only route, to the top.

"We've got to get better control," Simpson went on, almost to himself. "That fucking Fitch is a full day behind schedule. He sat on his ass
all day yesterday. The entire fucking day to medevac immersion foot
cases that are nothing but the result of bad leadership. Well, I didn't let
him. Teach him something."

Simpson poured himself another glass of wine and, rising from his
chair, gulped it down. He slammed the glass against the table. "That's
good stuff. Portuguese, isn't it? We ought to get another case of it." He
left the room and the others rose from their chairs as he went out.

Simpson continued to drink. After two hours of restlessly flipping
through the stack of papers on the makeshift plywood desk, he'd consumed nearly half a bottle of Jack Daniel's Black. He'd been up from
his chair six or seven times to look at the map tacked to another piece of
plywood that leaned against the damp canvas of the tent's side. He would
touch the coordinates of Hill 1609, Bravo's last reported position, and

try to assure himself they would be OK. Then, failing to find any comfort, and feeling his responsibility for a lot of lives, he would reluctantly return to the paperwork and refill his glass.

He knew he shouldn't drink so much, especially alone. But he was alone a lot. After all, he was the battalion commander. It was supposed to be lonely at the top. What did he expect, the easy camaraderie of the bachelor officers' quarters? But another voice reproved him. He ought to be on friendlier terms with the other battalion commanders in the regiment, or some of the regimental staff of his own age and rank. He'd tried. He'd asked Lieutenant Colonel Lowe, who'd been given Two Twenty-Four, over for dinner the other night. He'd broken out new cigars and some really good wine. But it had been awkward. Lowe had been playing football for Annapolis while Simpson was freezing his ass off in Korea, but here he was, three years younger than Simpson and at the same place. But that was just it—Annapolis. Simpson had worked his way through Georgia State and never had time to learn how to socialize. So he wasn't a socializer like Lowe or Blakely. Never was. Never would be. So what? So he was alone. So what? He wasn't here to have a good time. He was here to kill gooks.

He pushed the mass of paperwork slowly across the desk. In the clear space, he placed the glass of whiskey and the half-full bottle. The amber liquid reflected warmly back to him. Warm light. Deep and warm.

He kept going over Mulvaney's comments and questions during the briefing. Why did he have to get a goddamn cartoon character jackass like Mulvaney? He just couldn't be sure what Mulvaney was thinking —or what Mulvaney thought of him. Simpson had been certain that an old grunt like Mulvaney would be delighted when his headquarters were moved to Matterhorn. Mulvaney had even said it looked like there were gooks out there. Now, however, he felt he'd done something wrong, being out there and having to scramble to come back for Cam Lo. But Mulvaney had given the go-ahead. Simpson took a few more sips. Four days to open 1609. Had that been rash? God knows the men were left out there with a bunch of green reserve lieutenants. Soft on the troops. Moving too slow. There just weren't enough regular captains to go around. The whole goddamn thing stank. Marines were shock troops.

"Can openers," Liddell Hart had once called them. Or was it "lock open-ers"? He never remembered details like that, so he could never put pithy quotes into his reports the way he knew he ought to. But he knew his fucking tactics. Why should he have to remember pithy fucking quotes? The only can we opened over here was a fucking can of worms. Ma-laria. Jungle rot. Politicians. The nigras up in arms with this black power crap. He slowly and carefully measured out just a little more whiskey into his glass. Just a few more months to tough this one out. A battalion in combat. Hell, he was already thirty-nine. It was a godsend, a reprieve from the twenty-year final curtain. Now he'd have a chance to make full colonel—get a regiment. He smiled at the warm glass. No, not a division. You don't ask the gods for too much, or they'll put you down. But a regiment was possible, if he didn't screw this one up.

His stomach gave a lurch and he reacted by downing the rest of the whiskey. He refilled the glass.

Thirty-nine years old. Last chance. He knew he wasn't smart like Blakely, or colorful like Mulvaney. But he cared. He cared about im-mersion foot. He cared about security and cutting his casualty rate. But how do those things get you the notice of the commanding general? It stank. It all stank. Goddamn Bravo Company out there on a limb. He should never have let Blakely sweet-talk him and Mulvaney into it. Then the screwup about the rations. He hadn't caught it. Should have caught it. Supervise, supervise, supervise. That was the last "s" in BAMCISS: Begin planning, arrange for reconnaissance . . . or was it arrange for support? Make a reconnaissance. No, a plan. Damn. Memory never was that good. Shit. It's simple. You just go out there and kill the goddamned enemy. If that rations thing ever got out, there'd be hell to pay.

Blakely was transferring the supply officer who'd fucked up back to Da Nang. Not that the S-4 minded that. Hell, no. Officer clubs. Li-quor. Women. *Round-eyed* women. There was one blond who sold cars to the troops. Cars? Hell, Mercedes Benzes. A whole year's pay for one of them babies. Of course there'd be nothing on the supply officer's record. No sense making it hard on the guy. Blakely was using back channels to let people know they were letting the supply officer off easy and not putting it on his record. But if word ever got out, well, he could show he took immediate action by getting rid of the officer. Not that it was so bad. Hell, no one got killed or anything. Besides, they'd get Bravo Company out, make it up to them. He'd have steaks for everyone when they got back. In fact, with Bravo at VCB, the whole battalion would be here at the same time. He'd have steaks for the whole battalion and a formal mess night for the officers. Had 'em ever since the Royal Marines, goddamn it. Just like in the old days. That's the thing for morale. A mess night for the officers and steaks for the enlisted. Good fucking Marines, those kids. Not their fault. They'd like him in the end. They'd understand. No leadership. That wasn't anyone's fault either. You get these green-assed college kids, no experience. One day they're screwing government office girls in Washington and a week later they're dropped into the bush. What can you expect? Shit. They just needed some toughening up, that's all. Maturity. That's why he had to get back out in the bush again. Like those bunkers on Matterhorn. They'd have been slaughtered in an air raid or heavy shelling. You can't be too careful. Sure, it was hard on 'em—goddamn right it was hard. But that's what he was here for: to save lives. By God, all they needed was a good fucking jacking up. A little leadership.

He threw down the rest of the whiskey, grabbed his utility cap, and pushed through the blackout curtains into the night. Guided by the whitewashed stones that lined the path, he crossed over to the COC, the combat operations center. He pushed open the heavy door, surprising the watch officer, who was reading *Playboy,* and the three radio operators, two of whom were playing chess. The third was listening to the top-forty countdown from AFVN, the Army radio station in Quang Tri. Everyone scrambled to his feet.

"Get me Bravo Six," Simpson barked.

One of the radio operators began calling. Pretty soon Pallack's voice answered, and then Fitch came up. His voice was faint as a wraith.

"This is Big John Six. I want to know why you deliberately disobeyed an order and are sitting on your ass at checkpoint Alpha a full day behind schedule. I want a fucking good explanation or goddamn it you can explain yourself to somebody on Okinawa, because by God I'll have any commander's ass that can't do the job. Over."

The radio operators glanced sideways at one another. The watch officer began going over radio messages that had come in from division.

There was a long pause. "Did you copy me, Bravo Six?" Simpson insisted. "Over."

"Roger, sir. I copied." There was a break in the transmission. "We were fogged in all day. I kept waiting for that bird I'd requested. I have some bad cases of immersion foot, a body, and we're out of food. It was my judgment we could move faster if we had those problems taken care of. I'll take full responsibility for the delay. Over."

"You bet your ass you will. But that don't help me explain it to Bushwhacker Six. Over."

"I understand, sir. Perhaps if we knew what our mission was it would help the men move. Over." The distance and weak batteries made Fitch's voice waver and break.

"Your mission is to find, close with, and destroy the enemy. That's the mission of every fucking Marine." Simpson unconsciously pulled back his shoulders. He was aware of the staff watching him. "Now goddamn it you get to finding and destroying or I'll have you relieved for cause. You copy me, Bravo Six?"

"Roger. Copy."

"It's imperative—imperative—that you reach Checkpoint Echo by noon on Thursday. You'll await further orders there. Imperative. You understand? Over."

The radio was silent. Checkpoint Echo was where two rivers joined, the one coming from the mountains over which they were struggling and the other rushing down from another chain of mountains to their east. Fitch came up. "Sir, I'm looking on my map here and Checkpoint Echo is across the other side of some very steep stuff. Look, in this terrain I just don't think we can make it that soon. Over."

"Wait one."

Simpson darted over to the map, putting one finger on Bravo's position, neatly indicated by a pin with a large letter B on it. He then put his finger on the coordinates of Checkpoint Echo. His two fingers were approximately eight inches apart. Fitch was obviously shirking.

Simpson picked up the handset. "What are you trying to pull on me, Bravo Six? You be at Echo by noon or you'll spend your first month in Okinawa getting my foot out of your ass. You copy?"

"I copy."

"Big John Six, out."

In the damp and cold, thirty kilometers from VCB, Fitch lightly tossed the handset to the ground and stared into the dark. Relsnik fumbled for it and picked it up.

Hawke whistled. "Maybe when he sobers up he'll forget what he said."

Fitch grunted.

"Hey, forget it," Hawke continued. "What's he gonna do, Jim, cut your hair off and send you to Vietnam?"

Fitch smiled, grateful for Hawke's support, and wondered why he wouldn't be happy to be relieved. Just get out of everything. Still, he felt terrible. His fitness report would kill him. Any hope of getting a decent assignment once he left Vietnam would be crushed. To have started out so well, a company commander, and then be shit-canned back to the rear was something he couldn't bear. Fitch knew the Marine Corps well enough to realize that the word would get around. And in an organization as small as the Marines, he'd never be able to outrun it. No amount of explaining would help. It would only look like excuses. The real story, known by Hawke and the platoon commanders, would remain locked up in the jungle until they rotated home. By then it wouldn't matter. Fitch would be a joke.

Down on the lines Mellas and Hamilton sat on the back edge of their fighting hole. Hamilton had borrowed Mellas's red-lens flashlight to fill in another square on his short-timer's chart. It was a drawing of a delicate Vietnamese girl, her right leg cocked up above her head, exposing her vagina. Two hundred small numbered segments twisted around the girl in a spiral, ending with day zero on the sweet spot. "You know, Lieutenant," Hamilton said, "I truly think this girl here is beautiful. I mean I really do. She looks just like a girl I used to know back home."

"Get back, Hamilton. They all look the same from that angle," Mellas said, remembering a joke he'd heard. Then he felt that he'd somehow profaned the beautiful girl on Hamilton's short-timer's chart.

Hamilton leaned back on his elbows. "I wanted to marry her ever since the eighth grade."

"Why didn't you?"

"She married some guy who's an engineer at the plant. He had a draft-exempt job." Hamilton drifted off into his own world for a while, then returned. "I was with this friend of mine, Sonny Martinez. We'd come down from Camp Lejeune to their wedding. Sonny speaks pretty good English, but still a little fucked up. Anyway he gets Margaret's husband's attention at the reception and asks him, 'You been in Army before, hey?' 'No, I haven't' this guy answers. 'Why you not go to Army?' Hamilton's voice turned pompous and slow. 'Well, you see I have a very important job and, well, it's too important a job for me to go in the Army.' Well Sonny just shut up the rest of the day and I wanted to jump across the table and beat the bastard's eyeballs out."

Mellas laughed.

Hamilton raised his invisible toast glass. "Here's to Margaret and her fucking husband." He was silent for a moment. "Why is it that assholes like that always end up marrying the outstanding chicks?"

"I guess girls want security. Guys like you and me aren't too good a risk."

"Somehow I can't help thinking we're better guys, though."

"Unfortunately, women don't," Mellas said. He remembered the night Anne told him that she couldn't go along with this weird concept of morality he'd come up with about keeping his promise to the president. It had started as a wonderful meal in the New York apartment that Anne shared with two of her friends from Bryn Mawr, both of whom had made themselves descreetly absent. Anne had gone all-out, not only with the bacon-wrapped chicken livers and water chestnuts, but with real French-press coffee from a real French-press coffeepot that she'd brought home from her junior summer in Paris. Mellas had never seen one before. He thought that the best time to tell her about sending in his letter to the Marine Corps would be over coffee.

There was no best time. Mellas found himself standing with an empty coffeepot in one hand and two empty mugs in the other, looking at her beautiful backside. She was wearing the salmon-colored miniskirt that emphasized her small waist and hugged her bottom—the one that she knew drove him wild.

"You don't even *like* the president," she said. Exasperated, she whirled back to face the sink of dirty dishes. "You told me yourself that he's just a manufactured image. It's not like making a promise to a *person*."

"Yeah, but he's the *president*. American presidents don't lie to Americans." He felt foolish talking to her back. "He's like the representation of the—I don't know, of the Constitution, for Christ's sake. I swore to uphold the Constitution of the United States. I raised my hand and swore, so help me God."

She twisted around, her hands still on the edge of the sink. "You were a high school kid. You were *seventeen*."

"I was still me."

She turned back. "Oh, God," she said to the wall.

He looked dumbly at the pot and cups in his hand. Why was she mad at *him*? It was a sacred oath—and two of the guys he'd gone through training with at Quantico were already dead.

"Waino," she said, still looking at the wall, "Johnny Hartman got his doctor to say that knee he hurt in football would go out all the time. Jane's brother got *his* doctor to say that he was gay."

He said nothing.

She let out a long sigh. Her shoulders moved just that little bit back down where they normally sat. He realized that she'd been holding her breath. She went into her quiet voice, the one that he knew there was no arguing against. "You got into Yale Law School. You were *deferred*. In three years the war could be over, and if it isn't, you'll do your time as a lawyer. People would kill to get to where you are."

"People are *getting* killed. Better people that Johnny Hartman and Jane's brother."

She turned, this time slowly. She was trembling. The tears welling from her green eyes struck him dumb and made him feel guilty. "Yes!" she hissed. "Yes, yes, yes, yes! And you sent in the letter without even talking to me about it. You didn't even *think* to talk to me about it."

A month after that he was at the Basic School in Quantico, Virginia. He found it difficult to write to her, knowing that Marine training was totally foreign to her. She responded infrequently, saying that her new career kept her busy. Once, after he'd been in Quantico nearly three months, he called her to say that he could get up to New York on a three-day pass. She said that she had already planned something in Vermont. Two months after that he had his orders to Vietnam. He called her and said he had to see her before he shipped out. She said OK, but warned him not to plan on spending the night.

Beefed up from the training, hair cut to the skull, and in the uniform of a Marine second lieutenant, he made the long train ride from Virginia to New York. When he got to her apartment, her roommates told him that she was out on a date. He waited awkwardly, knowing that her roommates were trying to entertain him. Finally they went to bed. When she got home, she made tea. After an awkward half hour she told him he could sleep on the couch and she went to bed.

He'd been so frightened and desperately in need of comfort that he crawled into bed with her anyway. After two uncomfortable hours with her back to him, he gave up on sleep. He got up in the dark and struggled into his uniform in the over-heated apartment, the wool sticking to the sweat on his body. She watched him silently. He called a cab and packed his Val-Pak. When he was folding it together on the floor, he looked up to see her sitting on the side of the bed. She was wearing a long man's shirt. It didn't hide her panties. Apparently she didn't care.

"When's your plane?"

"Oh-five-thirty." He wished that he hadn't slipped into military time.

"You hungry?"

He stood up, pulled the Val-Pak upright, and lifted it. "No."

"Well . . ."

"Yeah." He couldn't take his eyes off her. He never could. "Bye."
"Bye."

He walked out the door, closing it quietly so he wouldn't disturb her roommates, and went down the stairs.

The cab was pulling up when he heard her running barefoot down the street, still in her long shirt. He stood there, paralyzed. She reached him, eyes brimming with tears, and gave him a hug and a quick kiss and then pulled back.

The cabby had picked up his Val-Pak and was back behind the wheel, giving them some time.

Anne sat down on the curb. "Go on," she said softly, looking across the empty street. "Go."

His last view of her was through the rear window of the cab. She was sitting on the dirty curb, bent over, her hands wedged between her face and her knees, shaking with sobs.

When they pulled out of sight of her, the cabby asked, not unkindly, "Going to Vietnam?"

"Yeah."

"Tough good-bye."

Hamilton was saying something that brought Mellas back to the present. "There must be some women, someplace, that think it's OK to be over here."

"You know any?" Mellas asked. He was uncomfortably aware of how bitter he was getting. It was as if some other person inside him sometimes used his vocal cords. He really hated women at some level, maybe because they stayed home and couldn't get drafted. Maybe it was the power they held over him because of his yearning to be with one, just to talk with one.

"No," Hamilton said.

"There it is," Mellas said softly to the dark wall of jungle. He turned to Hamilton. "Fuck it. I'm going to check lines." He left. Hamilton resumed staring at his short-timer's chart.

* * *

Around three-thirty that morning Fitch informed the actuals of the task ahead of them, the colonel's threat to relieve him, and the underlying threat of a court-martial. Mellas, enraged, offered to resign and go on trial with Fitch. "You get this thing out in the open and the Marine Corps would never stand for the bad publicity. They'd back down."

"Mellas," Hawke said, "this isn't some fucking sequel to *The Caine Mutiny*." Kendall and Goodwin laughed and Mellas had to smile in spite of his anger. "We got to be at Checkpoint Echo by tomorrow noon," Hawke continued. "That gives us about eight hours absolute maximum humping time to make Bravo, Charlie, and Delta." He turned to Fitch. "Ain't no way, Jim. I'd lose comm. Blame it on the batteries. Just skip a couple of checkpoints. We'll be fucking lucky if we get there by tomorrow night with straight beelining."

Fitch again began to bite his lower lip. "You don't think we can make them all, huh?" he asked.

"Jim, have you seen Hippy's feet?"

Fitch sucked in his cheeks, saying nothing.

"Maybe we could prep our route with the sixties," Kendall put in, "and lighten up on the mortar rounds."

"The last thing you'll shit-can is ammunition, goddamn it," Hawke said.

Kendall began to redden.

"That's all we've got left," Mellas said.

"That's right. And your life." Hawke took in a deep breath. "I want to impress on you boot motherfuckers just how far our asses are hanging out. All the grunts go to Cam Lo. So where does the artillery go, especially with no grunts to run security? Not only did they pull them out of Matterhorn, but yesterday we abandoned Eiger. That means all we've got is the eight inchers out of Sherpa. That's at their extreme range. Things get very wobbly at extreme range." He wiggled his hand for emphasis. "We all know the chances for air support in a monsoon: zilch point shit. So keep your fucking ammunition."

This was the first time Mellas understood that Hawke was afraid. It sent a tremor of fear through him. He imagined the company strung out in one of the rocky canyons, getting ripped apart by mortars, or struggling up a steep hillside, a .51-caliber machine gun across the valley raking them as they scrambled for cover where there was none. Mellas erupted. "Big John Six and his fucking Checkpoint Echo, that cocksucking son of a bitch. He'll actually fucking kill some of us just to make his goddamned checkpoint."

"There it is, Jack," Goodwin said. "You don't make general if you don't make checkpoints."

The rest of the day Mellas raged inwardly against the colonel. This gave him energy to keep moving, keep checking on the platoon, keep the kids moving. But just below the grim tranquillity he had learned to display, he cursed with boiling intensity the ambitious men who used him and his troops to further their careers. He cursed the air wing for not trying to get any choppers in through the clouds. He cursed the diplomats arguing about round and square tables. He cursed the South Vietnamese making money off the black market. He cursed the people back home gorging themselves in front of their televisions. Then he cursed God. Then there was no one else to blame and he cursed himself for thinking God would give a shit.

The day ended in despair. The country had become a series of jagged limestone cliffs that weren't shown on the map. It was impossible to get a bearing on anything in the dark forest. They couldn't even find the sun through the clouds. Hunger made their stomachs hurt and drained their limbs of strength, but they knew the only way to reach food and safety was to keep moving.

The next day was the same. As their resistance lowered, the jungle rot got more severe. Pus erupted from skin. Ringworm spread more rapidly, and several kids began to walk without trousers to avoid the painful irritation and chafing. That caused more cuts from the bushes and more exposure to leeches.

Pat collapsed, his legs quivering with exhaustion. Arran draped the dog on the back of his neck, holding Pat's legs over his shoulders, asking every hour or two for an emergency medevac. "You don't understand. Dogs don't have the same stamina as people. They just don't." It was the third full day without food.

Pallack wondered if dogs were smarter than people.

By the next day, some kids started eating the pulpy insides of various plants, not really certain what they were consuming. Others peeled bark from trees and chewed the inside. By early afternoon many were puking as they walked, fouling their own clothes or leaving sour-smelling patches of bile for those behind to avoid. Nothing helped.

Hippy kept thinking of the girl who had first told him about meditating one night when he was on liberty from Camp Pendleton. He tried to concentrate on the *now* of the pain. She had told him that if he was uncomfortable on his knees in meditation, it was only because he was thinking about the time stretching before him. "Are you able to stand it now?" she had asked him. "Yes," he replied. "And now?" "Yes" he had replied again. *And now,* the pain of putting his foot down hit him, but he could stand it. *And now,* on the other foot, but again he could survive. *And now. And now.* The hunger was nothing.

Mallory suddenly threw his heavy M-60 machine gun into the brush and flung himself down, holding his temples. He screamed for someone to help him. "My fucking head hurts," he sobbed. "Jesus Christ, my fucking head. Won't someone believe me?"

Mellas found him writhing on the ground. "It fucking hurts me, Lieutenant," Mallory sobbed.

A cry of "Corpsman up!" passed along the column. Doc Fredrickson came running, panting with the effort. Steam rose from his sodden clothing. "Oh, it's Mallory," he said, barely concealing his disgust.

"Well?" Mellas said.

"I don't know, Lieutenant. You got the same word I did. He's got a head problem. There's nothing physically wrong with him."

"You can't help him?"

"Do I look like Sigmund fucking Freud?"

Mellas took the handset from Hamilton's flak jacket and radioed for Sheller, the senior squid. "It's my character Mike with the bad head,"

Mellas said. The column kept moving. Everyone looked numbly at Mallory while stepping over him. The two Marines carrying Williams's body stopped when they saw him, the body swaying slightly between them. One of them spat, and they struggled off.

The radio hissed and Fitch came up. "Look, Bravo One, I can't stop this column for anything today. I'll send the senior squid back, but you be prepared to provide security. You'll have to catch up with us best you can, even if you have to drag the son of a bitch."

Bass arrived before Sheller. He toed Mallory. Mallory responded with a moan.

Mellas squatted down beside him. "Mallory, you've got to understand. We've got to keep moving. If you don't move, the whole company is in danger. I know it hurts, but just try and move. You've got to try."

"You don't understand, it fucking hurts me." Mallory sounded like a bewildered two-year-old.

Bass threw his rifle to the ground and grabbed Mallory by the front of his shirt, pulling him up to eye level. Mallory hung limp in his hands. Bass was screaming at him. "Goddamn it, Mallory, you fucking crybaby. We get left with shit like you and people like Williams die. You fucking coward. Walk!"

Mallory moaned, "I can't."

Bass, his face contorted, smashed his fist into Mallory's face. Mallory moaned and dropped to the ground.

"That's e-fucking-nough," Mellas said, furiously. "Goddamn it, Bass."

"There's nothing wrong with him. He's just fucking chickenshit."

"I'll decide that."

The two of them stared at each other. Bass reached down, picked up his rifle, and humped off down the trail. Skosh looked at Mallory, puzzled, then scurried after Bass.

"I'll talk to Bass, Lieutenant," Fredrickson said.

"I can't really blame him," Mellas said. "Look, tell Bass to take the platoon. I'll drop off with the last fire team while the senior squid checks him out."

Fredrickson hurried after Skosh and Bass just as Sheller arrived with Cassidy. Mellas briefed Cassidy while Sheller bent over Mallory, talking with him. The column disappeared ahead, leaving the small group alone. The Marines chosen for security nervously covered the trail around them. Sheller stood up, shrugging his shoulders. "I can give him a bunch more of Darvon, but he's been eating that shit like popcorn."

"Well, what in fuck do we do with him?" Mellas asked. "We're in no condition to carry him."

"Leave him," Cassidy said, putting his hand on Mellas's shoulder. Sheller looked at Cassidy in surprise.

"I can't leave him here," Mellas said. Cassidy winked and squeezed Mellas's shoulder. "You've got to, Lieutenant. We've got an entire company being jeopardized by this one individual. I ain't seeing any good Marines die because one chickenshit fucking coward refuses to hump."

"Well," Mellas said slowly.

"Grab his gun," Cassidy said to one of the Marines standing watch. "Get his ammunition too." They stripped Mallory of his machine-gun gear, leaving him his .45 pistol and pack.

"You can't leave me," Mallory moaned.

"Try me," Cassidy said. "I can leave a piece of shit like you any day of the week." He nodded his head up the trail. "Let's go before we get into trouble," he said.

The small group set off, a couple of the Marines looking back nervously. Cassidy grimly walked forward. After about fifty meters he stopped and nodded them into the brush. Everyone lay down. They waited about five minutes. Mallory came running wildly around the bend in the trail. Cassidy stuck the machine gun out, tripping him, and Mallory fell forward with a cry of fear.

Cassidy stood over him and Mallory looked up, only to have the heavy machine gun thrown at him full in the face. It chipped his tooth. Mellas winced.

"Get up, you coward," Cassidy said quietly.

Mallory, his lips and gums bleeding, whimpered like a dog. He picked up the machine gun and, in a strange shuffling half trot, headed up the trail toward the rest of the company.

"What're you waiting for," Cassidy growled at the other Marines, "a fucking skoshi cab?" Everyone hurried back up the trail to catch the company, fearful of being separated.

Nightfall found them halfway up the side of a deep valley with no room to form a perimeter. They dug in, looping the company in an oval over a protruding finger. If they were hit like this, they would probably be overrun.

They dug holes just sufficient to lie in horizontally. The fields of fire were cleared only a few feet beyond their holes. Mellas dragged himself from hole to hole, cajoling, joking, pointing out the danger, trying to encourage everyone to hack just a little more brush, dig just a little bit deeper.

When Mellas returned later to check on progress, he found most of the brothers gathered around Jackson's record player. Mole was there, as well as Broyer and Cortell. Mallory's machine gun had been positioned to cover an approach route up a small gulley, but Mallory was gone. So was Parker.

"Hey, Lieutenant, come on and have some supper," Cortell called out, "we're servin' a little Memphis soul stew."

Mellas laughed and walked up to the group, happy to be invited to listen. His heart swelled with pride at their good humor in the face of all the misery. They were listening to King Curtis doing "Memphis Soul Stew," the record moving unevenly as the tone arm jerked up and down with the warps.

Mellas was too tired to push the platoon to dig deeper. He joined with them and the music.

"Man, I'll never turn my nose up at a can of ham and moms again," Mole said, his body swaying slightly to the music. Mellas felt uncomfortable, not knowing what to say.

"Yeah," Cortell said softly, "and sprinkle it with a dash of"—he paused for effect, bringing his shoulders up—"canned ham and eggs. Oooh, man."

Mellas laughed. "And a full course of Tabasco sauce to kill the taste," he said.

There were murmers of "O-*kay*, Lieutenant" and "You got it," soft voices overcoming misery.

"I know Jesus said man does not live by bread alone, Lieutenant," Cortell went on, "but I never expected to have to prove it, man."

"Hey, how many records you got, Jackson?" Mellas asked.

"All depends on the table of organization, sir," Jackson said. "We got Second Fire Team with Cortell carrying the hard core, some Otis, a little James Brown." Jackson stopped and gave a pretty good imitation of James Brown doing an "eehhh" at the end of one of his lines.

"Whoa, bro." Mole laughed and touched his fist to Jackson's.

"And he got Wilson Pickett too," Jackson continued, "with yours truly packing the Marvin Gaye. Parker and Broyer now, they got the rest of the Motown. And Mallory, he's packing, uh . . ." Jackson noticed Mellas looking at Mallory's unattended machine gun. "Uh, he carries the instrumentals like King Curtis and Junior Walker."

"Memphis Soul Stew" died out, and the needle began rubbing back and forth against the paper record label, making a scratching sound. Broyer quickly lifted the tone arm, stopping the turntable.

"How's Mallory?" Mellas asked.

"How do you think, Lieutenant?" Jackson said. "He got his fucking mouth smashed in with a machine gun and his head hurts."

"And he ain't eaten for a week," Mole put in.

"I don't think Cassidy hit him in the face on purpose," Mellas said.

"Sheeit," Mole spat out.

"Well, I don't think he did it on purpose."

"Thing is, Lieutenant, it happened," Jackson said.

"Do you think there's going to be trouble?"

"Trouble?" Jackson looked around him, indicating their situation by opening his hands to the jungle and clouds. "What's trouble? It's just a different form of shit, Lieutenant." Faces that had been cheerful a moment before turned sullen. Mellas knew his presence had become inconvenient.

*   *   *

"I say waste the motherfucker," Parker said. It was almost dark and he was leaning back against the dirt of a shallow hole. China was sitting on Parker's left, looking into the forest, chewing on a stick, trying to ease his body's cry for carbohydrates. A light drizzle collected on his poncho and ran off in tiny streams. Mallory was on Parker's right, elbows on his knees, holding his head and staring blankly at the ground.

"We ain't wastin' nobody, Parker," said China.

"How you let a fucking pig like that live, huh?"

"I don't *let* him live. I got nothin' to do with him livin'. Or dyin'," he added pointedly.

"Henry'd kill the mother."

China noted the threat but said nothing. Henry might very well kill Cassidy, but that was where Henry was stupid. The knowledge that Henry would kill somebody if he was crossed, however, was also what kept him in command. China knew that if he got a reputation for being soft, he'd never take over when Henry rotated back home. Still, he couldn't just kill somebody. It was also too easy to figure out who had the motive in the company. It had to be done so it meant something. Either that or make it look like an accident. Ultimately, though, he didn't want to risk his weapons-smuggling operation.

"How you doing, bro?" China asked Mallory, changing the subject. He leaned over and looked across Parker's chest.

"It fucking hurts, China. You got to help me get out of the bush."

"We got to get *all* the brothers out the bush," China said, his voice rising. He despised Mallory and wanted to jerk him up by the collar and tell him to act like a man, but he also knew a good cause when he saw one. You just keep on moaning, Mallory, my man, he thought.

"You ain't going to do nothing about Cassidy beating on Mallory?" Parker asked. He was looking at a mosquito that was sucking blood from his arm.

"Course I'm gonna do something. But when the time be right." China slapped at a mosquito on his face.

Parker put his thumb on the bloated mosquito on his arm and burst it, spreading blood on his skin. "Blood, China."

"When the time be right."

"Tonight."

"No."

"Come *on*, man," Parker said angrily to Mallory. He stood up and slapped at a few more mosquitoes that were hovering around his face. "We better get back before Bass or College Boy finds us gone."

In the silence China could hear Jackson's record player. Jackson. If he could team up with Jackson, letting him organize the brothers in the bush, then he'd go back to the rear and start finding more Jacksons for the other companies. Man, an organization like that and they'd get fucking *tanks* to the brothers back home.

When full dark ended the 100 percent alert, Jackson was working on organizing his pack. He watched China walk up to Parker and Broyer and go through the handshake. Then he saw China coming for him.

China squatted down next to him. Jackson pulled a strap into place. "All we do, man, is pack and fuckin' unpack," China said. "I do that much packin' back home I be a *real* travelin' man."

Jackson smiled but didn't say anything.

"Where is back home for you, man?"

"Cleveland."

"O–*hi*–oh."

"Yep. Oh–hi–oh."

"You ever get high?"

"Once. In San Diego. This sister had marijuana."

"That shit be bad for the black man."

"I'm told it bad for ever'one." Jackson sighed, looking back six months into the past, seeing nothing but the small dark apartment, the funky red lava lamp, a black light making the fuzz picture of a girl in a paisley sari glow chartreuse—and Kyella. My God. Sweet Kyella Weed. He came back to the war. "Kinda fun, though."

"Yeah. That be its problem. The fucking British enslave millions of the yellow man with opium."

"I didn't get the shit from no Brit. I got it from a brother."

"Yeah, yeah. But that brother ain't doin' us no *good,* man. He doin' us *no* good. The Muslims, they don't like drugs. And they right. Drugs, they enslave millions of yellow people and the red man, too."

"China, I don't want be talkin' politics. I'm tired and I gotta fight a war on a empty stomach."

"That's right. A war against brown people. James Rado say the draft is *white* people sending *black* people to fight *yellow* people to protect the country they stole from *red* people. No black man should be forced to fight to defend a racist government. That be Article Six of the Black Panther Ten-Point Program."

"What good you terrorist friends in Oakland doin' 'cept makin' money writin' books? *Soul on Ice.* Sheeit. I don't see no brave-ass Panthers over here."

"That's the point. They ain't over here fightin' the white man's war."

Jackson's anger at being placed in positions he didn't like and from which he couldn't escape spilled out of him. "They ain't fightin' the *black man's* war. That's what they ain't fightin'. They just stirrin' up trouble. Just like you. I don't need you fuckin' shit, China. I don't need it." Jackson paused. "You know who the *real* people fightin' the black man's war are? I'm gonna tell you who. It that little girl go to school in Little Rock, wear a nice dress, scared shitless. She don't pack no heat, but that picture a her walkin' to school between federal marshals turned *hearts.* It those college boys gettin' murdered for registerin' voters. Yeah, white college boys. It people like Mose Wright." He paused. "I bet chew don't have a fuckin' idea 'bout Mose Wright do you, Mr. Black History?"

China threw his hands open in disgust. "OK. You be the preacher man. You tell me. Who Mose Wright?"

"You ever hear of Emmett Till?"

"Wha'chew think?"

"Yeah. I be seven and I see that puffy face with the eye hanging out in *Ebony* magazine and I never, *never,* forget that face. But *I* don't live in Mississippi. *You* don't live in Mississippi. Mose Wright, he Emmett Till's uncle, and *he live* in Mississippi where they hang you from a tree with you nuts cut off and throw you in the river with iron fan blades wrap 'roun' you black dead-ass neck. You speak up against that shit in Mississippi, you as good as dead. But Mose Wright, no education, no money, no nothin' except heart, he goes to the trial a those motherfuckers killed Emmett Till, rigged like it was, and he says 'D'ere!' And he point his fingers at the killers. Right there in that all-white courthouse. 'D'ere!' Right there, knowin' they'd be after him next, all alone, no help from the law."

"Yeah, shit man." China was momentarily stopped. Then he launched back. "Only those two chucks, they got off. They runnin' 'round loose today. They even make money *tellin'* 'bout it. They tell some white magazine that they done the killin' and that printed all over the country and they *still* get off."

"Sure. But this time everone *knows* and sees through. This time the light got shined on that fucked-up county courthouse. It got shined all over the fuckin' country. And why? Why this time? 'Cause that little black man and that pointin' finger a his."

"So what *chew* doing, black boy? They get off. You just gonna let shit like that go down? Do nothin'?"

"What I supposed do?"

"You can start by protestin' the way this fuckin' racist Marine Corps be run 'round here. We got brothers without R & R. We got fuckin' racist country-western crackers castratin' our brother Parker right in front of everybody, and that same fuckin' honky smash another our brothers in the mouth with a fuckin' machine gun, and you, *you* be movin' into *management.* You be part of the fuckin' problem, man."

"Look to me like chuck dudes humpin' and gettin' killed just like splib dudes," Jackson said, struggling to stay cool. "Chucks not gettin' any food, just like the brothers. We be about one out of twelve just like back home."

"How many officers in this regiment be brothers?"

"One."

"And you don't think it racist?" China asked.

"How the brothers gonna be officers if they don't be squad leaders?"

"How the brothers gonna be free if they don't stand together?"
Jackson locked eyes with China, and China stared right back.

Mellas and Hamilton were too tired to build a hooch, so they spent the
night lying next to each other in a shallow hole. It rained. They didn't
care. Gradually, the rain began to fill the shallow hole with water. Mellas
dreamed he was in a bathtub and the hot water had run out. He didn't
want to get out because it was even colder out of the tub. A long way
off, he could hear Hamilton's frightened voice. "Goddamn it, Lieutenant, you got to get up and move. Please, sir, get up and move."

Hamilton pulled Mellas to his feet. Mellas, in the stupor of hypothermia, slowly started to move. The world around him—the dark forest, his rifle, the rain, Hamilton—seemed incoherent, whirling. Hamilton
jumped around with him, grabbing him, turning him, the two of them
doing a macabre dance.

Mellas's body responded. It began to produce heat. His mind
started to clear. He stumbled off to check the lines, realizing that
Hamilton had probably saved his life.

Cassidy lay in the dark, listening to Lieutenant Hawke's deep even
breathing. He thought about how Lieutenant Mellas's warning had probably saved several kids from hypothermia. He smiled. He might have
made Marine Corps history as the only company gunny to have lost
men by freezing to death in a jungle.

He looked at his watch. 0438. Back home he would have already
been fixing a silent breakfast, trying not to disturb Martha and the baby
before slipping out the door. He'd start the engine and wait a moment
for it to warm up, watching the darkened house. Perhaps he'd check his
crisply starched uniform, or the boots or shoes he'd shined the night
before, and then he'd take one last look at the house before pulling away.
The few feelings that Cassidy did allow himself were either those he
could express openly for the Marine Corps or those that were intimate,
like his feeling for his family, which arose only in quiet moments when

he was alone, waiting for cars to warm up or waking in the dark and lying very still. Cassidy knew he was lucky to be married to Martha because she would never ask him to choose between the family and the Marine Corps. If he were forced to choose, he'd choose family. But he would hesitate.

This feeling for the Corps was why Cassidy was hurt so deeply when he found that the pin on one of his grenades had been bent straight. Gravity would eventually pull the grenade from the pin, and the grenade would explode. Cassidy moved out with the company that morning pretending nothing had happened, but he felt apprehensive and alone.

CHAPTER
NINE

It was the fifth day without food, and the company moved in a stupor, descending from the mountains into a valley. The air pressed down on them like a towel in a steam room. Hands burned from using ropes on the cliffs. Williams's body was putrefying faster as they descended to warmer air, and some fluid was already dripping out of the poncho. The skin on the hands had started to slough off. The feet had swelled within Williams's boots. He stank. Flies tormented the kids who carried him.

Hippy's feet grew worse. He took his bootlaces off to accommodate the swelling. He looked like a sleepwalker. He would murmur to himself, "Can you take this step now?" and then take the step. He repeated this procedure hour after hour, a spirit carried by crippled feet.

Mellas felt as if he were suffocating. He was nauseated but had nothing to throw up. His clothes clung like saran wrap. With everyone's electrolyte balance messed up, he worried about heat exhaustion.

They reached the valley, where a torrent of white water cut through the jungle floor to naked bedrock. Mellas decided to move in the water. Speed was now everything. Colonel Simpson had been calling Fitch every half hour for the past two days, telling him it was "imperative" that the company reach Checkpoint Echo by 1200 hours. The words kept repeating themselves in Mellas's head, like a song that won't go away. *It is imperative you reach Checkpoint Echo by 1200 hours.* Security lapsed. Maybe Marines were in trouble and they couldn't say over the radio. They swung east, sometimes chest deep in the swift water. Their penises shrank to nubs and their scrotal sacs pulled their testicles deep up inside them. Their arms grew weary, holding their weapons up out of the water.

Fitch told Relsnik to stop answering. It took far more juice to broadcast than to receive. In truth, there were only a couple of batteries in the whole company that had any chance of reaching another unit if the company got into the shit.

Mellas gave up on security. He pulled in the flankers who were moving in the jungle on both sides of the river and led the company straight downstream, Vancouver on point and Mellas behind him.

Occasionally someone fell. The current would then suck him under, his heavy pack and weapons dragging him down, until someone could reach him and help him regain his feet. Once it was Pollini. Mellas happened to be looking back at the column and saw Pollini miss Cortell's outstretched hand and fall backward into the river. He just watched, numb like everyone else. Then he threw his pack on the bank and started wading out to the middle of the river, grabbing Hamilton's hand and shouting orders to form a human chain. But they didn't move fast enough. Pollini went past them like an express train on the inside track. Mellas saw him surface, right in the middle where it was deep and fast, bouncing downstream. His helmet smashed against rocks, probably saving his skull from being cracked. Mellas watched him go down for what he thought had to be the last time, but Pollini hit a big rock and it spun him over toward the shallows.

Pollini just lay there. He was too far away for Mellas to tell if he was still breathing. The kids who'd tried to reach him with the human chain turned back exhausted. No one wanted to go the distance to get him. Mellas idly contemplated shooting him so they'd know for certain he had died. Then Pollini moved. He got to his hands and knees and stayed in that position for a long time, breathing visibly, the water flowing beneath his chest. Then he struggled to his feet, grinned, and waved.

Hamilton raised an imaginary glass and said, "Here's to you, Shortround."

Pollini hitched his pack up on his back and came grinning and splashing back to the column. Mellas whispered, "Shortround, you're a good fucking man."

*   *   *

The river swung in the wrong direction. Mellas and Vancouver struggled up the steep south bank and faced solid elephant grass and bamboo. Mellas seriously thought of just following the river wherever it went. That would be so much easier. But he and Vancouver waded into the tangle of stalks, both of them slashing with machetes. The platoon wearily climbed out of the water and followed them into the dank oven. The steaming towel of the air smothered them in its folds.

By late afternoon the day was dying beneath rapidly building clouds. Mellas leaned back on his pack, trying to keep the frag order out of his pounding brain, and watched huge clouds darken the treetops above him. If it rained, they'd be slowed even more. If it rained, the noise would cover them and they'd be cool. If they got hit in their condition, they'd never make it out alive. *It is imperative you reach Checkpoint Echo by 1200 hours.* A gust of cold wind suddenly swept through the sweltering jungle air. Then the first spattering of rain fell. Then it fell in a steady continuous roar.

The rain continued into the night. They stumbled on in the dark, the glowing green tip of the compass needle in Mellas's hand moving before him. Then Vancouver hit a trail that headed south. Checkpoint Echo was south of them. "Take it," Mellas said. "Fuck the ambushes." He figured that if he died he wouldn't have to worry about the fucking decision anyway.

Word came up the line that Hippy had stopped moving. When Mellas reached him, Hippy could say nothing. He stood upright, swaying between two friends, his machine gun still cradled on his shoulder. He was staring emptily ahead. Mellas finally spoke. "Can you keep going, Hippy? Just a few more hours."

Hippy looked at him from a long way away. Then he nodded. Mellas nodded back, watching Hippy's face. It was just the face of an eighteen-year-old kid with a peace medallion around his neck. Hippy wore a pair of wire-rimmed glasses, had straggly hair, and had the beginnings of a beard. An ordinary human face. Mellas had never really looked at one before.

*   *   *

They made it to Checkpoint Echo about an hour before dawn, formed a circle, and collapsed on the ground.

Lieutenant Stevens, the artillery liaison officer, being junior, had the early morning watch again when Fitch radioed in that Bravo Company was at Checkpoint Echo, back in communication, but with weak power sources, and waiting for further orders. He was requesting food and an emergency medical evacuation for about ten Marines, a body, and a German shepherd.

Twenty minutes later, Stevens briefed Lieutenant Colonel Simpson when Simpson made his customary visit before breakfast. Simpson asked when they'd arrived. Stevens, knowing that Fitch was already in trouble for being slow, tried to help out by saying that they'd reached Echo around 2200 hours the night before.

"Good. They had a good night's rest. Tell Lieutenant Fitch to build a zone and we'll get him in some fresh power sources. Also, send him this message." He paused while Stevens dug out a small green note pad. "Upon resupply proceed immediately Hill 1609. Prepare LZ for future use as Fire Support Base Sky Cap. Imperative you be there 1200 hours tomorrow. Code that," Simpson continued, "and I want those power sources delivered ASAP. That outfit's been candy-assing enough out there. I don't want any more excuses for them sitting on their butts."

Simpson started to walk out into the darkness.

"Uh, sir, what about the emergency medevacs and rations?" Stevens asked.

Simpson stopped. "Lieutenant, what would you do if you had command? You've got a company out in the bush under the guidance of completely inexperienced officers. They eat their rations too quickly and then run out because they are slowed down by immersion foot caused by their own neglect. As a consequence, they are at the moment way behind schedule in opening a very important fire support base. They are also, I presume, a little hungry and their feet hurt." He smiled at his joke. "If they succeed in building the LZ on Hill 1609 on schedule, they'll have all the helicopters they like by noon tomorrow. The first thing a

young officer has to learn is to take responsibility for his actions and to
have some pride. Pride, Lieutenant Stevens. It's what the Marine Corps
is built on."

Because of the Cam Lo operation, no Marine chopper could be
diverted to carry a few batteries to a company in the bush. Stevens con-
tacted every outfit he could think of. He finally found an Army Huey
that was free for the morning, having carried a general from Da Nang
up to Dong Ha. He talked the pilot into making a quick run.

At Checkpoint Echo, with K-bars, machetes, and Jackson's method of
throwing their bodies against the brush, they slowly opened a small patch
of crumpled, twisted vegetation in the broad valley floor. Above them
on all sides, the mountains towered dark and green, their tops hidden
by clouds.

Stevens's message to expect a Huey had come in the clear. The
order to create Fire Support Base Sky Cap had come coded. All the
actuals gathered around Relsnik as he worked out the code. When he
read the order there was stunned silence. Mellas pulled his map from
his side pocket and found Hill 1609. It was at the source of the river
that flowed from the mountains to their east down to Checkpoint Echo,
where it joined the river that they had followed the night before. He
looked at the peaks. Their tops were hidden by clouds. Goodwin came
over to him. "Where the fuck is it, Jack?" he asked. Mellas pointed. "Shit,
Jack," Goodwin said. One by one, each of the actuals looked at where
Mellas's finger was pointing. Upon seeing the location, Hawke went into
the hawk dance, screeching "Sky Cap! Sky Cap! Snark! Snark! Sky Cap!"
He cupped his hands and shouted "Sky Cap! Kahoo! Kahoo!" The cry
echoed back. He stopped and held up both hands toward the mountains
in the hawk power sign and gave two more cries of "Snark! Snark!" Then
he rested both hands on the top of his head and just stood there, his back
to the group, looking east toward the mountains.

Fitch took command. "Get your medevacs ready," he said. "We'll
be kicking off as soon as we get resupplied. We'll have twenty minutes
for chow. Don't let them go hog wild or they'll get sick. One C-rat, you

got me? One." Fitch again turned to squint at the barrier of green to their east. "Kendall, it's your turn to have point. You can't get lost going up a river." Kendall flushed, but then smiled when Fitch and the others grinned good-naturedly at him.

Jackson told Mellas that he didn't want to be squad leader any longer. "I just don't like telling my friends what to do all the time."

"You mean you can't take the heat. What do you want me to do, put Cortell in charge? Or maybe you'd like Parker making the decisions?"

Jackson looked at the ground, unwilling to meet the lieutenant's eyes.

"Do you think I give a flying fuck about how you feel right now?" Mellas went on. "I've got to have a good squad leader. I've *got* to have one."

Jackson fiddled with a grenade hanging from his belt suspenders. "Janc's probably been back from R & R over a week," he said. "He's just sitting on his ass at VCB. I only was supposed to have it temporarily."

Mellas's voice changed. "Goddamn it, Jackson, we need you."

Jackson looked up at Mellas. The idea made him stop. No one had ever needed him like this in his life. He tried to see it the lieutenant's way. Cortell was probably the only other guy in the squad who could lead it. He was so smart it was scary, but Cortell's kind of smart was deep smart. Out here, it was fast smart that counted: his kind. He'd felt OK being a fire team leader, but then Janc still carried the real load and took the consequences if he screwed up. That was just it. Janc never screwed up. Maybe he, Jackson, would, and if he did, he would never get another chance to lead again. But if he didn't lead now, he wouldn't get another chance either. He'd written home about being a squad leader. Imagine, him, in charge of twelve guys. His old man had never been in charge of anybody. Jackson looked at the lieutenant's young earnest face. Fuck China. "I can take the heat, Lieutenant," he almost whispered.

The two of them stood there, looking at each other, silent for perhaps three seconds. Then Mellas spoke. "You're the squad leader and I'm the platoon commander. Whether we like it or not, there it is."

"Yeah, there it is," Jackson said. He started toward his squad's sector and then turned to look back at Mellas. "But when Janc gets back, I quit."

"OK, Jackson. It's a deal."

Half an hour later they heard the sound of a helicopter. They strained to catch a glimpse. Someone shouted and pointed. The sound grew to a roar and a dark bulb flitted briefly across the clouds and was then lost. The roar returned. Fitch popped a smoke grenade and thick red smoke began to coil upward from the foliage. An Army Huey slick flashed overhead, then banked in a graceful climbing turn to the left.

"Big John Bravo, this is Bitterroot Seven. I've got a red smoke next to a blue line. Over."

FAC-man's voice came over the radio, assuring the pilot that they were by a river and it wasn't a trap. "Wind down here is negligible. Your best approach is from the south. Zone's secure. Over."

The helicopter, numbers gleaming, turned to the south, turned again, and made its approach. It set gently down, the air vibrating with the blades. The whine of the turbine ceased and the blades whiffled to a halt. The pilot, dressed in a crisp flight suit, stepped out of the bird. Cassidy had a work party ready to receive the supplies. Fitch and Hawke met the pilot at the edge of the rotor blades. Mellas, unable to hold himself back, walked out for a closer look.

A crew member handed out two boxes of batteries to two of the work party. A third Marine stepped up, waiting for his load of C-rations. Mellas saw the crew member shrug his shoulders. The Marine turned to look at Cassidy, stunned. Mellas rushed over to the small group who were just shaking hands with the pilot. "Hey, you got any food?" he burst in.

The pilot, a warrant officer about Mellas's age, looked at him. "No," he said puzzled. "Why? You guys out?"

"Well, no," Mellas lied. "Just wondered if maybe they threw on something."

The pilot looked around him. He seemed excited about being so far out in the bush and helping out another service. "Jesus, you guys smell," he said with a smile. "You been here long?"

"No," Fitch said. "We just got in this morning." He looked at Mellas and Hawke, obviously wondering what could have gone wrong with the resupply.

"This morning?" The pilot looked at Mellas. "Whatever possessed you people to hump down here at night?"

Mellas's chin was trembling. "We thought we'd avoid the heat," he managed to choke out. He turned and walked away.

"What's with him?" the pilot asked Fitch and Hawke.

"He's a little tired," Hawke said. "Had point all night. Don't take it personally."

"Sure. I can understand that."

"Say," Hawke added, "if you could do us another favor, we'd really appreciate a huss."

"Name it. I got to wait around while the general talks to your guys in Dong Ha. Glad to do something."

"Well, we got some guys that are due to go on R & R, things like that. Then there's another guy who's really overdue to go home. The company shouldn't be carrying him. It'd sure help morale if we could get them out."

"Sure. How many you got?"

"How many can you take?" Hawke asked evenly. "They're all fairly light."

The worst cases of immersion foot hobbled up to the edge of the landing zone. They exchanged their better clothing with those staying behind. By the time they were helped aboard by the crew chief, they looked very bad indeed. Cortell and Jackson struggled up to the side of the slick with Williams. They looked inquiringly at the crew chief and pilot, who were transfixed by the bloated discolored hands wrapped around the pole. The crew chief lost control and gagged but managed not to throw up.

"If there's not enough room," Cortell said, "we could tie him to the skids."

"No, it's not that," the pilot managed to say, still trying to hold his breath. He waved toward the chopper door. The Marines who were already aboard pulled the body in.

Corporal Arran carried Pat onto the chopper with him. Pat lay still, his eyes staring blankly, waiting for his handler to fix the hunger and sickness. He tried to lick Arran's hand.

The two Vietnamese Kit Carsons walked nervously onto the small zone. Everyone watched them silently. Most of the Marines had forgotten that they existed. The Kit Carsons crawled into the body of the chopper. The Marines on board ignored them.

Hippy had been waiting with the gun squad in the high grass at the edge of the zone. When the pilot climbed back into the chopper, he knew for certain that he was going home. He turned and handed Young his machine gun, as if exchanging colors. Then he grinned to break the solemnity. "Don't forget you're the only chuck left in guns," he said. "Since you can't wear a noose, maybe this will help." He lifted his peace medallion from his neck and handed it to Young.

He shook hands slowly with Mole. "They're all yours, Mole. Promise me, no Pancho Villa bullshit. You make sure they keep the fucking ammo in the cans and not all over their chests so it'll shoot when they need it." Mole nodded. "You hang in there, Mallory," Hippy said, and shook his hand, too. Mallory nodded rapidly.

Jacobs shook Hippy's hand and then offered to help him out to the chopper. Hippy refused the offer and walked out of the war one step at a time.

Twenty minutes after the chopper left, the company waded into the river, following Kendall. The clouds had lowered and a steady rain spattered the water. Within an hour they were moving between steep hills whose tops came into and out of view through the clouds. In another hour they were moving between low cliffs that got gradually higher as they moved east toward Sky Cap.

Late that afternoon, knee-deep in the rushing water, Parker collapsed, his contorted jaw clamping his teeth together. His scream echoed up and down the river between the rocky cliffs.

Mellas reached Parker before Fredrickson. Cortell was cradling his head out of the water. Parker's eyes rolled and blood dribbled down his chin from his lacerated tongue. Mellas tore off a branch and stuffed it into Parker's mouth. By the time Doc Fredrickson got there, the fit seemed to have passed. Parker was sweating heavily, even with the water flowing over his body. "Why didn't you tell someone you were epileptic?" Fredrickson asked softly.

Parker just stared at him, "What's epiletic?"

Fredrickson looked at Mellas, surprise on his face. He started shaking down his thermometer, his forehead creased with worry. "It ain't like anything I saw in Field Med," he said.

Fitch was on the radio asking what was holding things up. He ordered Kendall to push off, and the column began to move past them. Parker attempted to get up, but Fredrickson pushed him down. His temperature was 105 degrees.

The senior squid, Sheller, arrived. He, Fredrickson, and Mellas talked quietly where Parker couldn't hear them. Rain fell steadily, soundless in the river's roar. The clouds were at the cliff tops. If the whole company went back to the LZ at Checkpoint Echo, it would delay Sky Cap's opening by a full day. If Fitch sent Parker back with a single platoon, a single platoon might get hit in a canyon going back and a reduced company might get hit in a canyon going forward. They couldn't get Parker back to Echo before dark anyway, so an evacuation there was problematical before morning. Humping in the dark also increased the risk of injuries. Mellas suggested getting a bird to work its way up the river. Because the canyon walls blocked the PRC-25s line-of-sight transmissions, Relsnik couldn't contact battalion. Daniels managed to contact a forward air observer on a weather check above the clouds who acted as a relay. The word came back. Flying in a canyon with its erratic winds was risky—a blade could hit a cliff. Unless it was a clear emergency, they wouldn't risk a chopper and its crew. With malaria, dystenery, and many other tropical diseases, temperatures of 105 were common and not immediately life-threatening. They could medevac Parker when they opened the LZ on 1609.

Sheller asked, "You think you can hump, Parker?"

"What the fuck you think?" Parker spat out. "I got a choice?"

Parker rose shakily to his feet. There was sweat on his face, mixing with the rain. He picked up his pack, shrugged into it, and stepped off into the river.

"You think he's faking?" Mellas asked Sheller.

"You don't fake a temperature like that and a bloody tongue, sir. I think he's really sick. I'd turn the company around and medevac him from Echo."

"Nevah hoppin," Fredrickson said.

"There it is," said Mellas.

At dusk Fitch ordered Kendall to climb out of the canyon to find a safe position for the night. It was a difficult, dangerous climb that took two hours. One of Goodwin's men fell backward, badly bruising a knee, when a root he was holding pulled loose. Everyone breathed with relief that the man's back wasn't hurt—he could still carry his own gear.

At the top, Mellas met Kendall in the dark. He was guiding everyone to his position. "Nice job today, Kendall," he said.

Kendall nodded. "Hard to get lost in a fucking canyon," he said, "even for me."

Mellas laughed. He wondered why he had been so hard on Kendall. It wasn't Kendall's idea to be out here. Was it such a great failing not to be cut out to be a Marine infantry officer? Maybe in war it was.

Fog set in. They could hear the steady roar of the river far below them, an ominous and frightening noise because it would muffle the sound of anyone sneaking up on them. It had been their sixth day in a row without food.

Two hours before midnight, someone from Kendall's platoon screamed for a corpsman. A kid had suddenly gone into a fit, his temperature shooting dangerously upward. At two in the morning, Parker went into convulsions again. His choked screaming was that of a man no longer in control of his mind. When Fredrickson tried to take his temperature, Parker continued to jerk his head violently, saying "no" to someone who wasn't present, spitting out the thermometer. Fredrickson stuck it under his armpit. "One hundred and six, Lieutenant," Fredrickson said. "That's outside the body. His brain is cooking."

Parker started crying, "I don't want to die. Not here. Not here. I don't want to die."

Cortell clasped his hands and prayed. "You believe in Jesus, Parker, I know you do," he said. He poured water on the soaked field dressing that Fredrickson had placed on Parker's forehead.

Sheller arrived and looked into Parker's eyes with a flashlight. "Challand over with Third Platoon's got the exact same thing," he said. "It's nothing I ever seen. We don't get them cooled down, though, they'll die." He looked up at Mellas. "We'll get an emergency medevac this time for sure. The question is where."

Mellas's mind raced. Here above the canyon they were in jungle with 200-foot trees, and the fog came right to the ground. The canyon had narrowed considerably since Parker's first episode, but it had been clear of fog. It seemed the only choice. He remembered a wide spot just before Kendall took them off the river. He radioed Fitch.

Ten minutes later Vancouver was leading the way down to the river. Parker and Challand, the kid from Kendall's platoon, were both slung in ponchos. Parker kept moaning, so they stuffed part of his shirt in his mouth.

Mellas and Vancouver emerged from the jungle onto the canyon rim, somewhat ahead of the rest. They were a good forty feet above the river. Mellas's heart sank. Was the flat area upstream or down? He looked at his watch. Daylight in another hour. It had taken them two hours to make it to the river. He knew he was close, but what if he wasn't? They could be trapped in the river in the dark and moving in the wrong direction. They'd lose both Parker and Challand. It was his call.

He huddled over his map, hiding the dim red glow of his flashlight. The breeze made his back cold. He squinted into the dark, trying to identify any terrain feature that would help him make the right choice.

There was a loud groan and a sound of falling rocks as the litter bearers emerged from the jungle. Jackson came up to him. "Doc says we got to cool Parker off quick, sir. Parker ain't even making sense anymore."

"Get the rope," Mellas said. "We'll take him over the edge right here. I think we got to be close to the spot."

"Here?"

"Here, goddamn it. Get some security set up behind us."

Jackson put Tilghman, Amarillo, Broyer, and Pollini in an arc behind them to serve as a human trip wire against any NVA who might have zeroed in on their noise. He looped the rope around a tree, and he and Mellas dangled both ends into the darkness of the canyon. Mellas pulled it back up, relieved to find both ends wet. That meant that the first rapeller would reach the bottom safely. It also meant that the river was right next to the cliff, so the wide spot wasn't here.

Without being told, Vancouver wrapped the rope around his waist, walked out backward over the edge, and disappeared. Mellas crawled on his stomach, trying to watch Vancouver's descent in the dark. The rope slackened. Vancouver's voice floated up. "It ain't bad, Lieutenant. We even got some rock up out of the water."

Three others went over the edge to set up security, two upstream and two down. Then they lowered Parker and Challand to the water. Soon only a very frightened Broyer and Tilghman were left above to provide security where the rope was tied.

Fredrickson and Cortell undressed Parker except for his boots, leaving only his head out of the water. Challand, his fever having suddenly abated, sat by the river's edge, shivering uncontrollably. One of the squad mates took off his flak jacket and wrapped his arms around Challand, trying to warm him.

Mellas sent Vancouver and another kid upstream, and Jackson and another downstream. Jackson returned first. He'd found the wide spot.

They lifted Parker to the litter and carried him downstream, whistling for Broyer and Tilghman to come down the rope. Mellas told them to pull it down and wait there for Vancouver.

Mellas slipped and fell in the water three times before they finally reached the wide place. They laid Parker on his back on the rocks. He was fully conscious, the river flowing around him, cooling his body. Cortell knelt beside him.

"I been scared before," Parker said, "but I didn't think it'd be like this."

"You be OK. We get a bird in for you. Jesus be with you, brother."

Parker looked up at the darkness above him. His eyes closed. Then he reached out, grabbing for anything. Cortell took his hand, squeezing it hard.

"I don't want to die here, Cortell. I don't want to die here." He started moaning softly.

Mellas and Fredrickson looked on, the water running across the tops of their boots. Mellas's throat ached. He screwed up his eyes, forcing the tears back. He'd never watched anyone die.

"It'll be OK, Parker," said Cortell. "Brother, we just baptize you right here on the spot. Jesus wash all you sins away."

"I was going to kill the gunny."

"That's OK, Parker, so was I. You didn't."

"I rigged his grenade, but he must have found it. It was only luck I didn't kill him."

"That's OK." Cortell was slowly pouring water from his hands onto Parker's forehead. "We call that grace."

"I know I should never done it. That's why I got this fever." Parker rolled to his side, his elbow slipping on a loose rock beneath the water. He lunged for Cortell, who helped turn him on his back, cradling his head in the stream. He lay there and began sobbing. "How can I go to hell, Cortell? Forever. How can I? How can it be so fucking bad? Not like this. How can I go to hell?"

"You ain't goin' to hell. That where you been. You just ask Jesus to forgive you." Cortell gently poured another handful of water onto Parker's head.

"I can't."

"Then I will." Cortell let a third handful of water drain onto Parker's head. He placed his helmet on Parker's stomach. Then he bent over the helmet, hands folded, and closed his eyes. "Lord Jesus. Sweet Lord Jesus. You know this man Duane Parker who is about to come to thee. He has been a good man. He has seen some bad times. Now he asks you with all of his heart for you to forgive him so he might come to thee and thy glory. Lord Jesus, I know you hear me, even here in this river. Amen."

Cortell took his helmet off Parker's stomach and placed it on his own head again. He put one hand on Parker's chest and moved it in a slow rhythm.

"You know my sister," Parker said, "she's a cheerleader—of her high school. She live with our great-aunt now." Parker was breathing rapidly. "You tell her—you tell her I never much said anything nice to her—but I love her, huh. You tell her, Cortell."

"Sure. Don't worry. She know that." Cortell started singing a hymn. It was one that neither Fredrickson nor Mellas had heard: "Deep river, Lord . . . I want to cross over into campground . . . where all is peace."

Mellas filled a hand with water for a drink. But he just looked at it and let the water drain from between his fingers. Then he covered his eyes with his palm, his wet fingers against his forehead, to hide his tears.

They waited there, looking east for the first light, listening for the sound of a chopper. Just before dawn, Parker went into convulsions and died as the three of them tried to keep him from drowning. Challand was still alive when the medevac bird came up the narrow gorge, fighting the erratic wind currents, the rotar wash spraying water behind it like a hydroplane. It took out two bodies not yet on the planet twenty years, one living and one dead.

Word came back on the radio later that afternoon that the disease was called cerebral malaria. It was carried by an isolated species of mosquito found only in the mountains, and the usual pills didn't help against it.

The odds were high that others in the company had been bitten as well. Mellas felt shadowed by disease and madness.

The company made only three and a half kilometers that day. The gentle blue line on the map was a torrent on the ground. It ran between steep cliffs and through narrow gorges, and had sudden waterfalls that required the use of ropes. It was the only path to the horseshoe of mountains that cradled its source, one of which a general or a staff officer had named Sky Cap.

Fitch felt it would be best to climb out of the canyon to set in for the night. Blakely and Simpson disagreed. They had just sat through the fifth regimental staff meeting in a row during which they had to explain why Bravo Company wasn't where Mulvaney had been told it would be. The order was relayed by an air observer: "There will be no deviations from the line of march for any reason."

To leave the canyon and lie about their position would be suicidal. The artillery might assume the company was someplace else and drop rounds on it. Since the company was strung out in the canyon with no way of circling into a defensive position or digging into the rock, Fitch felt he had no choice but to keep moving. At one in the morning, a kid in Kendall's platoon slipped on a steeply pitched wet slab. There was a thud, a splash, and a suppressed moan. He had fractured his left tibia, and the broken bone was sticking through the skin. Fitch told Relsnik to lose communications, even if the battalion sent an air observer to act as a relay. They would wait for morning.

The company's position was so precarious that neither Hawke nor Mellas could sleep. All night, they sat huddled on a boulder, shivering in their damp clothes. Hamilton, however, lay sleeping on the rocks below them, his boots in the water.

"Imagine," Hawke said. "The first use of the column in the defense. We'll all get jobs at the Naval War College. We'll go down in military history."

"That's what I'm afraid of," Mellas said. "Going down."

The cliff rose behind them. The moon occasionally broke through the cloud layer, and a cold wind blew on their backs. The conversation came and went. Girls they knew. What they would do after they got out. Building a fortress on Matterhorn and then abandoning it. Whether the Rolling Stones were better than the Beatles. Anything but cerebral malaria.

"Did you hear that Parker tried to kill Cassidy?" Mellas asked.

"Yeah. Conman told me. It's all over the fucking company. Cassidy denies it. Says it's all black power bullshit, that Parker just wanted to show off."

"You believe Cassidy?"

"I believe Parker."

"Is there going to be trouble?" Mellas asked.

"Don't know. Depends a lot on whether Parker did it on his own."

"You mean China?"

"I mean China *if* Parker didn't do it on his own. But I don't know."

They listened to the water rushing past them. Hawke, looking sad, repeatedly traced a small pentangle on the rock beside him.

"You feel bad about not getting the company?" Mellas asked.

"I don't know. Sure. Sure, I wanted the company. But now I just want out of the fucking bush."

"Have you tried? Like getting a job at the operations center, like Stevens?"

"Do I look like a fucking Dictaphone? What the fuck you trying to do, Mellas, get rid of me?"

Mellas felt himself color slightly. He said nothing.

"Don't worry, Mellas," Hawke said, "you're so fucking boot, you'll still be here when I'm sucking down cool ones at O'Day's Bar. You'll have plenty of time to get a fucking company. For starters, you'll probably be Bravo Five if I ever do get my freckled ass out of here. Kendall's leaving in a few weeks. And Goodwin." Hawke chuckled softly. "Shit, Jack," he mimicked. "Scar. His lines are a mess, his paperwork's all fucked up, his radio procedure's a disaster, but the troops will follow him anyplace. *Anyplace.*" Hawke blew some air through his lips. "That's the problem with him. He's a fighter."

"That's a problem?" Mellas felt envious of Goodwin again, but his

envy fought against the warmth evoked by the image of Goodwin tugging on an earlobe and cackling about a third Purple Heart.

"In this war it is," Hawke said. "That's probably why it's so fucked
up. What you need in war is warriors, fighting, not little boys dressed
up in soldier suits, administrating."

"Then why don't you make Scar the fucking Five?" Mellas asked,
a little more hotly than he'd intended.

"Because Goodwin would be eaten alive in three minutes. And not
by the fucking NVA. You wouldn't, and you know it. In fact, I think you'd
thrive on the fucking politics."

They lapsed into silence.

After a while Hawke asked, "You know why we're really strung
out in this fucking death canyon?"

Mellas didn't know, so he just grunted.

"Because Fitch doesn't know how to play the fucking game. That's
why. He's a good combat leader. I'd literally follow him to my death.
But he's not a good company commander in this kind of war. He got on
Simpson's bad side because he got his picture in the paper too often and
never gave Simpson credit, which by the way he doesn't deserve, but
that's the point. The smart guy gives the guy with the power the credit,
whether he deserves it or not. That way the smart guy is dangling something the boss wants. So the smart guy now has power over the boss."

Mellas kept his mouth shut.

"It used to be if you were out in the bush operating independently
like we are, no one would second-guess the skipper. They didn't have
the radio power back then. Now they do, and the fucking brass think
they're out on patrol. And now the smallest units are run by the colonels
and generals, hell, right up to the president. Colonel and above used to
be the level where people dealt with all the political shit like congressmen on junkets, television, reporters, you name it. But now those guys
are running the show right down to this fucking river canyon and we're
in the politics too. And the better the radios, the worse it's going to get.
The politics is going to come right down to the company level, and
people like Fitch and Scar are going to be culled out and people like
you will take over."

"What do you mean 'like me'?" Mellas asked quietly.

Hawke sighed. "Shit, Mellas. I mean a fucking politician."

Mellas stiffened. "Is that what you think of me?"

"Yeah. That's what I think."

Mellas said nothing.

"Shit, Mellas, don't get your feelings hurt. I didn't say I didn't *like* you, for Christ's sake, or you're some sort of bad person. Although I will grant you the company you'll keep is going to be sleazier than average. Just accept that you're a fucking politician. So was Abraham Lincoln, and Winston Churchill. So was Dwight Eisenhower." He paused. "It ain't like they're bad people. And they all ran a pretty good war."

Mellas smiled ruefully. "You really think it's all about politics?"

Hawke blew air upward. Mellas could see his breath. "No," he said. "You better believe it ain't all about politics." He tossed a pebble into the stream and then looked directly at Mellas. "Simpson's right. All these arms caches we're uncovering can only be a tiny percentage of the total. That means there's a lot of gooks around here. A *lot*. How the fuck do you think all that shit gets carried in without trucks except by a lot of fucking backs?" He checked to see if he had Mellas's attention. "The caches we've found are stashed in a line pointing east from Laos to the flats. To pull off that political op at Cam Lo we had to pull back from Laos and the DMZ. Matterhorn controls the west end of Mutter's Ridge. Whoever controls Mutter's Ridge controls Route 9. If the NVA control Route 9 they can cut off Khe Sanh and VCB from the coast. They cut off Khe Sanh and VCB and they can take Camp Carroll. Then the gooks come down Route 9 with tanks and you can kiss fucking Quang Tri, Dong Ha, and Hue good-bye. That ain't politics."

The company started moving at dawn. It would be the eighth day without food. The kid with the broken leg was carried fireman style by friends who took turns. The senior squid gave the kid all the pills he felt his system could stand, to keep him from screaming. As the company moved forward, everyone passed a message scratched into the rocks: FIRST THEY SHAVED HIM. THEN THEY HUMPED HIM TO DEATH.

CHAPTER TEN

The canyon ended. The company stared upward at a wall of jungle-covered cliffs and terraces that rose out of sight in the fog. The top of the wall was Hill 1609. Their job was to turn it into Firebase Sky Cap.

Mellas's helmet fell from his head when he leaned backward and tried to see the top. He let it lie behind him and stared, stupefied, having no idea how they were going to climb the wall by nightfall. Fitch's voice came over the radio. Still deep in jungle, he could see nothing of what Mellas saw. "Come on, Bravo One," he said impatiently. "Let's move it up there."

Mellas waved a hand at Jackson, pointed firmly upward with one index finger, and put his helmet back on. Jackson, at the base of the cliff, nodded to Cortell and Broyer. Cortell gave him the finger. Broyer shoved his black plastic glasses back on his nose and took a deep breath, looking up the cliff a long time before he exhaled. Jackson slipped the squad's coil of nylon Goldline rope off his pack and passed it up to them. The two of them roped up, and Broyer started moving, his face against the cliff, pulling the rope up after him as Cortell paid it out. There seemed no place to go. Then Broyer found a root and tugged on it. It held—but vegetable holds were dangerous, and he knew it. He hauled himself shakily up to a narrow sloping ledge and tried to get secure with his butt up against the cliff and his boots on a nubbin of rock. He passed the rope around his waist in a hasty belay and then whispered as loud as he dared, "OK, I'm ready."

Cortell followed, pulled up by Broyer. Squeezing together on the ledge, leaning back on the cliff, they tied-in to exposed roots and put a friction loop over a barely adequate bump of rock. They then dropped the rope end down again and belayed Jackson, who was followed by Mellas, then Hamilton, then Mallory's machine gun, then Mallory, then the boxes of ammunition that Mallory and Barber, his A gunner, had been carrying, and so on until the next squad arrived with its own rope. Then Jackson's squad moved ever higher, repeating the process, but with different people leading. Soon the platoon was strung out in stages all along the cliff face. Fitch kept the rest of the company hidden in the jungle just in case there were NVA on top. Mellas knew it was the right thing to do, but he now regretted that his map skills had put First Platoon at the lead so often. His face and nose were pressed against the wet cliff, and he inhaled the smells of moss and dirt. A single NVA squad on the top could kill half the platoon before the kids could scramble down to safety. A single NVA machine gun across from the canyon could probably get them all. They were fucked.

Five hours later they were still climbing, surrounded by fog. Robertson and Jermain from Second Squad were now on point, with Jacobs close behind them, stuttering encouragement. Jermain had the squat M-79 loaded with fléchettes so he could at least spray anyone looking down at them and fire the weapon one-handed without having to aim. Robertson, who as a fire team leader could have ordered someone else to take point, hadn't had the heart to give the job to anyone but himself. He was now separated from his team by Jacobs, who himself had moved closer to the point position from his normally safer one behind the first fire team. Robertson was wondering whether to keep the safety of his M-16 off or on. If it was on and he fucked up, he'd be very likely to kill Jermain, who would certainly fall off the cliff, and, being roped into Robertson, take Robertson with him. On the other hand, if the enemy peered over the edge and Robertson didn't fire instantly on full automatic, because again he'd be one-handed, he might as well not even be carrying the damned weapon. He resolved the dilemma by nervously switching the safety on and off every minute or two.

Moving up the steep face of the cliff made silence impossible. If the NVA were waiting, Robertson thought, the two of them for certain—and probably the entire squad, including the lieutenant and Hamilton—would have to be written off in order to get the company out. Compared, however, with the constant draining pull against gravity and hunger, and the obstinate rock face the jungle now presented to them, death didn't seem so bad.

He saw that Lieutenant Mellas had reached a flat spot below him and was looking up. Robertson heaved himself and his heavy pack over a large rock formation. He stopped, breathing hard, perched precariously next to Jermain, who was sitting with his back against the cliff, looking upward, holding his M-79 above his head. Clearly, the small space was safe for only one of them. There seemed no place he could move. His face was flushed and felt hot and full. He knew that he was crying, because he had to keep wiping tears away to look for his next handhold.

The lieutenant pointed a thumb upward, nodding encouragingly. God knows how the guys behind us with the machine guns and mortars are doing, Robertson thought. Or the poor fucker with the broken leg and the ones carrying him. He turned to look upward into the fog. The cliff stood above him, unmovable, impossibly steep, its unseen top seemingly beyond reach. Slowly, with each breath, his anger grew: at the cliff, the bullshit, the hunger, the war—everything. He erupted in a frenzy of activity. He pumped his legs madly against the side of the cliff, scrambling for all he was worth on friction alone, moaning as he half-suppressed an angry scream. When he took off, he nearly shoved Jermain off the cliff, and Jermain actually raised the M-79 to club him but must have realized that he had Robertson on belay and didn't. Jermain paid out rope so that Robertson wouldn't be jerked short and fall. Robertson reached safety, just a few meters above Jermain, and apologized. Both of them were crying openly, like small children who needed to be fed and tucked into bed.

*   *   *

They reached the summit just before dark. It was a narrow razorback ridge of solid limestone, just wide enough for a single person to step along carefully, balanced between sheer drops on both sides. Obviously, no one had bothered to recon it. There was no possible place for a helicopter to land, much less an artillery battery.

Mellas, too, was crying with exhaustion and frustration when he radioed Fitch that there wasn't room for the rest of the company on top. Fitch regrouped the company on a small saddle just below the final cliff, packing it into a space that would normally have been occupied by a platoon. The company dug in and spent the night there. The next morning they climbed the trail blazed by First Platoon, using the ropes that had been tied in place—just as tired, but more confident, knowing First Platoon held the summit.

It took the entire day, using every piece of explosive the company had left, to blast a small niche for an LZ out of the solid rock edge of the massive sweeping cliff that plunged more than 2,000 feet into a river canyon on the north side of the mountain. They blew their final bars of C-4 just as darkness closed out any possibility of resupply.

The next morning they were hacking away at the rock with their E-tools. At around midday the fog temporarily cleared and Fitch radioed to VCB. Thirty minutes later they all silently watched a CH-46 come chundering up the long valley they'd taken days to get through. The perch they'd blasted and scraped from the limestone was just large enough for the chopper to put down its rear wheels. The front two-thirds of the helicopter hovered dangerously in midair as the pilot fought to hold the machine long enough to unload its cargo. This maneuver drew murmurs of respect for the pilot's skill. The tailgate came down, and a group of Marines ran out holding their helmets in the blast of air. No supplies came with them.

Marines from Third Platoon helped the kid with the broken leg aboard. The tailgate closed and the helicopter simply fell off the cliff, picking up airspeed until it could fly. It curved away and faded into the mist.

The Marines in the new group were full-fleshed and excited. Their camouflage helmet covers were conspicuously unripped, their jungle utilities bright green and brown. Hawke and Fitch walked up to them.

They could see pickaxes, power saws, large new shovels, bundles of C-4, even a surveyor's transit. A stocky first lieutenant, his silver bars gleaming on his collar, came over and shook hands. "Hi!" he said cheerily. "We're the Pioneers from Golf Battery."

Hawke and Fitch stared at him. Finally, Hawke spoke. "Well, if you're the pioneers, then we're the fucking aborigines."

An hour later the same helicopter returned, an external load of C-rations, ammunition, and explosives swinging beneath it in a net that streamed out behind it on a cable. The helicopter released the net on the tiny LZ, then, as before, looped around the mountain to hover with its rear end almost touching the LZ and the rest of it hanging in space over the edge of the cliff. The tailgate flopped down to the ground and another group of replacements came tumbling out, wondering where to run. They were followed by Jancowitz, who was wearing crisp new camouflage utilities and a red silk scarf that smelled of perfume. He was holding a case of canned steaks.

"I heard you guys might be hungry," he said.

Mellas could have kissed him but started stabbing at one of the cans with his K-bar instead.

The next day the choppers delivered hundreds of pounds of explosives, a tiny bulldozer, and three Marine engineers. It took the engineers several days to correct what the Marines of Bravo Company had thought was the mistake of selecting Sky Cap for an artillery base. What they didn't know was that long ago General Neitzel had figured out that he had the raw power to make the crooked places straight and would put his Marines where he wanted, not where nature would have allowed. The engineers simply blasted the top of the mountain down with plastic explosive and dynamite until it became wide enough to do the job.

The normal backbreaking routine of providing security for a fire support base was resumed. The long hungry march, now dubbed the

Trail of Tears Op, faded into the past. Days were filled with the nerve-racking tedium of patrols and nighttime listening posts, the stupefying work of laying barbed wire, hacking out fields of fire with K-bars, digging holes, improving positions, eating, shitting, drinking, pissing, nodding off, trying to stay awake. Still, it beat humping.

Sometimes Mellas would find time to sit alone at the edge of the cliff. On days when the peak was out of the clouds, he would look into North Vietnam. Black clouds moved slowly before him at eye level. Far below, he could see the jungle-covered impression of a small river that surely joined the Ben Hai River to the north. Along the way it gathered the rainfall from Sky Cap and Tiger Tooth, the huge mountain that towered above them to the southeast.

Because it took so long for security patrols to get off Sky Cap and back up, they didn't have time to cover the distance needed to reach the river, but its possibilities excited Mellas. Its winding path had the fascination of a deadly snake. Days passed, and Mellas kept coming back to the cliff's edge to stare at the river valley and daydream of glory and recognition. Then one evening he knew what he wanted to do.

Fitch was bantering with Pallack and Relsnik in soft whispers when Mellas poked his head inside the dripping ponchos. It was too dark to see anyone.

"I've got an idea, Jim," he said.

Fitch's voice came out of the dark. "OK. What?"

"You know the blue line just north of here that hits the Ben Hai?"

"Yeah," Fitch said uncertainly.

"Nagoolian's got to have all sorts of trails there. He had to in order to supply the attack on Con Thien last year. If they ever want to get Quang Tri, other than come right across the Z in tanks and get fucked up by Navy air and Army tanks and artillery, they've only got two alternatives: hold Mutter's Ridge, which means resupply via the trails along the Ben Hai, or kick us out of Vandy and the Rock Pile, barrel-ass down Route 9, hit Cam Lo, and take Quang Tri from the west."

"Mellas," Fitch asked patiently, "what do you want?"

"I think we ought to recon that valley. It's like a warehouse next to a freeway."

"The Ben Hai's no fucking freeway, sir," Relsnik said quietly.

"But it's got gook tollbooths every fucking klick," Pallack chimed in, "and dey ain't asking for no quarters either."

"I don't plan on going down the Ben Hai," Mellas said. He turned toward Fitch's voice. "It provides a good screening action in case someone's coming up the valley to hit us."

"Yeah, you'd be d' fucking screen, holes all over you," Pallack said.

Fitch was silent.

"It wouldn't hurt to show battalion we're taking some initiative," Mellas added.

After another long silence Fitch said, "OK. You got people crazy enough to go with you, be my guest. Take Daniels if he wants to go. How long you want to be out?"

"I figure three days."

Mellas dug out his map, and Fitch switched on his flashlight. Faint red light illuminated the interior of the hooch. Mellas saw Pallack and Relsnik curled up next to their radios in their poncho liners.

The next morning First Platoon had palace guard while squads from Second and Third platoons went out on security patrols. Security outposts disappeared into the jungle on the south side of the mountain or set up with binoculars on the cliff faces. Work parties were formed to lay more wire, burn garbage, and dig larger latrines. Mellas asked for volunteers. As he expected, almost everyone preferred the work parties. Also as expected, Vancouver was the first to say he'd go. He talked Daniels into coming. Mellas had to send the word out again for an M-79 man. Eventually Gambaccini showed up, saying he was coming only because Bass had mentioned to him that it was his turn to volunteer. Fredrickson felt honor-bound to go along, since he was still the only platoon corpsman.

They all took four hours to sleep that afternoon. Then they blackened their hands and faces and tied down their equipment.

In the darkness it took more than three hours to reach the jungle floor, by rope most of the way. Vancouver took point with an M-16 rather than his M-60 so everybody's ammunition would be compatible. He was followed by Mellas. Next came Daniels with the radio and Gambaccini with the grenade launcher. Fredrickson took up the rear, walking nearly backward, his M-16 pointing into the blackness behind them.

They moved silently beneath towering trees that rustled in the dark above them. Eventually they reached the stream and made their way north alongside it. They used its sound both to guide them and to mask their movements.

Mellas's senses were keenly alive. A thrill surged up his spine. He felt wonderfully powerful and dangerous. Vancouver on point. Four combat-tried Marines. Daniels backed with a battery of howitzers. If the clouds broke, jets from Da Nang or possibly from carriers in the China Sea might show up to support them. They could even call in the Air Force's Puff the Magic Dragon with its fiery streams of 40-millimeter shells from on high. He pictured his small team quietly stalking the enemy. A song from his college days rose in his memory, Ian and Sylvia, guitars driving, close harmony pushing the wildness, singing about outlaws: *They were armed. All were armed. Three MacLean boys and that wild Alex Hare.*

In the darkness Mellas could sense the stream slowing, indicating that the land had begun to broaden as they left the high peaks behind them. The underbrush also grew thicker, reducing their own already slow pace. Above, he could just make out the dark silhouettes of the huge trees against the barely perceptible lighter color of the cloudy night sky.

Suddenly Vancouver sank to one knee. Everyone quickly squatted, rifles outward in assigned sectors.

"Trail," Vancouver whispered.

Mellas moved forward in a low crouch. His hand felt packed mud. "Take it," he whispered.

The trail headed eastward, ever lower, and now they moved more rapidly away from Sky Cap. The trail was what Mellas had wanted. He'd been proved right. But it occurred to him that they might not be the only ones out tonight. He tried to force the nagging fear from his mind and concentrate on moving silently. Don't let water in the canteens slosh.

Check the taped metal on the slings. Heel down, feel for anything that could make noise. Try to keep the breathing even. What would happen, he wondered, if they ran into a major unit? He'd stupidly assumed that only small units would be on the trails at night. But Vancouver would see the enemy first. They'd pull back in time. It would be easy to envelop the five of them, however. What if one of them was wounded?

Mellas forced himself to think more positively. They'd find a perfect ambush spot. The gooks would come down the trail, talking, unaware. Daniels would give the word and the artillery would erupt. They'd uncover intelligence that would alter the whole division's strategy or foil an attack on Quang Tri. A medal. A story in the newspaper back home. But what if they didn't get set up in time and met the gooners head-on? What if some of them were wounded and the rest couldn't run?

Something ahead snapped, and Mellas's heartbeat accelerated as the shadow of Vancouver sank quickly to the mud. Mellas went down on one knee, eyes straining. The wind moved softly through the jungle, bringing the smell of damp rot. It also rustled the trees, filling the air with a steady hiss. Trying to hear anything was maddening. The failure to hear could mean his death. The fear made his heart pound and his breathing shallow and more rapid, all in turn making it more difficult to hear. No one moved. Everyone was waiting for an order from Mellas.

Mellas wanted to look at his map. If he could see the contour lines of Hill 1609 drawn on the map, it would help him feel that it and the company were still really there. In this darkness, it was a dream. There was only this ground, this smell, this small group of humans. He slowly reached for his map. Then he realized he'd have to turn on his flashlight to see it. To appear to be doing something, he slid his compass up before his nose and opened the case. The pale green glow of the needle's tip swung drunkenly, then steadied, rocking slightly. Guilty anxiety struck him. What if the snap up ahead meant a group just like them, waiting to open up the minute there was more sound? He silently closed the compass case. What good did a fucking compass do if you couldn't see where you were? He felt a hand tap his boot. "I don't think it was nothing, Lieutenant," Vancouver whispered.

Mellas knew he'd have to either move forward or decide clearly that this was the enemy and pull back into a hasty defensive circle. He also knew he could not do the latter without looking foolish. Another part of him finally took command and he whispered, "Let's go."

They rose to their feet. Carefully, they stepped forward. Heel down. Feel for something solid. Toe. Lift heel. Next foot. Heel down. Feel for loose sticks. Toe. Lift heel. They all moved the same way. Quietly. Slowly. The march of the reconnaissance team.

This march was not in four-four time. There was no time. There was forever. Trees creaked unseen above them. Direction became meaningless. The compass needle pointed only to darkness.

The flashes from the muzzle of Vancouver's M-16 seared their eyes. Ghostly trees stood silhouetted, exposed, as if by flashbulbs. Grotesque shadows leaped into being and died as everything went black again. Green spots plagued their night vision, the explosions echoing and reechoing in their ears.

Mellas had glimpsed the grimace of pain and fear on an NVA soldier's face.

They crawled backward, hearts pounding, panting with adrenaline. Mellas bumped into Daniels, who was pushing out to his assigned sector. He felt other boots touch his legs as Fredrickson and Gambaccini reached the circle. Mellas quickly whispered names. Everyone checked in OK.

The radio was frantically keying the check-in signal. Daniels keyed back the OK signal. The radio stopped.

"I only saw one, Vancouver," Mellas whispered.

"That's all I saw."

"Let's get the fuck out of here," Gambaccini whispered.

"Got to check the body for documents," Mellas whispered grimly.

"Oh, fuck, man."

They heard a moan.

"Oh, shit, he's alive," Fredrickson whispered.

"Now what do we do?" Gambaccini asked.

"Pump some more rounds into him," Daniels said.

"It'll give away our position," Mellas whispered quickly. "Throw a Mike Twenty-Six."

"There can't be just one of the fuckers out there," Vancouver said. "He's got to have friends behind him."

"I want the fucking documents. We need them for intelligence."

"Oh, shit, Lieutenant, fuck the fucking documents."

"Shut up, Gambaccini."

Mellas thought furiously. "Vancouver, go ahead and grease him with a grenade." That way the enemy would not be able to locate them. "When I give the word, we all move toward the blue line." He waited a moment. "Ready?"

"Yeah."

"Go."

Vancouver rose to one knee and threw the grenade. An arc of brilliant fire erupted down the trail as they scrambled for the river.

Again, they waited.

"Did you get him?" Mellas whispered.

"I don't know."

They waited.

Fitch came up on the radio, asking them to break radio silence. Mellas told him the situation in terse, barely audible whispers. They continued to wait.

"There's got to be more of the fuckers. Let's get out of here, Lieutenant."

"Goddamn it, Gambaccini, I want the documents."

Mellas, too, wanted to run, but he knew that bringing in solid information would make him look good. "I don't think there's any more of them," Mellas whispered. No one answered, since no one had been addressed. It was clearly Mellas's problem. The others would do as they were told. "Let's go check him out," Mellas finally said.

They crawled forward through the rotting sticks and fungus of the jungle floor. When they reached the body, Vancouver quickly pulled at the AK-47 that was attached to it with a shoulder sling. The man moaned.

"Fuck," Daniels whispered. "He's still alive."

Mellas sent Vancouver and Gambaccini to guard the approaches up and down the trail and went through the wounded soldier's pockets. He scanned the contents of the man's wallets with his red flashlight, trying to ignore the soldier's eyes, which were rolling with fear, pinkish brown in the red light. He was no older than Daniels or Gambaccini.

Fredrickson cut the kid's uniform open, revealing three bullet holes in his abdomen. There were gaping exit wounds in his lower back. Shrapnel from the grenade had smashed through his left leg and shattered his shinbone. Fredrickson looked up at Mellas. "He won't last but an hour or two. Less if we try to move him. Those are his guts coming out of the exit holes and I think that's part of his pancreas. The charts never look the way it really is, so it's hard to say."

Mellas wet his lips nervously. If only he could locate the soldier's unit. They could bring the sky down on it.

"We're going to pull back and wait for him to move," he said.

"What?"

"We'll pretend we're leaving. I want to see which way he crawls for help."

Mellas stuffed the wallet into his pocket and cut off the kid's shoulder patches with his K-bar. The kid's eyes darted left and right with fear as Mellas worked around him with the large knife. Mellas thought about cutting off the belt buckle but hesitated, wanting to appear more professional. "OK. Let's go," he whispered. He switched off the red light. It was like heat being taken away.

"You forgot the belt buckle, Lieutenant," Daniels said. "Ten cases of Coke in Da Nang, minimum." Daniels groped for the buckle in the dark and quickly cut it loose.

They moved off about fifty meters and Mellas formed them into a tight circle. After ten minutes of silence they heard a moan and then a very ordinary sound.

"Shit," Vancouver whispered, almost in disbelief. "He's fucking crying."

Mellas shut his eyes.

The crying didn't stop and was soon mixed with pleading foreign words. The sound cut through Mellas like a shaft of steel. The sobbing rose and fell in intensity. The pleading continued, a child crying for help, afraid to die.

"Jesus Christ, shut the fuck up," Mellas whispered aloud. The others were silent, waiting for Mellas's lead. "Shit," Mellas finally said. "Let's go find him."

The youth had managed to crawl nearly thirty meters from where they'd left him. Mellas turned on his flashlight, shielding it with his hand. The soldier had ground dirt into his mouth, and it had mixed with blood-flecked saliva in his teeth. He watched the Marines, eyes wide, lips pleading silently.

"Well, sir, it looks like his friends are east of here," Fredrickson said.

"Yeah," Mellas whispered.

There was an uncomfortable silence.

"Do you think he'll live?" Mellas asked.

"Won't make much difference anyway."

"How come?"

"Tigers. It's a pretty easy piece of meat."

"He'd die before then, wouldn't he?"

"Fucked if I know. I'm just an HM-three."

Suddenly the kid broke down and an anguished cry escaped his lips, followed by more frightened choking sobbing.

Fredrickson switched the safety off of his M-16. "It won't be the first time, sir," he said.

"No, don't." Mellas switched off his own safety. He pointed the barrel directly at the kid's head. The kid looked up at him, crying loudly, mucus running from his nose. Mellas switched the safety back on. "We can't," he whispered.

"Lieutenant, do him a favor. He's going to die."

"We don't know that."

"I fucking know it."

"Maybe we could get him back."

Fredrickson sighed. "We'd trail his guts all over the place. Even if he did live, we'd just have to turn him over to the ARVNs and they'd kill him slower than the tigers."

"We don't know that for certain." Mellas toed the kid gently.

Fredrickson placed the barrel of his rifle against the kid's head.

"Don't shoot him," Mellas said coldly. "That's an order, Fredrickson." He backed away from the boy. "He might make it. Maybe his buddies are real close."

"If they are," Gambaccini said, "let's get the fuck out of here."

"You going to leave him, Lieutenant?" Fredrickson asked.

"He might live," Mellas said. "There's a chance one of his guys could pick him up. They must have heard the firing." He struggled for more reasons. "It'd be murder."

Nobody said anything. The jungle had gone silent. Mellas no longer had any illusions about their vulnerability. They were alone, just as this single crying stranger at their feet was alone, their reason for being here probably not much different from his.

"East, sir?" Vancouver asked. "The way he was heading?"

Mellas didn't say anything. The others shifted nervously.

"Let's get the fuck out of here," Gambaccini finally whispered. "I'm cold."

There was a tense silence. Mellas could hear them all breathing, smell the sweat rising off them in the darkness. He felt Daniels next to him with the large PRC-25 on his back, scratchy whispers coming from the handset. Mellas rubbed his face, feeling the slight growth of his beard.

He knew it was no use pretending anymore. He was simply too frightened to push farther ahead into the darkness. "Daniels, tell Bravo we're coming in."

"All *right*," Gambaccini whispered.

"I ain't complaining," whispered Daniels, "but how come?"

Again there was silence as Mellas struggled for an answer. Finally he said, "Because I don't want to be out here any more."

* * *

All that night, Mellas didn't say a word beyond confirming Daniels's map reading. When morning came, Mellas expected the others to avoid looking him in the eye. Surprisingly, everyone kept offering him reasons he could give Fitch for coming in early. He could say that someone was ill or had turned an ankle. As they began to feel safer, climbing back up Sky Cap, the excuses for coming in grew wilder and more outrageously funny and the imaginary profits from the AK-47 and the belt buckle soared.

Mellas was unable to join the general levity. He couldn't look at Fredrickson. He knew Fredrickson thought he should have killed the wounded boy but didn't have the guts. He wondered if Fredrickson was right, just as he kept wondering if he was going to lie to Fitch about the mission.

When he arrived at the CP he found Fitch and Hawke sitting cross-legged eating C-rations. He pulled the Vietnamese kid's wallet out of his pocket, weighing it in his hand. "Sorry for aborting the mission, Jim. I don't know what to say for myself."

"Say you got scared," Fitch said. "Shit, confession's good for the soul. I told battalion you went out on a kill team, bagged a gook, and didn't have anyone hurt. A complete success."

"Great." Mellas kept looking at the wallet in his hand.

"Besides, it's good you came in early," Fitch said. "We're skying out to VCB tomorrow. Just got word."

Mellas continued to look at the wallet, saying nothing. Hawke, who had been watching Mellas through the steam that rose from his pear-can coffee mug, handed Mellas the cup. Mellas gave a brief smile and took a drink. His hand was shaking. Hawke said in a calm voice, "Something happened. You want to talk about it?"

Mellas didn't answer right away. Then he said, "I think I know where the gooks are." He pulled out his map and pointed to the spot, his hand still trembling.

"How do you know that, Mel?" Hawke asked.

"From the direction he crawled after he was shot." Mellas tossed the wallet down at Fitch. Then he dug into his pocket and pulled out the soldier's unit and rank patches. He looked at them, then at Fitch and Hawke, who were no longer eating. "I let him crawl toward home with his guts hanging out." He started sobbing. "I just left him there." Snot was streaming from his nose. "I'm so sorry. I'm so fucking sorry." His hands were now shaking with his body as he clenched the two pieces of cloth to his eyes.

CHAPTER
ELEVEN

The chopper's deck vibrated beneath them as they leaned back against the thin metal that separated them from several thousand feet of empty space. The trip from Sky Cap to Vandegrift Combat Base was like magic. Jungle-covered mountains that would have taken weeks to cross flashed beneath them in minutes.

Vancouver wondered if his gook sword or his space blanket had come in yet. Skosh was dreaming about R & R in Sydney and wondering what it was really like to have intercourse with a girl. Hawke was wondering if this might be his last time out in the bush, if maybe he could wangle a job in the rear. Fitch kept going over the events of the long march, preparing his case, worried sick about the disgrace of being relieved of command. He also wanted to get out of his filthy clothing and take a shower. China was counting the number of people ahead of him to pull KP duty and wondering what he could do to jump the line before the company skyed out on another operation. He needed time in the rear for organizing. Pollini was kneeling at a shot-out porthole watching the landscape slide beneath them. He wondered if any of his brothers or sisters were thinking about him. Cassidy wanted to sleep—to sleep and sleep and forget the shame of one of his own men wanting to kill him. Goodwin wanted to get drunk. So did Ridlow, Bass, Sheller, Rider, Tilghman, Pallack, Gambaccini, Jermain, and a lot of others. Jackson wanted to get stoned, as did Mole, Cortell, Broyer, Mallory, Jacobs, Fredrickson, Robertson, and Relsnik. Jancowitz fingered the now filthy red silk scarf he'd stuffed in his pocket, not wanting to look at it but not

wanting to throw it away. It still smelled faintly of Susi's perfume. He
didn't care how he did it, he just wanted to forget where he was.

Mellas, left behind with a squad to guide Kilo Company into the
lines, kept seeing the twisted face, running with snot, of the young Vietnamese soldier. He wondered why the kid had been out there alone in
the first place and whether there was a chance he'd lived.

While the chundering workhorse helicopters flew back and forth
between VCB and Sky Cap, sending out the freshly outfitted troops of
Kilo Company and picking up the ragged troops from Bravo Company,
Colonel Mulvaney was returning from a briefing at Dong Ha.

The stupid cordon operation was over, and Mulvaney was anxious to
be snooping and pooping, as he called it: interdicting the flow of NVA
supplies into the Au Shau Valley and toward Da Nang, screening the
NVA from the fertile plains to the east of them, and keeping open Route 9,
the only road running from the coast through the mountains to Khe Sanh
and Laos. If the NVA ever got their armor down that road on a cloudy
day, it would be Katie bar the gate.

"Is that Bravo coming in from Sky Cap, Corporal Odegaard?"
Mulvaney asked his driver.

Odegaard slowed the jeep as they passed the groups of two or three
trudging wearily alongside the muddy road. When they passed a Marine
with an Australian-style bush cover, brim turned up on the right side,
and a sawed-off machine gun, Odegaard said, "That's them, sir. There's
Vancouver, the guy who fucked up the ambush for them."

"Pull over when you get past those crates over there."

"Aye, aye, sir." Odegaard swung the jeep off the road and came to
a stop. Mulvaney watched two kids without trousers go by, waddling to
avoid irritating the ringworm that covered them from waist to ankle.
His experienced eye noted the rot on hands and faces, the state of dis-
repair of the mortars, and the way the kids' rotting uniforms hung off
their thin bodies.

"You want me to turn the engine off, sir?"

"No. Let's go."

Before they came upon Bravo Company, Mulvaney had been telling Odegaard one of his better sea stories. He didn't finish it and was silent all the way back to regimental headquarters. During the briefing, he said little. Toward the end the subject of who would supply the company for Bald Eagle–Sparrow Hawk duty came up. Bald Eagle was a company held on constant alert, combat loaded, at the edge of the VCB airstrip. It was there to instantly reinforce any unit in trouble or to exploit a tactical advantage. Sparrow Hawk was a platoon within that company for the smaller jobs, like getting recon teams out of trouble. No one liked the duty. The Marines spent their days doing make-work while ridden with anxiety because at any instant the company could be launched into combat.

"We had it last, sir," the commander of Third Battalion said.

"That makes it your turn, Simpson," Mulvaney said.

"Aye, aye, sir," Simpson said, writing it in his green pocket notebook, clearly unhappy, as it would leave him with only three companies.

After the briefing, Mulvaney headed for the door as soon as he saw Simpson and Blakely about to leave. "Why don't you stop by for a drink, Simpson?" he said.

Blakely, clearly not invited, nervously stubbed out his cigarette.

"It'd be my pleasure, sir," Simpson responded. "When would be convenient?"

"Right now." Mulvaney walked away.

Mulvaney was pouring two shot glasses of Old Forester when Simpson pushed through the flap of his tent. "You use water?" he asked, reaching into his little refrigerator. Simpson said he'd have it straight.

Mulvaney poured himself some water and dumped the shot of bourbon into it. He raised his glass. "To the Corps," he said.

"To the Corps," Simpson echoed. He tossed down the drink in a single motion and, seeming to realize what he'd done, nervously wiped his mouth with his hand.

"Sit, sit." Mulvaney motioned toward a chair. Simpson sat. Mulvaney leaned against the edge of his desk. He took another slow drink, then looked at Simpson. "We are engaged in a shitty war," he said slowly. "A shitty little war that is tearing apart the thing I love. Do you love the Marine Corps, Simpson?"

"Yes sir, I do."

"I mean do you really love it? Do you go to bed with it at night, wake up with it in the morning, see its sour side, see it when it's sick and tired, not just when it's glorious? Do you think about it all the time? Or do you think about where it's going to get you?"

"Well, sir, I . . ."

"Unh-unh. I'll tell you, Simpson. You think about where it's going to get you. You use it. Either that or you let someone else use you so it'll get *them* somewhere. I don't know which is worse."

"I, uhm . . ."

"Shut up."

"Yes, sir."

"And don't worry. It's all my nickel. And none of it's going into your fucking fitness report."

Mulvaney walked over to look at a framed photograph on the wall. It showed a Marine platoon in summer uniforms on a cold, rainy day. On it was written "New Zealand, July 1942." Mulvaney nodded toward it. Without looking at Simpson he said quietly, "Half of those guys are dead." He paused briefly. "A lot of them my fault."

He turned to look at Simpson. "America uses us like whores, Simpson. When it wants a good fuck it pours in the money and we give it a moment of glory. Then when it's over, it sneaks out the back door and pretends it doesn't know who we are." Mulvaney swirled the ice, watching it dissolve. "Yeah, we're whores," he continued, almost to himself now. "I admit it. But we're good ones. We're good at fucking. We like our work. So the customer gets ashamed afterward. So hypocrisy's always been part of the profession. We know that." Mulvaney narrowed his eyes and looked at Simpson. "But this time the customer doesn't want to fuck. He wants to play horsy and come in through the back door. And he's riding us around the room with a fucking bridle and whip and spurs." Mulvaney shook his head. "We ain't good at that. It turns our stomach. And it's destroying us."

Mulvaney was silent. Simpson looked at the bottle on the desk, then quickly back to his own empty shot glass.

"Did you look at Bravo Company when they came in today?" Mulvaney asked.

"I talked with their skipper, Lieutenant Fitch, sir."

"Did you see them, Simpson?" Mulvaney's voice started to rise.

"No sir."

"They looked like shit."

"Yes sir. I'll get right on it, sir. I'll talk with Lieutenant Fitch. I've been thinking of relieving him ever since he was on Matterhorn."

"It ain't Fitch, Simpson." Mulvaney took a deep breath and another drink. "They've been used. Badly. How long they been out in the bush?"

"By bush do you mean on a fire support base doing routine patrols or actually in the jungle on an operation?"

"I mean how long without regular food, regular sleep, safety, baths, *vitamins* . . ." The last word was a dangling question and an accusation. "I don't care what the fuck you have to do to get it, but I'm going to inspect Bravo Company's garbage cans tomorrow night, and I want them full of orange peels and apple cores."

Simpson pulled out his green notebook and wrote something down.

"Goddamn it, Simpson, put that away. If you can't remember this . . ."

"Yes sir." Simpson put the notebook back in his pocket.

Mulvaney turned from Simpson. When he spoke, he again addressed the photograph. "Simpson, I'm tired. I'm tired of being used. Killing for pay and politics is prostitution enough, but doing it this way sickens me. It sickens my soul, what's left of it." He slowly turned and pointed a thick forefinger at Simpson. "But you, you and that fucking Three of yours, you're one of the customers this time. But let me tell you something. I'll be goddamned if I'll let my troops play the customer's fucking game, even if the brass are."

Mulvaney was breathing heavily; his face was hot. He leaned over the desk. "The next time you tell me one of your companies is in good shape before I send them on an operation, by God you better not be lying. Now, get out of here. You're dismissed."

Simpson put his cap on and left, trembling.

Mulvaney swept the empty glasses from his desk with a cry of frustration. He sat down and watched the ice form puddles on the floor. Then he walked over to the picture on the wall and stood there looking at it for a long time.

Mellas arrived on the last chopper. With the others on his heli team, he shuffled along silently in a fog of fatigue. A particularly bad patch of his jungle rot was oozing pus. He wiped it on the sides of his trousers, where it mingled with the accumulations of many weeks. The trousers hung loosely from his waist. He'd lost twenty-five pounds. He was a bush Marine. He and his team walked as if they owned the LZ, but they were unaware of it. Mellas felt as though he was getting sick.

They arrived at the supply tent. Small groups of kids from the other platoons were lying out in the front on the wet clay, drinking beer. Mellas pushed aside the heavy canvas tent flap and walked in. Fitch, Hawke, Cassidy, and Kendall were there, along with a new second lieutenant. The new lieutenant looked up at Mellas and smiled, eager to please. Mellas, tired, ragged, hair touching his collar, did not smile back.

"Lieutenant," Cassidy said, "you look like you could use a beer." He reached underneath the table and pulled out a rusty can of Black Label. "Sorry it's just Black Mabel, but the good stuff gets picked off in Da Nang." He punched two triangular holes in the top and handed the beer to Mellas. Mellas took a long pull. The beer was warm, but it had the taste of good memories. He felt the stinging carbonation as it went down his throat. He chugged the entire can and sighed. "Thanks, Gunny." Cassidy was already opening another can for him.

Fitch was looking quite dapper again. His hair was cut and parted neatly on the side and he wore clean jungle utilities. Hawke looked clean, but it wasn't in him to look dapper. Mellas noticed that he was wearing a first lieutenant's bars.

"I'd like you to meet Paul Fracasso," Fitch said quickly. Mellas nodded at the new lieutenant, who was still beefed up from the Basic School and was wearing Marine-issue glasses. Mellas saw Fitch glance at Hawke. Suddenly he knew. They were going to give his platoon to this guy. Hawke was being transferred. He didn't say anything. It was what he had wanted. He'd even planted the seed with Blakely that day on Matterhorn. Now that his seed had grown to fruition, he was heartsick. He had no idea it would make him feel what he was feeling.

"Where's Scar?" Mellas asked, dropping his pack onto the floor.

"Back in Quang Tri to get the company pay," Hawke said.

"Oh, yeah. I almost forgot we get paid for this." Mellas took another long pull on the beer, finishing it. "Well, come on, get it over with." He knew it was unfair of him, but he resented the newcomer like hell.

"Right," Fitch said, tight-lipped. "Uh, Fracasso here will take over your platoon. You're now the company executive officer, Bravo Five. I thought you'd work out better than Goodwin."

"Great. Thanks." Mellas sat down on an ammunition crate and accepted another can of beer from Cassidy.

"Where you going, Hawke?" he asked.

"Three Zulu."

"Nice," Mellas said. He took another long drink. That meant Hawke would be working for Blakely as a staff officer in battalion operations. Blakely was no fool, that was certain. "Congratulations on your promotion, too."

"I've done my fucking time in the bush." Hawke sounded a little peeved.

"Didn't say you hadn't, Ted." Mellas drained the beer. Cassidy handed him another one, a slight twinkle in his eye. "Thanks, Gunny," Mellas said.

"Go on," Hawke said to Fitch. "You'd better tell the rest before he's fucking incoherent."

"The rest?"

"We've been assigned Bald Eagle–Sparrow Hawk," Fitch said.

"Is that like fucking Batman and Robin?"

Fitch smiled, watching Mellas take another long drink. "It's the code name for a company of Marines that stands by the airstrip. If someone gets in the shit, they drop us in to 'exploit' the situation."

"You can't be serious," Mellas said very softly.

The look on Fitch's face said that he was.

Mellas's teeth were clenched so tightly he thought he'd break them. "My fucking men can't walk," he said. "*I* can't fucking walk." He stood up and kicked his pack in frustration. The floor reeled beneath him.

There was the sound of another beer being opened, and Cassidy slid the can over the table to where Mellas was standing.

"Have another beer, Lieutenant. It'll take the edge off."

Mellas looked at the beer, watching the foam slowly ooze onto the tabletop. He felt so tired. "The men getting plenty of beer?" he asked.

"Sure," Hawke answered. "You can thank Gunny Cassidy. He bought a bunch of cases for each squad with his own money."

Mellas was touched by the gesture. "Thanks, Gunny," he said.

Cassidy grunted. "Can't have the kids without beer. If you're old enough to kill a man you ought to be old enough to drink."

Mellas slugged down the can. "How long before we get off fucking Bald Eagle?"

Fitch shrugged. "No telling. Until the regiment needs us someplace else or they drop us into the shit. The colonel thought it would give us a rest."

Mellas wanted to ask Fitch how sitting at the edge of an LZ waiting for some fat-ass to push a magic button and dump the company in the middle of a shit sandwich would be considered a rest. But he decided not to bother. What he wanted, more than anything else, was a shower. "Any clean clothes here?" he asked. Cassidy pointed to a number of open boxes stacked against the tent walls. The tent wobbled uncertainly around Mellas as he walked toward the clothing.

"Floor a little slippery, Lieutenant?" Cassidy asked slyly.

"You got me fucking drunk, didn't you," Mellas said. It took him a moment to locate Cassidy. "I'll be fucked." He took off his old clothes, not bothering to remove his boots. He looked a moment at his green underpants and threw them into the garbage along with the beer cans. For a moment he stood naked in front of everyone, with just his dog tags hanging on his sallow skin. He was struck by how vulnerable his body was.

Cassidy tossed him a new set of jungle utilities. They felt stiff, heavy, and the camouflage looked oddly bright compared with the set on the floor at his feet. He pulled on the trousers without bothering with underwear. He marveled at how thin his waist had gotten, how his ribs showed.

"Oh, and Mellas," said Fitch, "we need a man from First Platoon to stand KP next two weeks."

"Thank God," Mellas said. "You can have Shortround before he gets someone killed." He turned to Fracasso. "Come on Fricassee, or whatever your fucking wop name is, I'll introduce you to your platoon."

Simpson's hands were still shaking as he poured another glass of bourbon and told Blakely what had happened. Blakely laughed derisively. "Of course he told you it was off the record. He's not going to risk that star. Not now. Him and his fucking lost platoon from World War II. Look at the numbers, Colonel. We've got the highest men-in-the-field to men-in-the-rear ratio in the division. We're top in the battalion on man-days per month actively involved in combat operations. Our congressional inquiry rate is right next to zero. Our kill ratio's been climbing ever since I've come aboard. And don't think the right people at division and Third Amphibious Force don't know it." Blakely laughed again. "If he wrote up a bad fitness report on you, we'd take the stats and blow him right into retirement."

Simpson smiled tightly. "I guess I shouldn't be such a worrywart."

"You worry about the numbers. That's what the people who matter worry about. Mulvaney's an anachronism. Apples and oranges. Shit."

They both started laughing.

Mellas, wearing new jungle utilities, the creases still showing, led Fracasso to a flat stretch of mud that surrounded a single tent designed to sleep ten people. There were two other tents of the same size, each taken by the other two platoons. That left more than 100 unfortunates with less rank and seniority out in the rain. Some had rigged hooches as if they were still in the bush. Others simply threw down their packs, flak jackets, and weapons, claimed a small patch of wet clay for their own, and started drinking. Mellas knew that most of them would be too drunk or stoned to rig hooches and would sleep in the rain. At least drunk or stoned they'd get a full night of sleep.

Mellas walked over to Hamilton, Skosh, Fredrickson, and Bass. He introduced Fracasso and told them that he himself was moving up to XO to replace Hawke. Bass took it with the aplomb of the professional—another boot lieutenant to train. Mellas knew the squad leaders would take it less well. They didn't appreciate the Marine Corps' need to ensure that the higher ranks were filled with combat-trained officers. Once they had one broken in, they'd rather keep him.

Mellas shouted "Squad leaders up!" and the kids, some lying on their backs and already well on their way, relayed the call happily toward the gray sky.

Jancowitz was the first to arrive. "I hear you're leaving us, Lieutenant," he said.

"Yeah."

"Well." Jancowitz hesitated. "Congratulations on the promotion."

"It's no promotion, Janc. I'm still drawing the same pay. I suppose I'll get a few more coffee breaks when we're humping, but I'll still be humping with you guys."

"That'd be decent, sir."

Mellas felt like a turd. But this was his chance to move up. To be the executive officer this early in his tour gave him ample time to get a company.

Connolly came up to them, slightly bleary-eyed, a can of beer in his hand. "What's the new lieutenant like?" he almost demanded.

Mellas thought a moment. He could screw the guy right here by saying the wrong thing. He'd noticed the Naval Academy ring on Fracasso's finger—a lifer if he ever saw one. Jacobs arrived, just behind Connolly, with a silly grin on his face. Mellas just hoped Jacobs had enough sense not to smoke where he'd be caught. It would mean brig time and an automatic dishonorable discharge.

"Feeling pretty good, Jake?" Mellas asked, suppressing the little smile that crept around the corners of his mouth.

Jacobs immediately came down a little. "P-pretty good sir."

Mellas smiled at Jacobs's serious expression. "Now that I've got the power, if any of you jokers lose someone to the brig because they get caught smoking dope, I'll fuck your R & R quota and send you to Okinawa with all the lifers."

The group laughed.

"What's the new lieutenant like?" Connolly asked again.

Mellas scuffed the mud with his boot. "I think you guys have drawn a lifer. But I think he's going to be a good one."

"A fucking lifer, huh?" Connolly said. They all turned to look at the new lieutenant, who was talking eagerly with Bass. Bass and Fracasso saw them and walked over. Mellas knew that the next five seconds were among the most important Fracasso would ever live. They could certainly mean his career, and maybe even his life. In the next five seconds these three teenagers would decide if they'd work with him or not.

Fracasso was clearly nervous. The three squad leaders stared at him without any sign of welcome.

Mellas cleared his throat. "Well, I guess I ought to make a flowery farewell speech, but I'll be humping along with Bass in the rear of this sorry bunch of assholes every third day, so I guess maybe I won't." Mellas was surprised at his lack of articulation. "I, uh, I'll miss you guys." He couldn't look at them. "This is Lieutenant Fracasso. He'll be taking over."

Mellas pointed to each of the squad leaders and made introductions.

"Sorry to see you here, sir," Connolly said. "I'm already in the double digits before I get my ass out of here. I'm so short I need to stand on a helmet to take a piss."

Fracasso seemed momentarily taken aback, but he put his hand out to shake Connolly's. "*You're* sorry. Jesus. I've got over a year."

Connolly, followed by Jancowitz and Jacobs, shook hands. Fracasso had passed the test. It felt good to Mellas. He'd expected to be jealous. The platoon would be OK. He hadn't realized how he'd come to like these guys.

"One last thing before I go and Fracasso's stuck with you for good. Every man gets a fucking shower. There's a water point down by the river. You squad leaders make sure everyone gets there before you're all too fucked up and drown yourselves."

*　*　*

Two hours later Mellas was sitting in the mud, another warm beer in his hand. His body felt strangely light since he'd showered. It was his first shower since coming to Vietnam. The slight drizzle that was falling felt cool and refreshing on his face. He seemed to feel each individual drop of water.

It was dark, but all around him he saw vague shadows getting up from small circles of friends to walk away and take a piss. Then a figure would return—stumbling across one circle or another, finding its own—and sink down again into the small mass of dark shadows. Mellas thought it must have been like this with Genghis Khan and Alexander.

Mellas could have joined the other officers and staff members in the supply tent but felt a desire to linger with the platoon. He felt a new camaraderie with these kids. He knew it was sentimental, even mawkish, and he tried not to succumb to the loss he felt at moving a step up in the hierarchy.

His head ached badly, and he continually had to walk off into the bush to crap. Still, he was exceedingly happy. It was safe here. He hoped he wasn't coming down with dysentery. His new jungle utilities were already damp and muddy in the seat and knees and also slightly fouled from one of his trips into the bushes. He didn't care. If they launched the Bald Eagle the next day he could be dead. He kept pouring down beer.

With everyone getting shit-faced, China figured it was a good time to deliver the goods to Henry to be shipped back to Oakland or Los Angeles. The heavy seabag on his shoulder was awkward and its contents jabbed against his back and side. He was sweating heavily within two minutes of leaving the little airfield where Bravo Company was bivouacked. When he pushed in past the heavy canvas flaps that formed the door to Henry's four-man tent, he smelled mothballs still lingering in the material. He let the seabag down a little more quickly than he would have liked, and there was a metallic clunk as it hit the plywood floor. Henry was lying on his rack looking at a fuck book. He saw China and, after hesitating for just a moment, broke into a grin and got up and went through the hand dance. Two of Henry's friends were also there, and they did the same. It was good to be back with the brothers.

Henry found a warm beer and punched two holes in it with an opener. He raised it in a mock toast and upended it, chugging the contents in about five seconds. Then he sat down on his rack, reached under the rubber lady, and pulled out a small pouch of marijuana with some cigarettes already rolled. He lit one, took a long toke, and handed it to China.

"I don't do that shit," China said. He wasn't altogether sure it had been a friendly gesture. He'd talked with Henry before about black people enslaving themselves to drugs. Henry *knew* he didn't do that shit.

"Ah, shit, man. When you gonna get with the program, huh? This shit be just good fun. It don't hurt nobody."

"Yeah, OK. You go ahead then."

Henry passed the joint to one of his hooch mates and pulled up another can of beer, opened it, and handed it to China. China put his hands on his hips, looking down. Then he looked up at Henry. "You know I don't do that shit either."

Henry raised his eyebrows and looked over at the others. He held the can out from him, pulling his head back, and pretended to study it carefully. "What I got here, China? Devil in a can?"

China hesitated a moment. He really wanted that beer, but he knew that the Muslim brothers didn't drink. Then again, they weren't getting their asses shot off in a hot fucking jungle. He also knew that he'd have to stand up to his stated ideals. "Hey, Henry, you got a soda or somethin'?" he asked, trying to be casual.

Henry chugged the second can of beer, then walked over to the end of his bunk and pulled out a whole case of Coca-Cola. He levered open a can and handed it to China, grinning. "I got *ever*thing, brother."

China took it and sat down on the rack facing Henry, the heavy seabag on the floor between his feet. He drank the warm Coke. It tasted like summer back home. The joint got smoked down to where it was too hot to handle and one of Henry's friends put it in a silver roach clip. Henry had the last full pull before there was nothing left.

There was small talk, catching up, what brother made it home, what brother didn't. Then Henry fixed on China's eyes, a signal. "Parker really try and frag that racist bastard?"

China hesitated. "I think so."

Henry snorted. "Too bad he fucked up."

There were nods and murmurs of agreement.

China wasn't seeing the scene in the tent; he was seeing Parker being carried out of the perimeter in the dark, face bathed in sweat, fear in his eyes. He had tapped knuckles and given Parker a reassuring handgrip. That was the last he would ever see of Parker. He came back to the present. "I think the gunny must have spotted somethin'. He says it's all bullshit."

"Bull*shit* to that."

"Yeah." China didn't know what to do with his empty can. "Yeah, bullshit to that." He reached down to the seabag and unclipped the shoulder strap that also secured it's opening. "But I got somethin' here ain't no bullshit." He pulled out the barrel of an M-60 machine gun. Then he pulled out the back end, assembled it quickly, and handed it to the brother next to him. Then he pulled out an AK-47 and did the same thing. Then he pulled out a .45 pistol and handed it to Henry. Then he pulled out a second AK. He smiled. "For the brothers back home."

Henry pulled back the receiver on the .45 and looked through the barrel. His two friends were similarly fiddling with the AK-47s, which were rare in rear areas.

Henry smiled, almost sadly. "Where you get this shit, China?" he asked.

"We hit a big ammo dump. Me and some of the brothers been humpin' them in pieces ever since. I got the M-60 parts just sayin' mine worn out, little bit at a time, you know, and the .45, that's a combat loss. It was mine. I got me a new one."

Henry gave a sort of hummphh.

China looked at him. "Wha'chew mean, *hummphh?*"

Henry threw the .45 onto the end of his rack. "You think the brothers back home can't get they own firearms? Shit, man. All they need is money and they get all the fuckin' firepower they want. Don'chew remember you lived in fuckin' *Ah-mer-i-kuh,* China? We got more guns in Ah-mer-i-kuh than you mama got boyfriends she don't know they names."

China struggled to master his temper. The reference to his mother was a typical dozens insult. He wasn't about to let Henry know how close it had come to the truth. "Ever bit help, Henry."

"Sheeit." Henry stood up and walked over to a heavy, ornately carved Makassar ebony dresser he'd purchased in an illicit run to Cam Lo, a matching piece for an equally heavy and ornate trunk with which he'd replaced his standard-issue footlocker. "Besides, we don't get back to the world real soon those brothers back home have no fucking idea what to do with all that firepower. Sheeit, China. They be killin' each other over who get to be professor of Black Studies at You Cee Ell Ay. Sheeit. Killin' each other over who gonna be teacher to rich white girls and little China boys." He spun a combination padlock that secured a beautiful silver hasp to one of the drawers.

"That killin' be done by FBI undercover agents," China said.

"Sheeit, China. Get real, huh? That be nothin' but Slausens killin' Avenues." Henry pulled the drawer completely out, put it on the steel runway matting that served as the tent's floor, and started taking out clothes and other articles. Then he carefully removed a false bottom and motioned China over to look at it. There were dozens of small plastic packages, some filled with marijuana, some with blocks of hash, many with a slightly different, nearly white powder China thought might be heroin. Henry then carefully replaced the false bottom. "Wha'chew think that is, China?"

China didn't say anything.

Henry put the false bottom back and pointed a long graceful finger at it. "That be *green* power. I can turn that into so much fuckin' artillery we can start our *own* fuckin' war." He started putting the clothes and other articles back in. "You go trade them AKs to some rear-area cracker in Da Nang for some a that soda pop you like so much. Sheeit, China." Henry's friends broke into chuckles. One of them reached into a side pocket in his trousers and pulled up a wad of military payment currency, waved it just slightly while smiling at China, and then stuffed it back into the pocket.

China felt betrayed and foolish. He saw the amused eyes of Henry's friends looking at him. Henry had his head cocked slightly sideways and upward, looking at him. China held his gaze. "That shit be bad for the brothers, Henry. Malcolm X say to lay off that shit. The Panthers say to lay off that shit."

"Who says I be sellin' this shit to the brothers?"

"You don't tell me you just sellin' it to chucks."

"Naw. Maybe I ain't. So what?"

"That shit be bad."

"So we fuck up some white boys with it. People buy this shit be nothin' but dumb fuckin' animals anyway."

"That's what the mob say about sellin' shit to the black man."

"So now we gettin' even."

China set his lips tight. "You givin' all the money to the brothers back home?"

"Wha'chew think?" Henry's tone was edgy.

China didn't answer. If Henry was, he'd say yes, and if he wasn't, he'd still say yes. China knew when to drop something that needed dropping.

He looked down at the weapons, wondering what to do with them. Henry stepped in and rescued him. "Hey, man. It cool. It all cool. You just leave that shit with us and next time one'a the brothers get back to Da Nang we trade it for some good stuff with the Navy and Air Force boys and keep what we get for you next time you out of the bush. You done good, brother. You tryin'."

Henry's patronizing tone increased the humiliation. China put on a cool exterior. "Yeah. OK. I got to get back before I get missed too much." He turned to Henry's friends and went through the hand dance. "You brothers stay cool, OK?"

"Yeah. We be cool. You too, man."

China slipped out of the tent into the warm dark. He knew that in many ways he had experienced a serious defeat, and not just his own.

"You a lifer, Lieutenant Fracasso?" Jancowitz asked blearily. It was now well past midnight and the drinking had been going on for hours.

Fracasso seemed uncomfortable. Getting drunk with the men the first night wasn't how he had expected to take over command as a new lieutenant. "What do you think, Corporal Jancowitz?" he replied.

"Shit, Lieutenant. I don't know. Call me Janc." Jancowitz paused a little and Mellas could almost see the thoughts muddling around in his head the way he was muddling the beer around in the can.

"I really like the Marine Corps," Fracasso answered carefully. "Right now I think I'll be staying in."

"Goddamn, sir," Bass hooted. "It's about fucking time we got a lieutenant with some sense." Bass hiccupped at just the right moment to make them all laugh.

"Some lifers are OK," Jancowitz said with finality, "and some ain't."

"There it is," said Fredrickson. "I'll drink to that."

"Fuckin' A right you will, you squid asshole," Jancowitz returned.

"I said I would and I will, you jarhead asshole."

"And I said that's fuckin' A right. Aw, you're a good fucking squid." Jancowitz turned, smiled at everyone, and fell over backward, out cold.

"You see, sir?" Bass said. "No fucking staying power like us lifers."

"I guess not, Sergeant Bass," Fracasso said. He smiled awkwardly.

They sat in beery silence for a moment. Then the silence was broken by an animal-like scream.

"Fuckin' white-ass narco bastard. I'll kill him. I'll kill him!"

One of the groups in front of the large tent erupted in violent movement. Fracasso was instantly running to the fight. Mellas was so sick and weary he barely could get to his feet, but he lurched after Fracasso.

When Mellas got there a new guy was lying flat on his back, his face bleeding badly. Mellas saw the broken stubs of his two front teeth. Standing over him and breathing very hard was China. He had an E-tool in his hand.

"Don't you get enough fucking fighting, China?" Jacobs screamed. He came hurtling across the small circle at China and they both went down to the ground.

"He got a knife, brother. He got a fucking knife."

Mellas broke through the crowd and jumped on Jacobs as hard as he could. He saw Cortell, his high forehead glistening, come in for China and tackle him. Without any sign, both Marines stopped struggling.

"Anybody bleeding?" Mellas was breathing hard.

"Aw, shit, sir," Jacobs said, "I ain't got a fucking knife." He opened his hand, pinned to his side by Mellas. It showed a muddy harmonica. Several people laughed.

"First time I ever heard of assault with a deadly mouth harp," Mellas said. "You two OK now?"

"Yeah," China muttered.

"He didn't have to hit him with the fucking E-tool," Jacobs said.

"Fuckin' CID," said China. He meant the criminal investigation division. "Fuckin' cunt don't deserve to be alive."

Mellas stood and helped Jacobs to his feet.

"How do you know he was from CID?" Mellas asked China, ignoring the moans of the man on the ground. Cortell still had his hands on China's arm.

"He's a narc. You can smell the fuckers."

"He ask you for some dope or something?" Mellas asked.

"Yeah. He ask me for dope."

"Maybe he just wanted some. Did you ever think of that?"

"Why he ask *me*, huh? Why he ask *me*? A fuckin' chuck askin' a splib for dope. Shit, man. I don't even do that shit."

Mellas looked at the figure on the ground and bent down toward him. Fredrickson was already pushing in with his kit to start patching the guy up. If he went to the battalion aid station there'd be shit to pay and the company would lose both China and Jacobs. They were both too good to let go.

"Hey," Fredrickson said to the man on the ground. "What's your name, huh? You hear me?"

The man groaned a name.

"You in Bravo Company?" Mellas asked.

The man nodded.

"Were you asking about dope?"

The man shook his head.

"He's fuckin' lying, Lieutenant," China cried. The man gave a hoarse scream and went for China, but both Fredrickson and Mellas held him down. China had the E-tool positioned for a perfect butt stroke, sharp end toward the man. It probably would have killed him.

"You're a fucking fool," Mellas said quietly to the man on the ground. He heard Bass clearing the Marines out, sending them away from the fight. He turned to Jacobs and China. "I'll see you two tomorrow about this. Now go sleep it off."

Fracasso was standing there with his mouth wide open.

"Hey, Fracasso, don't worry about it," Mellas said. "They're just letting off steam."

He looked at the man on the ground. He had no idea whether the man was CID or not, but one thing was certain: he couldn't stay in the company. "Hey, look, whatever your name is, I'm going to transfer you out of the company. We can get it done, don't worry. You just keep quiet and this fight will never get on your record, all right?"

"I don't make deals," the man said, spitting out blood.

Bass shouted, "What?" He jumped on top of him. "You don't say fucking things like that to the lieutenant, you understand?" He started beating the man's head against the ground, rattling his body with his short solid forearms. "You fucking understand?" The man couldn't answer, because his head was being pounded into the ground.

Finally Bass stopped and started talking very quietly and very quickly, straddling his chest. "The lieutenant here just offered you two things. Your next promotion, if you want one, and your fucking life, because believe me, you fucking sneaky CID asshole, you'd last about one fucking hour on an operation if you don't make a deal."

"OK," the man croaked.

They took him to the supply tent, where Fitch was wearily catching up on paperwork by the light of a single candle. Fitch sent him back to the rear with a letter to Top Seavers the next morning, and that was the last they ever heard of him. Bass punished both Jacobs and China by taking them out of their place in line for KP duty.

* * *

The next day the company moved to a cluster of drooping tents that bordered a secondary landing strip. On the other side of the strip a stream meandered through a broad valley. Vandegrift Combat Base sat in the middle of that valley, between jungled ridges to its east and west. Across the stream on a small hill stood the bunkers and radio antennae of Task Force Oscar. No one in the company knew what Task Force Oscar did. The Marines could hear the sound of the generator that ran the air-conditioning and electric lights. Occasionally an Army helicopter would arrive and a high-ranking Army officer would be met by someone in a jeep to be carried 200 meters to the air-conditioned bunker or the small officers' club next to it. Civilians, looking overweight and out of place in Army fatigues without any insignia, came as well; they were probably from AID and the CIA, or journalists afraid to go out in the bush.

Upstream from Task Force Oscar was a contingent of South Vietnamese troops who apparently also did nothing. The Marines watched them with unconcealed hostility, hating them for sitting around while others died fighting their battles, hating them because their very existence served as part of the lie that had brought American troops to Vietnam in the first place. It was easier to hate a visible part of the lie than it was to hate the liars, who, after all, were their own countrymen: the fat American civilians and rear-area rangers who flitted back and forth with briefcases, sweaty faces, and shiny unused pistols. But the Marines hated them too. Some Marines hated the North Vietnamese Army and some didn't, but at least the NVA had the Marines' respect.

Caught up in the work of getting the tents into shape and cleaning out trenches, the Marines of the company could forget momentarily that they were waiting to be dropped into combat. But whenever a jeep came around the curve of the road a little faster than normal, or a helicopter rushed over their heads, fear and apprehension would return.

Mellas took the opportunity provided by his new position to ask if he could accompany Fitch to the next battalion briefing. Fitch agreed. The next morning the two of them entered the large tent that also served as a chapel and sat down on folding chairs. Hawke joined them. He had shaved off his mustache, and the sight almost made Mellas wince. It was a clear sign that Hawke was knuckling under to the rear-area chickenshit. Hawke was also wearing shiny new boots. Mellas whistled and pointed at them. Hawke flipped him the bird.

Major Blakely entered the tent and called everyone to attention. The colonel followed, striding briskly, nodding to Blakely to begin the meeting. Everyone sat down. Mellas looked sideways at Hawke, conveying the disgust he felt at the formal structure of rank and privilege. Hawke chose not to notice.

Blakely stood with his back to the rough wooden altar and announced the disposition of the companies. Then the staff NCOs began to read out their reports. Some of them seemed nearly illiterate, but others were highly efficient and professional, making suggestions that Mellas could see were crucial to the operation of the battalion rear. Father Riordan, the Navy chaplain, got up and announced the coming services for the various faiths, trying to be one of the boys.

At his appointed time, Sergeant Major Knapp rose, his slightly rounded body encased in starched jungle utilities, and began his part of the briefing. "Gentlemen, staff NCOs," he said. "With the entire battalion moving in, the battalion commander feels, and I agree, that we have to be extra careful about our standards of appearance. I expect the staff NCOs to have every man looking like A. J. Squaredaway. We've particularly noticed the proliferation of beads, emblems, hangmen's nooses, and mustaches." Knapp looked directly at Fitch and Mellas. "Mustaches are a privilege for E-5s or higher. They are to be closely clipped and not extended beyond the outer edge of the upper lip. Now I know we don't have as many E-5s as we do mustaches"—he chuckled good-humoredly—"so let's get that kind of crap cleaned up. I'll be talking directly to all the staff NCOs as the companies come in." Knapp smiled, turned to Blakely, and smiled again. "That's all I have today, sir."

"Thank you, Sergeant Major," Blakely said. Blakely turned to Simpson. "It's yours, sir."

Simpson nodded and walked up to the pulpit to address his command. His sleeves were rolled neatly, and his silver leaves shone on his collar next to the wrinkled red skin of his neck. He reminded Mellas of an irritable gnome. A rednecked gnome with a redneck Georgia accent, trying to act like gentry.

"Gentlemen, staff NCOs," he began. "First Battalion's going to get a goddamned chance to breathe. Then we'll be pushing off on the next operation. I can't tell you what that operation will be, but rest assured we'll be out in the bush either as individual companies, performing our constant task of hitting the enemy, interdicting his supply routes, uncovering his hospitals and ammunition caches, or"—he paused significantly —"we shall be working as we should, one entire massed battalion, kicking the hell out of Charlie in a major strike against his north-south supply lines." He paused to look at his men. Mellas was slumped in his chair, picking at some jungle rot on his hand. Fitch was writing something in his notebook. Hawke stared vacantly ahead.

"Gentlemen," Simpson continued, "we are under the happy circumstances that by tomorrow evening the entire battalion, less one platoon guarding the Khe Gia Bridge, shall be here in Vandegrift Combat Base. I have decided it is a splendid opportunity to hold a formal mess night, a gathering of the officers of the battalion in an evening of fellowship and camaraderie. The mess night will go at eighteen-hundred hours, with cocktails in my quarters, to adjourn to the officers' mess at nineteen-hundred for a meal that I am sure Master Sergeant Hansen will have prepared to be fit for a king. I expect everyone to look their best."

There was silence in the tent. People smiled nervously. The staff sergeants, who weren't invited, looked the most uncomfortable. Mellas turned to look at Hawke and conspicuously opened his mouth to mime shocked surprise. Hawke ignored him.

Major Blakely stood up. "I'm sure the officers who will be coming in from the bush, and of course all of us here, are going to be looking forward to Thursday night. I don't know if the younger officers are aware of it or not, but the tradition of mess night is one that goes back in time to our predecessors, the Royal Marines. To get a chance to do it while experiencing the intensity of combat is something that none of us will ever forget."

"He can say that again," Mellas whispered, looking straight ahead. He expected some reply from Hawke but got none. Hawke had taken out his notebook and was writing in it, an intent expression on his face.

After the meeting broke up Mellas stopped Hawke just outside the tent. "What the hell happened to your stache?" he asked.

"It fell off. What the fuck you think happened to it?"

"You didn't have to shave your fucking sense of humor off with it."

"Look, Mellas, the fucking Three and the colonel are on a big thing about beads, mustaches, hippy hairdos, and *hangman nooses*, so everyone in battalion had to shave. I'm in the battalion. Remember?"

Mellas's anger at the colonel flashed to the surface. "What's the fucking point? It's one small thing these guys can do that gives them some kind of pride, and these rear-area chickenshit fucks just take it away from them."

"Look, smart guy," Hawke said, "you push the colonel and the Three too hard and you're going to get into trouble. They're already just about as pissed as they can get."

"What they got to be pissed about?"

"Simpson went on record—more than once—about Bravo Company's objectives. He had to eat crow every time, in front of half the officers in the regiment, because of Bravo Company."

"He's the one that laid on the asinine fucking demands."

"That's beside the point, and you're smart enough to know it. The point is the colonel's been passed over for bird colonel once already. This battalion is his last fucking chance. If he doesn't make it, it'll be Bravo Company's fault. The Three is just a younger, smarter version of Simpson, and he isn't above making a few sacrifices to further his career either. And I don't mean personal sacrifices."

"So they're all playing politics. Nothing new to me."

"No, by God, I'll bet it isn't."

The two of them stood there facing off.

"I'm trying to tell you, don't fuck around with the guy," Hawke said. "First Battalion isn't high on Mulvaney's list right now, and Simpson thinks Bravo Company's the reason. You guys are going to make or break his career as far as he's concerned."

"Fuck him. I'll do anything in my power to keep that cocksucker from getting promoted." Mellas started to walk away.

Hawke grabbed him by the shoulder and spun him around. "You listen to me, you hotshot Ivy League piece of shit. I don't give a goddamn what you do to yourself, but you're not going to fuck up the kids in this company. Those are my fucking guys and I'll be goddamned if you or anyone else is going to fuck them up because of some personal vendetta. I don't give a shit how justified you think it is. I've walked a fuckload more shitty operations under that guy than you have." Hawke was breathing hard. "You just get one thing straight, Mr. Politician: the colonel controls the helicopters."

Hawke released Mellas's shirt. His hands were shaking. Mellas backed away, frightened. They stood there looking at each other, breathing hard. Mellas realized how close they'd come to a real fight, how he'd developed a hair-trigger temper. He could see that Hawke felt bad, too. Mellas wanted to reach out and touch him, say he'd been an ass. He couldn't bear the thought of Hawke not being his friend any more. The reference to his education and aspirations was especially hurtful. "I'll talk to Jim," Mellas said. "We'll clean up. I didn't mean to be an asshole about it."

Hawke was looking at the hills, not at Mellas. He fumbled in his shirt pocket. "I can't find a cigar," he said.

"It's good you can't find it," Mellas said. "You want to get your ass out of here and die of cancer a few years later?"

"You believe that bullshit?" Hawk asked.

"Uh-huh."

They looked at each other, both aware they were talking about death. Then Hawke spoke quietly. "I'm an asshole myself sometimes. The colonel's not the only one who's ambitious. Sure, I wanted Bravo Company when Jim got it. I had more time in the bush, and Jim made mistakes I'd already made and paid for, and I had to watch it happen all over again." His eyes went blank. Mellas sensed that he was replaying some terrible scene. Hawke snapped back. "I don't want it to happen again. You know what that means? What I have to do to play the game?"

Mellas nodded. "Ted, I don't want the company. I just want out of the bush."

"Let's at least not lie to each other," Hawke said.

"OK," Mellas said softly, "I want it too." Then he quickly added, "But I'd gladly hump under you, Hawke. Really. I don't want it that bad."

"I didn't think I did either."

There was an uncomfortable silence. "I got to get back," Mellas said finally.

"Sure."

Mellas walked away, dejected. He wanted Hawke's friendship in the worst way.

"Hey, Mel," Hawke called. Mellas, his hands in his back pockets, turned to face Hawke. "McCarthy and Murphy are both going to be in from the bush. You know the platoon commander who had the dead guy when we flip-flopped with Alpha and Charlie?"

"Yeah?"

"That's McCarthy. Murphy's the big guy who was on the LZ." Mellas looked a little puzzled.

"With the tic."

Mellas nodded.

"That's the mystery tour team. You want to come along? I'll sponsor you."

"Sure," Mellas said. "But what the hell's a mystery tour?"

"It's a fucking *drunk*, Mellas."

Mellas smiled sheepishly. "What time?"

When Mellas reached the company, he was greeted with more than a few sarcastic jeers.

"Lieutenant, you gonna send home for your dress blues for tomorrow night?"

"You officers getting your nails buffed so you don't fuck up the silverware?"

"They gonna start issuing tablecloths with the C-rats, Lieutenant?"

Mellas had to take the ribbing, and he knew it. Mess night was a dumb fucking idea. He went over to his rubber lady and lay down with a dog-eared copy of James Michener's *The Source*, for which he'd traded two Louis L'Amour shit-kickers. He tried to lose himself in ancient Israel.

He was interrupted by China. "Hey, sir, can we talk to you?" A tall black Marine stood behind China at the opening of the tent.

Mellas motioned them in. "What's on your mind?" he asked.

"Uh, sir," China said, pointing to his friend, "this is Lance Corporal Walker. We call him Henry. He's from H & S Company."

"Hello, Walker." Mellas held out his hand and they shook.

"We got ourselves a little sort of club," China went on. "We get together ever once in a while. Play some sounds. You know."

"Sounds nice," Mellas said, trying to be casual. He was beginning to feel uneasy, particularly with Walker, who scared him. He decided to be direct. "Cassidy said you had some sort of black power group you were involved in. Is that what he means?"

They both laughed. "Cassidy." China spat the name out. "That fuckin' redneck cracker don't know shit from Shinola. Black power. Sheeit. That's a word for a political movement and that's what it mean. Cassidy just a fuckin' bigot."

There was silence. Mellas wondered if he should tell them he used to be a member of SNCC, the Student Nonviolent Coordinating Committee, which organized students to go to the South for voter registration when he was a freshman at Princeton. That was before Stokely Carmichael threw the whites out and Mellas found other things to do with his time, like driving to Bryn Mawr.

China broke the silence. "We just got this club is all. It ain't no fuckin' black power harum-scarum. We got enough fuckin' violence round here. Besides, black power ain't about violence. It be about black people gettin' political and economic power. It be about self-*image* and *leadership* and gettin' the law to treat us the same as whites. That sound scary to you, sir?"

"Sounds like a good enough thing to me," Mellas said. He wished China would come to the point but was afraid to push him.

"Yeah, sir. It is a good thing. See, Henry here and me, we sort of run the meetins an' make the policy, you know?" China's husky voice seemed to hide his inner detachment. Mellas could see a twinkle of merriment in his eyes, as if there were another China sitting back from the conversation, watching the three of them and laughing his ass off. "Well, sir," China added, "we want to try and smooth out some of the differences between blacks and whites right here in our own area. You see, sir, we get a lot of literature from the brothers back home, and a lot of the stuff is hard stuff, man. *Hard* stuff. I mean they are advocatin' *violence*."

"I know," Mellas said. "I've seen some of it."

"Well, sir," Henry said, "some of the brothers they've had it right up to where they can't take no more. You know what I mean? Right up to they fuckin' throats." Henry's anger began to show slightly.

"So Walker and I was talkin' last night," China broke in, "that maybe we ought to do somethin' about it, so's we'd keep some of the brothers . . ." He paused. "Well, so we could stop somethin' like fraggin' from happening."

Mellas's eyes darted from one face to the other, looking for a clue to help him. It had never happened to him before, but he knew the protection racket when he saw it. He decided to play dumb. "You think someone's going to get fragged?"

"Us?" Henry said. "Naw. Not us. But then again that *might* happen. You take a guy like Parker, you know, the one they humped to death and wouldn't medevac. You remember him, Lieu*ten*ant?"

Mellas swallowed, wishing someone would return from chow to break up the situation. "Parker's death was an accident. No one knew what he had. We tried to get him out as soon as we could."

"As soon as a *white* boy got sick," China said. "And *white* boy, he gets out."

"I don't want to hear any more about it, China." Mellas said. "Challand barely lived himself, and it had nothing to do with his color. I don't want to hear anything more about it. I had to watch Parker die."

"What China mean, sir," Walker said, "is we on the edge of things around here. And lots of these guys maybe ain't so smart. And if they get fucked with enough, they liable do somethin' that gets themselves into trouble."

China said, "I mean, if it's OK to grease a fuckin' gook that don't fuck wit'chew at all, then why not waste some fuckin' bigot that be fuckin' wit'chew ever day of you life? That's fuckin' common sense."

"That's murder," Mellas said.

"Murder," China said. "Sheeit. We all a bunch of murderers. What difference it make if you kill a yellow man or a white bigot? You explain it to me, Lieutenant. You went to college."

"I don't see what all this has to do with me," Mellas said.

"We want to smooth things out before they get too tough," Henry said with an easy smile. "Maybe we can stop somethin' from happenin'."

"Go on," Mellas said.

"China here was tellin' me that some a the brothers have a thing out for Cassidy. Maybe some of them might lose they tempers and do somethin' that'd get 'em in trouble. We want to avoid trouble is all."

Mellas glanced quickly at the tent opening and waited for Henry to continue. Neither Henry nor China said any more. "Well, that's part of my job," Mellas finally said. "Avoiding trouble. How can I help out?"

"Nothin' special," China said. "Maybe just talk to Cassidy and tell him to ease up on harassin' the brothers. And maybe you ask him to apologize."

"Apologize?" Mellas snorted in disgust. "What the fuck chance do you think I have of getting Cassidy to apologize? And for what?"

"Try knockin' a man's teeth in with a machine-gun barrel," China said.

Henry added, "And maybe you slip someone the word about none of the brothers havin' to serve you dinner like fuckin' slaves tomorrow night."

"Look, Walker, I have nothing to do with that. I disagree with it, and I don't intend to go."

"You the one wanted to know how to help out. Avoidin' trouble. Sheeit."

"Walker, I don't have to take crap like that from you."

"That's right. You an officer and I a fuckin' snuff nigger."

"I didn't mean it that way."

"Sheeit." Henry turned to China. "What shit you feedin' me? He ain't no different than the rest of them."

Mellas's ears were burning. He looked at China.

"Reason we come to you, Lieutenant Mellas," China said, "was because we figured you'd be the only one we could talk to."

"I appreciate that, China," Mellas said. "I'll try to help. Just don't push me."

"We ain't pushin' nobody," China said. "We just trying to *explain* the situation is all." China looked over at Henry, then back at Mellas. "We on the edge, sir," he added.

"I'll see what I can do," Mellas said.

The two of them left. Mellas picked up his book but found it difficult to read. He stared at the cover, his body buzzing with the electricity of the encounter and the talk of trouble. But at the same time he was also slightly pleased. The brothers had come to him.

After chow Mellas wandered over to the sagging tent behind the combat operations center. It was already dark, and a soft drizzle was falling. He felt oddly content. Perhaps it was the beef hash he'd eaten and the steaming coffee he'd chased it down with. He tripped across several blown stumps and a couple of guy ropes before he stumbled into the tent. Hawke was alone, sitting on a cot and shining his new boots by the light of a candle. Only three of the six cots had mattresses. Hawke's old bleached boots were neatly placed beneath his cot.

"What you polishing your boots for?" Mellas asked. "You just got 'em."

"I'm getting a medal," Hawke said without looking up.

"Hey, no shit. Fanfuckingtastic. What you getting?"

"Bronze Star."

"Outfuckingstanding, Jayhawk." Mellas gave the hawk power sign and grinned. The thought of Hawke getting a medal filled him with pride.

"Yeah," Hawke said, trying to repress a smile, "I'm sort of proud of it."

"What'd you do?" Mellas asked.

"Oh, that fucking thing where I ran around in the open and called some arty in on some gook arty from Co Roc that was beating shit out of us at Lang Vei."

"I'd heard about that, actually," Mellas said.

"Really?"

"First day I got assigned to Bravo Company back in Quang Tri. The clerks were talking about it."

"No shit." Hawke let himself smile. "You know, Mel, I used to think a medal was a bunch of bullshit and I'd never really care. I was wrong. You get caught up in the little values of where you're at, I guess. So I'm proud of it. And I'm embarrassed about it. I know a lot of guys have done what I did and gotten nothing. Usually snuffs. Then there's the field grade officer who ran a mediocre supply dump in Da Nang and got the same thing." He started polishing a boot furiously.

He finally put the shined boot down and reached under the cot for his old jungle boots. He put them on, smiling grimly, then put his hands on his knees and looked at Mellas. "I'm tired of waiting for those two Irish assholes. I got six six-packs and a bottle of Jack Black. Let's get fucked up."

"OK by me," Mellas said.

"Mystery tour!" Hawke shouted at the top of his lungs and did the hawk dance. "Mystery tour!" He pulled the bottle of bourbon from his pack and poured Mellas and himself drinks in two heavy white coffee mugs. He raised his mug to Mellas's and at that moment the flap of the tent parted and the door was filled by the huge bulk of Jack Murphy. Mellas had last seen Murphy in exhausted sleep on the LZ that Bravo had flown to from Matterhorn. Behind him was McCarthy. Mellas tried to push away the image of McCarthy, shaking and asking for a cigarette, his men stumbling to join him with the body swaying between them. Then he saw Williams. Then Parker.

"Hey, hey, hey!" McCarthy pushed ahead of Murphy and he and Hawke started doing a noisy jig.

"You've both met Mellas," Hawke said, stopping to pour whiskey into two more mugs. McCarthy produced a fifth of vodka. Murphy had a half pint of Scotch and several small cans of sardines packed in olive oil, as well as a box of Ritz crackers.

An hour later they were giggling helplessly as Mellas stabbed at one of the sardine cans with Hawke's K-bar. Finally, in a rage, he started stabbing it randomly, squirting olive oil on his face and forehead.

"Fuck, Mellas, give up," McCarthy said, laughing.

After some more furious stabbing Mellas grabbed the oily can and smashed it against his forehead. "Aaahhh," he sighed as the oil ran off his chin. He sat down on the tent floor, his back against Hawke's rack, and shut his eyes.

"Goddamn it, Mellas," Hawke shouted at him, "you can't go to sleep now, we're just fucking starting." He began to slap Mellas lightly on the cheek. Mellas opened his eyes and grinned slowly. Hawke poured beer over Mellas's head. "We still got thirty-six beers to get through."

"Fuck you, Hawke. I was just resting my eyes." He looked up at the three friends. He knew he'd been let into the group.

Wonderfully, mindlessly drunk two hours later, the four lieutenants were sneaking in brief rushes up to the regimental motor pool, suppressing laughter. Hawke was leading them with hand signals learned at the Basic School, doing everything exactly to form. Their target was a half-ton truck.

"Keep your fucking ass down, Murphy," Hawke whispered.

Murphy giggled like a child.

"Fire team in the assault. Ready?" Hawke raised his arm. "Ho!" He pointed at the truck and the four of them rushed it. Mellas and Murphy piled into the back while Hawke and McCarthy scrambled into the cab and kicked over the engine. They roared off down the road toward the regimental officers' club.

Half an hour later, the movie at the small officers' club was interrupted by a wildly gesturing figure who tried to embrace the woman on the screen. The screen came down with a crash. Trying to make his escape in the dark, Murphy tripped over a power cord and pulled the projector off the table. Hawke shouted, "Retreat! Retreat! Abandon ship!" The mystery tour bolted for the door they'd staggered through twenty minutes earlier. Murphy panicked, still tangled in the electric cord. In the darkness and confusion he missed the door by two feet and took out approximately twelve square feet of fine wire insect screen.

As the four lieutenants piled into the truck, several officers shouted behind them, equally drunk. One of them pulled a pistol out and fired it into the air. He and two other dark figures jumped into a jeep and took off in pursuit.

The man with the pistol was waving it over his head, laughing and shouting, "Saboteurs! Saboteurs! Rape and pillage in the village!" He was about to fire two more rounds into the air just as the jeep bounced over a rut and the driver swerved violently to the side. The force of the turn and gravity pulled the heavy .45 down as it went off.

McCarthy, in the bed of the truck with Mellas, groaned and slumped to the floor.

Mellas immediately got sober—and very frightened. He knew they were in big trouble. He kicked in the rear window of the truck's cab and screamed at Hawke, who was driving. "McCarthy's fucking hit. We got to get him out of here."

Hawke turned to look at Mellas. The whites of his eyes were prominent. He then looked back to the road.

"McCarthy's fucking shot, I tell you."

Hawke turned the truck off the road, bouncing up a hill through low shrubs. It smashed against a blown stump, sending Murphy forward against the windshield and slamming Mellas up against the back of the cab. McCarthy came sliding forward, crumpling against Mellas.

They piled out and dragged McCarthy into the bushes, struggling uphill. The jeep roared past them down the road.

"Why you guys carrying me?" McCarthy asked suddenly.

"You ain't fucking shot?" Hawke asked.

"That fucker shot the half pint I was saving for the reentry. I got glass in my fucking ass."

They threw him to the ground, disgusted. McCarthy giggled and pushed himself uncertainly to his feet. The four of them walked through the bushes, eventually coming to a cleared piece of ground. A frightened voice shouted a challenge.

They hit the deck immediately.

"Don't shoot," Hawk called. "You'll be doing our country and the Corps a great disservice."

"I might, motherfucker," the voice shouted back. "Only I won't do my Corps fucking nothing. I'm in the Army. Come any closer and I'll blow your ass away."

"Where in the hell are we?" Mellas hollered.

"You think I'd tell you, you gook bastard?"

"Me, a gook bastard?" Mellas said to the others quietly. They were all giggling.

"Hey, Mellican sojah," Hawke called out, "me educated UCRA. You no shoot flendly countlyman. That numbah ten. You numbah one."

"You really Americans?"

"What the fuck do you think, asshole?" Hawke shouted sharply. "Is the pope Catholic? Do dogs lick their own balls?"

A pop-up flare shot out, casting eerie flickering green shadows over the landscape. The four lieutenants hugged the ground. Mellas caught a glimpse of the long barrels of an Army 175 battery that obviously ran its own security inside VCB's main defensive lines.

"Prove you're Americans," the voice called out.

"How the fuck we do that?" Hawke called back.

"Answer my questions."

"OK, but don't ask me nothing about fucking baseball. I hate fucking baseball."

"All right, where you guys from?"

McCarthy giggled. "Let me," he whispered. "East Padua," he cried out. "You know where that is?"

"East Padua? No."

Hawke cut in. "Hey, asshole, you're supposed to be asking the questions."

There was silence.

"All right, who's the secretary of the army?"

"I don't know," McCarthy replied.

"OK, then, who's the secretary of defense?"

Murphy answered, "Who the fuck cares?"

"I do," the voice answered.

"I don't know," McCarthy said.

"Who's the president then?"

"You got me beat," McCarthy answered. "I'm a gook."

"You must be fucking Marines. No one else could be so fucking stupid. Get your asses in here."

An hour later the mystery tour was at rest. McCarthy and Murphy were passed out on the exposed springs of two empty cots. McCarthy was naked from the waist down and his right buttock and thigh were swabbed red with Mercurochrome. The bullet had taken out a small piece of flesh from the right cheek. Pieces of glass lay on the floor. Murphy had performed surgery by pouring vodka on McCarthy's rear and picking the glass out with his K-bar. Mellas was heating coffee over a piece of C-4; he had thrown up and his face was pallid. The coffee was for Hawke, who needed to sober up enough to stand watch in an hour. Mellas's first mystery tour was over. It felt very good to be in.

CHAPTER
TWELVE

Morning started with the barking cough of a motor and the clank of treads as a tank headed for VCB's northern gate to escort the empty supply trucks returning to Quang Tri. Soon the grumble of truck motors vibrated through the ground to the wooden tent platform, rattling Mellas's very sore head. Pallack, who had the last radio watch, lit a ball of C-4 to heat coffee. A white-hot glare filled the tent.

Mellas cursed Pallack and pulled his poncho liner over his head. Fitch rolled onto his back and lay staring at the tent roof. The others, all completely clothed, including boots, moved stiff limbs and rolled from their air mattresses to the dirty wood floor.

"Anything happen on the nets?" Fitch asked.

"Naw," Pallack replied. "Same old stuff. Some super-grunts got in a jam up nort' of Sky Cap."

Fitch glanced quickly at Daniels, who pulled out his map. Rescuing reconnaissance teams was a primary mission of a Bald Eagle–Sparrow Hawk company. "Is that all you know about them?" Fitch asked. Mellas lay there listening under the poncho liner.

"Shit Skipper. Dey don't tell me what's happening all over I Corps. Call sign's Peachstate. Dere's a bunch of gooks all around 'em and d'ey can't move wit'out tipping the gooks off where d'ey are. Here's d'coordinates."

Fitch and Daniels checked the coordinates on the map. "Right where Mellas guessed," Fitch said.

"Maybe they'll use arty and yank them out, Skipper," Daniels said.

"Fuck," Pallack said. "Don't tell me dey're expecting *us* to get deir asses unjammed."

"What the fuck you think we're sitting here for?" Fitch said. "The artys all been pulled back for the Cam Lo op. If they get in trouble, we launch."

"Shit. If I'd a known I'd gotten scared last night."

Mellas moaned, threw back the poncho liner, and disappeared outside the tent.

"What's with him?" Fitch asked.

"He's caught Mallory's problem," Pallack said.

"Huh?"

"A bad head."

Fitch went to the COC to keep tabs on Peachstate. Around midmorning the word came down to put the company on standby. Mellas's bad head got worse. Everyone sat there. Waiting. Watching the sky. Listening for the sound of choppers. All the spare radios were tuned to the reconnaissance battalion's frequency so the company could listen to the team's progress. Cassidy passed out the hair clippers to the squad leaders.

At 1300 Peachstate made a break for it. At 1415 they were picked up by a Huey and got out with only one man wounded. By 1500 the Marines from Bravo Company were again filling sandbags at Task Force Oscar, rescuing knights one moment, serfs the next.

Mellas went to see Sergeant Major Knapp at the tent that served as the battalion office. He knocked sharply at the wood-framed opening and heard Knapp say "Come!" It was more of a command than an invitation.

Mellas entered, taking off his cap. Knapp looked up from a report and quickly rose to his feet. That embarrassed Mellas. The sergeant major was old enough to be his father.

"Yes, sir. Can I help you, sir?" Knapp asked.

"I hope so, Sergeant Major," Mellas replied. "Can I sit down?"

"Of course." They sat and Mellas toyed briefly with his cap, going over the words he'd already worked out. He waited for Knapp to say something first to break the silence, in this way putting himself at a slight power advantage by establishing an unconscious obligation on Knapp's part to make the situation agreeable. Mellas understood clearly that a second lieutenant nominally outranked but never outpowered a sergeant major. A sergeant major in the United States Marine Corps took shit from no one. This was going to be tricky.

Mellas could tell that Knapp was scrambling to remember which company he was from. Finally Knapp said, "I thought you folks were going to have to bail out that recon team. Close."

"Too close," Mellas replied. "I'd almost rather get launched right off the bat instead of standing by on that airfield." Mellas laughed casually. He'd have stayed on the airfield forever, and he knew it.

"I know what you mean, sir."

Again, Mellas waited.

"So, how can I help, sir?"

"Sergeant Major, it's about Staff Sergeant Cassidy, our company gunny."

"I can't imagine he's giving you a problem."

"Well, I don't know how to put this exactly, but I'm afraid for his life."

"How so?" The sergeant major leaned back, squinting slightly at Mellas, obviously not liking where this might lead.

"Can we treat everything I say in complete confidence?"

Sergeant Major Knapp hesitated. "As long as it's not in violation of the Uniform Code of Military Justice," he said carefully.

"OK." Mellas paused for effect. "On the last operation an attempt was made on Staff Sergeant Cassidy's life. The person involved, PFC Parker, blurted it out the morning he died of cerebral malaria. Cassidy never said a word about it. I never asked him. There is, therefore, no charge. Since the party involved is dead, I see no reason to make an inquiry. Do you?"

The sergeant major hesitated. "That might be a violation of the code."

"There would be no witnesses. No formal charge. It would only draw attention to racial unrest between one of your staff sergeants and a black PFC who died because a medevac bird was refused the day before by a battalion order."

The sergeant major jerked his head backward, almost imperceptibly. "Yes. I see what you mean."

Mellas continued. "I have it from certain sources close to radical black elements that Staff Sergeant Cassidy is still in danger."

Knapp took a deep breath through his nose, his lips compressed tightly. He exhaled. "Can I ask why, sir?"

"Staff Sergeant Cassidy isn't exactly tactful in the way he gets his job done." Mellas smiled. "Particularly with blacks."

Knapp smiled back. "I know what you mean."

"I think the best thing would be to transfer him out of the company," Mellas said. "They're asking for certain changes and an apology from Cassidy. I don't think I need to tell you the chances of that happening."

"He'd do it if he was ordered to."

"Yes," Mellas said. "And what would that mean for the authority of the rest of the staff NCOs?"

"Yes. I see."

Mellas let that sink in before going on. "Cassidy doesn't need to know anything about the transfer. It would defuse the situation. If we investigate, who knows where it will lead us?"

"And Lieutenant Fitch? What does he think of this?"

"You and I are the only ones who know. You can see what a bind that would put Fitch in, and the colonel, too, for that matter. The colonel would be obligated to start a formal investigation."

"Yes. I see, sir." Knapp drummed his neatly trimmed nails on the plywood table. He rubbed the back of his neck. "I could use someone to handle work parties here in the rear. The lines will probably have to be expanded, bunkers built. There's a lot to running a place like this, you know."

"I can sure see that, Sergeant Major. It's amazing how much has to get done and fuck all recognition for it." Mellas laughed lightly. "I remember being a guard on my football team and reading in the papers that somehow it was the halfbacks who scored all the points, not the team."

Knapp looked pleased by the remark. "Yes, sir. It ain't any different here either."

Mellas smiled. "Nope, no different," he said. "No matter where you go, it's still high school."

The sergeant major laughed. Mellas repressed a smile at the irony of Knapp's laughing at a statement that actually was about him.

"OK. I'll see what I can do, sir," Knapp said. "No promises. But we'd sure hate to have the death of a good Marine on our hands."

"That's the way I feel, Sergeant Major. I knew you'd understand."

"I appreciate your stopping by, Lieutenant." He stood as Mellas did, and they shook hands. The sergeant major walked with Mellas to the door of the tent.

"There's one other thing, Sergeant Major," Mellas said.

"Sir?"

"It might be a little awkward if any blacks had to wait on tables at mess night."

The sergeant major's smile disappeared. "If they've drawn KP, they'll do what they're told. We don't play favorites here."

"Of course not," Mellas said. "And I admire that you would accept the responsibility for a fragging rather than compromise your principles. Any board of inquiry would approve."

The sergeant major's breath was coming faster. He swallowed visibly. "I didn't mean I'd risk a fragging."

"Of course you didn't," Mellas said. "I know that, Sergeant Major. I know you don't like being put in this jam any more than I do. It's a tough place to be. I really do appreciate your help on this. Thank you, Sergeant Major."

Mellas turned and went out of the tent. He carefully adjusted his stateside utility cover and headed back to the airstrip. He had no doubt about what the sergeant major would do.

* * *

Several hours later Mellas and the other officers were running through
the rain to the large chapel tent. Hawke and McCarthy, the latter apparently none the worse for the glass in his rear end, were standing
outside in the drizzle. Hawke shook his head silently. An enlisted man
from McCarthy's platoon in Alpha Company, wearing a white coat
dredged up from Da Nang, trudged past them carrying a large pot of
soup. He managed to work enough of his right hand loose to give
McCarthy the finger.

"Suck out, Wick," McCarthy hissed back at him. The kid disappeared inside.

Candles lighted the interior, casting a flickering yellow glow over
everything. Tables were arranged in a large U shape and covered with
white cloths. The battalion communications officer stuck his head out
the door. "You better get in and find your place cards. We're all supposed to be standing by when the colonel arrives. Blakely's orders." He
scurried back inside.

Hawke sighed and walked in. The others followed.

The tent's ventilation flaps had been closed because of the rain,
and it was uncomfortably warm inside. Several enlisted men waited in
the rear, standing by their pots of food, sweating beneath their starched
white coats. Mellas noted that there were no blacks among them.

Shortround, at the very end of the line next to a large pot of string
beans, grinned broadly when he saw the lieutenants from Bravo Company enter the tent. Mellas was happy to see him but suppressed a grin
and just nodded quickly. Hawke gave the hawk power sign and
Shortround returned it, wiggling his fingers next to his hip, smiling
proudly to be included in Hawke's private joke.

Mellas found his place card opposite Hawke and between Captain Coates, the skipper of Charlie Company, whom he'd last seen passed
out on the wet LZ, and a new lieutenant from Alpha Company. The
new lieutenant and Coates exchanged pleasantries with Mellas, to which
he barely replied. This was Mellas's way of showing that he was here
against his will and was not enjoying himself. The conversation lagged,
and an awkward silence followed.

The tension was released when the Three walked in the tent, calling everyone to attention. Blakely's jungle utilities were starched stiff and his major's leaves shone in the candlelight. He stood ramrod straight and cut an impressive figure. There was no doubt in Mellas's mind that the fucking prig would be a general one day.

Simpson strode in, flushed with excitement and pride. "Gentlemen, be seated," he said crisply. The benches rumbled on the plywood floor as about thirty officers sat down. Blakely gave a brief talk on the tradition of mess night and raised his glass in a toast, and the official drinking began.

By the time they were through dessert, they had, for the most part, finished at least a bottle of wine each. Conversation had risen to a clamor punctuated by outbursts of laughter. No one noticed the colonel rise from his chair to give a toast, except Major Blakely, who clinked his glass to get the tent quiet.

Just like the fucking Rotary Club, Mellas thought darkly.

All the voices died down except McCarthy's. He was well into his second bottle of wine and was telling a new second lieutenant his favorite story about the Three. "'But we're fucking *out here*,' the skipper says. 'And I don't care what your goddamned map says, we're *out here* and you're *back there* and I tell you we see fucking lights on Hill 967.' But this fucking asshole tells us it's impossible and over the *radio* for shit's sake that we can't see what's in front of our fucking faces . . ."

The new lieutenant was tugging at McCarthy's sleeve and urgently nodding toward the head table. McCarthy turned darkly and leaned back, folding his arms. The Three announced that the colonel had something to say. His eyes never left McCarthy.

Simpson, mildly and happily drunk, gave a quick official smile. He spilled a little of his wine as he leaned forward with his hands on both sides of his plate. Then he stood straight, bringing his glass up with him. "Gentlemen. First Battalion Twenty-Fourth Marines has made a fine name for itself here in Vietnam. I am both humble and proud to address you, the officers who have contributed so greatly to that record." He lowered his voice and looked down at his dessert plate, where the ice

cream that had been flown in from Quang Tri that afternoon was melting. "And to remember those officers who contributed their most precious possession, sacrificing all they had, that the record might remain
proud and noble."

"He means the ones that got wasted," Mellas whispered to the new
lieutenant next to him without turning his head. Captain Coates touched
Mellas's boot with his own.

"We took command of this battalion at the commencement of
Operation Cathedral Forest," the colonel continued, "a drive deep into
the DMZ that resulted in significant findings of matériel, significant
contact, and significant kills. From Cathedral Forest to Wind River, at
the gateway to Laos. I'm sure many of you recall with fondness our
friends from Co Roc." About half of the officers laughed. Hawke wasn't
one of them.

"Well, we got our own artillery. Fire Support Base Lookout, Puller,
Sherpa, Margo, Sierra, Sky Cap." The colonel paused. "And Matterhorn." He looked at his silent officers. "We're building fountainheads
of steel right in the gooks' backyard. We're denying him the use of his
own transportation network, forcing him to go farther and farther west,
making his resupply more and more difficult for his operations in the
populated provinces to our south." Simpson paused here and changed
his tone. "We've been sitting on our asses around Cam Lo and in my
opinion abandoned our mission." He leaned across the table. "Well,
gentlemen, we are *through* with the political bullshit. From now on we'll
be back at our real job, closing with and destroying the enemy. Wherever he may be. And gentlemen, I know where he is. I know." He was
leaning on his arms and looking intently at them, his eyes darting back
and forth. Then he stood up for effect, head high, shoulders back.

Mellas raised his eyebrows, looking at Hawke across from him.

"He's around Matterhorn," the colonel continued. His eyes glit-
tered. He leaned forward again, his small red hands in fists on the table.
"Yes, goddamn it, Matterhorn. The gooks are there. Hiding. And by God
we're going to walk in there someday and kill every one of the yellow
sons of bitches. We were ordered off Matterhorn, against my will, and
against my own and my operations officer's best judgment, to fulfill the

wishes of some fat-assed politicians back in Washington. But every sign"—he emphasized his words with his fist—"every single piece of intelligence, every little contact"—he pushed back and smiled—"my fucking nose"—he touched it—"tells me that the NVA are in there, and in force. And that area is ours, gentlemen. We paid for it. In blood. And we'll get our due."

"That's bullshit," Mellas whispered to the new lieutenant. "There's nothing up there but leeches and malaria."

Coates elbowed Mellas in the ribs and glared at him. Hawke was staring stonily at his fork.

"We had to leave Matterhorn before our work there was finished," Simpson continued, "and Marines never leave their work unfinished. I promise you this, gentlemen: I'll do every goddamned thing I can to get this battalion where it belongs. That's where the fighting's going to be. That's where I want to be. That's where Major Blakely wants to be, and I know that's where every Marine in this battalion wants to be."

At this point McCarthy quietly belched, out of earshot of the head table.

"So, gentlemen," the colonel went on, "I'd like to propose a toast to the best goddamned fighting battalion in Vietnam today. Here's to the Tigers of Tarawa, the Frozen Chosen of Chosin Reservoir. Here's to the First Battalion Twenty-Fourth Marines."

The officers stood, echoing the toast. Then they sat down with the colonel, who received congratulations on his fine toast from Blakely.

Coates turned to Mellas, his eyes dancing with deep humor. "Cool down, Lieutenant Mellas. Colonel Mulvaney will never let him near the place. You don't commit an entire battalion to an area covered by enemy artillery that we can't go after because of political reasons. Add to that uncertain air support because of the weather. That's why Mulvaney pulled us out in the first place. Return to Matterhorn? Nevah hoppin."

Mellas was surprised. "Here I thought you were a lifer," he said, smiling.

"I am, Lieutenant Mellas. But I ain't stupid. And *I* also know how to keep my mouth shut."

* * *

Mellas awoke the next morning to hard rain slashing against the tent. Relsnik, on radio watch, was hunched in his poncho liner staring out into the dark. Mellas's first thought was hopeful. With rain like that, no choppers would be able to fly. Anyone who got into the shit would have to rely on something besides the Bald Eagle to get rescued. He wrapped the snoopy around his shoulders, never wanting to leave its security. He remained in a snug ball but was slowly losing a fight with his bladder. He gave up and ran out into the rain to piss.

When he got back inside the tent, Fitch was up, starting coffee.

"No way we can get launched today," Mellas said.

Fitch squinted into the darkness. He turned to his radio operator. "Hey, Snik, see if you can get a weather report out of battalion."

The weather report wasn't good. It was supposed to stop raining by midmorning. That meant the choppers could fly.

An hour later Mellas was at the supply tent, doing paperwork that ranged from writing press releases for local newspapers about the activities of local boys to handling inquiries about paternity suits from Red Cross workers to straightening out paycheck allocations to divorced wives, current wives, and women illegally claiming to be wives, mothers, and mothers-in-law. To Mellas it seemed as if half the company came from broken homes and had wives or parents who were drunks, dope addicts, runaways, prostitutes, or child beaters. Two things about this surprised him. The first was the fact itself. The second was that everyone seemed to cope with it so well.

A runner dropped off a small stack of papers and radio messages from battalion. Included were orders transferring Staff Sergeant Cassidy to H & S Company. Mellas marveled at Sergeant Major Knapp's efficiency. He looked back into the gloom of the tent where Cassidy and two helpers were trying to straighten out a mess of equipment and steeled himself for what had to follow. "Hey, Gunny," he said, feigning excitement and getting up from the table, "you've got orders out of the bush. Look at this." He walked back with the triplicate orders.

Cassidy looked at Mellas in surprise. "What? Let me see 'em." He furrowed his brow, reading the order slowly. It was a routine set, transferring a lot of people. His name was singled out by a neat rubber-stamped arrow. The words ORIGINAL ORDERS were stamped in bold capitals across the mimeographed sheet. "Well, I'll be fucked," he said.

"Where are you going, Gunny?" one of the Marines asked. Both of them were grinning broadly, happy that anyone was escaping the bush alive.

"Well, I'll be fucked," Cassidy said again. He sat down. "H & S Company. I didn't know nothing about it." He looked up at Mellas. "I don't see nothing about my replacement."

"He's probably coming in from division or someplace."

Cassidy said, "Well, sir, I'd like to go see what I'll be doing. No one told me nothing. I swear."

"Sure, Gunny, go ahead. I'll honcho this."

Cassidy sent the two Marines to chow, with orders to send two replacements back afterward. Then he walked off to see his new company commander.

Vancouver was one of the two Marines who managed to wangle work in the supply tent rather than fill sandbags in the rain. He and the other kid were soon rummaging through the damp, often mildewed bags of personal gear left behind by Marines who had rotated home or been killed.

"Hey, Vancouver," the other kid said. "Here's something that's yours."

When Vancouver saw the long rectangular box he felt a foreboding. It was his sword. It had been a funny shtick when he ordered it. He thought it had been lost for good. Now he said—but it was as if he heard someone else's voice saying—"Jesus Christ. Hey, it's my fucking gook sword. It's been here all along." He was tearing at the paper, pulling the long handle and sheath from the narrow box. He grabbed the hilt and, with a ringing sound, drew the sword from its sheath.

Mellas had turned at the sound of Vancouver's cry.

"Look at this mother, Lieutenant," Vancouver crowed. He was standing on top of two seabags, his feet spread apart, holding the sword in front of him. He took a quick slash at the air. "I'm gonna get some now," he said through clenched teeth.

By late afternoon word of Vancouver's sword had made its way through the entire battalion. A friend of Jancowitz's from H & S stopped by the sandbag detail to tell Jancowitz about it. Jancowitz had a feeling of despair which he couldn't identify and which he quickly forced back into the reservoir of other feelings he'd fought down for the past year and a half. "Crazy fucker," he said, smiling. "He'll get some, too. You wait and see."

"Yeah, he might," his friend told him, "but the gooks ain't hardly going to use swords. They ain't no fucking savages."

"Yeah, but Vancouver is," Jancowitz retorted. People laughed. His friend grinned and set off down the road. Jancowitz turned sadly back to his pile of dirt.

All day Bravo Company dug in the clay, filling the green plastic bags, trying to forget that at any second an officer in an air-conditioned bunker in Dong Ha or Da Nang could call in the helicopters that would carry them to some unknown spot in the jungle where they would die. They tried with every shovelful to forget that at any moment the company jeep might come tearing across the narrow airstrip, with Pallack shouting that someone was in the shit and Bravo Company was going to bail them out.

Jancowitz was as anxious as everybody else. He tried to think of Susi, but he was having a hard time remembering her face. He was embarrassed to take out his wallet in front of everyone and look at her picture, so he remained torn between wanting to do just that and not wanting to appear foolish. The guys would laugh and say she was just another fucking bar girl. He couldn't have taken that. He'd signed on for an extra six months of fear and filth just to spend thirty days with her. He threw himself into filling the next sandbag.

At 1700 they folded their E-tools and walked in twos and threes back toward their tents. Broyer had joined Jancowitz, his eyeglasses steaming slightly from the perspiration dripping from his forehead. "Hey, Janc," he said, wiping the glasses on his shirttail. "What we got an assistant general for anyway?" He was referring to the one-star general who resided at Task Force Hotel and whose red flag with a single gold star on it they had stared at all day while filling sandbags for his bunker. He put the glasses back on. They promptly slid forward. Annoyed, he pushed them back onto his nose, but then they started to steam up again.

Jancowitz didn't answer. He was thinking of Susi, trying to block out the smell of oil that had been sprayed on the road and the smoke that came from the efforts of a lone Marine who was burning shit with kerosene in three sawed-off steel barrels. Eventually, though, Broyer's question worked its way into his consciousness. He looked at Broyer. When Broyer showed up on Matterhorn, Jancowitz had been worried about his thin frame and hesitant way of talking. But he didn't worry about Broyer anymore—a good fucking Marine. "Fucked if I know, Broyer. General Neitzel probably needs someone to handle his paperwork."

"Way I hear it, he needs someone to handle his fighting. First order he gave was for everyone to button their utility shirts. Sheeit."

Jancowitz smiled, listening to Broyer, who was trying to make his "shit" sound cool. Jancowitz had been in-country when the previous general had arrived and had heard the same kind of bitching. Jancowitz had his own criterion for whether or not a general, or any other officer for that matter, was any good, and that was the number of times he saw the officer out in the bush with the snuffs. That's why he liked Colonel Mulvaney. He'd been out on the lines at VCB one night, raining like hell, dark as a motherfucker, when he heard this jeep coming up. He thought it was Hawke. So he hollered out, "What the fuck you doing out here?" He about shit his pants when it turned out to be Mulvaney, the commander of the whole Twenty-Fourth Marine Regiment. The old fucker had proceeded to ask him if he'd killed any rats, inspect his rifle, and tell him he was doing a good job.

"Lieutenant Mellas doesn't give a shit if we don't button our utility shirts," Broyer went on.

"Yeah. Only he won't stay in."

"You going to stay in?" Broyer asked after a moment.

"I don't know. I got this girl in Bangkok." Jancowitz smiled. "How about you?"

"I want to go to the University of Maryland on the GI Bill and get into government work." Broyer hesitated. "Maybe the State Department." He looked quickly at Jancowitz to see if there was any reaction. Then he smiled ruefully. "I thought being a Marine would look good on my résumé."

"What's a résumé?" Jancowitz asked. He saw that Broyer was surprised that he didn't know but was trying not to let on.

"You use it when you're looking for a job. It's a couple of pages that tells your experience, where you went to school. That sort of thing."

Jancowitz laughed out loud. He couldn't imagine why he'd ever need one of those to get a job.

They walked along silently for a while.

"I hear there's going to be a movie tonight," Broyer said. "And maybe even a Red Cross girl."

"That's an old rumor. They don't let Red Cross girls out of Da Nang. They say it's too dangerous. Such horseshit. They don't let the fucking Budweiser and air mattresses out of Da Nang either."

"But the movie isn't a rumor," Broyer said.

"I bet you it's a fucking cowboy show."

Broyer laughed quietly, and they walked along in silence again. Overhead they heard the gentle honking of some geese and they both looked up at a small flock of about six moving north. They stood and watched until the geese were lost in the clouds hiding Mutter's Ridge.

"Makes me homesick," Jancowitz said quietly.

"Me too," Broyer answered.

When they rounded the last bend before their tents by the airfield, Jancowitz said, "Well, I'll be fucked." Arran was sitting on the ground, leaning his back against his pack. Pat was beside him in the down position, head and reddish ears alert, panting quietly, watching the two of them approach. Pat looked questioningly at Arran, who said, "OK." Pat got to his feet and trotted over to greet Jancowitz and Broyer.

He put his muzzle right in Broyer's crotch, and Broyer giggled and started ruffling his fur. Then Pat danced away and circled behind Jancowitz, nuzzling up against the back of his knees, causing Jancowitz to giggle as well.

"Looks like he's singled you guys out," Arran called.

"Yeah, the old quitter," Jancowitz said fondly, rubbing Pat's head. "How long did it take for him to get back on his feet?"

"Aw, about a week. We just fucked off back at scout platoon, both of us getting fat and happy." He smiled and got to his feet, snapping his fingers quietly. "We were already dumb." Pat quickly moved into heel position. Arran turned to Broyer, nodding his head toward Jancowitz. "This crazy motherfucker got you broken in yet?"

Broyer grinned. "Yeah."

"You watch out for him, Broyer. Janc's the only other crazy motherfucker I know besides me upped for an extension in the Nam. Of course he did it for some chick in Bangkok, not someone who'd really stand by you." He squatted down and grabbed Pat on both sides of his jowls, putting his face right into Pat's nose, moving it back and forth. "Won't you, boy? Won't you, you dumb sheepdog?" He stood again. It was well known that Arran had extended his tour twice because the scout dogs couldn't be transferred to other handlers, and when their tour was over, they were killed. Someone back in the world had declared them too dangerous to bring home.

"You back with us for a while?" Jancowitz asked.

"Not as long as you're on Bald fucking Eagle, I ain't," Arran answered. "No need for a fucking four-legged radar set when they dump you right in the middle of the shit." He turned to Pat. "We're specialists, ain't we, Pat?" Pat wagged his tail.

"What're you doing here, then?" Jancowitz asked.

"We're going out with Alpha One Fifteen tomorrow. They're getting dropped in the east end of the Da Krong Valley. Lots of sensor activity." He stopped short and grinned. "You ain't supposed to hear that, otherwise I'd have to kill you."

"The fucking gooks already know about it anyway," Jancowitz said, not really joking.

There was an awkward silence. Janc realized that Arran had come over because he was going out in the jungle again and wanted to say good-bye.

"You'll be OK," Janc finally said. "Hell, you're the one's got Pat."

Arran grinned, looked down at Pat, and then looked up at the clouds, embarrassed. "Hope you motherfuckers don't get launched," he said. "We'll see you on your next op."

They watched Arran and Pat walk off. They all knew that it could be the last time.

At dinner that evening Blakely and Simpson walked to the head of the chow line where Marines on KP slopped large spoonfuls of food onto trays. One of the Marines splattered a speck of gravy on Blakely's sleeve. Blakely glared at him, unable to sop it up because both hands were holding the tray.

"Sorry, sir," the young Marine stammered.

Blakely smiled. "It's OK, Tiger. Just don't get so damn eager."

Blakely followed Simpson into the officers' and NCOs' mess. Someone shouted "Attention" and everyone rose. Simpson grunted "As you were," and everyone resumed eating, all conversation dulled temporarily until Simpson and Blakely got settled. Blakely got up soon after they had seated themselves and poured two mugs of coffee. He returned to his seat and said to Simpson, "I heard there was another fragging last night, down south. You hear about it, sir?"

Simpson looked up, washing down a mouthful of noodles with coffee. "Fuck, no. Who?"

"Some mustang lieutenant in Three Eleven. Three or four of the bastards rolled grenades under his rack while he was sleeping. Someone saw them running away. Black radicals. Nothing left for evidence but monkey meat."

"Fucking rear-area poags," Simpson said. "If any of that shit happens around here I'll string every black power son of a bitch up by his nuts." Simpson downed the rest of his coffee with a gulp. "We ought to send every black son of a bitch to the bush. That'd stop this shit." He looked at his empty cup. "How about a little of that pink Portuguese stuff?" he asked.

Blakely walked over to the cabinet where the colonel's case of Mateus was kept. He looked through the insect screen to where the enlisted men were eating. He noticed most of the blacks together in one corner. A few fine wrinkles creased his forehead. He broke the wine bottle's seal, pulled the cork stopper, and poured two glasses.

"May you be ten minutes in heaven before the devil knows you're gone," Simpson said, raising his glass and gulping a large swallow. Blakely was aware that Simpson prided himself on knowing many different toasts in different languages. He smiled appropriately and drank. Simpson drank some more. "Good fucking stuff," he said.

Blakely chose not to agree, rather than to disagree. After a moment he said, "Sir, did you ever think about maybe getting someone to watch your quarters at night?"

"You think I'm chickenshit?"

"No sir. But that fragging was the third one in the last two months." Blakely lowered his voice and leaned over the table. "I heard, strictly scuttlebutt, that someone tried to kill Cassidy, the new Area NCOIC we picked up from Bravo Company. That's why the sergeant major told me he got the idea to transfer him."

"Why aren't we investigating the fucking incident?"

"Apparently the black that did it was Bravo's cerebral malaria case. I'm not sure we want to stir that up."

Simpson nervously twirled the pink wine in his glass. "I'm glad to see there's some fucking justice in the world. That was smart of Knapp." He tossed down the wine. "I think I'll go check out the situation at the COC." He rose to his feet, and so did everyone else. He waved the others down with, "As you were, gentlemen."

Sitting alone in the tent he shared with his squad, Jancowitz didn't need to visit the COC to know what was going on in the regiment's area of operation. In his mind's eye he could see the units out in the bush setting their trip flares and putting out their listening posts. He watched as furtive figures, two by two, slipped beyond the lines, carrying their poncho liners and radios with them. He knew he could relax for the moment. There would be no "exploitation" by the Bald Eagle unit until daylight. A night helicopter lift took far too much planning. The units were on their own.

He took out his short-timer's chart and carefully filled in another day. He'd been in Vietnam twenty-two months. Well, really only nineteen and three quarters if you subtracted the first week of R & R in Bangkok, when he'd met Susi, and the two thirty-day leaves. He took out his wallet and looked at the picture he'd taken of Susi when she was asleep on his bed in the hotel. He tried to remember the smell of her hair, but that was even more difficult than remembering her face. All he could smell was the mothballs and oil of the sagging tent.

He walked down to the open pit that had been converted to a small outdoor theater. About a hundred people were sitting there on old crates and boxes. A slight drizzle was starting to fall, but it was warm, unlike the drizzle up in the mountains, and Jancowitz hardly noticed it. He put his hands in his pockets and waited for the movie to begin.

Nothing happened. The projector sat dumbly as the Marines waited for someone to arrive with the film.

Fifteen minutes later the crowd was becoming restless. Voices became louder. A beer can was thrown and one Marine jumped up to take the challenge, only to be pulled down by his friends. More beer was opened. A group of blacks had formed over to the left side of the theater. A white Marine got up to take a piss and had to walk through or around them. He asked one of them to move. It was Henry.

"Hey, mother*fuck,* I don't move for nobody 'less I want to," Henry said.

The crowd grew quiet.

Henry moved his face inches from the white kid's. The white kid stepped back but could go no farther because of some chairs behind him. Several white kids stood up and moved closer to him, offering silent support. Some of the blacks rearranged themselves, forming a semicircle to the side of the two who stood staring at each other. Jancowitz noticed that Broyer and Jackson were with the group, as was China.

Mole stood up on the far side of the open space where he'd been talking to Vancouver. The two of them looked at each other quickly, then averted their eyes. Mole started edging around the outside of the circle, keeping close to the clay wall of the pit.

Jancowitz had seen it start before. Everyone was scared not to be with his own race. Once fighting began, sides would be drawn and no amount of time together in the bush could break the barrier. Jancowitz had no idea what he would do, but he found himself walking quickly over to where Mole was moving around the outside edge of the circle, getting himself into position. Whites, feeling the same pressure as Mole, were gradually shifting to join their own color, no one wishing to be isolated when it happened. Jancowitz hissed at Mole. "Get the fuck out of here, Mole. You too, Vancouver. Just get the fuck out of here."

Mole looked over at the group of brothers forming at the side of the area, then at Janc. He shook his head, sadly, and continued toward the forming sides.

Jancowitz turned to see what Vancouver was doing. He, like Mole, understood that he was one of the best fighters and he had to support his color when the shit came down. He moved toward the group forming around the white Marine. Jancowitz could see that although they were all friends in the bush, here in civilization friendship was impossible.

Jancowitz ran up to the projector and jerked the cord of the small gasoline generator. The cough of the engine broke the silence. Marines of both colors looked to see its cause, to see if an officer had arrived, to see if there was some way out of the impending violence. Jancowitz turned on the camera and a brilliant white square appeared on the canvas screen. Then he calmly walked in front of the stream of white light and formed a shadow picture of a bird. A couple of people laughed nervously.

"All right, Janc," someone called.

"Is that all you can make is birds?"

"Fuck, no," he answered. He immediately began talking. "I got this girl down in Bangclap. Holy fuck you never seen a girl like this one." The shadows suddenly became two legs, spread wide apart. "Now I been in the Nam eighteen months and twenty-seven days." An erect penis, quivering, replaced the legs. "Of course I just got back from thirty days in Bangclap, you sorry motherfuckers." The penis went limp and there was laughter. "But then this girl." The legs reappeared and the penis began to slowly rise, fall, then rise again, egged on by the cheers of the Marines. "I'd lay forty miles of wire through the Au Shau Valley just to hear her piss over the phone." The penis went erect and cheers reverberated through the group.

The white kid who'd been trying to take a piss continued on his way with only a dark glance from Henry. Soon other kids stuck their hands into the stream of light, making their own figures on the screen, eliciting raucous and sarcastic commentary accompanied by the sounds of cans of beer being opened. Voices began to rise in a murmur of conversation.

Jancowitz sat down, still filled with adrenaline, feeling an immense longing for Susi, her clear brown skin and long black hair. Vancouver walked up to him and handed him a beer. "That was close, Janc. We'd been in the shit for sure, ay?" Jacobs also walked up and put his hand on Jancowitz's shoulder.

Then the screen went dark.

A groan arose from the crowd and people turned to look into the darkness behind them. A gunnery sergeant from base services was standing next to the projector with two large canisters of film under his arms.

"All right, who turned on the fucking generator?" The kids who'd been making shadow pictures sank quietly into the crowd.

There was silence.

The man spoke again, long years of authority in his voice. "If I don't get the wise guy that turned on this fucking generator there ain't going to be no movie tonight."

A murmur of discontent rose in volume. The gunnery sergeant shifted his eyes from side to side, surprised at the rebellion in the air, but even more determined to see his job through. "I don't care how long it takes, ladies, for one of you to come up here and tell me you started this generator, because I've seen this movie before. I'll give you one more minute, and then I'm leaving."

"Oh, fuck," Jancowitz said quietly. He rose, tired, and faced the man. "I started the fucking generator, Gunny. Movies were supposed to go at 1930 hours, so I thought I'd start them on time."

"Come up here, Marine."

Jancowitz slowly walked up to the gunnery sergeant. He could smell liquor on the sergeant's breath. The gunnery sergeant took out a notebook and pen. "I want your name, rank, and unit, Marine. And then I want your ass out of the area. Is that clear?"

Jancowitz gave him the information he wanted and walked away. Vancouver came to join him, but Janc told him to go back and watch the movie. He felt like being alone.

As Jancowitz walked down the dark road toward the tents he thought of Susi, feeling that somehow he'd sacrificed her, or some part of her in him. Behind him he heard the movie start. He turned to see, on the screen, an unshaven man wrapped in a Mexican poncho, his arms at his sides near a pair of six-guns, a thin cigarillo clamped tautly in his mouth. The music rose in pitch as the man walked toward the corral fence, where other men were seated, all with weapons ready to use. The screen burst into violence as the man pulled his pistols and shot all the men on the fence. A mocking cheer rose from the Marines. Jancowitz turned around in disgust and continued walking. He'd been right—another fucking cowboy show.

China, his mouth slightly open in reflection and wonder, watched Jancowitz disappear into the darkness. He realized he'd seen something very brave and wise. "Fucking Janc, man," he kept saying to himself in his mind. "Fucking Janc." It occurred to him that he and Janc had been in the bush together ever since he had arrived in the Nam but he'd never really talked to Janc. He suddenly wished Janc were his friend, but he knew it was impossible. He looked over to where Henry was sitting with a group of blacks, basking in their admiration. Henry seemed to grow in stature while China himself got nowhere. China's face began to burn again at the memory of Henry's disdain for the weapons, and of how his friends had chuckled. China knew that for now it was Henry's game and he himself had to play ball. He'd lost way too much ground and didn't know how he could recover it.

While Jancowitz was walking away from the movie, Pollini was standing on a crate washing a huge aluminum pot in steaming water. Wick, the Marine from McCarthy's platoon, was working next to him. Their heads were at the same level, although Wick's feet were on the ground.

"Never thought I'd love scrubbing pots," Wick said.

"Not me," Pollini said. "The lieutenant told me I only had to do KP for a month."

"Only a month?" Wick shot back. "You get a whole fucking month? McCarthy only gave me a week. I only got two days left and if Alpha ain't out in the pucker weeds by day after tomorrow, I got to go with them. How come you get a whole month?"

Pollini shrugged and grinned—his response to any situation he felt he couldn't handle.

"I'll tell you why you get a whole fucking month," Wick said, clearly angry at the injustice of the situation. "It's because they don't want your ass out there with them, that's why."

"It was my turn," Pollini said hotly.

"Fuck. Your turn. Nobody gets KP for a fucking month. Ain't nobody can kiss enough ass to pull that one off." Wick started cleaning the huge pot again. "Shortround," he said, "you got it made. Everyone else begging to get to the rear and you got people trying to get you there. Man, you got it made."

Pollini kept grinning. "Yeah. I guess I do," he said.

"Why'd you up and join the Marine Corps anyway, Shortround?"

"My father was a Marine," Pollini answered proudly. "He fought in Korea."

"That explains it."

"That explains what?"

"Why we lost the fucking war in Korea. I bet you're a chip off the old block, ain't you?" Wick laughed again, enjoying himself.

There was no response from Pollini. If Wick had looked, he would have seen that Pollini was gritting his teeth in pain and fighting to hold back tears. In Pollini's hands was a large steel serving ladle. He whipped it around with both hands, catching Wick across the left cheek and the bone above the left eye. Wick screamed in pain, his hands reaching for his face, and Pollini picked up the pot full of hot water and threw it at him. Then he ran out of the mess tent into the darkness, swinging the heaving ladle at another Marine who was running in.

Wick was standing up, blood and soapy water running down his face.

"Jesus Christ," the Marine said. "What happened to you?"

"Shortround hit me with a fucking ladle."

"Sweet Jesus," the Marine said, awed. "I'll get the squid."

"I don't want any goddamned flap over it. I'll get my own squid to look at it."

"If you say so. What the fuck happened?" Other Marines on KP had crowded into the tent where the pots were washed.

"Nothing," Wick said angrily. "Just clear the fuck out of here and let me finish the goddamned pots."

"Sure." The others left Wick alone, staring at the overturned pot that lay on the muddy floor. He reached down for it. "Sorry, Short-round," he said quietly.

Mellas and Goodwin decided to go to the new officers' club at Task Force Oscar. They went to get Hawke, but Hawke had just bought a case of beer. They decided to have one warm-up drink together outside Hawke's tent, avoiding a couple of new officers who had just arrived from Quang Tri.

An hour later the three of them had not moved. The case was now three-quarters gone. "Can you beat that," Hawke was saying, staring into his beer.

"Can you beat what?" Mellas asked. His tongue was beginning to get in the way of his words.

"I mean can you beat the fucking Three getting a medal for hanging out in a Huey when we got into that shit sandwich by Co Roc?"

"Fucking insanity." Mellas spat, and it landed in the half-empty case instead of nearby, where he'd aimed. "I still haven't gotten any word on Vancouver's and Conman's medals."

"They're snuffs. It takes longer."

"There it is, Jack," Goodwin said.

Hawke opened another can of beer and Mellas watched the foam spill satisfyingly over the sides and onto his hands. "The medal was for rallying a demoralized company and risking his life to coordinate its extraction under fire. Captain Black didn't get zip for going in and pulling Friedlander's ass out of the shit."

"Shit is right, Jack," Goodwin said.

"The war's run by a bunch of assholes," Mellas said.

"How do you know?" Hawke asked.

"We get fucking killed and they sit in Paris and argue about fucking square tables and round tables."

"Those are diplomats, not assholes," Hawke said.

Goodwin popped open another can of beer and lay back on the ground. A light mist fell on his face.

"They're in charge of the fucking war, aren't they?" Mellas said.

"Right, right," Hawke said, nodding.

"And the war is so fucked up it has to be run by a bunch of assholes. Right?"

"That's fucking right, Jack," Goodwin said. Hawke agreed.

"So . . ." Mellas said.

"So what?" Hawke asked.

"So . . ." Mellas finished his can of beer. "I can't fucking remember what I was trying to prove, but the people that run this fucking war are a bunch of assholes."

"I'll drink to that. Goddamned right." Hawke leaned back, chugging the remainder of his beer.

"I'll drink to anything," Goodwin said fuzzily.

A silence followed. The damp wind moved gently through the dark, rippling tent walls, causing an occasional light leak to flutter briefly.

Mellas let out a long contented burp, his head spinning happily, not really aware of where he was except that he lay in some wet grass in a light drizzle.

The sustained heavy slapping of an AK-47 on full automatic sent the three of them flat on their stomachs, their beer cans thrown aside. People came piling out of the tents around them, running for the bunkers, some hopping as they struggled into trousers. The AK opened up again and a ricochet spun over the three lieutenants' heads with an almost lazy hum. Hawke was clutching the case of beer, protecting it from possible damage from the bullets.

Shouts arose from the battalion area.

"What do you think?" Mellas asked, his head spinning. Hawke shrugged and popped open three more cans of beer. "If it's fucking sappers, they're after the fucking helicopters. And I ain't a fucking helicopter. But I don't ever remember sappers doing one-man attacks."

The three of them sat up, watching the confusion. Blakely went sprinting across to the COC bunker, head bent close to the ground, shouting directions to people. He disappeared into the bunker.

"Hey, Jayhawk," Goodwin said.

"Uh?"

"What kind of medal you think the Six and Three will get for this one?"

"Navy Cross," Hawke said, "or possibly higher." Hawke raised his hand to his lips and gave a jeering raspberry of a bugle call.

A small figure came creeping up behind the BOQ tent. They all froze, realizing they were without rifles; the bravado of the beer was gone. The man, his back to them, was creeping up on the tent.

Goodwin moved very slowly, motioning to Hawke and Mellas, indicating that they should roll in his direction. He pointed into some high grass behind him.

The figure continued to creep along the back of the tent. "Hey, Lieutenant Hawke," the figure whispered to the tent. "Hey Lieutenant Jayhawk, it's Pollini, sir."

"Shit, Jack," Goodwin moaned.

"Shortround, you fucking numby," Hawke hissed. "Get over here."

Pollini turned around. "What are you guys doing in the bushes?" he asked loudly. He groped his way toward them. He was carrying the AK-47 Vancouver had brought back from Mellas's aborted reconnaissance.

"Over here, Pollini," Mellas whispered fiercely. "Where the hell do you think you are, Central fucking Park? Get your ass down before someone sees you."

"Oh, Lieutenant Mellas, sir," he said aloud. He walked over and sat down. Hawke grabbed the AK-47 from Pollini, who smelled like a grape factory on strike in a heat wave. His eyes were clouded over and a little drool was forming at the side of his mouth.

Mellas was furious with him. "This stunt could land you in the brig for months. What do you think you're doing?"

Pollini scratched his head and then said brightly. "Just shooting up the place."

"Why, Pollini?" Hawke asked.

"Wasn't that right?" he answered. "Isn't that what a shit bird does?" He stood up, weaving badly. "Oh, here, sirs." He dug into his pockets. Out came a loaded magazine. "Here's what makes the little fucker go bang." He started laughing.

Goodwin pulled him to the ground.

Pollini suddenly broke into sobs, the start of a crying jag. He curled up in a ball, sobbing, "I don't want to be a shit bird. I wanted to be a good Marine. I want my father to be proud of me."

"Who said you were a shit bird?" Mellas asked, feeling suddenly awkward about all the times he'd poked fun at Pollini. "Hey, you can't cry like that," he said softly. "Hey, Pollini, don't cry."

Through the sobs came the story.

Mellas had a hand on Pollini's back. He didn't know what to do. He turned to Hawke. "But why would he get so upset? To go after a guy with a fucking soup ladle?"

"His father was killed in Korea."

Mellas moaned. "Isn't the shit of this war enough? We still have to deal with shit from Korea?" He shook his head slowly. Did it have to go on and on and on?

Pollini eventually fell into a stupefied sleep. The three lieutenants finished the case of beer, watching the battalion area return to normal. Long after it was quiet, Goodwin threw Pollini over his shoulder, Mellas took the rifle, and together they walked toward the landing zone and put Pollini to bed.

The next day Mellas took him off KP.

The same day, the Bald Eagle was launched into combat. But not without complications.

The battalion surgeon, Lieutenant Maurice Witherspoon Selby, USN, was sick and tired of the mud, the lack of ice, the unsanitary conditions, and the monotonous round of malaria, dysentery, ringworm, infected leech bites, jungle rot, crotch rot, sore backs, sore legs, and sore heads. He was particularly tired of PFC Mallory's sore head. Mallory had just returned from an examination by the lone psychiatrist at Fifth Med in Quang Tri with a note saying he had a passive-aggressive personality and he'd have to learn to live with his headaches. He also had a note from the Fifth Med dentist, who had put on temporary caps and said that Mallory was fit for duty but should see about getting a bridge when he got back to the States.

"Look, I'm busy," Selby said to Hospitalman First Class Foster. "Just give him some more Darvon and get him out of the sick bay."

"He seems pretty riled up, sir."

"Goddamn it, I've looked at his ugly head until I'm blue in the face. I was training to be a surgeon, not a psychiatrist." Selby reached for a bottle of aspirin and slugged down four, not bothering to take any water. "Now you tell him that sick bay goes at oh nine hundred, and let me do some work. You got that, Foster?"

"Yes, sir." Foster paused as Selby sat down behind the crude desk, his hands over his face. "Sir?"

"What, Foster?"

"Will you see him at oh nine hundred? I don't think he's going to take one of us squids giving him more Darvon. He's eating the stuff like candy anyway."

"What do you want me to do, hold his fucking hand? I've got a bunch of people out there that I *can* cure, and I'm sick of seeing him. No. I won't see him."

"Yes sir." Foster walked to the entrance of the tent. Mallory was sitting on a bench, his forehead in his hands, gear strewn beneath his feet. His flak jacket and .45 lay across his pack.

"PFC Mallory," Foster said.

"Yeah."

"I talked with Lieutenant Selby and he said there wasn't really anything he could do for you."

"That's what they all say. What's going down around here, huh?"

Foster sighed. "Mallory, I don't know what else to tell you. If there's nothing they can do in Quang Tri, there's sure not anything we can do here."

"My fucking head hurts."

"I know that, Mallory. All I can do for you is give you—"

"Fucking pills." Mallory stood up, screaming, "I don't need fucking pills. I need help. And that motherfucking doctor is fucking me over and I'm tired of it. I'm tired, you hear me?" He began to whimper. "I'm so fucking tired."

Selby walked through the partition. "You get out of this sick bay right now, Marine," he said, "and if your ass isn't out that door in five seconds, I'll have it for disobeying a direct order."

Mallory, visibly in pain, screamed and reached for the .45 at his feet. He pulled back the action. "My fucking head hurts and I want it fixed." The pistol was pointed at Selby's stomach.

Selby backed slowly away. "You're going to be in a heap of trouble over this, Marine," he said nervously.

"My head hurts."

Foster started easing toward the door. Mallory turned the pistol on him. "Where you going?"

"Let me go find the colonel or someone. Maybe they can do something about it. What do you think, Lieutenant Selby?"

"Oh, yes," Selby said. "Maybe we could send you to Da Nang. Maybe Japan. I had no idea you—"

"You shut up," Mallory said. "You had no *idea*. That right. You had no *idea* until I stand up here with a gun barrel poked at you fat face. You sure as shit have no fucking *idea*."

"Look, I'll write up an order right now, sending you to Da Nang."

"You can do that?"

"Sure I can. Foster here can get it all typed up, can't you, Foster?"

"Yes, sir. That's right."

"All right. You start typing," Selby said to Foster. It was clear that Mallory's anger was cooling. Selby could also see that Mallory was no longer sure about what to do with the pistol or how to get out of the situation.

Foster put three forms with carbon paper between them into a typewriter and started pounding away. Selby stood stiffly next to Foster's table, trying to summon up enough courage to glare at Mallory. He ended up pretending to read what Foster was typing.

Hospitalman Third Class Milbank, returning from breakfast, came whistling up the small path to the aid station. He stopped short when Foster shouted, "Sick call doesn't go until oh nine hundred, Marine."

"What?" Milbank said. He could see Foster through the open doorway, with Selby standing nervously by him.

"You know the rules, Marine. Oh nine hundred. We're under a lot of pressure here. Now clear out."

"Sure." Milbank walked off the path, puzzled. He walked quietly to the side of the tent. It was absolutely silent inside. Then he heard a hostile voice. "Where you going?"

"I have to look up the right coding on the order." Foster's voice answered, a little too slowly and clearly. "It's in that book over there."

Milbank carefully peeked beneath the wall of the tent. It ended about half an inch above the ground. He could make out the bleached boots of a bush Marine and a helmet among some gear with the medevac number M-0941 on it. A medevac number consisted of the first letter of the man's surname and the last four of his serial number. Then he saw the .45 held in a black hand. M—Mallory. It was that morose fucking machine gunner with the headaches, from Bravo Company.

Milbank ran to the mess tent and found Staff Sergeant Cassidy scraping the remains of his breakfast into a garbage can. "Mallory's got a .45 pulled on Doc Selby and Foster," he said. "Over at the battalion aid station."

"You get Lieutenant Fitch right now," Cassidy said. He ran for the aid station.

Milbank didn't know which way to go. He spotted Connolly and shouted at him. "Mallory's pulled a fucking gun on Doc Selby. Get your skipper up here right away." Everyone in the place stopped eating. Connolly looked at his cup of coffee and closed his eyes, then ran for the airstrip.

Cassidy reached the battalion aid station with Milbank close behind him. "You can see him through the crack under the tent," Milbank whispered. Cassidy merely grunted. He went to the ground and peered up through the narrow open space between the tent wall and the ground. He saw Mallory's jungle camouflage trousers and then the underside of the .45.

He walked calmly around the tent and through the door. Mallory, surprised, took a step backward.

"Give it to me, Mallory," Cassidy said.

"I tell you, my head hurts. I'm getting outa here."

"Give me the fucking pistol or so help me I'll jam it down your scrawny fucking throat."

Mallory shook his head, then seemed to collapse into a whimpering child. "It hurts me."

Cassidy walked over, took the .45 away, and tossed it at Selby, who put his hands in front of his face rather than catch it. The pistol clattered to the floor. "They don't work without magazines in them, Lieutenant Selby, *sir*," Cassidy said. He looked at Mallory, his hands on his hips. "And you, you fucking excuse for a man, I ought to tear your head right off." Cassidy suddenly lashed out with his fist, sinking it into Mallory's stomach. Mallory doubled over. Cassidy, cooling down, picked up Mallory's .45, went to Mallory's pack, and found a magazine, which he inserted into the butt. He pointed it at Mallory. "This one's loaded, fuckhead. Now get up."

"I got my rights," Mallory muttered.

"That's all that's saving you, puke," Cassidy said. "Now move."

Cassidy walked Mallory past a crowd of Marines to an empty steel conex box and roughly kicked him inside. He had just rammed the steel pin into the hasp of the heavy door when Fitch and Pallack came roaring up in the jeep. Major Blakely came running over from COC.

"What the fuck happened?" Fitch asked.

"It's that puke Mallory."

"What's going on here, Sergeant Cassidy?" Blakely asked, panting after his run.

"Like I was telling the skipper here, sir, it's PFC Mallory. He pulled his .45 on Lieutenant Selby over in the sick bay. I locked his ass in this cargo box."

"I guess he won't cause too much trouble in there," Blakely said, smiling.

Fitch smiled hesitantly, took his cap off, and stroked his hair. "Anyone hurt?" he asked.

"No sir," Cassidy answered.

"Well, we can't just leave him in the cargo box," Fitch said, half questioningly.

"Leave him there for now," Blakely answered quickly. "Do some good to see someone locked up for a crime around here. Besides, we got another situation developing I want you to sit in on."

Fitch carefully put his cap back on. "We'll talk about it later, Sergeant Cassidy," he said. He and Blakely walked away.

Cassidy tossed the .45 to a Marine from H & S who was in the crowd. "Schaffran, shoot anyone that tries to let this fuckhead out. Just make sure he doesn't roll over and die in there. He doesn't come out until I say so." Cassidy walked off.

"Not even to piss, Sergeant Cassidy?" Schaffran called after him.

"Till I say so, numbnuts."

Schaffran looked at the pistol, sighed, and sat down in front of the box.

*   *   *

Twenty minutes later Mellas received word to put the Bald Eagle on alert. It was another reconnaissance team, call sign Sweet Alice. They were fighting a running battle with a company-size unit just south of Matterhorn. Sweet Alice had six Marines.

Mellas radioed the news to the work party over at Task Force Oscar. Something deep within him stirred as he watched the Marines run down the hill from where they'd been filling sandbags. Entrenching tools and shirts in their hands, they streamed across the damp airstrip, running for their gear, running possibly to their deaths.

"*Semper Fi,* brothers," Mellas whispered to himself, understanding for the first time what the word "always" required if you meant what you said. He remembered a discussion at his eating club with his friends and their dates one night after a dance. They were talking about the stupidity of warriors and their silly codes of honor. He'd joined in, laughing with the rest of them, hiding the fact that he'd joined the Marines several years before, not wanting to be thought of as whatever bad thing they thought a warrior was. Protected by their class and sex, they would never have to know otherwise. Now, seeing the Marines run across the landing zone, Mellas knew he could never join that cynical laughter again. Something had changed. People he loved were going to die to give meaning and life to what he'd always thought of as meaningless words in a dead language.

Mellas's knees were quivering. His hands shook as he buckled down the straps on his pack and tested the springs in his ammunition magazines. "Make sure everyone's canteens are full," he said to each platoon commander. "You never know when we'll be getting water next."

Fracasso was walking back and forth like a caged animal. In his hands were several plastic-covered cards on which he had written the directions for calling in artillery fire and air strikes.

"Don't worry about it, Fracasso," Mellas said. "When you need artillery, you'll get it called in. Just remember they need to know three things: where you are, where the gooks are, and then you just tell them if they're long or short." Fracasso laughed, looking at his carefully prepared cards. "Put them in your pocket if it makes you feel better," Mellas said, sounding more combat-wise then he felt.

He and Fracasso both turned at the sound of someone running up to them. It was China. "They got Mallory in a fuckin' cage like some kind a animal," he screamed at Mellas. "They ain't gettin' away with shit like that."

Mellas put his arms up, palms toward China. That gesture cooled China down a bit. "He pulled a fucking pistol on a goddamned Navy doctor," Mellas said evenly. "What do you want me to do about it, change the fucking rules for you?"

"They don't lock him in no cage like no fuckin' animal. That's the fuckin' *rules*."

"China, we don't have time for this bullshit. We got somebody in the bush in a shit sandwich. Mallory can fucking wait."

"But the pistol didn't have no magazine in it."

This was news to Mellas. "What? You sure?"

"Yes sir. One of the squids told me, and it makes sense. I know Mallory. Mallory wouldn't shoot nobody."

Mellas didn't know whether to believe this or not. Even if he did believe it, what could he do about it?

"You don't believe me, just call up those fuckers that helped Cassidy put him in the cage," China said.

Thoughts crowded into Mellas's head. Maybe the alert wasn't a go. They'd suffered through no-gos before. Mellas looked around. The company was formed into heli teams. Goodwin was walking slowly down the line of his platoon, joking, bantering. Kendall was sitting tensely by his radioman, Genoa, staring at the hills across the airstrip. He saw Bass checking his own gear, a sure sign that everyone else's was ready.

"OK, China," Mellas said. "I'll see if I can get the Jayhawk on it. You better have it fucking straight." He picked up the handset of the radio. "I want to talk to character Hotel, the Three Zulu. This is Bravo Five. Over."

There was a long wait. The battalion operator came back up. "The Three says character Hotel is busy. Over."

"Did you ask Hotel if he was busy?" Mellas asked. "Over."

"Wait one." There was another pause, shorter than the first.

Then Major Blakely's voice came over the hook. "Bravo Five, this is Big John Three. We've got a Bald Eagle alert and you better be getting that mob ready to fly. Over."

"Roger that. Bravo Five out."

Mellas looked at China. "I'm stuck," he said.

"Shit," China said. He turned away, disgusted.

"Look, China," Mellas said. "Even if we can get Lieutenant Hawke to get Mallory out of the cargo box, you know he's still in deep shit even if it wasn't loaded." Mellas knew that whoever he sent to find Hawke had to be trusted to come back for the launch. At the same time, it had to be someone China trusted.

"China," he said, "so help me if you don't make it back in time for this launch, I'll fuck with you so bad you'll never have seen such fucking-with. Now get going."

China took off full tilt up the road. Goodwin and Ridlow came running to Mellas. "What in fuck's going on?" Ridlow growled, looking at China's disappearing backside.

"Mallory pulled a forty-five on the battalion surgeon."

"I know that. Relsnik told us."

"The pistol wasn't loaded. I sent China to tell Hawke to try and get him out of the cargo box."

"Cargo box? Fuck," Ridlow said slowly. "That fucking nigger couldn't break out of a cellophane bag."

"Who the fuck wants him sprung?" Goodwin asked.

"Guess, Scar."

"Ah, shit," Goodwin said. "China's one of my best fucking gunners."

"He'll be back."

"You want to lose some money on that?" Ridlow asked.

"He'll be back," Mellas said. He looked down the road, wishing he could be certain. He saw Fitch and Pallack driving up in the jeep. It skidded to a stop and they both jumped out.

"I just saw China shagging ass down the road," Fitch said. "What the fuck's going on? The company ready to go?"

Mellas told him it was and explained what China was doing. "I believe him," Mellas added. He looked at the cynical faces around him.

Fitch hesitated a moment. He turned to Pallack. "Go pick up China and take him wherever he wants to go. And then get his ass back down here. We need fucking gunners."

Pallack jumped into the jeep and spun down the road, slinging mud and water behind him.

Fracasso, Goodwin, and Kendall were already moving in on Mellas and Fitch, their notebooks out. Mellas pulled his own notebook out. His hands were sweating. Jesus Christ, please just make it another false alarm. Mellas felt as if he were on a conveyor belt that was slowly moving him toward the edge of a cliff.

Fitch spread his map out on the ground. "Here," he said, pointing to a spot circled in red. "A recon team, call sign Sweet Alice, is in contact right now with a company-size NVA unit. Scar, you patrolled this valley. You too, Mellas. What's it like?"

"Thick as shit, Jack."

Mellas nodded agreement. "Elephant grass and bamboo," he added.

Fitch licked his lips. "If we get the word to launch we're going in hot, take them on their flank from the west. Right here." His finger was almost on the red line of the circle. "We'll have gunships but arty is probably out. Extreme range."

"We went in first last time," Ridlow said.

Fitch ignored him. "What do you think, Scar? Can we get a bird in?"

"Yeah."

"We went in first last time," Ridlow said again.

"Shit, Ridlow, I know. I also know why fucking platoon sergeants don't usually attend the actuals meetings."

Ridlow smiled. "Just looking out for my men's best interests."

People laughed and Fitch grinned.

Mellas looked at the tableau of friends around him. Some of them would very likely be dead in an hour. Fracasso, who was barely old enough to drink, really showed his fear. He was writing everything he could in his notebook, bouncing up and down in a crouch, his teeth bared in a tense grin. Goodwin, the hunter, was nervous, like a runner before a race, possessing some primitive ability to lead men into situations where death was the understood payoff. Kendall, worried sick, his face pallid, his helmet already on his head, was leading a platoon that didn't trust him. Fitch, at age twenty-three, had already worn responsibility that most men only debated about. He was now taking 190 kids into battle, and his decisions would determine how many came back. The kids: dreaming of R & R, or remembering the R & R from which they'd just returned, some savoring a memory of smooth brown skin pressed against their own, a few remembering wives left behind at antiseptic airports. And Mellas: in less than an hour there could be no Mellas.

The radio crackled to life.

"It's a go, sir," Relsnik said gravely.

Everyone looked at everyone else.

CHAPTER
THIRTEEN

The kids filed quietly to the edge of the strip to wait for the helicopters. Other Marines stopped to watch them, wanting to say an encouraging word yet not daring to break into their private world—a world no longer shared with ordinary people. Some of them were experiencing the last hour of that brief mystery called life.

Pallack skidded the company jeep to a stop and he and China ran for their packs and weapons. They trotted heavily to where the company waited.

China came up to Mellas, his machine gun on his shoulder. "Jayhawk said he'd do the best he could. If the pistol wasn't loaded, he'd get him out."

Mellas really didn't care. "Good," he said. He was trying to figure out from which side they should come in on the gook company and whether or not they'd have any choice, not knowing the wind conditions.

"Sir," China said. "Lieutenant Hawke told me to tell you this too." China stopped.

"Well, what the fuck did he say?"

"He said, sir, to make sure I tell you both things. That you ought to solve you own fuckin' problems and not dump them on other people." China paused. Mellas kept his lips compressed. "And that you'd better get you ass back here when the shit's over so he can kick it for you." Mellas broke into relieved laughter.

China snorted. Mellas noticed that he didn't have his pistol, which all machine gunners carry for protection. "China, where's your fucking forty-five?"

"It got ripped off, sir."

Mellas and China looked at each other a moment.

"Goddamn it, China, why lie now?" Mellas said sadly. He'd heard the rumors about the blacks sending parts back to the States. He pulled his own pistol and holster off his belt and threw it to China. China looked at it and started strapping it on. He turned without saying anything.

Sergeant Ridlow, who had just returned from a final check of his platoon—tightening loose straps, saying a gruff, encouraging word—had watched the last part of the exchange with China. "He's not chicken-shit," Mellas said, watching China checking out his machine gun.

"None of them are, Lieutenant," Ridlow said.

Mellas looked down the rows of heli teams, feeling cut off from his old platoon as he watched Bass and Fracasso making sure everyone was ready. Just days before, he had been their platoon commander, lifting off from Sky Cap. War made a mockery of his previous concept of time. He watched the leaden sky for the arrival of the helicopters. Anne's face floated into his memory. He knew she never wanted to see him again, but here she was, perhaps the last good thing on his mind.

"Here they come," somebody shouted.

Suspended in the sky were tiny black dots. The sight sent a trembling, sick dread into Mellas's guts. His knees wanted to collapse and his body wanted to run. The black dots peeled off as they came closer, turning into twin-rotor CH-46s, coming around in a single line to land from the south. Mellas wanted them to crash, to fall out of the sky. They were coming to kill him. For no reason. And he was going to step aboard. Again he felt the conveyor belt carrying him toward the cliff.

The first chopper settled in on its rear wheels. Kendall and the first heli team jogged across the mud and disappeared into the tailgate. A second chopper dropped its ramp and another heli team from Kendall's platoon ran aboard. Then a third chopper pulled up, and a fourth, and the choppers kept coming and the kids kept disappearing. Then there were no more heli teams left but Mellas's and one other, and then Mellas was running, the weight of his pack thumping against his back. He ducked his head beneath the rotor blades, pounded past the crew chief, and settled on the metal deck. It was still cold from the altitude.

The chopper shuddered with increased power and became clumsily airborne. That moment of false security, waiting on the airstrip, was cut off forever.

It was about thirty-five kilometers northeast to the red circle on Fitch's map. Mellas watched the Rock Pile and the Razorback, two towering rock formations that dominated the landscape around VCB, slip behind them. He kept taking compass readings, trying to keep his bearings straight. He wondered what would happen if he just refused to get off the helicopter. They'd have to fly him back to Quang Tri. He'd be tried and convicted. But he'd be alive. He worried anxiously about whether or not the LZ would be hot.

The chopper lurched sideways. Mellas pushed himself to his knees, fighting against the acceleration of the turn and the slanting deck. He stumbled to one of the shot-out portholes and stuck his head out, squinting against the rushing air, trying to see why the pilot was making such fast turns. The machine gunner on the starboard side was leaning out into space, the big .50-caliber pointing downward. The crew chief was on the port side on a second machine gun, craning his neck to see, but tilted too far above the horizon to do any good. The bird suddenly righted itself, then went into a sickeningly fast descent. The roar increased. Then Mellas heard the whiplike sound of bullets snapping through the air. The starboard .50-caliber opened up. Then the gunner spun backward, the plastic of his helmet shattered, his face a mess. He slumped to the floor, his throat tangled in his intercom wire.

Everyone wanted out of the chopper, including Mellas.

The bird hit the deck and the ramp swung down. The Marines started to hurtle out. The pilot panicked and took off before all of the Marines were on the ground. When Mellas reached the exit the bird was already six feet off the ground and gaining speed. He was shouting at the crew chief, "Keep this fucker on the ground, goddamn you. Keep this fucking bird on the ground." He leaped off into space and hit the ground hard. The bird continued roaring for altitude behind him. The last kid on the chopper looked anxiously behind him, gulped, and hurled himself into space to join his friends. He and his pack, which weighed almost 100 pounds, hit with a sickening thud. Mellas watched the leg bone give way and bulge out beneath the trouser leg. The kid's scream could be heard above the roar of rifle and machine-gun fire.

Mellas shouted. "You bastard, you fucking bastard." He lifted his rifle to fire a burst at the disappearing helicopter, but some inner strength froze his finger before he pulled the trigger. He ran instead to the hurt kid, shouting for a corpsman, and began to drag him and his gear away from the landing zone. Another Marine came up to Mellas and together they pulled the writhing kid into the relative cover of some elephant grass. They left him and ran on ahead, catching up to the advancing platoon, which Goodwin had spread out on line. He was moving it in quick squad rushes toward the enemy.

The firing stopped. Two Huey gunships that had been laying down machine-gun fire just to their north looped up in a curve and roared over their heads. There were a couple of desultory shots from M-16s. An M-79 grenade launcher fired. Then came another random burst of fire. Then silence, except for occasional shouts. Mellas went running behind Goodwin's platoon, crouching low, fighting his way through the thick elephant grass. Everyone had stopped, waiting, sweating, panting. Mellas met Goodwin coming the opposite way. There was a burst of M-16 fire, but nothing answered it.

"Everything's OK back there, Scar," Mellas said. "One Oley with a broken leg." Mellas had automatically shifted into radio code.

"Fitch stopped us," Goodwin said. "I think the little fuckers dee-deed."

It was over.

Mellas kept jogging along parallel to the company's line. Everyone lay tensely on the ground, M-16s and machine guns pointed ahead. As he reached the left end of the line, he started passing his old platoon. They smiled at him. He ran past. Chadwick was on his back, blood covering his chest. He gave Mellas a thumbs-up and grinned, knowing he was on his way home. Mellas ran past him. He came upon Doc Fredrickson, who was working on a new kid Mellas had never even met. Mellas kept running. He reached Fitch, who was on the radio.

"They pulled out. Over. No, I can't tell which way, Stevens, goddamn it. We can't see shit in this stuff. Over. To the north. I understand that. It would be suicide chasing them in this shit. Over. They're not *running*, goddamn it, they're *retreating*. They'll be laying on the ground and we'll be standing. They'll chew us up."

There was a pause. Mellas heard another voice come on the radio but couldn't understand what it was saying. Then Fitch said, "My mission priority is to get that team out safely and our wounded medevaced. We can't chase them, sir, if we have to carry bodies with us. Over. Aye, aye, sir. Bravo Six out." He turned to Daniels. "You got the fucking fire mission going yet?" Daniels was talking on the hook and just nodded. "We got to circle them up, Mellas," Fitch said. "The recon team has five Oleys. That's out of six and the other one is Coors. I'm sending Scar to pick them up. We'll lift them out of the zone. Big John Six is going bug fuck. How's it look down there?"

"OK. I didn't see any Coors. A couple of bad Oleys."

Fitch grunted, relieved.

Mellas set the company in around the LZ and soon had everyone digging holes. Goodwin took two squads and reached the reconnaissance team in ten minutes. It took them twenty minutes to make it back to the zone, struggling under the weight of the dead body and one kid who was shot through both knees. The rest of the team managed to walk out under their own power. The leader, a big lieutenant, had grenade fragments in his left leg. He came up to Fitch and Mellas.

"Thanks," he said. "I thought I'd kissed my ass good-bye."

"It's OK," Fitch said. "What the fuck happened?"

"It was my fault." The big man let out a long quivering sigh. He started shaking, the pressure off.

"Want a smoke?"

The lieutenant shook his head. "Up there." He pointed to Matterhorn, its base looming above the valley, the top hidden by clouds. "I spotted some movement two nights ago. I thought I could work in closer to see what it was."

"Tubing! Tubing! Incoming!" The cry resounded throughout the circle. People scrambled for cover.

"Oh, fuck," Fitch said. The three of them lay flat on the ground, none having had time to dig a hole.

Six explosions, almost simultaneous, rocked the area just outside the perimeter.

"They're up there, all right," the lieutenant said. "I saw two machine guns. They're dug in on that hill to the right. There's a burned-out helicopter on it. With that many heavy machine guns my guess is we may have a company up there. I wanted to check out the other hill, but—"

"Incoming!" someone shouted.

Mellas was digging furiously. Six more explosions walked across the interior of the company perimeter. The NVA gunners had the range. There was no doubt in his mind that there was a company. No smaller unit would hump the mortar ammo.

"Get the fucking fire mission going, Daniels!" Fitch shouted. "They've got our fucking number." Fitch immediately switched to the two circling gunships and directed them to find the mortars if they could.

"We can't get a mission going if the choppers are in the way," Daniels shouted, frustrated. "And the rate of fire will be slow because of the range. They'll burn their barrels up if they shoot too fast with max charges."

"I don't give a fuck about their barrels. You call in the goddamn mission."

Everyone was throwing dirt, cursing, scratching at the earth. Again there were six explosions. Someone screamed.

Mellas dug. At the same time he was timing the pattern. He figured at least two mortars firing three rounds, or maybe even three firing two. With barely enough dug out to get his body in lengthwise, he pushed his face into the soil, feeling naked and exposed.

"Here come the birds!"

Two Huey medevac slicks came shooting in over their heads from the south. FAC-man popped a green smoke grenade and was moving with his radio on his back, talking to the lead bird as it swung up away from the ground and made a looping turn to come back into the zone.

Off to the north, muffled by the distance, they could hear the deep-throated roar of machine gun fire from one of the two gunships that Fitch had sent over toward Matterhorn.

The big lieutenant ran, limping, across the landing zone. The lead chopper hit the earth hard. Marines loaded the wounded. The lieutenant waited for the second chopper, helped more of the wounded aboard, threw the dead body inside, and climbed on the skids. The chopper was just getting airborne, its nose tipped down as it gained forward speed, when six more mortar rounds hit. The explosions hid the chopper from view. Then it cleared the smoke at the far end of the zone and lifted into the air.

"Let's get the fuck out of here," Fitch said. "Goddamn it, Daniels, get us some fucking smoke." Daniels already knew that he couldn't effectively counter the mortars. His only hope was to lay a smoke screen between the company and the ridgeline to the north. The shells, however, weren't striking where he'd called for them. With Eiger abandoned, he was forced to use the 8-inch howitzers on Sherpa, but they were at the edge of their range. At that distance the shells were subject to winds and temperature differentials he could only guess at. He hoped that where they did land would be good enough. He looked uneasily at the clouds hiding the tops of the ridges.

Bravo Company split into three columns and moved into the protection of the jungle. A final NVA mortar shell found the tail of Kendall's platoon before they reached the cover of the trees, and two more Marines were wounded, but these weren't emergency medevacs and could be carried. The company had medevaced six kids, none of whom had died, and had rescued Sweet Alice, the reconnaissance team. If they got their other two wounded out by morning they'd have lost no one. They all felt proud. Drained, yet oddly content, they dug in, feeling protected by the thick jungle. In the morning they would be skying out, mission accomplished.

Colonel Simpson, too, felt proud and flushed with success. "I knew the little bastards were there," he kept crowing. He and Blakely had just returned to the combat operations center from the regimental briefings, where congratulations had been warm and plentiful. He reached for the hook, calling Bravo Company once again.

Hawke heard Relsnik's voice over the squawk box that enabled everyone in the COC to hear the conversation. Hawke imagined Fitch's eyes rolling. It was at least the fifth time since the fight that the colonel had wanted to talk with Fitch.

Hawke continued plotting air observer and sensor sightings. He didn't like the look of them. Too much activity, right where the colonel wanted it, right where Bravo Company was.

Simpson asked, "You say you can see them? Over."

"We sent our Foxtrot Oscar up a tree to call in fire and he says they're digging in on Helicopter Hill. Matterhorn's covered with clouds. We can't see anything on it." There was a slight pause filled with background static. "Sweet Alice told me they're probably well entrenched on Matterhorn in our old bunkers. Over."

Hawke looked to see if Blakely and Simpson had any reaction to Fitch's statement. They didn't show one.

"They've split their forces." Simpson turned excitedly to Blakely. "I think we ought to exploit the situation."

Blakely picked up the hook. "Bravo Six, this is Big John Three. What do you estimate the enemy size at? Over."

"Like I said, the Oscar type from Sweet Alice told me he thinks maybe a company. We can only see maybe fifty or so on Helicopter Hill, but there's got to be at least twice that on Matterhorn just to cover the perimeter. Besides, the mortar rounds come in sixes. Over."

"How many do you *see*, Bravo Six?" Blakely replied. "Not how many do you guess. Over."

"Fifty," was Fitch's terse reply. The handset keyed off and then on again. Fitch's voice was controlled and without intonation. "Sir, one of my O types did a lot of patrolling down here and he says we've got a good Lima Zulu at—from Comiskey Park—up two-point-two, left one-point-seven." Fitch was telling them the location of a landing zone using the radio brevity code for the day. "We can hump over there, it's below the cloud layer, and get out without exposing the wingies to a lot of mortar fire from Matterhorn or Helicopter Hill. Over."

"Wait one, Bravo Six." Blakely turned to Simpson. "You say anything about lifting them out, sir?"

"Fuck, no. Not with the gooks with their tails between their legs and me with three companies ready to kick ass."

Hawke stopped putting marks on the map.

"Bravo Six, this is Big John Three. Hold off awhile. I want you to wait at your present pos until you receive a frag order from us. You copy? Over."

"Roger, copy, Big John Three. Bravo Six out."

Blakely walked briskly over to the map. Simpson followed him. They stood looking at it, aware that everyone's eyes were on them.

"We've got a known platoon-size unit, maybe more," Blakely said. "A fresh company of Marines who know the enemy territory like the back of their hands. And damn near a battalion in reserve."

"I knew the bastards were there," Simpson said. "No one would listen to me. I'm ordering Bravo Company into the assault. I'll go confirm with Mulvaney right now. I bet he's just eating boiled crow." Simpson laughed, high on excitement and success.

Blakely could see that this was an opportunity. He knew they had only a little time before the enemy consolidated on the two hills, but he also knew Fitch couldn't leave his wounded behind without protection and this would weaken his assaulting force. If there was a company up there, as Fitch suspected, attacking it would be foolish. They had no surprise, no local superiority, and no real firepower, with all the artillery batteries pulled back because of the Cam Lo operation. It would take time to shift a couple of batteries back out that way, but that would of course leave the other battalions with less support, and that wouldn't be done unless Mulvaney agreed.

On the other hand, it was the first time in a couple of months they actually knew where a sizable unit was. If he could keep Simpson under control, they might be able to do some real damage. Meanwhile, they had to keep Nagoolian fixed. And they would have to commit the battalion, for which they needed Mulvaney's OK. That wouldn't be easy. Mulvaney had been criticized before about getting too aggressive, and his bitching about the Cam Lo operation hadn't scored him any points with the brass.

But people also got criticized for not being aggressive enough, and that was far worse. The log would show a unit of fifty on Helicopter Hill. Blakely had learned that younger officers tended to overestimate the size of the enemy force they were facing, so maybe there were thirty gooks up there. But the enemy was digging in, probably with machine guns, and certainly had mortars. Thirty on Helicopter Hill meant at least seventy or eighty on Matterhorn. Still, with air support, a fresh company of Marines could easily take them. A vague thought about the difficulty of fixed wing support with monsoon clouds surfaced in his mind but was quickly repressed by the thought that helicopter gunships could get in there. They'd done it earlier today, after all.

Obviously they didn't need the fucking hill. They'd abandoned it themselves. But Blakely knew that the fight was no longer about terrain; it was about attrition. Body count. That was the job, and he'd do it. If there was a company up there, a battalion couldn't be too far away. And if he could fix that battalion in place using the battalion's three remaining rifle companies and any others that Mulvaney could spare, they'd have a field day. They could bring in the B-52s from Guam, flying well above the monsoon clouds, and cream the little bastards whether they could see them or not. There would finally be something tangible to report instead of these infuriating dribbles of kills and casualties they'd been turning in for weeks.

Blakely began calculating lift capacities and artillery positions. They were too far inland for naval support, even from the *New Jersey* and its big sixteen-inchers. It would take time to move the artillery to compensate for the inconsistent air support, but they could do it. That meant they had to get Nagoolian to stick while they shifted artillery around—if he could get Mulvaney to go along with it.

He came back to the present at the COC, aware that Simpson was ready to act, but that was about all. "Sir, before we see Mulvaney, maybe we'd better have a sketch of a plan worked out," Blakely said. "This could involve a lot more than just the battalion, you know, if your hunches about the gooks prove correct."

"Yes, by God, you're right."

The two of them walked out of the COC and over to Simpson's tent. Simpson reached for a bottle of Wild Turkey and poured himself a shot. "This could develop into something really big," he said, smiling, trying to hide his nervousness. He got a glass out for Blakely, but Blakely refused. Simpson suddenly felt embarrassed. He hadn't really been thinking about the booze; it was just a natural thing to offer someone a drink. Now he didn't know whether or not to drink the shot he'd poured. God, he couldn't be drinking—not when a company had recently been in contact with the enemy and was maybe about to go into the assault. He put the bottle away, looked at the shot glass sitting on his table, ignored it, and walked over to the map. "We'll have to move some artillery batteries if we've got a sizable force there," he said, trying to regain his command of the situation. He felt like a fool.

"Sir," Blakely said, "what do you think the chances are of Mulvaney letting you commit the battalion to retake Matterhorn?"

"What do you mean? You mean he might turn us down?"

"Not if we do it right." Blakely walked over to Simpson's map. "Look, sir, Matterhorn is at the ultimate limits of our artillery protection, as you just pointed out, but it's well within range of the gooks out of Co Roc or anywhere else inside Laos. But we can't attack their artillery without political OK."

"That's no problem," Simpson said. "We'll get it. We'll be suppressing fire to help one of our units on this side of the border."

"It's not the approval that's the problem, sir," Blakely said. "It's the process. To get approval we'll have to submit all our reasons why we want it, before we need it." He paused. "Or we'll have to have some good reason for needing it when we want it."

Simpson reached for the shot glass and tossed down the whiskey. This fucking political bullshit, he thought. God*damn,* did it fuck things up. He wasn't exactly sure what Blakely had just said, but he was certain he didn't want to submit a plan to division that involved moving artillery batteries that would be firing into Laos. The recon team was already rescued, and its leader just *thought* there was a company around. That wasn't good enough. It would look stupid and it wouldn't go. God*damn* these fucking politicians. He knew the fucking gooks were right where he'd always figured. Now he couldn't do anything about it. He slammed the empty shot glass down on the plywood. "Fuck!" he said. "We'll have to just fly 'em back home, won't we?" He looked at Blakely but saw no dismay or anger. "Or don't you think so?" he asked, looking at his operations officer through narrowed eyes.

"Like I said, sir, a reason for needing it when we want it."

"Go on."

"Mulvaney's an old grunt. Nothing but an overweight platoon commander with birds on his shoulders. He'd leap at a chance to get in there and kick ass if he had any excuse at all. But he's not about to take any major plan in to division. You know the scuttlebutt as well as I do. He's none too popular up there. On the other hand, our job is to kill gooks. If we let an opportunity like this go by, we could look pretty chickenshit. You've got complete tactical control. You don't need to talk to anyone to do something that doesn't commit other forces you don't control or screw up your current mission. Your log shows fifty gooks. You've got a fresh company, and you know Fitch is probably overestimating the number anyway. It's more like twenty-five or thirty. On the record you've got a three-to-one superiority, and probably a five-to-one. We've got all we need to take them. If we find out there are more and we already have a company in action? *Then* you've got a story you can take to Mulvaney."

Simpson was pacing back and forth, nodding nervously as he listened to Blakely. "Yes, goddamn it, I see," he kept saying.

"I say we commit Bravo now, a perfect exploitation of the success you had this afternoon. If we've got gooks up there, like you've been telling everyone, then we'll find out for sure when Bravo hits Helicopter Hill. If things get too tight, we'll just walk them back to that LZ Fitch told us about and yank them out."

Simpson stopped pacing and looked at the map.

"If we wait around," Blakely went on, "we'll end up watching Nagoolian fade across the border. You'll never prove your case. Commit Bravo and prove your point. Then Mulvaney's got to let you commit the rest of the battalion to support them. Once Bravo's engaged, it'll be just what Mulvaney needs to get his ass off the dime: a bunch of grunts fighting like hell and a bunch of grunts waiting to wade in and help them. Otherwise he's liable to back off, worry about patrolling his fucking firebases. He's still in Korea taking hills. It's attrition that counts in this war. Turf doesn't mean jack shit."

Simpson felt the nervous chill that men feel when faced with decisions that they know can bring the fulfillment, or the ruin, of their dreams and ambitions. He paced back and forth. He kept looking at the map. He wanted a drink but knew he couldn't take one in front of Blakely.

"Sir, the sensor reports confirm what you've suspected all along as well. Your case is airtight."

"Goddamn it, Blakely, let me think."

Blakely kept silent.

After about three minutes Simpson leaned over, his knuckles on the plywood table, and looked up at Blakely. "All right, by God, we'll do it." His eyes were shining with excitement. Then he reached for the glass.

After making the decision to attack, Blakely and Simpson both grew concerned that sending Bravo in right away might be too hasty. It would require a platoon to move the wounded to a safe LZ. This could entail an assault with only two platoons, which would look bad if it failed. They could, of course, take the risk of guarding the wounded with only a squad, but if the squad was overwhelmed, and they had evidence from Sweet Alice that a company was in the area, that would be even harder to explain. If they tried to medevac the wounded they risked losing a chopper, and that wouldn't look good either. They both knew that bold moves might have been all right for Stonewall Jackson or George Patton, but this was a different kind of war. They played safe.

The first frag order told Fitch to send a platoon to the LZ with the wounded. Fitch sent Mellas off with Fracasso, who was jumpy after having gone into a hot zone on his first day of command. Mellas humped along in the rear with Bass, shooting the shit, happy to be back with his old platoon. He watched with satisfaction as Fracasso led the platoon to the LZ, accomplished the medevacs, and guided the platoon back by a different route to link up with the rest of the company, now in position closer to the ridge. There, Fitch had set the company in on a small rise of ground, fifty meters inside the protective cover of the jungle. The jungle edged a broad patch of elephant grass on the valley floor immediately below the approaches to Matterhorn.

This all took until nightfall, giving the NVA plenty of time to dig in on Helicopter Hill.

The second frag order came at twilight. Long before Relsnik finished decoding the order it was apparent that an assault was being ordered.

Goodwin sauntered up to the CP group. He was eating a can of spaghetti and meatballs mixed with a package of Wyler's lemonade powder. "What's up, Jack?" he asked Fitch.

"We're going to take the hill at first light."

"Matterhorn?"

"No. Helicopter Hill."

Goodwin whistled. "Just like in the movies," he said.

"Let's hope so," Fitch replied, spreading his map.

Looking at Matterhorn and Helicopter Hill as an attacker, Mellas wondered how he could have been so frightened when he was defending it. Steep fingers led up to the top, divided by deep, heavily jungled gullies. To stay in contact as they advanced, they would have to move in single file. But to move the entire company single file would take hours, exposing them to mortar attack and a possible flanking movement. To attack from the west, north, or south exposed them to automatic weapons fire from the bunkers on Matterhorn. To attack from the east would mean channeling their attack into a narrow front, perfect for defensive machine-gun fire and mortars. Then there was the support problem. They'd have to rely on air.

One plan was scratched. A second was proposed, and then a third. It grew darker. They huddled over the map with their red-lens flashlights. Every plan had a flaw. After three hours of debate they finally realized that there was no perfect plan. Somebody was going to get killed.

Mellas sat down with his head in his hands, rubbing his eyes, wishing fervently that Hawke was still with them. He now regretted telling Blakely that Hawke wanted out of the bush and that the battalion might lose him if Blakely didn't act fast—this was a big part of the reason why Hawke wasn't with them. It was all absurd, without reason or meaning. People who didn't even know each other were going to kill each other over a hill none of them cared about. The wind picked up slightly, bringing the smell of the jungle with it. Mellas shivered. He couldn't figure out why they didn't just quit. Yet they wouldn't.

They finally decided to move Fracasso's First Platoon and Kendall's Third Platoon up a long finger that led south from the main ridgeline, starting just east of Helicopter Hill. When they reached the main east-west ridgeline, First Platoon would attack westward and hit Helicopter Hill from the east. They would be supported by Kendall's platoon, which would also act as the reserve. Kendall would set up on a little hump just behind First Platoon's line of departure, from where they could fire over First Platoon's heads. Goodwin's Second Platoon would simultaneously move up a narrower finger that paralleled the one the main body would take and was just to the west of it. Instead of joining the main ridgeline, however, the narrower finger led directly into the south side of Helicopter Hill. The Air Force's defoliation had not been as successful on that finger, so there was good cover almost to the top. Goodwin was to get on line, draping his platoon across the top of the finger and down both sides, if possible without being detected, and attack from the south when Fitch felt the enemy was fully engaged with First Platoon on the east side. In this way Second Platoon would be concealed longer and, once released, would be exposed to fire from Matterhorn itself, which was directly to the finger's west, for the shortest possible time. Approaching in the dark would eliminate fire on Goodwin's platoon from Matterhorn before the assault, but only if they weren't detected. In fact, a large part of the plan depended on Goodwin's getting into position undetected. When daylight broke and the assault began, Goodwin's platoon would quickly be mingled with NVA troops on Helicopter Hill, and the NVA on Matterhorn would probably have to hold their fire.

Of course the main issue was the defenders of Helicopter Hill itself. Still, Fitch hoped the dead branches of the defoliated jungle just below the hill might give some concealment and cover if they could attack during the poor light of early morning. That meant everything had to go at dawn, and, he hoped, with the clouds low to the ground. On the other hand, if clouds were close to the ground, there was no hope for air support.

"Fucking brilliant," Mellas said. "It took us three fucking hours to figure out we'll just charge the motherfuckers." It was almost with relief that he threw himself into planning the mechanics of departure lines, timing, air coordination, and smoke and hand signals.

They filed out into the blackness of the jungle at 0100, emerging an hour later into the high grass on the valley's floor. Low clouds, drizzle, and darkness hid Matterhorn and the ridgeline completely. Mellas felt as if his map and the dim red spot of his flashlight were the only reality in a darkness that oppressed not only sight but the mind as well.

They reached the point where Goodwin's platoon was to veer off to the west to begin moving up its assigned finger. Everyone quietly dropped his pack. This was so everyone could save energy on the climb, free themselves for instant and fast movement when the action started, and avoid unnecessary noise. They took only water—canteens topped to prevent the sound of water sloshing—and two cans of food, carefully wrapped in socks to avoid the sound of cans clinking together. Ammunition was carefully placed in cloth pockets. Faces were smeared with clay and dirt.

Even unburdened of their packs, they moved very slowly. The tiniest sounds rang out like bells. Unseen branches slapped at their eyes. The cold fog enveloped them. The kids cursed beneath their breath as they groped for the ground in front of them. They silently cleared limbs from their faces, biting back the need to vent their anger at the pain.

They crawled over downed trees, squeezed through thick brambles. Moving quietly in the dark takes a great deal of time. Too much time. Dawn was breaking.

An explosion ahead of the main body sent everyone down to his stomach. A long wailing scream hung in the air. Samms, directly behind Mellas, rose to his feet and whispered, "Shut the fucker up, somebody. Shut that son of a bitch up." First and Third Platoon had lost the advantage of surprise.

The scream stopped abruptly.

The stillness of the jungle after that anguished sound was like ether-laden cotton, numbing, oppressive, dangerous. Everyone wondered what had happened to cause such pain, and how it had ended.

It had been ended when Jancowitz shut his eyes and jammed his fist into the hole left by the blown-away lower jaw of the kid who had been on point. The shrapnel from the DH-10 directional mine had taken out his eyes and lower jaw but had left his vocal cords intact. One foot had been ripped off as well.

Jancowitz pulled his bloody hand from the mess around the kid's throat. A piece of jawbone with two teeth in it caught on the opal ring Susi had bought for him. Fredrickson rushed up and pinched the spurting carotid artery with one hand while he fumbled to stuff a thick bandage pad against the stump of the lower leg.

Jancowitz touched Fredrickson on the shoulder and shook it gently. "Let him die, Doc," he said.

Fredrickson hesitated, then let go of the artery. The blood oozed out quickly, no longer spurting.

"Who was it?" Fredrickson asked quietly, blood smeared on his face. The face before him was unrecognizable.

"Broyer."

Fracasso, who had been anxiously watching Fredrickson's efforts, backed away involuntarily, bumping into Hamilton. "Excuse me," Fracasso mumbled.

They wrapped Broyer's body in his poncho and put his black plastic glasses in the pocket of his utility jacket. They then rolled the

poncho's edges for hand grips. Fredrickson put the medevac number in
his notebook along with the cause of death.

Fracasso put Jacobs's squad on point. They continued moving
awkwardly forward to get into position for the assault, knowing there
would be no surprise in their favor. Their main hope now shifted to
Goodwin, if only he could work his way up undetected.

The fog swirled around them. The fear of mines dogged every step.
Broyer's body slowed them considerably.

Big John Six was frantic.

"It's damn near oh eight thirty. They were supposed to be at their
FLD three hours ago. I knew I should have shit-canned that goddamned
Fitch."

Hawke listened, knowing that Fitch would have been extremely
fortunate to make the FLD—the final line of departure—on time. He
was more worried about the weather than Fitch's failure to kick off on
schedule. Air support, holding in tight circles within easy striking distance of the target, had to have clear weather and had to strike before
running short of fuel.

Captain Bainford threw his pencil across the bunker and leaned
back in his chair to look at Simpson and Blakely. He'd had four F-4
Phantoms waiting above the clouds, but they had gone bingo fuel and
had to return to base. He cursed about Fitch's inability to stick to a schedule. One of the radio operators picked up Bainford's pencil.

"What about the Navy?" Simpson asked.

Bainford sighed. "I'll try, sir. But they got to be able to see what
they're bombing, just like everyone else." Bainford went back to the
radio, trying to drum up another flight to wait above the towering clouds
that hid the western mountains.

At that moment Goodwin was quietly spreading his platoon out in a
long frontal line, preparing to move from the cover of the trees up the
defoliated slopes of Helicopter Hill. He keyed the handset to signal his

arrival. Fitch checked his watch. The company had been moving nearly eight hours without rest or food. Fitch could only guess how far away he was from his own final line of departure.

Robertson emerged from behind a thick cover of bush and caught movement in a tree from the corner of his eye. An NVA soldier was taking a piss, holding on to a branch and making patterns on the ground below him with his urine. Robertson said, "Oh, shit," and fell backward, firing his M-16. At the same time, a second NVA soldier in the tree let loose with a long burst from his AK-47. The one who had been taking a piss jumped to the ground, running hard. His friend toppled over backward with Robertson's bullets running up the inside of his body.

The radios crackled to life.

"We're committed," Fitch said. "End radio silence. Over."

The company surged forward, still in single file, behind Fracasso, who emerged from the shelter of the jungle onto the defoliated crest of the main ridgeline and went running across, down the north side, spreading the platoon in a single line behind him as he went. He stopped, setting them in place, and then returned to the center, moving in a crouch behind them as they lay looking intently at their objective.

Helicopter Hill's bald outline wavered in the gray fog. It had changed considerably, having been made into an auxiliary LZ by the artillery battery, the trees blasted clear for forty or fifty meters from the crest, and all the remaining trees and brush killed by defoliating chemicals. The NVA had also built bunkers that were plainly visible near the top of the hill, which was about 100 meters above the ridge on which Fracasso was crouched. The ridge sloped gradually upward from him toward the west. About 300 meters from where he was, it merged into Helicopter Hill, which rose abruptly and steeply from the ridge, like a large knuckle. From the map, and from interviewing everyone he could, Fracasso knew that the much larger bulk of Matterhorn stood behind Helicopter Hill, about 600 meters to its west, hidden from his view. Matterhorn's summit, with its flattened LZ and abandoned artillery positions, was about 200 meters higher than Helicopter Hill. That was within rifle range and Fracasso didn't like it. For now, however, he had other things to worry about.

Kendall and Samms set Third Platoon into position, packing everyone on the small hump behind First Platoon in tiers, thankful they had gone into the hot zone first the day before yet feeling guilty and anxious for the Marines of First Platoon, who lay silently on the ground in front of them. Mellas joined Fitch and the command post group on the top of the little hump.

Bass and Fracasso moved from kid to kid patting rumps or legs, checking equipment, going over the smoke and hand signals for the twentieth time, comforting them with the thought of jets standing by even though everyone knew the clouds would keep the jets away. Maybe the skipper won't send us in without air, they thought. That hope died when Fitch picked up the hook. "OK, Bravo One. Pop smoke when you want fire. Good luck. Over."

"Aye, aye, Skipper," Fracasso answered. Everyone lay staring ahead at the dead shrubs and defoliated trees on the hill. Fracasso looked down the line to where Bass was crouched with Skosh. Bass was looking at him, waiting for the signal to go. Fracasso crossed himself. Then he stood up and waved his arm forward toward the hill. Bass imitated his signal for those who couldn't see Fracasso. Every Marine rose to his feet, switched off his safety, and walked forward. There would be no running. To reach the summit of the hill in a state of exhaustion would mean almost certain death. They walked, waiting for the enemy to open fire.

Mellas, watching First Platoon's backs, kept asking in a whisper, "Why? Why? Why?" At the same time, immense excitement gripped him. He turned to Fitch. "You don't need me here. I'm going with First Platoon." And not knowing why himself, he ran to catch up with the slowly moving platoon.

Running to rejoin them, he felt overwhelming joy. It was as if he were coming home from a lashing winter storm to the warmth of his living room. The sky seemed brilliantly blue and clear, although he knew

it was overcast. If he didn't move his legs faster, his heart would out-
pace his feet and burst. His heart, his whole body, was overflowing with
an emotion that he could only describe as love.

He came up beside Bass, panting from the run, and settled in on
the southern downhill side of the ridge, a few meters to Bass's right. Bass
had placed himself between Jacobs's squad, on his left, and Jancowitz's
squad, which held the middle position of the line and was draped over
the ridge. Fracasso had given Jancowitz the middle position because of
the skill and experience it would take to keep the squad from splitting
in half if gravity and fear pulled people in its middle downhill from the
ridgeline. Fracasso had placed himself just off the ridgeline on the
northern side. There he could see where Jancowitz's right flank met
Connolly's squad, which held the far right of the line, and endeavor to
keep the two squads from splitting apart. At the same time he could pop
up over the top of the ridge and see where Jacobs's squad was, although
he was relying heavily on Bass to keep them formed up with the rest of
the line.

They were about 100 meters from the base of the hill when a
machine gun opened up from low on the hill, lacing a long line of bullets directly down the crest of the ridge, swaying slightly to both sides
of the crest. The line of Marines hesitated only for a moment, ducking
more from instinct than anything else. The three squad leaders, Bass,
and Fracasso immediately pushed forward to maintain the deliberate
walking pace. The whole line continued forward with no one right on
the ridge's crest where the machine-gun bullets kicked up mud. The
gun was well placed. It denied the easiest approach to the hill, forced
the attackers onto steeper ground on the sides of the ridge, and wid-
ened the gap between them.

Fracasso ran forward of the line, just off the north side of the ridge,
where the machine-gun bullets flew over his head. Hamilton ran beside him with the heavy radio. Then Fracasso popped a red smoke grenade and Hamilton radioed for Third Platoon to open up behind them.

The morning air was shattered by the combined fire of forty rifles
and three machine guns. First Platoon surged forward, now running in
short bursts of speed, the kids throwing themselves to the ground to fire

upward, then moving again, ever higher. The ground on the side of the hill was churning with the bullets being poured into it by Third Platoon. The Marines of First Platoon hit the steep bank, the line of advance folding in on itself in a crescent, and moved up the slope in disciplined short bursts—a movement that had been drilled into the Marines from their first day at boot camp. Some of them were shouting to keep their spirits up; some were shouting from sheer excitement. A few fired their rifles up the slope, but most simply held their fire, knowing that the angle was poor.

About twenty-five meters up the hillside Fracasso popped a green smoke to signal Third Platoon to stop firing. Fitch called off the fire of Third Platoon to avoid hitting his own men.

There was a second or two of silence.

Then Helicopter Hill exploded with the steady, ear-splitting fire of heavy machine guns and the flat clatter of the solid automatic AK-47 and semiautomatic SKS rifles of the North Vietnamese Army. Now the ground beneath First Platoon's feet spat up dirt and mud, some of it tinted dark red.

Mellas ran forward, throwing himself behind rocks, scrambling across exposed patches, and then lunging again for any sort of cover from the fire pouring down on them. All of his being was wound up in his pumping heart and the rapidly rising heat of the blood coursing through his brain and legs. The kids were running and dodging in groups of two and three. Fracasso was trying hard to keep the platoon together. Connolly's squad, on the north side of the ridge, was bunched together, leaving a large gap between it and Jancowitz, who had half his squad on one side of the ridge and half on the other. Jacobs, on the south side, had his squad moving forward in rushes, two fire teams shooting while the third scrambled forward.

The NVA, no longer pinned down by Third Platoon's fire, maintained its own fierce fire. The world seemed to turn over as Mellas watched soft flesh run against hot metal. What, moments before, had been organized movement now disintegrated into confusion, noise, and blood. The attack might have looked as if it were still being directed by the leaders, but it wasn't. It went forward because each Marine knew what to do.

Mellas was transported outside himself, beyond himself. It was as if his mind watched everything coolly while his body raced wildly with passion and fear. He was frightened beyond any fear he had ever known. But this brilliant and intense fear, this terrible here and now, combined with the crucial significance of every movement of his body, pushed him over a barrier whose existence he had not known about until this moment. He gave himself over completely to the god of war within him.

A burst of machine-gun bullets cracked over his head as he ran parallel to the contour of the hill to try and help get the squads back together again. He heard screams for a corpsman. He ran toward the sounds and found Doc Fredrickson already there. Two kids were down, one still breathing raggedly, the other shot through the upper teeth, a gaping exit hole in the back of his head. The two remaining fire team members were still moving upward against the fire. Mellas ran after them. He saw Jacobs crouching behind a small outcropping as he moved forward against a machine-gun emplacement.

Young scrambled up beside Jacobs, set the bipod at the end of his machine-gun barrel on a small hump, and began a steady fire against the NVA machine gun. This enabled the two remaining kids from the fire team to keep crawling up the hill, grenades in their hands.

"Where's Jermain?" Mellas shouted at Jacobs. "We need a fucking M-79." Jacobs turned and looked down at Mellas, who was just below him. He pointed. Mellas raced away, using the steepness of the hill for cover. Bullets passed over his head. He found Jermain crawling cautiously upward through the thick bushes, his stubby M-79 grenade launcher pushed out in front of him.

"We need grenades," Mellas shouted. "Machine-gun bunker. Jacobs is going after it." Mellas turned around, not even looking to see if Jermain would follow and not thinking for a moment that he wouldn't. Jermain ran after him.

The earth was spattering on the front of the small hump and on both sides of Young. His teeth were bared and his face was contorted with fear as he and the NVA machine gunner locked on each other, bullets flying between them. But Young continued firing in short disciplined bursts so as not to overheat his barrel, leaving the others free to move. Jermain shouted at Robertson and two new kids in his fire team above him to get down. Then he stood up, exposing himself to the fire, and began to pump grenades at the opening of the bunker. The NVA machine gun stopped firing.

Then Robertson and the two other kids crawled to their knees and scrambled up to the side of the bunker to finish it off. Mellas was already running away, having done all he could. He didn't see one of the kids crumple to the ground, shot in the back from a hidden hole to the right of the bunker. Robertson rolled forward into the cover of the bushes, throwing both his grenades into the open hole and killing the two North Vietnamese who were firing from it. Without grenades, however, he was now ineffective against the bunker with the machine gun. He lay on his back and cradled his rifle on his chest. The machine gun opened up again. Young responded. This left Jacobs to figure out what to do next.

Mellas ran behind Jancowitz's squad. They were bunching up, making it easier for the NVA gunners, and the terrain was forcing them, unwitting, toward the easier but far more deadly approach of the top of the ridgeline. Mellas saw Bass and screamed at him, "Get those stupid fuckers off that ridgeline." Bass nodded, gasping for air, and ran forward, Skosh dogging his heels with the radio.

Mellas moved straight up the hill. Pollini was there, frantically trying to clear his weapon. Pollini kept looking above him, not at his weapon, jamming the action over and over again.

It took no time for Mellas to figure out the trap. The bushes directly in front of Pollini had been cut away from the ground level up to about two feet, and then the branches had been left in their normal state. It was a clear field of fire for a machine gun that would chop down the advancing man's legs, causing him to fall into the bullets. "Give me that fucking rifle, Shortround," Mellas shouted. His voice was barely audible above the noise. Pollini handed Mellas the rifle as if it might explode any second. He looked at Mellas wildly, then looked downhill to what seemed like safety. Then he grinned at Mellas. "It's jammed, sir."

Mellas quickly saw that Pollini hadn't seated his magazine completely and the upper edge was blocking the passage of the bolt. Mellas shook his head and snapped the magazine into place. He fired a short burst. The hot shell casings poured out, hitting Pollini on the side of the face. That snapped Pollini back to the situation at hand. He grinned and reached for his rifle, once again looking uphill through the tunnel of cleared brush.

"You OK, Shortround?" Mellas asked.

Pollini smiled, gulped, and nodded. "Yeah. Fucking stuck, huh, sir?"

"Yeah, well, it's unstuck now. You watch it. There's a fucking machine gun right above you." Mellas moved away, looking for Jancowitz.

Pollini scrambled to his feet and darted up the hill. He ran straight up the carefully cleared path, disappearing from Mellas's view before Mellas could tackle him.

The machine gun opened up, and Mellas lunged behind a small lip as the bullets chopped up mud and branches. The gun stopped. In the brief silence he heard Pollini shout, "I'm hit. I'm hit."

Mellas hugged the earth when the gun started again, hoping Pollini would crawl back. He didn't.

Bass came around the side of the hill. "Who's hit?" he asked.

"Shortround," Mellas said, crawling backward toward Bass, who was leaning on his side against the steep slope. Skosh was crouched at his feet trying to listen to the radio, one hand over his exposed ear.

Bass looked up the hill. "There's a fucking machine gun up there, sir."

"I know. Shortround's alive. I heard him yell."

"Me too," Bass said. "But it's suicide to get him from here. We'll work around it. It's dug in but it's not in a bunker like the other one. Maybe a Mike twenty-six."

Doc Fredrickson came scrambling into the relative safety beneath the hill's crest where the three of them crouched. He leaned back against the hill, chest heaving, and stared down the long ridgeline where several bodies lay exposed. He wasn't listening to the conversation.

Mellas turned to Bass and grinned. "What do you think, Sergeant Bass? Is it worth at least a Navy Commendation medal if I go get him?" Mellas intended this as a joke but realized he was partially serious.

Bass looked at him. He was not in a joking mood. "You'll get killed up there, Lieutenant. Don't do it."

Mellas was suddenly determined to get a medal; moreover, it was his fault that Pollini wasn't on KP duty back at VCB. He turned to Fredrickson. "Wait here until I get him down." Fredrickson was still catching his breath and didn't respond.

Bass said, "OK, sir, I'll try and give you some cover. If you get killed I'll put you in for a posthumous Bronze Star."

"It's a deal."

Up until this moment, Mellas had felt as though he were in a movie. Now, faced with the consequences of his decision, he sensed that the film was about to break in two: sudden, searing white light, and then nothing.

He watched Skosh and Bass crawl slowly into place to his left. He nodded at them and they raised their rifles over the lip of the hill and opened up. Mellas whirled to his feet and went charging over the small crest, throwing his body forward on the ground, firing blindly uphill, hoping to keep the machine gunner's head down as he crawled forward.

Pollini was sprawled on his back, feet pointing uphill toward the machine gun. Mellas hit the ground below Pollini's head. He reached up and tried to pull Pollini downhill by dragging on his utility shirt at the shoulders. The machine gun opened up as soon as Mellas stopped firing. Mellas tugged but couldn't get sufficient leverage to move Pollini's weight. He cursed. He tugged again. He couldn't move him. Bullets snapped past his ears. He fired a last desperate burst from his M-16 directly over Pollini's body and scrambled up beside him. He turned himself around and threw himself on top of Pollini, hugging him face-to-face. Wrapping his arms around him he jacked the two of them sideways on the steep hillside and then quickly rolled downhill, pulling Pollini on top of him as he rolled. Mellas felt bullets impacting all around him. With every roll he hoped it was Pollini and not him who would catch the bullet.

Suddenly the earth gave way and he fell over the embankment. Fredrickson was waiting there. He pulled Pollini free. Pollini's breathing had stopped. There was blood coming from his mouth. Bass and Skosh came running around the corner of the embankment and the three of them watched in silence. The objective of taking the hill and the terrific noise and confusion raging about them were forgotten as they watched Fredrickson try to save Pollini's life.

Fredrickson was blowing air into Pollini's mouth, spitting out blood and vomit between breaths. He did this for at least a minute, then looked up at the other three, defeat on his face. He moved aside some matted, bloody hair on the top of Pollini's head and exposed a small round hole. Mellas remembered that, at the top of the hill, Pollini's helmet had been behind him on the ground.

"There's nothing I can do for him, sir," Fredrickson said, grief and helplessness showing on his face. "He's got a bullet inside his head someplace. I don't see no exit hole."

Mellas nodded and looked at Bass and Skosh.

"Fucking Shortround," Skosh said quietly and turned away, his jaw working, looking uphill.

The machine gun opened up, its heavy rounds slamming through the air. They heard grenades going off. Then silence. Then the machine gun opened up again.

Mellas forgot about Pollini and ran off toward the sounds. He came upon Amarillo, who was crawling forward, and joined him.

Sweat ran down Amarillo's face. "Janc, sir," he said. "He is going after that gun. He has Jackson's team with him."

Mellas could see nothing of Jackson or Jancowitz. He looked behind him. A new kid was hunched over in a little ball, a bullet through his shoulder and neck. Mellas didn't even know his name.

Amarillo saw Mellas looking at the dead Marine. "He is too boot from ITR. He goes running up against the machine gun."

Mellas didn't answer. Both of them overcame their desire to stay hugging the earth and scrambled forward.

Jackson was moving his team in small rushes, closing in on the gun. No Marines were firing. "Where's Janc?" Mellas shouted.

Jackson pointed ahead. "He took off around the side, sir. We don't know where the fuck he's at." Mellas now understood why no one was shooting.

They heard roaring bursts of fire and yelling to their left, but Mellas barely registered this. It was Goodwin's platoon, just released by Fitch.

In the midst of the roaring they caught glimpses of Jancowitz's head above the bushes. He was running directly along the contour of the hill, taking the NVA machine gun from the side. He fired a burst from his M-16. A man next to the machine gunner turned his AK-47 on Jancowitz, but Janc kept running forward.

Jackson saw the gunner turn the machine gun toward Jancowitz. He scrambled to his feet and charged up the hill screaming, "Janc, you stupid motherfucker. You crazy stupid motherfucker."

Jancowitz released the spoon of his grenade as the gunner got the machine gun turned around and opened up on him. Janc seemed to throw the grenade and go down simultaneously, bullets bursting out of the back side of his flak jacket. Then his grenade went off—like a sudden hand clap in an empty room.

Cortell went running after Jackson, firing quick bursts at the gun pit. Then, as if jerked by an unseen hand, Cortell's neck snapped backward and his helmet went spinning into the air behind him. He sank to his knees, staring stupidly at his rifle, which he was holding horizontally in front of him. Then he collapsed forward, ending up with his bare head on the ground like a Muslim at prayer.

Jackson kept running forward, trying to reach Jancowitz. Mellas reached Cortell and rolled him over on his side. Cortell's knees were still folded up against his stomach in a fetal position. Blood was running off his forehead and his hair was matted with it. He was gritting his teeth in pain. "Janc got him, sir," Cortell wheezed. "Janc got him. Oh, Janc. Oh, Lord Jesus." Mellas grabbed Cortell's gauze bandage package from his belt, ripped open the paper, and slapped it on what looked like a furrow starting at his forehead and going back over the top of his ear. He put Cortell's hand on the bandage, pressing it down hard. "Don't fucking move it," he said.

He turned back uphill. He passed Jancowitz's body. Blood was still oozing from beneath the back of his flak jacket. A dark black patch was slowly spreading into both trouser legs. Three facts registered simultaneously: the machine gun was silent, Jancowitz was dead, and the opening had to be exploited. Mellas turned to his left and saw Goodwin already moving toward him with an entire squad. Goodwin, his natural fighting instincts functioning faster than Mellas was thinking, was already rushing into the gap where the machine-gun fire used to be. Within seconds he and five other Marines were behind the line of holes and bunkers. China, scrambling up the steep slope with the heavy machine gun against his chest, slammed into the earth at the edge of the former NVA machine gun's position. He began laying fire over the NVA fighting holes to Goodwin's right. Mellas immediately saw what China was doing. He kept running. He shouted at Goodwin, who didn't seem to hear him. He ran. He made hand signals at the Marines behind him, redirecting them behind China, taking advantage of the fact that the enemy could no longer stand up long enough to take aim and fire because of the stream of China's bullets. He caught Goodwin's eye, pointed at him, and then pointed left. He pointed at his own chest and then pointed right. Chaos slipped momentarily into order.

With Second Platoon now pouring through the gap and coming at the NVA from behind them, it seemed as if a heavy weight had been removed. "They're on the top! I see Scar on the top!" The cry passed all around the hillside. Fracasso and the Marines of First Platoon surged forward. Mellas was exhilarated. All his fear had left him. He ran straight up to the hill's crest, Marines appearing all along the line in small groups and surging through the line of holes. Those NVA soldiers who hadn't been trapped in position were moving in rapid but disciplined flight down a finger to the northwest. What just seconds before had been mad scrambling now turned into methodical and cautious destruction. Grenades were rolled into holes and tossed into the openings of the crude log bunkers. As each NVA position fell, the one next to it became vulnerable. Any NVA soldier trying to break for the jungle was immediately killed by fire from several directions.

Mellas met Goodwin at a short trench leading to the dark opening of a bunker. Both had their grenades out. They looked each other
in the eye briefly, then Goodwin nodded and they both swung in front
of the opening, threw their grenades, and dived to the side as the blast
came ripping out of the entrance. They crawled in together, firing short
bursts on automatic. Mellas was flat on the deck and Goodwin was just
behind him in a crouch so that they could fire their rifles at the same
time.

There was no one inside.

Mellas started to laugh and rolled over on his back, looking up at
the roof of the gloomy bunker.

"You two guys having fun, ay?" Vancouver was peering through
the entrance at them, smiling. His face was streaked with sweat; his
machine gun was steaming. His sword was sheathed. "Nagoolian went
thataway." He pointed toward Matterhorn.

Mellas crawled out and sat on top of the bunker, his legs quivering so that he was unable to stand. The battle was over. There were
pitifully few dead enemy soldiers to show for it.

Goodwin moved off to set in his platoon. Ridlow, wounded in the
leg, lay on the hillside, pallid with shock, and waited to be helped up
to the LZ. Mellas, still shaking, trotted down the hill to guide in the
Marines of Third Platoon, who were racing forward to set up for a possible counterattack.

Mellas passed Pollini. His eyes were frozen open. He remembered
Pollini's voice as he cried out, "I'm hit." How could he cry out if he'd
been shot in the head? A guilty sickening thought wrenched Mellas's
stomach. Pollini's head had been pointing downhill. Could *he* have shot
Pollini when he was firing wildly upward, trying to keep the machine
gunners' heads down?

Mellas stared at Pollini's blank eyes. He sat down beside him,
wanting to ask, wanting to explain what he'd done: that he really had
wanted to save him, not just add a medal to his list of accomplishments.
He had pulled Pollini off KP because he wanted to do right by him. He
hadn't meant for him to end up dead. But he could say none of it. Pollini
was dead.

Mellas tried to put down the thought that he could have killed Pollini. It must have been the gook machine gun. He wanted to leave the doubt behind, buried with the bullet in Pollini's brain, but he knew he never could. If he made it out alive he'd carry this doubt with him forever.

CHAPTER
FOURTEEN

Victory in combat is like sex with a prostitute. For a moment you forget everything in the sudden physical rush, but then you have to pay your money to the woman showing you the door. You see the dirt on the walls and your sorry image in the mirror.

Thick fog made twilight of midmorning. It hid the Marines on Helicopter Hill from the sniper fire now coming from the bunkers that Bravo Company had built on Matterhorn. But the fog also kept the helicopters from evacuating the wounded. The Marines dragged their dead friends to a shallow pit near the top of the hill. Mellas and Fitch sat in the dark interior of the bunker Goodwin and Mellas had taken. The fog hung silver-gray in the entrance hole.

Fitch started crying in small silent sobs, the tears running down his dirty cheeks and dripping on the map that lay between him and Mellas. Relsnik was transmitting medevac numbers, identifying the dead and wounded. "Zulu Five Niner Niner One. Over."

A bored voice came back over the radio. "I copy Zulu Five Niner Niner One. Over."

"That's affirm. Bravo Niner One Four Niner. Over."

"Hey, is that a Coors too? Over."

"That's a rog. These are all Coors. Did you copy that last? Over."

"Roger, I copy Bravo Niner One Four Niner. Give me the next one. Over."

And Relsnik did, reading them off one by one. The numbers would eventually lead a somber man, sickened by the job he had to do, to some woman's door, to let her know that her husband or son would be coming home wrapped in rubber. The body would arrive in the early morning hours so that the people at the airport wouldn't be disturbed.

As he listened to Relsnik's voice—Pollini, Poppa Seven One Four Eight; Jancowitz, Juliet Six Four Six Niner—Mellas retreated inside himself. How could it be possible? He analyzed his own moves from the moment he had started helping Pollini with the M-16. He'd warned him. But Pollini had gone up. He'd heard Pollini cry, "I'm hit." Can a man with a head wound do that? But where else was Pollini wounded? What difference did that make? But Pollini had been lying with his head downhill. How did he get that way? An M-16 would surely have exploded his head, wouldn't it? But what did a 7.62-millimeter NVA bullet do?

Mellas kept part of his mind focused on the physical. Was it his bullet or not? That was a yes-or-no question, and he had to decide on the answer. The question that was not yes-or-no was why he had been there with Pollini in the first place. He could have stayed with the CP group. But he'd wanted to help. He'd also wanted to see what the experience was like. He'd found it unbelievably exciting. He'd wanted glory. He could have left Pollini there. Maybe Pollini would still be alive if he had. But he'd wanted to help. He'd wanted a medal. He was the one who had gotten soft and let Pollini off KP. If he'd stuck to his guns, Pollini would be alive at VCB. But Pollini had wanted to be with the company and do his share. Mellas could also have let Fredrickson, or someone else, crawl after Pollini, or waited until the fighting was over. But he'd wanted to do his share. He'd also wanted a medal.

Mellas tried to imagine Goodwin in the same situation. There would have been no conflict. Scar would have wanted to help *and* he'd have wanted a medal. Helping and a medal were both good things. The fact that Pollini was dead didn't make the desire for a medal wrong, did it? What's fucking wrong with wanting a medal? Why did Mellas think it was bad? Why was he so confused? How did he get this way? From where did he dredge up all these doubts? Why?

He sighed. He simply wasn't Goodwin. He was himself—and filled with self-doubt.

Mellas's reverie was broken by the faint sound of voices crying, "Tubing." Fitch and Mellas looked at each other, waiting silently for the explosions.

"Wait one, we got incoming," Relsnik said to the battalion radio operator. He put the handset down beside him. Pallack curled up a little. There was no sound. Then they felt the vibrations through the earth. Then, no sound again.

"Sounds like they hit down the south side," Mellas said, wanting to break the silence.

"The gooners can't adjust in the fog," Fitch said. "Just keeping us honest, I guess."

They waited a minute longer. Silence. Fog. Relsnik picked up the handset and continued reading the list of medevac numbers. First and Second platoons had each lost six. Five kids were in serious need of a medevac and another twelve, though not in danger of dying, were fairly useless. Then there were fourteen who had received slight flesh wounds or nicks from shrapnel. They included Mellas, whose right hand had taken some of the blast from Jancowitz's grenade. It looked as if he'd fallen on gravel.

Normally, small wounds wouldn't be reported, but Fitch had had enough of normality. He told the senior squid, Sheller, to report every nick and scratch on the hill so the medical bureaucracy could grind out Purple Hearts for as many Marines as possible. "Two Hearts and they're out of the bush. Three and they go to Okinawa to sort socks. I'll be goddamned if I'll stand in their way quibbling over how wounded they got to be to qualify. Every fucking scratch, you understand?"

Sheller undertook the task with grim pleasure.

"Wait one," Relsnik said. He turned to Fitch. "Battalion wants a confirmation on that body count."

Fitch sighed. "We haven't killed any more. Tell them it still stands at ten confirmed and six probable."

"Roger that." Relsnik keyed the handset. "Big John, this is Big John Bravo. That's affirmative. Ten confirmed and six probables. Over."

There was a pause, followed by a new voice. "Wait one. I'll put him on." Relsnik sighed and handed the handset to Fitch. "It's the Three."

"This is Bravo Six. Over," Fitch said.

He held the handset close to his ear, making it difficult for the others to hear, but his answers indicated that apparently the body count was too low. "That's affirmative. We did send people out beyond the holes to count. Sir, we were attacking fortified bunkers. Over."

The handset blurted static, and the Three's voice came over. "Look, Bravo Six, they had to be hurting to leave those two open-belt seven-point-six-twos behind." Relsnik had radioed in about the two captured machine guns. One had been taken by Vancouver. The other was the one that Jancowitz had died taking. "I think you easily have twice the probables you've reported. Over."

"Tell him you killed d' whole fucking Three Hundred Twelfth steel division, Skipper," Pallack said. Fitch held a hand up, annoyed, trying to listen to the Three.

"Yes, Big John Three, you're right on that. Over."

"OK, Bravo Six. We'll see what we can do here. How's everything up there? Over."

"We only got enough ammo for one heavy counterattack, and we need water. How we looking on those medevac birds? Over."

"We've got them standing by, Bravo Six. Over."

"I've got five emergencies up here. If they're not out before dark they're going to be dead. You tell the fucking zoomies that. Over."

Blakely's voice was curt, controlled. "Bravo Six, I suggest you leave the air evacuations to the forward air controller. I understand you've had a tough day, but you know as well as I do that flying in this kind of weather is idiotic. Over."

Mellas burst out, "What the fuck is sending a company of Marines out in this kind of weather?"

Fitch waited for Mellas to finish before he keyed the handset. "I understand. Anything else? Over."

"We're preparing a frag order for you ASAP. Big John Three out."

* * *

At the top of the hill wraithlike figures moved slowly toward the trench where the dead lay in rows, their weather-bleached boots sticking out from beneath dark ponchos made slick by the fog. Cortell waited for them there. His head was bandaged. When he felt that all who were coming had gathered, he pulled out a small pocket Bible and read some verses aloud. Jackson was silently mouthing, "Janc, why did you do it?" Fracasso stood uneasily behind Cortell. At the Naval Academy, no one had ever talked about what to do afterward.

Fracasso had asked Jackson to take over the squad. Jackson refused. Puzzled, Fracasso talked things over with Bass, who told him the probable cause. So Fracasso switched Jackson and Hamilton, giving Hamilton the squad. Jackson hoisted the heavy radio over his flak jacket. He'd made his deal; he'd stick with it.

The daylong twilight faded. The medevac birds weren't coming. Kids who'd been drinking their water in anticipation of a resupply were sorry they hadn't been more sparing. Down in the bunker where they had pulled the serious cases, Sheller watched helplessly as the dwindling IV fluid drained into the wounded. When the other corpsmen left the bunker to dig in for the night, he quietly slipped the IV tubes from two unconscious kids and poured the fluid into the bottles hanging above the others.

Merritt, a rifleman from Goodwin's platoon, was watching him. He was one of three wounded who were still conscious. "What are you doing, Doc?" he whispered. His torn clothes were plastered to his body by drying blood. Dirt was in everything, and there was no way to clean it out. The squids just poured antiseptic in with the dirt. A candle flickered, disturbed by the damp air as Sheller sat down. "Just changing your oil and water," he said, smiling.

"You took it from Meaker."

Sheller nodded.

Merritt stared up at the slightly rotting logs that formed the roof of the bunker just four feet above his head. He smelled blood and abandoned fermented fish sauce and rice. "Is it wrong to want to go home so badly?" he asked.

Sheller, smiling gently, shook his head. Merritt took a labored breath. The pain in his intestines, where he'd been hit by two bullets,

one shattering his pelvis, nearly drove him into blissful unconscious-
ness. But he fought off entering that dark realm, afraid he would never
want to come back.

"Does it mean Meaker will die?"

Sheller looked over at the two kids he'd picked for death. He didn't
want to answer Merritt's question. He wanted to lie, even to himself. "I
think you'll all make it," he said.

"Don't fucking lie to me, Squid. I don't have time for it." Again
Merritt took a quivering breath, biting back the scream that wanted to
erupt whenever he filled his lungs. "If I'm going to live because of
Meaker, I want to know it. And I want to live."

Sheller put his hand on Merritt's uniform. "The thing is, we might
be wasting plasma on Meaker. He keeps bleeding inside and I can't stop
it. You're not bleeding as fast as he is."

Merritt looked at Sheller. "I'll never forget it, Squid. I fucking
promise." Then he turned his head toward Meaker's unconscious body.
"Meaker, you dumb son of a bitch," he whispered. "I ain't never going
to forget it."

Meaker died three hours later. Sheller and Fredrickson dragged
him out of the bunker and stacked him on the foggy landing zone with
the rest of the bodies.

In the battalion operations center Simpson and Blakely debated whether
or not to press the attack against Matterhorn the next day. The kill ratio
looked bad—thirteen Marine KIA against only ten confirmed NVA
bodies. If they could continue the action, there was a chance that they
could get the ratio up to something more reportable. But how many of
the enemy were on Matterhorn? Was it a full force or just a rear guard—
or an advance guard? Fitch could report only that he saw movement in
the bunkers, but there was no way of telling how many NVA were inside them. And now it was pitch black up there. At this moment, the
NVA could be reinforcing or withdrawing.

"There's only one way to find out," Simpson said grimly. "We've
got to attack. At first light."

Blakely knew Simpson was right. If the NVA reinforced during the night, an assault by Bravo Company would surely go badly, but those were the breaks. They were there to kill gooks. If they ran into a buzz saw, Mulvaney would get the whole fucking regiment involved and finally kick some ass up there. If the gooks had taken off for the border and it was only a rear guard, then Bravo could handle it and Simpson would look foolish not to have pressed the attack, even if it was just to get more information. That was the right move. No one could second-guess them. If they kept Bravo sitting on the hill, that could be perceived up at division as a lack of initiative.

There was the problem of artillery and those goddamn bunkers they'd left behind. The 105 batteries had all been pulled back to support the Cam Lo operation. The 8-inch howitzers on Sherpa had barely been able to reach the valley to the south of Matterhorn. Moreover, even if they could be moved closer, a direct hit from an 8-inch shell would probably not collapse one of those bunkers. Blakely had seen Bravo Company build them. Maybe it had been hasty to pull out of there so fast. Those were the breaks. In any case, it wouldn't look like an unsupported attack, especially since Bravo had been the one to fuck up the air support during the initial assault and no one had lodged any complaints. And if Bainford could keep some fixed-wing on station and they did get a break in the clouds they could lay in some snake and nape and watch those kill ratios climb.

At 2335 Fitch received the order to attack Matterhorn.

The lieutenants stumbled and crawled to Fitch's bunker through the foggy blackness. Their faces appeared in the entry hole lit by Fitch's red-lens flashlight. First Goodwin, haggard but still quipping. Then Fracasso, shaken, wearing his partly shattered glasses. Finally Kendall, apprehensive, knowing it was his turn for the next dangerous task.

Again they argued and struggled over how to take the hill. They interviewed all the kids who could remember anything about the details of the bunkers they'd built, the layout and hidden gates of the razor wire they'd put in place. Again they were hampered by terrain and weather. But now they were also hampered by their own wounded and dead. "We can't take the wounded with us on the assault," Fitch said. "We've got to secure this hill."

"And split our forces exactly like the fucking gooks did?" Mellas argued. "That's the only reason we were able to get up here in the first place. We've got to pack our wounded with us."

"Maybe we could leave a squad?" Goodwin said.

"A squad can't cover this whole fucking hill," Fitch said. "Besides, if they got in trouble we'd have to send back a platoon from Matterhorn to help them, if we had a platoon to send back. Then we'd be split in three, one on each hill and one in the saddle between them. All three would get the shit kicked out of them."

"There it is," Fracasso said, suddenly understanding the phrase.

They finally agreed with Fitch. An entire platoon plus the command post group would stay with the wounded on Helicopter Hill. Two platoons would assault Matterhorn. If the two assaulting platoons got into trouble, Fitch could send two squads from the platoon guarding the wounded. This would leave just a single squad guarding the wounded. If both assaulting platoons were in trouble, however, that risk had to be taken.

"Why not just wait until we have enough horses for the job?" Mellas asked.

"The Six feels we'll loose the initiative."

"You mean he's afraid the gooks will dee-dee and we'll be stuck with thirteen dead and forty wounded and only a worthless hill and ten confirmed to show for it," Mellas said.

"There it is," Fitch said.

They settled on a plan that would use the fog and their knowledge of the terrain to their advantage. Two platoons would work their way through the razor wire in the darkness and attack just before dawn. It was Kendall's turn for the hard stuff. Goodwin and Fracasso called Fitch's flip of the coin to see who would join Kendall. Fracasso lost.

"Who did you put in Janc's place?" Mellas asked Fracasso.

"Hamilton. Jackson wouldn't take it. So I made him my radioman."

"They're both good men," Mellas said.

Everyone was silent, looking at the map in the circle of dim red light.

"Maybe all the gooks have dee-deed across the border," Fitch said.

"Yeah," Kendall answered.

Vancouver was the first to touch the wire. He gently pushed it upward, testing it, searching for the gate he knew was there. The wire resisted. He backed down. He crawled slightly to the left and tried again. Connolly, Jacobs, and Hamilton were doing the same thing.

The rest of First Platoon waited, heads buried in the damp earth, almost afraid to breathe. Fracasso listened anxiously for a static burst, which would signal that Kendall and Third Platoon were through the wire and in position.

Kendall had led his platoon quietly west through the jungle, aiming for the south side of Matterhorn. He stopped and looked at his compass. The luminescent needle swayed, then steadied. It always pointed north. Always. But what good did that do if he didn't know whether the hill was in front of him or to his right? He gulped and shoved the compass back into its pouch on his belt. Cold panic welled up in his stomach. If they were going south . . . No, they were going west, toward Laos. But if the ridge ran south, it could be leading his platoon prematurely up the slope of Matterhorn before they could get into position on the south side. He tapped the shoulder of the kid ahead of him. "Bear a little to the left," he whispered.

Kendall's platoon began heading away from Matterhorn.

Hamilton suddenly felt the wire give easily. He felt further and located one of the stakes around which the wire was loosely secured. He crawled backward, leaving tiny scraps of a C-ration box as he went. The dull white of the cardboard could be seen up to a foot away.

The word passed back to Fracasso. Then, as agreed, Connolly began to crawl through the gate, remembering each turn as he went, leaving a trail of cardboard. Vancouver followed, pushing his machine gun before him; his sword was tied firmly to his leg so it would make no noise. The rest followed, praying that the fog they'd cursed so many times in the past would now save them, praying against all odds that no one would be waiting for them beyond the wire, praying that the NVA had retreated in the night.

Samms, at the rear of Kendall's column, figured out that Kendall was headed away from Matterhorn. Furious, he started keying the handset to get Kendall's attention. Fracasso mistook the keying of the handset to mean that Kendall was in place. He tapped the person in front of him. Three taps. Third Herd's in place. The taps went up the line.

Connolly emerged from the far end of the gate and began crawling to the right. The blackness, the crawling, the fear—none of it would ever end. At the same time, he didn't want it to end. What followed would be far worse.

Kendall heard the handset keying furiously and knew that he'd been caught doing something terribly wrong. He immediately stopped. The word passed up in low whispers.

"We're going the wrong fucking way."

Kendall, crushed by a sense of failure, groped backward along the column. His radio operator followed. They met Samms, and there was an intense flow of barely audible words. "What the fuck are you doing? I ought to shoot you right here. Now, goddamn it, you are going to follow me until we reach the fucking wire, and if I hear so much as a fucking sound you're going to get blown away." Kendall dropped back into the center of the platoon. Samms led the way, retracing their steps.

Dawn would arrive in minutes. The Marines of First Platoon were lying in the mud, trapped between the wire and the enemy bunkers, waiting. Fracasso was frantic. Kendall was supposed to begin the attack. What the fuck was Kendall doing? He looked at his watch, holding it so close to his eyes that the dial was blurred. In a few minutes the light would start coming.

All along the line, there was anguished perplexity. What happened to Third Herd? Why were they waiting in this fucking death trap?

Fracasso wanted to cry. He wanted to turn around and crawl back through the wire, but he knew that the platoon would never make it out before daylight. Halfway in, halfway out, he'd lose most of them.

Then Fracasso noticed the faint white of the dial of his watch, mingling with the glow of its phosphorescent hands. Daylight had not waited.

"Holy Mary, pray for us now," he whispered. *And at the hour of our death.* He lurched to his feet and roared as he threw the grenade he had been holding in his right hand. All along the line, the platoon threw their grenades as hard as they could, aiming for their former bunkers. Explosions ripped across the hill, lighting fierce and frightened faces. Fracasso, firing his M-16 on full automatic, ran screaming up the hill, covering the short distance between them and the bunkers in about five seconds.

"They're fucking empty!" he shouted as he approached the first one. "They're fucking empty!" The entire platoon surged along beside him, and everyone felt a great weight lift from his back.

Then, from the new holes just above the old bunkers where the NVA unit, reduced in size, had moved during the night, bright fire blazed out of the gloom. Fracasso, singled out by at least five riflemen as the leader, went down instantly.

When the fire erupted from above the empty bunkers everyone wanted to crawl underground. Several kids, in fact, went down on their knees. Had the others done the same, the attack would have stopped, and the outcome would have been a disaster. But the attack went on—not because of any conscious decision, but because of friendship.

Jackson went running forward, more to see if Fracasso was alive than for tactical reasons. Vancouver saw Jackson heading for the lieutenant and decided that even if the platoon were in a hopeless shit sandwich he'd be goddamned if he'd let Jackson run forward alone. So he kept going. Connolly, seeing Vancouver charging forward, did exactly the same, although his mind cried out to him to merge with the great welcoming earth beneath his feet. He wouldn't abandon a friend to go it alone. Neither would any of the others.

Jackson, who'd been nicked on the arm by the concentration of fire on Fracasso, saw Vancouver surging ahead, shell casings flying from his machine gun. Jackson couldn't let him go alone, nor did he see any advantage in trying to crawl back through the wire. He kept running forward, though forgetting to fire his weapon.

A man in good condition can run 100 meters in about twelve seconds. Uphill, with rifles and ammunition, a flak jacket, a helmet, water, grenades, heavy boots, and maybe a last can of pecan roll, the run takes a lot longer. There were approximately twenty-five meters between the old bunkers and the new fighting holes from which the NVA soldiers were firing. It took approximately five seconds to cross that deadly ground. In that time, one-third of the remaining thirty-four in the platoon went down.

Then attackers and defenders joined together and bellowing, frightened, maddened kids—firing, clubbing, and kicking—tried to end the madness by means of more madness.

Vancouver jumped into a hole with two small NVA soldiers, firing his machine gun right up against their chests, his muzzle blasts lighting the three of them as if by strobe lights. One of them, before he died, put a bullet through Vancouver's left arm, shattering the bone above the elbow. Vancouver clawed his way out of the hole, mad with pain but trying to reach the top of the hill. When he emerged from over the lip of the flattened top of Matterhorn, he saw the commander of the NVA unit shouting his men across the LZ to aid those defending the east approach.

Vancouver saw the NVA officer look at him in surprise. Even in the predawn gloom Vancouver could see that the officer was no older than Mellas or Fracasso. The young man reached for his pistol, which was tied with a lanyard around his neck and rested in a shoulder holster. Several others, seeing the large Marine, his arm dripping blood, turned their AK-47s on him.

Vancouver, unable to raise his machine-gun barrel because of his crippled arm, went to ground beneath the lip of the LZ. He rolled to the left, freeing the ammunition belt to enter the gun's receiver. He rested the barrel of the gun on the lip of the LZ and pulled the trigger. The officer went down, wounded, and a knee of one of the soldiers firing at Vancouver was shattered. Vancouver began to pump short steady bursts across the flat LZ, forcing the NVA reinforcements to work their way around the hill the long way.

The NVA officer, shouting, crawled to reach a former artillery pit. Soon two soldiers carrying a drum-canister machine gun joined him. The officer directed their fire against Vancouver. A burst of bullets tore the earth around Vancouver's eyes, forcing his head down as the bullets sucked across the flat table between them. As Vancouver's head went down the officer shouted something and a group of his men rushed across the LZ.

Vancouver suddenly understood the game.

As long as he could keep firing, the reinforcements were slowed, giving the platoon time to break through the line of holes. He looked behind him and saw Connolly running for a fighting hole with a grenade, and two other Marines on their knees firing at the hole to keep its occupants' heads down. A minute was all that was needed. The defenses would be pierced. If Third Platoon made it in time, they'd overrun the enemy lines.

The five NVA soldiers were now halfway across the LZ.

Vancouver poked his head above the rim of earth and emptied his belt at them. Two went down wounded. Two hit the earth voluntarily and crawled for another empty artillery pit. One turned back to join the officer and the machine-gun crew, who continued firing at Vancouver.

Vancouver's left shoulder was torn apart by one of the gun's bullets. His arm, already wounded, became a bloody, floppy, uncontrollable appendage.

One-handed, he fumbled awkwardly to reload his machine gun. Large spots of gray-black obscured the feed tray and cover. He shook his head, trying to clear his vision. His single hand wouldn't work right. It felt clumsy and slow. He heard Bass screaming at him but couldn't understand the words. He heard Connolly's grenade go off and saw

Connolly rise from next to the hole and fire a burst into it. Muzzle blasts winked in the gloom along the line of holes.

The NVA officer shouted again. The two soldiers in the other gun pit rose once more to move toward Vancouver. Another group emerged from the same pit as the officer.

Just a few seconds were all Bass and Connolly needed.

Vancouver pulled his sword from his side. He had never really expected to use the damn thing. He'd had fun joking with the new boot lieutenant and Bass and the gunny about it. He slipped out of his gun harness and emerged over the lip of the flat ground of the LZ snarling, his face black, his helmet fallen off, blond hair matted with blood. His left arm hung helpless, but in his right hand he held the sword raised above his head. He would run and scream for thirty seconds, and then it would all be over, one way or the other.

The NVA soldiers at the machine gun couldn't turn it on Vancouver, because he was already between their two comrades who'd started running across the LZ toward him. Both of them were now going down under his hacking sword.

A short, thickly built sergeant from the second group of NVA soldiers ran straight for where Vancouver and the two others were fighting and then stopped short. Vancouver finished the second soldier off and turned to attack the sergeant. The sergeant pointed his rifle and fired three quick shots. Two went into Vancouver's stomach. He sank to the ground. The sergeant fired again. Vancouver shuddered and crumpled over. The man waved his squad forward, running for the edge of the landing zone. One of the two NVA soldiers whom Vancouver had attacked cried weakly for help. Vancouver, his face in the mud, heard him and knew they would die together. That felt appropriate somehow.

The small group of NVA reached the edge of the LZ just as Samms fought his way through the wire on the south slope. Wild with despair and shame at having left First Platoon to go it alone, he hurled himself against the wire, not bothering to find the gate. Bullets churned the dirt around him; the dim light was foiling the NVA's aim. Samms tore at stakes, pulled the wire up, and shouted to his men through the gloomy fog. Finally, he tore free. Bleeding from his arms and legs, he rushed past the empty bunkers, heading for the line of new holes above him. Miraculously, bullets slammed past him.

Samms saw the NVA reinforcements silhouetted against the gray dawn light. Lunging to the earth, he fired two quick bursts, watching the flight of the tracers he had interspersed after every five bullets. He quickly adjusted his aim, sending the bullets into the small group of reinforcements. Luckily for Bravo Company, Samms thought, the NVA were thirty seconds too late.

The rest of Third Platoon went swarming past him as he emptied his magazine. His radioman, also bleeding after being torn by the wire, flopped down beside him. Samms, heedless of the radio operator, ran forward, heading toward the fire coming from First Platoon.

Some NVA soldiers were backing up the hill, firing as they went. Others stayed in their holes, fighting until the last.

Samms scrambled over the top of a small acclivity on the side of the hill and came into full view of First Platoon. One of the new kids snapped his rifle around and fired a quick burst.

Cortell jumped on the newbie, shouting, "Friendlies! Friendlies on the left!"

Samms stared at the two of them. Two bullets were in his chest, one stopping his heart. "You dumb fucking numby," he said calmly as sick blackness swirled into his brain and his hands and forearms started to buzz. He sank to his knees and curled over in a ball like a child going to sleep.

The rest of Samms's platoon came storming around the shoulder of the hill. Some stopped when they saw him lying there. Bass shouted at them, pointing at the breach in the NVA lines with his short-timer's stick. The kids from Third Platoon, feeling disgraced at having let First Platoon down, charged through the gap, firing as they ran. They surged across the LZ, which was deserted now, and descended on NVA holes from above and behind. Whistles shrilled. Within seconds the NVA were retreating in an orderly fashion down the west slope of Matterhorn toward Laos.

Bass ran after Third Platoon, knowing he'd have to stop them from chasing the enemy all the way down the hill and exposing themselves to counterattack. Skosh, with a rib broken by a nearly spent bullet, struggled to follow Bass. Kendall, not knowing what to do, was following his platoon.

"Get them set up for a counterattack!" Bass yelled at him.

Kendall nodded and started shouting at them to stop and set in. Bass ran back to First Platoon to try to set up a defense, directing people with his stick, waving it in the air, pointing with it to weak spots. He saw Vancouver's body and the bloody sword. He turned Vancouver over quickly, saw the familiar face of the dead, and ran on, calling to Hamilton and Connolly to link up with Kendall's platoon at both ends.

Skosh, his chest still heaving, stopped to pull the sword from Vancouver's hand. Vancouver looked like a dog that had been run over. "You big dumb gunjy fucking Canadian," Skosh said. He keyed his handset. "Bravo, this is Bravo One Assist."

Pallack answered immediately. "Go, One Assist."

Skosh keyed the handset. "The big Victor's dead. Over." He let up on the handset.

Pallack quietly repeated the message to Fitch and Mellas. It was as if the company's soul had been taken away.

A minute later they heard the ominous sound of distant mortar rounds firing out of tubes. Then the NVA mortar rounds came whistling down out of the luminous gray sky.

The wounded lay exposed along the east side of Matterhorn. The mortar shells walked with fiery feet among them, occasionally stumbling on one, leaving a meat-red footprint. Some of the wounded tried to crawl for cover. Others, unable to move, watched the sky in numb terror or simply shut their eyes, praying for a friend to reach them and drag them to safety. Their friends came.

With insufficient personnel to man the company's original perimeter, Bass moved everyone into the NVA's holes. There, the kids huddled against the earth and waited for the shelling to stop, and then, perhaps, for the counterattack to start.

Bass had another concern beyond the counterattack and evacuating his wounded. If attacked, they would be firing on their own dead who lay on the slope of the hill. Even dead, they were still Marines. He remembered Jancowitz giving his life to break the ring of interlocking fire that stopped the first assault on Helicopter Hill. He knew what Vancouver had done for them. The dead, for Bass, were not dead.

"Fuck it," he said to Skosh. "If they attack now we'll fight 'em down there."

He rose from his hole just as three NVA shells erupted in a quick series. Shrapnel and dirt tore through the fog. "Everyone up! Everyone up! We're not done yet. We got work to do, Marines. Get up!"

Frightened kids peered at him from their holes. He was waving his short-timer's stick. "Get up! We're going to get the bodies. Get up!" He ran down the slope. They all rose from their holes, even Skosh with his broken rib.

It looked like an assault in reverse. Through the exploding shells they called to each other, some with rebel yells, some shouting, "Fuck it! Fuck it all!" They ran for their dead. Some fell to the flying shrapnel. They were picked up, having barely touched the earth, and dragged back up the hill with the dead bodies. In one minute the slopes were cleared.

Then, as if God had pulled a curtain, the fog lifted completely. The Marines on Helicopter Hill saw Matterhorn standing naked before them. Little figures in camouflage green scurried here and there, dragging other little figures in camouflage green behind them or walking with others hanging on to their shoulders.

"Get those fucking birds, Snik," Fitch shouted gleefully.

Mellas could see Bass clearly, on the top of Matterhorn, pointing his short-timer's stick at something, shouting at someone.

With the fog gone, however, NVA on the ridge north of Matterhorn began laying automatic weapons fire in with the mortar explosions. All movement on the LZ was stopped.

Fitch and Mellas looked at each other hopelessly. The birds couldn't come in unless the weather was clear. But if it was clear, the NVA had the Marines pinned down with automatic weapons.

Then a cry went up from those on Helicopter Hill. "Tubing! Tubing!" The Marines had been digging a second perimeter inside the first— they no longer had enough men to defend the outer one—but they stopped and began burying themselves in the dirt. They waited for the time it took between the sounds of the tubing, which went in a direct line to their ears, and the time it took the rounds to complete their high arcs. The mortar rounds crashed harmlessly, far down the hillside. Then the Marines were up again, digging furiously to complete the new perimeter.

Mellas felt a sickening dismay. The sounds of the tube pops had come from a different direction from the first ones.

Mellas ran down to the lines, diving into Goodwin's hole, from which he hoped to hear the second set of tubings and help Daniels with a cross bearing.

"You've got to hand it to them little fuckers," Goodwin said to Mellas, waiting for the next volley of mortars. "They're fucking pros. Too bad they ain't on our side."

"Just wait a while," Mellas said. "They were on our side twenty-five years ago."

"No shit. Who switched sides, us or them?"

"I think it was us. We used to be against colonialism. Now we're against communism."

"I'll be goddamned," Goodwin said matter-of-factly. "Whatever we're against, Jack, they're fucking pros."

Mellas held up his hand, listening intently for the next sounds of tubing. As soon as they came, he took a bearing and radioed it back to Daniels on Goodwin's radio. Then he waited for the mortar shells to complete their slow, high trajectory. He watched the top of the cloud bank that swirled beneath the two hilltops and obscured the valleys below them. Matterhorn seemed unattached to the earth, an ugly bulb rising out of silvery gray. Then the shells hit—all over and inside the perimeter. The Marines curled down, hands over their ears, and tried to squeeze inside their helmets.

The shelling continued for fifteen minutes. Just fifteen minutes. Then it stopped.

Mellas waited two minutes. He peered over the edge of the crater and then got up to check the damage. He found the senior squid already out patching someone up. Goodwin reported two more killed: they'd both been in the same hole. Otherwise, there were only minor shrapnel wounds.

Mellas walked back to Fitch's hole. Relsnik looked up, his face working. Pallack was looking away.

"What is it?"

Fitch broke the silence. "Bass is dead," he said quickly. As if he were trying to atone for this terse announcement, he added, "We don't have enough effectives to cover both hills. As soon as we get the wounded off of Matterhorn, I'm pulling One and Three back here."

It took Mellas a moment to register both pieces of information. Even then his next question was automatic. It was all he could say to fill the emptiness.

"How?" he asked numbly.

"Shrapnel. He bled to death."

Mellas turned around and walked back to the edge of the lines facing Matterhorn. It was quiet. Matterhorn floated serenely above the fog. He saw Bass on Matterhorn just weeks earlier, teaching him, joking with him, bitching to him. Bass wrapping him in a blanket one day after a patrol when he was so cold he couldn't stop shivering. Fixing a cup of coffee. Talking about home. The Corps. Bass. Dead. On this fucking wasted piece of earth.

Goodwin came up behind Mellas and put a hand on his helmet and rocked it back and forth. He didn't say anything.

"Thanks, Scar," Mellas finally said.

Mellas's throat ached. Tears crowded close behind his eyelids. But the ache was never released and the tears never broke through. Emptiness filled his soul.

"Hey!" someone shouted on the south side of the perimeter. "Here come the birds."

Out of the fog to the south, a single CH-46 climbed upward toward the zone on Matterhorn. Someone on Matterhorn popped a red smoke grenade. The smoke spread slowly through the air, like blood in water.

Lazy puffs of darker smoke curled around the chopper as it came in—more mortar rounds.

Leaving the radios, Mellas picked up Fitch's field glasses and perched on a small mound. He watched Jackson standing all alone in the middle of the zone, directing the chopper with hand signals, the radio on his back, while mortar shells burst around him. With Fracasso and Bass both gone, Jackson took charge. There had been no orders and no questions.

Mellas watched the chopper settle in. Crewmen piled out while the Marines from Bravo Company ran up, carrying the wounded in any way they could manage, and throwing them into the tailgate. While crew members pulled the bodies forward, the Marines continued to run into and out of the bird with more dead and wounded. Then the chopper lifted, beating the air, as Marines ran from it and scattered for shelter. A figure appeared at the closing tailgate, hesitated a moment, then jumped out into space and tumbled to the ground. It looked like Jacobs. The wry thought entered Mellas's head that Jacobs had probably stuttered too badly to get the pilot to stay on the ground, but then he felt bad for having such a thought. He watched as Jacobs lay there for a second; then someone darted out into the exploding mortar rounds and tugged on him. Then they both were up and running for cover.

"Fucking Jake, man," Mellas muttered out loud. "He actually jumped back into this shit."

He watched Jackson calmly direct another chopper in. Then the clouds closed out the zone and he could see no more.

A third chopper came straining up the south side of Helicopter Hill. Everyone listened to its progress. Pallack was talking to the pilot on the radio, and the senior squid was preparing the previous day's wounded for evacuation. Two of the five original emergency cases were still alive. One of them was Merritt, still saying he wasn't ever going to forget this. Sheller said he wouldn't either. Sheller and the corpsmen from Second

Platoon put Merritt's foul-smelling body on a poncho strung between two sticks and carried him down to a torn piece of flat earth on the east side of the hill, away from the automatic weapons fire, to wait for the chopper.

Mellas watched the chopper emerge from the fog. Pallack popped a yellow smoke and the mortar shells once again started falling on Helicopter Hill.

The pilot was talking to Pallack in a calm, steady voice. "OK, son. Where are they shooting *from?* I know where they're shooting *at.* Over."

"The finger just to our north, sir. Also tubes to d' northwest and due west just about on d' border. Over."

"OK, son. I'll bring her in from the southeast. You're sure that fucking hole is big enough to get me in? Over."

"Yes, sir. I walked right across it. It's a nice big flat space. Over."

"Nice big flat ain't helping me much. How about some numbers? Over."

"One nice big flat spot, sir," Pallack said. "Over."

"I ain't in the fucking mood for kidding around. Over."

Pallack didn't want to tell the pilot how small the zone was; he was afraid the pilot would turn around and not try it.

"Goddamn it, son, now I know you think I'm going to fly away if it's too small, but so help me, if you don't tell how big a spot you've got there, I am turning this fucking machine around. Right now. Over."

Pallack hesitated. "Ten meters, sir. But d'ere's no fucking wind. Over."

"Shit." The word was muttered, not intended to go over the air. Nevertheless the chopper kept coming in. Mellas could see the pilot, a large overweight man, probably a field-grade officer, hands moving deftly at the controls, large sweating face packed into the narrow plastic helmet. Mellas couldn't help thinking of Santa Claus.

By now small arms fire from the finger to the north could be heard crackling through the air above the landing zone; the chopper was flying straight into it. A second volley of tubing sounded through the fog, and everyone who was waiting for the chopper flattened out against the mud. More shells exploded on the hill.

Sheller was sitting next to his wounded men, rubbing his face. Ridlow, still chalky white and with clammy sweat on his face, was bantering about whether or not to leave his .44 Magnum with Goodwin, but he and Goodwin were both worried. Ridlow had passed out twice from loss of blood.

The pilot started talking as if to keep his own mind off the danger. "Normally I wouldn't do this, son, but I was held up by some wild-ass redneck staff sergeant right outside Delta Med who told me to drop off a huss for you guys when I went in or he'd shoot me out of the fucking sky." The pilot laughed. "You know that character? Over."

"Yeah. It's d' gunny," Pallack said. "He would, too, sir," he added. "You're much better off with us. Over."

"That's what I figured, son." The radio lapsed into static.

The fire intensified, but the bird kept coming in a slow, straight, exposed approach. More mortar rounds hit the hill behind the backs of the evacuation party. The bird loomed up on them out of the fog, its blades whapping and pounding, its turbines screaming. Suddenly there was chaos as the bird shuddered, hovering above the tiny level space on the side of the hill, its blades barely missing the earth on the uphill side. Mellas saw that bullets had perforated the clear canopy around the pilot. The copilot was slumped over, held up only by his seat belt, his plastic helmet shattered and broken.

The chopper hit the deck and the crew chief started throwing out bags as Sheller and Fredrickson, with the help of others, shoved the critically wounded into the belly of the bird. In seconds the chopper was moving and the kids on the ground were diving for holes, not caring what was in the bags. The next salvo came just as the chopper started curving away, gaining speed rapidly as it moved with gravity, sliding southward toward the valley. A hand poked out of one of the chopper's broken portholes. It held a Smith & Wesson .44 that barked out six heavy shots at the north finger.

Mellas lifted his head from the earth. He darted down to the satchels, hollering for help, and began dragging them up the hill to the bunkers. Inside the bags were several cases of IV fluid, several cases of machine-gun ammunition, fifteen gallons of water, a case of hand

grenades, and, in a Marine seabag stuffed with melting ice, two cases
of Coca-Cola.

"D' fucking gunny, man," Pallack said.

First and Third Platoons filed back onto Helicopter Hill three hours
later, having had to walk at the pace of the wounded for whom there
hadn't been room on the medevac birds. Connolly had Vancouver's
sword. He walked up to the CP and handed it to Mellas.

"What the fuck am I supposed to do with it, Conman?" Mellas
asked, feeling its weight.

"I don't know." Connolly looked out into the fog. "All I know is if
it went back with Vancouver, someone who didn't deserve it would take
it. At least you could trade it for something."

"That doesn't seem right," Mellas said. "Maybe we ought to send
it home to his father," he added lamely.

"What father?" Connolly said. "He wouldn't want that, sir. What
you think a fucking Canadian is doing in an American war if he had a
home and a father he wanted to go back to?"

Connolly sat down in the mud and stared past Mellas, across at
Matterhorn. "He was my fucking brother, sir." He started crying. Mellas
looked at the sword, unable to speak. Tears were running over
Connolly's mouth and chin. He kept wiping them away with his filthy
hand, smearing his face. He looked up at Mellas. "He was my fucking
brother."

Mellas put the sword in the CP bunker. Then he walked down to
First Platoon's position and took over the platoon without even asking
Fitch.

There were now fifteen bodies stacked on top of Helicopter Hill, stiff
with rigor mortis, several of them mutilated by a mortar shell that had
exploded in their midst. Goodwin's platoon had lost fifteen: eight
killed and seven medevaced. The other wounded of his platoon stayed
behind and were still capable of fighting. Kendall had lost fourteen: six

killed and eight medevaced, with ten others left behind functioning with minor wounds. First Platoon had twenty left out of forty-two—the addition of Mellas made it twenty-one. Of those, half had minor wounds but were still able to fight. With the CP group and the mortarmen, that left ninety-seven effectives in the company. Fifteen gallons of water divided by ninety-seven was roughly a pint and a quarter for each Marine. Everyone also got half a can of Coke.

The time was only 1015.

They redistributed water, food, and ammunition from the dead, including the NVA. Some Marines kept the NVA water in separate canteens from their own. Others just dumped the two together. It made little difference. Machine gunners met and split their remaining rounds evenly.

All day they sat or stood in their holes, staring at the fog. Every so often someone would shout "Tubing!" and they would squeeze down, knees up to their helmets, waiting for the sounds that would let them know they weren't the ones who were hit.

By evening, as a result of the hammering by the NVA mortars, Mellas's mind was running out of control. At some point he'd taken a second flak jacket off a dead body and put it on over his own. His mind wouldn't stop calculating: if one flak jacket will take fifty percent of the flak, then two will take seventy-five percent. If I wear three, that will be eighty-seven and a half percent, and four will be ninety-three and three-quarters percent. He would keep this up until his fogged mind could divide no further; then, for some reason, he would start up again. If one will block half, then two will block three-quarters . . . He tried to shut the calculations off. He walked from hole to hole talking to people. But then he would hear the tubing, and he would know more shells were on their way. He would scramble for the nearest hole and once again go through the numbers, waiting for the explosions. He remembered a lecture about how mortars are fairly ineffective against troops that are dug in. But the lecturer hadn't mentioned the psychological effect on the troops.

At dusk Fitch called an actuals meeting in the bunker. Kendall arrived before the others, very subdued. Word about his fuckup had spread all over the hill. He looked guiltily at Relsnik and Pallack and mumbled a greeting to Fitch. He sat down in the darkness, his arms holding his knees close to his chest, to wait for the others to arrive.

"How're you doing?" Fitch asked.

"OK, Skipper."

"The platoon?"

"A few more shrapnel wounds, nothing serious. They're tired. Real thirsty. We haven't slept in two nights."

"No one else has either," Fitch said, sighing.

"I didn't mean it that way, Skipper," Kendall said.

"Sure, I know." Fitch smiled. "Hey, I really know. Don't worry about it."

They were both silent. They could hear one of the listening posts checking out the radio before leaving the lines. "Bravo One, Bravo One, this is Milford. Comm check. Over." Since Milford was a town in Connecticut, the speaker was one of First Platoon's LPs.

"I got you Loco Cocoa, Milford." This was Jackson's voice, saying he could hear the transmission loud and clear. "Hey, the actual says he wants to talk to you before you head out. Over."

"Roger One. He coming down here? Over."

"Wait one." There was a pause. "That's affirmed. He says he'll be there in zero three. Over."

"Milford out," the voice acknowledged.

Fitch chuckled. Kendall knew that Fitch was trying to raise his spirits. "Mellas thought he wanted to be the Five," Fitch said, "but I think he's much happier as Bravo One Actual. He'd rather be checking out his LP than up here at the actuals meeting."

Kendall merely nodded. His world was in his memory. Bass waving his ornately carved stick, shouting, trying to organize the top of the hill, doing Kendall's job. Fracasso's body being tossed onto the helicopter. The quiet condemnation of his platoon as he led them back to Helicopter Hill.

The awkward silence was broken when Goodwin crawled in through the doorway.

"It's colder than a well-digger's ass in January," he said. "Why I left my fucking pack behind I'll never fucking know. Some dumb-assed idea from some fucked-up officer."

"Hey, Scar," Pallack said. "You get your third Purple Heart today?"

"You ain't shitting, Jack." Scar crawled over to Pallack and pulled down his filthy collar. "Look at that. A wound, right? A fucking shrapnel wound, right in the neck. I got the squid writing me up right now. That's it, you sorry motherfuckers." He paused for effect. "Okinawa."

"I can't see no fucking wound, Scar," Pallack said.

"That's because it's fucking dark in here, Jack."

"You really going to take a third Heart for that, Scar?" Relsnik asked. "And go back to Okinawa?"

"You're fuckin' A right. You can't have no nervous wreck leading the troops."

"How's the platoon?" Fitch broke in finally.

"Shit, Jack. How do you think?"

Fitch didn't answer.

"They're all right," Goodwin finally said. "We're going to freeze our fucking nuts off tonight, though."

"You just hope that's all that happens." Fitch turned to Pallack. "See if Mellas is on his way up here yet."

Sheller crawled in, and they went back to bantering about Scar's Purple Hearts until Mellas crawled through the narrow trench that led into the bunker.

It felt warm and very secure compared with once again sitting down on the lines with the platoon.

"Any word on relief?" Mellas asked before he had even settled into position. He pulled his muddy boots and legs up underneath him and pushed his back against the musty earth of the bunker.

"Alpha and Charlie were supposed to be dropped into the valley this afternoon," Fitch said. "But the weather fucked it up. Maybe tomorrow morning. They say they're doing everything they can. Meanwhile, we just have to hold the hill. They weren't too happy about us abandoning Matterhorn."

"I didn't see any of them up there," Mellas said through clenched teeth.

"No one's blaming us," Fitch said quickly. "At least not over the radio. I told them we didn't have enough men to hold Matterhorn and we had the stretcher cases to protect here and a smaller perimeter."

"So what's he doing about it, Jack?" Goodwin asked. "If the fucking fog don't lift we'll be out of Hotel Twenty tomorrow night."

"Hotel Twenty?" Fitch asked. "Get the fuck back. Where'd you pick that up?"

"Ain't you been to fucking school, Jack? H two O. That's water. You remember the stuff. You used to drink it back in the world. Turn a little fucking handle in the kitchen and it was sort of clear and had funny bubbles in it."

"And you didn't have to fuck it up with halazone," Mellas said.

"Naw, d'fucking government fucked it up for you at d'plant," Pallack put in.

They laughed for a moment and then became quiet. Sheller broke the silence. "I've got to have water for the wounded in a safe place where I can get to it. It helps keep people from going into shock."

They agreed on a plan for collecting and redistributing the water, saving a portion for the wounded.

Very faintly through the dirt they heard a cry of "Tubing!" No one spoke. A few seconds later two dull thumps reached them through the earth.

"Must have overshot," Kendall said.

"No shit," Scar answered.

Fitch quickly broke in. "We can thank the fog for one small huss. The gooks have got to hump their mortar rounds just like us. They won't be shooting up too many without being able to adjust."

"Unless there's a lot more people packing mortar rounds than we think," Mellas said darkly. "Listen. My fucking head seems to do numbers all day long, so I've been counting mortar rounds. We seem to get three at a time from three different positions. That's nine at a crack. Today they were pumping them in about every ten to fifteen minutes. That's about forty an hour. So twelve hours of shelling today—that's four hundred eighty rounds. Add about forty or fifty from when they were hitting Matterhorn and you're up over five hundred. That's two hundred fifty men at two apiece, and at three each it's one hundred sixty-six and two-thirds."

"Hey, Jack, we got some of the two-thirds thrown over the side of the fucking hill." Goodwin laughed, as did the others.

Mellas continued, focused on the math. "But that's just sixty-ones. They've been hitting us with eighty-twos and I think some of the big shit on Matterhorn the other day could have been from a hundred-twenty. So eighty-twos weigh, what, six or seven pounds a round? The fucking hundred-twenties must weigh around thirty. So it could be a lot more than two hundred fifty guys. And that's only counting what they've shot so far." He scanned each face in the group. "So either we've got a company that's all out of mortar rounds and packing their fucking bags tonight"—he paused—"or we've got real trouble."

"You know, Mellas," Fitch said mockingly, "you should have been in intelligence instead of on this fucking hill with us dumb grunts."

"Military intelligence is a contradiction in terms," Mellas said.

"Nice fucking news, sir," Pallack said. "Why don't you take your adding machine and go home?"

Contrary to Mellas's opinion about the effectiveness of military intelligence, G2, division intelligence, had over the past several days come to the same conclusion he had. Through analyzing information from the pockets of dead NVA soldiers, sightings by air observers who had managed to get between the clouds and the ground, and the reports of reconnaissance teams huddled against the rain on hilltops with Star-lite Scopes, infrared sighters, binoculars, and their own straining ears and eyes, division was pretty sure that an NVA regiment was moving east from Laos to secure the high ground along Mutter's Ridge north of Route 9. A second regiment was moving parallel to it through the Au Shau Valley to the south. Division assumed that there would be a third regiment moving down the Da Krong Valley between the two others, but so far there had been no sightings.

By taking Helicopter Hill, Bravo Company had put itself directly in the northern regiment's line of march. This forced the NVA to either blast Bravo out or isolate it like a tumor and move around it, hammering it with mortars and perhaps artillery. The only alternative was to take an extremely slow and difficult detour through the jungle-choked valleys beneath the ridgeline. So G2 was betting that the NVA would attack Bravo—but not until it could mass sufficient forces.

This was going to be a race. Division assumed that the NVA would assume that the Marines knew what was happening. The Marines considered the NVA to be professionals and gave them due respect. It was no accident that they had decided to move in when the Marine artillery was pulled back for the Cam Lo operation. The high card in the Marines' hand, however, was that the NVA probably didn't know how quickly the Marines could put it all back into place if they got a break in the weather. The NVA, moving within the confines of the ridgeline, would be safe as long as the clouds held. Since the North Vietnamese moved on foot, the weather didn't affect them as much as it did the Marines, and they would be in a position to overrun Bravo in the next day or so. If the clouds lifted, the superior mobility of the Marines would enable them to intercept the NVA, fix them in place, and inflict considerable damage. The longer Bravo held out, the better the chance of a good regiment-size battle, doing considerable damage to the NVA. At worst, the Marines risked losing a company. No one liked that, of course, but a company of Marines with their backs against the wall wouldn't be any picnic even for a far larger NVA unit. Even in the worst-case scenario, the NVA would pay a very heavy price. And in this war, attrition was what was important.

The intelligence staff's assessment was professionally and capably relayed up to General Neitzel and down to the regiments.

Mulvaney had been keeping a close eye on First Battalion ever since the Bald Eagle was launched. But he also had two other rifle battalions to worry about, and even though G2's assessment made sense, he wasn't about to start shifting bodies all over hell and creation until he knew he really had something. He started as many balls rolling as he reasonably could, knowing he had a hundred kids with their asses hanging out. But they were Marines. That's what they were there for. He knew G2 was right. If the NVA stopped to take out Bravo Company, a tempting target for any commander, they'd pay dearly. If he couldn't get his other battalions into position in time, Bravo would also pay. What bothered Mulvaney was that he knew the NVA felt they were buying something worth the price: their country.

He could no longer say the same for the Marines. That kind of clarity was a thing of the past. What was the military objective, anyway? If they were here to fight communists, why in hell wasn't Hanoi the objective? They could easily put the communist leaders out of their misery and end all this crap. Or just throw a bunch of Army divisions across the northern and eastern borders in defensive positions, which would multiply their force capabilities at least threefold. They'd keep the NVA out of the country with about one-tenth of the casualties. The South Vietnamese could sort out the Vietcong. Hell, since Tet last year, the Vietcong were already sorted out. The Marines seemed to be killing people with no objective beyond the killing itself. That left a hollow feeling in Mulvaney's gut. He tried to ignore it by doing his job, which was killing people.

Major Blakely felt the same as Mulvaney, but with two notable differences: Blakely was more excited, because he didn't have two other battalions to worry about; and this was his first war, not his third. Also, Blakely never reflected on what was being purchased or why it was being purchased. Blakely was a problem solver.

He knew Bravo was at risk. He'd put Bravo at risk, and he didn't particularly like the fact that he had. And although he'd seen dead kids being dragged off the choppers, he'd never actually been there when they'd died. For this reason, he found it hard to respect himself. This was a war for captains and lieutenants, and he was already too old, thirty-two. He didn't know and felt he would never know, unless he could somehow get involved, if he had what it took to lead a platoon or a company in combat.

Mellas would probably have said that Blakely didn't have what it takes, but Mellas would have been wrong. Blakely would have performed a lower-level job just as well as he performed his current job— competently, not perfectly, but well enough to get the work done and stay out of trouble. He'd make the same sorts of small mistakes, but they'd have a smaller effect. Instead of sending a company out without food, he might place a machine gun at a disadvantage. But the Marines under him would make up for mistakes like that. They'd fight well with the imperfect machine-gun layout. The casualties would be slightly higher, with slightly fewer enemy dead, but the statistics of perfection never show up in any reporting system. A victory is reported with the casualties it takes to secure that victory, not the casualties it would have taken if the machine gun had been better placed.

There was nothing sinister in this. Blakely himself would not be aware that he'd positioned the machine gun poorly. He'd feel bad about his casualties for a while. But reflecting on why or for what wasn't something Blakely did. Right now the problem before him was to engage the enemy and get the body count as high as possible. He wanted to do a good job, as any decent person would, and now he'd finally figured out a way to do so. He might actually get to use the entire battalion in a battle all at one time, an invaluable experience for a career officer.

Around 0300 one of Goodwin's listening posts started keying the hand-set furiously. Mellas heard Goodwin's voice come up quickly on the net. "Nancy, this is Scar. Whatja got? Key it once for every gook. Over."

The handset went wild. Mellas lost count.

"Jackson, get down there and get everyone up," Mellas said. "We got trouble."

"Why me?" said Jackson.

Mellas said, "RHIP, Jackson. Besides, you won't show up so much in the dark."

"You'll live to regret this, Lieutenant," Jackson whispered.

"I hope I fucking do."

Jackson slipped off, and soon Mellas heard the urgent whispers start down the line.

Fitch's voice came over the air, calling to the listening post. "Nancy, this is Bravo Six. If you think you can make it in, key your handset two times. Over."

There was no answer.

"OK, Nancy," Fitch continued, "we've got everyone alerted. You just get down on the fucking ground and stay there until we say different. Over."

Nancy responded by keying the handset two times.

A tiny dribble of dirt ran down the side of Mellas's fighting hole, pattering against his damp back. He could see nothing beyond the small mound of earth beside his hole. A quiet wind whispered with the fog through the jungle. The radio blurted out the sounds of other handsets keying furiously. "OK, you other Lima Poppas," Fitch radioed. "Get your asses back in if you can."

Mellas took the radio and crawled down to the lines to alert everyone that the LPs were coming in. Jackson was coming back up. "You *do* shine in the dark, Lieutenant," he said, crawling rapidly past.

Rider and Jermain were on LP. Everyone strained tensely. Then a whisper came: "Honda." A voice whispered back: "Triumph." Then there were the sounds of rapid scrambling on the hillside and a slight grunt as someone piled into a fighting hole. Then a second scramble and a second grunt. Safe.

Mellas had just slid back into his own hole when the night was hacked open by a roar of small arms fire in the jungle below them. The fog lit up with the barrel blasts.

"Bravo Two," the radio crackled, "this is Nancy. They got us spotted. We're coming in."

The fierce sound of the NVA's 7.62-millimeter weapons punctuated the lighter but more rapid firing of the Marines' M-16s.

"Nancy, goddamn it, don't get up and run." Goodwin was pleading with his LP not to break cover. "You'll get shot. Keep your cool, Jack. We'll get your ass out of it. Over."

"We're coming in, Scar, goddamn it," the radio answered. Then the firing stopped.

The handset keyed on and a voice different from the previous one came over the hook. It was a voice unused to the radio—a frightened, lonely voice.

"Uh, Lieutenant Goodwin, sir," the voice whispered, "can you hear me?" There was the brief static of the transmission key being let up.

"Shit, Jack. Lemon and Coke. Over."

The voice came back. "Roscoe's dead, I think." There was a long pause of blank transmission as the kid held the key down, not knowing that he was keeping Goodwin from answering. "Oh, Jesus, get me out of here, Lieutenant." He let up the key.

"Just start crawling backward, OK? Just keep low and start crawling backward. Over."

"But the radio's on Roscoe's back."

"Leave the fucking radio. Screw up the channel knobs. Crawl into the fucking weeds, dig in, and wait there. We'll get to you. Don't worry. Over."

There was a long wait. Then the handset keyed again. "I can't get the fucking radio off," the voice whispered, desperate.

Goodwin's voice became commanding. "This is an order, Jack. Switch the frequency and leave the fucking thing. They can't circle around you, because they'd be shooting their own guys, so crawl backward away from them and lay low. Once they get into the shit with us they ain't going to be looking for no lone Lima Poppa. As soon as it's light and the attack's over we'll come get you. Now move, goddamn it. Over."

Again there was no answer. Then the voice whispered, "Lieutenant, please get me out of here. Please, sir."

Jackson moaned softly and whispered, "We can't, you dumb son of a bitch. Just start shagging ass."

"Please, Lieutenant Scar, get me out of here," the voice came again.

Suddenly three hand grenades exploded in rapid succession, showing faint flashes through the dark jungle.

"Nancy, Nancy, this is Bravo Two. If you're OK, key the handset two times. Over." Goodwin repeated the question three times before he gave up.

* * *

The company waited, but the attack never developed.

"That LP saved our necks," Mellas said in the quiet that immediately followed.

"At least for tonight," Jackson replied.

They both knew they lived because two men had died. This was, of course, exactly why companies put out listening posts.

There were perhaps fifteen minutes of silence. Then, from all around them, tiny muffled clinks came from the jungle. It was the sound of digging.

Mellas called Goodwin on the radio. "Hey, Bravo Two, you hear people digging? Over."

"You ain't lying, Jack. Over."

Fitch's voice came up on the net. "Bravo Three, this is Bravo Six. How about you? Over."

Kendall answered softly. "Yeah. Down on the finger that Two came up the other day. Over."

"Shit, Jack," Goodwin broke in. "We just got our asses surrounded. Over."

"You're a military genius, Scar. Over," Fitch grumbled.

"How many Purple Hearts you got, Jack? That's the sign of a fucking military genius. Over."

Kendall shut his eyes and tried to remember every small detail of his wife's face, her body.

Mellas started praying silently so Jackson wouldn't hear him. "Dear God, I know I haven't prayed except when I'm in trouble, but dear God, get me out of here, please get me out of here." All the time he was praying, his mind was racing, casting about for an escape route, deciding he'd leave the wounded, leave the platoon, anything, just to reach the protection of the jungle.

Mellas was hit by the overwhelming, shattering knowledge that it was very likely he was going to die. Here on this filthy piece of earth. Now. Life had barely started, and so terribly and surprisingly soon it would be over.

CHAPTER
FIFTEEN

In the morning, when the fog turned to dull gray, the Marines began to shift in their holes. Some had laid their ponchos out behind their holes to collect dew. That didn't work, but they licked the ponchos anyway. A couple of jokes were passed. Mellas scrambled across the top of the hill to Goodwin's hole. Goodwin was standing upright in it, only his head and shoulders exposed. He wore his belt suspenders and was testing the springs on his magazines. His face was troubled.

Mellas squatted down next to Goodwin's hole. "Going after your LP?" he asked softly.

"Yep." Goodwin climbed out of his hole and worked the action of his M-16.

"The gooners can't be more than a hundred meters from here," Mellas said.

"I know, Jack." Goodwin turned and looked into the fog.

It was the first time Mellas had seen Goodwin so serious. A sudden rush of feeling swept over him. "Hey," Mellas said. "Take it easy out there, huh?"

Goodwin turned and looked at Mellas. "We going to get our asses out of this shit sandwich?"

Mellas shrugged his shoulders. "All we need is a clear day."

They both looked up at the clouds, just visible in the early light. Goodwin looked at Mellas. "I don't know about you, but I'm fucking thirsty." He then put two fingers to his lips, gave a shrieking whistle, and shouted out, "Hey, you gunjy fuckers. Get your asses up here." He turned to Mellas and grinned. "I asked for volunteers and they all said they'd go. But Roscoe and Estes were both from First Squad, so First Squad will go get them."

He hollered out again. "Goddamn it, Robb, get them up here." He turned back to Mellas. "Knowing how scared they were last night, I figure they couldn't have gone more than thirty or forty meters outside the lines." The squad moved silently and slowly up to Goodwin's hole.

China was sliding the bolt on his M-60 slowly back and forth. Part of him was crying out about how stupid it was to risk his life going to retrieve a couple of dead chucks, but another part of him was making sure the machine gun worked perfectly. He looked toward the top of the hill and saw the religious nut, Cortell, sitting by the dead bodies. The fool just couldn't see that he'd adopted the white man's religion. But there was something about Cortell that China envied—Cortell was sure where Parker had gone. China slammed home the bolt and looked at Goodwin. Jesus, the white cracker moonshine hillbilly son of a bitch took this *Semper Fi* shit seriously. Here he was about to get his ass shot off doing *Semper Fi* bullshit while Henry was back at VCB doing business. The image of Parker trying to hold back his fear swam into China's consciousness. He saw Vancouver heading off in the night to work his way down to the river, and Doc Fredrickson wiping Parker down to keep him cool.

He watched Goodwin silently counting them, pointing his index finger at each one as he did. It occurred to him that Goodwin probably mouthed the words when he read, too. Goodwin nodded to the squad leader, Robb, and then crouched low. Ten meters beyond the holes, Goodwin went directly to ground and started crawling. Robb was three meters behind him. Then it was China's turn. He went.

Mellas watched until the entire squad had crawled into the fog and disappeared. The entire hill waited for the firefight. An hour dragged by. Goodwin wasn't talking on the radio. Cortell came and sat next to Mellas, saying nothing.

Eventually Mellas spoke. "You pray about shit like this, Cortell?"

Cortell looked at Mellas from under the bloody bandage around his head. "Sir, I pray all the time."

Within an hour the squad was back, dragging two bodies. Mellas noticed that the LP's radio was gone. When they reached the lines, Goodwin gave the senior squid the dead kids' water and then went through their pockets. "Hey," he shouted, holding up a single dark green C-ration can, "fucking beef stew."

Being besieged is like any other variation of war. Behind the immediate terror of killing one another is tedious, spirit-destroying boredom. The fog remained thick that morning, and the NVA shelled them only a few times. The NVA were probably afraid of hitting their own men who were dug in around the Marines. This gave everyone a lot of time to think.

Mellas wandered alone to the stack of bodies on top of the LZ. All he could see were the bleached boots of the veterans, with their sickly yellow nylon tops, and the black boots, with the dark green tops, of the new guys. Paper tags had been wired to boots and wrists.

The senior squid squatted beside Mellas. He was holding what looked like photographs in his hand.

"What you got there, Sheller?" Mellas asked.

"Snapshots. Off the bodies. I need your OK to throw these. Division standing order is to make sure nothing risqué goes home with the corpse."

"Risqué?" Mellas asked through clenched teeth.

Sheller hung his head, embarrassed. "It's just something they say to do, sir."

Mellas went slowly through the photographs, his hands trembling. There were pictures of dead North Vietnamese: blasted, blackened bodies. One picture was of a body with no head, sitting bolt upright in a fighting hole. A kid from Goodwin's platoon was posing next to it, smiling, with the head in the crook of his arm. There was a picture of three dead American kids all squeezed into one fighting hole. On it, written with a ballpoint pen, was "Snake, Jerry, and Kansas." One picture was of a beautiful Thai girl lying naked on a bed in a hotel room. Mellas looked at it for a long time, noticing her black hair floating across the sheets, her smooth brown legs modestly hiding her vulva. The fragile beauty amid the carnage took his breath away.

"That one bothered me," Sheller said.

"He extended, didn't he, to see her again?"

Sheller nodded.

"Burn 'em all."

Sheller calmly took out a Zippo and lit the snapshots. They watched the photos slowly curl in the heat, change color, then burst into flames. And they watched the naked body of a bar girl in Bangkok do the same. No one knew her name, other than Susi, so no one could tell her that Janc had died. She would find that out when her next letter came back stamped DECEASED.

Mellas went back to his fighting hole and scrunched down inside it, trying to stay warm. The two flak jackets provided little help. Jacobs came up to him to ask if the birds were coming.

"Believe me, Jake, if I get word about a fucking bird being able to land here, even so much as a tiny sparrow, or even a tufted nuthatch, or a hairy-chested widow maker, I'll let you know."

Then Mellas noticed that there was an ear stuck in the rubber band on Jake's helmet. He went cold. "What's that on your helmet?"

"An ear, sir," Jake said offhandedly.

"Get rid of it."

"Why the fuck should I?" Jacobs asked hotly. "This f-fucking b-bastard killed Janc, and I know because I threw his goddamned b-body down the hill."

"You know you could go to jail for mutilation."

"Go to jail? F-fucking jail. Who's going to go to fucking jail for k-killing Janc? Th-they ought to go to jail, the ones that made up the fucking rules."

"Throw it away right fucking now. And you'll bury the bodies, too."

"I ain't burying no g-gook body. No sir."

"Come on Jake, let's go look at them."

Jacobs silently followed Mellas down to the lines. They looked down the steep slope where the bodies of the dead North Vietnamese kids had all been thrown after the assault. They lay there, some with eyes open, arms and legs askew, rigid, seeming oddly uncomfortable. One body had been hacked at with a K-bar. It also had one ear missing.

"Who hacked the body up, Jake?" Mellas asked softly. "Look, I know they killed some of us, but we killed some of them, didn't we?"

Jacobs nodded, looking down at the ground. Mellas remembered laughing once with him about how they'd both been altar boys. "I hacked it," Jacobs said. He reached up and tore the ear from his helmet and hurled it down at the bodies. "I just r-ran down the hill and hacked it. I don't know why."

They stood together watching the fog. Jacobs's eyes glistened with tears, but he held them back. "Fucking Janc," he said.

Gambaccini came up. Two ears were pinned to the crown of his bush cover. "I cut ears too, sir," he said. "If you put Jacobs in the brig, then I did it too."

Mellas shook his head slowly. "Gambaccini, I don't give a rat's ass about the dead gooks. Just get rid of the ears so you don't go to jail." Mellas started to walk away. "But you can help Jake bury the fucking bodies."

When Mellas had moved some distance, he glanced back. The two of them were still standing there, looking down at the corpses. Then Gambaccini took the two ears and, curling a finger around each like a skipping stone, sent them sailing one after the other into the fog.

There came a moment during the lull when Mellas, lost at the center of the swirling fog, knew beyond any ability to lie to himself that he had, indeed, killed Pollini—and he was overwhelmed by an emptiness that knocked him to his knees. Slumped in his wet hole, cocooned by two flak jackets, he broke. He was the butt of a cruel joke. God had given him life and must have laughed as Mellas used it to kill Pollini, to get a piece of ribbon to show proof of his worth. And it was his worth that was the joke. He was nothing but a collection of empty events that would end as a faded photograph above his parents' fireplace. They too would die, and relatives who didn't know who was in the picture would throw it away. Mellas knew, in his rational mind, that if there was no afterlife, death was no different from sleep. But this cruel flood was not from his rational mind. It had none of the ephemerality of thought. It was as real as the mud he sat in. Thought was just more of the nothing that he had done all his life. The fact of his eventual death shook him like a terrier shaking a rat. He could only squeal in pain.

His mind jumped in. We'll escape. Play dead when they finally overwhelm us. Don't use the knife—play dead and use the confusion of that last assault to cover your escape. You'll be alive! Leave these Marines and this false notion of honor. Get into the jungle with the rest of the animals and hide and be alive. Alive!

But the terrier shaking him by the neck laughed. And then? A career in law? A little prestige? A little money? Perhaps a political office? And then, dead. Dead. The laughter turned him inside out, exposing his most secret parts. He lay before God as a woman opens herself to a man, with legs apart, stomach exposed, arms open. But unlike some women, he did not have the inner strength that allowed them to do such a thing without fear. There was no woman's strength in Mellas at all.

The terrier shook him again and Mellas was painfully alive. Stripped to a scream, undressed to a cry of pain, he sobbed his anger at God in hoarse words that hurt his throat. He asked for nothing now, nor did he wonder if he'd been bad or good. Such concepts were all part of the joke he'd just discovered. He cursed God directly for the savage joke that had been played on him. And in that cursing Mellas for the first time really talked with his God. Then he cried, tears and snot mixing together as they streamed down his face, but his cries were the rage and hurt of a newborn child, at last, however roughly, being taken from the womb.

Mellas's new insight didn't change anything, at least on the outside, but Mellas knew he wouldn't play dead. He'd been playing dead all his life. He would not slip into the jungle and save himself, because that self didn't look like anything worth saving. He'd choose to stay on the hill and do what he could to save those around him. The choice comforted him and calmed him down. Dying this way was a better way to die because living this way was a better way to live.

The senior squid came crawling into Mellas's hole, covered with blood and vomit from the wounded. "I just had to get away," he said. He slid in next to Mellas to watch the jungle and the fog. Mellas knew that his own existential crisis didn't mean shit to Sheller. And he suddenly knew where Hawke got his sense of humor. He got it from observing the facts. What a great joke—that Mellas would probably get a medal for killing one of his own men. It seemed appropriate that the president would probably get reelected for doing the same thing on a far larger scale. Then a new voice within him started to laugh with God.

He became aware that he was laughing out loud when he saw Sheller looking at him quizzically. "What?" Mellas asked, still laughing.

"What's so funny, sir?"

Mellas laughed again. "You're a fucking mess, Sheller. You know that?" He kept laughing, shaking his head in wonder at the world.

Tedium marked the passing of the hours. The kids fought their desire to sleep. Just before noon the fog lifted slightly, hovering a few feet above Matterhorn and giving enough visibility for a bird to get into Helicopter Hill. Fitch immediately radioed for the resupply birds.

Helicopter Hill, however, was also in plain sight of the NVA mortarmen, who started firing, easily adjusting their shots. When the Marines heard the projectiles leaving the tubes, they knew they had only a few seconds to get deep while the rounds were making their large arcs over to Helicopter Hill. The mortar rounds came down, the ground shook, and the pressure hit eardrums and eyeballs. It wasn't sound or noise, because it wasn't heard. It was felt. It was pain.

The Marines huddled in their holes and felt the concussions. They held their ears. Dirt rained on their helmets and stuffed their nostrils. One kid from Third Platoon was hit by a shell that landed on the lip of his hole. They dragged him into the bunker that held the few canteens of water being saved for the wounded. Everyone else was out.

The birds were on their way when the fog closed in again. The helicopters were unable to find the landing zone and turned back after running short of fuel.

The shelling stopped.

Boredom, fatigue, and thirst set in again.

Goodwin was restless and moved down below the line of holes facing Matterhorn. Occasionally, through the fog, he could see the bunkers First Platoon had attacked the morning before. He sat down with his rifle and adjusted its sights. Resting it against a log, he settled in to watch and wait.

An hour passed. Goodwin had the patience of a born hunter. He lived in no-time, leaving it only briefly to shift his body.

The fog moved in and closed Matterhorn from his view. Twenty more minutes passed. The fog lifted again. A tiny figure could be seen trudging between two bunkers. Goodwin squeezed off a round. The bullet kicked up dirt below the figure. The man started running. Goodwin aimed above him to compensate for the distance and fired three more quick shots. The third one clipped the man in the leg and he went down. Excitement coursed in Goodwin's throat. He quickly adjusted his sights for the distance and wind and fired two more rounds. He couldn't tell where they hit. That was a good sign, because if they hit flesh they wouldn't kick up mud. Small arms opened fire from Matterhorn. Goodwin heard the crack of the bullets in the air around him before he heard the sound of the discharges. The bullets thudded into the hill above him, sending the Marines diving for their holes, joking and cursing Goodwin, who was hidden below them, readjusting his sights again.

Two figures darted out of a bunker and dragged Goodwin's target away. Goodwin, enraged, opened up on full automatic, but the M-16 rode up with the recoil. He saw a tracer bullet make a flat orange arc that seemed to be sucked quickly into the hill above the three NVA soldiers. "Fuck. We need a fucking M-14, Jack."

The fire died down. Goodwin went back to the lines and began trading straight bullets for tracers, alternating one for every four in his magazines. Then he and a couple of others slipped just below the holes and set up at a different location. At that distance, the tracers, being lighter, wouldn't impact exactly where the bullets did, but he could estimate about where the heavier bullets would go and knew he'd still have a better chance of correcting for range and wind. He also knew that the tracers would give away his position.

Mellas wandered down to see what was happening. Goodwin was sitting there, leaning over his rifle, as patient and as still as a cat waiting by a mouse hole. Fifteen minutes passed. Mellas got bored and went back to his side of the hill.

Two hours passed. The fog closed back in again, making it safe to walk or sit aboveground. Kids talked, whittled, and dug elaborate shelves and steps in their holes. Several went down and helped Gambaccini and Jacobs dig graves for the dead NVA, simply for something to do. Many dozed, thankful to have nothing to do but wait in their holes. All of them looked at the sky every few minutes, like cargo cultists waiting for deliverance.

Two and a half hours more passed. Mellas crawled down to check on Goodwin. Goodwin was still waiting over his rifle. Mellas lay down beside him. Goodwin talked without taking his eye from the rear sight. "That little bastard's just about to poke his head out that hole. I can feel it."

Mellas squatted there, looking across the hill, which came into and went out of view in the swirling gray. Ten minutes passed. He thought about the man inside the bunker across the way. The bunker was one that Jacobs had built. It was dug in deep, with eye-level just aboveground, logs interspersed with dirt, runway matting, sandbags—unless it was hit right on top, even a 500-pound bomb wouldn't hurt someone inside. Infantry would be required. Mellas didn't want to think about this anymore.

He got bored again and left. Close to 1500—half an hour after he'd left Goodwin the second time—he heard the single crack of the M-16, then two more shots in quick succession. "Scar got one." The cry came floating over the hill. Mellas ran across the top, ducking in case there was return fire.

"I got the little fucker," Goodwin said as Mellas threw himself down beside him. One of the kids providing security with Goodwin handed Fitch's binoculars to Mellas. Through them, he could see the dead soldier being dragged back into the bunker. "I got him right in the high part of the throat," Goodwin said matter-of-factly. "I knew he'd have to come out and piss sometime."

"Nice shot," Mellas said. "You gonna try for another one?"

"Beats humping."

The fog cleared for a moment, exposing the top of Helicopter Hill to the NVA again. A single AK-47 rattled briefly. The Marines scrambled into their holes. But the AK-47 was even less accurate at long range than the M-16.

Mellas lay flat on the ground, thirst battering his brain. His lips and tongue felt like cotton. He noted the obvious fire discipline of the NVA. They could reach quite accurately with their 7.62 machine guns but didn't fire them: like the Marines, they did not want to give away key defensive positions. But the NVA had no compunction about firing their SKS rifles and AK-47s, particularly from the little finger running northeast from Matterhorn.

Goodwin poked his head over the log after the firing stopped. "They don't know where we're at, Jack," he said quietly. He crouched and duckwalked away from the log, screened by the dead bushes; then he stood straight up and, looking directly at Matterhorn, took a piss. Then he walked back and settled on his stomach behind the log. He rested the rifle on the log and leaned his cheek against the stock. "See that fucking bunker with the little bush to the left, two over from where we shot the gook?" he said to the kid with the binoculars.

"Yeah," the kid answered. They were both ignoring rank and the usually obligatory "sir."

"I saw someone move in there and I'm going to kill him."

Mellas looked at Goodwin, then across at Matterhorn. He exulted in Goodwin's prowess. He wanted to kill as well, but knew he wasn't nearly as good a shot and would embarrass himself. Nor did he have Goodwin's uncanny patience. Mellas didn't hate the NVA. He wanted to kill the enemy because that was the only way the company would get off the hill, and he wanted to live and go home. He also wanted to kill because a burning anger inside him had no place to go. The people he had hated—the colonel, the politicians, the protesters, bullys who'd shamed him in childhood, little friends who'd taken his toys when he was two—weren't available, but the NVA soldiers were. At a very deep level, Mellas simply wanted to stand on a body that he had laid low. Watching Goodwin with more than a little envy, he had to admit that he wanted to kill because part of him was thrilled by killing.

At Vandegrift Combat Base the battalion staff was huddled around several large maps.

"What do you think, Lieutenant Hawke?" Simpson asked. "You've operated all around there."

"Like I said yesterday, sir, it's triple canopy all the way up the ridge and it's lucky to make three klicks a day, and then they'll be totally disregarding security."

Captain Bainford spoke up. "The AO says the closest place, before the cloud cover socks things in, is Hill 631." He pointed to a gently sloping hill in the broad valley south of Matterhorn. "That's only nine klicks from Matterhorn. I can't believe it would take three days."

Hawke exploded. "You can't believe it because you've never fucking been there."

Bainford looked hurt and glanced over at Blakely and Simpson. Stevens started looking for something to do.

"Sorry, Captain Bainford," Hawke said. "I guess I'm personally invested. I didn't mean to take it out on you."

"That's OK, Hawke," the air officer replied, clearly happy to seem magnanimous. "I understand how it is."

The fuck you do, Hawke thought. He tried to think of something constructive. Then he realized he could do no more than they could. Neither Blakely nor Simpson had slept much since the attack on Matterhorn, and it showed, particularly in Simpson. They'd worked hard. Supplies had to be detailed and ranked by priority; choppers, trucks, and loading parties had to be coordinated; fixed-wing air support had to be organized and briefed, not just to help Bravo Company but for every insertion of every company in the battalion. The same went for artillery from the 8-inch howitzers on Sherpa to the 105s now around Cam Lo, down to the battalion's own 81-millimeter mortar platoon. All had to be prepared to move, to be picked up by choppers, to be moved to a new position that had to be secured by infantry, supplied with ammunition, water, and food. They'd done all this. Everything was ready to go, including two additional companies op-conned from Third Battalion that were going to be dropped in to cut off any retreat by the NVA. But they were held up, just as everything else was, waiting at landing zones for the clouds to rise high enough for the pilots to see their way into the mountains.

Hawke was thinking that if they didn't get a clear day soon, Bravo Company would be out of water and ammunition and would have to abandon the hill. Then they'd have to fight their way through a regiment. There would be nothing left of them. The colonel had been right, Hawke thought ruefully. There were fucking gooks around Matterhorn.

Captain Bainford was angry with Hawke. Just because Hawke had been in the jungle with the fucking ground pounders, he acted like God Almighty's gift to the Marine Corps and treated Bainford like a child. These fucking grunts couldn't appreciate the burden of being personally responsible for several million dollars' worth of aircraft.

Lieutenant Stevens wished he could catch some sleep. For the past forty-eight hours, he'd been standing around answering stupid questions about how far 105s and 155s could shoot. He wondered if they were going to be able to get the two eight-inch guns moved to Eiger along with Golf Battery. Get those eight-inchers in there and they'd shoot the motherfuckers right through the slits in their bunkers. You couldn't beat an eight-inch for precision. Those poor fucking grunts on that hill, man. Gook eighty-twos for two solid days now.

Major Blakely was frustrated. He'd put together a perfect operation, and now the fucking weather had closed him out. It was shaping up to be two Marine battalions taking on a gook regiment in a running fight. Too bad Fitch had made the blunder of splitting his forces. And then to pull back to the lower hill. A classic fuckup. They should have been screaming bloody murder to get a regular captain to replace Fitch. Sure, it was a mistake not to blow those bunkers on Matterhorn, but then that was hindsight. At the time, the Cam Lo cordon was a big deal and it had been a nightmare scrambling to keep up with all the changes. They'd been watching that combined operation with the ARVNs right up to the White House. Vietnamization. Horseshit. If Blakely were at the Pentagon, there'd be no bullshitting about the ARVNs being able to take on the NVA or this pacification crap. You had to get in there and scrap—with American firepower and guts. That was the only way to do it. He smiled to himself. Grab them by the balls and their hearts and minds will follow. Whoever had said that had *been* there.

Lieutenant Colonel Simpson was worried sick. If he didn't get Bravo Company's ass out of the crack in the next three days they'd be too dehydrated to fight. They had enough ammunition for maybe two more firefights. If the NVA mounted an attack of any length, it would run them dry of ammo. But that was probably the little bastards' strategy. Simpson pictured the little gook colonel, eating rice in his command bunker, looking at maps with strange Chinese writing on them. That little bastard was going to sit there and wait for the company to run out of water. If Bravo Company tried to break out, he'd have them by the short hairs. But if the fog held, just for another day, Simpson would have an entire regiment fixed in place. Then, if it cleared, he could call in the jets and have a field day. If Bravo Company took too many more casualties, though, it was going to look bad no matter what the outcome. That didn't seem fair.

"We've all done what we can," Simpson said, still looking at the map. "I suggest we catch some rest before dark. It might be a long night."

Everybody took him up on the suggestion except Hawke, who had the watch until 2000 hours. When he was relieved, he went to the regimental O-club to start a private mystery tour.

When Colonel Mulvaney pushed through the screen door of the O-club he recognized Hawke standing at the bar. There were already four empty shot glasses in front of him. Mulvaney walked over to him and threw a wad of pink military payment currency onto the bar, saying,

"You're Hawke, aren't you?" He asked the bartender for drinks for himself and Hawke before Hawke could respond.

"Thank you, sir," Hawke said.

"My pleasure." Mulvaney leaned his heavy bulk over his forearms. "I see they got the wire mesh repaired," he said.

Hawke studied his shot glass.

"Seems some young officers tied one on and disrupted a movie."

"Did you find out who it was?" Hawke asked.

Mulvaney watched Hawke in the mirror. "No. But they also stole a truck. One of my staff officers at the club had a little too much to drink himself and he put two bullet holes in it. He got a letter of reprimand."

"That's too bad, sir."

"Too bad?"

"I mean, for him. I mean shooting a pistol inside the perimeter of a base like this is a little foolish."

"So is stealing a truck."

"Yes sir," Hawke said. He hung his head.

Mulvaney leaned his back against the bar and looked at the groups of officers drinking at the tables. "Well, the screen's fixed. The truck's OK." Mulvaney turned to Hawke, who was still looking down at his glass. "But just between you and me, Hawke," he said, very evenly and quietly, "it was a stupid fucking thing to do. It could have ruined the careers of some good officers, and we need all the good ones we can get. If I could kick your butt all over this bar without having to get involved in a goddamned court-martial I'd do it."

"Yes sir," Hawke said.

Mulvaney softened. "Goddamn it, Hawke, are you Irish or what? I got to drink all these things by myself?"

"No sir." Hawke looked up at him. "Sir, I'm sorry."

"Forget it. I've been there too." Mulvaney was pointing to a package of Beer Nuts with his left hand, but he was also seeing Jim Auld moaning in the sand on the banks of the Tenaru, his eyes pleading for help, a bloody socket where his arm had been before the Japanese antitank gun had taken it off. "You just got to remember to get the shit out of your system someplace where you won't get in trouble."

Mulvaney opened the package and spread the Beer Nuts on the bar in front of them. He popped them into his mouth as he talked, downing the whiskey half a shot glass at a time. "My wife tells me I shouldn't drink so much but, goddamn it, what's the sense of having tax-free whiskey if you can't drink more than the ordinary son of a bitch?"

"I agree, sir." Hawke took another drink and picked up several of the nuts. "Sir," he asked, "you got any word on the relief for Bravo Company?"

"Naw. Nothing new. Fucking monsoon." Mulvaney gave Hawke a reassuring smile. "Don't worry about them, Hawke. They'll make it OK. There's been worse situations."

"Yeah. We read about them all the time in glory-filled history books."

Mulvaney wanted to tell Hawke about the Chosin Reservoir, but he knew Hawke didn't want to hear about it any more than Mulvaney had wanted to hear about Château-Thierry when he was a lieutenant. Everyone's war was the worst. "No need to bad-mouth bravery just because you're pissed off and tired," Mulvaney finally said.

"I'm sorry, sir. It just slipped out."

"Slipped out? Bullshit. What lieutenant worth his fucking salt isn't pissed off and tired? I'm pissed off and tired too, but then I'm the bastard that makes the decisions, so I don't have any right to bitch about it." Mulvaney chuckled.

Hawke didn't respond as Mulvaney would have liked. Instead he put his glass down and turned to face him. "Why was it necessary for Bravo Company to go into the assault, knowing we're in monsoon season?"

Anger quickened Mulvaney's pulse. He wanted to tell Hawke how Simpson had ordered the assault without consulting him, how Blakely had pre-briefed the division staff informally, cutting off any chance of countering the order. But Simpson and Blakely reported to Mulvaney. He was responsible. It was the code. "We thought it was a chance to kill some gooks," Mulvaney said. "That's our job, Hawke. You knew that when you came aboard."

"Yes sir, I did." Hawke took another gulp of whiskey.

"Look, Hawke, I think you're a hell of an officer and I'm not going to bullshit you. Bravo Company's up there either because of a fuckup or because of a brilliant tactical move. It all depends on the body count. That's the kind of war we're in."

"Which fuckup?" Hawke asked. "There were a lot of them."

"Officially it will be Fitch's. He split his forces, abandoned a key position, and got his ass into a jam. He's a reserve officer. His career's not at stake."

"You really think Fitch is that dumb?"

"I told you the way it will read, not what I thought. Christ, Hawke, you really think *I'm* that dumb? The fucking kid had too few men to do what was asked and still provide security for his wounded. You think you're the only fucker's ever been to war around here?"

"Sometimes it looks that way."

"Well, you ain't. Grow up and quit trying to find blame like everyone else around here. Just get the fucking job done."

"Yes sir."

There was drunken laughter from one of the groups of officers throwing dice for drinks.

"I didn't want to preach to you like some sort of fucking bishop," Mulvaney said.

"I guess I brought it on myself, sir."

Mulvaney felt a barrier growing between him and Hawke. He felt lost, lonely, heartsick.

"It's the situation," Mulvaney said, pushing a Beer Nut with his thick finger.

"There it is, sir," Hawke said.

"Don't give up on me, Hawke," Mulvaney said. He grinned. "Tell you what. You promise to go regular, I'll see you get a fucking rifle company." He watched Hawke visibly react and then regain control.

"I'm out of the bush, sir, and I don't ever want to go back. But thank you, sir."

Mulvaney studied Hawke closely. "Don't try and bullshit a salty old fucker like me, Lieutenant, because I've been there. A Marine rifle company. Two hundred twelve Marines—two hundred twelve of the biggest hearts in the world. And you're barely old enough to stand in a bar and drink." He paused. "It'll be Bravo Company if it's open."

He watched Hawke catch his breath.

Hawke was saved from having to answer because just then Corporal Odegaard, Mulvaney's driver, shouted through the door, "Colonel Mulvaney, sir, Bravo Company's in the shit again."

Mulvaney gulped the remainder of his whiskey, put his big hand on the top of Hawke's head, and gave a couple of barely perceptible little pushes. "Think about it," he said. "We need you." Then he strode quickly out the door, Hawke on his heels. He knew without a doubt that Hawke had just gone regular.

The attack started with the NVA coming up on the company radio net. "Fucky you, Bahvo, fucky you. Fucky you, Bahvo, fucky you."

"Goddamn it," Mellas said to Jackson. Goodwin's LP had failed to scramble the frequency knobs on the radio. "They're jamming the net."

"Yeah, well, fuck you too, you fucking gook," they heard Pallack snap back over the net.

Mellas grabbed the hook. "Bravo, this is Bravo Five. Get everyone switched off right fucking now. We'll get you the new freak ASAP."

"Fucky you, Bahvo, fucky you."

Firing broke out in a roar just below Kendall's lines. It was his LP.

"Fucky you, Bahvo, fucky you."

The radios were useless. The LPs were isolated.

Mellas shouted at Jackson above the racket. "Get your ass up to the CP and get us a new freak." Jackson immediately heaved himself out of the hole and crawled off in the darkness. Mellas did the same but headed toward his LP. "Hartford in!" he shouted. "Hartford in! The radio net's fucked up. Get your asses in here, Hartford. Friendlies coming in!"

A burst of fire ripped out of the jungle below him, the muzzle blast glowing strangely in the fog. Then there was the roar of the M-16s from the listening post. There was an indistinguishable shout and then someone was yelling the password: "Lemonade, Lemonade, it's fucking Jermain, goddamn it. Lemonade, we're coming in." Another roar of fire cut off his words, but Mellas heard the sound of running and scrambling through the brush, and then another M-16 on full automatic.

Up at the CP, Fitch was sick with dread. All the radio net could do was sing, "Fucky you, Bahvo, fucky you," jamming all transmissions. He scrambled out of the bunker to find out what was happening. Pallack and Relsnik followed after him, dragging the radios.

Down at Third Platoon, Lieutenant Kendall was crouched in his hole. The roar of the firefight at his listening post drowned out every thought in his head. Genoa, his radio operator, watched him anxiously, wishing Samms were still alive. He hoped the lieutenant would stay in the hole and give him an excuse to do the same thing.

Goodwin grabbed his rifle and headed downhill to his center squad's machine-gun position. There, even if he couldn't talk on the radio, he could at least direct the fire of one of his three biggest weapons and be in the middle of the fight. His radio operator, not knowing what Goodwin had in mind, scrambled after him shouting, "Friendlies, friendlies! It's Scar and Russell."

Goodwin had doubled the size of his listening post to increase its odds of survival and hold down the jitters. The four kids on the LP, hearing the sound of firing on both sides of them, bolted for the lines. They ran uphill, flailing at the thick brush and tree limbs, panting, their legs cramped from lying on the damp ground, guided forward by eerie green and white flashes that brought brush and trees into and out of their sight. They broke out into the cleared field of fire below the lines and started shouting the password just as one of Goodwin's men threw an M-76 fragmentation grenade. It bounced down the hill toward them. The kid who threw it immediately shouted, "Jesus. I'm sorry. It's a fucking grenade." None of the four heard him as they kept panting up the slope. Three seconds later the grenade exploded. One kid from the LP caught the bulk of the shrapnel along his right side. The three others crawled over and dragged him up the hill shouting, "Corpsman! Corpsman!" Goodwin stood up and waved his arms, forgetting that they couldn't see a thing in the dark, and shouted, "Over here, you stupid motherfuckers, over here." Guided by Goodwin's voice, they dragged the wounded Marine into the machine-gun hole. The platoon corpsman crawled over to work on the first of the many wounded who were to come. No one gave a damn about what had caused the explosion that wounded the boy. The Marines were all too grateful to be inside the lines with their friends.

The firefight with Kendall's LP died out. The Marines stared into the dark and fog. Goodwin crawled from the machine-gun position to a point about ten meters to the left and behind it, his radiomen crawling after him, the radio still spewing nonsense. Then Goodwin lay on his back and shouted at the sky, "Remember it's claymores first, then grenades and Mike-seventy-nines. And don't waste your shotgun rounds." Goodwin's voice steadied nervous movements all around the hill. "Nobody fires a rifle until you hear mine," he continued. "Any of you fuckers give away a machine-gun position before we need it, you won't draw KP for the rest of your tour." Then he whispered to Russell, "Let's get the fuck out of here." He broke into a scrambling crawl, heading for the machine gun again, Russell right behind him, just as brilliant flashes of light erupted from the jungle, the bullets hitting where Goodwin and Russell had lain on their backs.

Then the entire hill was quiet. Everyone waited. The silence hung like smoke over their heads.

Mellas crawled back to his hole and waited for Jackson to return with the new radio frequency. He toyed with the safety on his M-16, wondering if he'd be killed, feeling very alone and afraid, wishing Jackson would hurry back, worrying about him, worrying about getting the company up on the new frequency.

Kendall crouched in his hole thinking of his wife, wondering if the kids on the LP were still alive, wishing that Fitch would tell him what to do. He imagined Genoa's disdainful stare. He looked up over the edge of his hole into the blackness.

Jackson, with the new frequency on the radio, crawled back toward Mellas's hole, praying no one would hear him and shoot him accidentally.

A very frightened Pallack, who had to carry the new frequency down the lines, followed him out of Fitch's hole. "Hey, it's Pallack," he whispered, hoping he was near someone. There was no answer. No one wanted to give away his position. "Goddamn it, now, it's me, Pallack, d' Romeo carrier. Don't shoot my ass. OK?"

No one answered.

"Hey, Scar. I'm coming down. OK?"

No answer.

Pallack lay flat in the mud, face buried, wanting never to move. The cold fog moved across his back. Why in the fuck was he the fucking company radio operator? He swallowed and continued crawling down-hill, gravity pulling the blood to his face.

"Hey, it's Pallack," he whispered again, tentatively. Jesus fuck, the lieutenants do this every night? No wonder they're so fucked up. "Hey! It's me. Character Poppa from d' CP," he whispered again.

"Goddamn it, Pallack, what do you fucking want?" someone hissed.

"Tell Scar to come up on fifteen point seven," he whispered.

"Fuck, Pallack."

Pallack was already crawling away as fast as he could.

The main attack started with an explosion at the far end of First Platoon's lines, not small arms fire. "Zappers!" Fredrickson whispered. He swal-lowed. NVA sapper units were elite troops who carried satchel charges filled with several pounds of TNT that they used to clear paths through barbed wire and destroy bunkers. They also hurled these into fighting holes. Satchel charges didn't leave a corpsman much to work with.

Another series of satchel charges were hurled by the North Viet-namese sappers as they rose from where they'd been silently creeping forward in the dark. At the sound of the satchels going off, the NVA infantry burst from the cover of the bush and came running uphill, heavily laden with grenades, rifles, and ammunition, fighting the same gravity that the Marines fought, their lungs gasping for the same damp air, their bodies hurled forward by the same adrenaline and fear.

Goodwin opened up with his M-16, not waiting for Fitch's orders, and the entire hill went off like a chain of gunpowder. The night turned phosphorescent orange and green, and the roaring sound of the weap-ons seemed to squeeze everyone's brain down to the size of a fist. First the entire line erupted with the claymores going off, detonated by the Marines in their holes, spewing wide arcs of steel balls at groin height. Then the Marines rolled grenades beneath the legs of the advancing enemy. Tracers, green for the NVA and orange for the Marines, criss-crossed in front of the lines.

Mellas crammed his fists against his ears, not to block the over-powering sound but to try and hold thoughts in his head, figure out what to do, and not let fear send him quivering into the bottom of his fight-ing hole, hoping for the mercy of God. No intelligible sound could be heard above the sustained explosion of a Marine rifle company fight-ing for its life.

The machine gunners laced fire horizontally across the lines, set-ting up a curtain of moving steel through which the advancing NVA soldiers had to struggle as if in slow motion. Still they came forward, silently, laboriously, bravely. Some made it to the line of fighting holes. The rest were slaughtered by staggering firepower.

The North Vietnamese who'd survived the storm of fire were crawling and darting among the holes, hurling satchels, firing their rifles. The entire hill disintegrated into the confusion of 300 human animals, white, brown, and black, trying to kill each other to save their skins.

Then the sound of the battle changed. The explosive roar dissolved into sporadic bursts; cries of excitement and pain, previously drowned out by the noise, could be heard; and there was the occasional explo-sion of a grenade. Fitch, who could hear nothing until now, was imme-diately asking for situation reports. Mellas and Goodwin reported in. There was nothing from Kendall.

"Where the fuck's Three Actual, Pallack?" Fitch fumed. "They should've been up by now."

"Fucked if I know sir. I gave 'em d'freak."

"You're sure they got it?"

"I heard Genoa tell me he had it."

Genoa had indeed heard the frequency, but in the darkness he couldn't see clearly enough to switch the dials, and Kendall's red flashlight was in his pack at the bottom of the ridge, where they'd left it three days earlier. Genoa had twirled the knobs as fast as he could but still couldn't pick up the frequency. When the fight erupted, he forgot the numbers. Kendall hadn't listened in the first place, expecting the radio operator to take care of it. Genoa kept trying different combinations, futilely turning the tens counter one way, the ones counter the other.

"I can't get Bravo on the hook, sir," he said desperately.

Kendall nodded, his lips pressed together. "We've got to find out what's going on," he whispered.

Genoa didn't answer. He had no desire to find out what was going on.

"We got to find out what's going on and report to the skipper," Kendall said. He took a deep breath and crawled out of the hole. Genoa watched in dismay, then crawled after him, as was his duty.

Flurries of sporadic fire and occasional explosions still erupted in the night. The NVA were trying to get back out, now that their satchel charges had been delivered.

"Campion," Kendall whispered to his second squad leader.

No one answered.

"Campion, it's me, the lieutenant," Kendall called out softly.

There was a long wait, then a tense whisper. "Here."

Kendall rose to a crouch and started running toward the sound. Genoa followed him.

The two NVA sappers lying on the ground knew the English word "lieutenant" and opened up with their AK-47s as soon as they heard the movement. Unable to see their target, they both sprayed their bullets in an arc about four feet off the ground. Two of the bullets caught Kendall and Genoa across their chests. They fell to the earth, gasping in pain, each with one lung collapsing and filling with blood, but neither of them was dead.

Campion had seen the muzzle flashes of the two NVA and opened up on automatic. His partner did the same, and they each threw a hand grenade. Then they waited tensely. They heard nothing except the lieutenant and his radio operator gasping for air.

"Corpsman!" Campion shouted. He and his friend crawled out to find them.

The firefights died down. The cries for the corpsmen ceased. People waited for the morning light, their ears straining to hear the one broken stick or swish of cloth against grass that would save their lives. The North Vietnamese who remained inside the perimeter crawled desperately, slowly, rifles in front, trying to beat the sun, trying to make no sound at all. Tension and fear bound the different men on the hill together like wire.

Every so often a North Vietnamese soldier tried to make a break for it. There would be the slapping sound of an AK opening up, followed by the sound of a hand grenade or an M-16.

The night wore on. Marines stretched their ponchos out beside their fighting holes, hoping to collect a little of the mist that swirled around them. Down below the lines, a wounded NVA soldier began to moan.

After brief whispers to make sure it wasn't a Marine, Jacobs and Jermain threw a couple of grenades at the sound. "That'll sh-shut the f-fucker up," Jacobs said. It did.

Mellas, still suffering from diarrhea after the long march to open Sky Cap, felt an urgent churning inside his intestines. He tried to control it, not wanting to shit inside the hole but afraid to leave it. "I got to shit," he finally whispered to Jackson.

"Shit? We ain't eaten for two days, Lieutenant. I always knew you were full of it."

Mellas tried squeezing his buttocks together with all his strength. "I can't hold it," he said.

Jackson didn't say anything. Mellas dragged himself cautiously over the edge of the hole, his rifle in his hands. He duckwalked about two feet from the edge and pulled his trousers down, staring into the darkness, listening through the wind. He was facing uphill. The feces flowed from him like liquid paste, spattering the back of his trouser legs. He realized that the continual shitting, even of paste, meant he was losing fluid faster than those without diarrhea.

Then he heard a scrape. He squatted there, the shitty paste running down his thighs, too frozen with terror to move or make a sound.

A soft light was gradually beginning to filter through the fog. Mellas could make out the darker outline of his and Jackson's hole three feet to his right. Again there was a faint scrape. Mellas could barely discern a wounded North Vietnamese soldier. His clothing clung to his chest, sticky with blood. Mellas could see that the hand holding the rifle was back by the NVA soldier's hip, just starting to come forward in the crawl. The soldier had run out of darkness at the wrong moment.

Mellas threw his legs out behind him, landing in his own feces, and fired on full automatic. The M-16 flashed. At first the bullets did not seem to reach the man, whose eyes stared, frozen, at Mellas. But then the man's chest shuddered and his head snapped back unnaturally. Mellas moaned, his face in the earth, thanking God he was still alive, not caring that he'd killed a man.

Jackson had spun around, rifle ready to fire. "You all right?" he whispered.

"Yeah," Mellas answered. He crawled away from his shit, trying to keep the rest of his body from being covered with it. He wiped it off his stomach and thighs with his hand, then rubbed his hand in the mud to clean it. He moved to his knees and pulled his fouled wet trousers back on.

Mellas crawled up to the dead man. He'd hit him right between the eyes and twice in the tops of the shoulders. Mellas himself felt too shaky to stand but forced himself into a crouch. Everything seemed to work fine. He felt proud of himself. Right between the eyes.

When it got lighter, he and Jackson moved down the lines, going from hole to hole to evaluate the damage. The little open bunker that Young had constructed of logs and branches to house his machine gun had been destroyed by one of the satchel charges. Mole was sitting on the pile of logs and leaves. He stared into the hole, tears streaming from his eyes. "It's Young, sir," he kept repeating. "Little Young."

The satchel charge had left very little of the three kids who'd shared the position. Flesh was plastered against the logs and sides of the hole. The machine gun was twisted.

Mellas could only stare at it as if it were a picture puzzle, unable or unwilling to make sense of it. Jackson stood behind Mole, put both hands on Mole's shoulders, and gently rocked him as he sat there, his feet dangling into the pit.

They pulled ponchos off the dead Marines' belts, which were still attached to their pulped torsos, to provide body sacks. They had no idea if the correct body parts would make it home to the correct wives or parents. The best they could do was put together one head, two arms, and two legs. Helping to haul the dead up to the edge of the little LZ, Mellas noticed kids licking their ponchos. His own tongue felt thick and cottony. He looked down to see if any moisture had collected on the ponchos of the dead he was hauling, but quickly repressed the impulse. He reached the pile and dropped the body parts with the rest. Mellas wondered if it had eventually been like this in the concentration camps. Had they reached the point where horror had no force? He hurried back to his hole and licked his own poncho, tasting the rubber, getting no satisfaction.

Mole volunteered to take over the critical machine-gun position, now known to the NVA. He moved his own gun from a less critical point to Second Squad's position. He had to scrape blood and pieces of flesh from the walls of the pit with his K-bar.

The bodies of the dead North Vietnamese were tossed down the side of the hill with those from the previous fights. They stiffened into awkward angles as rigor mortis set in. Soon the flies were at them.

After checking everyone for immersion foot, making sure everyone took his malaria pills in spite of the difficulty of swallowing, and redistributing ammunition from the dead, Mellas stopped at the bunker where Kendall and Genoa were panting for air. In the candlelight inside the dark bunker, Kendall's smooth face was chalky white. His eyeglasses had been pulled off and he looked younger without the protective yellow lenses. He lay on his side, gasping like a fish out of water. Genoa was the same.

Kendall tried to smile. "I guess—someone shouted—or I did." The words came in short tortured gasps, but Kendall wanted to talk, to forget the fact that he was dying.

Mellas looked at Genoa, who was barely conscious although his eyes were wide and terrified. He was wheezing steadily. Sheller, who was working on another wounded kid behind the two of them, caught Mellas's eye, looked up meaningfully at the fog and then at Genoa, and slowly shook his head.

Kendall gasped again, then went on. "And I—I said—It's lieutenant —hah—" He tried to laugh but spat up blood instead.

Mellas gently wiped the blood and spittle away. Then he wiped it on his trouser legs, which were still damp from his own shit.

"Now," Kendall continued, "wasn't that—stupid—fucking thing." He gasped for air. "Genoa, too—my fault—sorry."

"You're forgiven," Mellas said, smiling. "I guess some people just got to learn the hard way. Besides, it couldn't be too stupid. You'll get to go home and see Kristi, and Genoa will be fucking his brains out in California." He reached out, took Kendall's wrist in his left hand, and put his right hand on Kendall's forehead, as if checking a child's temperature.

Kendall looked at Mellas, his eyes moving rapidly back and forth. He felt so alone. He looked at Genoa. They were on their sides so that the blood and fluid would collect in the bad lung, leaving the good one to struggle for air. But the good lung had to pump twice as fast to get enough oxygen. Both he and Genoa were straining with the effort.

"You think—any birds—today?" Kendall gasped.

Mellas grinned and sat back on his knees. "Everyone thinks I'm the fucking air traffic control around here," he replied gently. "Sure they'll get in. As soon as the fog burns off."

"Fog," Kendall gasped. He went back to concentrating on his breathing. He wheezed, pulling in the air, panting as if he'd just run a footrace. Sudden fear swept across his face. "I—always wondered how I'd—die," he wheezed.

"Hell," Mellas said. "You won't die. A fucking chest wound is nothing to fix up."

"Mellas—I—don't even have a kid. I don't—hardly know—what—it's like—to be married—only—four fucking weeks." It was taking Kendall an intolerably long time to get through his thoughts. Mellas wanted to leave him and get back to redistributing ammunition and figuring out how to cover the approaches now that Young's machine gun was gone along with most of the ammo.

"Mellas?"

"Yeah, Kendall."

"Mellas—don't shit me. No choppers—I'm dead."

Mellas bit his lip, not saying anything. He looked into Kendall's eyes.

"Don't shit me—OK?"

"No. I won't, Kendall."

Exhausted, Kendall said no more. He went on struggling for air.

Sheller came over and squatted between Kendall and Genoa, removing the IV fluid bottle from Genoa and transferring it to Kendall. He looked over at Mellas. "We're running out of this shit. I'll start losing guys if we do. Where is it on the priority list?"

"At the top," Mellas said. "Right up there with ammunition."

"It'd better fucking get here soon."

Mellas went back to his hole and sat there, Jackson to his left, Doc Fredrickson to his right in another hole. They stared into the fog, listening to the sounds of digging all around them. The NVA weren't leaving.

All they could do was sit in the fog and listen to the digging and to Kendall and Genoa panting. Mellas stared at the gray nothingness before him. He kept trying to think of how he was going to work his way back to VCB when they got overrun.

Mellas again counted machine-gun rounds. Enough for about one minute of firing—and that included the two captured Russian 7.62s. They'd evenly redistributed the rifle ammunition and come up with about one magazine per man. It took only three quick bursts on automatic to empty one. Mellas wondered if he should save all his ammunition, not fire at all, and crawl away through the darkness and terror when the NVA hit them. Marines never leave their dead or wounded. They'd never expect a single Marine to break the code and slip by them. He'd hump right out to VCB and safety. He'd hump right out of the war.

The fantasy kept returning, with new details. But it remained a fantasy. A more dominant part of him would adhere to the code. He'd die before he'd abandon anyone. Nor would he surrender. The lecture from the Basic School floated into his memory. "A Marine never surrenders as long as he has the means to resist. And we teach you fucking numbies hand-to-hand combat. So if your hands are blown off, you can surrender—only you'll have to raise your legs." They had laughed.

There was no getting out. From time to time, that thought would overwhelm him like a wave. There was no getting out. Worse, he'd choose to stay and fight. He was going to die here in the mud. He was going to die and, unlike Kendall, he would never know what it was like to be married for even four weeks. He too would never have a child, never do work that gave some satisfaction, never see old friends again. Maybe someone would pick up what remained of his body and ship it home, but whatever inhabited that body would end, right here, in this hole, slumped over his rifle or shitting in his pants, just like the rest of them.

All day the thirst chewed at everyone's throat, clawed at temples, pounded the head with dehydration. Get me water. All around, fog. Fog is water, but it gave no relief.

There was a series of loud metallic clanks. The entire hill tensed. The clanks were muted, then stopped. No one knew what they had been.

Fitch came down and squatted by the hole, asking how everyone was doing. His eyes were sunken and dark from dehydration.

"We're thirsty," Mellas said. "Don't the troops get beer and ice cream every day in Vietnam?"

Fitch chuckled. "I got good news and bad news. They're landing two companies from Two Twenty-Four north of us this morning and two more as soon as they can. Three Twenty-Four is being dropped in east of us. They'll be taking hills on Mutter's Ridge and then we'll get in a couple batteries of one-oh-fives." He paused. "And Alpha and Charlie hit the valley south of us five minutes ago."

"No shit." Mellas felt excitement and hope stir. "Where?"

"That's the bad news. Because of the clouds, they had to land them two days from here—if they don't run into the shit themselves."

"You think they will?"

"Remember your little number game with the mortar rounds?"

Mellas said nothing.

CHAPTER
SIXTEEN

Forty minutes later, Charlie Company made contact with the NVA. Murphy's platoon, on point, was ambushed in the bamboo. The NVA rigged two ten-pound DH-10 directional mines to a tree, waited as long as they dared until the Marines got close, pulled the pins, and ran, covering their retreat with automatic weapons fire. Duck soup, as the old expression goes.

One Marine died and another lost a leg. Murphy had to leave a squad to medevac them, effectively losing fourteen.

On the hill, the Marines of Bravo Company heard everything. Mellas ran to the CP to hear Charlie Company's position report. They were still six kilometers away and 4,000 feet below Bravo, with the NVA in between.

Fitch looked at Mellas. They both knew that without Charlie Company's ammunition, there would be about one minute of fire. Then it would be knives. Then it would be over. Fitch hung his head between his knees momentarily, then looked up. "We might not make it," he said.

"I know," Mellas answered.

They couldn't express what they were feeling. It had to do with eternity, friendship, lost opportunities—with the end.

"You ever get down around Los Angeles?" Fitch asked.

"Sure."

"If we make it out of here, why don't you look me up? I'll buy you a beer."

Mellas said he would.

"God," Fitch whispered. "A beer."

Fitch pulled the company into the smaller circle of holes. There were no longer enough Marines to defend the outer perimeter. Mellas tried to ease the pain in his throat and tongue by licking the dew on his rifle barrel. It didn't work.

"Imagine dying of thirst in a monsoon," Mellas wisecracked to himself as he walked up the hill to see how Kendall and the other wounded were getting along. He passed the growing stack of bodies.

Genoa was gone. Mellas knelt beside Kendall, who was panting like a runner, staring into empty space, and concentrating everything he had on keeping up the relentless pace of his breathing. He was clearly in pain. Sheller had decided against morphine for fear that it would sedate his breathing and kill him. Kendall nodded toward the clay, wet with blood and spume, where Genoa had lain.

"You're nowhere near as bad as Genoa was," Mellas said.

"My fault," Kendall gasped.

"We've already been through that. It wasn't," Mellas said. He hesitated, struggling with himself, wondering if he could help or if he would just be indulging in self-pity. Then he took the plunge, hoping for the best. "Hell, I may have been the one who shot Pollini."

Kendall stared at him for several seconds, taking it in, breathing hard. "Tough one—hell—tough ones—bring home with us." Then he fell silent again except for the tortured rapid panting. But he had a slight smile on his face.

Mellas smiled back. "The skipper says they've got two birds on standby at VCB and another bird waiting on Sherpa."

Kendall nodded. Mellas crawled out into the daylight before he could break down in front of him. He hurried over to the CP. When he got there Fitch and Sheller were huddled intently, away from the radio operators. Mellas joined them. Fitch pursed his lips, then motioned Mellas to sit down.

"You tell him, Sheller."

The senior squid, his face no longer round, turned to Mellas. "It's the water, sir. I've got kids going down with dehydration. They're starting to lose blood pressure and faint. We're losing effectives."

"So?" Mellas opened his hands and spread his arms, leaving his elbows at his ribs. *What the fuck can we do about it?*

Fitch broke in. "We can take the IV fluid we're giving to the wounded and give it to the effectives to keep them effective."

Mellas was silent, conscious of what that meant for the wounded. He swallowed. "Who's going to decide who doesn't get the IV fluid?"

"It'll be me," Fitch said grimly. "No one else."

Sheller looked at Mellas, then down at Fitch's hands, which were trembling.

"Fuck, Jim. You don't get paid enough to make choices like that."

"Yeah, and I'm too young and inexperienced." Fitch laughed, on the edge of losing control. He put his hands underneath his armpits, probably to hide the trembling. "You're the numbers guy, Mellas. If we can't see, and our fucking heads hurt too much to think, and every time we stand up to shoot we feel like fainting, how the fuck are we going to defend the wounded? How many wounded live this way versus that way?"

Mellas shook his head. "Jim, it ain't about numbers. How are you going to decide?"

"I'll start with the worst off."

"Like Kendall?"

"Like Kendall."

"Jesus Christ, Jim," Mellas said. He was suddenly near tears, but crying was impossible. He felt his jaw tremble and hoped the others wouldn't notice. "Jesus fucking Christ." Then, to his shame, he hoped to hell Fitch wouldn't die so he himself wouldn't have to take over.

* * *

That afternoon Fitch ordered half of the remaining IV fluid to be distributed evenly to everyone in the company. The order was disobeyed. No one would take it. Fitch called the squids together and ordered each of them to pick five kids from every platoon who were already ineffective or about to go ineffective because of thirst. They submitted the names. Fitch and Sheller scurried from hole to hole, ordering those kids to drink, checking their names off the list. Others watched with very mixed feelings.

Mellas was among the others. Thirst was driving him mad, but he hadn't been picked. There was nothing to do but sit in his fighting hole with Jackson, who also hadn't been picked, and pray for a break in the weather. But the fog stayed, cloaking them like wet gray wool.

A little later, when it became apparent that the choppers wouldn't be able to get in, Fitch called for Goodwin and Mellas. They found him sitting cross-legged, staring into the fog to the south. He had combed his hair and neatly rolled his muddy shirtsleeves to his upper arms.

He motioned for them to sit. "We're going to get the fuck out of here." There was a mischievous glint in his eye and Mellas couldn't help smiling.

"How, Jack?" Goodwin asked.

"I've been counting bodies," Fitch said. "Warm, cold, you name it. We pair up the walking wounded so they can help each other. We sling the stretcher cases between four guys, one for each leg and arm. The wounded that can't walk but can hang on will go piggyback on the biggest guys we got. The smaller guys take the dead over their shoulders. That'll leave us with eight guys free, not counting the three of us, so that makes eleven." He was looking down into the fog. "We stay here and it's hand to hand for sure. The wounded will get slaughtered. I say fuck that bullshit."

He looked at each of them, trying to judge their reaction. Both of his lieutenants were steady, listening. "Scar, you and I and four machine guns will go in front with all the gun ammo. The walking wounded get most of the rest of the ammo. They'll form a wedge behind us. Mellas and two others are tail-end Charlie with M-79s and all the fucking grenades in the company to keep the gooks off our backs. Everyone else gets half a magazine and stays on semiautomatic. We'll be going down-hill and it'll be balls to the wall until we hit Charlie Company. The sides of the wedges will hold ground while we hustle the wounded through. Mellas, you'll be the plug at the other end as we collapse the funnel." He looked at the two lieutenants. "What do you think?"

There was a long pause.

"It isn't exactly what strategists would call elegant," Mellas finally said.

Fitch laughed.

"When we gonna leave, Jack?" Goodwin asked. "This place is getting on my nerves."

"Just after dark. The gooners'll be getting ready to attack and won't expect it."

"And if someone gets separated?" Mellas asked.

"We'll wait for him. We're all going out together."

"You know what that means?"

"You're goddamned right I do. And you're tail-end Charlie, so it's most likely you we'll be waiting for."

"Hell of a good policy, Jim."

"Next to Column in the Defense, the Funnel Breakaway could be my greatest contribution to military science yet," Fitch said. There was a smile around the corners of his mouth. They all broke into laughter.

The laughter fed on itself. Soon the three of them were roaring, making up outrageous tactical theories. They were still laughing when the first of the rockets came slashing up from the fog below. They scrambled for the bottom of Fitch's hole, jumping in together, still laughing. "Rockets," Mellas said. "What'll they think of next?" They all broke out laughing again. At least the mystery of the strange clanks had been solved.

Fitch told Sheller to save just enough IV fluid for the wounded for that night, knowing that either they would be low enough under the cloud cover to get medevaced or it would be raining. Or they'd be overrun and dead and they wouldn't need it. So he ordered all the rest to be given out. Everyone got about four gulps of the flat, salty liquid. It tasted of rubber stoppers.

Mellas stayed with Fitch, listening to the radios. At one point Fitch stiffened and his head jerked up. Then Mellas too heard the sounds of a firefight, far off to the east.

"It's got to be someone from Three Twenty-Four," Fitch said. On Daniels's radio they could hear Mike Company's forward observer calling for everything he could get.

"The mission grid is coming now, sir," Daniels said excitedly. "Seven-four-three-five-seven-one."

Fitch jabbed his finger at the coordinates. More than six kilometers. Forever.

"We can't do a fucking thing here," Mellas said helplessly.

"Yeah," Fitch said. "We're the princess and they're the dragon slayers."

Mellas looked at Fitch. "The fucking bastards," he said. "We're nothing but fucking bait. Bait." Mellas whirled and stalked off down the hill.

An hour passed, and with it his anger. He reached down and grabbed some damp clay, making a fist, squeezing it into a ball until his forearm trembled. Then he let the earth go, watching it plop down to the wet clay of his fighting hole. He began to stroke the clay, moving his fingers over it lightly, caressing it. He felt a sense of beauty and longing for the damp muddy ground that would have moved him to tears, but he was too dehydrated to cry. He yearned with all his heart to be able to see that clay for just one more day and then one more day after that.

Jackson knew what Mellas was thinking and stared quietly ahead, not wanting to embarrass the lieutenant by watching him. Mellas stopped feeling the ground and folded his arms over the chest of his two flak jackets. "I'm a hell of an inspiration, aren't I?" He gazed down at the backs of his muddy hands. He tried to wipe away tears that hadn't come, smearing more dirt on his face.

"We can't all be Chesty Puller, sir," Jackson said.

Mellas took a deep sigh, then another, blowing the air out with puffed cheeks. "Hey, Jackson, will you show me how you brothers shake hands?"

"Huh?"

"You know. All that bap bap bap shit."

Jackson looked at Mellas, not sure if he was serious. When Mellas didn't look away, Jackson rolled his eyes upward and said, "You just never tell anyone how you learned this, OK?"

Mellas grinned and held his fist out. After five times Mellas still hadn't mastered the intricate movements.

"Almost there, Lieutenant," Jackson said, fist out again. "Almost there."

Mellas sighed. "It just doesn't feel right."

Jackson smiled. "It never will."

"Why not?"

"You ain't black."

Mellas suddenly felt self-conscious, even stupid, for asking Jackson to show him the handshake. "I always thought deep down we were the same," he said.

"We are the same. Hell, I got two white great-grandpas, just like you. It's just that we seen things differently so long we ain't able to talk about it much."

"Try me."

"No way, Lieutenant." Jackson folded his arms. "You think someone's going to understand how you feel about being in the bush? I mean even if they're like you in every way, you really think they're going to understand what it's like out here? Really understand?"

"Probably not."

"Well, it's like that being black. Unless you've been there, ain't no way."

Mellas shifted his feet, pulling one boot out of the muck with a sucking sound. He saw Mole, down on the lines, stand up next to his hole to try to piss. It wasn't going well. Mellas couldn't remember when he had last peed, but he did remember that then it had been a brown dribble. He heard the sound of tubing. Mole hurriedly zipped up his fly and scrambled into his hole. Three shells blasted the top of the landing zone. Mellas removed his hands from his ears and waited. Mole got up again to finish trying to pee. Mellas watched him idly, along with Jackson, wondering if anything would come out.

When Mole gave up, Mellas turned to Jackson. "Hey, Jackson. Before we get split up, I want to ask you something. If you think I'm an asshole for asking it, just try not to get mad at me for it."

Jackson didn't say anything.

Mellas plunged in. "I think guys like China, and maybe even Mole, are sending weapons home. Mole can't lose as many machine-gun parts as he says he does."

Jackson chuckled. "I think that operation got shut down." He looked out at the fog, his eyes twinkling. "Let's say by better business practices."

"What?"

"The word among the brothers is that they're not doing it any more, sir."

Mellas wanted to probe but held back. It was sufficient to know that the rumor was true and that no action needed to be taken. After a brief silence Mellas asked, "Is there going to be serious trouble? I mean back home. You know, with serious weapons."

Jackson said nothing.

"I got this feeling that somehow I should be involved, but I can't do a fucking thing."

"You can't."

"Nothing?"

"Just leave us the fuck alone." Jackson was looking him right in the eye and had spoken with kindness. Even though Mellas was an officer, and white, at that moment Jackson was just someone close to his own age who shared the same hole. "You really don't understand it, do you?" Jackson said.

"I guess not."

Jackson sighed. "Shit, Lieutenant. We might be dead in an hour or two, so I guess this isn't any time for fucking around not saying what we mean. You OK with that?"

"Not with the being dead in a couple of hours part," Mellas answered.

Jackson snorted approval. "OK, sir." He paused. Then he said, "You're a racist."

Mellas swallowed and looked open-mouthed at Jackson.

"Now hold on." Jackson said, obviously marshaling his words. "Don't get all excited. I'm a racist too. You can't grow up in America and not be a racist. Everyone on this fucking hill's a racist and everyone back in the world's a racist. Only there's one big difference between us two racists you can't ever change and I can't ever change."

"What's that?" Mellas asked.

"Being racist helps you and it hurts me." Jackson looked out at the distance. They were both quiet. Then Jackson said, "You know, China's really got it right. We got to overturn a racist society. No easy thing." He brightened. "There's another difference between us racists."

Mellas kept quiet.

"Some of us racists are prejudiced and some aren't. Now you, I'd say you're trying not to be prejudiced. Me too, and Cortell, and even Mole, though he'd never admit it. Hawke's not prejudiced, flat out. Not being prejudiced is the best any of us can do right now. It's too late about being racist."

"I don't get it."

"How many black friends you got back in the world?"

Mellas paused and looked away into the fog, embarrassed. Then he faced Jackson. "None."

"Righhht," Jackson said with a smile. "And me, I don't have any white friends. We won't be free of racism until my black skin sends the same signals as Hawke's red mustache. The way it is now, you can't look at me without thinking something more, and me, I can't look back without the same attitude."

Mellas was starting to understand.

"We'll know we're free of racism when every white person has a black friend," Jackson said. Then he laughed out loud. "Hey, you're the math guy, Lieutenant. That means every black person has to have seven or eight white friends. Ooh-wee. Ain't no way. We're a long way from that." His voice went quiet. "A long way."

"You got me good," Mellas said. He smiled. "So what do we do?"

He waited while Jackson thought a moment. "It's like the way you like China," Jackson said. "You have to stop that shit."

"What's wrong with liking China?"

"Ain't nothing wrong with liking China. Everyone likes China. That's why he's so good at his organizing shit. What I mean is the *way* you like China. I mean he's your nigger."

The barb silenced Mellas.

"You know what an Uncle Tom is, right?" Jackson said, fingering the hangman's noose around his neck. "A sort of Stepin Fetchit?"

"Yeah."

"Well, that's somebody's nigger." Jackson's long fingers began drumming against his dirty camouflage. "That's some chuck's idea who lived in Hollywood in 1935. But now we got guys like China. They wear the Afro even when it gets them in trouble. Shit, to *get* them in trouble. And they throw shit into whitey's face every chance they get. Well, you know something? You know who they are? They're the niggers of people like you, that's who they are. Every time they stand up and tell you to get off their backs, and that the whole fucking society is built up by racists and pigs, little white students living off daddy's cash in Berkeley or Harvard stand up and say 'That's right on, *boy,* you tell us guilty white pigs what's happening. I am *with* you. You are *my* nigger.' Only none of them are about to integrate any of *our* schools. None of them are about to move south and sit on the juries and stand up for the black man. And none of them are getting shipped home in rubber bags either. In fact, soon as this war heated up, all the rich white kids forgot all about civil rights and started worrying about getting their asses drafted."

Jackson stopped talking. He was trembling with anger. He took a deep breath and exhaled.

"Well, I'm nobody's nigger," Jackson went on. "I'm not some college student's fucking nigger and I'm not some movie man's fucking nigger. I'm going to be my own nigger."

"If you're your own nigger how come you let China talk you into refusing to take over the squad?"

"He didn't talk me into it. I didn't have anywhere else to go. If I take the squad, I'm the system's nigger. If I stay where I am, I'm China's nigger. It's like I can't stand up or lay down. Anyways I turn I'm someone's nigger. That's why I took the radio when Lieutenant Fracasso offered it to me and why I'm packing it now." He snorted. "So I ended up in between and looking like *your* nigger." He snorted again. "Seems it's the best I could come out and still be my own nigger." He looked at Mellas, a hint of inquiry on his face. Mellas understood that Jackson was trying to see how he was taking it.

He stared into the fog, envisioning the many times he'd joked with guys like Jackson. Then he saw Mole, turning his face around to him after cleaning his machine gun on Matterhorn when Cassidy had shaved Parker. And then Jackson, throwing his body against the bamboo to build the useless LZ and then standing in the open with the NVA shells coming in, evacuating the wounded from Matterhorn. And Mole again, staring at the machine-gun bunker where Young was blown away and agreeing to take it alone, frightened, but knowing it was a key point in the defense, now revealed to the enemy. He realized guys like that didn't need his help at all. All he had to do was get out of their way. "I blew it, Jackson," he said. "Sorry about that."

"Shit, sir. You didn't blow it any worse than the rest of us. Me and Mole only just figured it out when you and the other lieutenants was up all night making that fucked-up plan to take Helicopter Hill."

They looked at each other and started laughing.

"A fucking sneak attack by Scar," Jackson said between giggles. "Sheeit."

They grew quiet again.

"So if white people leave you alone," Mellas said, "where's that going to leave you guys? White people do control our society. Rich white people in fact."

"Yeah," Jackson said, "and rich niggers, too. Look who's fighting this fucking war: poor white and poor black. And the occasional goddamned fool like you, begging the lieutenant's pardon." He paused and his eyes went to the jungle below them. Mellas let him think. Then Jackson turned to him. "We've got to handle our own problems," he said. "All you got to do is start treating us like everyone else. It's as simple as that. We don't need nothing special. Oh, yeah, we got people who are going to fuck us up. Fuck us up good. They'll be pissed off and throwing shit around and smashing things. And you got 'em too. Look at fucking Cassidy. But we don't need any special fucking help. We're people. Just treat us like people. We're no dumber than you and we're no smarter." He looked over at Mellas. "Although we do do better music."

Mellas laughed.

"Let us solve our problems the same way everyone else does," Jackson went on. "We might even make some mistakes. We're people, Lieutenant, just like you." Then he made a fist and held it out to Mellas. "We're just treated different." He was nodding in encouragement. Mellas smiled and tapped Jackson's fist with his own, and once again they went through the hand dance. Mellas still did it awkwardly, but he laughed with pleasure.

Two rockets lashed out of the jungle, sending everyone deep into his hole. Goodwin radioed in, reporting one more wounded.

Daniels brought an artillery mission crashing in from a 155-millimeter howitzer battery. Beautiful rolling volleys of sound washed over them from the jungle. Mellas grunted in satisfaction. He hadn't known that the 155s had been moved within range. "At least they're finally doing something for us niggers," he said.

Stevens and Hawke had been up all night pushing staff from various organizations to move a 105 battery to FSB Eiger about ten kilometers southeast of Matterhorn. It was at extreme range to support Bravo Company, but it could cover the companies moving to Bravo's aid from the south and east. They also talked the regimental staff into moving two 155s there. It was these two 155s that Daniels was directing. They'd wanted to move a 105 battery to Sky Cap, but that move was made impossible by the same fog that prevented all helicopter flights to Helicopter Hill. Eiger, at least 2,500 feet lower than Sky Cap, however, was clear of clouds and building ammunition and other supplies rapidly.

Simpson and Blakely hovered over the shoulders of the radio operators, leaping on every report that came in from Alpha and Charlie companies. They were moving at an agonizingly slow pace. "If they don't get their asses in gear, Three Twenty-Four will beat us to it," Simpson muttered grimly. "How are the replacements doing?"

"They're on the LZ, sir. Everything's standing by."

On the edge of the muddy landing zone at Vandegrift Combat Base, every new replacement who had come into the battalion was waiting in the slow drizzle. Cardboard boxes, each containing four glass containers of IV fluid in a protective wood carton, were stacked next to the kids, along with boxes of ammunition and C-rations, all covered with rubberized canvas tarps to keep the cardboard from crumbling to mush in the rain. A small water tank on wheels also stood in the rain, wrapped in a cargo net that would be hooked to the underside of one of the choppers. Rumors that Bravo Company was getting slaughtered had grown enormously. The kids were pale with fear and cold, unable to eat.

At division headquarters at Dong Ha, Colonel Mulvaney was meeting with General Gregory Neitzel, commanding officer of the Fifth Marine Division; Willy White, commander of the Twenty-Second Marines, the artillery regiment; and Mike Harreschou, CO of Fifteenth Marines, another of the division's three infantry regiments. An aide walked in with a slip of paper. "Excuse me sir," he said. "Mike Three Twenty-Four is in contact at 743571." The aide didn't know the protocol: whether to hand the slip of paper to Mulvaney, whose company it was, or to the general.

Mulvaney spared him the decision by grabbing the paper from his hands. "Unknown-size force. Goddamn it." He turned to the aide. "I want an estimate of size as soon as you can get it."

"Aye aye, sir." The aide left.

The general and the artillery commander quickly moved to the large map on the wall. "Right here, Willy," the general said, his finger pointing to the coordinates. "Just about where we figured. How's that battery at Smokey doing?"

"They ought to be ready to fire within the hour, sir."

"Good." General Neitzel turned to Mulvaney. "Mike, what do you think?" he asked.

"It's our gook regiment, no doubt about it." Mulvaney went to the map and with a thick finger pointed out the locations of enemy contact. There was Charlie Company's ambush incident just to the south of Matterhorn. Then there were two firefights with Lima and Alpha companies, and Mike Company was in a fight right now. All those fights formed an arc. Mulvaney completed the circle that the arc implied, roughly outlining the area that held the NVA regiment.

"Willy," the general said, "if I were to authorize your First Battalion to pile in a few more artillery pieces, could you put them to work anyplace?"

"Yes sir. If I can get some grunts for security. We could put a battery here on Hill 427, due south of Matterhorn. Eiger could support it, and vice versa, although I'd sure like to get something up on Sky Cap again." He stopped short of mentioning the decision to abandon all of the artillery bases in the western mountains, like Sky Cap, in order to support the political operation in the flatlands. "It's mighty close to the goddamned Z, though, and I'd need good security. We'd need air or maybe counter battery from Red Devil to stop getting shelled by the gook artillery across the Ben Hai." Red Devil was the call sign of an Army eight-inch heavy artillery unit. "Those gook hundred twenty-twos were designed as naval guns and they can reach us, but we can't reach them with our one-oh-fives." He paused, stroking his chin. "Assuming we get political clearance to fight back."

Neitzel grimaced. "I'll take care of that."

Harreschou and Mulvaney exchanged a look.

"Maybe a battery of one five fives on Lookout," White continued. "They'd have the reach. That would take a little longer, though."

"How long?"

"Tomorrow afternoon?"

"Tomorrow morning," Neitzel insisted.

"I don't know, sir."

"We'll get you extra lift capacity with some Army CH-47s out of Phu Bai."

"We'll try it, sir. It's fast, but we'll go for it."

"It's crucial," Neitzel said. He walked to the map and went over the situation with them again, as if reassuring himself about the strategy. The NVA had attacked from out of Laos with three regiments, along three separate corridors, taking advantage of the pullback from the far west that had been necessitated by the political operation at Cam Lo. They had also been encouraged by the fact that just before Christmas the Army's 101st Airborne Division had been pulled from the area completely because of fierce fighting in the central highlands. What they didn't know was that the 101st had just been ordered into the Au Shau Valley. That unit could move extremely fast, given its airlift capacity. That left the Fifth Marine Division handling the two northern thrusts: the central one in the Da Krong Valley and the northern one on Mutter's Ridge. Mulvaney's Twenty-Fourth Marine Regiment had the northernmost of the three NVA advance routes, by virtue of the fact that it was already there. His Second Battalion, Two Twenty-Four, with four rifle companies, was being moved into the valley north of Matterhorn. The NVA would not want to move north against a Marine battalion that was waiting for them. They'd push up against the Marines like water hitting a dam. They'd concentrate in front of that dam, making themselves vulnerable to artillery, which was indifferent to the weather once it was in place, and to Arc Light attacks out of Guam, whose B-52s flew well above the weather and dropped their bombs using radar. Simpson's three remaining companies of One Twenty-Four were moving into a mirror-image position on the south side of Matterhorn. That would stop the NVA from moving south, just as Two Twenty-Four would stop them from moving north. Third Battalion's Mike Company was already in contact with the NVA regiment, and Three Twenty-Four's remaining companies would be hitting the NVA within hours. This would stop any forward movement east along the ridgeline. The NVA would be forced to retreat west. But Bravo Company, sitting on Helicopter Hill, blocked the only easy route to the Laotian border.

Neitzel then looked at the situation from the enemy's point of view. The NVA needed to use the high ground of the ridge. Trying to move through the jungle in the valleys below the ridge would be a nightmare for any infantry unit. If the NVA commander didn't move fast enough, he risked getting cut off, or cut in two, by a pincer movement from the Marine battalions to his north and south. As long as the NVA commander felt safe from air strikes, he could stay on the ridge, holding the high ground, making the Marines pay dearly for every hill. But he too knew that weather changes. His best option had to be to overrun Bravo Company and clear it from his path. That would be a propaganda victory and would spread all over the newspapers in America, making the whole northern thrust a political success—and political and propaganda victories, not attrition, would win the war for the north. In addition, eliminating Bravo Company would give the NVA control of the western end of Mutter's Ridge, allowing an orderly withdrawal.

General Neitzel's problem was getting everything into place in time.

He turned to the other infantry commander. "Harreschou, I want Fifteenth Marines to bottle them up in the Da Krong."

Colonel Harreschou nodded, trying to imagine how he was going to turn the fucking regiment inside out to get it into position in the Da Krong before the NVA broke out onto the coastal plain. He bit his lower lip. The other two colonels were silent. "OK, sir. You know as well as I do what that's going to take."

"I know," the general answered. "Like I said, with the 101st involved we think we can get some of their lift capacity. I'll shift our forty-sixes north to help out Mike and you get the Army forty-sevens."

Harreschou grunted. The big Army CH-47s had much more lift capacity than the CH-46s of the Marines, which were built smaller and had folding rotor blades to fit on carriers. That meant they'd need fewer of them than the 46s, but what if none were available and Neitzel had the 46s committed to the north? Harreschou didn't ask what he should do in that case. There was no answer and, as usual, he knew the Marines would make it work.

Colonel White cleared his throat. "I've got a lot of firebases hanging out there, Greg."

"I know it, Willy, goddamn it." Neitzel paused. The divison's other infantry regiment, the Nineteenth Marines, had just returned from an operation in the south. They were ragged and exhausted, but they could at least hold firebases, even if they had to split companies. The artillery-men themselves could fill in on the perimeters where there weren't enough infantrymen. On the other hand, with the gook regiments en-gaged, they wouldn't have enough capacity to also threaten very many firebases. "You'll have grunts from Nineteenth Marines. They're pretty beat up, but they ought to be able to provide firebase security."

White nodded.

Neitzel turned to look at Mulvaney. "When Bravo took that ridge away from their advanced elements it really set the gooks up. That was good work, Mike."

"Dumb luck, Greg," Mulvaney replied. "And I mean dumb." The sarcasm wasn't wasted on Harreschou, who cast a quick glance at his old friend Mulvaney. They'd been together with First Division at Inchon. In fact, Mulvaney had served as Neitzel's Three when Neitzel had Two-Nine during the Laos cluster-fuck; that was why he wasn't afraid to risk a sarcastic comment. Willy White had been to Amphibi-ous Warfare School with Neitzel, and both of them had been young officers on Saipan. The Marine Corps was small, and personal relations often helped cut through the usual bureaucratic behavior and chicken-shit that went with all military units, including the Corps.

"Luck, I'll grant you," the general said, not picking up on Mul-vaney's sarcasm. "If Sweet Alice hadn't gotten into the shit we'd have never launched the Bald Eagle. Bravo would never have assaulted the ridge. Shit, Mike, I know you're worried about Bravo up there. Sure it's risky, but that's what the gooks don't expect of us. We've been too cau-tious. War is risky."

He sat down in his stuffed leather chair and leaned back, looking at the operations map, his hands clasped behind his head. "I don't think Nagoolian has the slightest fucking idea what we can deliver around that hill once we get these batteries shifted around. The whole fucking sky is going to fall on him." He looked up at Mulvaney. "Can Bravo hold?"

Mulvaney knew that Neitzel knew what was being asked. He also knew why. They were here to kill their country's enemies. If this worked, they were going to kill a lot of them. "They'll hold," he said.

Neitzel watched Mulvaney intently for a moment; then he stood and walked over to the map. "Nagoolian thought he'd trapped a company," he said to no one in particular. He planted a large fist on the map right over Matterhorn. "We're about to trap a regiment." He turned to face the three men. "Let's just pray the bad weather and Bravo hold for one more day."

While the paperwork and helicopters shifted artillery batteries, matériel, and tired Marines through leaden skies, First Lieutenant Theodore J. Hawke collapsed on his bunk in the BOQ tent. Exhausted as he was, he couldn't sleep. He went over in his mind the myriad of details. Nowhere could he find a spot where he could be of any use.

Hawke sat up suddenly. Stevens, who was unlacing his boots and about to pass out, looked at Hawke, puzzled, but said nothing. Hawke began to drag equipment out from beneath his bunk.

"What the fuck you doing?" Stevens asked, yawning. He sat there with a boot in one hand.

"Packing."

"What for?"

"It's like the nesting instinct. I get it once a month."

"Be that way," Stevens said. He dropped his boot to the floor and lay back with a sigh. "My aching fucking feet," he moaned.

Hawke smiled as he began to put on his old bleached-out jungle boots. He picked up his .45, which had been lying on the floor in its holster and was already rusting. He looked at it disgustedly. He took it out and worked the action, then snorted. From the sound of it, there would be plenty of spare rifles. He slung on his cartridge belt with its canteens and belt suspenders and reached for his helmet and flak jacket. He carefully rolled his old stateside utility cover and put it in one of the voluminous pockets on the sides of his trousers. He attached his pear-can cup to the outside of his pack.

Stevens sat up. "You're not going up on the hill, are you?" he asked. Hawke was stuffing his poncho liner into his pack and didn't bother answering. "What will the Three say? I mean, did you clear it with him? Leaving your post without permission is serious shit, Hawke."

"Stevens, the Three needs a Three Zulu like a fucking satyr needs a dildo. There's two boot lieutenants up there and zero staff. Count them: zero. And a fucking herd of newbies scared shitless down here at the LZ. Besides, I already asked the Three."

"Jesus," Stevens said, obviously surprised. "Hard to believe he let you go."

"He didn't."

Hawke walked out the door into the rain. He trudged down the muddy road toward the landing zone, feeling the familiar weight of the pack, the rain beginning to seep into his clothing, the mud and water squeezing in through the metal eyelets in his boots, making his socks wet. Mulvaney could keep his fucking company, he thought sadly and bitterly. There was only one company as far as he was concerned, and it was being destroyed while he did nothing but watch.

The feeling of action lasted the ten minutes it took Hawke to get down to the large LZ. Two CH-46 twin-bladed helicopters sat side by side on the airstrip, their fuselages scarred and pockmarked from hard use, their long rotor blades drooping in the rain. They looked abandoned. On the ground nearby were about forty replacements, huddled miserably beneath their ponchos.

Hawke could barely see across the little airfield. The clouds were so low to the ground that the rain seemed to materialize in the air around their heads. He realized that a chopper couldn't even find *this* airfield, much less Bravo Company, more than 3,000 feet higher in the mountains. And in five hours it would be dark.

He sat in the mud, knees pulled up beneath his poncho, and wondered what he'd just done. He was disobeying a direct order, throwing away a career, to sit helplessly on this fucking piece of wet earth. He pulled his poncho tighter around his neck.

After about ten minutes he realized that two pairs of very black, very new boots were standing in front of him. He looked up. Two kids were shifting their weight back and forth, uncertain about the protocol of interrupting what was obviously a bush Marine in what was obviously an attempt to enter oblivion.

"You with Bravo Company?" one of them finally asked.

Hawke contemplated them quietly, noting how well-fed they looked. Finally he said, "Can either of you think of any other fucking reason why someone would be sitting here in the rain?"

That brought two tentative smiles.

Then Hawke noticed something. "You got any machine-gun ammo someplace?"

One of the kids said, surprised, "No. I'm an oh-three-eleven," referring to the military occupational specialty code of a Marine rifleman rather than the code of a machine gunner.

"I don't give a fuck if you're a goddamned nuclear weapons expert. Did anyone give you any fucking machine-gun ammunition to carry?" Hawke was no longer lethargic.

"Uh, no, uh—"

"Lieutenant," Hawke filled in for him.

"Sorry, sir. I didn't know. I just—"

"Who's in charge of this cluster-fuck?"

"Uh, I am, sir. There's none of us above PFC, but I shot expert at Pendleton, so the guy with the radio—the one that has Shore Party on his sweatshirt—he put me in charge."

"You're through being in charge."

"Yes sir."

"From now on you will be known as Jayhawk Zulu."

"Uh, yes sir. Jayhawk Zulu."

"Can you find the battalion COC bunker?"

"I think so, sir."

"I want you to find a staff sergeant named Cassidy. You tell him the Jayhawk wants him down on the LZ as soon as he can get here with as much machine-gun ammunition as forty very well-fed boot motherfuckers straight out of ITR can carry." He paused. "And I mean *barely* carry. He'll do the interpreting."

The kid started to leave, but Hawke stopped him.

"And a hundred sixty canteens full of water."

"One hundred and sixty, sir?"

"Do I have to do the fucking math for you? Four times forty. OK? Counting the two everyone has on now, that's only six each."

"Aye aye, sir."

"If you don't get Cassidy here before this fog lifts, I'll kick your boot ass into Laos." He smiled at the kid and then gave him the curled talons sign and roared out, "Hawk power!" The kid gave his friend a quick glance and ran for the COC.

Within an hour Cassidy had joined Hawke at the LZ and every replacement was laden with machine-gun ammunition and water to the point where he could barely move. Hawke or Cassidy would walk up to each one and have him jump up and down. If the kid looked too lively they'd throw another belt of ammo across his shoulders until his knees were just short of buckling. Then Cassidy left and they were all sitting in the mud again, covered with ammunition and canteens.

"Don't fucking worry," Hawke joked with them. He began to speak in a sonorous monotone. "Come unto me all you who are burdened and heavy laden." Smiles appeared. He quickly turned on them. "But I ain't giving you fucking sinners any rest." He turned to one of the replacements who had cracked a smile. "You think I'm fucking Jesus or something? Do I look like Jesus to you?"

"Uh, no sir," the kid said. But others were now also trying to hide smiles.

"Maybe you think I look like the Virgin Mary?"

"No, sir. Not even—no, sir!"

"Not even a little bit?"

"No, sir," the kid roared out.

"Shit. And I even shaved this morning."

Smiles were breaking out.

Then Hawke turned serious. "You'll be relieved of all your burdens, believe me. All you have to do is make it from the back of the chopper to someone's hole. I don't think you'll find that too difficult under the circumstances."

As usual, the combination of Hawke's sarcastic Boston twang and his natural empathy had the crowd well in hand. He kept staring out beyond the airstrip, however, looking for a break in the weather.

He saw a break at about 1500. The constant rain let up, and soon he saw the base of the hills, about a kilometer from the airstrip. He stood up, ran over to the CH-46s that sat at the runway's edge, and roused a crew member who was asleep inside.

It took him a few minutes to persuade the man to call the pilots. At one point the man asked Hawke who the fuck he thought he was.

"I'm Captain Theodore Hawke, Twenty-Fourth Regiment assistant operations officer," Hawke lied, "and goddamn it, if you don't get some fucking pilots in these birds ASAP I'm going to have you and them standing tall in front of Colonel Mulvaney explaining why they let one of his companies get overrun because they wouldn't fly in some ammunition when we requested it."

"Yes, sir," the crewman answered. By this time several other crewmen had shown up and were watching the scene silently. "I don't know the call sign for the O-club, sir."

It took a few minutes, but the crewman got the frequency and call sign and raised a bored bartender. After some initial confusion about who was calling for what, a voice came on the radio that the crewman had switched over to speaker mode. "What the fuck's going on, Weaver?"

"Sir, I got the Twenty-Fourth Regiment's assistant Three here wondering why we're not flying. Over."

"Tell the son of a bitch that we're not flying because those fucking clouds have rocks in them. Over."

"Uh, sir, he's right here listening in. Over."

There was a pause. "Who is he? Over."

"He's, uh, Captain Hawke, sir. Twenty-Fourth Marines' three shop. Over."

"Captain? Put him on. Over." The voice sounded confident.

Hawke was handed the crewman's earphones with their attached microphone. "What the fuck is going on here, Captain? This is *Major* Reynolds."

Outranked, even if he really had been a captain. In for a penny, in for a pound. "Sir, I have a company of Marines that need resupply and the weather's cleared. Colonel Mulvaney wants these birds flying right now."

"Captain, the weather hasn't cleared. I'm looking at it right here, right now. And these birds aren't flying if we don't have the weather hold lifted by Group. I don't care what the fuck some grunt colonel thinks. I've got several million dollars worth of aircraft at risk here. Is that clear? Over."

Hawke didn't answer. He'd heard the shit about "several million dollars worth of aircraft" before. He handed the headset back to the crewman and began running across the airstrip for the O-club. In three minutes he burst through the screen door, dripping with sweat because of the heat trapped by his poncho. Faces turned from drinks, dice games, and cards to look at him. It wasn't hard to spot the pilots. Four of them, all in flight suits, were at the same table. Just right for bridge.

He walked over to their table. "Is one of you Major Reynolds?"

A rather overweight man with a florid face pushed back his chair and looked up at Hawke. "I'm Major Reynolds." Then in a mocking tone, "Captain Hawke, I presume?"

"Sir, I can see the foothills. That's one klick of visibility."

"And I can see about a hundred feet of those fucking hills, and that's a hundred feet of visibility—up," Reynolds answered, pointing at the ceiling. "And that's here at two hundred fifty feet above sea level. Your fucking company is at over five thousand feet above sea level. No fucking way, Captain. Not until we get VFR and a weather clear from MAG-39."

"You don't know what it's like at five thousand feet unless you go there."

"I don't need to go there to know what it's like. We had a weather bird out there an hour ago and it's souped in from here to fucking Burma." He looked at his three comrades with a slight smile. "We're in constant contact with Captain Bainford from First Battalion, and it's his guys up there, not yours. He's also got an enlisted forward air controller right on the spot. I think between us we'll get the job done"—he paused slightly—"when it's possible. Now just kindly let us do the flying, Captain."

The sudden rage of the combat infantry veteran flashed through Hawke. His hand went to the butt of his .45, but the pistol was hidden beneath his poncho. The fact that he would have to hike up the poncho to reach the weapon slowed him down just enough. For some reason, the image of Hippy, his M-60 cradled on his flak jacket, struggling through the bush on those ravaged feet, hit him. Breathe, he thought. He did. Then he thought again. Then he plunged.

"I'm not a captain and I'm not the assistant Three at Regiment. I'm Lieutenant Hawke, First Battalion S-3 Zulu and the former executive officer of Bravo Company. My guys are out of water and out of ammo and they're dying up there. They need help." Eyebrows went up from all four of the pilots. "I don't know fuck about flying, but I do know fuck about trying. You guys going to sit here playing cards or you going to try?"

There was a long moment of silence. The pilots knew better than Hawke what was being asked of them. Under these conditions, groping nearly blind just above the trees because that was the only airspace in which they could see, one slight error in navigation, one second of inattention, one slight temperature shift that turned clear air into impenetrable fog, and they would see the side of the mountain for about one second before it killed them and all the Marines on board.

Hawke made one last desperate stab. "Marines are in trouble. You afraid to help them?"

A younger first lieutenant pushed back his chair. "That fucking does it," he said. He slapped his cards down and stood up. Hawke feared that he'd pushed too hard. But the pilot looked over at his bridge partner, obviously his copilot. "What do you think, Nickels?"

"Fuck." Nickels threw his cards on the table, faceup, and rose to his feet, followed by the first lieutenant.

"Well, Major?" the lieutenant asked. "I believe we've been called chickenshit."

The florid man sighed and threw his cards onto the table. He rose from his chair, calling out to no one in particular, "Anyone got a fucking jeep? I don't feel like walking to my own funeral."

And that was the true origin of the story, which later made the rounds of the Twenty-Fourth Marine Regiment and the Fifth Marine Division, that a grunt lieutenant had walked into the regimental O-club and pulled his pistol on four zoomies and threatened to kill them if they didn't fly the mission to save his old outfit.

The story that made its way around Marine Air Group 39 and the Fifth Marine Air Wing was that four pilots disobeyed a weather hold to snake their way up a 7,000-foot mountain with only thirty or forty feet between their wheels and the trees in a driving monsoon rain to rescue a Marine company that was surrounded by an NVA regiment.

CHAPTER
SEVENTEEN

FAC-man picked up the radio calls from the two birds long before they could be heard. He was amazed. It didn't seem possible for a chopper to find them. He had just told Bainford the ceiling height, and Bainford had told him they'd have to wait, that it was too dangerous to fly.

Mellas ran crouching behind FAC-man up to the LZ, where they both piled into a nearby hole. A single sniper round passed over their heads. "I don't know what the fuck's going on, sir, but we got two birds down in the valley trying to find us. They say they got reinforcements and ammo. Captain Bainford told me they were all on weather hold." Just then the radio hissed.

FAC-man listened. "That's a neg, sir. Still can't hear you. Over."

He and Mellas sat silently. Mellas motioned for FAC-man's radio and switched quickly to the company frequency. Pallack answered.

"This is Five Actual," Mellas said. "Tell everyone we have a bird trying to find us. I want total silence. Over." Soon the entire perimeter was quiet, everyone waiting in the fog, not wanting to hope.

After a few minutes Mellas saw FAC-man tense, look to the south, and pull out his compass. Mellas's ears were so damaged by the recent combat that he heard nothing except a high-pitched ringing that seemed to have settled permanently inside his head. "Magpie, Magpie, this is Big John Bravo. I have rotor noise bearing one seven niner. I repeat, bearing one seven niner degrees." FAC-man looked at Mellas, then shook one clenched fist in excitement. He was grinning. Something came over the radio. "That's affirmative, sir." There was another pause. "Magpie, this is Big John Bravo FAC. We have about"—he squinted, looking up at the clouds—"forty feet." Then he hung his head. Mellas realized that by telling the truth, FAC-man might doom the company because the choppers would turn around, but that not telling the truth might doom the choppers. He caught FAC-man's eye and gave an understanding nod. The FAC-man smiled and looked up at the sky again. "There it is, sir," he said quietly.

Then FAC-man tensed again, sighted on his compass, and keyed his handset. "Magpie, I have rotor noise now bearing one eight five. Over."

In his mind's eye, Mellas watched the choppers moving westward past the spot where FAC-man had first heard their rotor noise, then turning north to try to come back. That would probably put them just west of the Laotian border. If they could get up to altitude and stay on their northward course, they'd miss the hills to their south. But they would probably overfly Helicopter Hill and Matterhorn in the clouds. If they stuck close to the ground, they could crash into either hill. Mellas hoped fervently that they were flat-hatting across the top of the jungle.

"You're good, Magpie. I still have you bearing one eight five degrees. Stand by for my mark."

There was another intense interval, this time filled with the steady drone of rotor blades augmented by the whine of turbine engines. Then, just above them, obscured by fog, two choppers flashed across the sky. FAC-man jumped to his feet and shouted into the handset, "Mark! Mark!"

He and Mellas watched the choppers disappear. The Marines on the hill were silent. Everyone listened to the whining engines and the clattering of the choppers' blades clawing at thin mountain air during the sharp turn. FAC-man yelled compass bearings and ran to the center of the LZ at the same time. "I got you at zero three zero." He'd pause. "Zero three five." He'd wait. "Zero three five, holding. Yes sir. That's it, sir, a ridge bearing roughly zero niner zero. It's just to our Echo about one hundred feet below us."

Finally a huge fuselage loomed out of the clouds, belly exposed as the pilot brought it up, rear wheels down, fighting its way, engines firing full-on to hold the steady descent. Then it bounced in and the new replacements were rushing, falling, stumbling, and crawling for the sides of the LZ as the air erupted in automatic weapons and machine-gun fire from both Matterhorn and the finger to the north. Mellas had his compass out and coolly took a bearing on the sound of the machine gun on the north finger. He found the spot on his map. "Got you, you bastard," he said.

The first chopper lifted off, and the second one piled in right behind it. Again, dark figures hurtled from the rear ramp, stumbling under immense weight, falling, crawling, and scrambling for safety. Then, to Mellas's amazement and joy, one of the figures stood up on the landing zone and raised his right arm in the hawk power sign. Mellas also stood up, yelling jubilantly. "Goddamn it, Hawke, over here. Over here."

Hawke turned and, weighted down with ammunition and water, ran jerkily toward Mellas. Mellas's heart sang as Hawke collapsed into the hole. Marines on the hill risked getting killed to run over to Hawke, laughing, shouting, slapping him on the back.

Then the mortar shells came slamming down again.

During a lull in the shelling Mellas ran across the LZ and jumped into the hole Hawke was digging for himself. Mellas took out his K-bar and started stabbing at the hard clay, helping Hawke dig, unable to suppress a broad smile.

"So what the fuck are you doing here?"

"I got bored," Hawke said.

"Ah, I think you got sentimental."

"So I'm a bored sentimentalist." Hawke grunted and tossed another shovelful of clay.

Again they heard tubing. They went down low in the shallow hole. The shells shook the ground beneath them and black smoke irritated their nostrils. The explosions jolted them, and their eyes ached from the pressure waves.

"Nice fucking place you've got here," Hawke said. He threw more shovelfuls of dirt, then said, "Fuck it. Deep enough." He jabbed the shovel into the earth and curled back into the hole.

"Hey, Hawke," Mellas said. "You got any water? I'm dying of fucking thirst."

Hawke pulled a canteen from its pouch. "Well, I'll be fucked," he said. He showed the canteen to Mellas. There was a small shrapnel hole in it.

"Better than a hole in your fucking ass."

"Yeah, but it was the one with the Rootin' Tootin' Raspberry."

He handed Mellas the half-empty canteen. Mellas took a long drink, gulping it down, wanting to swim in its tart sweetness. He finally stopped, smiling, with a contented sigh. "I always was a Baron von Lemon fan, but Rootin' Tootin' Raspberry will certainly do."

"Well, Baron von Lemon is very hard to get this year," Hawke said.

Another explosion hit, only fifteen feet from their hole, followed by four more. Mellas felt as if he were in a heavy black bag being beaten with unseen clubs. Smoke replaced oxygen. They couldn't talk. They endured.

Then the explosions shifted to another part of the hill. Hawke calmly took out his tin-can cup and a small chunk of C-4 and started making coffee. He looked up at Mellas, who was watching him intently. "It's the ever-flowing source of all that's good and the cure of all ills," Hawke said. He lit the ball of C-4 and brought the water to a boil. When the coffee was ready he gave the cup to Mellas.

Mellas took a sip. Then he closed his eyes and took another. He sighed and handed the steaming coffee back to Hawke. "When's Delta getting here to relieve us?" Mellas asked.

"Fucked if I know. Do I look like—"

"A goddamned fortune-teller?" Mellas said. "No, but you're supposed to be the Three Zulu, whatever the fuck that is."

"It's nothing. And if I was Delta Company I'd never get my ass up here."

"You came," Mellas said, suddenly serious.

Hawke's brief pause acknowledged Mellas's thanks. "Yeah," he said quietly, "but I'm crazy. I couldn't fucking stand it any more."

"That bad, huh?" Mellas said.

"Oh, hell," Hawke said. "I don't know. A consummate politician like you might even like it back there." He tried to smile.

"It'd beat humping," Mellas said. "I'm out here freezing my nuts off in a jungle and dying of thirst in a monsoon."

Hawke looked up at the sky. "The Six and the Three are saying you abandoned your packs. That's why you're cold and ran out of water and food. Then you fell asleep on the lines last night."

"They can't be serious," Mellas said slowly.

"'Fraid so. Simpson was talking about relieving Fitch again."

Mellas stood up and shouted, "What the fuck's the matter with him? What the fuck's the matter with everybody? These guys only fought a fucking week with no sleeping gear, no food, no water, and that fucking asshole *thinks* they were sleeping. We're the ones who should be insane, not that drunken bastard." A shell exploded, but Mellas no longer cared if it hit him or not.

"Sit down before you get fucking blown away," Hawke said, pulling at him.

Mellas sat down. He wanted to strike out at someone. "It's a fucking blatant lie. Our LP took the first hit, just like in the books. No one was asleep. I fucking guarantee."

"You took more casualties overall than you got confirmed."

"What does he want us to do? Send out another squad or two and have them killed counting dead gooks so it'll even up his goddamned reports to division?"

"I don't know what he wants, Mel. I just know what he says." Hawke was playing with a stick and he paused to flick some mud with it. "You all right?" he asked. "I mean personally?"

"Yeah," Mellas answered. "I got some metal in my ass and hands but you can't tell it from the jungle rot."

"I don't mean that way. I mean about Bass and Janc and all."

"I'll get over it." Mellas looked away from Hawke, up into the blank and now nearly dark sky.

"I doubt it."

"How the fuck do you know?"

"I just know," he said.

"How's Mallory?" Mellas asked, changing the subject.

"Diddy-bopping around. Waiting for his court-martial. Waiting to go to the fucking dentist. That'll probably be in six months or so."

"How long did he stay in the box?"

"I got him out about three hours after you left," Hawke added.

"Thanks."

"Don't mention it. I just hope you have to be his goddamned character witness, not me."

"You have any trouble?"

"I just told the snuffy on guard I was taking over. Blakely ranted and raved about going behind his back, making him look bad, making Cassidy look bad, the Marine Corps, military justice, you name it. Then he went to the O-club."

They both laughed. Then Mellas remembered Hawke, boots shined, notebook out, trying to look good at the battalion briefing. He looked down at the mud. "Hawke, I know what it took. Thank you. He's nobody you want on your bad side." Then he grinned. "Especially since you turned into a lifer."

"Next time do your own goddamned rescuing, that's all I ask," Hawke said, a little sharply.

"They going to throw the book at him?" Mellas asked. He was trying to figure out why Hawke was angry.

"He pulled a goddamned pistol on a fucking Navy officer who's screaming his fucking head off."

"It was fucking empty."

"It's still a fucking pistol," Hawke said. "You've already been out here too long. Ordinary people think pistols are dangerous. They don't stop to look if there's a magazine in it or not and laugh at the joke. The doctor's pissed and he wants Mallory's ass. And he'll get it. Several years' worth."

"Maybe Mallory was out here too long, too," Mellas fired back. "The fucking Navy doctors were the ones that kept sending him back."

"I don't want to talk about fucking Mallory," Hawke said.

They heard more tubing pops in the distance. "You won't have to," Mellas said and pushed himself against the side of the hole, once again

Karl Marlantes

waiting for the explosions. These were so close that afterward Mellas's ears rang and Hawke just stared straight ahead at the opposite wall of the hole, with blood trickling from his nose and his mouth hanging open. They looked at each other, saying nothing. Then Mellas pulled out a notebook and began work on the supply list for the next bird.

"Mellas, stop for a second, huh?"

Mellas looked up, straining through the ringing in his ears for whatever Hawke had to say.

"I resent the shit out of you calling me a lifer."

Hawke's words lodged like a heavy weight in Mellas's stomach. "I was just kidding," Mellas said.

"I resent the shit out of it," Hawke repeated.

"I'm sorry," Mellas said. "I didn't mean it. My usual sarcasm." He tried to think of how he could make it up to Hawke, but the words had been said. Mellas could only be forgiven. "Sometimes my mouth runs off faster than my brain," he added lamely.

"Than your heart, Mellas," Hawke said. He was still visibly angry. "What the fuck do you think a lifer is? Do you really think he's the same guy these kids think he is? It's fucking easy for your kind. You'll go back and be the fucking lifer's superior for the rest of your life. What's a guy like you even doing here? Slumming? These so-called fucking lifers don't have any place to go like you do. And neither do the fucking snuffs. For most of them this is it. This is the top of their little hill. And people like you fly over it and shit on it. Goddamn superior fucking assholes."

"I didn't mean to be putting people down," Mellas mumbled.

"Just don't put down the good ones like Murphy and Cassidy. You're going to go to law school. Where the hell's Cassidy going to go? Here he counts for something. And you shit on it."

Mellas's own temper was starting to rise. "What am I supposed to do, feel sorry for him? I suppose I should feel sorry for the colonel and the Three, too."

"Look. The colonel's an asshole. The Three's an asshole. Fine. I agree. All I'm saying, Mellas, is don't you ever wonder *why* they're assholes? Do you think they enjoy spending every minute of their tiny lives worried that someone's going to shit on them because one of their companies didn't make a checkpoint on time? I'm not saying to forget that they're assholes. I'm just saying when you call someone a name, have some compassion. Label the shit out of them, but who they are and who you are is as much about luck as anything else."

Mellas and Hawke were both looking at the dirt in front of them, unable to let their eyes meet.

"I guess I forget my place sometimes," Mellas finally said, giving Hawke the flicker of a smile.

Hawke smiled too. "Shit. Turn a good fucking sermon into a joke, Mellas." He tucked his hands under his flak jacket and looked at Mellas. "Mellas, you've got everything I wish I had. It just makes me jealous to see you so fucking give-a-shit about it."

"*I've* got everything you wish *you* had?" Mellas broke into laughter that was half a cry of pain. "Hawke, I've got *nothing.* Jack shit."

"You've got brains, you know where you're going, how to get there. You call that nothing?"

"One minute you're making me feel like a turd for being insensitive and now you're telling me I've got talent and you're envious."

"I didn't say you were fucking perfect."

Over their laughter they heard the distant sound of mortar tubing. They hunkered down and waited. Mellas was counting seconds to see if the flight time was the same as for the last bunch. It was different. The shells landed near the top of the LZ, causing only a mild thud.

"Hawke," Mellas said quietly, "you know we might be dead tomorrow."

"Shit," Hawke said. "Tonight." Then he smiled. "You ain't going to get killed, Mellas. You've got too far to go."

That evening, the siege lifted. But there were no thundering hoofbeats, no flashing swords, and no bugle calls. The air simply reached a certain temperature and humidity and the fog vanished. Matterhorn stood before them, greenish-black in the dying light. The kids rose from their fighting holes and cheered. NVA small arms and mortar fire soon pushed them back into their holes, but everything was changed. The helicopters could fly.

And they did. They came flying through the automatic weapons fire and the exploding mortar shells. Ashen-faced replacements ran for the nearest holes, staggering under their loads of extra ammunition, IV fluid, water, and food. Corpsmen and friends of the wounded ran in the opposite direction, ducking into and out of the trembling fuselages, stacking live bodies, running for cover from the one NVA machine gun that had revealed itself on the northeast finger and was systematically stitching bullets into the landing zone. Then the pilots pushed throttles forward and the choppers took off, curving out of sight, taking the happy wounded with them, including a triumphant, grinning Kendall.

Just before dark a single platoon from Delta Company arrived and took a position between Mellas's and Goodwin's platoons. That evening, while friendly artillery fire plastered Matterhorn and Daniels laid down protective fire that surrounded Bravo Company and the Delta Company platoon like smoky armor, the kids drank Kool-Aid and Pillsbury Funny Faces and ate C-rations, happily throwing occasional dirt clods at one another. As far as they were concerned, it was fucking over.

For General Neitzel, however, it wasn't over, and time was running out. He radioed Colonel Mulvaney at VCB, urging him to move even faster.

Mulvaney, however, knew that the window of opportunity was closing. The NVA command must have recognized its vulnerability by now, and the gook regiment was probably heading for Laos as fast as it could go. Neitzel's prayer that the weather would remain bad and give him one extra day hadn't been answered. The fog had lifted too soon. Mulvaney chuckled. Too many of those goddamned kids in Bravo Company had been praying against Neitzel, he thought proudly. No, the NVA would see the advantage gone and scatter to regroup in Laos, as always. The NVA could wait for years if they had to. It had been chancy all along. "Risk," the general had said, hoping Bravo would slow things up enough to get the entire Twenty-Fourth Regiment engaged.

It would have been a hell of a fight. But with the choppers grounded the Marines just couldn't move fast enough.

The NVA were putting a rear guard on Matterhorn to keep the high ground as they pulled back, but otherwise the northern part of the operation was over. With their northern flank exposed, the two units moving down the Da Krong and Au Shau valleys to the south would also be called back. No need to push when time was on your side, Mulvaney mused. That was the problem. The NVA had forever. The Americans had until the next election. Still, it had cost only half a company of Marines to fuck up a major thrust. Since the entire division had been involved, all the casualties and deaths in Bravo Company would be compared with a full division, and the daily briefing would simply say "light casualties." The action wouldn't even get into the newspapers. Thwarting a major enemy offensive *before* it got going just wasn't news. Reporters cared about hot stories and Pulitzers, neither of which resulted from battles that involved only light casualties. Heavy casualties made hot stories and supported antimilitary politics. Over time, continual bad news will discourage any civilian population, and Americans had the lowest tolerance on the planet for bad news. Mulvaney grunted. He had to hand it to the gooks. They have us coming and going, he thought.

He left for evening chow, knowing there would be a lot of backpedaling in the morning. Neitzel had his dick hanging out all over Quang Tri province and not a goddamned thing to show for it. Mulvaney chuckled again. He'd probably have to do some quick backpedaling himself.

In Lieutenant Colonel Simpson's tent, no one wanted to chuckle. Both Simpson and Blakely felt the opportunity trickling away, like sand trickling through their fingers. "Hawke was right," Simpson growled. "The place to be is in the fucking bush, not sitting on our cans moving goddamned artillery around. Hawke was right to go up there."

"I think he ought to be reprimanded for abandoning his duty station, if not fucking court-martialed," Blakely said quietly but firmly.

"You're just an old woman, Blakely," Simpson said. He poured himself another bourbon and tossed it down quickly. "I say we move the CP to Helicopter Hill. Direct the operation from right smack in the middle."

Blakely immediately thought how that might look to an awards review board. He dismissed the idea as foolish, then thought about it again. He knew, even if the old buzzard didn't, that the show was just about over. With a high chance of fixed-wing air, escape to the DMZ blocked, two battalions of Marines moving in from the south and east, and a reinforced company sitting right smack on the NVA's line of supply, Nagoolian would be heading back to Laos. The gooks weren't idiots—at least, not the North Gooks. But they probably would defend Matterhorn to cover their withdrawal. Some value might be squeezed out of that.

"Maybe you've got a point, sir," Blakely said.

"Goddamned right I do," Simpson said, pouring himself another bourbon. He offered the bottle to Blakely.

Blakely was looking at his empty glass, not at the bottle, and thinking quickly. He began talking, still staring at the glass. "Given the casualties from Bravo Company," he said carefully, preparing his case, "the poor kill ratio, falling asleep on the job—the list goes on—it would look almost imperative that a good battalion commander personally take control of a leadership situation as badly out of hand as that."

Simpson looked at Blakely, still holding the bottle of bourbon out to him. Then he slowly withdrew it.

Blakely let him think.

"Major Blakely," Simpson said after a long silence. "I want the CP group ready to move to Bravo Company's position tonight."

"Tonight, sir?"

"You heard me. Tonight. Get Stevens to gin up a bunch of arty illumination and tell Bainford we'll only need one chopper." He touched the top of the bottle as if it were a talisman. "And I want an assault prepared for Matterhorn first thing in the morning."

"By who, sir?"

"By Bravo Company. They need to redeem their honor and get their pride back."

*　　*　　*

The battalion CP group arrived on the hill around 2200. They immediately occupied Fitch's bunker, moving Fitch and his CP group into an open hole near the LZ.

Around 2300 Mellas led a reconnaissance. He moved the squad slowly and silently until he felt he was close to the enemy positions. He called in an illumination round. In the swaying greenish light he saw the line of abandoned holes that the enemy had dug all around Helicopter Hill. The NVA had probably withdrawn to the bunkers on Matterhorn as soon as the weather cleared, knowing the jets would be coming.

Mellas was back by 0100. "They've fucking dee-deed and we'll be out of here tomorrow," he told Fitch and Goodwin. Goodwin grinned. Fitch, however, was tight-lipped. He'd just crawled back from his former bunker, now occupied by Simpson and Blakely.

"What's the matter?" Mellas asked when he noticed Fitch's mood. "Those cocksuckers didn't relieve you, did they?" He was suddenly afraid his friend would be leaving. "Hawke told me about the packs . . ."

Fitch shook his head. "Nothing so good as that." Goodwin and Mellas looked at each other, puzzled. Then Fitch said in despair, "We've been ordered to take Matterhorn. Daylight assault at first light."

Mellas, fearful, took a breath. "We can't take these guys up there again," he whispered. Goodwin stood up, outlined against the faint light of the night sky. He was looking in the direction of Matterhorn, even though it could not be seen.

"The colonel says we've lost our pride, getting kicked off that hill," Fitch said, "and now we're going to get it back." He was trembling again.

"He's insane," Mellas said. "We're still way under strength, even counting the new guys."

Fitch tried to think of something to say to his two lieutenants. "We're supposed to get fixed wing."

Mellas and Goodwin just stared at him.

He tried again. "Maybe it's not so insane. I mean to keep the initiative someone has to move into attack position in the dark. The rest of Delta isn't here yet. So it's up to us."

"Fuck that shit, Fitch," Mellas said. "The only reason they can't wait a day is because they're afraid the fucking gooks will leave." He filled his lungs with damp cool air and then let it out, trying to control his temper. "Fuck 'em and their goddamned body counts. I've counted enough fucking bodies."

Goodwin backed Mellas up. "These guys have come through too much shit to be killed by a fucking madman." He rubbed his hands on his bloody trousers. He'd been hit that morning but had said nothing. "Listen," he added, "this is no joke. I know I like to joke around, but this is serious." He paused to make sure Fitch and Mellas understood he wasn't kidding. "I say we kill the motherfuckers. We wait until the shit starts coming in and then toss in a couple of frags. They can both die fucking heroes. I'll write them up myself."

"I'll help you," Mellas said.

Fitch shook his head. "You know you can't do that, Scar. It's murder."

"Murder," Scar said bitterly. He waved his arm in an arc, indicating the hill and its remains. "What's the difference?"

Fitch, suddenly overwhelmed, put his face in his hands and bent almost double over the map before him. "I don't know the difference," he muttered. "Just don't fucking bother me." His hands were shaking again.

After a moment of quiet Mellas said, to no one in particular, "We can blame war on orders, which means we can blame it on someone else. You have to take personal responsibility for murder."

"I don't know what the fuck that means, Mellas," Goodwin said.

"I didn't until a few days ago," Mellas answered. He thought of Pollini and the dead soldier above his hole, both killed—or murdered—by his hand.

Fitch raised his head. "There's no way around it unless you want to commit mutiny," he said. "I'm not about to do that. When I get out of here I want to screw my brains out. I don't want to go to jail."

Mellas picked at the calluses on his hands. He kicked softly at the mud and sighed. He knew Fitch was right. "All right," he said, "let's see what kind of fucked-up plan you come up with this time, Jim." He and Fitch looked at each other and started laughing.

Goodwin shook his head and then joined them. "It ain't going to be the flying fucking wedge, Jack."

*   *   *

Once again they worked over the bleak options. By 0300 they had a plan. Goodwin would go up the narrower east side with Second Platoon. Mellas, with a platoon made up of the bulk of the replacements and the remnants of First Platoon, a squad from Third Platoon, and the mortar squad, which was now carrying only rifles, would take on the broader south slope. They'd attack together, the southeast shoulder of the hill shielding them from one another's fire. Conman would take the remaining Marines from Kendall's platoon, now not much larger than a squad, and six of the replacements, and secure the northern finger. That was to stop the sniper fire they'd taken on the previous assault and, in particular, the machine gun that had given away its position to shoot at the choppers. The back of Goodwin's assaulting platoon would be exposed to its fire. Cortell would take over Connolly's squad. Fitch and the company CP group would set between Mellas's and Goodwin's platoons, and advance behind them so that Fitch could at least have a chance of seeing what was going on. Delta Company would fly in to protect the battalion CP group and lay down a base of fire. Third Squad of First Platoon, now under Hamilton, along with Mole and his A gunner, would circle around to the west and kill the NVA who ran off the hill or prevent reinforcements from arriving if the assault bogged down.

Mellas made Jacobs his platoon sergeant and gave Jacobs's squad to Robertson, who had been the leader of his first fire team. Then he called all of the squad leaders together and repeated the plan. He felt it would be better to keep the squads intact, even if they were all about half their former size. That, however, gave him and Jacobs five squads to control instead of three.

Connolly gulped at being given the responsibility for what remained of Third Platoon and taking out the machine gun on the ridgeline. He wished he had been a bad squad leader instead of a good one. He wished Vancouver were still with him to help. He wished he didn't have so many totally green kids. He wished he were back home.

Mellas noticed his reaction. "Conman, I know you can do it. Otherwise I wouldn't have given it to you."

Connolly stopped gulping, but Cortell spoke up after Mellas had finished the brief. "I'm not goin'," he said. "I won't take over Conman's squad."

Everyone looked at him silently.

"Call me a chickenshit motherfucker, but I ain't goin' up no hill 'cause some crazy honky out to make general over my black ass. I ain't goin', man, and I won't be the only one."

Nobody blamed him. He had been wounded in the head and could have jumped on the bird that brought the battalion CP group in that afternoon, but he had stayed.

"OK, Cortell," Mellas said. "Who do you want to take the squad?"

Cortell had expected a different reaction. He was taken aback. He looked around. No one spoke.

"Rider," he finally said.

"Go get him."

Cortell hesitated. Then he whirled angrily and headed toward the lines.

Mellas felt the fear of those huddled near him in the darkness. "Anyone else who's got an excuse that'll get him off the hill can take it," Mellas said.

People shuffled their feet, looking at the ground. Jacobs spoke up. "J-Jermain's got an R & R and his arm is f-fucked up from that scrap metal in it."

"Please, Jake," Mellas said. "Before I get killed, just once call it shrapnel." The others laughed softly. "You have someone else who can handle the M-79?" Mellas asked.

"I'll carry it myself," Jacobs replied.

"OK." Mellas looked around. "Anyone else?"

No one spoke.

Rider crawled up to the group, looking worried. His hair was scorched, his eyebrows were burned off, and he had salve all over his face. "Lieutenant, I hear we're going to make the assault tomorrow. Cortell says everyone's going crazy and he's going to get medevaced."

"There it is, Rider," Mellas said.

Waiting for the coming assault was different from waiting for the previous ones. It was as if they'd already thrown their lives away.

Mellas kept thinking about girls he wished he'd known better. He remembered a dance thrown by the Boston Rugby Club. He'd gone up to Boston from Princeton with two friends from the rugby team. They both had girlfriends at Radcliffe, one of whom had fixed Mellas up with her roommate. They'd worn tuxedos; the girls, long dresses. It was snowing, soft gentle snow. After the dance they'd gone to a house on a lake and curled up before a fire. The other two couples drifted off to bedrooms, leaving Mellas alone with the girl. He could tell that she was afraid he was just another animal from the rugby team. Mellas himself was afraid she'd think he was clumsy because he didn't know what to do. They had sat there, nervous, unable even to talk to each other, and had wasted that precious moment.

Mellas wanted to reach out across the Pacific and apologize. He didn't remember her name. She didn't know he was in a hole about to die. War was breaking life apart and splintering it, so there were no second chances and all the first chances were wasted. Mellas also saw Anne crying. *She* had turned her back on *him* their last night together. How could she be the one crying? But now he'd never be able to explain how he felt, explain how it hurt, find out why she did it, apologize for his lack of understanding, or cry out at her for hers. They were torn apart and separate, with no second chances.

He saw himself rolling down the hill with Pollini; he saw the neat hole in Pollini's head. Then he remembered Bass whittling on his short-timer's stick, and Vancouver leaning over him and Scar in the empty bunker and saying, "Nagoolian went thataway."

Once, later that night, Mellas whispered, "You all right?" He meant Bass, Vancouver, and Pollini. Jackson thought Mellas meant him and answered that he was. Mellas wondered why Jackson had said that.

The radio whispered with the sound of Goodwin checking an LP. Even before an assault, war's tedious tasks went on uninterrupted.

The fog hung thick and heavy as the kids formed into a single line on the south side of Helicopter Hill. Mellas felt as if the clouds above him were slabs of slate. The kids were fatigued and filled with despair at the insanity of it all. Yet they were all checking ammunition, sliding bolts back and forth, preparing to participate in the insanity. It was as if the veterans of the company, succumbing to this insanity, had decided to commit suicide. Mellas, sick with exhaustion, now knew why men threw themselves on hand grenades.

He silently inspected his platoon. Many of the kids were strangers to him, but others were familiar friends. He'd pull on someone's loose canteen, tug a hand grenade that was carelessly placed, going through the routine of inspection as a mother tidies her children before they leave for school.

Mellas heard someone trudging down the hillside toward them. A ghostly figure came out of the dark fog, an M-16 on his shoulder, full bandoleers of magazines across his flak jacket. "Well, Mel," Hawke said, "where's my fucking platoon?"

Mellas could only shake his head. Words failed him. Finally he said, "You take Third Herd, Hawke, with Conman. It's not much more than a squad. The idea is to hold down the sniper fire on Scar's rear from that northeast finger. There's a machine gun there." He pulled out his map and the flashlight with the red lens. "I think it's right here," he said, pointing at the place he'd calculated. "You'll probably have to clear some bunkers." He looked up at Hawke's intense dark eyes. "Thanks for coming, Jayhawk. I hope you don't get fucking killed."

"Why do you think I'm taking the platoon that's not going up the fucking hill?" Hawke turned and walked down the line of men, holding up his fingers in the hawk power sign.

"Hey Lieutenant Jayhawk, you're going to get your ass shot off," someone called.

"Only if the fucking gooks have invented a bullet that shoots underground."

Hawke had the kids laughing at death.

Pallack's voice came over the PRC-25s. "OK, Bravo One, Two, and Three. Kickoff time."

The company walked off into the black jungle as the artillery shrieked above them and exploded into Matterhorn, shaking the ground. The light from the exploding shells was reflected and softened by the fog and came to their eyes as pale glimmers.

They passed Cortell and Jermain, Jacobs's M-79 man, sitting on a log watching them.

"Good luck, you guys," Cortell said sincerely. Jacobs said thanks. So did a few others. Nobody thought badly of them. Jermain watched his friends file by, silently shaking his head, as if telling himself, "I won't go. Not this time. This time it's crazy."

Jermain and Cortell watched the last man disappear. They said nothing for at least three minutes. Then Jermain spoke up: "I feel kind of shitty."

"Me too," Cortell said. There was another silence.

"You think we go to heaven when we die?" Jermain asked.

"I don't think nothin'. I *believe* Jesus take care of us when we die." Cortell looked at Jermain. "Believin's not thinkin'."

Jermain took that in for a while. "What if you're wrong?"

Cortell laughed. "What if *you* wrong? You been worse off than me all you life. I got the safe bet, not you."

"I didn't say I didn't believe."

"No, you just playing it safe and not choosin'. Jesus don't want you to play safe. You don't get anyplace if you don't choose."

"I don't want to go nowhere but back to the world."

"Yeah, I be right there with you," Cortell said. He was silent for a moment. Then he said, "Ever'one here think it easy for me. I be this good little church boy from Mississippi with my good little church-goin' Mammy, and since I be this stupid country nigger with the big faith, I don't have no troubles. Well, it just don't work that way." He paused. Jermain said nothing. "I see my friend Williams get ate by a tiger,"

Cortell continued. "I see my friend Broyer get his face ripped off by a mine. What you think I do all night, sit around thankin' Sweet Jesus? Raise my palms to sweet heaven and cry hallelujah? You know what I do? You know what I do? I lose my heart." Cortell's throat suddenly tightened, strangling his words. "I lose my heart." He took a deep breath, trying to regain his composure. He exhaled and went on quietly, back in control. "I sit there and I don't see any hope. Hope gone." Cortell was seeing his dead friends. "Then, the sky turn gray again in the east, and you know what I do? I choose all over to keep believin'. All along I know Jesus could maybe be just some fairy tale, and I could be just this one big fool. I choose anyway." He turned away from his inward images and returned to the blackness of the world around him. "It ain't no easy thing."

The platoon was well into the jungle when Mellas saw Jermain, holding an M-16, break past him. Jermain handed the rifle to Jacobs and took back his M-79 grenade launcher and the vest filled with grenades without saying a word. Jacobs turned around and grinned at Mellas, his face lit by an illumination round. Jermain kept moving forward, refusing to turn around.

"Hey, Jermain," Mellas finally whispered during a halt.

Jermain turned around, looking chagrined.

"Don't look so fucking hangdog," Mellas said gently. "Did Cortell come too?"

"Yeah. Crazy motherfucker started praying and shoved off without asking me if I'd come or not. So I shoved off, too. Crazy motherfucker."

"You or him?" Mellas asked.

Jermain laughed. "Fucked if I know, sir."

"Well, I'm glad you guys came. I hope you make your R & R."

"Me too, sir."

They kicked off again. Mellas put Robertson on point with Jermain and three new kids, knowing that Robertson and Jermain had scaled Sky Cap together and were tight. Between them, they could probably handle the green ones.

The newbies were starting at every little sound. The artillery barrage grew louder as they neared Matterhorn. Robertson slowed to one pace at a time, inching toward the edge of the jungle. The entire line waited as Robertson's squad inched forward, feeling for the dangerous open fields of fire that Bravo itself had cleared.

Gradually the fog turned gray with the coming of dawn. Then Robertson held up his hand. He turned and whispered something that Mellas couldn't hear through the roar of the artillery. Mellas knew they'd reached the edge of the trees. He scrambled forward in a crouch. Robertson was on his belly, peering out just a meter short of the cleared ground.

Before them stood Matterhorn, now ugly and barren, swathed in the sweet-sick smoke of the artillery. Mellas could see the large gaps torn in the wire during and after their previous assault. He could also see First Platoon's former bunkers. He moved the platoon into a long assault line just inside the jungle and radioed Goodwin to link up. When Goodwin radioed that he had contact with Mellas's right flank, Mellas radioed Fitch. He told Fitch they were at the final line of departure.

The kids lay on the ground, rifles in front of them, sweating, some taking nervous sips of water and Kool-Aid from their canteens. The artillery stopped. They heard the rest of Delta Company coming in on choppers, which were met with only desultory rifle fire. Still, Mellas felt frightened. He watched the hill anxiously. The artillery had been useless against the fortified positions. Nice work on those bunkers, he thought ruefully. Now it all depended on whether or not fixed wing could take them out with napalm and 250-pound or maybe even 500-pound bombs.

They waited. Nothing happened. Mellas's fear overcame him, and he reached for the hook. "Bravo Six, this is Bravo Five. Where's the fucking fixed wing with the snake and nape? Over."

"It's supposed to be on its way. They're having trouble with the weather. Can't see the fucking hill and going too fast to risk coming in lower."

"Fuck," Jackson whispered.

Mellas radioed Hamilton, who had continued westward to position his squad to stop any NVA reinforcements or to kill any NVA retreating from Matterhorn. The going was terribly slow. "Get your asses moving," Mellas said fiercely.

Hamilton rogered.

Mellas lay in close to Jacobs and Jackson. They waited. Mellas wanted to shit again. His bowels felt like they were full of wet tissue paper.

Jackson felt the radio pressing his chest into the earth. This made it uncomfortable to breathe, but at the same time he felt good to be pressed so close to the ground. A strange insect walked in front of his nose. It occurred to Jackson that in the insect's world the events of the day would go unnoticed. His mind flipped back to the world, to his family, to his neighborhood in Cleveland. Bringing lunch to his dad at Moe's Tire and Retread. His mother laughing with the customers as she styled their hair at Billie's Cut and Perm. Like the insect, they too lived in a separate world.

Mellas checked on Hamilton again. He was still several hundred meters from his destination. This irritated Mellas, and he let Hamilton know it. He checked in with Fitch. "Goddamn it, where's our fucking airplanes?"

"I don't know, Five. Out," Fitch said curtly.

Mellas crawled backward. Jackson followed him. They moved in a slow crouch behind the long line of Marines. "We're waiting for snake and nape," Mellas would say, touching kids on their shoulders. "We're waiting for the fixed wing. They're going to napalm the shit out of the hill with snake-eye bombs." The kids grew less jittery.

He and Jackson reached Cortell. Cortell looked up at Mellas. "I'm crazy, Lieutenant. I'm a crazy cotton-pickin' idiot."

"I think so, too," Rider said, grinning.

"Hey, man," Cortell replied, "I do the thinkin' 'round here. I think you bein' squad leader went to you head."

Rider smiled and shrugged his shoulders.

Jackson knelt beside Cortell and the two of them touched fists in the hand dance, looking at each other solemnly.

"Hey, brother, we in a real nightmare," Jackson finally said.

"You just trust in Jesus," Cortell said. They both knew these might be the last words they would exchange. "But keep you fuckin' rifle out of the mud, too." They touched hands again and Jackson turned to follow Mellas down the line.

Mellas and Jackson returned to their original spot next to Jacobs. The hill was deadly quiet. No air stirred. The thinning artillery smoke tinted the blasted mud gray.

Jacobs opened a packet of Choo-Choo Cherry, poured the dark red crystals into his hand, and popped them into his mouth. His hand ran red where the sweat on his palm dissolved the crystals. He handed the package to Jackson, who also took some. Jackson's lips turned reddish purple.

The radio hissed. "Foxtrot Whiskey coming in. Get your fucking heads down. Over." The word passed along the line. Then a rushing scream filled their ears and the huge bulk of a Phantom fighter-bomber slashed so closely above their heads that they felt the wake turbulence. It disappeared across the top of the hill. As this sound died away, it was replaced by the chatter of a lone automatic weapon.

"How come they didn't drop nothing?" Jake asked. He had taken out his Instamatic camera.

Mellas shrugged.

A second jet came in above them. Snake-eye bombs—four tiny eggs, dark against the gray sky—dropped from its wings. The bombs suddenly blossomed four-petaled tails that arrested their rapid movement, allowing the jet to roar safely out of danger before they hit.

The bombs exploded harmlessly on the other side of the hill.

Mellas was on the radio instantly. "Those stupid motherfuckers are bombing the wrong place. Tell them to drop five hundred. Over."

"I hear you, Bravo Five," Fitch replied. "We're telling. Out."

Another Phantom thundered overhead. Mellas watched in disbelief as four more snake-eyes floated harmlessly out of sight.

"Goddamn it, Skipper, they're missing the fucking hill!" Mellas shouted.

Goodwin was on the radio, too. "Please, for God's sake, please tell them they're hitting the wrong target. If they don't hit those bunkers we're going to get creamed. Over."

Mellas sank back into the ground. Again the jets passed overhead, with a shattering noise. Again they wasted their precious cargo on the jungle.

Jake turned around and looked at Mellas, his eyes wild with frustration and fear.

"What the fuck can I do?" Mellas nearly shouted at him.

Fitch was pleading with Captain Bainford's radio operator. Bainford eventually came up on the hook. "I tell you one of the pilots reported a secondary. Over."

"I don't care if he reported hitting the Glorious Revolution Ammunition Factory, you're missing the fucking target. Over."

"Look, Bravo Six, you have to try and see things from their perspective. They're going five hundred miles an hour and it's foggy. It's a hell of a job. Over."

"You get them on fucking target or I'll open up on them, so help me God. Over."

"We'll see what we can do. Big John One Four out."

A single jet came in, only a few hundred feet above them. Two long sausage-shaped cylinders tumbled out. These were the napalm.

The cylinders fell out of sight, moving at 500 miles an hour across the top of the hill, uselessly searing the jungle with the flaming jellied chemical. A second jet followed. One of its canisters caught the top of the hill just inside the circle of bunkers. Orange flame mixed with intense black smoke washed across the dark earth of Matterhorn's LZ. But there was nothing to burn there.

Mellas grabbed the hook. He switched off the company frequency. He came up on the battalion frequency and started shouting. "Goddamn it, you tell those stupid motherfuckers to drop two hundred meters. I say again. Drop two hundred meters!"

"Bravo Five, this is Big John Three. You clear the fucking nets. We're controlling the fixed wing. They said the last drop looked right on. Now get off the net. That's an order."

"Goddamn it, I tell you they can't fucking *see*. I'm right here! They're hitting the wrong fucking target!" Mellas rolled over and moaned.

The two planes came in again, and again the napalm sprayed uselessly several hundred meters to the northwest of the hill. Then they didn't come in any more.

Fitch's crisp voice came in over the company net. "That's it. The weather's closed them out. We had another flight on station, but Big John says they won't be able to run them. It's too dangerous in this weather."

There was a pause.

"Too dangerous," Mellas said to no one.

Fitch came up again. "OK, that's it. No more air. Show's over. Let's go. Over."

"Bravo One, roger," Mellas said, handing the receiver to Jackson. Goodwin rogered and so did Hawke.

And then Mellas stood up.

His hands were shaking. The blood pounded so hard in his throat that each heartbeat hurt. His thighs felt too weak to keep his knees from folding. His empty insides still churned with the desire to eliminate watery feces. He gave the signal and walked forward into the nakedness of the hillside. The others walked with him, emerging from the trees in a single quavery line.

CHAPTER
EIGHTEEN

The long line of Marines moved forward in silence, breaking and bending on the blasted ground, wavering around shattered stumps, forming up again. Their breathing became labored as they climbed the steep slope.

"Keep walking," Mellas was saying to himself. "Don't run. Keep walking."

Twenty meters. He glanced over his shoulder to see if there were any stragglers. The jungle behind the Marines already looked, as usual, impenetrable. Twenty-five meters. A kid stumbled momentarily, pitching forward. He caught himself. The line moved upward. Twenty-eight meters. Maybe no one was up there. Thirty meters. Only the sound of breathing could be heard as they walked up the hill.

The bunkers seemed miles above them.

Mellas slipped backward on the slope but caught himself. He was still thinking: Keep walking. Don't panic. Maybe no one's there. Don't run. Keep it all until you need it. Maybe no one's there.

The tension was like a balloon being filled to its bursting point. With every step more air was forced in. Until the agonized rubber burst.

The bunkers winked light, and the ground around the Marines seemed to come alive. The air was split by bullets and by the sound of AK-47s, SKS rifles, and Russian-built RPD 7.62 machine guns. Almost immediately, Fitch gave the signal for Delta Company on Helicopter Hill to open up. There was a mind-numbing roar as Delta poured bullets above the heads of the advancing Marines of Bravo Company. Mellas heard the bullets cracking and snapping over his head and watched them hit all along the line of bunkers. Adrenaline surged through him. Then he became aware of the cries of those who were being hit.

Mellas tried to shout above the roar: "Let's go, goddamn it. Let's go!" He churned forward, Jackson scrambling to his left. A rush of machine-gun bullets hit the mud in front of them, and they both dived for the earth and clawed their way to a log. Out of the corner of his eye Mellas saw Robertson dive for cover in a shell crater. One of Robertson's squad members, however, was left kicking on the earth behind him. Another Marine grabbed the kid's legs and started to pull him to safety, but the advancing machine-gun bullets cut the second kid down. He curled over in a fetal position, holding his abdomen. Then he lay still.

Mellas raised his head above the log to start forward. Bullets kicked mud and rock fragments into his face and cracked and snapped over his head. Mellas pushed his face into the ground. It was suicidal to go farther.

The attack, barely started, came to a complete halt.

Another of the new kids from Robertson's squad darted from cover and tried to reach the two others lying in front of him. He was shot through the chest. Jacobs raced out after him, and Mellas yelled for a corpsman. Doc Fredrickson came running across an open space and dived behind the shelter of the log while Jacobs brought the kid back in behind it. The entire sequence took approximately five seconds. The kid Jacobs had pulled in was dead.

There were now four of them and a body huddled behind the log. Mellas was mumbling and praying aloud, although no one could hear him: his face was pressed into the ground. Why, God, why didn't they drop the napalm? Why didn't they hold off until the weather cleared and just burn the fucking hill down? Why are we doing this now? Why doesn't somebody move?

The air was alive with noise, bullets, and madness. They had now lain behind the log for more than thirty seconds.

Jermain came running across to the group behind the log. Bullets ripped past him. "There's no fucking room for you, Jermain," Mellas shouted, but Jermain ignored him and kept coming. Jermain piled on top of Mellas and Jackson, knocking the air from Mellas's lungs.

He made it, Mellas thought.

Jermain's chest was heaving and his eyes were darting back and forth wildly. But he had made it without being hit. That thought kept picking at Mellas's mind. Mellas started to turn his own face toward the earth again, trying to ignore the firing, and letting the noise and confusion immobilize him, but Jermain shouted, "I know where the fucking gun is, Lieutenant."

Mellas wanted to shout back at him, *So fucking what? I'm not going up there. I'm not going up there so some fucking colonel can get a fucking medal.* Instead, he said, "Well, shoot at the motherfucker," and pressed his face down into the wonderful earth.

Jermain rolled off Mellas's and Jackson's backs to the end of the log. He fired a grenade, then ducked down again as the earth in front of the log and several hundred meters behind it exploded with machine-gun bullets.

Fitch was shouting over the radio. Jermain popped up and fired a second round, and then a third. Mellas couldn't hear, above the noise, what Fitch was saying. He covered one ear. Fitch's voice said, "What the fuck's going on over there? Two is pinned down. They can't move. Three's run into at least five positions on the finger. The whole front of the goddamn hill is laced with fucking machine guns. What the fuck's happening over there? Over."

Mellas was panting. He didn't know how to answer. He heard a sharp cry and turned around. Jermain, shot through the shoulder, reeled and fell on top of Jackson, blood running from beneath his flak jacket. Jackson shoved him off, and the blood spattered on Mellas. Fredrickson reached across and stuffed a wad of battle dressing into the exit hole in Jermain's back while Jacobs grabbed the M-79 and, enraged, started to fire at the machine gun Jermain had taken on.

Mellas looked at the blood on his arms and hand, and at Jermain's contorted face. Suddenly he seemed to be floating above the scene, watching the entire company. Everything was in slow motion and fuzzily quiet.

Jermain was probably going to die.

An explosion from Goodwin's area rocked the hill.

They'd now been behind the log slightly more than a minute.

Mellas floated high above the hill. He saw the line of Marines stretched out below him, some kicking or contorted in pain, some lying still. He saw the people he knew, still alive, trying to stay alive, behind logs, in small defilades, many lying flat on the ground and attempting to merge with the earth. He studied the bunkers. He saw the inter-locking fire as if in a drawing. He saw the machine gun Jermain had attacked—and he knew. He floated back to a tactics class at the Basic School where a redheaded major said that junior officers were mostly redundant because the corporals and sergeants could take care of just about anything. But there would come a time when the junior officers would earn every penny of their pay, and they would know when that time came.

Mellas came back to the hill. His time had come.

He saw the smoke from the burning napalm. He saw what would open the door through the interlocking fire, and it was right in front of him, shooting at him.

Mellas keyed the handset. "Bravo Six, this is Bravo Five. Over." As if from behind his own shoulder, Mellas watched himself telling Fitch the situation calmly over the radio. He seemed to be reading lines. He was no longer there but somehow directing the scene from above or beside it.

Mellas didn't wait for an answer. He handed the receiver to Jack-son. Why Jermain? Why the one who volunteered while the shit-birds stayed in the rear? Why were his friends dying? There seemed only one way out of the nightmare. The single machine gun was the way.

"Gun up," Mellas yelled. "Get a fucking gun up here." Somehow he had to draw the machine gun's fire.

A new kid ran forward with an M-60; an ammo humper scrambled after him with the heavy steel boxes of ammunition belts. The gunner's eyes were wild with fear and pain. He had been shot in the left calf. Mellas could see flecks of blood coming off his soaked trouser leg. Still he came lurching forward, running hard. He lunged in on top of Fredrickson, then rolled over just as the ammo humper piled on top of them. His eyes were very white against his black face. It occurred to

Mellas that if this kid weren't here he would probably be hotdogging on his high school's basketball court.

"You start shooting that fucking bunker. That one right there," Mellas shouted, pointing straight ahead. "Don't let up." The new kid nodded. He moved, leaving blood behind. Mellas could see it spurting rhythmically. An artery, he thought abstractedly. Maybe the kid had three or four more minutes of consciousness.

The kid leaned the M-60 over the log, cradling it against his shoulder. The machine gun barked. Then it settled into the disciplined, barrel-saving short bursts of the trained gunner. Mellas felt relief. He silently thanked some instructor at Camp Pendleton.

The NVA gunner answered. The duel grew in intensity. The roar increased. The two new kids just kept firing, eyes squinted almost shut, as if squinting could protect them from the bullets.

Mellas redirected Jake's M-79 fire to a second bunker just to the left of the NVA machine gun. He intended to use the projectiles to blind the people inside with smoke and mud. "You keep firing at the fucking entrance. No place else, no matter what I do," he said. Jacobs nodded and loaded another projectile. Mellas pulled a grenade from his suspenders and whispered, "Dear God, help me now." He felt that this was possibly his last moment of life, here behind this log with these comrades, and knew it was indescribably sweet. A longing sadness arose with the fear, and he looked one more time at his comrades' intent faces. He wet his lips and said good-bye, silently, not wanting to leave the safety of the log and their warm bodies.

Then he stood up and ran.

He ran as he'd never run before, with neither hope nor despair. He ran because the world was divided into opposites and his side had already been chosen for him, his only choice being whether or not to play his part with heart and courage. He ran because fate had placed him in a position of responsibility and he had accepted the burden. He ran because his self-respect required it. He ran because he loved his friends and this was the only thing he could do to end the madness that was killing and maiming them. He ran directly at the bunker where the grenades from Jake's M-79 were exploding. The bullets from the M-60 machine gun slammed through the air to his right, slashing past him, whining like tortured cats, cracking like the bullwhip of death. He ran, having never felt so alone and frightened in his life.

He passed the large gap in the barbed wire and kept going. The bunker was only fifty meters above him now. He kept waiting for the bullet that would end the run and would let him rest. He almost wanted that bullet so he wouldn't have to continue with the awful responsibility of living. But he ran. He zigzagged. He twisted. His breath came in painful gasps. He saw a shallow hole just above the bunker and to its right. He prayed. He pictured himself striving for it, saw himself from above, small and puny on the vast terrible hillside, his legs churning. The hole loomed large above him. He hit the hole and rolled, catching a glimpse of movement from the corner of his eye. He twisted around, bringing his M-16 to bear at the same time, and was on the point of pulling the trigger, knowing he was doomed. Then the movement solidified into a person wearing a bloody head bandage. It was Cortell—with three new kids. They had followed him.

Mellas came to his feet, releasing the spoon on the grenade he'd been carrying. He rushed toward the door of the bunker, praying that Jacobs would have the sense to stop firing as he closed in on it. Mellas reached the door and ran past the bunker, throwing the grenade inside. He rolled to the right as Cortell came running after him, dropping in a grenade of his own. The two grenades went off almost simultaneously.

Mellas rolled to his feet. He looked behind him in bewilderment—and then with joy. Jackson was running toward him. Behind Jackson was another fire team. To their right, another group was charging the machine-gun bunker while it still received the new gunner's disciplined fire. The whole platoon was swarming up the hill after him. Far off on the right flank of the assault, Mellas saw Second Platoon scrambling to keep up, Goodwin running in front, waving them forward.

Mellas's heart surged with wonder.

Bullets were now flying uphill from the Marines and downhill from the NVA. They were so thick that at one point Mellas heard two bullets collide and then ricochet with a singing buzz parallel to the crossing fire. The air was filled with roaring and screaming. Then farther down the slope Mellas saw, looking like rag dolls, those who hadn't survived or wouldn't survive. Some twitched fitfully. Two were crawling toward the defilade. The others lay still, in awkward positions.

Three minutes had passed since the opening shot.

From Helicopter Hill it looked like a textbook assault. In fact, it was. Blakely was pacing up and down in excitement. Simpson, his eyes pressed to his binoculars, was clenching his jaw so tightly that his neck muscles stood out in cords.

Mellas was running hard to his right, shouting as he went, trying to get his platoon to move toward Goodwin's. The fight had disintegrated into the mad actions of individuals. Noise, smoke, confusion, and fear prevailed. Mellas rounded a slight knob and saw Goodwin about 100 meters away, running parallel to the hill with the radio receiver in his hand, his radio operator scrambling after him to keep the cord slack.

Jackson handed Mellas the receiver. "It's Scar, sir."

Mellas could barely make out what Goodwin was saying, because of the noise and Goodwin's wild panting. "There's a gun—edge of the LZ—fucking us up good, Jack." There was more machine-gun fire. Mellas saw Goodwin go down and then get up. "Got to get the motherfucker—with grenades," Goodwin shouted. "Don't move toward it."

Just as Goodwin was speaking, Mellas saw Robertson pop up from a shell hole and disappear across the lip of the LZ. He was amazed to see Robertson so high above the rest of them. Goodwin was moving upward beneath the lip of the LZ with five others, carrying two grenades each. They couldn't see Robertson; they had no idea he was there. Mellas reached for the receiver. Just as he started to shout, "Goddamn it, Scar, I've got a man up there," Goodwin sprinted forward, away from his radio. The five Marines followed in a rush.

Robertson popped up, running across the LZ toward the same bunker Goodwin's group was after, in full view of everyone except them.

Robertson reached the bunker's top just as twelve hand grenades came sailing over the lip of the hill. He tried to stop short, his arms flailing in the air. He threw his own grenade away and tried to sprint to safety. The grenades began going off in a sustained explosion, obscuring him.

Mellas, still holding the handset, shut his eyes. The smoke cleared slightly. The machine-gun opened up again. Mellas heard Goodwin cursing over the radio.

Then Robertson appeared again. All alone, inside the ring of enemy fighting holes, exposed, he ran back to the machine-gun bunker. He dropped in two grenades, then stood calmly taking a third from his suspenders. He pulled the pin and tossed it in. Just then, fire and smoke erupted from the bunker beneath him. He sank to his knees, twisting slightly, and fell out of sight.

Mellas knew he was dead.

"Robertson got the bunker, Scar. I watched it go up," he radioed.

Goodwin immediately started moving his platoon forward.

Then, from Helicopter Hill, Mellas became aware of a faint sound of cheering. The cheering filled Mellas with white-hot rage. He turned to look behind him. Marines were firing at bunkers, trying to maneuver up on them from the sides. The North Vietnamese were obviously finished but still kept firing at the Marines from holes on the lip of the LZ.

Mellas's fury gave him the cunning of an animal. He forgot everything that had happened before this moment. He knew only that he wanted to kill. He didn't care who or what he killed.

He shouted at Hamilton over the radio. "Goddamn it, get fucking moving. These bastards are going to start running off this hill and I fucking want them. Move! Move! Move! I want these fucking gooks killed. You hear me? Over."

"Aye aye, sir," Hamilton's voice crackled back. Hamilton was gasping for breath.

Mellas headed for the open holes above the covered bunkers. He knew that now the work would be dirty and methodical. There would be no more cheering. It occurred to him how much the NVA must hate them, not to get up and run.

Jacobs joined Mellas and Jackson. His face was streaked with black powder, mud, and sweat. His Instamatic dangled against his flak jacket.

Mellas was directing fire teams and individuals, watching as position after position was destroyed. He moved cautiously, in quick rushes, with long waits in between. Jackson and Jacobs followed his every move.

Suddenly a man rose from a hole above them and threw a grenade.

Mellas was transfixed by the sight. The small black object seemed to hang suspended in the air above him.

"Grenade! Chi-comm!" Jackson yelled. Mellas saw the grenade explode. Two small objects hurtled past his head, one on each side. Then the world went black as the explosion enveloped him. It slammed him backward, nearly pulling his head from his neck. He sank to the ground, giving in to the blackness; the sounds of the firing and confusion whirled away from him. Dying was a huge relief. For the first time, he felt safe.

Jackson crawled forward to reach Mellas and called for Doc Fredrickson. Mellas's face was covered with blood, powder burns, and bits of solder. Jackson shouted again, but Fredrickson was out of hearing, moving among the bodies left behind in the initial wild run up the hillside. Jackson started shaking Mellas. "Sir, sir. You OK?" He kept looking around for help. The radio was yammering in his ear, but now he or Jacobs, not Mellas, had to make the decisions.

Jacobs crawled up to Jackson.

"J-Jesus. I-is he all right?"

Jackson was still shaking Mellas and saying, "Sir. Sir." He turned to Jacobs. "I don't know. I think he's dead. Fuck."

Jacobs cursed.

"It's your fucking platoon now, Jake. What we going to do?"

Jacobs had no idea. A burst of rifle fire sent bullets snapping above his head. He saw Fredrickson running to another body far below. Then the NVA soldier in the hole above them popped up again and threw another grenade.

"Chi-comm!" Jacobs shouted. He and Jackson grabbed Mellas by the legs and tore down the hillside, dragging him facedown. As they ran down the hill the grenade followed them inexorably, moving with gravity, as if linked to them. Jackson finally figured it out and shouted, "Stop!" He and Jacobs dug their heels in. They buried themselves against the inert Mellas and the deadly canister bounced on past them. It exploded about half a second later, just below them. Neither of them was hurt.

Jacobs turned Mellas over, faceup. He tore open both of Mellas's flak jackets and put an ear to his chest. "I can't hear fuck. God *damn* it." Then Jacobs pulled off Mellas's helmet, took his canteen out, and poured grape Kool-Aid all over Mellas's face, washing some of the mess away. He kept shaking the canteen, emptying the remaining drops on Mellas's eyes, which were shut tight with black powder, solder, blood, and dirt.

The world again became black for Mellas. He felt the cool stickiness and smelled the sweet grape odor of the Kool-Aid. Then there was the sound of firing and screaming all around him in the darkness. He felt, rather than heard, someone shouting and pulling at his flak jackets and helmet. He tried to move. He couldn't. He tried to open his eyes and finally managed to open one. He saw gray light. The nightmare was continuing. He could not wake up. He wanted to return to oblivion. There were sounds of voices shouting, heard as if underwater. He again came back to the gray light. He knew that he had something to do with or for those voices. He became aware of Jackson lying on top of him, shielding him from fire. He realized that the grenade had been faulty, splitting in two down its soldered seam instead of shattering into deadly pieces. He became aware that Jacobs was shouting over the radio, lying on his back next to him and Jackson, staring upward at the sky, probably talking with Fitch. "Ah, f-fuck, Skipper, I think he's Coors. G-grenade. Right in the face. No c-corpsman. What do I do now? Over."

"Will you get off me?" Mellas said quietly to Jackson. "I can't fucking move."

Jackson rolled off, tangling the handset cord around Mellas's neck, so that the handset was nearly pulled from Jake's hand. This forced Jake to look at Mellas.

Jake saw Mellas open one eye. "J-jesus fuck, Lieutenant," he said in relief. "I thought I was g-going to have to take the platoon."

"Thanks," Mellas said. "It's nice to know you'd miss me." Mellas's face felt raw, as if there were no skin on it. He couldn't open his right eye. He assumed he'd lost it.

He noticed the purple liquid on his hand as he tried to wipe his eyes clean. "I told you I hate fucking Bugs Bunny Grape," he said.

Jackson was looking up the hill. His eyes opened wide. "Oh, fuck," he whispered. "Chi-comm!" A third grenade came bounding down the hill. Jackson and Jacobs pulled Mellas with them, tripping over each other. They hit the dirt as the grenade exploded. A sudden concussion hit them. There was a puff of dirty smoke, and then the smell.

They started to scramble back up toward the hole. Jackson pulled out a grenade and flipped it in a hook shot, arching it over the edge of the lip in front of the hole. It exploded.

They waited a moment. Mellas's head finally cleared.

Again a deadly black canister came sailing over the lip in reply, and the three of them scrambled for safety. Jacobs started parallel to the hill but slipped. He clawed at the steep slope to try to stop his downward momentum. The grenade was sliding down the hill with him. Jacobs cried out in frustration and terror. His fingers raked the muddy clay; his boots churned against the embankment. His eyes grew wide. "I can't f-fucking st-stop!" he cried.

The grenade went off. Mellas and Jackson both turned their faces to the earth. When they turned around again, half of Jacobs's neck was laid open by the shrapnel. They ran down the hill, grabbed him by his shirt and web belt, and dragged him sideways to a tiny depression in the ground, hoping it would give them shelter. Blood was spurting from Jacobs's throat. He was trying to stop it with his hands. Mellas pushed them aside and put his own hand into the long narrow hole, feeling the warm throbbing of the blood, the tiny bubbles of air escaping from

Jacobs's lungs. Jacobs could make no sound. Only his eyes could express the terror of that last moment.

Mellas cried out and shoved his filthy fist hard against the severed carotid artery, trying to stanch the blood. Then the light went from Jacobs's eyes and the terror vanished. Mellas rolled away from him. He looked at Jackson in bewilderment and anguish. Blood dripped from his hand. "Jake? Jake?" he said, questioning, accusing, grieving.

Another chi-comm rolled down the hill. They threw themselves to the ground, and the grenade exploded. They were still alive, for no particular reason. Jackson went yelling up the hill, the heavy radio, seemingly forgotten, on his back. He had a grenade in his right hand and a rifle in the left. Mellas, with sudden clarity, saw the solution. One of them should not duck. He ran to Jackson's left. Jackson hurled the grenade with a moaned curse, then hit the dirt, waiting for it to explode. Mellas did not hit the dirt. He kept running. The grenade went off. Mellas felt invulnerable to it. As the smoke cleared, Mellas threw himself to the ground just at the edge of the lip. A young North Vietnamese soldier pushed his head out of the hole. There was another kid with him, but that one was slumped, inert, against the back wall of the hole. The young NVA soldier pulled another grenade. He cocked his arm back to throw it. Then he saw Mellas's bloodied, blackened face and the rifle pointed squarely at him.

Mellas watched the young man's face change from determination to horror to resignation. Still Mellas did not pull the trigger. "Just don't throw the fucking thing," he whispered, knowing the young North Vietnamese soldier could not hear or understand him. "Just don't throw the fucking thing and I won't shoot. Just give up." But Mellas saw hatred fill the young man's face. That hatred had kept him in his hole, fighting, beyond any possible hope of survival. And even now, Mellas thought, the kid must have guessed that if he didn't throw the grenade Mellas wasn't going to shoot. But he threw the grenade anyway, his lips curling back from his teeth.

Fuck you, then, Mellas thought bitterly as the grenade sailed toward him. He pulled the trigger and the M-16 responded on full automatic. The bullets ripped through the kid's chest and face, blowing the backs of his lungs and brain out. Mellas put his head down on top of his rifle and moaned, "I told you not to throw it, you fucking asshole." The grenade exploded, scattering shrapnel all along Mellas's left side. He was still wearing two flak jackets, so only his buttocks and legs took the jagged metal.

Jackson found him there, still lying on top of his rifle, a few seconds later.

"You all right, Lieutenant?"

Mellas nodded. He painfully rose to a half crouch, using his rifle to push himself up. Marines were gathering beneath the lip of the landing zone. All that remained to be dealt with were a few isolated holes on top, where small groups of North Vietnamese had taken cover.

"They're running!" he heard someone shout. "They're fucking running!"

At last.

His eye felt as if a nail were being hammered into it. His legs were burning. He limped up to the two dead North Vietnamese soldiers who had been throwing grenades at them. They looked about fifteen or sixteen years old. He poked one with his rifle and there was a movement, a twitch. He pulled the trigger, forgetting that he still had his M-16 on automatic, and fired three bullets through the kid's head before he could stop.

His rage was gone, and in its place was an inert, sick weariness. Mellas now knew, with utter certainty, that the North Vietnamese would never quit. They would continue the war until they were annihilated, and he did not have the will to do what that would require. He stood there, looking at the waste.

Below the west ridge, Hamilton's work was just beginning. "They're coming off the hill," he shouted. "Goddamn it, hurry. Let's go!" He and Mole emerged from the jungle onto the defoliated ridge. They threw themselves down, and the rest of the squad scrambled to join them. Hamilton was pointing excitedly at a small group of figures who were trotting in an orderly fashion off Matterhorn. Mole set the bipod of the gun down on the earth. His A gunner crawled next to him holding the long belt of bright copper bullets away from the feeder assembly. Mole began to fire. Two of the figures went down. The others scattered.

"We're getting some, Lieutenant," Hamilton said happily over the radio. He saw a small hillock just in front of them. He tapped Mole on the shoulder. It would be a perfect place to command the entire finger. He stood up and ran, the radio on his back. Mole started after him.

A rocket-propelled grenade slashed violently out of the jungle where the NVA had taken cover. It exploded in front of Hamilton, killing him instantly.

Mole shouted Hamilton's name. He tossed his gun to his A gunner, grabbed Hamilton's body, and dragged it back to their original safe position. The rest of the squad followed him. Mole wasn't about to get his ass killed because some fucker went bloodthirsty on them.

The fight for the LZ moved into its final phase. The south and east slopes were covered with Marines methodically killing anything that moved. Fitch and the CP group were walking up the south slope. Hawke and Connolly, who had captured the NVA machine gun, were covering the exposed northern slope, firing at the retreating enemy with careful short bursts. Three groups of NVA, unable to escape, had set up positions in the old Golf Battery artillery pits. One of the groups had a machine gun that was keeping the Marines at bay, covering the top of the hill with its fire.

Mellas radioed Hawke. "I'm sending a baseball team around to the north to get behind that fucking gun. You'll see character Charlie with a bandage on his head instead of a helmet. Don't shoot his ass. Over." Mellas looked up at Cortell, who was nodding, his filthy bandage unraveling slightly.

"You tell him to pop some smoke when he gets there so we don't shoot him. Over," Hawke returned.

Mellas relayed the message, and Cortell nodded again. Mellas pulled his last smoke grenade from his belt suspender and gave it to Cortell.

There was a sudden explosion nearby. The three of them flinched. There was yelling in Spanish. Amarillo had thrown two grenades into a bunker just below them and was now crawling rapidly inside. There was a brief spatter of shots from his .45. Everyone waited anxiously, watching the entrance of the bunker.

The familiar camouflage of the Marine jungle utility emerged, back first. Amarillo was pulling a shrapnel-mutilated body out of the bunker behind him. The shots had all been fired into the man's skull.

Then a ricochet from the NVA machine gun spun crazily over their heads. "OK, Cortell. Get going," Mellas said.

Cortell crawled off to join his squad. Mellas poked his head above the hole he and Jackson shared with the two dead North Vietnamese boys. He pulled one of the bodies down, stuffed it into the bottom of the hole, and stood on it to get a slightly better view. The LZ was deserted save for Robertson's body, which lay sprawled by the side of the blasted machine-gun bunker.

No trees remained on Matterhorn. The thick bushes that he and Scar had first tumbled into when they arrived were burned away. The entire beautiful hill was shorn, shamed, and empty.

Mellas saw Goodwin poke his head briefly above the lip of the LZ. Goodwin ducked down again when machine-gun and rifle fire from some nearby positions opened up on him. Goodwin radioed Mellas.

"How we gonna get that fucker, Jack?"

Mellas explained that Cortell was working his way behind the position. It would be a matter of time. The remaining enemy were trapped.

Occasionally a Marine would pop up, apparently desultorily, unload half a magazine in the direction of the enemy machine gun, and get back down.

Mellas saw Cortell's red smoke. He stood up, shouting, "Don't shoot. Cease firing. Cease firing." Goodwin did the same.

Cortell's bandaged head appeared momentarily above the crest. The seven kids left in the squad jumped above the lip of the LZ, threw seven grenades at the machine-gun position, and jumped down, out of sight. The gunner started to turn the barrel to meet the new threat. The grenades went off in and around the shallow pit, causing a series of shock waves that hammered Mellas's eardrums.

Immediately Goodwin was rushing across the LZ toward the smoke from the explosions. A stunned NVA soldier struggled to turn the machine gun on Goodwin but couldn't move fast enough. Goodwin, like a panther making a kill, was on top of him, firing his M-16. The remaining NVA in nearby gun pits stood up, weaponless, eyes filled with terror, and raised their hands. They were cut down in seconds as every available weapon on the hill turned on them.

Mellas, still standing on the dead boy's body, slumped his head forward and rested his bloody, stinging face on the cool clay. Jackson leaned back, resting his radio against the side of the hole. "We won," Jackson said.

Mellas simply nodded inside his helmet liner. His helmet was motionless against the clay. He reveled in the feel of the cool earth against his chin and mouth. Soon, however, the wind made his damp utility shirt too cool for comfort. He dragged himself from the hole and started shouting at various fire team leaders to organize the defense in case of a counterattack. Then he remembered Hamilton, waiting in ambush down below.

"Bravo One Three, Bravo One. Sorry I rushed you in so much. Why don't you get up here and set in from eight to ten. Twelve is due north. Over."

There was a long silence.

"One Three, this is One Actual. Did you copy? Over."

Mole's voice came over the radio, trembling. "Character Hotel is Coors. Over."

Mellas's hands started shaking. "Any others? Over."

"We got two minor Oleys. Over."

"Can you get everyone in without help? Over."

"Yeah. Over."

"One out." Mellas handed Jackson the handset.

The hill was theirs.

Jackson leaned over and put his head in his hands.

Mellas limped to the edge of the LZ and watched Mole struggle up the hill with Hamilton slung over his back.

Mole dumped Hamilton at Mellas's feet. "Sorry, sir. I know you was tight." He walked away, leaving Mellas standing over Hamilton's body.

Mellas silently emptied Hamilton's pockets. He found a letter from Hamilton's mother. In it she'd written, "Don't you worry, Buster, you'll be home soon and it will be all over." Mellas hadn't known Hamilton's

nickname was Buster. He felt he had never known Hamilton at all—
and never would know him.

Mellas's left leg throbbed with the shrapnel, and his right leg
burned. Blood caused his trousers to stick. He felt a sharp, pulsing pain
in his blinded eye. If only he could sit down, just sit down and do nothing. But the defenses had to be set in.

He struggled to his feet. An explosion slammed against him. He
hit the dirt, rolling next to Jackson. They both looked up to see greasy
smoke drifting across the LZ. Someone was shouting for a corpsman.
"Mine! A mine," someone shouted from Goodwin's sector. "The place
is fucking mined!"

"Jesus shit," Mellas muttered.

He stood up again. The land around him had become toxic. He
didn't know where to step.

Still, the company had to be set in. Mellas went to his knees, crawling so he could see the signs of a buried mine or trip wire as he went from
hole to hole. The kids, too, just wanted to sit. Mellas joked with them,
cajoled them, threatened them. Eventually they started to dig into the hill,
throwing dead bodies from holes, re-digging half-buried trenches. Others were struggling up the hill with dead Marines or helping to move the
wounded so they could be evacuated. Fitch called for volunteers to clear
a small section of the hilltop for a medevac bird. Soon a line of Marines
formed and slowly crawled across the area with their K-bars in front of
them, probing for mines, watching for trip wires. One kid was blown open
from the abdomen when his knee set off a pressure device his knife had
missed. They threw what remained of him onto the pile.

Fitch called an actuals meeting. Mellas made his way around the
rim of the LZ. Smoke choked and nauseated him. It drifted sluggishly from
the hill to join the heavy gray clouds rolling endlessly away toward Laos.

"Nice work, Mel," Fitch said. He was haggard and drawn. Hawke
and Goodwin were both sitting with their elbows resting on the inside
of their knees. They were staring into space.

"Hamilton got killed," Mellas answered. "He used to carry my
radio." He had no idea why he was talking. He just had to tell someone.
"Is Conman OK?" he asked Hawke.

Hawke nodded.

Fitch looked at Mellas more closely. "You need to be medevaced," he said.

Mellas didn't answer. With his good eye, he was looking across at Helicopter Hill. He saw people with bright green uniforms looking at them through field glasses.

"The fucking bastards cheered," Mellas said very softly.

"Hey," Hawke said, touching Mellas's shoulder. "It's OK. They didn't know."

Relsnik walked over with the radio and gave Fitch the handset. "Big John Six, Skipper," he said.

The colonel's voice was crisp, businesslike. "Roger, Bravo Six. I want a full body count and after-action report. We have your medevac birds standing by. That zone of yours safe yet? Over."

"Not yet. Over," Fitch said flatly.

"Magnificent. I wish I'd had a movie camera, that's all I can say. Big John Six out."

Fitch tossed the handset onto the ground next to Relsnik. "He wishes he'd had a fucking movie camera," he said. He stared across the little dip toward Helicopter Hill.

Mellas followed Fitch's gaze, his mind filled with tumbling images. The company too weary to go on, but going on. Watching helplessly as the bombs fell on the far side of the hill. The stupid cheering—as if combat were a Friday night football game. Simpson's incredible order, on the long march to Sky Cap, that there would be no more medevacs. Hippy, crippled. The insane pushing. The stupidity. The blood pumping from the new machine gunner's leg. Jacobs's throat. For what? Where was the meaning?

Mellas's good eye focused on the little figure in the clean jungle utilities. He saw only the colonel. The 600 meters separating them shrank to nothing. Mellas decided to kill him.

He limped slowly away from the group. "Hey, Jack," Goodwin shouted, but Fitch put a hand on his arm, holding him down. Hawke watched Mellas, a puzzled expression on his face. Mellas walked down the hill through Hawke's lines. He barely acknowledged the greetings of Conman and the Third Platoon as they dug in.

Just beyond the lines, Mellas chambered a round and put the rifle's selector on safety. He pushed into the brush, down onto the finger, moving closer to the other hill, not caring about the danger. He found a log and adjusted his sights for the distance, taking pleasure in the fact that he was doing just what he'd been taught on the rifle range. He settled in. The flat gray morning seemed eternal. Time was meaningless. There was only the small figure of the colonel, high above him now on the defoliated hillside. He pushed the selector to full automatic. With the tracers, Mellas was sure to get him. He leaned over the rifle, twisting his neck sideways so his good eye was sighting down the barrel. The colonel turned away from him. Mellas waited. He wanted the bastard to see the tracers coming at him before they ripped him apart, so he'd know, just as Jacobs had known. The colonel was still talking. Mellas waited as patiently as an animal. Time stopped. Only this one task. Wait for the bastard to turn around so he could see the bullets coming. Then Simpson started to turn.

Mellas heard someone yell hoarsely behind him. Hawke landed on him in a headlong dive, forcing the rifle forward as Mellas jerked the trigger. The bullets tore the earth in front of them. Mellas, in a fury, reached out to hit Hawke. Hawke rolled away, kicking hard, knocking the rifle from Mellas's hands. Mellas swung his fist, hitting Hawke square in the face, and stood up to look for his rifle. Then Hawke was on his feet, standing in front of him, breathing hard, his rifle pointed just to Mellas's side but obviously ready to defend himself.

"Goddamn you, Hawke. Goddamn you to hell!"

Hawke said nothing, watching Mellas, on his guard.

Mellas began shrieking. "That bastard killed all of them. He sent us up here without air so he could watch a show. He watched us while we died. That bastard doesn't deserve to live. God damn you, Hawke. God damn you and your fucking—your—oh, God damn us all." He sank to the ground and stared at nothing.

Hawke put his hand on Mellas's shoulder. "Come on, Mel, the counterattack could hit us any minute."

Mellas followed Hawke back up the hill.

CHAPTER
NINETEEN

The counterattack never materialized. The NVA were heading to Laos, covering their retreat with well-placed infantry and mortar units.

A medevac bird beat its way up the valley, and Pallack talked it in. Three NVA mortar rounds bracketed the chopper, sending the Marines who were dragging the wounded aboard to the ground. They immediately rose and got the wounded aboard and then ran for their holes, holding their helmets against the rotor wash. The helicopter dived off the edge of the LZ and soared downward into space, picking up airspeed. Another bird made it in and took the last of the emergency cases. Then the fog returned. This stopped the shelling, but it also stopped any further medical evacuations.

The day was spent in weary stupefaction, hauling dead American teenagers to a stack beside the landing zone and dead Vietnamese teenagers to the garbage pit down the side of the north face.

The senior squid told Fitch that Mellas's right eye was seriously injured. If the eye wasn't already lost, it would be without immediate surgery. The only place where that could happen was on one of the hospital ships. Mellas told Fitch that with Conman probably needing to take Third Platoon when Hawke went back to battalion staff, he didn't feel comfortable turning First Platoon over to either Jackson or Cortell. No matter how much combat experience they had, they were still only nineteen. Besides, Fitch and Goodwin would be the only officers in the company. In reality, although he didn't say it aloud, Mellas had simply grown too fond of everyone to leave the platoon facing danger without his help. He refused to go. Fitch knew that Mellas was right about the lack of leaders, and as far as he could tell the eye was already lost. So he let Mellas stay.

That evening Mellas and Jackson pulled some splintered plywood over their hole, shivering like two wounded animals in the cold wind that moaned out of Laos. Jackson would occasionally shudder with stifled sobs. Mellas stared with his good eye into the blackness, enduring the pain in his leg and the throbbing in his other eye. He had tried reading the C-ration boxes earlier, and it felt awkward and uncomfortable. He consoled himself by imagining what he would look like in a Hathaway shirt ad. Then the sense of fear and loss coiled up from his stomach where it had lain waiting and he wished fervently that he had taken Sheller's advice and tried to save the eye. He prayed.

Mellas crawled out of the hole to check lines at 2030. He returned at 2230, dragging his leg. At 0030 he started out again.

"I'll go, Lieutenant," Jackson said. "I can keep someone awake just as good as you can." Mellas didn't argue. He immediately dozed off with the radio against his cheek.

Jackson crawled from beneath the plywood into a cold wind. He could sense that the clouds were higher, moving swiftly eastward, even though he couldn't see them. In the blackness around Matterhorn the jungle lay breathing quietly after the convulsive fury of the morning. Jackson felt as if the jungle were resting, preparing to make its own assault on Matterhorn when these destructive insects left it to clean its own wounds. The jungle would slowly creep up the hill, covering it with new green skin, once again sheltering the exposed clay and rock, hiding the garbage thrown down its sides, softening the artificial lip of the LZ, and rounding Matterhorn smooth once again.

Jackson squatted there, close to the solid sleeping earth, feeling its healing powers. Unexpected tears came to his eyes. "Hamilton," he whispered. "I'm sorry. I'm so fucking sorry, man." He was openly weeping now. He knew it was foolish to talk out loud to a dead person, but he felt that he somehow had to apologize to Hamilton for still being alive and so happy about it. Hamilton had wanted to get married and have children. Now he wouldn't and Jackson would.

The burst of crying passed. Jackson stayed there a little longer, feeling the damp wind on his wet face. He wiped his face with his hands, which were hot and cracked from dirt, dehydration, and infection. He couldn't shake off a persistent gnawing anxiety as he crawled away to check the lines. Why did Hamilton die and he live? When he finished checking all the holes, he didn't feel like going back to the hole under the plywood. Something compelled him to climb upward to the deserted LZ.

When Jackson tripped the mine, the explosion jerked Mellas back to the darkness and the cold. At first he thought it might be someone from the CP group. Then he heard Jackson's frightened wild cry. "Help me! God help me! Please—someone help!"

Mellas slung the radio on his back and crawled toward Jackson's voice, whispering "no" over and over. He reached Jackson just after Fredrickson, who was holding Jackson down, trying to get hold of his thighs. Jackson was screaming.

"Help me hold the fucker down, Lieutenant," Fredrickson said. "Goddamn it, Jackson, stop moving."

Mellas lay down over Jackson's heaving chest, whispering, "You're going to be all right, Jackson. You're going to be all right."

"Sheller," Fredrickson shouted to the senior squid, who was already crawling through the blackness. "I need some goddamned IV fluid and something to cut off these arteries." Sheller appeared with a bottle and IV tubes as well as his kit. While Fredrickson was doing what he could to stanch the bleeding, Sheller jabbed a catheter into Jackson's arm and held the glass of fluid as high in the air as he could. Jackson calmed down, his terror and panic diminishing as the two corpsmen got his faltering system working again. Mellas glanced down Jackson's body. Fredrickson was working on pulp below Jackson's knees. There were no feet.

"You're going to be all right, Jackson," Mellas kept repeating. "You're going to be all right." Jackson moaned and passed out.

Mellas didn't pray, but his mind once again soared above the landing zone, seeing all of I Corps below him, and went looking for something better than God—a good chopper pilot.

* * *

At the MAG-39 airfield just outside Quang Tri, First Lieutenant Steve Small was losing at acey-deucey to his copilot, Mike Nickels. It seemed to Small that the present game of acey-deucey had never started and never ended. It was as much part of life at MAG-39 as the sand, sweaty flight suits, ten-cent bourbon, gritty sheets, guilty masturbation fantasies, crappy movies, and underlying anxiety that the next flight was the one where the gook .51 was going to rip a hole right up your anus and out of your mouth.

Small's CH-46 waited in the dark, its twin rotor blades drooping with their own weight. Crew members dozed on canvas stretchers amid machine-gun ammunition and boxes of IV fluid. Small's chest armor, hanging from his shoulders, seemed heavier than usual. Maybe he had overdone it at the O-club. On the other hand maybe he hadn't drunk enough. He'd flown that damned bird so many hours it didn't make any difference if he flew it fucked up or not. The thing seemed to fly itself. Its whirling blades and sickening lunges entered his dreams at night, along with its beauty when it slipped off a mountaintop or slid in to a perfect landing in a small zone, the grunts grinning at him, rushing up to get their goodies, or staring dull-eyed in relief as they threw on board what remained of their friends.

The ready-room radio squawked, and the man on watch put down his hot rod magazine to answer it. Small and Nickels listened tensely. Small checked his watch. It was 0217. No hope of daylight. Big John Bravo again. One Emergency. Matterhorn. Weather terrible. The same fuckers that had carved out that goddamn canary perch on Sky Cap. The same dumb sons of bitches he'd flat-hatted over all of western Quang Tri Province to take that crazy redheaded grunt lieutenant and his overloaded replacements up to the biggest shit sandwich he'd seen in almost ten months of combat flying. And the bastards were still at it. Jesus fucking Christ, he thought. Then he wondered why the Christian deity was so much more satisfying as a swearword than the Jewish deity of his childhood. It had all started when he found out that Art Buchwald was in the Fourth Marine Aircraft Wing in World War II. What was he fucking thinking? All this was running through his head as he and Nickels ran for the door. There was no question of not trying.

Their running steps awoke the crew. Small immediately began going through start-up procedures while Nickels radioed for artillery clearance so they wouldn't get shot out of the air on their way past the big Army 175s at VCB and the eight-inchers firing night missions out of Red Devil.

The engines whined. The blades turned clumsily. Instruments glowed in front of the two pilots. Small taxied out onto the runway. The fuselage trembled; the roar increased to the point where only the radios inside their helmets could be heard. The bird moved forward in the darkness and lifted gently from the earth. Stray lights rapidly grew dim behind them in the mist, then disappeared. They were in total blackness save for the dim green glow of the instrument panel.

Small was sweating but not from heat. It was going to be a pisser.

He got a bearing from Nickels and settled in at 6,000 feet. Black clouds obscured the sky above him. Below, unseen but clear in his imagination from countless daylight missions, were the plains with their elephant grass, bamboo, and slow sluggish rivers. Then came the mountains.

"Try and get Bravo up on their company push," Small told Nickels over the intercom. He was straining to catch a glimpse of anything familiar, to let him know how close to the ground he was—how close to death.

"Big John Bravo, Big John Bravo, this is Chatterbox One Eight. Over." Silence. Maybe the stupid grunts didn't know that Group had changed the call from Magpie, standard operating procedure to keep gook intelligence guessing. Small didn't like Chatterbox. It sounded too cute. He didn't feel cute.

"Big John Bravo, Big John Bravo, Chatterbox One Eight. Over."

There was a burst of static. "They must be able to hear us," Nickels said. "Too weak to reach us on their company push."

Small looked at a dog-eared card on a clipboard strapped to his leg. He dialed to the battalion frequency, knowing that the battalion operator would probably have the big aerial up. "Big John Bravo, Chatterbox One Eight. Over."

Relsnik's voice, amplified by the Two-Niner-Two antenna, came out of the blackness into the helmets of the two pilots. "Chatterbox, this is Big John Bravo. We got you Loco Cocoa. How you? Over." Small smiled at hearing Loco Cocoa for loud and clear. That was new to him. Lemon and Coke last week. Lickety Clit two weeks before.

"I got you fine. I don't know where in hell you are. Over."

"We're on Matterhorn, sir. Over."

Small cursed under his breath. Goddamn kids on the fucking radios. Where was the goddamn FAC-man? He took a deep breath to control his temper and fear. "I know you're on Matterhorn, Bravo. I mean I can't *see* you. It's fucking dark up here. Turn on a goddamn light."

There was a long pause. A new voice came up on the radio. "Chatterbox, this is Bravo Six. We've been taking mortar fire all day and we're a little reluctant to light fires. Over."

Well, I'm a little reluctant to fly fucking blind in the goddamned mountains, Small thought to himself. He knew Bravo had had the shit beat out of it lately. "What's your ceiling like there? And where's your FAC? Over." There was another pause. Leave it to a fucking grunt to have no idea how high the clouds were.

The answer was more like a question. "Hundred and fifty feet, Chatterbox? Over."

"Fuck."

Inside the dimly lit bubble the two pilots looked at each other. One hundred fifty feet at 100 miles an hour took less than a second.

Fitch's voice came over the radio. "We got your sound, Chatterbox. You're to our Sierra Echo. Bearing one-four-zero. Can you come up on the company freak? Over."

"Roger. See you there. Over."

Small immediately corrected the helicopter's direction and twisted knobs back to Bravo's frequency, clearing the battalion net for other traffic.

They got back in contact again. "You give me a mark when I pass overhead. OK?" Small radioed. "How am I doing for course? Over."

"Still to our Sierra Echo," Fitch returned. "Keep coming. Over."

The bubble vibrated green and red in the darkness. Small pictured an imaginary Bravo Six, somewhere below him, in a muddy hole, straining to hear the faint lawnmower rattle that meant life or death for a wounded grunt. The radio spat out "Mark!" Small banked immediately but saw only blackness.

"I didn't see a fucking thing, Bravo. Over," Small radioed back, already straightening the bird to horizontal and coming back toward the place where he had heard "mark," all the while watching his altimeter and his roll and pitch indicator. "How high above you do you think we were? Over."

Again the long pause. Again the tentative answer. "Six hundred feet? Over."

"We got any other fucking mountains to worry about around here?" Small snapped to Nickels.

Nickels answered immediately. "Dong Sa Mui at fifty-one hundred feet. About two klicks to the northeast. Other than that, Matterhorn's about it for four klicks."

Small muttered under his breath.

He asked the grunts to try artillery illumination rounds. They lit up only the fog.

"What the fuck's wrong with your emergency case, Bravo? Over," Small asked, almost absently, as he was trying to think what to do.

"He's got both his legs blown off. Over."

Why even bother?

"I can't find you fuckers without any lights on the LZ. Isn't there some way you can hide some? Over."

Again the silence. "We could put some heat tabs in helmets. Over."

Jesus, a fucking grunt that could think. A fucking miracle. "Good. Put them in a twenty-meter circle. You got it? Ten meters radius, exactly. Otherwise I won't know how far above the fucking thing I am. Over."

There was a wait. Then Bravo Six came up again. "Chatterbox, it'll have to be thirteen and a half meters diameter. The rest of the area is mined and we can't guarantee it." There was a pause and blip of static as Fitch let up on the key. Then he was back. "But if you want to risk it, we'll risk making the circle. Over."

Small switched over to the intercom and spoke to Nickels. "Mined? Can you believe this fucking shit? They want me to hit the top of a fucking mountain in the dark, in the fucking fog, and the goddamned LZ is *mined*? And all this to get some poor bastard that probably would rather be dead anyway. At least I would. Jesus Christ. Both fucking legs."

"Better than both balls."

"I ain't so sure. What's he going to do back home? Fuck cantaloupes for the rest of his life?" Small was trying to imagine what thirteen and a half meters would look like compared with twenty, and trying to get that into his head so if he did see it he could guess how high above the LZ he was.

"OK, Bravo. Don't risk the mines, but get the fucking circle made. I don't have all night. And when I say pop a Willy Pete, I don't care if they mortar the fuck out of you, you pop a goddamned Willy Pete. You got one? Over."

Bravo Six said they did.

They collected heat tabs from all over the company and placed their helmets in a circle around Jackson and the two corpsmen. When the pilot gave the word, China and Conman ran from helmet to helmet with cigarette lighters, igniting the heat tabs. A blue circle of light, ghostly in the fog, grew around Jackson, the helmets hiding the flickering blue flame from all directions except directly above.

The huge helicopter rushed in just a few feet above their heads. The rotor wash tipped over two of the helmets, and dark figures rushed to hide the two heat tabs, throwing them back in with bare hands.

Mellas heard the pilot mutter over the radio. "Jesus Christ, Bravo. I'm right on top of you fuckers. OK, coming around. Get that man ready. I got your heat tabs. Over."

"Can you believe this, Nickels?" Small said, switching to the intercom. "I actually said 'I got your heat tabs.'" Holy shit, he thought to himself, thirteen and a half meters.

"OK, Bravo, coming around," he radioed. "You pop that Willy Pete when I tell you. Over." Small looked over his shoulder into the blackness behind the chopper, but the dim circle was lost in the clouds again. Totally blind, he felt, more than he piloted, the big bird around to come at the LZ again, keeping that faint picture of glowing blue in his mind. He straightened the chopper out slowly and came back down to the same altimeter reading. He changed the pitch and attitude. The helicopter roared alone in the blackness.

Suddenly, like a marsh ghost, a quavering blue oblong appeared, moving fast, too fast, changing to a circle, changing too fucking fast, too fucking fast. "Now, goddamn it. Now," Small yelled.

"Now," Fitch shouted, and Pallack popped the spoon on the white phosphorous grenade and threw it into the zone. Sudden brilliant white light stabbed at the men's eyes. The huge whirling black mass crashed into the zone with an anguished screech of buckling metal. The front wheels gave way and the bird lurched sideways, nosing in, pivoting on the buckled wheels, twisted by the torque of its blades. Then it lurched sideways and came to a stop, its tailgate jammed.

The crew chief came crawling out over the barrel of a .50-caliber machine gun, shouting. The litter bearers hoisted Jackson in through the narrow opening, handing the plasma bottle to the side gunner. Fredrickson and Sheller, seeing Jackson safely inside, scrambled back and dropped to the mud as the blades of the chopper gained speed. Fredrickson picked up two bloody objects and threw them through the side opening: Jackson's boots, his feet still in them.

Then the mortar shells started homing in on the burning phosphorous. The helicopter skimmed across the landing zone and disappeared, falling downhill into the darkness. "Get off the top of the fucking hill," Fitch shouted, unnecessarily. Everyone was running for cover. Conman tried to extinguish the burning phosphorous. It broke into smaller pieces and he screamed in pain when one of them burned a tiny hole into his leg. It went through the muscle and didn't stop until it reached the bone.

Mellas spent the rest of the night trying to understand why Jackson had lost both legs while he himself seemed to bounce from near miss to near miss. He felt that somehow he had cheated. Then he laughed softly. What was he supposed to do, stand up and get blown away to make things up to the dead and the maimed?

He thought of the jungle, already regrowing around him to cover the scars they had created. He thought of the tiger, killing to eat. Was that evil? And ants? They killed. No, the jungle wasn't evil. It was indifferent. So, too, was the world. Evil, then, must be the negation of something man had added to the world. Ultimately, it was caring about something that made the world liable to evil. Caring. And then the caring gets torn asunder. Everybody dies, but not everybody cares.

It occurred to Mellas that he could create the possibility of good or evil through caring. He could nullify the indifferent world. But in so doing he opened himself up to the pain of watching it get blown away. His killing that day would not have been evil if the dead soldiers hadn't been loved by mothers, sisters, friends, wives. Mellas understood that in destroying the fabric that linked those people, he had participated in evil, but this evil had hurt him as well. He also understood that his participation in evil was a result of being human. Being human was the best he could do. Without man there would be no evil. But there was also no good, nothing moral built over the world of fact. Humans were responsible for it all. He laughed at the cosmic joke, but he felt heartsick.

The next morning Mellas crawled from his hole to make his round of the perimeter. He went from hole to hole, kidding, trying to lighten everyone up. He poked fun at Conman for trying to handle burning phosphorous with his bare hands. Conman flipped him the bird and looked pleased that Mellas was acknowledging his sacrifice. Some of the kids began to open C-rations with the tiny can openers that hung with their dog tags. Others brewed coffee. Several were digging a hole to shit in away from the lines.

All around Mellas the ridges and peaks stood clearly against the lightening sky. The jungle in the valley below him was no different from when he'd first arrived: silent, gray-green, at once ancient and ageless. But it was no longer a mystery. It contained rivers that he'd waded across and fought in. There were also hilltops whose approaches and slightest contours he knew intimately, and bamboo patches, beaten down and forced back, already starting to rise again. And there was a trail, now beginning to grow over, soon to disappear. It was another ordinary day in the world of fact. But it was different because the mystery had been slightly penetrated and Mellas saw things differently.

He stopped at the CP to find out about Jackson. Fitch said he was still alive.

Four Phantoms roared across the top of the hill, shattering the dawn with noise, just as artillery fire erupted in the valley to the northwest. "That's the prep for Speeding Home Kilo," Fitch murmured to no one in particular. Soon, four CH-46s circled into the valley to the north. Everyone in the CP group listened in on Kilo's frequency as the lead platoon commander reported a cool zone.

"D'gooks are making fucking hat," Pallack announced. Everyone smiled. Mellas guessed, however, that Kilo's job would be to sit astride the escape routes. They'd be busy soon enough.

Hawke joined them and Fitch passed his coffee around the circle. They decided to build a new LZ out of sight of the NVA observers, between Matterhorn and Helicopter Hill, to evacuate the walking wounded like Mellas. Mellas gave Conman the platoon and was helped down the hill to the new zone, where he collapsed.

He lay there semiconscious. Anne floated through his mind, and he awoke to feel the hidden sun on his face, or the cool mist—and to an emptiness and a longing for her unlike any he'd ever felt. But he knew it was useless to think of getting back together, and that was months in the future anyway. There were white girls in Sydney. Round-eyes. Maybe he'd go to the outback. A quiet farm with sheep. Maybe he'd fall in love there. Maybe he'd save his eye. Everything seemed to be part of a cycle as he stared into the gray nothingness above him, hearing the wash of distant waves on a warm beach, feeling the sun pulling his body upward like evaporating rain.

Then he remembered Vancouver's sword, still in the CP bunker on Helicopter Hill. He got two of the walking wounded to come with him for security.

Stevens was on watch in the little bunker. A work party was just finishing a larger bunker for the CP group. Mellas could see the colonel and the Three talking with Bainford, looking at something off to the north, their maps out. He nodded to Stevens in the gloom, crawled over to the corner, and pulled out the sword.

"That yours, Mellas?" Stevens asked in amazement.

Mellas eyed him for a long moment. "I don't know," he finally said. "I really don't know."

"Yeah. OK," Stevens said. "You guys did a hell of a job yesterday."

Looking at Stevens with one eye made Mellas aware that he had taken seeing for granted. Now, this way, he saw Stevens differently from before. He couldn't get mad at Stevens for the comment. Stevens was just Stevens, a cog in the machinery, trying to be nice. And Mellas was just Mellas, another cog, deciding not to get angry. He didn't much like being a cog, but there it was. He smiled at his silent conversation. "Thanks," Mellas said.

He returned to the new LZ and fell asleep with the sword beside him.

Someone was kicking his boot. Mellas opened his good eye. He was flooded with ugly anger at being disturbed.

It was McCarthy. Alpha Company was winding through the small landing zone. "Wake up, you silly fucker," McCarthy said. "It took me forever to find you with that goddamned bandage wrapped around your face."

Mellas, smiling, reached a hand up to McCarthy. McCarthy's radio operator was smoking impatiently. "Where the fuck you going?" Mellas asked.

"West. Two Twenty-Four set up a blocking position right on the Z at the Laos end of the valley. We'll be the hammer. Charlie Company's kicking off to our north right now. They're pulling you guys out this afternoon." He paused. "You guys had a rough time, didn't you?"

"Yeah," Mellas agreed. "Nothing unusual, though. 'Light casualties' I believe it's called back in the world. All you have to do is report it as a battalion action and the percentage lost thins to nothing. Who's going to hold Matterhorn?"

"Why should you care? You'll be skating on board the *Sanctuary*, dazzling round-eyed nurses. Maybe we'll get in another mystery tour when this fucking op's over."

"Who's holding fucking Matterhorn?" Mellas demanded, rising to his elbows, his good eye beginning to spasm.

McCarthy shrugged. "No one," he said.

Mellas sank back to the ground and lay looking at the sky. No one. Finally he spoke. "Be careful, Mac."

"Don't worry about me," McCarthy said.

Mellas looked at him. They both knew McCarthy was going into a fight that afternoon, the same day Mellas was leaving it all. It was another cycle, another wearying, convulsive rhythm, and if it wasn't Mellas it was McCarthy, and if not McCarthy someone like McCarthy, forever and forever, like an image in facing mirrors in a barbershop, deeper and deeper, smaller and smaller, curving with time and distance away into the unknown, but always repeating, always the same. Mellas thought that if he could smash one of those mirrors, then this agony would stop and he'd be left alone to dream. But the mirrors were only thoughts, illusions. Reality was McCarthy, standing above him, a friendly face, his radioman impatient to get going because they'd have to hump extra fast to catch up with the rest of the platoon.

"Good luck," Mellas said.

McCarthy waved and trudged after his radio operator. He turned and waved again. Mellas kept thinking, Don't get killed, damn you, don't let yourself get killed.

CHAPTER
TWENTY

The medevac helicopter flew eastward. It flashed across a white beach and then out over the South China Sea. Eventually a white ship with large red crosses on its superstructure and hull appeared below. The chopper tilted back, its blades pounding the air, and set down on the deck. Corpsmen ran inside and hauled the wounded out on stretchers. A nurse in fatigues was holding a clipboard, looking at medevac tags and wounds. She was rapidly sorting the wounded into groups. The most severely wounded were being shoved to the side as the less wounded were stripped of weapons, boots, and clothes and rushed into the interior of the ship.

The nurse grabbed for Mellas's tag, not really looking at him. "I'm all right," he said. "Those guys over there are a lot worse off than I am."

"You let me run triage, Marine." She looked up at his bandages. She had a coarse, red face, small eyes that seemed sleep-deprived, and heavy eyebrows. She wore her hair in two short stiff pigtails. "Most likely to survive go first," she said. Mellas realized that the idea was to maximize the number of men who could return to combat.

"What's this?" she asked, pointing at Vancouver's sword.

"It's a friend of mine's."

"All weapons, Marine," she said, motioning for the sword.

"I'm a lieutenant."

"Sor-*ry*," came the sarcastic reply. "Look, *Lieutenant*. I'm busy. All weapons—even stupid souvenirs."

"The fuck it's a souvenir."

"What did you say, Marine? You know you're talking to a lieutenant in the United States Navy, don't you?" That rank was the equivalent of a Marine captain.

"Yes, ma'am." Mellas gave her a sloppy nonregulation salute, his hand curved over limply. "How do I know I'll get it back?" he asked, still holding the salute, waiting for her to return it.

The nurse glared at him. Then she shouted over her shoulder, "Bell, take this man's weapon."

"I told you—"

"You obey orders, Lieutenant, or I'll have your ass on report." She moved off to the next man, reading his medevac tag, writing on her clipboard.

Bell, a hospital corpsman, came over and took the sword. He looked at it appraisingly.

"How do I know I'll get it back?" Mellas asked again.

"You pick it up when you get orders back ashore, sir."

"I want a receipt."

"Sir, you're holding up the process. We got Twenty-Fourth Marines in the shit and—"

"I'm *in* the Twenty-Fourth Marines. I want a fucking receipt."

"We don't have any receipt forms for swords, Lieutenant. It'll go with the rifles. It'll be all right."

"I've had three of my men pay for their goddamn rifles because some fucker in the Navy sold them to the gooks. I want a receipt and I want it now."

Bell looked around for help. He spotted the nurse and went over to her. Mellas saw her set her lips tight, then say something to Bell. Bell returned. "You'll have to wait, sir. The lieutenant says she's busy."

When the last stretcher disappeared inside the ship, the nurse walked over toward Mellas, holding herself rigid. "Now what's the problem, Lieutenant?"

"Ma'am, the lieutenant would like a receipt for the lieutenant's *weapon*, ma'am."

"A receipt. I see." She looked down at her clipboard. "Mellas, Second Lieutenant, Bravo Company, First Battalion Twenty-Fourth Marine Regiment. Correct?"

"Yes, ma'am," Mellas replied.

"I'm going to issue you a direct order, Second Lieutenant Mellas, with HM-1 Bell as a witness. If the order isn't obeyed, I'm going to place you under arrest for disobeying a direct order. Is that perfectly clear?"

"Yes, ma'am," Mellas said tightly.

"Lieutenant Mellas, give your weapon, that sword, to HM-1 Bell and get your ass down to the officers' ward. If you're not moving in ten seconds I'm placing you under arrest. As it is, I'm putting you on report for disrupting triage."

Mellas knew when the machinery had him. He gave Bell the sword.

In the officers' ward another corpsman collected Mellas's reeking uniform, but Mellas wouldn't let him take the boots. He tied them to the end of the bed and glared at the corpsman. When he felt the boots were safe, he found a basin, filled it with warm water, and with a deep sigh put both feet into it. Sometime later he was brought back to reality by the voice of another corpsman. "Debriding, Lieutenant," he said. Mellas reluctantly removed his feet from the basin.

They put him on a gurney and wheeled him deeper inside the ship. There they gave him a local anesthetic and he watched them pick metal, dirt, and cloth from his legs, snip off dead flesh, then clean and rebandage the shrapnel wounds. "The rest will come out on its own," the surgeon said, already looking at the next problem on the list, wiping his hands. A corpsman wheeled Mellas back to his bed. He had to wake Mellas up to get him into it.

He jerked awake, his heart pounding, upon hearing his name. He took a gulp of air and searched frantically for danger with his good eye. A nurse with red hair whose name tag read "Elsked, K. E." was standing over him. Like the triage nurse, she wore the twin bars of a Navy lieutenant. She was curt. "You're due in the operating room in five minutes, Lieutenant." She looked at his bandaged legs. "Can you walk or do you need help?"

"Whatever's efficient," Mellas answered. He crawled out of the bed and walked, his legs stiff. She led the way down the passage, turning occasionally to see how far behind he was.

Mellas watched her every move, noticing her hips and the outline of her bra strap beneath the crisp white synthetic material of her dress. He longed to catch up to her and touch her, make contact with someone soft, someone who smelled clean and fresh, someone warm. He wanted to talk to someone who knew how he felt, who could talk to the lost, lonely part of him. He wanted a woman.

The nurse directed two corpsmen to arrange Mellas on an operating table. She wouldn't look him in the eye. Mellas regretted being sent to this place, where his sudden flood of longing had no possibility of fulfillment. She thinks all I want to do is stick it in her, he thought bitterly. Of course I do, but there's so much more. He laughed aloud.

"What's so funny?" one of the corpsmen asked, moving a huge machine that hung from a track overhead. He positioned it carefully over Mellas's face.

"Between the emotion and the response, the desire and the spasm, falls the shadow," Mellas said. He attempted a smile.

The red-haired nurse turned to look at him intently.

They held him down by the shoulders and an older doctor came in. He peered into Mellas's eye and injected a local anesthetic next to it. The nurse washed the eye, cleaning out the dirt and powder that had mixed with the ointment that Fredrickson had shoved into it. A piece of shrapnel had laid open Mellas's eyelid. Another piece had gone into the skin just above the bridge of his nose, stopping against the skull. Mellas was tense with fear of what was coming. He looked up at a large black machine on tracks above him. It had large thick glass lenses and a stainless steel needle about six inches long that narrowed to a very fine point. The machine started to glow through the lenses, which magnified the doctor's eyes, peering back at him. Then the lenses covered the brilliant light, and the light seemed to penetrate Mellas's brain. The steel needle came out of the haze of light, and the doctor moved dials that moved the needle. The redheaded nurse's hands pressed down on Mellas's forehead and chest. The needle went into Mellas's eye. He held on to the gurney and tried not to scream.

Bit by bit, the chips and flakes of the defective hand grenade were picked from Mellas's eye. Then the surgeon put two stitches in the eyelid.

"You're incredibly lucky, Lieutenant," the doctor said. He was already pulling off his mask. "Two of those slivers were just microns from severing the optic nerve. You'd have lost your eye." He pushed the machine back. "You won't see normally for a week or so. Keep a patch on it for a while, but you'll be able to return to your unit in about a week." He turned and began washing his hands. Mellas felt as if he'd just been notified of his own hanging.

He was wheeled back and he slept.

When Mellas awoke he climbed out of the stiff sheets and hobbled to the passageway. The cold steel beneath his feet vibrated from the ship's engines. He hailed a passing corpsman and asked where the enlisted men were. He was pointed in the right direction and limped off. He found Jackson in a ward with about a dozen other wounded Marines, all hooked up to IV bottles. Jackson was awake, staring at the wall, propped up against the headboard with a blanket over his legs. There were no bumps at the end of the blanket.

Mellas suddenly didn't want Jackson to see him. He wanted to walk away and blot Jackson from his mind.

A corpsman came up to Mellas. "Can I help you, uh . . ."

"Lieutenant," Mellas finished for him. "I'd like to see one of my men."

"Sir, we're not supposed to have visitors except between fourteen and sixteen hundred hours. These guys are still pretty critical."

Mellas looked at the corpsman. "Doc, he was my radioman."

"If one of the fucking nurses comes in, I ain't covering for you," the man said and stepped aside.

Mellas approached the bed. Jackson turned his head slightly, then looked away.

"Hi, Jackson. How you doing?"

"How the fuck you think?"

Mellas took a breath and nodded his head. He didn't know what to say. It was clear that Jackson didn't want to see him.

"Look, Lieutenant, just get the fuck out of here."

Other Marines, who'd been half-listening from nearby beds, went back to reading or fiddling with the tie strings on their light blue pajamas.

Mellas, also in pajamas, standing alone, felt suddenly naked. He seemed to be a petitioner at Jackson's stumps. "Jackson?"

Jackson turned his head again, looking coolly at Mellas.

"Jackson, I . . ." Mellas tried to keep some dignity, not wanting to break down in front of everyone. "Jackson, I'm sorry it happened to you."

Jackson turned back to the bulkhead. Then his lips started to quiver. "I lost my legs," he said, his voice shaking. He started to moan. "I lost my legs." He turned to Mellas. "Who's going to fuck someone with no legs?" His voice rose and he broke down completely. "Who's going to fuck a goddamned watermelon?"

Mellas backed away a couple of steps, shaking his head, feeling he'd done something wrong for still being whole, for having collapsed, for letting Jackson do the hole-checks. He wanted forgiveness, but there was none. Jackson was now thrashing back and forth, shouting. Corpsmen rushed to hold him down, and one shot a needle into his thigh. "You better get out of here, Lieutenant," the corpsman said.

Mellas limped into the passageway. He listened to Jackson's muffled screaming until the drug took effect; then he walked slowly back to the officers' ward.

He slept and slept, waking up only for meals. When he finally had enough courage to visit Jackson again, he found someone else in the bed. Jackson had been flown to Japan.

Between bandage changes Mellas took long showers, ignoring the Navy's plea to take short ones. Then he slept some more. He occasionally saw the nurse from triage. They studiously avoided each other. He also saw the red-haired nurse coming into and out of the ward. He couldn't help watching her. To his displeasure, she seemed to be on good terms with the triage nurse.

He tried to engage the red-haired nurse in conversation, but it was clear that she was on duty and had little time for it. She was polite and would occasionally give him a warm smile after checking on his eye. Soon they were having short conversations. He found out she, too, was from a small town, but in New Hampshire, and that they both used to like to pick blackberries. Although he was grateful for the brief conversations, what he wanted was to have her enfold him in her arms and hold him so tightly that it would be as if they had crawled inside each other. It wasn't to be.

Within a couple of days his wounds were no longer bleeding and he was asked if he wanted to eat his meals in the officers' mess. He accepted.

He walked hesitantly into the polished wooden interior wearing his old boots, fresh jungle utilities, and a gold second lieutenant's bar on one collar. Filipino mess men were putting the final touches on tablecloths. The tables were set with gleaming silver and white china. Mellas looked down at his scarred boots against the carpeted deck. One of the Filipinos motioned him toward a table for eight with four lighted candles as a centerpiece. He sat down. The chairs around the table filled with nurses, seven in all.

Mellas's heart hammered with joy at sitting next to these women. He tried to contain his excitement by rubbing his hands over the tablecloth. Several of the nurses tried to talk with him, but he couldn't respond intelligently. He was struck dumb. All he could do was stuff food in his mouth, look at them, and laugh. They were talking about commissaries in Manila and Sasebo, and about leaves in Taipei or Kuala Lumpur. Some made innuendos about male officers while the others giggled.

Mellas wanted to touch them. He wanted to reach out across the table and put his hand over their hearts and on their breasts. He wanted to put his head on their shoulders, smell their skin, and absorb their femininity.

But they were older than he was, and they outranked him. They were also uncomfortable, assuming that he was horny. This was true, but it was not the whole story. Eventually their talk among themselves became less awkward, eddying around and over him, ignoring the problems and opportunities caused by the fact that they were women and he was a man. Finally they made their excuses and left Mellas alone. The Filipino stewards cleared the tables. One brought him fresh coffee.

He saw someone getting up from a chair across the room. It was the red-haired nurse. She seemed to hesitate, then walked over to Mellas's table.

"Mind if I sit down?" she asked.

"Please do," Mellas answered. He tried to think of a joke about the empty chairs around him but couldn't.

"How's the eye?" She sat down and leaned closer to him, inspecting the bandage.

"OK."

"You like coffee, huh?" she asked. She smiled warmly. She had let down her hair from where it usually sat on the top of her head. It reached almost to her shoulders.

Mellas opened up like a flower. He found himself telling her every detail of how to make coffee with C-4 explosives. They both talked about home, about growing up in small towns. She kidded him about paraphrasing Eliot just before the eye operation, but then she said, "Somehow I felt that I was the shadow."

Mellas cleared his throat and scraped his boots on the rug beneath his chair. "Well, not exactly. I mean you were part of it. You really want to know?"

"Sure." She smiled as if to say, We're all grown-ups here.

"Out in the bush," he said, "it's first the bang and then the whimper. Then you end up here and it's all whimper and no bang." He immediately regretted this attempt at being clever.

"Not so funny," she said.

"You're right," Mellas said. "Sorry." He paused. "I just get tired of being politely treated like a sex offender."

"You think we don't get tired of every kid that comes mooning in here out of the jungle, desperate for it?"

"'It' being sex."

"I didn't think it was necessary for me to spell it out for you."

"No, I can spell real good. Listen. S-E-X. Right?"

She smiled sarcastically. "Clever."

"Yeah. Clever." He looked at his coffee mug. "It's what every red-blooded American tiger wants, isn't it?" He cocked his head, looking at her. He saw Williams, slung from a pole. "It's only natural, right?"

"Sure," the nurse said, not unkindly.

The calm, kind way she said "sure" made Mellas realize he was talking with an actual human being who cared. It defused his anger at being perceived as a threat and at his own failure to tell her that he just wanted to make friends. He stared at his mug.

She sat back and looked at him somewhat quizzically.

"They know they can't have s-e-x because enlisted men don't fuck officers," Mellas said. "Maybe all they want is someone to be a woman around them instead of fake men with fake-men talk. They just want a real woman to smile at them and talk to them as though they were real people instead of animals."

"You'd see it differently if you were in our shoes," she said.

"And you'd see it differently if you were in ours," Mellas replied.

"There it is," she said. She looked him in the eye and smiled warmly. "Look, I wasn't trying to be prissy." He noticed that her own eyes were green.

Mellas could see that she was trying to connect with him. He melted and smiled back.

"You've got to understand what we do here," she said. She started to reach her hand toward him on the table, but checked it and put both hands on her coffee cup instead. "We fix weapons." She shrugged. "Right now you're a broken guidance system for forty rifles, three machine guns, a bunch of mortars, several artillery batteries, three calibers of naval guns, and four kinds of attack aircraft. Our job is to get you fixed and back in action as fast as we can."

"I know. I just don't feel very much like a weapon right now."

"How often do you think I feel like a mechanic?" she shot back. Then she softened. "It's not why I became a nurse." She put her palms to the sides of her forehead and rested her elbows on the table. "I *do* get so tired of it all." She looked up at him, no longer a Navy nurse, just an exhausted young woman. "There's too many kids coming on board," she finally said. "They're lonesome. They're in pain. They're scared of dying." She paused. "We can only patch the bodies. For all the other"— she searched for a word—"stuff, well, we try to keep our distance. It isn't easy."

"There it is," Mellas said. She was stirring up all the feelings he'd had when the meal started. He was afraid he'd say something wrong and she would leave, so he said nothing.

She broke the silence. "They're sending you back to the bush, aren't they?"

Mellas nodded.

She sighed. "It's like I do my job well, and the result is sending you back to combat."

"Kind of a bind."

"Nothing like going back to the bush."

Mellas smiled at her again. He felt understood. He felt that he could talk with her.

"It's different this time," he said. "I know what I'm in for." He swallowed, looked up, and then exhaled briefly. "I'm afraid to go back." He looked at her, worried that he may have overstepped a boundary, revealed too much. He ran his open palm over his unbandaged eye, shutting out the soft light of the wardroom. Images flooded in: stiff twisted bodies, the terror on Jacobs's face, a leg pumping blood.

"Remember that feeling you got picking blackberries?" he asked. "You know, with friends, and maybe somebody's grandmother who's come along and she's going to make pie when you get home, and the air's so warm it's like Mother Nature is baking bread."

She nodded, smiling. "I remember."

"There used to be a great patch," Mellas continued, "near the garbage dump of this little logging town where I grew up." He smoothed the tablecloth. She waited for him to continue. "It's like a car suddenly roars down on you with six beefy guys in it. You stand there next to this old kind woman with your berry bucket in your hand and you're suddenly a little scared. All the guys have been drinking. Their faces are covered with masks. They have rifles. One takes the berry buckets and throws them down on the side of the road. They shove you around. Then they take you to the dump, laughing a little, as if they're expecting some fun. You're instructed that you're all going to play a game. Here's the rules." Mellas carefully pressed a butter knife into the white tablecloth. "The men, that is the boys, have to crawl through the dump from one end to the other. Whenever we come across a can whose lid we cannot see, we must pick it up and show it to the men with the rifles. If the can turns out to be empty, we can continue. If it turns up unopened, then we get killed. We get down in the garbage. The dump always has a fire smoldering. The smoke makes you puke and cough. The old grandma's job consists of bringing water to any of us who come up with a pleasing or clever way of revealing the can. We even get ribbons if we're particularly clever. Of course, if we refuse to pick up any cans, then we have to stay crawling in the garbage forever, or at least until the strange men . get tired of their fucking game."

Mellas had to force the last sentences out between clenched teeth. He was bending the butter knife against the table, his knuckles white. "And one by fucking one"—the knife bent slowly—"the guys you picked berries with get killed. And you just keep being clever." He rocked forward with each word. "And the game goes on and on and on."

He looked up at her, the knife in his hand. The same rage that had caused him to whip out his K-bar and slash plants rose inside him. He wanted to lash out and cause pain. He pushed the knife's point into the tablecloth and with both hands bent the blade ninety degrees.

This clearly scared her. She rose. "I'm sorry, Lieutenant," she said. "Maybe I—" She started to say something more, but stopped.

Mellas was bewildered at what had just happened. "I'm the one who should say sorry," he said. He nervously placed the bent knife next to a plate, wanting it out of his hand. It looked very odd there. "It just spills out. I feel really stupid."

She reached across the table and put her hand on his. "Don't be hard on yourself. It might be what gets you through." She pressed his hand quickly a couple of times. "God knows we all need something." She looked at him for a moment. "You take care of yourself out there." Then she walked rapidly through the hatch.

Mellas was alone with his pounding heart and his inexplicable rage. He knew that he'd destroyed the one chance he had to talk with the one woman who'd offered him what all the others were afraid to give. He wanted to run to her, grab her, talk with her about love and friendship. Instead he grabbed a handful of the polished silverware from the white tablecloth and hurled it against one of the plushly upholstered couches that lined the bulkhead. A Filipino mess man stuck his head out from the swinging doors of the galley. Seeing Mellas standing there, fighting for control, he quickly pulled back inside.

Mellas finished his coffee in silence. He could see his reflection in the polished wood paneling. It was obscure, a little distorted, but it was him, as he was now, alone.

Mellas wanted off the hospital ship.

Mellas was afraid to go back to the bush.

Mellas had no place to go.

His orders arrived in the morning. He was to return to his unit by 2000 hours the next day. So, with the arrival of this mimeographed sheet with his name on it, his feet had touched the ground. Time flooded back into his life like an unexpected but inevitable tide. He'd been on the ship five days.

He set out to get back his rifle and Vancouver's sword.

The sailor at the weapons locker looked bored. His weapon? His M-16? It must have been sent on to Fifth Marine Division. Here it is on the list. A sword? No idea. They don't do swords here. They're not considered weapons.

Mellas raged. The sailor sympathized. Mellas demanded to see someone. The sailor turned him over to the chief. The chief turned him over to the supply officer. The supply officer called up the records from the files. The records showed no sword. Don't worry, it's probably gone to Fifth Marine Division with the rifles. Did he have a receipt? Here, fill in this missing equipment form. After all, it is a weapon.

Mellas returned to the ward dejected, feeling powerless.

At dinner that night he was subdued. Everyone at the table knew he was going back to the bush the next morning. He would soon cease to be a problem. Everyone was polite. The red-haired nurse wasn't there.

Around midnight Mellas gingerly pulled his clothes on over the bandages and went to look for her. He stepped into the faintly trembling steel passageway. The gradual swell of the South China Sea, along with the vibration of the engines, came up through the soles of his boots. He headed into the interior of the ship, through a labyrinth of passageways, down ladders that led to unknown spaces.

During the past few days, just as he'd watched girls disappear down strange streets and into unknown houses in high school, he'd watched where the nurses disappeared to when they went off duty. Also he remembered that the red-haired nurse was Lieutenant K. E. Elsked.

Now, in the heat and stillness of the echoing decks and passageways lit by dim red lights, Mellas quietly worked his way closer to the center of officers' country. He knew that the area where the nurses lived was off-limits to him. Nevertheless, he nervously pushed ahead. A corpsman and then a sailor passed him. Both looked at him but said nothing, because he was an officer. Mellas continued down the passageways. His boots, pliable from hours in water, whispered softly against the metal beneath them. He turned a corner in the passageway and went by an open door. Inside he glimpsed an older, gray-haired officer, bent over a small desk. With a start, Mellas realized that this was the captain of the ship. He hurried by and worked through a bewildering maze of turns, not certain where he was, trusting to instinct that he'd eventually find Lieutenant Elsked's quarters, with her name over the hatch.

Eventually he did.

His heart was thumping in his throat. If she reacted badly, he would be in serious trouble. He looked up and down the empty passageway, swallowed, then knocked.

After a moment there was a muffled question to someone else, then a louder "Who is it?"

Mellas didn't know how to answer. He'd never actually told her his name. Would she remember it from the operating room?

"Who is it?" a second, harsher, voice repeated.

"Uh, it's me." Mellas felt lame. "The Marine lieutenant." He paused, then quickly added, "T. S. Eliot."

There was a muffled, annoyed, "Who?" from the second voice, then a responding "It's OK. I know him." There was a pause. "I'm afraid you do, too."

The door opened. Lieutenant Elsked, clutching a white terry-cloth bathrobe around her, peered out.

"What in the world are you doing here?" she whispered.

"I got to talk to you about something."

"What?" she whispered. "You're going to get in real trouble."

"Let me in, then."

She tightened her grip on the robe, closing it more firmly.

"Please," Mellas whispered. He looked at her, pleadingly. "It's not what you think. I need help." He saw her fingers relax slightly. "I need someone who knows the machinery around here. I mean the social machinery."

She paused a moment. "OK." She opened the hatch. "God, the things I do for my country."

Mellas slipped in.

She turned on a desk lamp. "Sorry, Kendra," she said.

Mellas looked over to see the nurse from Triage on the lower bunk. She looked back, her jaw tight.

"I believe you two know each other," Lieutenant Elsked said impishly. "Second Lieutenant Mellas, United States Marine Corps." She nodded her head slightly toward Mellas. "Reserve, correct?" She had a hint of a smile. "Meet Lieutenant Dunn, United States Navy." She pulled a chair out from under the desk. "Now that you've been introduced, maybe you could both relax." She sat down and pulled her bathrobe tighter around her knees. She leaned back and put her hands in the bathrobe pockets, clearly amused. "Neither of you is as bad as the other one thinks," she added.

Dunn glared at Mellas. She pulled her blanket up around her shoulders and turned her back on him to face the bulkhead.

Mellas looked at Lieutenant Elsked, who gave a little shrug as if to say that she'd given it a try. She looked down for a moment at her bare feet. Mellas couldn't help following her gaze. His eyes lingered a split second on her calves before resting on her red toenails.

"Well, T. S.?" Elsked said, looking up warmly. "Or can I call you Waino? Funny name."

Mellas felt himself blush with embarrassment, because she obviously had been told all about his encounter with her roommate—and with happiness, because she knew his name.

"Waino's fine," he said.

"Mine's Karen. Bet you didn't know that."

"No I didn't, Lieutenant Elsked."

"You can call me Karen when I've got a bathrobe on."

There was a pleasant, awkward pause, broken by the decidedly noisy shifting of Elsked's roommate.

Mellas plunged in. "Somebody's stolen my sword."

Dunn threw back the covers from her head and turned to face Mellas. "I'm sick and tired of that damned sword. Now turn your ass around and walk out of here. If it wasn't for Lieutenant Elsked, I'd have you arrested."

Mellas felt his usual rage begin to uncoil, but this time he controlled it. He turned to Elsked. "I need your help. I've gone to everyone I can think of. It's disappeared. I don't have a receipt. There's no way of tracing it. An HM-1 named Bell was the last one I saw it with."

"What's Lieutenant Elsked supposed to do about it, Lieutenant?" Dunn said.

Mellas took a deep slow breath. He kept his eyes fixed on Elsked's.

She watched him clinically. "I thought maybe you'd know how to find it," he said. "If you asked around—you know, asked some of the corpsmen—maybe they've seen it. Somebody's got to have it."

"OK. I'll ask around on my shift tomorrow."

Mellas shook his head. "It can't wait. I've got orders for tomorrow." Fear made his stomach plunge.

Elsked looked at him carefully. "How much longer have you got to go?"

Mellas's mind stopped. "What day is it?"

Elsked laughed. "Thursday, April third, unless it's after midnight. This Sunday's Easter."

Mellas was looking at his right hand and moving his fingers. "Three hundred four days and a wake-up," he finally said. It was like a life sentence. "If I stay awake all night. Otherwise it's two wake-ups." He forced a smile.

Her face showed kindness. "That's a long time."

"Yeah."

"The eye OK?"

He nodded.

"Legs?"

He nodded again.

The light in her eyes grew warmer. She looked down at her legs again. Mellas's eyes followed. Her legs were very well shaped.

"Why is the sword so important?" she asked.

"Somebody died . . ." Mellas stopped. He saw Vancouver breaking up the ambush, probably saving his life. How many lives were owed to this warrior? "I don't know. It just is." He paused. "You had to be there."

"Jesus, it's a souvenir sword," Dunn said. She had been putting on a blue bathrobe beneath the covers. Now she got out of the berth, her body rigid beneath the robe.

"It's sort of hard to explain," Mellas said. It angered him that Dunn thought the sword was trivial, but he held it back.

"You better believe it's hard to explain," Dunn said. Her small eyes were narrowed even further. She grabbed a set of utilities and a pair of small black shoes with thick rubber soles. "Come *on*, Karen."

"Where are you going?" Elsked asked her.

"To get the duty officer." Dunn turned her back and put her pants on underneath her bathrobe. She turned around, holding together the opening of the robe.

"He hasn't done anything wrong," Elsked said quietly but firmly.

"Just off-limits, is all. Not to mention disobedience of a direct order and disrespect for a superior officer." Dunn sat on the bunk and pulled on a pair of khaki socks and her shoes, fumbling to hold her robe closed. She rose to her feet.

"Kendra, hey, he just asked for some help. What's the big deal?"

"Maybe I don't like swords. Maybe I don't like him. He's off-limits and way out of line." She moved toward the hatch.

Mellas put his hand on the hatch, almost as if to bar Dunn's way. His insides quivered. He tried to make his voice controlled and calm. "Please, Lieutenant, ma'am." He held one hand out to her, palm up, fingers spread, as if to ward her off. "Believe me, I didn't come here to cause trouble. I admit I'm off-limits. Look, I can't explain why it's so important. Please. I just came here to ask Karen—Lieutenant Elsked—for help, and I think it's up to her. If she says no, I'll leave. I'll even leave if she says yes. I'm leaving tomorrow. I'll be out of your life. I might even be out of mine." He turned back to Elsked and blurted out, "Karen, I've got to have that sword." If throwing himself at Dunn's feet would have helped, he would have done it.

Elsked saw this, and compassion flashed across her face. She slowly nodded. She got up and reached for her uniform. "Go wait in the wardroom," she said to Mellas. "There's always some coffee brewing there. I'll meet you as soon as I can." She turned to Dunn, who'd been watching them with compressed lips. "So relax, already. OK? He's harmless." She looked back at Mellas. "At least to us."

Mellas reached the safety of the officers' mess without incident, but his heart was still thumping. He poured himself a mug of coffee and began to wait. An hour passed. He drank two more mugs. He read magazines distractedly. Nurses and doctors filed in as the watches changed. Some nodded or said hello. The room emptied. He started on a fourth mug. Another hour passed.

Then Elsked walked into the paneled room. She had the sword in her hand. Her eyes were shining and she was breathing hard, her breasts noticeably moving up and down.

"You got it!" Mellas cried. He rushed up to hug her, then slowed and stopped.

She handed it to him, almost formally, as if in a presentation. He took it. "God, Karen. Thank you." Mellas grabbed it by the hilt and squeezed it hard, his eyes wet with triumph and gratitude. He held the sword up in front of both of them. "I feel like Sir Francis Drake," he said, suddenly self-conscious.

She laughed. "Well, if you really want to, I'll touch you on both shoulders with it, but I didn't exactly feel like Queen Elizabeth when I knocked on the hatch of the good doctor who bought it off of HM-1 Bell." She laughed. "But I was Bloody fucking Mary when it came to getting the deal reversed."

"I'll bet you were," Mellas said and laughed. He looked down at her and realized that she was a good six inches shorter then he. "It belonged to a guy in my platoon named Vancouver. He died with it, running across an LZ trying to take out some gooks coming across from the other side. He saved the assault. He . . ." Mellas, to his own surprise, started to choke up. "He . . ." He wanted to go on, but the choking sadness filled his lungs and eyes and stopped his tongue. He couldn't speak.

"It's OK," Karen said. She touched him lightly on his forearm. "He was a friend. You miss him, like the others." She gently grasped his forearm and held on.

Mellas could only nod, tears streaming down his face.

"I knew it was important. You don't have to explain it. I'm glad I could find it." She held him in her gaze and then released his arm.

Mellas smiled. The choke hold was gone. "I don't think you know what you did," he said.

"Actually," she answered. "I think it's just the opposite."

Mellas looked at the sword. "Yeah. It's like I think we're going to need it someday or something. Crazy, I guess."

"No. Healthy."

He looked directly into her eyes, and they looked back, clear and warm.

"I probably won't see you again," he said.

"Let's hope not." She tried to smile but managed only a shaky twitch. "God knows you're better off if you can stay clear of here." She bit her lower lip. "Will you be all right? I mean . . ." She faltered. "You know what I mean—not physically."

Mellas nodded several times. "I will now," he finally managed to say. She reached out for him and kissed him quickly on the cheek. He grabbed her with his left arm and squeezed her to him, the sword still in his right hand, caught between them. He wanted to merge with her. He tried to bury his head against her soft red hair. She pushed him away gently but firmly. He saw that her eyes were moist as she turned and walked quickly away.

CHAPTER TWENTY-ONE

The day Mellas had been medevaced, Bravo Company filed off Matterhorn and climbed back up Helicopter Hill to be evacuated. All the holes they'd dug were taken by Delta Company and battalion headquarters.

Fitch looked around nervously. The kids sat down. Some saw friends of theirs and went over to try to slip into their holes, but most of the company just remained exposed, lying on their backs in the wet clay.

Blakely crawled out of the command bunker when the radio operator reported Bravo's arrival. He could see that there was no fight left in them. Yet he couldn't help being thrilled, remembering the assault. Blakely regretted that he couldn't have been a young lieutenant and participated in it. Yet at the same time he felt immensely proud of his own part. It was staff work, but he knew that it was important and he was good at it.

Right now he had two shitty jobs to do. The first was to tell Bravo to go back down the hill. He couldn't move Delta Company, because they needed to be on the LZ as the reserve and exploitation element. To leave Bravo on the hill would crowd everything and invite casualties from the mortars. Besides, if they were dug in down on the saddle, that would eliminate the NVA's easiest approaches to both hills.

He watched Fitch and Hawke walk wearily toward him. Fitch's radio operator was about three paces behind them, shouting something at one of the troops from Delta Company.

"Lieutenant Fitch," Blakely said, reaching out to shake his hand, "I'm sorry you walked up here." He explained that all the birds were tied up moving troops and artillery and that Bravo would have to spend the night in the saddle between Matterhorn and Helicopter Hill.

"Oh, boy," Pallack said, just audibly.

Blakely looked at him, a little irritated at this lack of respect.

"Sir, my men are beat," Fitch said. "You're asking them to build another perimeter, in an exposed position. We could barely keep them awake last night."

"I'm not surprised," Blakely said. It angered him that with such an unprofessional attitude Fitch somehow always managed to come out smelling like a rose. The colonel was tickled pink over the assault. Everyone in the division, right up to the general, had been watching this one. No one had seen any of the sloppy leadership, the disrespect, sleeping on watch, and getting stranded without food and water.

"Oh, boy," Pallack said again.

"Lance Corporal Pallack, that's enough," Fitch said. "Go tell Scar to get everyone water, food, and full ammunition. I'll join you later."

"Aye, aye, Skipper." Pallack looked briefly across the chasm of hierarchy and class that separated him from the major, then turned back toward what remained of the company to do his job.

"I want to talk to you two," Blakely said. He turned and walked toward the entrance of the bunker, leaving Hawke and Fitch looking at each other.

"What's he going to do?" Fitch asked. "Make us assault the hill again?"

"He just might," Hawke answered. "With Delta defending."

They followed Blakely in.

Blakely said that he could have Hawke court-martialed for leaving his post. "I guess you also know I'm not going to," he added to Hawke. "Why didn't you just come and tell me?"

Hawke was silent.

"Do you have anything to say for yourself before I dismiss you?"

"For my*self*? No sir."

"OK, then. The colonel wants to see you. He's over by Delta's CP. I want to talk with Lieutenant Fitch alone."

"Aye, aye, sir." Hawke left to see Simpson.

When he'd gone, Blakely told Fitch that Simpson was transferring him out of the battalion. It was only out of kindness and in recognition of his recent assault that Simpson wasn't going to relieve him of his command for cause. Fitch could consider himself transferred once they got back to VCB. Goodwin would take over until Mellas got back, and Mellas would have the company until they could get a regular.

Over at Delta Company's CP, Simpson said he was putting Hawke in for a Bronze Star.

When Hawke rejoined Fitch and Pallack next to Fitch's old bunker, he heard cries of "Tubing!" People everywhere scurried into holes. The mortar rounds came crashing in. Marines huddled in their holes, holding on to their helmets, praying, trying not to think, hear, or feel. Hawke crouched low next to the bunker entrance, staring out at his old company.

Fitch and Goodwin walked side by side, leading the company silently off the hill. The Marines of Bravo Company followed, in silence, giving no apparent thought to the mortar shells, walking with their rifles slung on their shoulders. Exhausted, they were as indifferent as if the falling shells were rain.

Some Marines from Delta Company poked their heads up from their holes and watched their comrades, as Hawke was doing. Some shook their heads and muttered, "Crazy motherfuckers." Some let out a low whistle. Most were silent.

Emotion constricted Hawke's throat. He suddenly understood why the victims of concentration camps had walked quietly to the gas chambers. In the face of horror and insanity, it was the one human thing to do. Not the noble thing, not the heroic thing—the human thing. To live, succumbing to the insanity, was the ultimate loss of pride.

The next afternoon, after the battalion staff was withdrawn, the company was ferried back to VCB. It was Sunday. Father Riordan, the battalion chaplain, thought it would be comforting to hold a memorial service. The colonel and the Three readily agreed, even though regular services had already been held that morning.

* * *

Goodwin had to bully everyone into going. Supply dropped off new uniforms. The company walked down to the canvas bag showers next to the stream. Unfortunately, when they washed off the dirt and crusted blood and pus, their jungle rot oozed fresh pus onto their new uniforms. Still, it was a pleasure to be able to squeeze the pus out and watch it run clean and yellow-white and soak into the clean crisp cotton of the new jungle utilities. There was bitching, but the clean water, the new clothes, and a hot meal held it to a minimum.

At 1550 Fitch and Goodwin walked over to the muddy area where the troops were pitching their shelters. "OK. You got ten minutes to get over to the chapel," Fitch said. "We'll see you there. After chapel, you're on your own until oh eight hundred tomorrow." He looked around. His company was pitifully small. Then he looked down, unable to talk, his shoulders slumped.

"Look, you guys," he added. He tried to smile. No words would come. His nose began to run. The muscles in his throat ached. Then he reached up and took his cap off. "Look . . ." he croaked weakly.

People rose from the ground. Those with caps on took them off and remained standing, some with hands folded in front of them, looking at Fitch standing there beneath the leaden sky.

Fitch put his cap on and walked toward the chapel.

At the service Father Riordan led everyone in a hymn. Most of the blacks didn't know it and neither did half the whites.

Riordan introduced Simpson.

Simpson surveyed the freshly washed young faces in front of him, feeling a stir of pride and valor. He stood with both hands behind his back, his legs slightly apart, and told them how proud he was of every one of them, how proud of those who had sacrificed everything. "It was a textbook assault. In the very best traditions of the Marine Corps." He paused, searching for words that could convey how he felt. "I don't know if you know it, but I keep a bulletin board in my quarters that has all my units listed on it. If one of my units does a particularly outstanding job, I put a gold star next to it so everyone that walks in there can see it. I've only put two gold stars up there the entire time I've been in-country. Well, this morning I added two more. One for the eighty-one-millimeter mortars, my personal weapon of opportunity, and one for Bravo Company." He looked at the faces looking up at him. "There's never been a prouder commanding officer." He sat down, holding back the tears that flooded his eyes.

Father Riordan stood.

"Let us bow our heads in prayer." He waited for the shifting and rustling to stop. "Our Heavenly Father, we ask thee to take the souls of these departed young men who in the past several days have died for their country, giving that last greatest gift that any man can give that others might have the taste of freedom, the chance to worship thee in the way in which they . . ."

Whispering had already started in the back of the tent. "Hey Gambaccini, you wops listen to this shit all the time?"

"This is a fucking travesty to Jesus."

"Our colonel's a fucking gold star mother."

"Hey, Scar, can we get the fuck out of here?"

". . . comfort and solace to the dear ones left behind by these our departed comrades in arms. Let them know that their sacrifice was not in vain, but grant, loving Father . . ."

"Fucking loving Father wasn't cutting *us* any slack up on the hill."

"I ain't angry with God, but He sure as shit must be pissed at me."

"Cortell, you get up there and show that mackerel how to preach, man."

There were also some who said nothing, like Mole and China.

The colonel retired at about midnight, thinking it had been a pretty good day. At 0200, shadowy figures crept to the downhill side of his quarters. In front, the Marine assigned as security guard fought hard against dozing off. He heard someone shout down on the mud path by the supply bunker. "Whoooeee, we can be some kind of *fucked* up." Then another one joined in. "Hee ya. *Sheeit*, man." Laughter floated up the path. He watched two black Marines slapping hands. The guard smiled.

The iron pipe caught the guard across the side of his face, caving in his jawbone and dislodging five teeth. A second one came from the other side, catching him above the eye. He sank to his knees and was hit again across the neck. His moan was stifled by a dark hand, and he was gradually lowered to the muddy ground.

There was a quick flurry of activity. The two supposed drunks ran out of sight. The two pipe wielders ran in the opposite direction. Someone coolly lifted the flap of the colonel's tent and tossed in a grenade. Then he, too, ran quickly into the darkness.

The clunk of the grenade on the floor startled Simpson awake. He made a muffled, frightened grunt—and ran. He fell over the tent's ropes and slipped in the mud in the dark, desperately trying to beat the explosion. He dived into the mud outside, covering his head.

Nothing happened.

He looked up, feeling foolish in his muddy underwear. He saw his security guard slumped on the ground. "Duty officer!" he shouted.

The heavy door of the COC bunker opened and a shaft of light spilled onto the ground before the blackout curtain closed it off. Stevens came running.

"Get a fucking corpsman," Simpson shouted. "My guard's been bushwhacked."

"You all right, sir?"

"Get a fucking corpsman."

Stevens turned around to one of the battalion radio operators who was running up to him. "You heard him, get a squid." The kid went running for the battalion aid station.

Simpson was trembling. "Someone tried to fucking frag me. I heard the grenade come in. It was a dud."

"Holy shit, sir," Stevens said. The two men stood watching the colonel's tent. "You sure it's a dud, sir?" Stevens finally asked, afraid the colonel would ask him to go look.

Simpson stood still a moment, his muddy underwear turning cold. "Fuck yes."

Others were coming out of the COC bunker. One had a flashlight. Then two others came running from the aid station. The corpsman also had a flashlight. Simpson took the light and walked into his quarters.

Lying on the floor was a grenade with the primer taken out. Wrapped around it was a sheet of paper. Simpson took the paper off and smoothed it out. It was a mimeographed company roster, with names, ranks, serial numbers, and tour rotation dates. It was Bravo Company. Names had been heavily crossed out with a ballpoint pen. Neatly typed next to them were words like murdered, crippled, maimed, blinded . . .

Simpson crumpled the paper. Blakely burst into the room. "You all right, sir?" he asked.

"Yes, goddamn it. A lot of good your fucking security guard did."

"He's pretty badly beat up, sir."

"He deserves it. Probably asleep. I ought to fucking court-martial the puke." He handed Blakely the grenade.

"The primer's out," Blakely said.

Simpson looked at him coldly.

"I'll get it in for prints," Blakely said.

"Don't bother. You know the chances of that." Simpson turned on the light. He handed Blakely the crumpled paper.

Blakely swallowed. He handed the roster back to Simpson. "Sir, I suggest action be taken immediately."

"What?" Simpson asked.

"Disarm Bravo Company until we get them out in the bush again. Collect all grenades, all weapons. Put extra men on guard duty. My quarters too."

"OK. Get Staff Sergeant Cassidy in here. They were his men. And get Lieutenant Goodwin up. It's his company."

Within half an hour Cassidy was standing with three Marines from H & S and sadly surveying the pathetically small tent city of ponchos and prone bodies that was his old outfit. Some kids were sleeping exposed to the rain where they'd passed out drunk. Then he set his jaw.

Goodwin had refused to help him. "OK. Everybody up. Wake up in there. Everybody out of the rack."

Kids groaned. Some looked at their watches: 0300. Fear struck. Somebody was in the shit so bad that they were being sent in again. The fear raced through the squalid mud compound. But Marines must be in trouble. They'd go.

"Someone in the shit, Sergeant Cassidy?" someone asked.

"Yes," he replied grimly, "Bravo Company."

Kids shivered in the drizzle. Some pulled on flak jackets for warmth.

"I want to see all the acting platoon commanders," Cassidy said. Three former squad leaders walked up to him: China, for Second Platoon; Connolly, First; and Campion, Third. Three concerned faces looked at Cassidy.

"Someone beat the colonel's guard tonight. Almost killed him." He looked straight at China as he talked. "A good fucking Marine. Three more days until he would have rotated out of this fucking place. And some assholes beat the shit out of him because he drew guard duty. Some real proud dudes."

China stayed cool. Connolly and Campion exchanged glances.

"A dummy grenade was tossed into the colonel's quarters. It had the Bravo Company roster on it." He paused. "With some modifications."

"Like what, Gunny?" Connolly asked.

Cassidy was still looking at China. "Like the ones who'd died for their country had their names crossed out and the word 'murdered' was typed in."

"You think someone from Bravo Company did it, Gunny?" China asked, wide-eyed.

Cassidy hated China but at the same time admired his cool. "I don't think anything," he said. "I've got orders to collect all grenades, weapons, claymores, everything. I want them stacked up in piles right here, by platoon."

"What kind of shit is this, Gunny?" Connolly said. Others had gathered around the group of four and echoed his protest.

"Just do what you're told, Conman."

"I earned that fucking rifle."

"Yes, you did. You all did." Cassidy clenched his teeth. He looked at their drawn, haggard faces, their dead eyes. He looked around him at the squalor, saw the kids he'd humped with through the heat and cold, now shivering in the darkness, puzzled, angry. He wanted to cry out to them to make this easier on him.

But no one moved.

"Am I going to have to take them away from you?" Cassidy asked.

"You ain't wrong, Gunny," Connolly said. He walked over to his hooch, pulled out his rifle, and threw it in the mud. He then sat down and stared at it.

"Pick it up, Conman."

"Fuck you, Cassidy."

Cassidy strode over, towering above Connolly, who continued to stare at the muddy rifle. Then Connolly wrenched around, reached into the sagging hooch, and pulled out Vancouver's modified machine gun. He threw it into the mud. "There. The fucking asshole can have that too." Tears welled up in his eyes and he tried, unsuccessfully, to blink them away.

Cassidy stared at the gun lying in the mud.

"I want all the grenades too, Conman," Cassidy finally said.

"That's right. You fucking bastards want everything, don't you?"

"Where's your fucking pride, Conman?" Cassidy said softly.

"I left it on that fucking hill we just abandoned."

Cassidy wheeled away. His parade-ground voice came back. "Goddamn it now, I want all ammunition and grenades piled neatly. I want the rifles stacked in an orderly manner. I want the stacks right here."

Some kids began to move for their weapons. Then China said, "Uh-uh." Everyone stopped. China reached for his machine gun and threw it into the mud in front of him. He stood erect above it. Others did the same. Soon the area was littered with grenades, rifles, ammunition belts, bandoleers, claymores, and captured weapons.

"How about our fucking can openers, Gunny? That little chicken-shit fuck want our John Waynes?"

"I got a needle in my sewing kit. You want that?"

Cassidy stood alone, saying nothing. Eventually he motioned to his team from H & S to collect the weapons. The Marines from Bravo Company, disgusted, started crawling back into their hooches or rolling up in wet ponchos on the ground.

China continued to stand over his machine gun, waiting. When one of the H & S Marines approached it, China kicked it away. The kid stood up. "Look, man, this ain't my idea." He bent over for the gun again. Again China kicked it aside. The kid turned to look at Cassidy, who hadn't noticed the exchange, then turned back to China. "Hey, come on. Just let me get this shit over with. I ain't got nothing against you."

"You touch that gun and I'll kill you."

"Christ, don't get personal about it."

China leaned over. "Ain't nobody gettin' my machine gun but Cassidy. You pick it up and you gonna get fucked with real bad, whether I be here or not."

"All right. All right." The kid moved on.

Cassidy had noticed. He walked up to China.

"How come Schaffran didn't pick up your gun?"

"He didn't want to."

"Did you threaten him, you fucking puke?"

"How can I threaten somebody? *I* ain't got no weapons."

Someone snickered. Cassidy was aware now that everyone remaining was watching him to see what he would do. He and China stood there, eyes locked.

"You gonna do your *duty*, Cassidy, and pick up my gun?" China asked softly.

Cassidy looked directly into China's eyes. His hands began to tremble. Then he bent over to get the machine gun.

China kicked it away. "Parker," he said.

Cassidy stood up. His voice quivered with anger. "If you think I'm going to order you to do something so you can refuse it, become a fucking martyr, and hang around in the rear waiting for trial with the rest of the vomits you call your friends, then you got another think coming."

He reached again for the gun. Again China toed it aside. "Broyer," he said.

Cassidy stood. "I lost friends too, China."

"How a fucking cog have a friend? How a fucking cog ever be a man?"

Cassidy clenched his fists and saw China steel himself for the blow. Cassidy hesitated, struggling to restrain his anger. "Manhood's something you'll never understand," he said. He stooped down and picked up China's machine gun.

"You make me sick, cog." China walked away toward his hooch, leaving Cassidy with the muddy weapon. The rest of Bravo Company turned their backs on him.

Some, however, did not forget him.

"It's time to off the motherfucker," Henry said. "Now."

"We seen 'nough killin'," China said quietly.

Henry stood up and whirled around. "Man. Do I have to listen to you *we-seen-'nough killin'* shit, like I'm some kind of small boy look wonder-eyes at big daddy home from the wars? You know who you been killin' out there don'chew? You own brothers. Yeah. You own brothers. That's who you been gettin' you *'nough killin'* with. Well, I say we finish with that shit. We gonna do some killing our own. And *for* our own."

China could see that Henry had most of the brothers with him. Still, some of them, like Mole, looked to China to say something. China's rhetoric failed him.

"You gonna just sit on you ass while that racist cracker throw our brother Mallory in the fucking conex box like some kind of animal?" Henry asked. "And then *you* run you ass up that fuckin' hill like you some kinda nigger Audie Murphy and half you fuckin' company get killed for nothin', and *he* send you fuckin' Coca-*Colas*, like you on some sort of football team? Hey, man. And then cut you balls off by takin' you rifles. You don't think maybe that fuckin' lifer hasn't been practicin' violence on you? Or you just turnin' white in more ways than one? Maybe you daddy be a white motherfucker and leave you all them white spots."

The familiar taunt made China clamp down his teeth so hard that he was afraid he'd break a molar. He knew what Henry was doing, and he knew that too much was at stake to give in to his rage.

Henry strutted over to the Makassar ebony trunk and opened the heavy lid. "You think about it, brother, while I fix us up some good brother Roogie and try and understand why you so fucked up." He carefully removed the clothing and other items in the trunk to reveal a beautifully crafted box with a sliding drawer. He opened the drawer and took out a silver bong with a crystal water bowl and an ornate cigarette roller and some paper.

China took the plunge. "You the one that's fucked up. Wha'chew think you gonna accomplish killin' one more fucked-up God-and-country pork chop? He just a fuckin' cog in the machinery. He *crawled* in front of me, man."

Leaving the lid to the trunk open, Henry simply smiled at China. He coolly walked over to the matching dresser, removed the false bottom in the drawer, and pulled out a small plastic bag of marijuana. Then he took a diamond-inlaid silver cigarette lighter from the top drawer. Still smiling, he turned to face China. "You the one give him you gun. He cut off you fuckin' balls, the way I see it."

China rose to the bait, but not in the way Henry wanted. "You think I'm not ready to roll on them suckers? You think I don't see they a bunch of sick motherfuckers?" China turned to the other brothers, not even addressing Henry. "What you people think this is, some sort of gang bullshit? We not about just goin' out and doin' violence to cut up some people for the hell of it. We about stoppin' things at the source of the evil. The *source*. We got to overturn a racist society. If it come to a fight, it gonna be a *real* motherfucker. We can't let them get us one at a time."

He turned to Henry, who'd sat on his cot and was carefully building a joint with the ornate roller. "You think I'm not souped up for a motherfucker over this? You think that I don't know payback gonna be a motherfucker for that racist cracker? But payback gotta come right. All that happen wit'chew is they throw you black ass in another conex box just like Mallory. They do worse for you. They throw you upside down in one of those fuckin' punishment holes like they do the gooks, and you be in so deep they have to pump sunshine to you all the way from Texas." That got a laugh from the other brothers, and China started to feel better. "They send you so far out in the bush they gonna use rock apes to carry you mail." Then China pounded his fist on his palm. "We got to get power. One dead Georgia cracker a drop in the bucket over here. I left dead Georgia crackers all over that fuckin' hill. And dead brothers too. Dead people ain't worth shit. They just big nothins."

"Power," Henry sneered. "Sheeit." He licked the glue on the joint and smoothed the paper into place. "You and you jive fuckin' talk, China. Mao say power come from the barrel of a gun. That dude know where it's at. Wha'chew gonna do? Go back to the world and sing 'We Shall Overcome'?" Now Henry got the laughter.

"Spare me," China said.

"Well, wha'chew gonna do?" Henry coolly licked the cigarette paper along the seam, sealing it shut, watching China through narrowed eyes. "I can just see China singing 'We Shall Overcome' as he walks in for his cyanide shower."

Henry's friends now chimed in.

"Hey, Henry. You tell him."

"Yeah, China. How come you not runnin' with us no more?"

"Hey, come on, brother. What's into you? Huh, man?"

"Nothin' into me," China fired back at them. "I been out in the fuckin' bush tryin' straighten shit out while you jive-assed mothers in here talkin' about revolution. I *workin'* revolution."

"*You* spare *me*, brother," Henry said. "Just 'cause you ain't figured a way get you ass out of the jungle." He laughed. "If you really workin' revolution, then you better start right here. You frag the motherfucker. That way we teach those fuckin' bigots that payback start right away. They gonna fuck with us, we gonna fuck with them worse." He put the joint in his mouth and started striking at the flint of the lighter.

China, his senses heightened from months in the bush, smelled the lighter fluid. It annoyed and slightly nauseated him. "I told you there's no point. He just a little cog in the works. Besides, we get our own point across without killin'. We need to arm the black man for *de*fense. We ain't about murderin' people. We maybe pop a smoke under his ass some night or maybe put a note on it like we did for the colonel."

"You gonna write another note?" Henry asked. He blew out a long exhalation of smoke. The others laughed. "Later for that, huh. *Way* later."

He handed off the joint and then turned his back on China and reached under his cot. He pulled out a fragmentation grenade. "This ain't no smoke," he said, tossing it lightly up and down in his palm. He tossed it over to China. "I think you chickenshit to use it."

Nobody laughed.

China knew in a flash of insight that once again Henry had him coming or going. If he did what Henry wanted, Henry was the leader. If he didn't do it, he was disgraced, and Henry was still the leader.

"We see who's chickenshit," China said. He pulled the pin of the grenade and everything seemed to go in slow motion for him. He was so weary of slaughter that his own didn't matter any more. It was the same tired suicidal feeling he had walking off the hill in the mortar fire. He was only dimly aware of people shouting, running, scrambling for the door of the tent. "He's fuckin' crazy, man! A fuckin' frag goin' off! Jesus Christ!" China, his tongue on his lips, concentrating on the count, tossed the grenade back to Henry and watched the spoon fly off toward the side of the tent.

Henry, his eyes wide, tossed the grenade back to China and dived out of the door for the wet ground.

China threw the grenade into Henry's open trunk, slammed down the heavy lid, and threw a flak jacket on top of it. He dived for the far side of the tent behind a pile of seabags, flinging himself down, rolling off the runway matting of the floor, facedown onto the dirt just beneath it at the edge of the tent, covering his head with his hands and arms.

The explosion pounded his ears and body.

He lay on the damp dirt. The silence and darkness were gradually filled by painful ringing in his ears, then by the smell of TNT. His head ached. But he was unharmed. He heard the excited babble of voices outside the tent. He stood up. Someone opened the now ragged flap of the ruined tent.

Henry walked in. He struck the lighter and coolly looked at the splinters of his once solid ebony trunk, at his shrapnel-pitted dresser, the ripped seabags. "You gonna pay for this, China."

China knew Henry wasn't talking about the furniture. He also knew that although Henry's image had taken a hit, power always trumped image—and, he was beginning to learn, ideology. Power was the ability to reward and punish. Henry could reward with money and drugs. He could punish by withholding money and drugs. A nice combination. Ultimately, however, Henry wielded the power of punishment held only by a self-selected few. He was willing to murder. China knew that if a man could kill *some*one, everyone knew that he could kill *any*one. The only way to stand up to that kind of power was to be willing to die.

China walked back to the company area, uneasy and apprehensive.

CHAPTER TWENTY-TWO

A helicopter carried Mellas the thirty miles from the hospital ship back to reality, dropping him to the ground at the Dong Ha airfield. From there, he hitched a ride on an Army truck thirteen kilometers south, across a dreary wasteland of abandoned rice farms, to Quang Tri, the location of the division's administrative rear. Mellas could tell that the Army driver was curious about him. After all, Mellas had a patch over one eye, several boxes of cigars under his arm, and a sword hanging from a complicated strap over his shoulder.

Finally the driver could contain himself no longer. "Where'd you get the sword?" he asked.

Mellas was amused. "Out in the bush," he said.

"Ah."

There were some things he couldn't tell the uninitiated. For them, the bush should, and would, remain a mystery.

In Bravo Company's unpainted plywood office a clerk was pecking at a typewriter. He had his shirt off and sweat glistened on his broad back, which also bore the scar of a bullet exit wound. Cigarette smoke curled limply upward in the humid coastal air. Above the clerk, covering the entire back wall, was a blown-up picture of a beautiful model in a girdle and brassiere advertisement. A note had been handwritten by the model on the large poster in neat round script. "To the men of Bravo Company, First Battalion, Twenty-Fourth Marines. You're doing a great job.

Love, Cindy." It was dated February 1967—just two years earlier but in some ways a bygone era.

The clerk told Mellas that Fitch was leaving for Okinawa in the afternoon and filled him in on the staged fragging, the note wrapped around the grenade, and Simpson's disarming the company. He also said that Cassidy had come to the rear, ostensibly to say good-bye to Fitch but more to drink himself into oblivion after having to be the one who actually took the weapons. Then the clerk said that the company would be skying out tomorrow for Eiger, and that Hawke had been given command. According to scuttlebutt, Mulvaney himself had given Hawke the job. Mellas said he was glad. Then he walked over to supply to get new gear for the bush. There he was told he'd have to sign for a deduction from his paycheck in order to pay for his old rifle before they would issue him a new one.

"The fucking Navy has the goddamned thing."

"I'm sorry, Lieutenant, but I'm not paying for the fucking thing. If you ever want to go home you better have all your fucking bills paid. They ain't paid, we don't endorse your orders. I don't care if you stay here the rest of your life."

Mellas paid $127.

He left with his new rifle and trudged over to another supply tent to rummage around for his seabag. When he found it he went through the contents, looking for items he'd want to take to the bush. He smiled as he held up several of the green T-shirts and boxer shorts his mother had dyed, remembering how he had asked Goodwin about whether or not to wear underwear in the bush. He threw the underwear into a trash can and headed for the staff club to forget where he would be in twenty-four hours.

The staff club had improved since he and Goodwin had last been there, drowning their fears. A fancy Akai tape deck was now sitting on the bar. The bar itself had some nice new inlay work, and several new beer signs rolled, sparkled, and advertised sky-blue waters from out of the gloom. Newly installed, high on the wall behind the bar, was Vancouver's sawed-off machine gun. It was flanked by two captured Russian machine guns.

Staff Sergeant Cassidy sat alone at a table, a bottle of Jack Daniel's Black Label in front of him. No one else was in the club. Gunny Klump, the manager, had gone out to do errands, leaving Cassidy to mind the store. Mellas said he could use a beer, and Cassidy disappeared behind the bar. He emerged with an armload of cold wet cans, which he set ceremoniously on the table in front of Mellas. "No sense in getting up and down except to piss," he said. He was already well along on his own mystery tour.

Mellas reached for one of the cans, punched two holes in it, and chugged the beer down. Then he opened another can and leaned back in the chair. He noticed an air conditioner half installed in the plywood wall. "Air-conditioning," he mused. "Not bad."

"Yeah," Cassidy muttered. "Klump figured he'll get people in from the other battalions once the spring heat hits. It'll help the profits."

"Here's to fucking profits," Mellas said, lifting his can. He chugged it, thinking of both Hamilton and the $127.

"I guess you heard about the skipper," Cassidy said.

"I'm sure it all looked nice and voluntary."

"You can't fool the fucking troops," Cassidy muttered. He took another drink of whiskey, and his grip tightened on his shot glass until his knuckles showed white through his jungle-rot scars. "I should have been up there with you. It was when you needed me worst."

Mellas was tempted to tell Cassidy who had gotten him transferred, so that he wouldn't feel so bad. He saw that Cassidy was looking up at Vancouver's machine gun, polished and oily, displayed beneath a large fleur-de-lis imposed on crossed rifles, the emblem of the Twenty-Fourth Marines: *Les Braves des Bois Belleau.*

"I've had to do a lot of shitty jobs since I've been in the Corps, sir," Cassidy said. He brought his gaze back to Mellas. "But the worst thing I ever had to do was go from man to man and collect their rifles. Twenty years ago anybody try and take a Marine's rifle he'd been fucking plugged. Shit, five years ago."

"Times change," Mellas muttered. He thought about the girl in the girdle and brassiere advertisement.

"I had to go from man to man. Some of them I'd been with on Wind River and Co Roc and the DMZ op. And I had to search them like fucking prisoners." Cassidy turned his watery blue eyes on Mellas. "Well, I did it, because it was my job. But I didn't like it, Lieutenant. I could feel them hating me." He stopped, noticed that he was clenching his fists, and slowly straightened his fingers. "I guess that's why I had to get the fuck away from there."

Mellas and Cassidy got drunk.

It was just after noon when Mellas left Cassidy passed out at the table and dragged himself back to the company office. He pulled himself wearily up the back stairs to where two cots were separated from the rest of the office by a hanging wool blanket. He knew he would have a pounding headache as the day wore on—unless he could keep drinking. Could he keep drinking forever? He threw himself onto a cot. The wool blanket felt hot and scratchy beneath his sweaty cheek. His mind, and the floor beneath him, whirled. He again felt as if he were on a conveyer belt heading for a cliff. Every minute brought him one minute closer to tomorrow, and tomorrow he'd be back in the bush. His mind, unwilling to face the thought, closed down.

At VCB the newbies' tension about the coming operation was already palpable. The old hands, like China and Mole, talked quietly to each other or simply cleaned their rifles and machine guns over and over—they had learned how to keep disturbing feelings at bay. They ate. They drank beer. They elaborately concocted cups of coffee. They tried to get on KP duty. They smoked marijuana. They joked. They thought of girls back home. They masturbated.

The new black kids were especially drawn to the two black machine gunners, taciturn gods of the bush who wore dark green hangman's nooses around their necks. China would hold court, engage them, talk a little politics, laugh off any fears they expressed. Mole spoke only to China and the other old hands. The items on his personal agenda did not include making new friends.

China and Mole were cleaning their machine guns near the opening of a large ten-man tent with a packed mud floor, which they shared with eighteen other black Marines. In the front of the tent, when the

flaps were pulled fully back onto the roof, they could get enough light
to see what they were doing and still be out of the rain. But the rain had
become less constant. The Vietnamese spring was coming, and it would
be followed by the relentless dry season.

They had their guns completely broken down and were meticu-
lously cleaning each component. The air smelled of Hoppe's No. 9
powder solvent, sent from home in response to many anxious requests,
the combination of burning diesel fuel and shit from the latrines and
mothballs from the tent canvas. Mole looked up from his gun and chuckled softly. "I'll be goddamned, China. Looky what we got coming up
the road."

China looked and smiled, seeing Arran and Pat. Pat was at a loose
heel, padding along silently, as always, tongue out just slightly, looking
as if he were on a Sunday stroll. His red ears flicked forward when he
heard Mole's voice. Arran, noticing the ear flick but unable to hear anything, followed the direction of the ears. He saw Mole and China and
raised his shotgun high in the air with one hand, grinning.

Arran touched fists with China and Mole. Pat sat down, still in heel
position.

"I thought you was out in the fuckin' Au Shau or some badass place
like that," China said.

Arran grinned. "All over. Coming back to you guys. I hear we're
skying out tomorrow."

The two gunners nodded but said nothing.

Pat started whining, wanting to break heel. He had tuned in on a
figure coming up the road. It was Hawke. Pat whined again. Arran
laughed and released him. Pat bounded down the road to greet Hawke.
Soon the two of them were roughhousing together, Hawke hugging the
dog's strong neck, cradling it in his arms and moving Pat's head back
and forth, while Pat kept trying to nuzzle into Hawke's crotch and at
the same time rub his own sides, catlike, against Hawke's thighs.

Hawke, still laughing at Pat's antics, reached the three Marines.
He motioned for China and Mole to remain seated.

"Enough, OK," Arran said to the dog. "Show the skipper some
respect." His tone then altered just slightly. "Sit." Pat immediately was

on his haunches, panting happily. "He sure as hell likes you, Skipper," Arran said. "Not everyone gets a greeting like that."

Hawke was rubbing Pat's head and ears. He looked up at the three Marines. "Yeah. I'm real glad to see you two back," Hawke said. "Feel blind out there without you." Then he put a hand on Mole's shoulder and sidled between Mole and China, poking his head into the interior of the tent without saying anything to them. He pulled his head back and turned to the two gunners. "I got word you chased some chucks out of the tent."

"I'm out of here," Arran said, grinning. He snapped his fingers softly and Pat stood.

"Oh-four-thirty in the supply tent," Hawke said.

"Aye, sir. Nice to be back." Arran left, Pat padding along at his left side as usual.

The three watched for a moment as the dog and handler walked away.

"Well?" Hawke asked.

"Nobody chased no one, Skipper," China said.

Hawke looked at him for a while. "Uh-huh."

"No, honest Injun, sir. They just left on they own."

Hawke thought about it for a while. "You know, China, I don't give a fuck about *congregating*. Never did. Everyone's going to turn green when we board those choppers tomorrow." He unconsciously looked skyward. "You guys ready?"

They both cocked their heads to the side, and Mole shrugged his shoulders.

"I need you to keep the newbies steady. OK?"

"We can do that, sir," China said.

Hawke looked at them, nodding almost imperceptibly. "Good. Thanks."

The two gunners watched him walk away down the road. "He's decent," Mole said.

"Yeah," said China. "He is. We got lucky for once."

"China, you think we should tell him?" Mole said in a low murmur.

China shone the beam of his smile on his friend. "Say what? Tell him what?"

"Get real, China. About Henry offing Cassidy."

"That be old shit. They ain't doin' nothin'."

"I don't know," said Mole.

"Hey, man. No way, brother. I been talkin' to those guys, and they see what I mean 'bout the Panther brotherhood. We startin' here in the Nam and we bringin' the true grit back home. We be tested in the fire, and tested under fire—"

Mole cut him short. "Just you stop, China. Just for once dispense with the revolutionary country preacher bullshit. Henry don't give a shit 'bout you Black Panther mumbo jumbo. He just need the brothers to be retailing while he wholesaling. If he have to kill Cassidy to stay in charge, he gonna do it."

China looked down on the parts spread out on Mole's poncho. "He just don't get it," he said softly.

"*You* just don't get it."

Mellas was awakened by the slight scraping of a boot on the plywood floor. His heart started pounding. He was covered in sweat and his head ached. Fitch, who was looking down at Mellas, sadness on his face, had deliberately scraped the boot so he wouldn't put Mellas into combat overdrive by waking him too abruptly.

"Hi, Jim," Mellas said.

Fitch sat down on the opposite cot. "You fucked up, Mellas?"

"Naw. Just had a few beers with Cassidy is all. What time is it?"

Fitch looked at his watch. "One o'clock."

"You're already on civilian time."

"Never left it," Fitch said.

Mellas swung his feet to the floor. His head was hot and pounding. He ran his hands through his hair, feeling sweat in it. He wiped them on his new stiff trousers. "I did manage to save my fucking boots," he said, looking at their familiar whiteness.

There was an awkward silence. "I guess then you heard I was leaving," Fitch finally said.

"Yeah." Mellas didn't know how to go on talking about it. He saw Fitch flush slightly, probably taking the silence as condemnation, so he said, "I'm real glad you're getting out."

"Me, too." Fitch forced a half smile and there was another awkward silence.

"When you leaving?" Mellas asked.

"Six o'clock. Getting the big bird out of Dong Ha. I ought to be in Oky by day after tomorrow."

"Laundry officer, huh?" Mellas smiled.

"Socks and T-shirts division."

"You could have gone to Mulvaney about this. It's a bum deal."

"I'd have to go through Simpson."

"Shit, Skipper. Back channel. You must know that's how it works."

Fitch looked away, toward the plywood wall, assuming the familiar thousand-yard stare. Mellas supposed that an entire movie was unreeling inside Fitch's mind. Fitch finally turned and looked into Mellas's good eye. "I don't want to go back to the bush. I'll do anything to stay alive."

He started stuffing gear into an already bulging seabag. He combed his hair, bending slightly to look into a steel mirror nailed to a two-by-four. Then he carefully put on a neatly starched stateside utility cover. His single silver lieutenant's bar gleamed, newly polished.

"Still dapper Dan," Mellas said.

"There's a place in Da Nang called the White Elephant," Fitch said, taking the cover off and smoothing his dark hair, "and it's got round-eyed pussy in it. Red Cross girls, stewardesses. Air-conditioned. There's even a goddamned German girl who sells Mercedes to AID fat cats. And in about three hours I'm going to be there getting fucked up, and I'm going to forget I ever saw this place."

He hoisted the seabag onto his shoulder. Mellas stood up, shakily. There was a sudden clutch in his throat. He could see Fitch's lips quiver, then go into the tight, pursed expression that Fitch used to hide his feelings from the rest of the company.

"You take care of yourself, Mellas," Fitch said. "I'll write and let you guys know what happened to me."

"We'd like that."

"You tell everyone to look me up when they get back to the world. You know it doesn't matter if they're snuffs."

"They know it."

They stood there looking at each other. Mellas was incredibly happy that Fitch had made it out alive.

Just before dark Mellas bought a bottle of Jack Daniel's from Gunnery Sergeant Klump and hitched a ride over to MAG-39, where he caught one of the last birds heading out to VCB. The empty, darkening land rolled beneath him. He thought of Cassidy, scared, getting drunk in the dim staff club. If it had gotten that bad, he'd better talk with the Jayhawk about it. Then he thought of Fitch in the brightly lit nightclub called the White Elephant, where American girls carried on with overweight AID and CORDS personnel. Then he thought of himself, heading for the dark jungle-covered mountains. Ten more months to go, he mused. Five more Trail of Tears ops. Five more Matterhorns. Mellas now knew that there was nothing special about Matterhorn and the Trail of Tears op. Both were just ordinary war.

Ten minutes later the chopper had reached the mountains and the jungle sea rolled in ever larger swells over the first of the foothills. Mellas pulled out his map—this was now a compulsive habit—and got his bearings as a prominent peak flashed beneath him, a river winding in a tight S-curve around it. Then they were over the next upthrust of hills, now higher and more rugged.

Mellas untied Vancouver's sword from the side of his pack and crawled over to an open porthole, squeezing past the door gunner, who was watching him while at the same time idly moving his eyes back and forth across the ground below. When Mellas reached the porthole, the blast of the air threatened to pull the patch off his eye. He tugged it back into place and then knelt, leaning into the rushing air, holding the sword out in front of him. Mellas looked at it for about half a minute, remembering. Then he threw the sword into the twilight.

He watched it falling behind them, twisting, catching a glint of the dying light before it merged into the vast unbroken gray-green below. Mellas then unfolded his map and carefully marked the spot where it had fallen with a cross, printing "VS," Vancouver's sword, next to it.

The door gunner shook his head. "You fucking grunts, man," he shouted at him. "Crazy motherfuckers."

Coming up on VCB in the early evening, Mellas felt the nostalgia that many people feel on coming home, no matter how squalid the setting. Below him a few lights, careless of NVA rockets, blinked out from behind the blackout curtains.

When he got out of the chopper a small group of field-grade officers from division staff were there, waiting to be picked up, with briefcases in hand and .45s in shiny black holsters. Mellas walked silently on the dark road toward the battalion area, passing the tents where he'd awaited the launching of the Bald Eagle. A company from Nineteenth Marines was there; the Marines were whittling, writing letters, cleaning rifles, and playing cards to counteract boredom and fear. The air was noticeably warmer than it had been the last time he'd been at VCB.

He reached Bravo Company's supply tent. Someone had made an attempt to straighten its sagging exterior. The interior was in good order, with seabags stacked neatly in the back on wooden pallets to keep them off the mud. The old writing table was there, with two candles burning on it. Three strangers sat inside.

"Can we help you, Marine?" one of them asked sharply. He was beefed up and obviously had just arrived from the world. He had a knife stuck in his boot. Mellas wanted to groan.

"Fuck," Mellas said. "Is this Bravo Company or what? I'm Lieutenant Mellas. Where's Hawke and Scar?"

The three strangers stood up.

Mellas sloughed off his pack, undid his belt-suspenders, and let everything fall with a thud to the metal runway matting beneath his feet.

"Welcome back, sir," the man said. "We've heard a lot about you. I'm Staff Sergeant Irvine and this is Staff Sergeant Bentham, and this is Lieutenant LaValley, sir." He hesitated a moment. "We heard that you lost the eye."

"So did everyone else," Mellas said.

Mellas shook hands with each of them, playing the role of silent wounded hero. He could see that the new lieutenant was in awe of him, just as he himself would have been in awe of a veteran a couple of months ago. Their reaction meant nothing to him now, other than informing him that tales of Matterhorn had probably been exaggerated far beyond anything he could have concocted, and that the new kids would be jittery as hell.

Mellas dug into his pack and pulled out the bottle of Jack Daniel's. "Any word on what's happening?"

The new lieutenant told him that they were going to Eiger and would spend about a week there guarding the artillery battery. Charlie Company would be dropped into the river valley north of Eiger at the same time and would move north. After a week the two companies would flip-flop. Alpha was already on Sky Cap with Delta Company sweeping the Suoi Tien Hien River valley just to its immediate east.

"When we leaving?" Mellas asked.

"Oh-six-hundred tomorrow."

Mellas grunted. "Then I guess I got time tonight to get fucked up." He held the bottle up to the new lieutenant and the two new staff sergeants. "Anybody want some? It's your last chance."

They each took a small shot in a coffee mug or canteen cup to show Mellas that they were friendly.

"You think the zone'll be hot when Charlie hits it?" the lieutenant asked, holding his mug between his knees and leaning forward.

"Do I look like a fucking gypsy?" Mellas wisecracked. "Naw. I don't think so." He looked at the amber liquid, reflecting the candlelight. "How're the troops?"

"We got a lot of boots, Lieutenant." It was the other staff sergeant, Bentham, who'd spoken up. Mellas looked at him, surprised. He talked as if he'd been in combat before. Mellas was thankful for that. He'd probably made sergeant on his last tour, then had gotten promoted to staff back in the world, and had been shipped out here as soon as his two years of grace were over.

"Which platoon you got?"

"I got Third Platoon. I have that until we get one more lieutenant."

"And you two?" Mellas asked the others.

"I'll be honchoing Second Platoon with Lieutenant Goodwin," the staff sergeant with the knife in his boot answered.

"And I've got your old platoon," LaValley said, smiling.

"They ain't mine," Mellas said, laughing. "You can blame all your troubles on a guy named Fracasso. Of course I'll take credit for anything they do that's good."

"From what I hear they never really had much time to feel like they were Lieutenant Fracasso's bunch," LaValley said.

Mellas swirled the whiskey. "Naw. He was one hell of a good guy. They were his platoon all right." He looked at LaValley, feeling a wave of sadness. Then he tossed down his whiskey and grinned, despite the empty hole in him that the whiskey couldn't fill. "Don't you worry about it. They'll be yours in no time. After you've been here awhile you can tell a winner from a loser in one second flat. You don't have anything to worry about."

Mellas tried to include everyone as he spoke, and he was sure everyone felt included. But he knew that the Jayhawk could also tell a winner from a loser. The guy with the fucking knife in his boot was going with Scar so that Scar could keep him from doing too much damage.

"As for me," Mellas added, "I'm going to go find a couple friends of mine and get knee-walking, commode-hugging drunk. And if I'm at all successful you might just have to take the company tomorrow while the skipper and executive officer try to regain consciousness."

He left them laughing and walked outside to look for Hawke and Goodwin. He saw a lone Marine walking up the road, with a towel around his neck and a soap container in one hand. Probably on his way to a final shower before the op.

"Lieutenant Mellas," the kid shouted, "we heard you was back." It was Fisher.

"Jesus Christ, Fisher. I thought you were back in the world. What do we have to do to get *out* of this fucking place?"

"Beats me, sir. I think we have to get killed."

They both stopped short at the words; then they both laughed.

They shook hands, grinning hugely.

"You OK? I mean, down there." Mellas nodded toward Fisher's crotch.

Fisher brought him up to speed on his operation and recovery from the leech.

"You mean everything works?" Mellas asked.

"I ain't shittin' you, Lieutenant," said Fisher. "At least everything works in Japan. Goddamn but I'm in love with Japanese women. They treat you real decent, sir."

"So I've heard," Mellas replied. "I'm glad you're OK. I mean it, Fisher. I'm really glad."

"Yeah. Thanks, sir," Fisher said. Then his expression changed. "I heard about you guys getting in the deep shit."

Mellas didn't want to talk about Matterhorn. "You got your old squad back?" he asked.

Fisher understood. "What's left of them," he said. "It's still Second Squad, I guess." He kicked at a mud clot. "Shit. Sixty-seven days to go. I'm a double-digit midget." He grinned at Mellas. "I'm so short I can swing my legs sitting on my flak jacket. In fact I'm so short, when I wear it, it drags on the ground. How many you got, Lieutenant?"

"Three-hundred-three and a wake-up." He pointed his finger at Fisher's face. "And don't give me any shit."

"Shit, Lieutenant, you still ought to count in months."

Mellas laughed, genuinely glad Fisher was getting short. He thrust the boxes of cigars at Fisher for him to hand out to the company and contined up the road. When he got to the BOQ tent he found McCarthy,

Murphy, Goodwin, and Hawke laughing around a footlocker with three bottles opened on it.

"Roll up for the magical mystery tour!" he sang. "I'm coming to take you a-way-y."

Two officers he didn't know groaned. One of them was trying to sleep. "Holy Christ. Another one."

"Hey!" McCarthy shouted. "It's Mellas. With a fucking patch!" Murphy hugged Mellas and lifted him off the floor while Mellas held the bottle of whiskey above his head. Murphy set Mellas down and McCarthy grabbed the bottle from him. "Blessed be God, forever," McCarthy said, holding it up to the light. "For our good and the good of the Corps." Mellas flipped him the bird.

"Scar and Patch," Hawke said. "I don't have a company. I've got a fucking animal act."

"Well, take your fucking act someplace else," the disgruntled would-be sleeper said. "I got a watch to stand in three hours."

"No fucking stamina," Hawke shot back. He stood and carefully put his stateside utility cover on his head, adjusting it in a steel mirror that hung on one of the tent poles. "Come on," he said. "Cassidy's in Quang Tri. Let's go over to his place and let these fine staff officers sleep."

Cassidy slept in a neat little room with its own exterior entry in the back of the S-4 tent. It was dark. Hawke eventually found a candle and lit it. He sat down on Cassidy's cot.

"By the way, Hawke," Mellas said, "congratulations on getting the company." He held out his hand. "It's number fucking one as far as I'm concerned."

"Thanks, Mel." Hawke leaned back on the cot. "It's funny though. It's like a different company."

"I know what you mean."

McCarthy handed Mellas and Goodwin mugs filled with whiskey. "Quit mourning over your fucking lost company," he said. "You're wasting my goddamned time."

"Then let's get this mystery tour on the road in *my* company jeep," Hawke said. "Who's sober enough to drive to the O-club?"

Mellas looked around. "I guess I'm about it," he said.

"Good," McCarthy said. "You sit in the back and catch up with us. I'll fucking drive."

Soon all five of them were sitting around a table at the crude regimental O-club, a hasty barricade against reality. A small generator hummed steadily, providing flickering light. The bare plywood walls still had the grade stamps showing. Exposed studs oozed pitch. A battered dartboard was nailed to one of the walls.

They stuck candles directly onto the table by melting puddles of wax. Then they ordered five drinks apiece, the only way to avoid squabbling over who would get the honor of buying the last round. McCarthy and Murphy stood at the bar while the bartender measured out twenty-five shot glasses of whiskey and placed them on two large trays. Holding the trays out in front of them, McCarthy and Murphy made their way between tables. McCarthy had a package of Ritz crackers in his teeth. Hawke took the crackers and opened one end while the shot glasses were placed on the table. McCarthy went back for two pitchers of water and five larger glasses that he set on the table in front of Hawke.

Hawke had been counting the number of crackers in the package. "Here," he said. "Seven each. Except I get eight because I'm the company commander." He passed the package over to Mellas, who took his seven and passed it on to Goodwin. Hawke picked up a pitcher and started to silently question them in turn about their preferences for how much water they wanted in their whiskey, holding up one, two, or three fingers. When everyone had been served, he raised his glass and said, "*Semper Fi*, motherfuckers," and threw down the first drink.

Soon Mellas was deliciously high, so that the bourbon tasted smooth and cool while simultaneously warming his belly. It was a magical contrast. He was well aware of the moment, in spite of the bourbon. He knew that the five of them had shared experiences no one else had shared or would share. He also knew it was unlikely that all of them would live to share such a moment again. Indeed, he could be the one missing. All the gaiety in the world—all the shouting, all the pain-numbing drunkenness—

would not conceal that lurking thought. But the lurking thought was what made him aware that this moment was precious.

"Hey, Mel," Hawke said, "when we get back to the world we ought to go into business or something. Shit, all five us. Wouldn't that be a gas?"

"With what we know, all we could do is compete with the Mafia," Murphy said.

"The only business you could ever run is a fucking bar," McCarthy said. "But I'd run one with you."

"I'll drink to that," Hawke said, lifting his glass. "That's it. A fucking bar." He hiccupped. "A special fucking bar." He giggled. "We'll call it the Bunker."

"Naw," Mellas said. "Not sophisticated enough. Call it Ellsworth."

"Fuck you and your sophistication, Jack," Goodwin said. "We want a fucking bar, not some fairy discotheque."

"That's right," McCarthy said, "and to get a drink there you have to park your car four hundred meters away and cut through solid bamboo and elephant grass with a machete to find it."

Mellas thought for a moment. "Only you don't give the customers any fucking maps," he said. "No maps!" He started to slap his palm on the table with each word. "No fucking maps!"

"But you could have one smoke grenade," Hawke said. "That way if you give up, a chopper can take you back to the parking lot free of charge."

"Charge the fucking bastards, Jayhawk," McCarthy said. "Jesus. I don't know about you and business. You can't make money if you're going to be a softy."

The banter about the Bunker got louder and more outrageous. Make the customers throw bits of food to the rats and pop leeches on the tables. Make them fill a hundred sandbags as a cover charge. Make them squat on their haunches or sit on a wet floor. Make them get their water by licking the overhead pipes. Make them piss in the corners. Make them walk back to the parking lot only to find their cars stolen. Soon all five were standing, stamping their feet, and chanting, over and over, "No resupply! No medevacs! No maps!"

Finally Hawke sat down. The rest followed. "It'd never work," Hawke said, taking a drink.

"Why not, Jack?" Goodwin asked.

"The government would never give us a license to blow up half the customers."

There was a moment's silence. Then Murphy raised his glass. "Here's to the Bunker," he said. His head jerked up toward the raised glass.

"And all the customers," Hawke said.

There was another silence while they toyed with their glasses. "Ah, fuck you guys," Murphy said. "You don't know a good time when you have one."

"Typical fucking lifer, Murphy," Mellas said. "Every shitty thing's a good time for you guys. That's why the government will always get you to do its shitty jobs for it." Mellas tossed back the rest of his drink and put the glass on the table. "You're fucking fools."

Everyone was quiet. McCarthy was clearly suppressing a smile. He caught Hawke's eye and then looked toward Murphy. Mellas didn't pick up on the fact that he was sailing in treacherous waters.

"Someone's got to do the shitty jobs, Mel," Murphy said, wrapping his hands around his empty glass.

"Well, I've done all the shitty jobs they'll ever get me doing. I'm getting the fuck out. Fuck you *and* your government, if you're dumb enough to stay in."

"How in the hell do you expect the fucking Marine Corps to ever get its shit together if you chickenshit assholes fuck off and leave it because you figure you can make more money someplace else?"

"Suck out, Murph. All the fucking money in the world wouldn't keep my ass in the Crotch."

"So why are you leaving?"

"I fucking hate it, that's why," Mellas said. "I'm sick of the fucking lies and covering the lies with blood."

"I'll drink to that," McCarthy said, and belched.

"That's no fucking answer," Murphy said. His beefy arms rested in pools of spilt bourbon. The others were sitting back in their chairs, silly grins on their faces, watching Mellas and Murphy pair off, the hare and the bear. "You guys take off and leave it to the liars and the ass-lickers and the troops get fucked over worse. You're just chickenshit to stand up in public with a goddamned short haircut because you're afraid you'll never get laid."

Instead of accepting that the gibe hurt because it was true, Mellas lost his temper. "You stand the fuck up," he said, rising from his chair. His fists were clenched.

McCarthy pulled him down by the back of his utility jacket. "Jesus, Mellas, Murphy will kill you. Just because he hit a fucking sore spot doesn't mean you have to become a human sacrifice over it."

"Murphy's right," Hawke said. "Since you been in the Corps, Mellas, how many women you dated that have gone to college and aren't southern?"

"Fuck all, that's how many," McCarthy answered for him.

"Right," Hawke said. "You go up to D.C. and there's all sorts of college girls working for all sorts of government offices, but you're there in your short fucking haircut and you're a nigger in Georgetown if ever there was one."

"Thank you, Theodore J. Hawke," Mellas said. "Another pea-green philosopher." He thought of Karen Elsked and felt empty.

Hawke leaned back in his chair. "You think I'm lying? In six months, you two"—he was pointing at Mellas and McCarthy—"six months after you're out of the Corps, if you get out of this place alive, you'll be goddamned long-haired commie intellectuals telling everybody how fucked up the war is and how you knew all along. And you know what? You'll be lying. Lying so you can get ahead in their world. You'll be wearing your hair down to your ass, smoking dope, and marching and protesting and wearing fucking beads and sandals just like the rest of them. And you'll be doing it for no other reason than to make the girls like you."

"Fuck off, Hawke," McCarthy said.

"I won't fuck off." Hawke leaned back into the table. "You'll both be afraid to go back to the world and tell all those assholes that you were good fucking Marines. Oh, you weren't Marine legends. You weren't even the best. But you were good. And you'll try to tell everyone how bad you were and how sorry you are so you won't have to explain how it really is. How good it can feel to do something so bad."

"You're fucking drunk," McCarthy said, "but I'll drink to that." He did, draining his glass and then smacking it down on the table. "I fucking volunteered."

"Didn't we all?" Mellas said. He stood and raised his glass, nearly falling in the process. "Here's to the fucking volunteers." Everyone solemnly stood. Hawke was weaving uncertainly. Murphy and Goodwin were leaning against each other. They touched glasses and drank. Then Mellas turned and looked directly at Hawke. He held his empty glass in front of his face and, looking over it at Hawke with his good eye, quietly said, "Bravo has died. Bravo is risen. Bravo will fight again." Then he raised the glass above his head. "Mea culpa," he added.

Hawke's eyes focused for a moment and he solemnly made the sign of the cross. "Absolution," he said, somewhat slurred. His eyes became unfocused again. Mellas smiled his thanks, and he and Hawke clinked glasses. Mellas looked for a moment at his empty glass and then let it drop to the floor. It broke. He took a full glass and held it above his head while he made a complete turn. Then he dipped his thumb and two fingers into the whiskey and began to anoint those around him with solemn ceremonial movements of his wrist, chanting, "Dulce et decorum est pro patria mor-r-i. Dulce et decorum est pro patria mor-r-i."

Hawke knelt down and stuck his tongue out. McCarthy solemnly placed a piece of cracker on it. He picked up a whiskey glass with both hands and began to pour the contents slowly on Hawke's head. The whiskey dripped down Hawke's face. Then McCarthy made the sign of the cross over Hawke's head and chanted, "In the name of the colonel and the Three and a do-nothing Con-n-gress."

Hawke knelt there with his tongue out, catching the amber liquid as it dribbled down his face. McCarthy then held up his fingers in a V—the peace sign—and turned slowly around, his arm raised high over his head. He intoned to the now silent crowd, "Peace. My peace I give you." Then, with his thumb and two adjoining fingers together, high above his head, he turned a complete circle, saying, "Deliver us from every evil and grant us peace in our day." After that he took the empty glass, looked at it for a moment, and shattered it against the wall. Hawke threw himself over backward and lay on the floor, spread-eagled, staring drunkenly at the ceiling.

"Hey, Jack," Goodwin said, "this party's getting too fucking religious."

In Cassidy's room they passed around some beers. They felt the closeness that arises from sharing, as in passing a peace pipe. Hawke talked about his number-one squaw. She'd written him a letter saying that she had a new boyfriend and that she couldn't go on writing to him, because she was opposed to what he was doing. The five of them drank to her continued good health and moral fiber. Mellas could tell that Hawke was hurt badly, but Hawke didn't let on and drank with everyone else, mocking the end of the relationship.

Eventually the beers were finished and Goodwin, Murphy, and McCarthy wandered out to get two hours of sleep before pushing off on the operation. Hawke and Mellas were left alone. Mellas was bone-weary and his head was spinning. He wanted to sleep but knew this was their last night together before their new formal relationship added a layer of complication. Tomorrow Hawke would be the skipper and Mellas the executive officer.

They fiddled with the empty beer cans in an embarrassed silence. Finally Mellas gently tossed his empty beer can at Hawke and said, "You scared about going back to the bush?"

"Why you think I'm fucking drunk?"

They were silent a moment.

"I'm glad you got the company, Ted. It would have been a disaster if I'd have gotten it."

Hawke smiled and shook his head. "Mellas, you dumb shit, you didn't have a chance of getting it. You're still a boot motherfucker."

Mellas smiled and nodded his head in agreement. "Yeah, but it still would have been a disaster."

"Fuck, Mellas. You'll make first lieutenant in another month or so, then a few months after that you'll be short and all you'll want to do is go home. So that's when they'll offer it to you, when you won't want it any more. But there won't be any better alternative, so you'll take it on. And you'll be the best alternative."

Mellas laughed, pleased and embarrassed at the praise. "Anyway, it'll be a pleasure to work with you. In fact, I'd seriously think about opening up that fucking bar with you if we make it back to the world." He laughed briefly through his nose. "The Bunker. I'd let all the vets watch the customers through one-way mirrors."

Hawke leaned back and smiled at the roof of the tent. Then he sat up, suddenly sober. "It's a fucking fantasy, Mellas. At least for eighteen years."

"What do you mean?"

"I went regular."

"No."

"Yeah," Hawke said. He tried to sound lighthearted. "Wrapping myself in Marine Corps scarlet and gold."

Mellas said nothing.

Hawke fumbled for the right words, looking at his crumpled beer can rather than at Mellas. "You know. Shit. I don't know what the fuck I'd do once I got back to the world. You're different. You'll go to fucking law school or something and walk right on up to the top. Me? Shit. There's good people here. Mulvaney. Coates. Cassidy. Even Stevens. He tries." He looked up at Mellas. "Good guys. Good officers."

"If I hadn't thrown my fucking beer can at you I'd toast you." Mellas lay back on the rack and stared at the folds of the tent above him, watching the play of shadows from the single candle. "Murphy's right. The troops get fucked even worse if the good guys don't stay in."

Mellas thought in silence about the old Bravo Company, now gone, scattered to hospitals in Japan or the Philippines, or in rubberized body bags on commercial airliners heading across the Pacific toward home.

"Tell me something, Hawke," Mellas said, not looking at him but just watching the shadows on the ceiling. "Before you become Bravo Six"—he couldn't resist adding a small bite—"and a regular"—Hawke flipped him the bird—"why did the colonel send us up the fucking hill the second time?" Mellas's voice started to tremble. It caught him by surprise. "The gooks weren't running. Delta Company could have done it."

Hawke took some time before he answered. "Because you volunteered. He'd cut the order for the assault but at the last minute he told Fitch that he'd switch in Delta if Fitch didn't want to do the job."

Mellas sat up. The tears that had started to form when he began talking about the assault were shut off, but his throat constricted. "What?"

"Simpson told Fitch he had two choices: get the company's pride back for abandoning Matterhorn, which is why there had to be another assault, or be a yellow-livered dog and let Delta Company clean up Bravo's mess." He paused. "And all that entails. You know how small the Marine Corps is."

"If I'd known Fitch volunteered, I'd have wanted to kill him, too," Mellas said quietly, almost musingly.

"And if you'd been faced with the same choice, you'd have volunteered just like Fitch," Hawke said.

"I know it," Mellas answered.

"You still feel like killing Simpson?"

"Naw. You know I went crazy up there. He was just doing his job." Mellas lay back on the cot. "I just wish he'd do it sober." He laughed and Hawke joined in. Then they lapsed into silence.

"The funny thing is," Mellas said, "I still like Fitch. I'd have gone up the hill with him even if I knew."

"Before or after you would have killed him?"

"Both."

The two were again quiet. The alcohol blurred Mellas's vision and threatened to pull him into sleep. Then he surfaced again. "He still volunteered us, the poor fucking bastard. He'll carry that a lot longer than a bad fitness report. And here I've been feeling bad because I enjoy killing people."

Hawke laughed quietly. "At least you're over the hump on that one. It's the people who don't know it who are dangerous. There's at least two hundred million of them back in the world. Boot camp doesn't make us killers. It's just a fucking finishing school." He gave a bitter laugh. "I remember my ex-fucking squaw telling me it was inconceivable— that was her word, *inconceivable*—that she could ever go to Vietnam like I did, no matter what the consequences. This was just before she went to Europe for her junior year and met her new boyfriend."

With one hand Hawke crushed the beer can he was holding. He began to work the mangled can back and forth, twisting it, bending it. Mellas didn't say anything. "None of them have ever met the mad monkey inside us," Hawke added. "But we have."

"There it is," Mellas said.

Hawke's voice became softer and softer. "Maybe we could have an amusement park across the street with a ride called the Mad Monkey." He lay across the cot, feet on the floor, eyes closed.

"You're about to crash, Jayhawk," Mellas said gently.

"Fuck if I am," Hawke mumbled. "I'm just resting my eyes."

They both laughed at the old joke. Then Hawke's breathing became slow and regular.

"Hey," Mellas said. "Jayhawk."

"Hmm."

Mellas lifted Hawke's feet up on the cot, put a poncho liner over him, and blew out the candle. The tent was plunged into blackness. Mellas made his way through the rain and darkness to the Bravo Company supply tent and rolled up in his poncho liner. He fell asleep on the metal runway floor, listening to the wheezes and grunts of the sleeping strangers who would soon share his life so intimately.

Someone was shaking him awake.

"What the fuck is it?" he whispered, his head aching badly.

"It's me, China, sir."

"Goddamn, China, what the fuck do you want?" Mellas rolled over. His wounded eye was pounding even worse than his head. He wondered what he'd done with the patch, or whether he'd lost it someplace. Then he found it on top of his head.

"Lieutenant Mellas, you got to help. They's gonna be trouble tonight."

"What do you mean?"

"I mean I think they's gonna to be someone killed," China whispered.

Mellas heard a scraping sound outside the tent behind China. Then a match was struck and he saw Mole lighting a candle. Mole's face, like China's, was tense and worried.

Mellas said, "Oh, fuck, I got to piss. Give me a fucking second." Mellas stood outside the flap of the tent and peed into the darkness and cold. When he returned, China and Mole were talking in low whispers. The others were sound asleep, except for the new lieutenant, who was staring at the three of them wide-eyed, but keeping out of things. Mellas led them outside.

"Now what the fuck's going on?" Mellas whispered. He was fully dressed, not having undressed when he had collapsed on the floor.

"It's Cassidy, sir," China said. "I think they gonna frag him tonight. I wanted to just throw a fuckin' fake in, you know, to make a statement, but they gonna waste him instead. They said a fuckin' pop won't get nothin' done."

"But Cassidy's in fucking Quang Tri," Mellas said. "What the fuck can I do about that?"

"No, he's not, sir. He's come back. We saw the lights on in there tonight."

China's words jerked Mellas's spine straight. "Jesus Christ," he whispered. "The Jayhawk's in there."

Mole, startled, looked at China. "That's why we couldn't find him."

Mellas started running. He could think only of getting Hawke out of Cassidy's rack. He felt sick and wanted to throw up but kept running.

Mole flew past Mellas, his longer legs moving even more swiftly, sprinting with everything he had to reach Hawke. China, who was stockier, came behind. All three were filled with a dread that pushed them like a hand on their backs, racing with them, as the low ground fog swirled beneath their running feet.

The explosion ripped through the air and sent Mellas ahead even faster, running as he had never run before, but burdened by despair.

Dark shadows flitted away from the tent. Mellas rushed through the entrance just behind Mole. He could see nothing inside. He smelled the sickening, burning odor of TNT. Mellas stumbled over to the rack where he had laid Hawke. The grenade had gone off directly beneath him. Pieces of mattress ticking still hung in the air. What remained of the torn mattress was sticky with blood. He tried to feel where the bleeding was coming from, running his hands over the limp body. "Get a light!" he screamed. "Get a fucking light!" Hawke was lying facedown. Mellas located Hawke's head and felt his neck for a pulse. There was nothing. He felt beneath his body for his chest and encountered only warm pulp. He'd been laying facedown when the grenade went off beneath him.

Mellas heard footsteps outside, and then a flashlight shone in through the door. The light shone on Hawke's face. His eyes were open. He must have heard the grenade clunk to the floor just before it exploded.

China was trembling in the doorway of the tent with the flashlight. Mole was talking to him quietly, his arm over China's shoulder. They both looked at Mellas, terrified.

Mellas began to shake. Unable to control the shaking, he squatted on his haunches, steadying himself on Hawke's rack, looking at Hawke's open eyes. There was no Hawke behind them.

"Bye, Jayhawk," he said, and closed the eyes.

He stood and looked at Mole and China. He wanted to beat them senseless, cut their tongues out, for keeping quiet until it was too late. He wanted to scream accusations of murder and send them to prison. At the same time he knew that nothing would be gained but more bitterness. Justice in the midst of war was a scrap of paper in the wind. If he implicated Henry, he would drag in China and Mole, and he didn't want to do that. Their only sin was the one he'd committed too often himself, not speaking up. Besides, he liked them, and the company couldn't afford to lose its two best machine gunners. He was suddenly aware that he was thinking like the company commander. He had 200 Marines to take care of. Everyone could deal with his own conscience. Mellas truly no longer cared about justice or punishment—at least, he no longer cared about the kind the courts stood for. Revenge would heal nothing. Revenge had no past. It only started things. It only created more waste, more loss, and he knew that the waste and loss of this night could never be redeemed. There was no filling the holes of death. The emptiness might be filled up by other things over the years—new friends, children, new tasks—but the holes would remain.

Mellas saw Hawke's tin-can cup hanging on his belt suspender over the back of a chair. He unhooked the cup and stuffed it into one of his own pockets. "You two had better get out of here," he said quietly to Mole and China as he walked out past them.

Mellas stayed around for the inevitable hullabaloo. Bravo Company, to a man, stonewalled, as did he. All he knew was that he'd been asleep when the grenade went off. Any investigators would have to find their way to Henry on their own. If they didn't, so be it. If they did, there'd be insufficient evidence to bring about a trial, much less a conviction. Moreover, there was a war to fight, and no one would benefit from a long and time-consuming murder investigation.

When the hullabaloo died down, Mellas walked alone to the edge of the deserted landing strip and lay down in the mud. He cried until he could cry no more. Then he just lay there, empty, alone beneath the slowly graying sky.

Goodwin finally found him and helped him up. They walked to the COC bunker, where Blakely informed them that Mellas would be the new company commander until a captain arrived. If Mellas did a good job, maybe he'd get a company of his own later—maybe even Bravo Company. His first task, however, once Eiger was secured, would be to help the S-1 write up the investigation of the accidental death.

CHAPTER
TWENTY-THREE

The operation kicked off at 0600 as planned. By 1000 the company was set in and Mellas had three patrols out. Only with the coming of evening and its soft fading light could he finally be alone. He hid behind a blasted stump and he tried to think about meaning. He knew that there could be no meaning to someone who was dead. Meaning came out of living. Meaning could come only from his choices and actions. Meaning was made, not discovered. He saw that he alone could make Hawke's death meaningful by choosing what Hawke had chosen, the company. The things he'd wanted before—power, prestige—now seemed empty, and their pursuit endless. What he did and thought in the present would give him the answer, so he would not look for answers in the past or future. Painful events would always be painful. The dead are dead, forever.

Mellas longed to go out on patrol, back to the purity and green vitality of the jungle, where death made sense as part of the ordered cycle in which it occurred, in the dispassionate search for food that involved loss of life in order to sustain life. He thought of the tiger that killed Williams. The jungle and death were the only clean things in the war.

The warm evening was a harbinger of the post-monsoon heat that would soon follow. Mellas felt the dark night beginning to enfold him like a woman's arms. The listening posts were out. So were the major stars, brilliant in the sky. Toward Laos, lazy green NVA tracers and antiaircraft fire floated beautifully above the horizon. The NVA were trying to kill an American pilot, but the distance made the effort seem no more than a slow-motion fireworks display. Mellas felt a slight breeze from the mountains rustling across the grass valley below him to the north. He was acutely aware of the natural world. He imagined the jungle, pulsing with life, quickly enveloping Matterhorn, Eiger, and all the other shorn hilltops, covering everything. All around him the mountains and the jungle whispered and moved, as if they were aware of his presence but indifferent to it.

He started to fix coffee, knowing he'd need the caffeine to stay awake through the night, and it would soon be too dark for him to heat anything safely. Hawke's old pear-can cup felt familiar and good. Mellas had found comfort in it several times already that day as he carefully and mindfully brewed coffee, remembering Hawke. When he finished making the coffee he took a careful first sip; the edge of the cup was heated to a satisfying lip-burning temperature.

He became aware of someone, down on the lines below him, tapping out a rhythm on a drum made from a C-ration box. It was a strange, wild, strong rhythm. It grew loud, then soft, but it was always fierce. Then soft voices, chanting in a weird atonal harmony, rose like spirits from the earth below him. As the rhythm became stronger, the voices became more intense, although not really louder. Gradually he could make out the words of the chant, as if he had tuned in to its frequency. The words chilled him but at the same time lifted his soul skyward.

The voices were chanting the names of the dead.

If it's good enough for Jacobs, then it's good enough for me.
If it's good enough for Jacobs, then it's good enough for me.
If it's good enough for Jacobs, then it's good enough for me.
Good enough for me. Good enough for me.

The voices chanted on. With each new name the rhythm would be altered to fit the syllables. Mellas walked slowly down the hill to find the chanters, being careful not to spill his hot coffee. They were Conman, Mole, and Gambaccini. Mole was drumming the C-ration box. The three of them were staring into the darkness, lost in their rhythm. Mellas sat down. He didn't disturb them.

He heard a slight noise behind him and looked up. China was standing there listening and watching. Mellas moved over slightly and patted the ground next to him. China sat down. Mellas lifted the hot tin-can
cup in a silent toast to Hamilton. He handed it to China, who took a
drink and handed it back. Neither said a word.

If it's good enough for Shortround then it's good enough for me . . .

Each of the names evoked a remembered face, an outstretched
hand reaching down from a rock or across a rushing stream—or a look
of fear as a friend realized that death had come for him.

If it's good enough for Parker then it's good enough for me . . .

Mellas tried to shake off the other images: the burned bodies, the
smell, the stiff awkwardness beneath the wet ponchos. He couldn't. The
chanting went on, the musicians giving in to the rhythm of their own
being, finding healing in touching that rhythm, and healing in chanting
about death, the only real god they knew.

Mellas didn't sleep that night. He sat on the ground and stared out
to the northwest, toward Matterhorn. He watched the mountains sub-
tly change under the shadows of clouds cast by a waning moon as it
moved across the sky until the shadows began to fade with the coming
of light in the east. He tried to determine if there was meaning in the
fact that cloud shadows from moonlight could move across the mountains and yet nothing on the mountain would move or even be affected.
He knew that all of them were shadows: the chanters, the dead, the living. All shadows, moving across this landscape of mountains and valleys, changing the pattern of things as they moved but leaving nothing
changed when they left. Only the shadows themselves could change.

GLOSSARY
OF WEAPONS,
TECHNICAL
TERMS, SLANG,
AND JARGON

actual   Specific person commanding a unit, as opposed to just the unit in general. For example, if someone calling on the radio said, "This is Charlie One," this would mean that it could be anyone on the radio, usually the radio operator, calling from First Platoon of Charlie Company. If the person said, "This is Charlie One Actual," it would mean that the speaker was the actual commander of First Platoon. "Put your actual on" meant "I want to talk to your commanding officer."

A. J. Squaredaway   Marines used made-up names to personify conditions or standards. A. J. Squaredaway meant looking sharp. There were others. Joady was the guy screwing your girl back home and Joe Shit the ragpicker was the opposite of A. J. Squaredaway.

AK-47   Standard-issue automatic weapon used by the North Vietnamese Army and the Vietcong. It fired a 7.62-millimeter bullet at a lower velocity than the M-16. It was much less accurate than the M-16, but far easier to maintain under jungle conditions; and in close-in jungle fighting, accuracy at a distance was not a significant factor.

Arc Light missions   "Arc Light" was an Air Force operation that used B-52s based on Guam. These B-52s were modified to carry thirty tons of conventional bombs, which were guided to the targets by ground-control radar. The missions were most often flown at night against enemy base camps, troop concentrations, and supply lines.

arty   Artillery.

ARVN   Army of the Republic of Vietnam, the South Vietnamese army—allies of the United States.

ASAP   As soon as possible.

Avenues   A gang of the 1960s in Los Angeles.

baseball team   Radio brevity code for a squad (thirteen Marines).

Basic School, the   Lowest-level Marine Corps officer school, where all Marine officers, including Marine pilots, are given the basic education needed to run a rifle platoon and company. It is located in Quantico, Virginia, and its name is abbreviated TBS.

basketball team   Radio brevity code for a fire team (four Marines).

battalion   A battalion, usually about 1,200 to 1,300 Marines and sixty naval medical personnel, had four rifle companies, and one larger headquarters and supply company (H & S) that held the 106-millimeter recoilless rifles, the 81-millimeter mortars, and the supply, maintenance, communications, mess, medical, and administrative personnel. Each battalion usually had a specific 105-millimeter artillery battery attached to it permanently from the regiment's artillery battalion. A battalion was usually commanded by a lieutenant colonel, often called a "light colonel." That rank is designated by a silver oak leaf. In the Marine Corps during the 1960s, command of a battalion was critical for advancement to high rank.

battery   Artillery unit roughly equivalent in size to a rifle company. A battery in Vietnam had six 105-millimeter howitzers. One battery was normally assigned to one infantry battalion and whenever possible was situated on the highest ground in the area it was intended to support.

The battery often sent out forward observers to move with the infantry to help call in artillery missions. All Marine infantry officers and non-commissioned officers (NCOs) can call in artillery fire; however, lacking detailed knowledge of the immense amount of technical difficulties faced by artillerymen, they are usually more impatient than the forward observers.

bingo fuel   Out of gas.

bird   Any helicopter, but for the Marines it was usually a CH-46 helicopter.

blowing a dump   Destroying an ammunition supply storage site (or ammo dump) by setting off explosive charges in the midst of the ammunition.

Brown, H. Rap   A 1960s black radical and defense minister of the Black Panther Party.

Butterbar   A second lieutenant, often new and inexperienced, so called because the rank was designated by a single gold bar.

CAG   Acronym for combined action group. This was a small group composed of Marines and local militiamen called popular forces (in slang, ruff-puffs, from Republic of Vietnam Popular Forces) that was placed in a small specific area to protect villages from intimidation and terror. This idea achieved considerable success, and the Marines who fought in CAG units were brave and competent, having to operate on their own away from traditional unit structures. Unfortunately, following the iron law of manipulation—that if a system can be invented, a countersystem can be invented—Marine infantry commanders would often "volunteer" shirkers and troublemakers for duty with CAG to get them out of their own units.

C-4   Composition C-4 plastic explosive was used for virtually anything from cooking coffee to blowing up ammunition dumps and clearing landing zones. It came in white bars about one foot long, one inch thick, and three inches across, wrapped in olive drab cellophane. It could be safely dropped, cut, pulled into long cords, or stuffed into cracks. It was detonated by blasting caps, which had to be carried in special small wooden boxes and were much more dangerous. When ignited in the open, C-4 burned with an extremely hot white flame but did not explode. Its primary use in this configuration, strictly against policy, was for heating C-ration cans. When detonated by a blasting cap, C-4 was a powerful explosive. A thin cord wrapped around a two-foot-diameter tree would cut the tree in two, although a preferred method was to put one charge slightly higher than another on opposite sides and cut the tree between the two offset blasts.

CH-46   Twin-rotor assault helicopter called the Sea Knight, used by the Marines for assaults, resupply, and medevacs. It had a crew of five: pilot, copilot, crew chief, and two aerial machine gunners. It had a long fuselage and a ramp at its tail where Marines got on and off. This ramp was pulled up to serve as the rear door when the CH-46 was airborne. Depending on the altitude, temperature, how many gunners were carried aboard, and how much risk the pilot was willing to take, a CH-46 would carry from eight to fifteen Marines as far as 150 miles. In emergencies more people were carried, but then the risks went much greater. Alternatively, the CH-46 could carry about two tons of "external load," slung beneath it in a cargo net. Its maximum speed was approximately 160 miles per hour. The CH-46 Sea Knight was smaller and carried less load than the more familiar CH-47 Chinook used by the Army, although the two helicopters looked similar. Because of the requirement for folding rotors and efficient storage aboard ships, the Marine CH-46 was not capable of carrying the heavier loads that the Army CH-47 helicopter— with its permanent rotor blades and larger engines—could manage. The Marine Corps depended primarily on the CH-46 to deliver its units to combat. The CH-46 also doubled as the supply and medevac workhorse because the Marines were insufficiently supplied with the more mobile and versatile Huey.

CH-47   Twin-rotor turbine-driven helicopter called the Chinook and used by the Army. It was made by Boeing Vertol and from a distance looked like a very large CH-46. Its crew consisted of a pilot, a copilot, a crew chief, and one or two waist machine gunners. The Army chose the CH-47 as more of a workhorse supply vehicle and depended on the smaller Hueys to deliver its infantry units into combat.

chi-comm Hand-thrown antipersonnel fragmentation grenade used by the NVA and Vietcong. It had a wooden throwing handle and a round cylindrical form; hence the nickname "potato masher."

chopper Any helicopter.

chuck Among Marines in the bush in Vietnam, a non-derogatory term for a white Marine, used by both races, as in "He's a chuck dude." It was more along the lines of jive talk, like calling someone a cat. It most likely was derived from "Charles," also slang for "the man." It was usually opposed to "splib," commonly used slang for a black Marine.

CID Acronym for criminal investigation division. The Marine Corps CID was responsible for investigating and uncovering criminal activity taking place within Marine units. Major concerns during the Vietnam War were drug dealing and fragging. Agents, in many cases civilians, often worked under cover posing as ordinary Marines. They had roughly the same standing among Marines as narcs or snitches did among civilians who used drugs. Most Marines saw drug use in rear areas as a victimless crime and the penalties—long prison terms and dishonorable discharges—as unfair. Drug use in the bush, where lives could be lost as a result of failure to perform, particularly on watch, was discouraged through what could politely be described as self-policing activities.

claymore Popular fan-shaped antipersonnel land mine that used composition C-4 as its explosive. It produced a directional, fan-shaped pattern of fragments and was usually placed aboveground in front of a fighting hole or alongside a trail for an ambush. When detonated, from a fighting hole using an electric detonator wire, the M18A1 Claymore delivered 700 spherical steel balls over a sixty-degree fan-shaped pattern that was more than six feet high and fifty yards wide by the time the fragments reached fifty yards out. It was named after a large Scottish sword by its inventor, Norman A. MacLeod. One side of the mine was inscribed with the bold embossed words, THIS SIDE TOWARD ENEMY.

CO   commanding officer.

COC   combat operations center. This was usually a tent with sand-bag walls, or, if the unit had been in place long enough, a bunker made entirely of sandbags with a roof usually made from steel runway mat, also covered with sandbags. It contained all the maps, radios, and personnel that ran a battalion or regimental combat headquarters. It was the tactical nerve center of the battalion or regiment.

company   During the Vietnam War a Marine rifle company consisted of 212 to 216 Marines and seven Navy hospital corpsmen. It was designed to be led by a captain (two silver bars), and at the beginning of the war the majority of companies were. By 1969, however, many were being led by a first lieutenant (one silver bar); and during intense periods of fighting, a second lieutenant (one gold bar) could end up running a company until a higher-ranking replacement arrived. The company consisted of three rifle platoons and a weapons platoon. The weapons platoon was designed to have a second or first lieutenant in charge and consisted of nine M-60 machine-gun crews and three 60-millimeter mortar crews. But in the jungle and mountain fighting during the Vietnam War, machine guns, which were originally in the weapons platoon, were attached directly to the rifle platoons, usually one per squad. This left only the 60-millimeter mortar squad as the entire weapons platoon, usually led by a corporal or sergeant who reported directly to the company commander. Companies usually operated with 160 to 180 Marines, because of attrition.

conex box   Short for "container, express." A conex box was a heavy corrugated-steel shipping container about eight feet long, six feet high, and six feet wide. One end was hinged and could be opened like a heavy door to facilitate loading.

Coors   Radio brevity code for "killed in action." These codes changed frequently.

cordon and search   Operation in which an entire village or even an area (if enough troops were used) was surrounded: i.e., "cordoned off."

Units were then sent in to search the houses and hiding places for NVA or Vietcong. If any were flushed out, they could not escape through the ring of surrounding troops.

CORDS   Civil Operations and Revolutionary Development Support. A hybrid civilian and military organization under the Department of State that was formed to coordinate the U.S. civil and military pacification programs. Some of its personnel actively tried to make pacification work, exposing themselves to danger, but far too many were seen as rear-area fat-asses.

corpsmen   Navy medical personnel assigned to Marine units, the equivalent of the Army medics. They provided the first medical care received by a wounded Marine and were highly respected. Many sacrificed their lives trying to save wounded Marines. At full strength, every Marine rifle company had two Navy corpsmen assigned to each of the three platoons, and one additional senior corpsman, usually an HM-1, their boss, assigned to the small company command post or CP. Because of shortages later in the Vietnam War, many platoons got by with a single corpsman, and companies got by with HM-2s instead of HM-1s.

CP   A command post. Technically, the term refers to a spot on the ground where the company or platoon commander set up with his radio operators and staff. An equally common use of the term referred to the group of people, not the place, as in "the CP group." In a typical Marine company in Vietnam, there was no "post"—that is, no physical structure such as a bunker (as seen in movies). Instead, there were just fighting holes like those on the lines or, when a unit was on the move or in action, simply any place from which a company or platoon commander would direct the unit.

C-ration   Often called C-rats or by less neutral nicknames. The standard C-ration, used beginning in World War II and believed by most Marines in Vietnam to have been packed at the same time, came in three "styles" or "units," contained in thin cardboard boxes. The B1 style had a single small can, the size of a tuna fish can, full of chopped ham and eggs, ham slices, beef, or turkey loaf; and a larger can of fruit, such as applesauce, fruit cocktail, peaches, or pears. The B2 had larger cans of beans and wieners, spicy meatballs, beefsteak and potatoes, spaghetti and meatballs, and ham and lima beans (considered inedible except under extreme duress). This package also contained a small can of pound cake, pecan roll, or fruit cake, and cheese spread (caraway and pimento) and thick crackers. The B3 unit contained meat loaf, chicken and noodles, spiced meat, and boned chicken. All three styles also came with an accessory pack containing a white plastic spoon, instant coffee, sugar and nondairy creamer, two Chiclets, cigarettes in a four-smoke mini pack (Winston, Marlboro, Salem, Pall Mall, Camel, Chesterfield, Kent, and Lucky Strike), a small roll of toilet paper, moisture-resistant paper matches, and salt and pepper.

Crotch, the   Slang for the Corps, the Marine Corps.

cumshaw   A bribe. Pidgin English, from Chinese (Amoy) *gamsia*, an expression of thanks.

dee-dee   To run away or exit quickly. From the Vietnamese *didi mao*, "go away." One example would be "Let's dee-dee," meaning, "Let's get out of here fast." Another would be "The enemy dee-deed," meaning that they left quickly.

division   Large unit, approximately 13,000 to 14,000 Marines, usually commanded by a major general (two stars). It included an artillery regiment, three infantry regiments, and supporting units such as engineers, heavy artillery, intelligence, reconnaissance, and supply.

DMZ   A demilitarized zone. In Vietnam the DMZ was a zone about five kilometers (just over three miles) wide on both sides of the seventeenth parallel, established by a treaty that attempted to disentangle the French forces from the Vietminh forces. It came to form the border between North and South Vietnam. The Ben Hai River ran through its center in its eastern half. The eastern end stopped at the China Sea. The western end stopped at the Laotian border.

dozens   The dozens is an African-American oral contest in which two competitors, usually males, go head-to-head in usually good-natured, ribald trash talk. Example: "Your momma's so fat I had to take two buses to get on her good side." They take turns insulting each other or their adversary's mother or other family members until one of them has no comeback.

DShKM .51-caliber machine gun A Soviet machine gun similar to the American .50-caliber Browning machine gun, although its round had a somewhat longer case. The initials stand for Degtyraov and Shpagin, the two people most instrumental in the weapon's development. The K is for *krupnokalibernyi*, large caliber, and the M is a development model designation. This weapon was used extensively by the North Vietnamse Army as an antiaircraft device, primarily for shooting down helicopters.

elephant grass Huge stalks of bamboo-like grass. It grew higher than a man's head in thick, nearly impenetrable stands that could cover an entire valley floor. Its sharp edges drew blood.

E-tool Entrenching tool. A small folding shovel about two feet long, carried by all combat Marines. Designed primarily to dig fighting holes, it was also used to dig latrines, bunkers, and firing pits and to clear brush for fields of fire. On rare occasions it was used as a weapon.

executive officer, XO The second in command of a Marine company. The XO handled the administrative details of the company and acted as general counsel to the commanding officer (CO) and platoon commanders. On combat operations, the CO and the XO were usually physically separated so that if the commanding officer was hit the executive officer would probably be able to take command.

FAC The forward air controller, an enlisted man from the air wing who was attached to a company-size unit to coordinate all air support from resupply to bombing and strafing. An officer pilot usually occupied the same position at battalion headquarters. The Marine Corps pioneered close air support tactics and procedures in World War II, and the close working relationship between Marine Air and Marine Ground is a specialty of the Marines.

FAC-man Nickname commonly given to the enlisted forward air controller.

fire team   Smallest unit in a rifle company. A fire team was designated to be four riflemen, but under combat conditions, because of attrition, fire teams quite often consisted of only three riflemen.

Five   In radio code, the company executive officer, the second in command; for example, Bravo Five.

flat-hatting   Flying extremely close to the ground.

FLD   The final line of departure, an imaginary line behind which the assaulting troops wait for the signal to move forward. Once this imaginary line is crossed, the unit is irrevocably committed.

football team   Radio brevity code for a platoon (forty-three Marines).

foxtrot whiskey   Fixed-wing aircraft (as opposed to helicopters). Marine Corps, and occasionally Navy or Air Force, fixed-wing jet aircraft delivered almost all the close air support.

fragging   Murdering someone, usually an unpopular officer or sergeant, by throwing a fragmentation grenade into his living quarters or fighting hole. The Marine Corps had forty-three fragging incidents during the Vietnam War, although not all ended in fatalities.

frag order   Fragmentary order. This term has nothing to do with fragging. It was an addendum to a larger original order. Frag orders were usually more prevalent than original orders and were done for the sake of efficiency (at least as far as issuing orders was concerned). For example, an original order might have told a unit to enter a certain valley, destroy what it found, and return. A frag order could amend that original order, telling the unit to continue the mission for another week, or to proceed to a certain place, with the same mission but without having to repeat everything over the radio.

G-2   Also, G2. Division intelligence. American military organizations designate staff functions and organizations with letters and numbers. G stands for a division-level staff, R for regimental level, and S for battalion level. Staff functions are designated by numbers: 1 for administrative, 2 for intelligence, 3 for operations, and 4 for supply. So, at the division level, the intelligence staff would be G-2 and at the battalion level it would be S-2. The officer in charge of that staff function would be called "the S-2," or "the Two." Major Blakely, as head of operations at the battalion level, is called "the Three," because he is in charge of battalion operations, S-3.

grid coordinates All military maps are divided into one-kilometer squares (that is, each side of a square is six-tenths of a mile). A baseline point is established and designated 000000. The first three digits refer to the distance east from the base in tenths of a kilometer, and the last three refer to the distance north. For example, grid coordinates 325889 would refer to a point 32.5 kilometers (about 20.3 miles) east and 88.9 kilometers (about 55.5 miles) north of 000000.

gunjy Slang for zealous and combative, or overly zealous and overly combative, depending on the context and the tone of voice. It is probably derived from "gung ho," a Marine expression borrowed from Chinese meaning "work together."

gunny A company gunnery sergeant. During the Vietnam War, with the companies operating at long distances from headquarters, the company gunny was usually the highest-ranked noncommissioned officer out in the bush. The company first sergeants, one rank higher, usually handled administrative functions in permanent headquarters at locations like Quang Tri. The company gunny, who reported directly to the company commander, handled most of the supply functions and had a strong tactical and personnel advisory role. Although the gunny was not directly in charge of the platoon sergeants, who reported to their platoon commanders, he had a very strong dotted-line relationship with the platoon sergeants. A gunny's "request" was the equivalent of an order. A platoon sergeant could go around the gunny by working through his commanding officer, but this was exceedingly rare. In peacetime the company gunny would normally be an E-7 gunnery sergeant, but because of wartime shortages this position was often filled by E-6 staff sergeants.

H & S Stands for headquarters and supply.

heat tabs   Blue 1, 3, 5-Trioxane (sometimes called trioxin) wafers about one inch in diameter that could be placed in the bottom of "field stoves" made by punching holes in C-ration tin cans. Because the heat tabs didn't oxidize well in the field stoves, they gave off noxious fumes that stung the nose and eyes. Heat tabs also took too long to heat anything. In the bush, most Marines preferred to cook with C-4 plastic explosive, often digging apart claymore mines (this was very dangerous and strictly forbidden) to get something less noxious with which to heat their C-rations.

heli team   The weight, or load, that a helicopter can carry varies with the altitude and temperature. The higher the altitude and temperature, the lower the possible load. Although tactically it would be most effective to load entire organizational units, most often tactical units had to be divided into units called heli teams in accordance with the weather and altitude. Upon arrival in the landing zone, the heli teams would immediately disband, and the Marines would re-form into standard tactical units such as fire teams, squads, and platoons.

HM2   Also HM-2: hospital corpsman second class. Sheller, the senior squid, has this rank.

HM3   Also HM-3: hospital corpsman third class Fredrickson, the platoon corpsman, has this rank.

hooch   Any shelter, permanent or temporary. A hooch could be anything from a rough plywood building in a rear area to a couple of rubberized ponchos strung together over some communication wire out in the bush. Sometimes spelled "hootch."

Huey   The UH-1 single-rotor helicopter. There were several variations, such as UH-1B and UH-1G, ranging from a "slick" (which had little armament and firepower and was used for evacuating the wounded and inserting ground forces) to a "gun ship" (which was armed with rockets, machine guns, or 20-millimeter cannons and was used for close air support). Hueys had many uses, including close air support, medical evacuations, inserting and extracting reconnaissance teams, and transporting high-ranking officers. The Army used them as assault helicopters, and Army airborne and cavalry units had the use of many times more Hueys than similar-sized Marine units.

humping   Aside from the obvious sexual connotation, humping meant hiking out into the bush with seventy or more pounds of gear on one's back, the normal weight carried by the Marine infantryman. "They humped me to death" was a common complaint about being forced to do more walking than one thought reasonable.

huss   A favor granted by a superior or by the system in general. Example: "He caught a huss when he got out of the bush to pick up the paychecks."

IFR   Stands for instrument flight rules. These "rules" were procedures and standards put into effect whenever visibility was so limited by bad weather or darkness that the pilot had to rely on flying with instruments. When IFR was not in effect, VFR—visual flight rules—would be used.

immersion foot   Condition in which the foot becomes numb and then turns red or blue. As the condition worsens, the feet swell and open sores break out, leading to fungal infections and ulcers. If left untreated, immersion foot usually results in gangrene, which can require amputation. Immersion foot develops when the feet are constantly cold and damp and are enclosed in constricting footwear. It is also known as trench foot.

ITR   Stands for infantry training regiment. Upon graduation from boot camp, Marines are assigned their military occupational specialty, or MOS. They then undergo training in their MOS at various bases. Those assigned an MOS of 03, infantry, went on to the Infantry Training Regiment at Camp Pendleton, California. "Oh-three" was far and away the most common Marine MOS.

John Wayne   Small thumb-size can opener that folds the blade against itself and is usually worn with the Marine's identification tags (dog tags). Its official military designation is the P-38 can opener.

K-bar   Knife with a seven-inch blade and a wrapped-leather handle. It looked like a large bowie knife and has been standard issue to all Marines since World War II. It could be a lethal and effective weapon, but it was most often used for numerous more utilitarian jobs, such as cutting brush, opening cans, whittling short-timer's sticks, and cleaning fingernails. The name is of obscure origin, but the likely source is "Knife Accessory Browning Automatic Rifle."

KIA   Stands for killed in action.

Kit Carson scout   North Vietnamese and Vietcong soldiers who surrendered were offered the opportunity (and good pay) to become scouts for Marine units, using their knowledge of NVA tactics and the terrain to help direct the Marine units on operations. Often these men were disillusioned with communism and fought from idealistic motives, but sometimes they were simply cynical mercenaries fighting for whoever would pay them the most. They were generally regarded as traitors by the Marines, however unfair that image may have been.

KP   Stands for kitchen police, i.e., the menial chores of running a kitchen: peeling potatoes, washing dishes, etc. Usually, in peacetime, KP is considered something to avoid and is often assigned as a punishment for mild infractions. In Vietnam, however, if a Marine got KP duty, he got out of the bush and into a place of safety, so the punishment became *not* allowing the Marine to get KP duty.

lifer   Someone who is making the military a career. "Lifer" was quite often a derogatory label, obviously connoting a prison sentence. It also implied that the lifer put career, military rules, and decorum above the welfare of the troops.

Loco Cocoa   Loud and clear. Any other combination of L and C, such as Lime and Coke or Lickety Clit, that struck a radio operator's imagination could also mean loud and clear.

louie   Slang for lieutenant.

LP   A listening post, usually a team of two Marines placed outside the defenses at night with a radio. Their job was to listen (since they could not see) for enemy movement and warn their unit of an enemy attack. All Marines on LP hoped they could hear the enemy coming, give their warning, and make it back to safety or simply hide in the jungle until the fight was over. They were well aware, however, that the job was sacrificial. A company in the jungle would normally have three LPs out at the same time, one in front of each platoon.

LZ   A landing zone for helicopters. Such zones ranged from uneven, often sloping, cleared patches of ground deep in the jungle or elephant grass, whose diameter was only about twice the expected chopper's length, to larger, better-constructed zones on permanently occupied hilltops. LZ could also refer to something as sophisticated as a large, permanent, often blacktop area at a rear base that accommodated several choppers at the same time.

M-16   Standard-issue automatic rifle used during the Vietnam War. It fired a 5.56-millimeter spitzer boat-tail bullet at a very high velocity, the object being to wound rather than kill. (Wounds tax an army's medical and personnel systems more than kills do.) The M-16 is still in use today, but the bullet is slightly heavier (62 grains versus 55 grains) and is fired at a slightly slower velocity (3,100 feet per second versus 3,250 feet per second).

M-26   Standard-issue fragmentation grenade during the Vietnam War. It was also referred to as a "Mike twenty-six," or a "frag" (as opposed to a "smoke" or an "illume") It weighed 21 ounces, and looked like a fat egg with an olive drab smooth steel skin. It came with a "spoon" on the top—a spring-loaded arming device that was activated by removing a wire ring holding the spoon to the grenade's side. Once the ring was removed, the thrower had to keep the spoon in place by holding it against the grenade with his hand. Once the grenade was thrown, the spoon was released and started a chemical reaction that set the grenade off in four to five seconds. The grenade was filled with coiled perforated metal, which blew into pellet-like projectiles that could kill people within a radius of about fifty feet. The effective killing radius of the grenade, however, was actually only about ten feet. An average Marine could toss an M-26 thirty or forty yards. The explosive was composition B, a mixture of mostly TNT and cyclonite (or hexogen).

M-60 machine gun   Standard-issue Marine machine gun in Vietnam. Its maximum range was 3,725 meters (2.3 miles), although its effective range was closer to 1,100 meters (about 0.7 mile or twelve football fields). It fired the standard NATO 7.62-millimeter round (.308 caliber) using linked belts with 100 rounds each. These belts were often carried crossed over the body, but in jungle warfare carrying them that way would expose them to small sticks and leaves, which would stop the firing, so the belts had to be contained in metal cans that were very heavy and very awkward to carry. The M-60 was designed to be manned by three Marines: a gunner and two assistants to help carry the ammunition. In Vietnam, however, because of attrition, the teams were usually only two men. A good gunner could fire 100 rounds per minute at a sustained rate. Firing at the gun's maximum rate of 550 rounds per minute would soon generate too much heat and destroy the barrel. The M-60 had a folding bipod on the front of the barrel and weighed 18.75 pounds. Marines loved this weapon and generally admired the guys who carried and fired it.

M-79   Grenade launcher that looks very much like a short, fat shotgun. It can fire high-explosive grenades (HE round), heavy buckshot (shotgun round), or fléchettes, small arrowlike projectiles, in a wide arc, so it is a very good jungle weapon where targets are hard to locate quickly.

MAG   Marine Air Group.

Marine amphibious force (MAF)   Two or more Marine divisions plus necessary Marine air support. During the Vietnam War the MAF was led by a lieutenant general (three stars) and based in Da Nang. It reported operationally to MAC-V, Military Assistance Command Vietnam, headed by an Army general (four stars) located in Saigon. For administrative and logistical support it reported to the commanding general, Fleet Marine Force Pacific (three stars), located in Hawaii. MAC-V reported to U.S. Pacific Command, headed by a four-star admiral.

mast   See **request mast.**

medevac   Medical evacuation.

MIA   Stands for missing in action.

mike mike Millimeter.

Mike 26 The M-26 hand grenade.

montagnard From the French for mountain dweller. In this context, any person belonging to one of the many indigenous tribes that inhabited the western mountains and jungle of Vietnam.

motor-T Motor transportation. Support troops that operated and maintained trucks and other vehicles used primarily to move people and matériel on the ground. This vital function is often overlooked, much as football fans overlook linemen who seldom score, but without whose contribution no team can win.

mustang Officer who came up from the enlisted ranks.

Mutter's Ridge Strategically important east-west chain of high hills in northern Quang Tri province that paralleled the DMZ. The origin of the name is uncertain, but it has been attributed to several Marines named Mutter, most prominently Staff Sergeant Alan Mutter, USMC, who was killed there. The name has also been attributed to the radio call sign of Third Battalion Fourth Marines, which fought an early battle there. Mutter's Ridge paralleled Route 9 for most of its eastern half and was vital to the control of Route 9 and the valley of the Ben Hai River to the north, another access route to penetrate from Laos and North Vietnam into the Quang Tri plain. In the novel it extends much farther west than it does in reality.

Nagoolian Usually a name for the enemy, specifically the North Vietnamese Army, but often used to designate any Vietnamese unit or even a hypothetical individual. It is derived from Nguyen, the most common Vietnamese name.

NCO Noncommissioned officer.

NCOIC Noncommissioned officer in charge.

NIS Naval Investigative Service. This organization was like the detective force of the Navy, as opposed to the shore patrol, whose members acted more like uniformed police. NIS also was involved in covert operations that attempted to find criminal activity such as drug dealing.

numby or numbnuts   A stupid or incompetent person. Numby is pronounced "nummy."

NVA   North Vietnamese Army, the regular army of the People's Republic of Vietnam, a well-equipped and well-trained regular fighting force, in contrast to the VC or Vietcong, which was a guerrilla force.

Oley   Radio brevity code for wounded in action.

on line   When not fighting, infantry units normally move in columns, one man behind the other. In the jungle, there is almost no other way to move and maintain any control. When men who are in a column have to engage an enemy in front of them, they would be able to use only the fire of the first two or three people, otherwise the others could get shot in the back. The solution is to "go on line." This means that the column spreads out in a long line facing the enemy so that every rifle can be brought to bear on the enemy without the risk of shooting a friend in the back. This maneuver was easier to think about than to accomplish while under fire, particularly in a jungle, where visual contact could be lost within twenty feet.

OP   Stands for outpost. An OP served the same purpose as a listening post (LP) but was used in daylight. It was less frightening than an LP because one could see as well as hear and smell and the company usually had small units patrolling out beyond the OPs; these units afforded the OPs extra protection and warning time.

op-con   Verb formed from *op*erational *con*trol. Often, Marines will simply switch units from one command to another if that serves a tactical situation. For example, if a company from one battalion found itself operating to support a company from a different battalion, the battalion commander of the first company would hand over operational control to the commander of the second battalion, thereby eliminating the useless and even possibly destructive delays and misunderstandings that could arise if the two battalion commanders had to coordinate with each other. The first battalion's company would thus be "op-conned" to the second battalion.

OV-10   The OV-10 Bronco was a two-engine, twin-boom observation and close-air-support plane. With its twin booms and large connecting horizontal stabilizer it looked much like the old P-38 Lightning. It carried four M-60 machine guns and two 4-missile Zuni pods outboard on each wing, as well as smoke rockets. It could also be configured for small bombs.

patrol   Mission assigned to a smaller unit. A patrol involved walking outside the sight and rifle range of the larger unit and would range anywhere from five to ten kilometers (about three to six miles) and last up to a full day, depending on the terrain. Patrols were used to locate the enemy and enemy supplies and to destroy them or fix them in place until reinforcements could arrive. Patrols also were used to screen the enemy from approaching the larger unit and give warning if an enemy approach was detected.

platoon   Three squads form a platoon. During the Vietnam War a platoon was designated to be forty-three Marines, but in combat conditions the platoon was usually manned at levels in the low to mid-thirties. A platoon was supposed to have either a second lieutenant (one gold bar) or a first lieutenant (one silver bar) as its leader, a platoon sergeant (four stripes), a platoon guide (three stripes), and the platoon leader's radio operator. In Vietnam by the late 1960s, there was a shortage of staff NCOs, so three-stripe sergeants often became platoon sergeants. Platoon guides were often done away with, and a second radio operator was added (along with a second radio) to assist the platoon sergeant—who in mountain and jungle fighting often operated independently from the platoon commander. Both the platoon sergeant and the platoon commander led squad-sized patrols.

poag   An overweight rear-area do-nothing. The term is derived from the time when the Marines were in China before World War II. They were issued candy (Baby Ruth, Tootsie Rolls, etc.) to supplement their rations. Sugar and other sweets were rare commodities in China, so the troops found the candy useful for barter in towns. The Chinese word for prostitute sounded something like "pogey." Thus, the candy became "pogey bait" and the expression eventually became Marine slang for junk food and candy bars in general.

point The first man in front of a column is said to be the point man or simply the point. The act of being the first in the column is called "walking point." It is probably the most frightening and nerve-racking job, short of an actual assault, that an infantryman does—and some claim it's worse than an actual assault.

poncho liner Thin blanket of camouflaged nylon (5 feet 8 inches by 6 feet 10 inches) quilted to a polyester fill. It was tied, by attached strings, underneath a Marine's rubberized-canvas poncho to provide warmth. It was most often used as a blanket, the only source of warmth for most Marines in the field.

pos rep Position report.

PRC 25 Pronounced "prick twenty-five." This was the AN/PRC 25 FM radio used by all Marine infantry units in Vietnam. It used early solid-state technology and weighed about twenty pounds, with its battery. It was carried like a backpack by the radio operator. It had 1.5 watts of power and could broadcast three to seven miles, depending on the terrain. Unfortunately, high hills blocked the signal, making it less effective in the mountains. Also, although the radio itself was waterproof, the handset was not. The handset looked like a black 1960s telephone handset attached by a long spiral cord. When the radio was turned to maximum volume, a person could hear easily with the handset a couple of feet from the ear. The handsets were often wrapped in plastic to protect them from the constant rain of monsoons. Radio operators were prime targets, easily spotted by the large FM antenna, which also identified the person closest to the radio as the unit leader.

R & R Stands for rest and recreation. Marines were given a five-day R & R once during their thirteen-month tour of duty in Vietnam. Because some places were more popular than others, the most desired places to go on R & R were allocated according to how much time a

Marine had spent in-country. Sydney was a first choice among white Marines. Bangkok was a favored choice among black Marines. Hawaii was a favorite of married Marines. Some Marines waited until their twelfth month in order to get enough seniority to go where they wanted.

radio alphabet code Because letters can often be mistaken when transmitted orally, the military adopted a standard code designating each letter: Alpha is "A," Bravo is "B," and so on through Zulu for "Z." Because NVA intelligence units would intercept radio messages, Marines were leery of saying last names over the radio, so Jones would become "character Juliet," Smith would become "character Sierra," and so on.

radio brevity code An unsophisticated but continually changing shortcut code used for concealing information from the enemy in speaking over a radio. For example, beer brands could be used to designate different categories of casualties: e.g., "Coors" for killed in action, "Oley" for wounded in action. After a short time a new system would be established, such as cigarette brands: "Camels" would mean killed in action and "Luckies" would mean wounded in action. A few days later professional quarterbacks would be the general category, so Namath could mean killed in action; Hornung, wounded in action; and so on. Brevity code was applied to anything that was dangerous to transmit in the clear. For example, "cars" would be the brevity code to transmit locations. A specific car name would refer to a designated grid coordinate. The person radioing in a position would say, "From Cadillac up two point four and right three point one." The listener would go to the designated "cars" grid coordinate for the day and calculate (in kilometers) from there to locate the transmitting party. Sending one's location in the clear would invite artillery or rockets to that location.

radio unit designators To confuse enemy intelligence when transmitting the names of units, a battalion-size unit would have a radio name that it changed frequently. For example, here the First Battalion of the Fourteenth Marines is designated "Big John." Bravo Company of the First Battalion would thus be designated "Big John Bravo." The First Platoon of Bravo Company would be called "Big John Bravo One." At the company level, for convenience, the battalion designator would be dropped.

The company would just be Bravo, and the First Platoon would be Bravo One. First Platoon would be Bravo One. First Squad in the First Platoon would be Bravo One One, and so on.

Red Dog   Radio brevity code for any squad-size patrol.

regiment   Traditional core unit of the Marines, about 4,000 Marines. It consisted of three infantry battalions, one artillery battalion, and supporting staff and was usually commanded by a full colonel, often called a "bird colonel" because the rank is designated by a silver eagle. When someone is asked what unit a Marine served with, the answer will usually be in the form of the individual's regiment, such as "Fourth Marines," "Ninth Marines," or "One-Nine," meaning First Battalion Ninth Marines. Regiments can be shifted to various divisions or task forces, depending on need. Command of a Marine regiment is a very prestigious position.

regular   The Marine Corps divides its officers into two categories: reserve and regular. A reserve officer has USMCR placed after his name and rank; a regular officer has only USMC placed after his name and rank. All enlisted personnel are regulars, unless they specifically join a reserve unit after active service. Reserve officers are expected to serve three or four years of active duty and then either join a reserve unit or quit the Marine Corps altogether. The bulk of junior officers are reserve officers, the exceptions being graduates of the Naval Academy and some graduates of Naval ROTC who have already chosen the Marine Corps as a career. If a reserve officer wants to make the Marine Corps a career, he "goes regular" and is then viewed very differently by the Marine Corps personnel system. He no longer has a set time commitment to the Corps, but is expected to serve at least twenty years until retirement, and in most cases longer. In exchange, good positions such as command of company-size or larger units and advancement in rank are easier to attain. Very few reserve officers ever attain a higher rank than first lieutenant or get assigned to career-enhancing positions.

request mast   Every Marine has the right to request an interview with his commanding officer. The term "request mast" hasn't changed since the days when Marines served on wooden sailing ships and the interview took place "before the mast."

RHIP   Rank has its privileges.

Route 9   A mostly dirt or gravel two-lane highway that connected the coastal plain around Quang Tri to Vandegrift Combat Base, Khe Sanh, and Laos. During the Vietnam War it was the only easy way to cross the mountains and supply Marines operating in them with land-based transportation. It also ran through the only easy way to get from Laos into the populated coastal lowlands, and was the most direct way for the NVA to reach Quang Tri, particularly with armor; hence, it was of immense strategic value.

RPD   Ruchnoi Pulemet Degtyarev, one of the lightest and most effective machine guns ever produced, was the standard machine gun used by the NVA and the Vietcong. It used the same 7.62-millimeter bullet as the AK-47 and the SKS. Beneath the barrel, it had a 100-round drum that contained the belted ammunition. The drum protected the ammunition from getting fouled by jungle dirt and plants, further increasing the RPD's effectiveness. This weapon could fire about 150 rounds per minute for an effective range of around 800 meters (about half a mile). The bipod is permanently attached but can be folded alongside the barrel for ease in movement. The RPD weighed 19.4 pounds fully loaded.

RPG   Stands for rocket-propelled grenade. This is a small rocket with an explosive head that can be fired by a single man. It is very effective and is still used in Iraq by the insurgents.

RTO   Stands for radio operator, from "radio telephone operator," a defunct name no longer used by the time of the Vietnam War.

scuttlebutt   Gossip, rumor. A scuttlebutt is a water fountain on a ship, a place where people congregate and exchange informal talk.

Semper Fi   Short for *Semper Fidelis,* Latin for "always faithful," the Marine Corps motto. It means always faithful to the country's call, but for Marines it primarily means always faithful to each other.

senior squid   The Navy hospital corpsman assigned to a company headquarters who is in charge of the corpsmen assigned to the platoons in the company. The table of organization rank called for a hospital corpsman first class (HM1 or HM-1), a naval petty officer equivalent to a Marine staff sergeant (E6 or E-6). Each Marine company had one senior hospital corpsman at the company headquarters. Tactically he reported to the company commander, but administratively he reported to the battalion surgeon, a Navy doctor, usually a Navy lieutenant. In Vietnam, because of shortages, this post was often filled by a lower-ranking hospital corpsman second class (HM2 or HM-2), the equivalent of a Marine sergeant (E5 or E-5), and there was often only one corpsman to a platoon.

shit-kicker   A paperback western novel.

shit sandwich   A particularly tough firefight.

short-timer   A standard tour of duty for a Marine in Vietnam was thirteen months. Around month eleven or twelve, most Marines began behaving differently. At this time, in contrast to the previous months, they could entertain the hope that they were going to get through alive and unscathed, but this hope destroyed the earlier psychological numbness and fatalistic thinking of the combat infantryman that had made fear easier to deal with. Short-timers' behavior took all sorts of forms, like wearing two flack jackets, refusing to come out of a fighting hole to urinate, or refusing to brush one's teeth (on the assumption that brushing made one's smile too bright). Some of these behaviors were consciously opera buffa, but others were a result of serious psychological disturbances.

short-timer's stick   Wooden staff from three to five feet long and about two inches in diameter. It was marked in some way each day, elaborately or simply, depending on the skill and taste of the carver. A few contrarians would mark all the days at once and then lop off a mark for each day that passed, until the lucky ones carried just a stub. The sticks served as walking sticks, canes, tent poles, and even weapons in a pinch. Some of the short-timer's sticks were works of art.

sick bay   This was where the battalion medical staff was available for nonemergency illnesses and injuries. The term also meant the activity of providing routine medical care, as in "Sick bay will be at 0830 hours every day."

Six   Radio code for the commanding officer of a unit the size of a company or larger.

skipper   Casual term of affection and respect used by Marines to designate a company commander, no matter what his rank. Sometimes it is used for the leader of larger formations, such as a battalion or Marine Air Group or squadron. In the Navy, it refers to the commanding officer of a ship or boat, no matter what his rank, and has much the same connotation.

Skoshi cab   A small Japanese taxi. "Skoshi" means small or little in Japanese. Small Marines often were nicknamed Skosh, for example, Bass's radio operator.

SKS   Standard-issue semiautomatic weapon used by the North Vietnamese Army and Vietcong. It fired the same 7.62-millimeter bullet as the AK-47, but it did not fire automatically: the trigger had to be pulled for each shot. Being longer than the AK-47, it was much more accurate.

snoopy   Slang for a poncho liner, so called because one could hide under it in the jungle when "snooping around." The name also evoked, comfortingly, the cartoon beagle Snoopy.

snuff or snuffy   A young Marine of low rank.

Slausens   A gang of the 1960s in Los Angeles.

splib   Among Marines in the bush during Vietnam, this was a nonderogatory term for a black Marine. It was used by both blacks and whites as a rather "hip" way of identifying an African-American, usually a male. A common example is "He's a splib dude" for a black Marine, in contrast to "He's a chuck dude" for a white Marine.

squad   Unit designed to consist of thirteen Marines: three four-man fire teams and a squad leader. Usually, however, it operated with about ten or eleven Marines. A squad was designed to be led by a sergeant (three stripes), a noncommissioned officer with at least four years of experience or more; in Vietnam, though, most squads were led by corporals (two stripes) or even lance corporals (one stripe), most of whom were teenagers.

squid   Slang for a Navy hospital corpsman. The Navy provides all the medical services for the Marine Corps. (The Army, by contrast, has its own medical services; the Army equivalent of a corpsman is called a medic.) Corpsmen wore Marine uniforms and trained for service with the Marine Corps in special schools run by the Navy at Marine Corps facilities called field medical services schools ("Field Med" for short). The table of organization called for two corpsmen for each platoon, but there was often only one.

stand to   Most attacks come at dawn or dusk, when the light is favorable enough for the attacker but makes him hard for the defender to see. For this reason all Marines would be required to man (stand to) their fighting holes at these critical times.

super-grunts   Reconnaissance Marines. Reconnaissance personnel were all volunteers who operated far from friendly units in very small groups. Only highly recommended and experienced Marine infantry personnel were selected from the rifle companies; hence the half-derogatory, half-admiring nickname "super-grunts." Marines still in rifle companies had mixed feelings about reconnaissance teams. On the one hand, these teams were admired because they were brave, were frequently sent on dangerous missions, and had already proved themselves as ordinary grunts. On the other hand, they lived in relative comfort in the rear when they weren't out in the bush, and if they got into trouble they sometimes had to be bailed out by a rescue operation, which usually involved a firefight. There were two levels of reconnaissance: division and force. Force reconnaissance personnel received more extensive training than division reconnaissance personnel; for example they were all highly trained scuba divers and parachutists. Force recon is generally considered to be the crème de la crème of the Marine Corps, equivalent to (although the Marines would say better than) the Navy's SEALs.

TAOR   Tactical area of responsibility. A geographic area assigned to any unit for which that unit has sole operating authority and responsibility.

TBS   See Basic School.

Three   The officer in charge of the staff tasked with planning operations. Major Blakely is in charge of First Battalion's operations staff, S-3, so he is called "the Three."

tubing   When an armed mortar shell is dropped into the mortar tube, an explosion propels it from the tube toward its target. The sound of this explosion is very distinct and is called tubing. Usually, if one hears tubing, there are several seconds before the round hits, because the sound of tubing arrives much faster than the high-arcing mortar round itself.

twelve and twenty   A Marine's tour in Vietnam was thirteen months, as opposed to the Army's standard tour of twelve months. The thirteenth month was added because initially Marines were transported to Vietnam and back by sea, and the two voyages took roughly a month. Even though the Marine Corps later adopted the Army's practice of moving personnel by air, the tour of duty remained unchanged. However, there was an unwritten policy that no Marine would spend his last ten days in Vietnam out on an operation. Marines would often get so nervous and spooked, worried that they would die just before they were to be sent home, that many stopped functioning. This unwritten policy of getting out of the bush on one's "twelve and twenty" was generally adhered to.

utes or utilities   Camouflaged trousers and jackets used by Marines in the jungle. Also called jungle utilities, cammies, and jungle utes. Marines referred to their working non-dress uniforms as utilities; the Army referred to them as fatigues.

VC   Vietcong, the guerrilla army based in South Vietnam and supplied by the North Vietnamese. The Vietcong were the "peasants in black pajamas" of folklore, but this force ranged in quality from "peasants" to well-equipped cadres virtually indistinguishable from a traditional regular army. Early in the war the Vietcong had nationalist as well as communist elements, having grown out of the Vietminh movement that opposed French colonial rule. The Vietcong were purposefully virtually eliminated as a fighting force by the North Vietnamese during the Tet Offensive of 1968. They were deliberately thrown into battle, inadequately equipped or inadequately trained to withstand American firepower, while the regular NVA units, better equipped and better trained, were held back. This was done because the North Vietnamese government feared that the Vietcong would form an opposition to its eventual rule.

VCB   Vandegrift Combat Base, located in a small valley in the eastern side of the Annamese Cordillera about midway across Vietnam. VCB was originally called LZ Stud the primary LZ from which the Marines and the 1st Air Cavalry division launched their relief of Khe Sanh. When the Marines withdrew from Khe Sanh, they turned LZ Stud into a forward staging area from which smaller units of company size could be inserted into the mountains. The Marines named it after the hero of Guadalcanal General Alexander Archer Vandegrift, recipient of a Medal of Honor and the eighteenth commandant of the Marine Corps.

VFR   Stands for visual flight rules, operational standards and procedures that are in place when flying conditions are good enough that pilots need not rely on instruments.

wake-up   It was extremely important, psychologically, to know exactly how many days a man had left until his tour of duty was over and he could leave Vietnam. However, there was an ambiguity. Do you call the day you board the plane for home your last day in Vietnam or your first day out of Vietnam? This was resolved by calling that day a "wake-up." It didn't count as in or as out, and this was the most accurate way of expressing how much time was left until the date of departure. (That date was called the RTD, "rotation of tour date," by the Marines, and DEROS, "date eligible for return from overseas," by the Army.) It is the day you wake up in Vietnam, but the day you go to sleep somewhere else.

WIA   Stands for wounded in action.

XO   Stands for executive officer.

Numerical Terms

.44 Magnum   Staff NCOs (four stripes) and higher ranks could carry personal firearms of their choice, and a favorite was the Smith & Wesson Model 29 or Colt .44 revolvers designed to fire the powerful .44 magnum cartridge. (Another favorite was the slightly smaller .357 Magnum.) The original .44 Magnum revolver was developed jointly by Remington, which developed the .44 cartridge (actually a .429), and Smith & Wesson, which beefed up its standard .44 Special to accommodate the cartridge. The weapon was developed in the 1950s but did not become widely known to the general public until later, because it was carried by Clint Eastwood's famous character Dirty Harry Callahan.

.45   Standard-issue .45-caliber semiautomatic pistol. It was issued during the Vietnam War to officers, noncommissioned officers, corpsmen, and machine-gun and mortar crews. It was developed by John Browning in 1905 as a result of Marine action against the Moros in the Philippines, where it was found that a .38-caliber revolver, without a direct hit to either the heart or brain, could not stop a man who had bound his limbs and body with vines or ropes to stop bleeding and prevent shock. The .45 fires a very heavy bullet, at low velocity, and will knock a man down when it hits him in nearly any part of the body. The disadvantages of the .45 are that it has only a few shots before having to be reloaded and that it is notoriously inaccurate. The reputation for inaccuracy is somewhat unfair: because of their far shorter barrel lengths all pistols are less accurate than rifles, and accuracy up to fifty feet is quite good with a skilled shooter. Mastery of the weapon, however, is difficult. It has immense recoil that puts the next shot off target; and accuracy requires sighting time and a steady hand, both of which are often lacking in combat. In Vietnam, most junior officers, corpsmen, and even machine gunners carried both .45s and M-16s. Controversy still rages over the .45. In 1985 the U.S. military replaced it with the 9-millimeter Parabellum semiautomatic pistol, but the Marine Corps still retained the .45, though not as standard issue. Reports from Iraq indicate that the 9-millimeter is too light, and demand for .45s, which, among their other virtues, can penetrate concrete blocks and still kill someone on the other side, has risen sharply in that theater.

46 See CH-46.

47 See CH-47.

60-millimeter mortar These mortars are referred to as "sixties" or "sixty mike mikes." The weapon consisted of a 12.8-pound tube 2 feet 5 inches long and 60 millimeters in diameter; a 16.4-pound bipod; and a 12.8-pound base plate. It could fire a 3.1-pound high-explosive round in a high arc a distance of just under 2,000 yards at a rate of eighteen rounds per minute until the tube got too hot. The blast radius of the projectile was about thirty-five feet. All Marine companies in Vietnam carried three sixties, and the rounds, usually two per man, were carried by every Marine in the company.

81-millimeter mortar The M29 81-millimeter mortar was a smoothbore, muzzle-loading weapon with a high angle of fire. The mortar platoon was located in the battalion H & S company and was most often used by the battalion commander to support ongoing operations when air or artillery was not available. The 81-millimeter could be carried by men on foot if it was broken down into a three-man load: a fifty-one-inch tube and sight, bipod, and base plate. In total, it weighed about ninety-three pounds. It could fire about twenty-four rounds in one minute, but because the barrel heated up, its sustained rate of fire was about two per minute. Its effective range was about two and a half miles. Each round weighed about fifteen pounds.

82-millimeter mortar The Russian-designed, slightly larger version of the very similar 81-millimeter mortar used by the Marines. It can be broken down and carried by a three-man crew. There was a rumor that this mortar was designed as it was because in a pinch it could use the slightly smaller U.S. rounds, but U.S. mortars could not use its slightly larger rounds. An 82-millimeter mortar round weighs about six and a half pounds and carries a terrific explosive wallop. It has an effective range of about two miles. It is very effective in hilly terrain, as it shoots in a high arc. (Standard artillery, by contrast, usually cannot fire in high arcs but has far greater range and even heavier rounds.)

105   The M101 105-millimeter howitzer was the standard artillery piece used by the Marines in Vietnam. It had a maximum range of 11.27 kilometers (about seven miles). Its maximum sustained rate of fire was about three rounds per minute. (More than six rounds per minute would cause the barrel to burn up.) The figure 105 millimeters refers to the diameter of the barrel (and therefore of the projectile), about 4.1 inches.

120-millimeter mortar   Soviet-designed, it fired a thirty-four-pound round up to three and a half miles. It took a crew of five or six to operate, and weighed about 375 pounds. It could be broken down and packed by the infantry, but it was often packed on a two-wheel carriage if the terrain permitted. It was greatly feared because its explosive power was much more destructive than that of the 82-millimeter mortar.

155   The M114 155-millimeter howitzer. The diameter of the barrel and projectile was about 6.1 inches. The 155 had a bigger range—14.6 kilometers (about nine miles)—than the 105. It also carried a much bigger punch; its projectiles weighed ninety-five pounds, nearly three times the weight of the 105-millimeter projectile. The 155 was already obsolete at the time of the Vietnam War, having been put into service in 1942, but its replacement was self-propelled and couldn't be used in the jungle or easily transported by helicopter, whereas the older but lighter version could. For every four batteries of 105-millimeter howitzers, there was one battery of the larger 155-millimeter howitzer.

175   The M107 self-propelled 175-millimeter gun. The diameter of the barrel was about 7.1 inches, and the high-explosive projectile weighed about 174 pounds. This gun could fire almost thirty-three kilometers (twenty miles). The Marines in western I Corps most often used Army 175s when there was no other available support, but did not use them for close support because at long ranges the 175 was not nearly accurate enough. For heavy close support the Marines relied on the eight-inch howitzer, which fired a 200-pound projectile nearly seventeen kilometers (ten miles), but with far greater accuracy. I once saw an

artillery FO, First Lieutenant Andrew Sullivan, put an eight-inch howitzer round through the slit of an NVA bunker from around seven miles'
distance with only two adjustments. (Andy was only 300 yards from the
bunker.)

782 gear   Standard-issue Marine combat gear, mainly the pack, poncho, utility shovel, ammunition belt, and suspenders.

ACKNOWLEDGMENTS

I would like to thank Barbara Lowe, Ken Pallack, Greg Neitzel, and my wife, Anne Marlantes. There were dark moments when I felt like quitting but pressed on because of their constant support and encouragement. I would also like to thank: Gisèle Fitch, for covering so many bases when I was writing the early drafts; Michael Harreschou, who encouraged me when I wrote well and beat me up when I didn't; Albert LaValley, Arthur Kinney, Waverly Fitzgerald, and Joyce Thompson, who taught me the mechanics of writing fiction; Sherman Black, Ladene Cook, Lloyd Hanson, and James Lynch, who taught me to love literature; Kama, who typed the first clean draft for next to nothing; and Tom Farber, the publisher, and Kit Duane, the senior editor, of El León Literary Arts, who first brought *Matterhorn* to reality. Finally, I would like to thank Jofie Ferrari-Adler of Grove/Atlantic for his fine editing; Morgan Entrekin of Grove/Atlantic for seeing the novel's literary value and taking the risk of publishing it; my agent, Sloan Harris of ICM, for his support and advice; Susan Gamer and Sunah Cherwin for their fine copyediting; and Don Kennison for his proofreading. Many of the novel's characters are named after friends, which explains why some of the above names may look familiar.